ALTERATIONS

a graphic novel by
Ray Xu

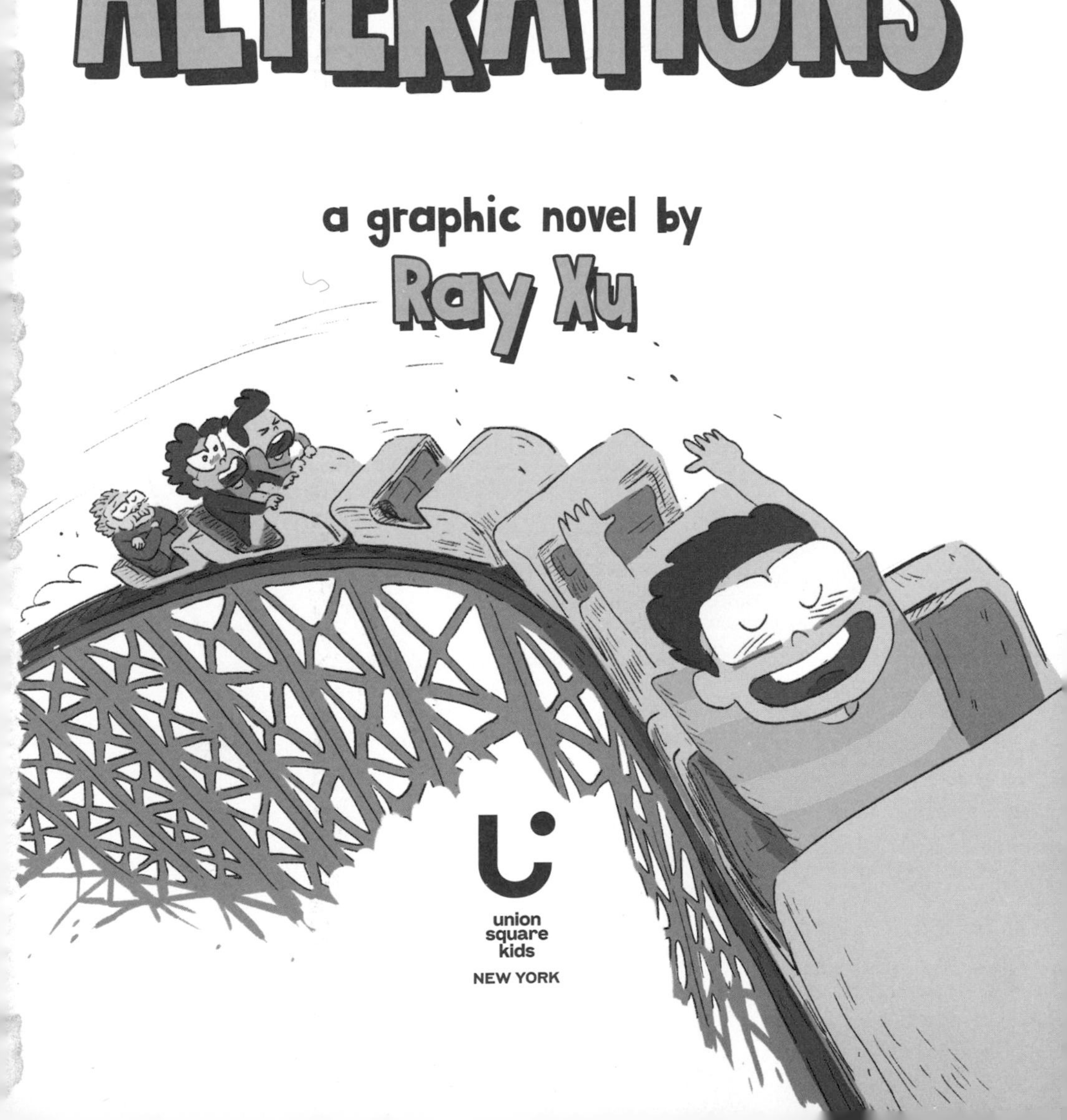

union
square
kids
NEW YORK

For Mom, Sis, my wife Sapna,
and my sons Atlas and Hayden.

union
square
kids

NEW YORK

UNION SQUARE KIDS and the distinctive Union Square Kids logo are
trademarks of Union Square & Co., LLC.

Union Square & Co., LLC, is a subsidiary of Sterling Publishing Co., Inc.

© 2024 Xuxu Studios Inc

ISBN 978-1-4549-4584-0 (hardcover)
ISBN 978-1-4549-4585-7 (paperback)
ISBN 978-1-4549-4586-4 (e-book)

Library of Congress Cataloging-in-Publication Data

Names: Xu, Ray, author.
Title: Alterations / by Ray Xu.
Description: New York : Union Square Kids, 2024. | Audience: Ages 8-12 |
    Summary: "A semi-autobiographical middle-grade graphic novel about a
    Canadian-Chinese boy who feels invisible at home and in school but longs
    to stand out"-- Provided by publisher.
Identifiers: LCCN 2023009612 | ISBN 9781454945840 (hardcover) | ISBN
    9781454945857 (paperback) | ISBN 9781454945864 (epub)
Subjects: CYAC: Graphic novels. | Self-confidence--Fiction. |
    Self-realization--Fiction. | LCGFT: Graphic novels.
Classification: LCC PZ7.7.X76 Al 2024 | DDC 741.5/971--dc23/eng/20230417
LC record available at https://lccn.loc.gov/2023009612

For information about custom editions, special sales, and premium purchases,
please contact specialsales@unionsquareandco.com.

Printed in India

Lot #:
2 4 6 8 10 9 7 5 3 1

10/23

unionsquareandco.com

Lettered by Rob Leigh
Cover and interior design by Liam Donnelly

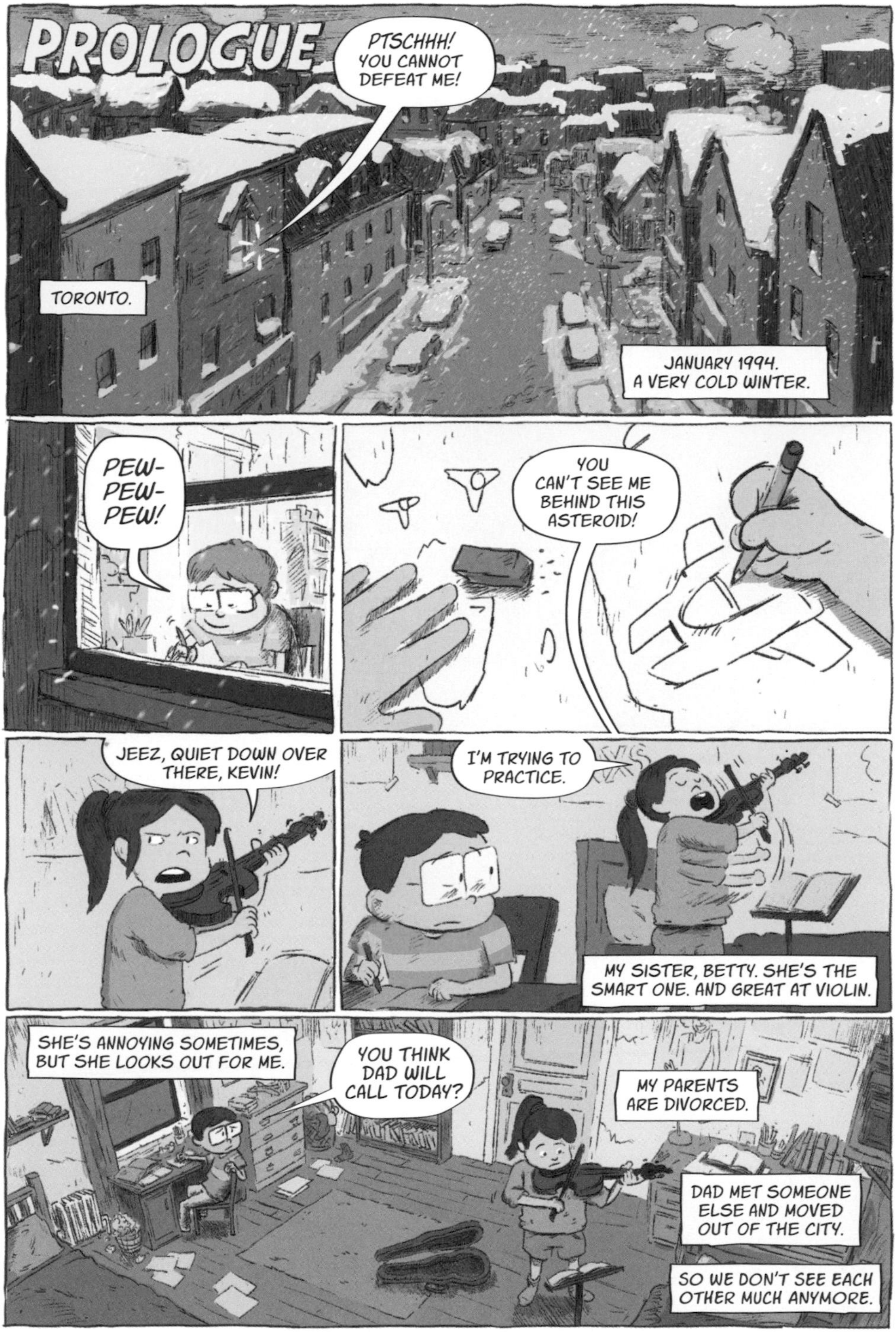
PROLOGUE
PTSCHHH! YOU CANNOT DEFEAT ME!
TORONTO.
JANUARY 1994. A VERY COLD WINTER.
PEW-PEW-PEW!
YOU CAN'T SEE ME BEHIND THIS ASTEROID!
JEEZ, QUIET DOWN OVER THERE, KEVIN!
I'M TRYING TO PRACTICE.
MY SISTER, BETTY. SHE'S THE SMART ONE. AND GREAT AT VIOLIN.
SHE'S ANNOYING SOMETIMES, BUT SHE LOOKS OUT FOR ME.
YOU THINK DAD WILL CALL TODAY?
MY PARENTS ARE DIVORCED.
DAD MET SOMEONE ELSE AND MOVED OUT OF THE CITY.
SO WE DON'T SEE EACH OTHER MUCH ANYMORE.

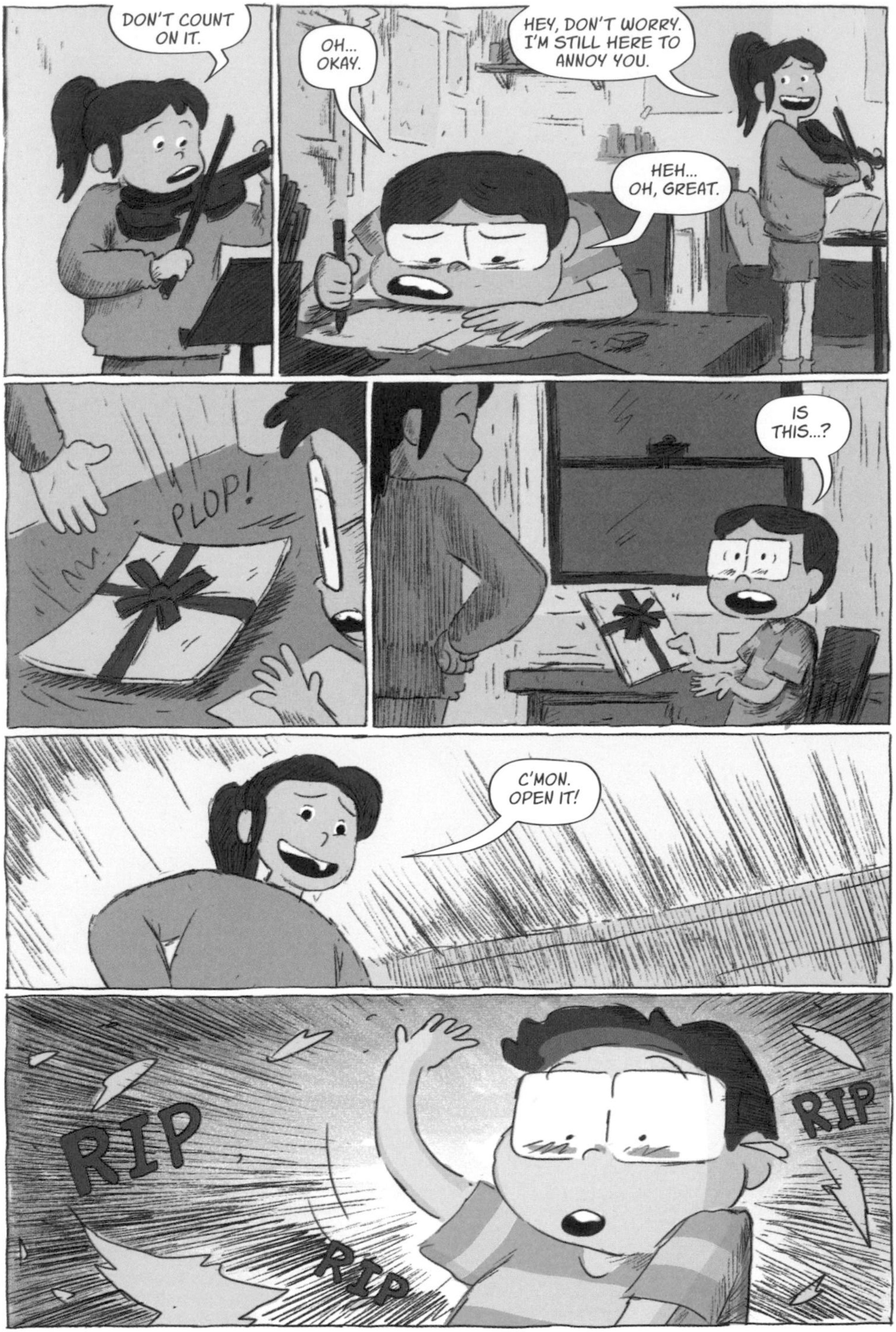

DON'T COUNT ON IT.
OH... OKAY.
HEY, DON'T WORRY. I'M STILL HERE TO ANNOY YOU.
HEH... OH, GREAT.
PLOP!
IS THIS...?
C'MON. OPEN IT!
RIP
RIP
RIP

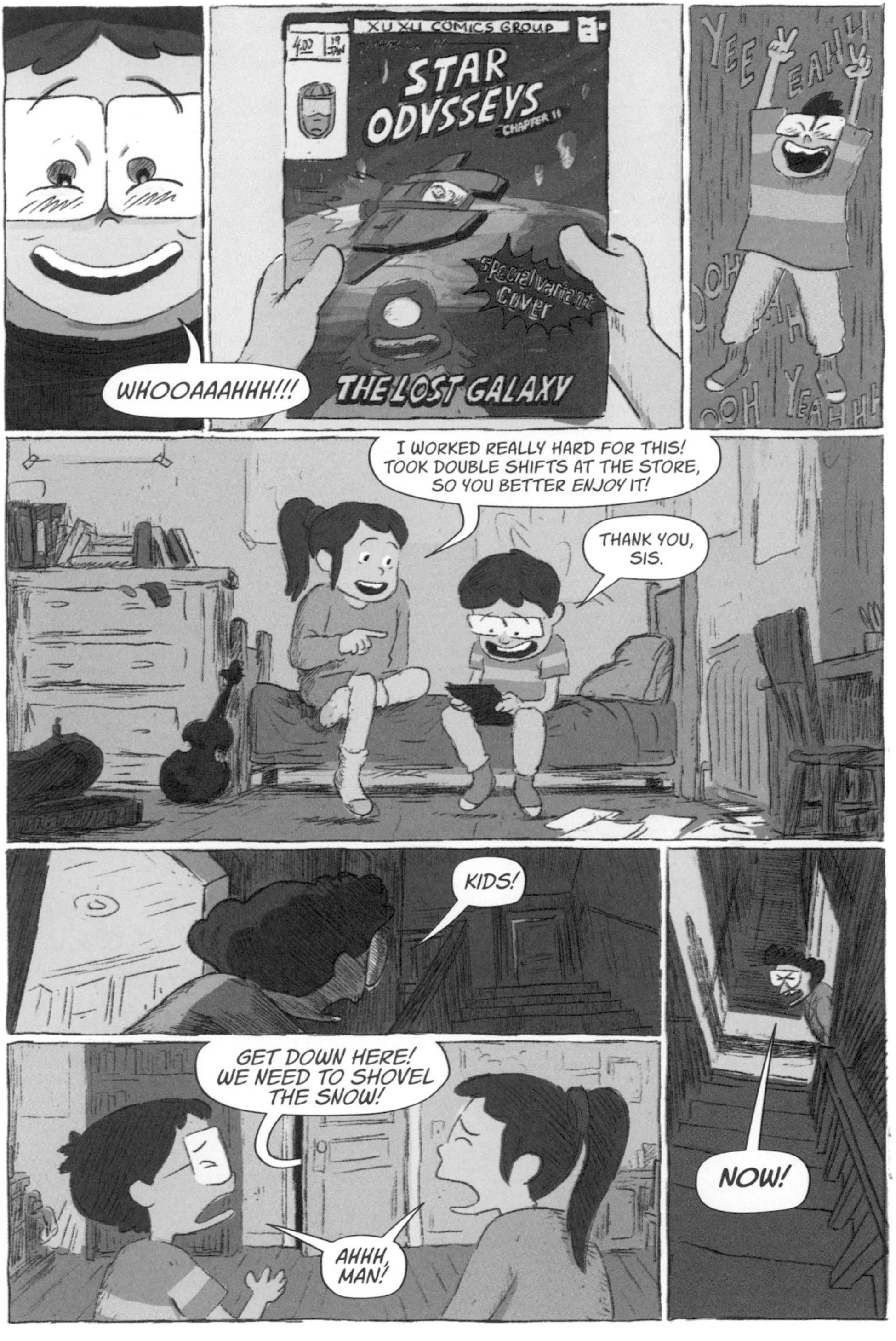
WHOOAAAHHH!!!
XUXU COMICS GROUP
4.00
19 JAN
STAR ODYSSEYS
CHAPTER 11
SPECIAL VARIANT COVER
THE LOST GALAXY
YEEEAHH
OOH AHH
OOH YEAHHH
I WORKED REALLY HARD FOR THIS! TOOK DOUBLE SHIFTS AT THE STORE, SO YOU BETTER ENJOY IT!
THANK YOU, SIS.
KIDS!
GET DOWN HERE! WE NEED TO SHOVEL THE SNOW!
AHHH, MAN!
NOW!

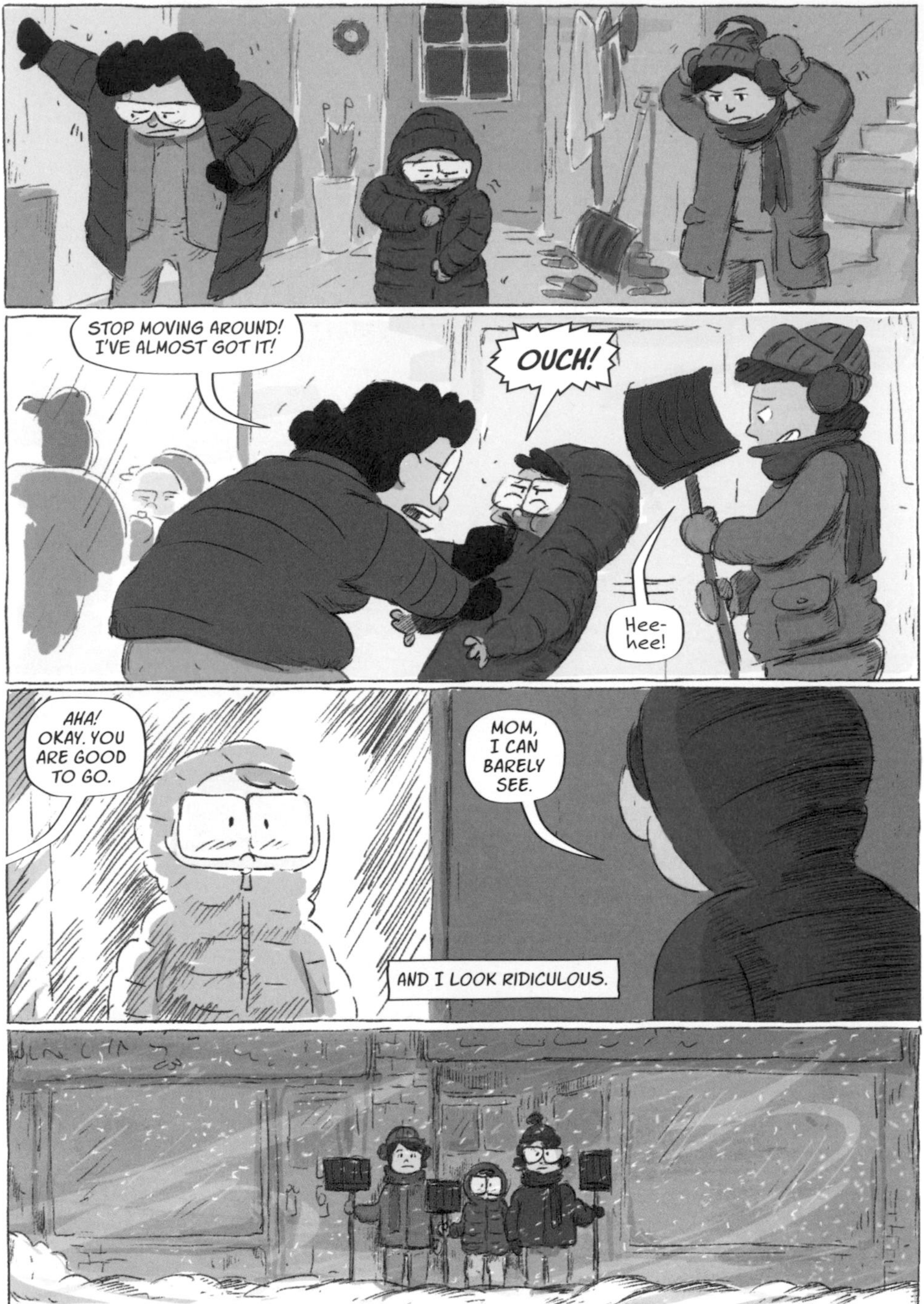
STOP MOVING AROUND! I'VE ALMOST GOT IT!
OUCH!
Hee-hee!
AHA! OKAY. YOU ARE GOOD TO GO.
MOM, I CAN BARELY SEE.
AND I LOOK RIDICULOUS.

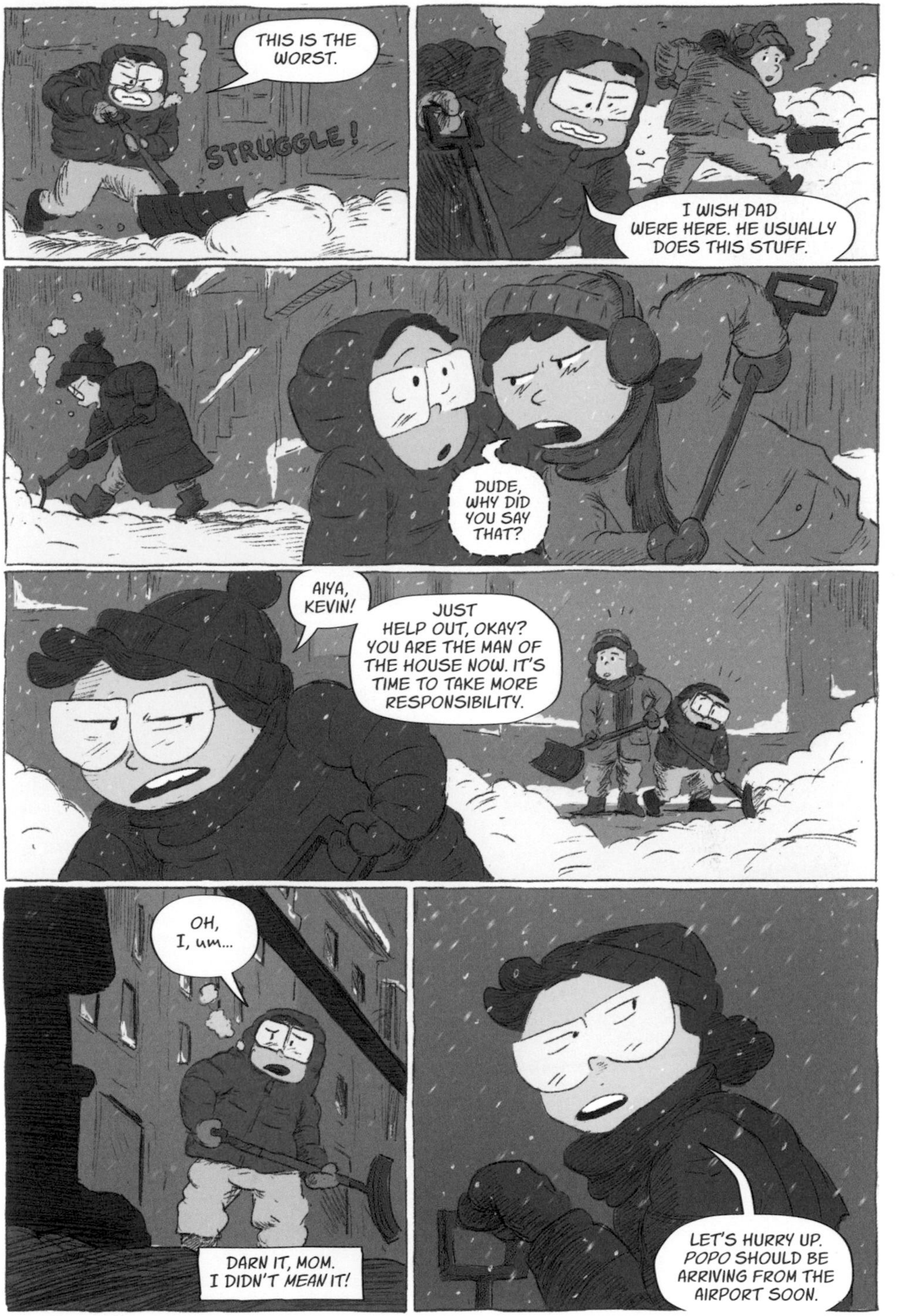
THIS IS THE WORST.
STRUGGLE!
I WISH DAD WERE HERE. HE USUALLY DOES THIS STUFF.
DUDE, WHY DID YOU SAY THAT?
AIYA, KEVIN!
JUST HELP OUT, OKAY? YOU ARE THE MAN OF THE HOUSE NOW. IT'S TIME TO TAKE MORE RESPONSIBILITY.
OH, I, um...
DARN IT, MOM. I DIDN'T MEAN IT!
LET'S HURRY UP. POPO SHOULD BE ARRIVING FROM THE AIRPORT SOON.

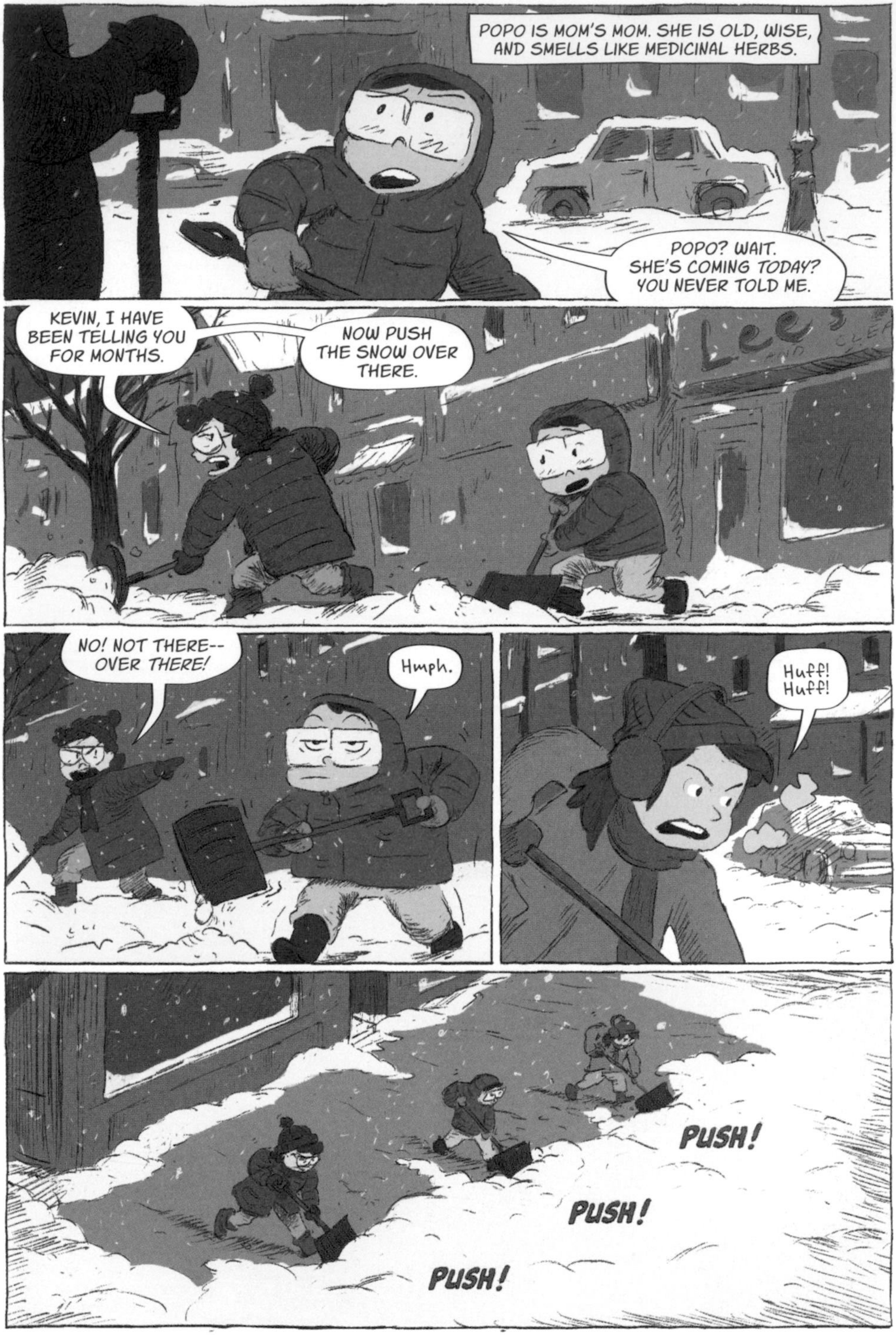
POPO IS MOM'S MOM. SHE IS OLD, WISE, AND SMELLS LIKE MEDICINAL HERBS.
POPO? WAIT. SHE'S COMING *TODAY*? YOU NEVER TOLD ME.
KEVIN, I HAVE BEEN TELLING YOU FOR MONTHS.
NOW PUSH THE SNOW OVER THERE.
Lee's
NO! NOT THERE-- OVER THERE!
Hmph.
Huff! Huff!
PUSH!
PUSH!
PUSH!

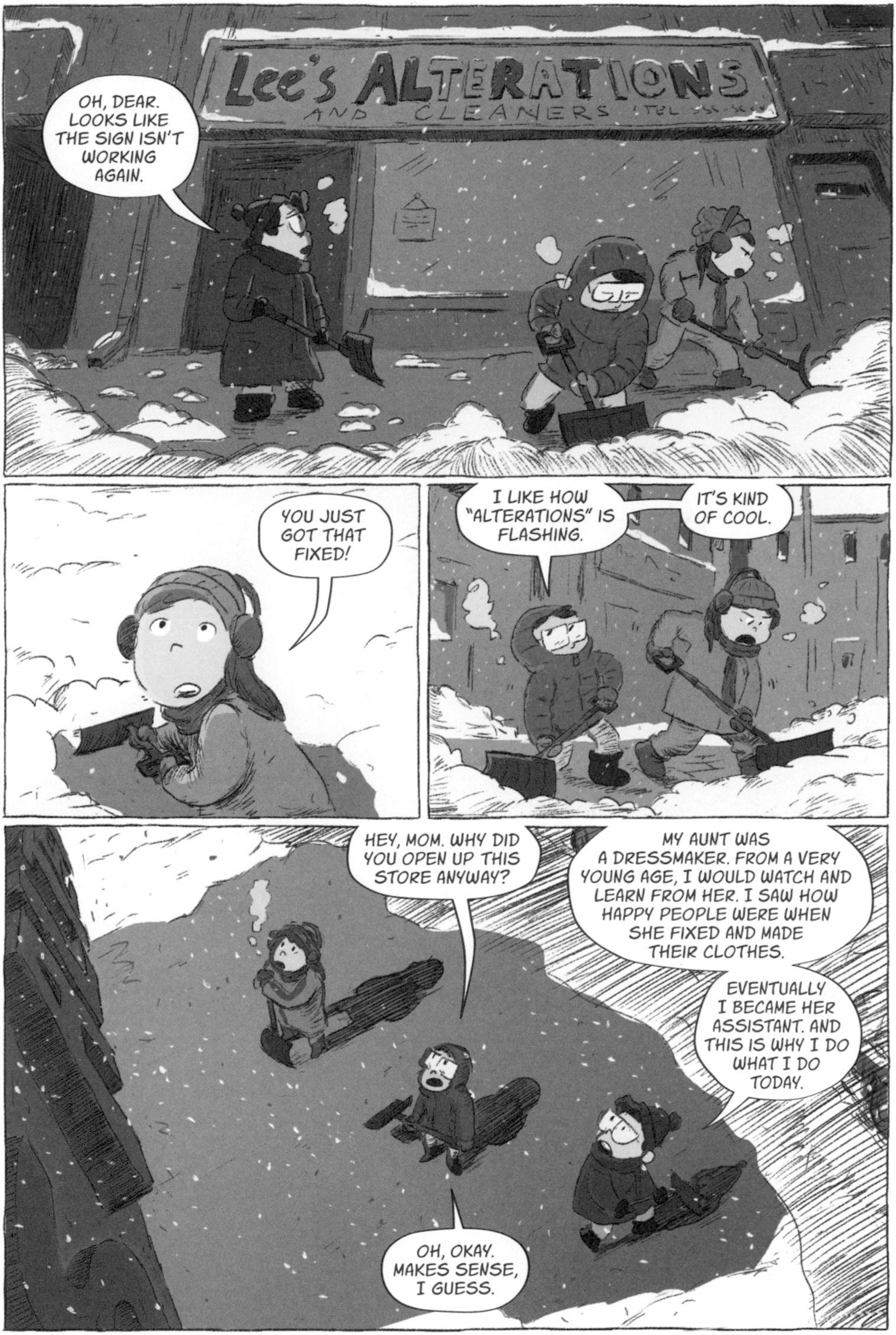
Lee's ALTERATIONS AND CLEANERS TEL
OH, DEAR. LOOKS LIKE THE SIGN ISN'T WORKING AGAIN.
YOU JUST GOT THAT FIXED!
I LIKE HOW "ALTERATIONS" IS FLASHING.
IT'S KIND OF COOL.
HEY, MOM. WHY DID YOU OPEN UP THIS STORE ANYWAY?
MY AUNT WAS A DRESSMAKER. FROM A VERY YOUNG AGE, I WOULD WATCH AND LEARN FROM HER. I SAW HOW HAPPY PEOPLE WERE WHEN SHE FIXED AND MADE THEIR CLOTHES.
EVENTUALLY I BECAME HER ASSISTANT. AND THIS IS WHY I DO WHAT I DO TODAY.
OH, OKAY. MAKES SENSE, I GUESS.

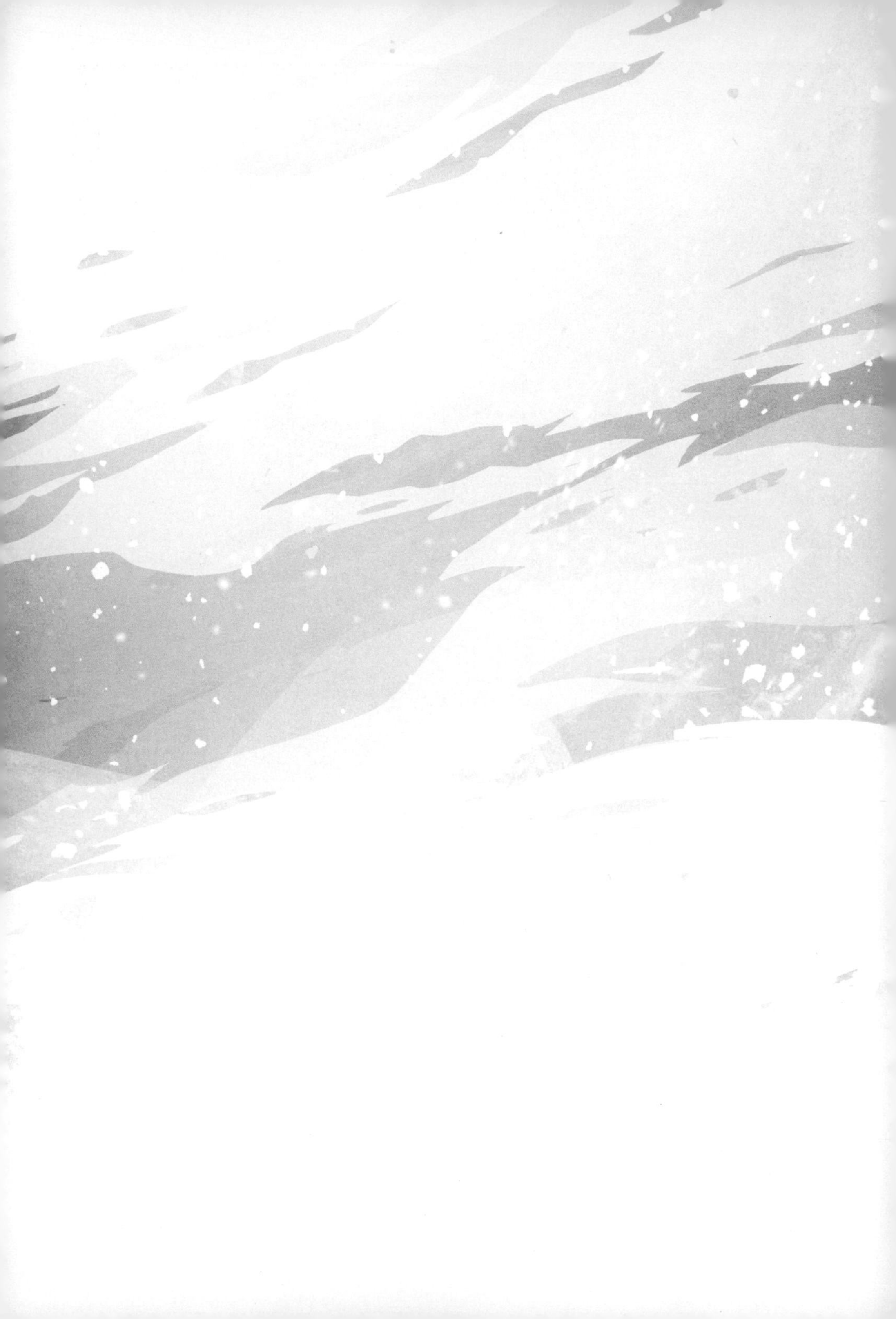

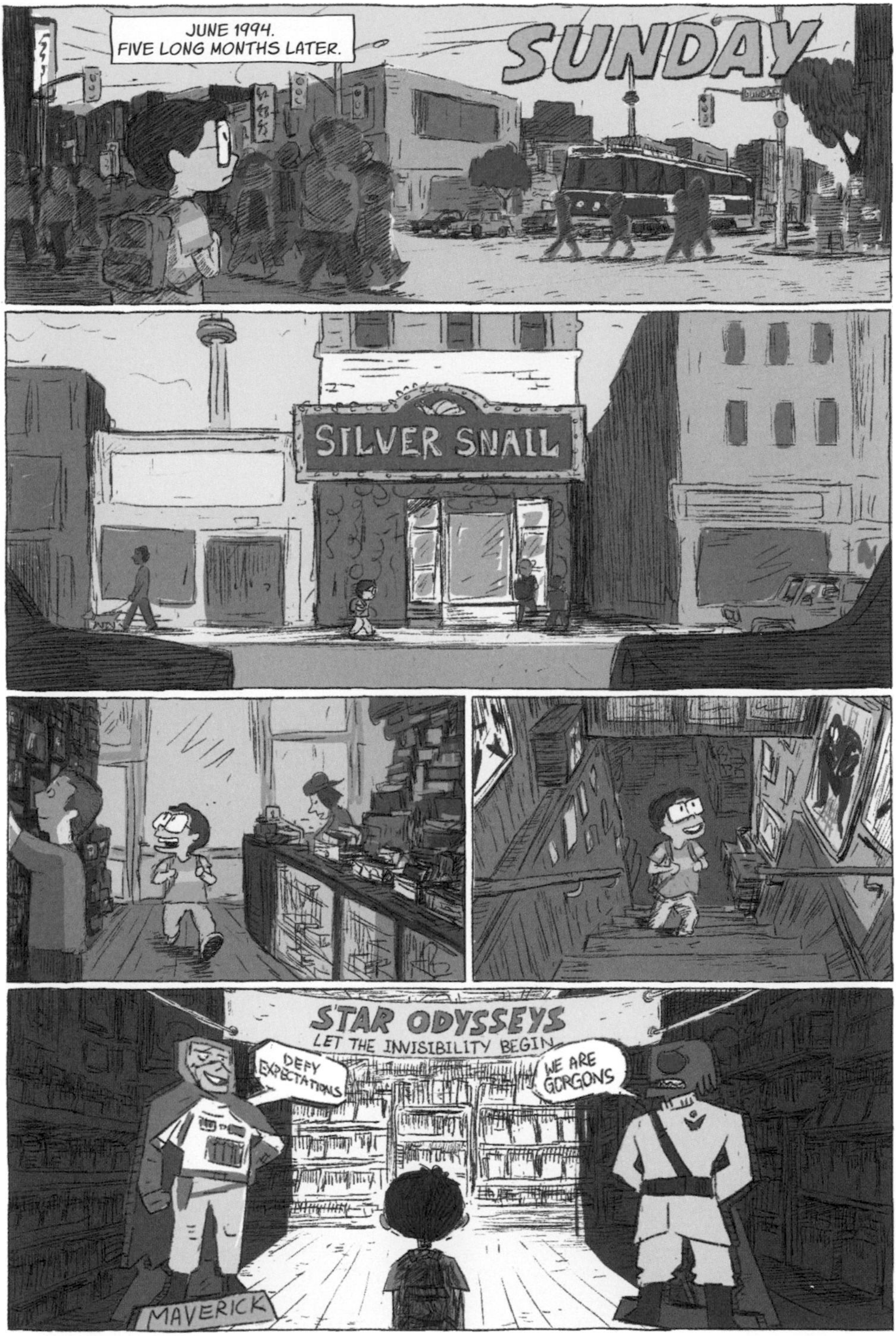
JUNE 1994.
FIVE LONG MONTHS LATER.
SUNDAY
SILVER SNAIL
STAR ODYSSEYS
LET THE INVISIBILITY BEGIN
DEFY EXPECTATIONS
WE ARE GORGONS
MAVERICK

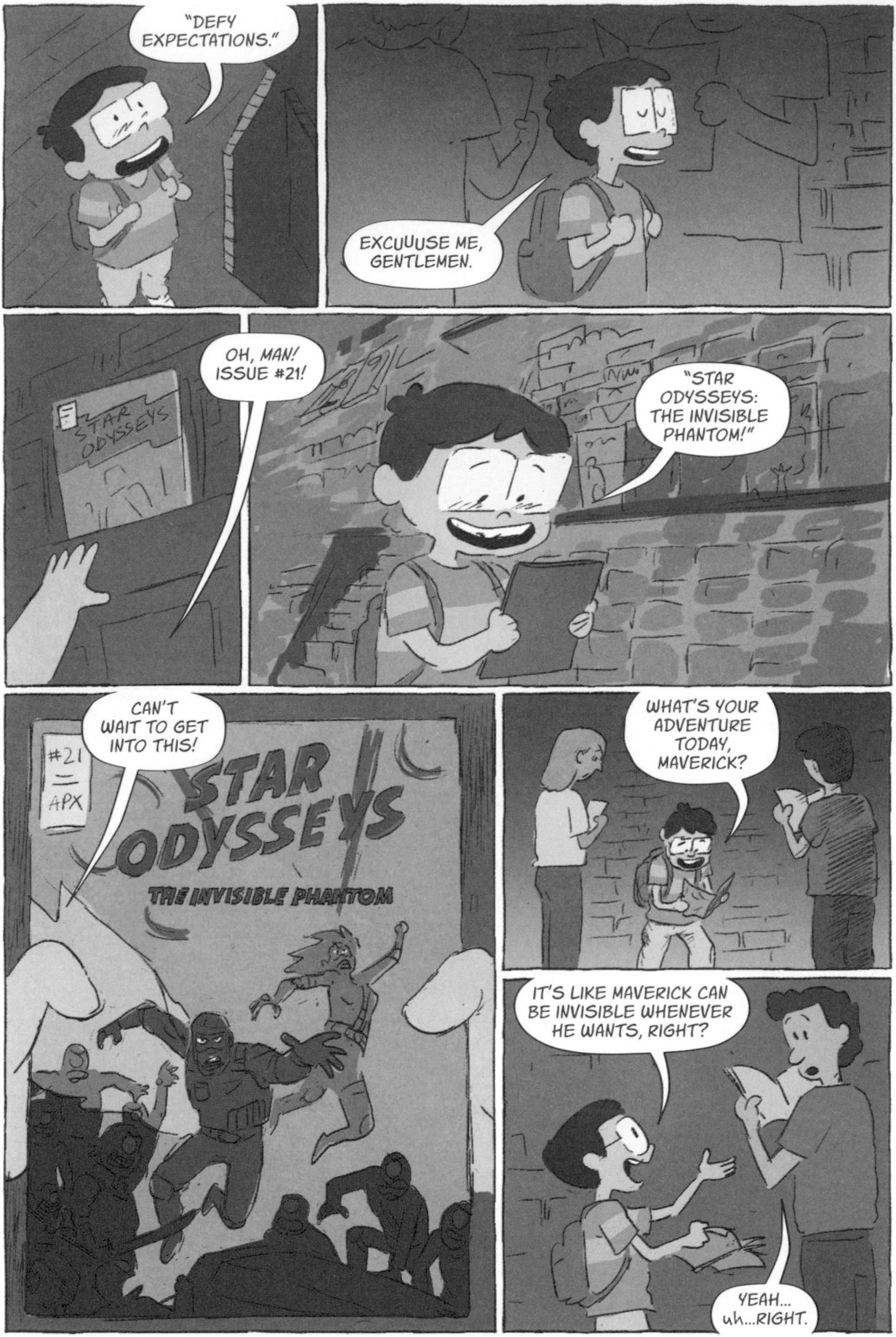
"DEFY EXPECTATIONS."
EXCUUUSE ME, GENTLEMEN.
STAR ODYSSEYS
OH, MAN! ISSUE #21!
"STAR ODYSSEYS: THE INVISIBLE PHANTOM!"
CAN'T WAIT TO GET INTO THIS!
#21
APX
STAR ODYSSEYS
THE INVISIBLE PHANTOM
WHAT'S YOUR ADVENTURE TODAY, MAVERICK?
IT'S LIKE MAVERICK CAN BE INVISIBLE WHENEVER HE WANTS, RIGHT?
YEAH... uh...RIGHT.

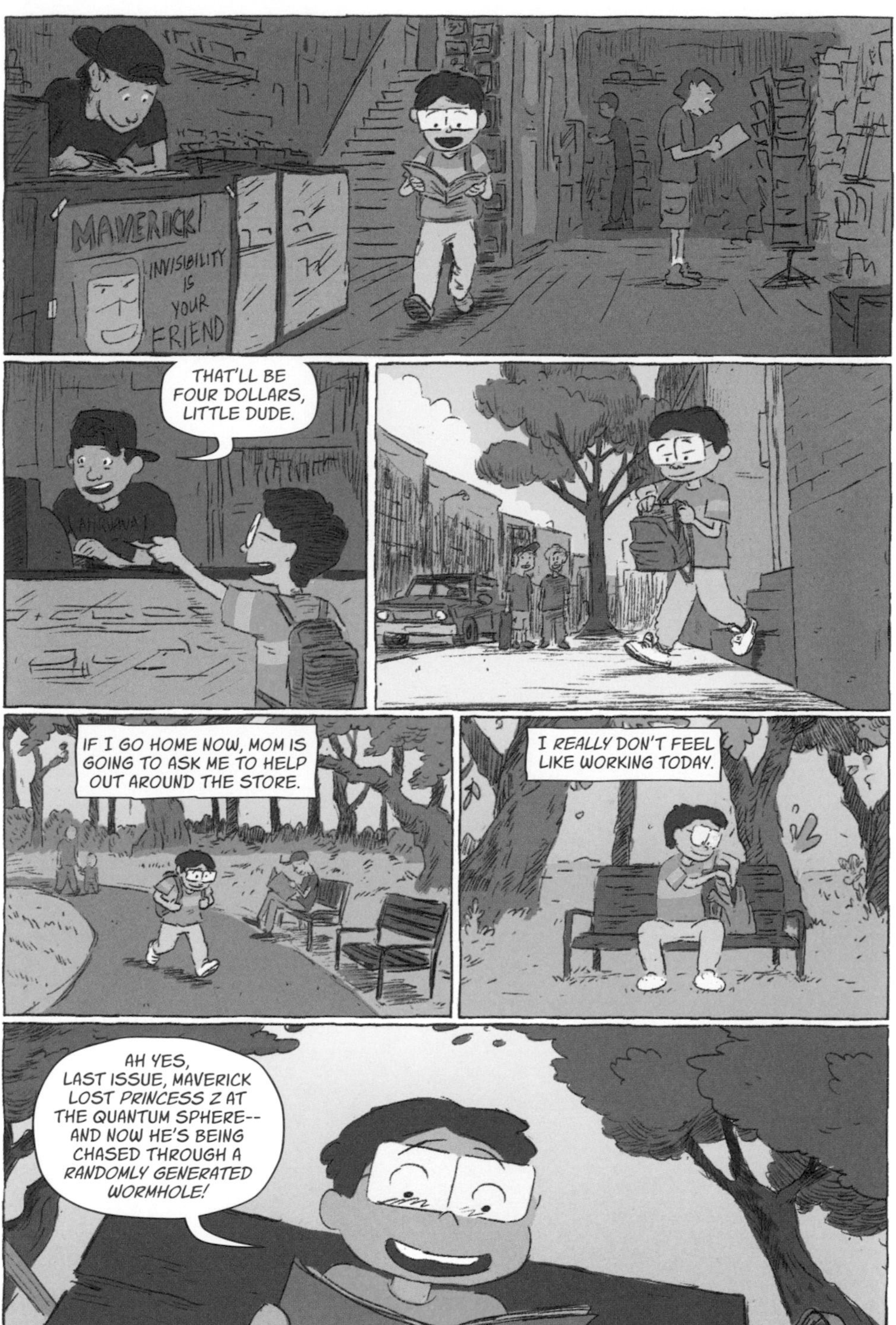
MAVERICK
INVISIBILITY IS YOUR FRIEND
THAT'LL BE FOUR DOLLARS, LITTLE DUDE.
IF I GO HOME NOW, MOM IS GOING TO ASK ME TO HELP OUT AROUND THE STORE.
I *REALLY* DON'T FEEL LIKE WORKING TODAY.
AH YES, LAST ISSUE, MAVERICK LOST *PRINCESS Z* AT THE QUANTUM SPHERE-- AND NOW HE'S BEING CHASED THROUGH A *RANDOMLY GENERATED* WORMHOLE!

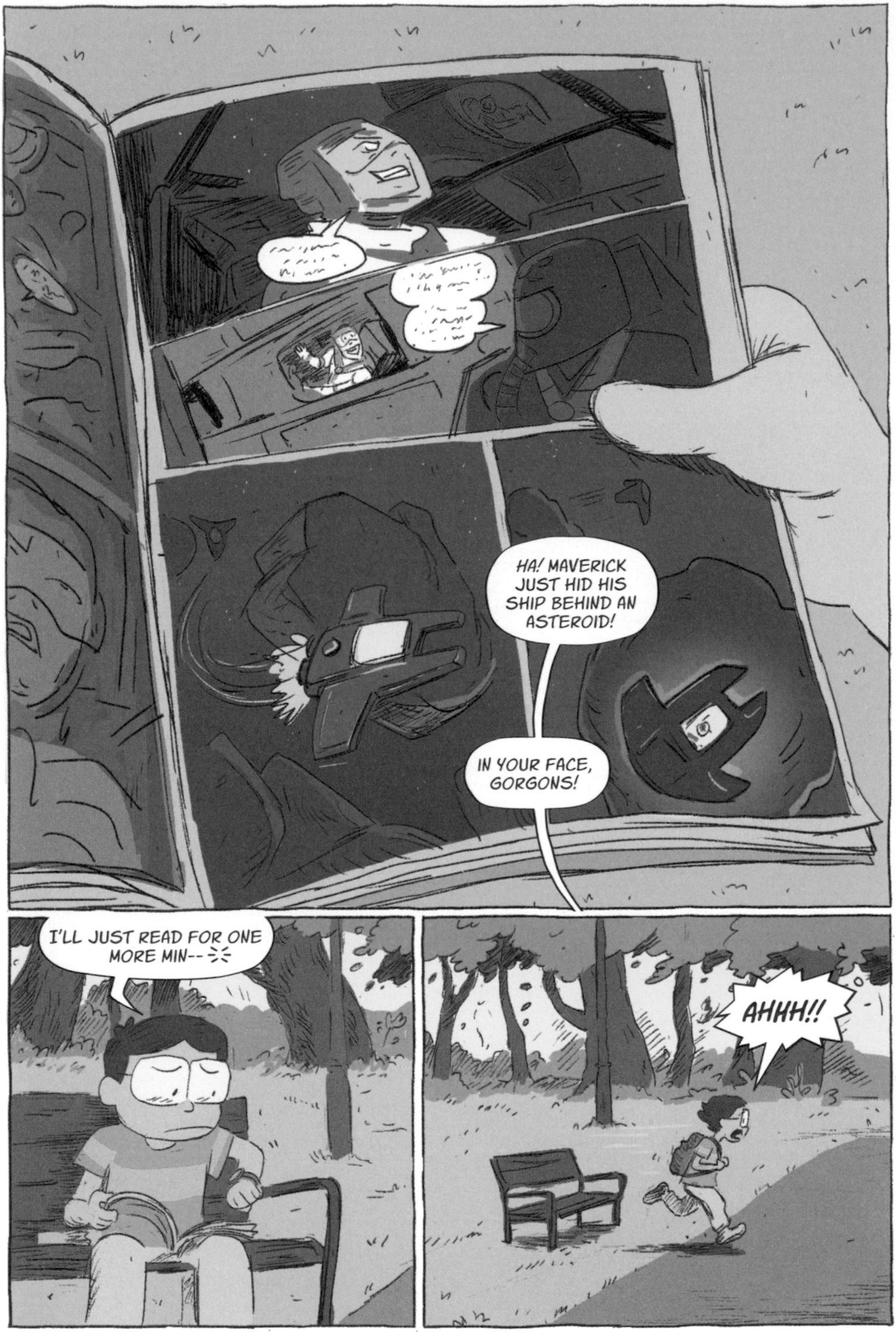

HA! MAVERICK JUST HID HIS SHIP BEHIND AN ASTEROID!
IN YOUR FACE, GORGONS!
I'LL JUST READ FOR ONE MORE MIN--
AHHH!!

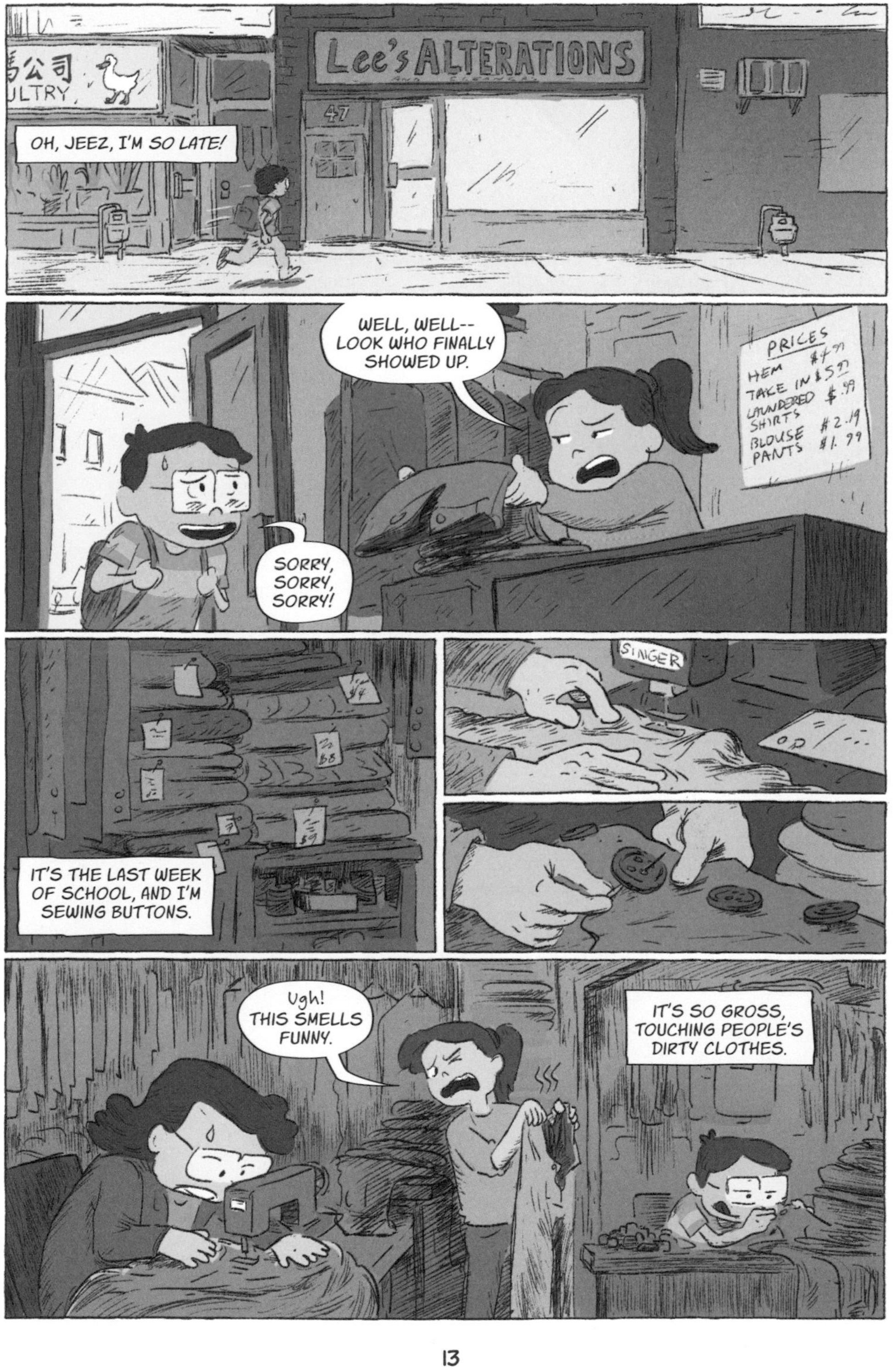
Lee's ALTERATIONS
47
OH, JEEZ, I'M SO LATE!
WELL, WELL-- LOOK WHO FINALLY SHOWED UP.
PRICES
HEM $4.97
TAKE IN $5.97
LAUNDERED SHIRTS $.99
BLOUSE $2.19
PANTS $1.99
SORRY, SORRY, SORRY!
SINGER
IT'S THE LAST WEEK OF SCHOOL, AND I'M SEWING BUTTONS.
Ugh! THIS SMELLS FUNNY.
IT'S SO GROSS, TOUCHING PEOPLE'S DIRTY CLOTHES.

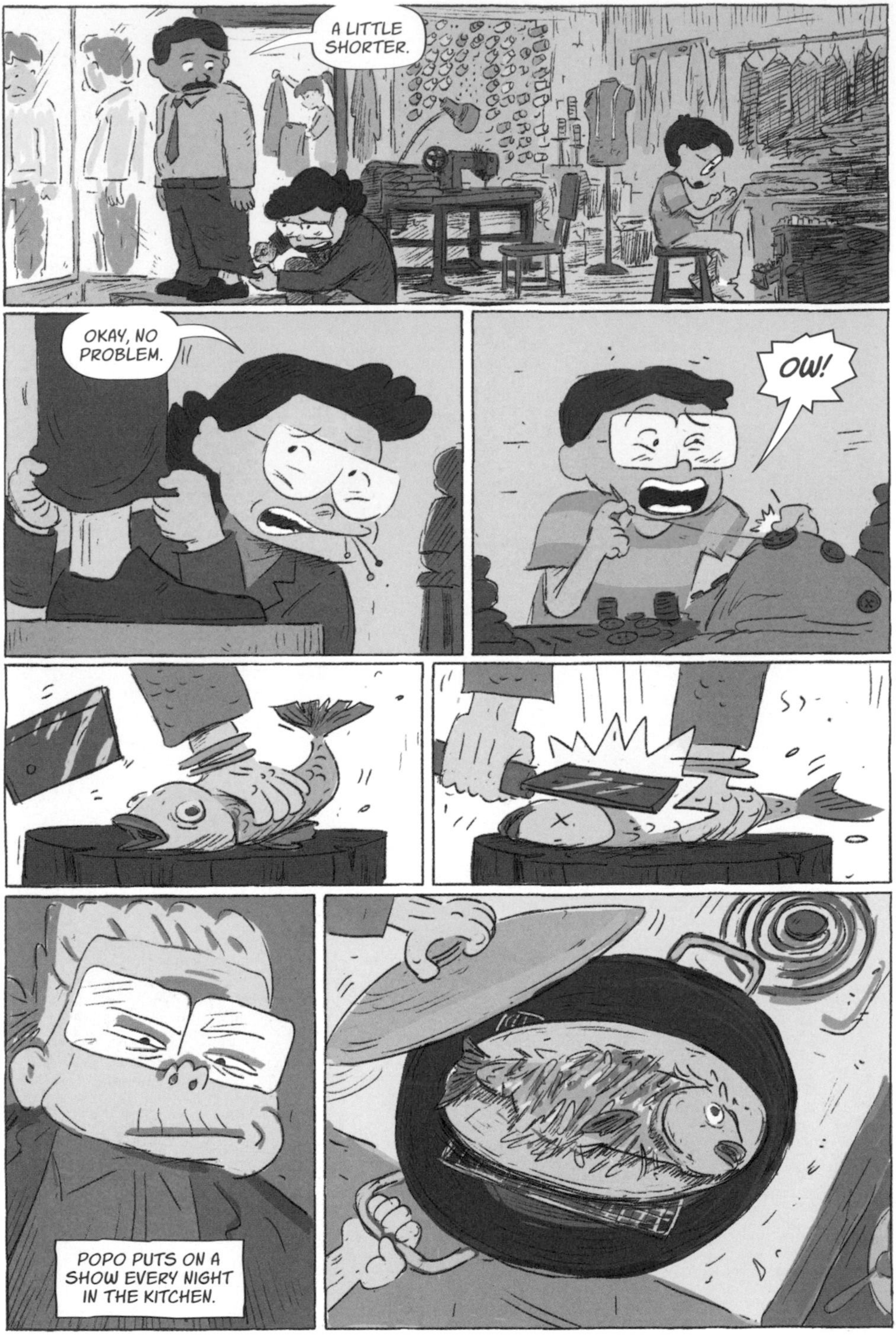
A LITTLE SHORTER.
OKAY, NO PROBLEM.
OW!
POPO PUTS ON A SHOW EVERY NIGHT IN THE KITCHEN.

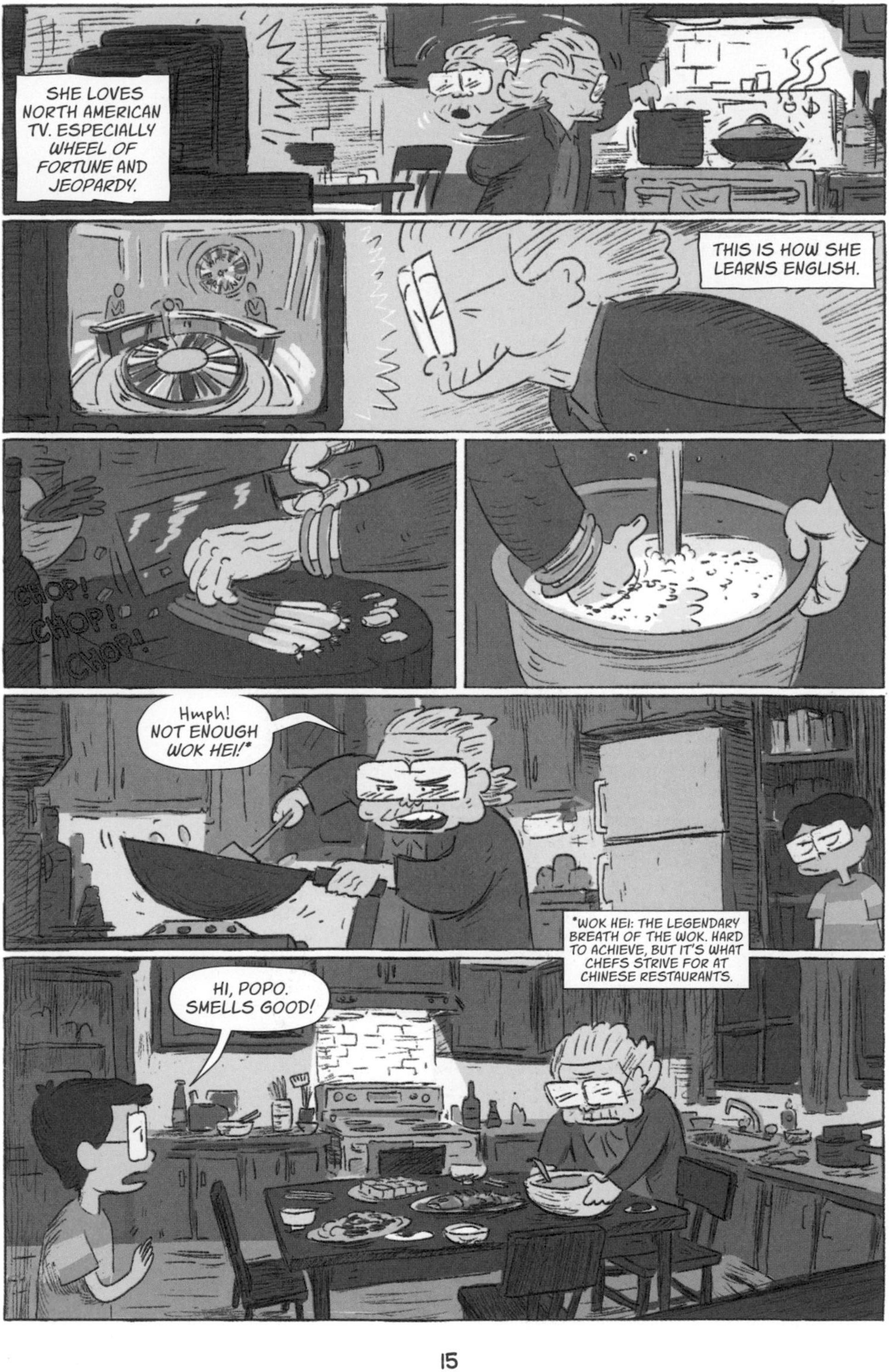
SHE LOVES NORTH AMERICAN TV. ESPECIALLY *WHEEL OF FORTUNE* AND *JEOPARDY*.
THIS IS HOW SHE LEARNS ENGLISH.
CHOP! CHOP! CHOP!
Hmph! NOT ENOUGH *WOK HEI!**
*WOK HEI: THE LEGENDARY BREATH OF THE WOK. HARD TO ACHIEVE, BUT IT'S WHAT CHEFS STRIVE FOR AT CHINESE RESTAURANTS.
HI, POPO. SMELLS GOOD!

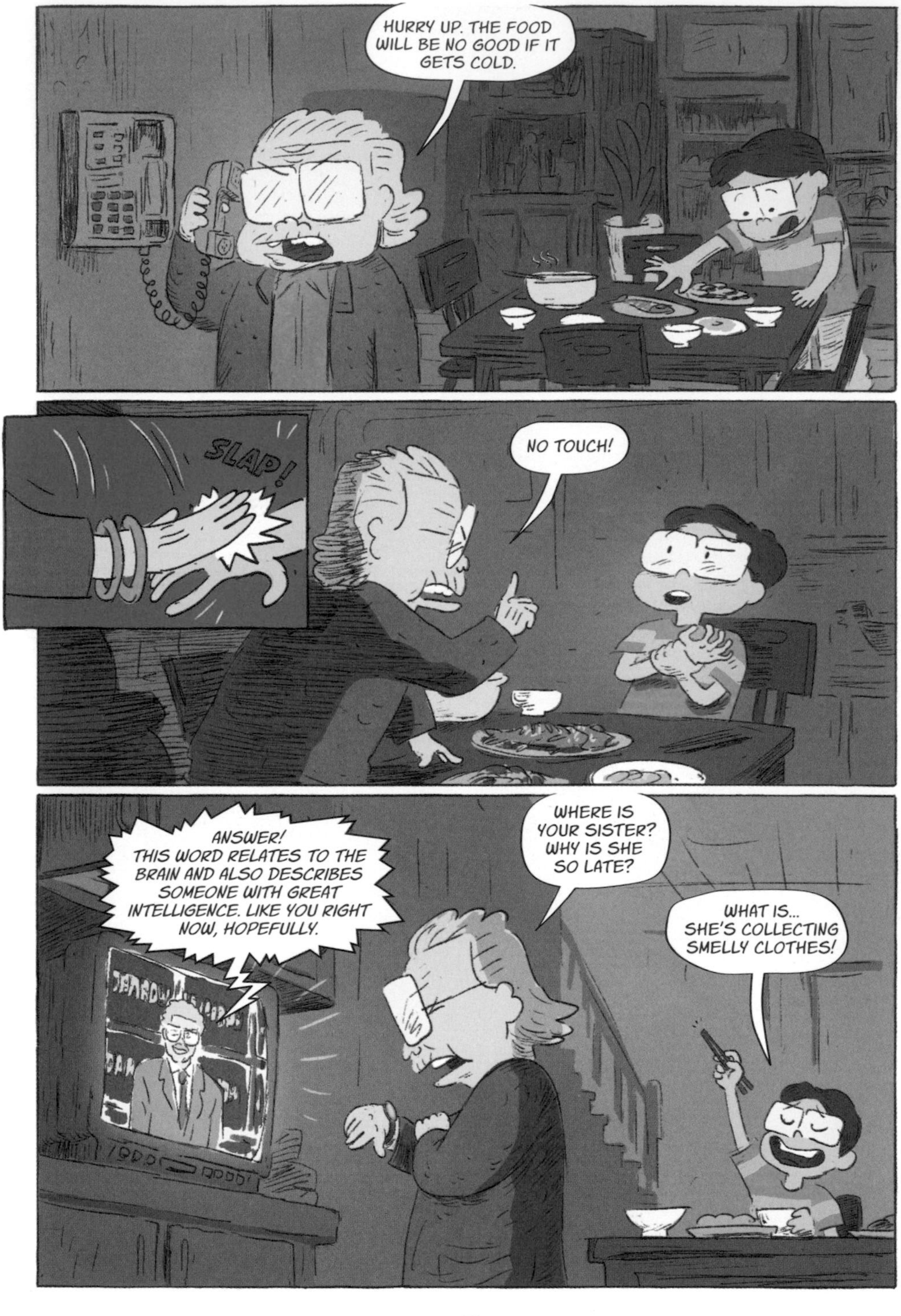
HURRY UP. THE FOOD WILL BE NO GOOD IF IT GETS COLD.
SLAP!
NO TOUCH!
ANSWER! THIS WORD RELATES TO THE BRAIN AND ALSO DESCRIBES SOMEONE WITH GREAT INTELLIGENCE. LIKE YOU RIGHT NOW, HOPEFULLY.
WHERE IS YOUR SISTER? WHY IS SHE SO LATE?
WHAT IS... SHE'S COLLECTING SMELLY CLOTHES!

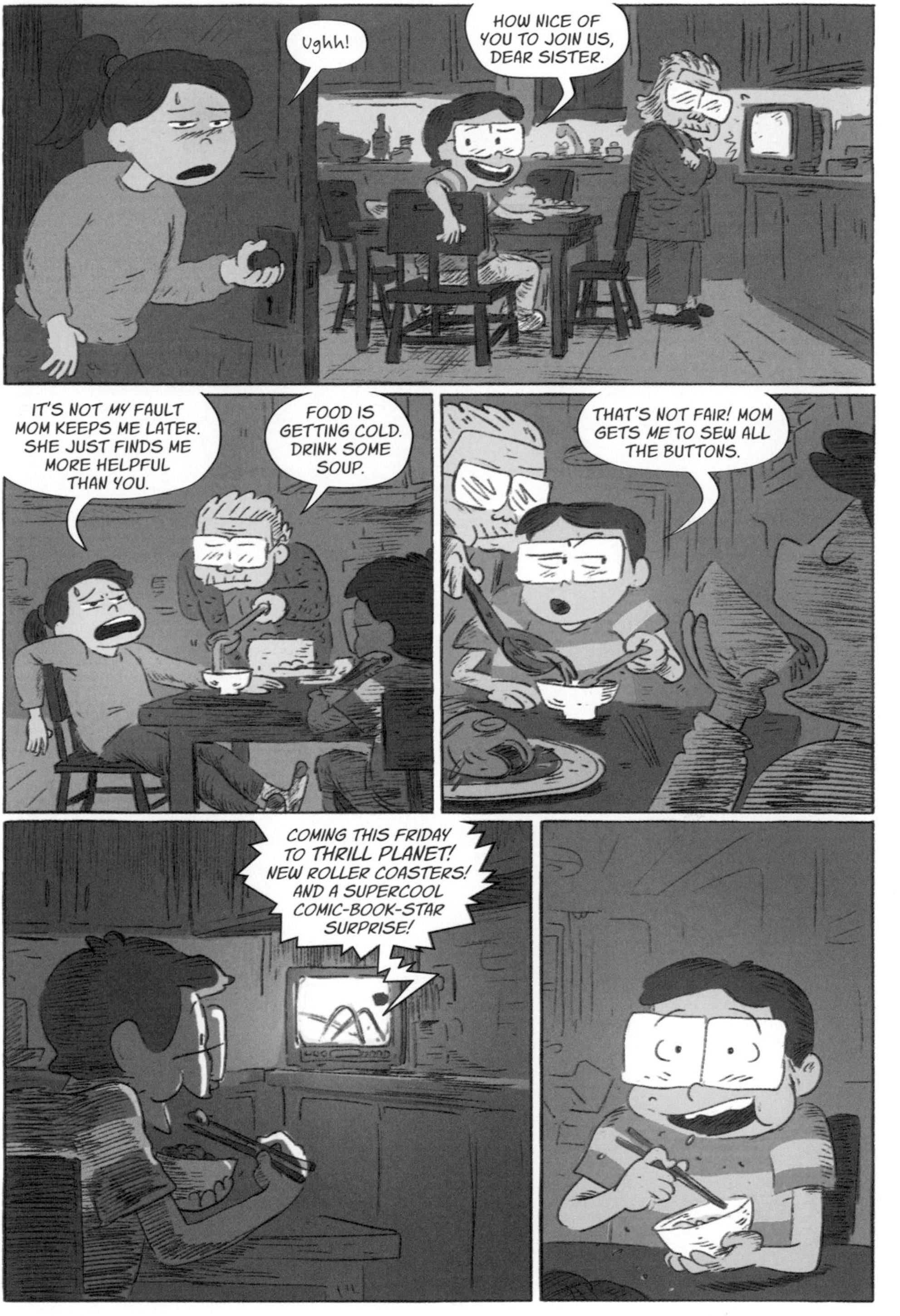

Ughh!
HOW NICE OF YOU TO JOIN US, DEAR SISTER.
IT'S NOT MY FAULT MOM KEEPS ME LATER. SHE JUST FINDS ME MORE HELPFUL THAN YOU.
FOOD IS GETTING COLD. DRINK SOME SOUP.
THAT'S NOT FAIR! MOM GETS ME TO SEW ALL THE BUTTONS.
COMING THIS FRIDAY TO THRILL PLANET! NEW ROLLER COASTERS! AND A SUPERCOOL COMIC-BOOK-STAR SURPRISE!

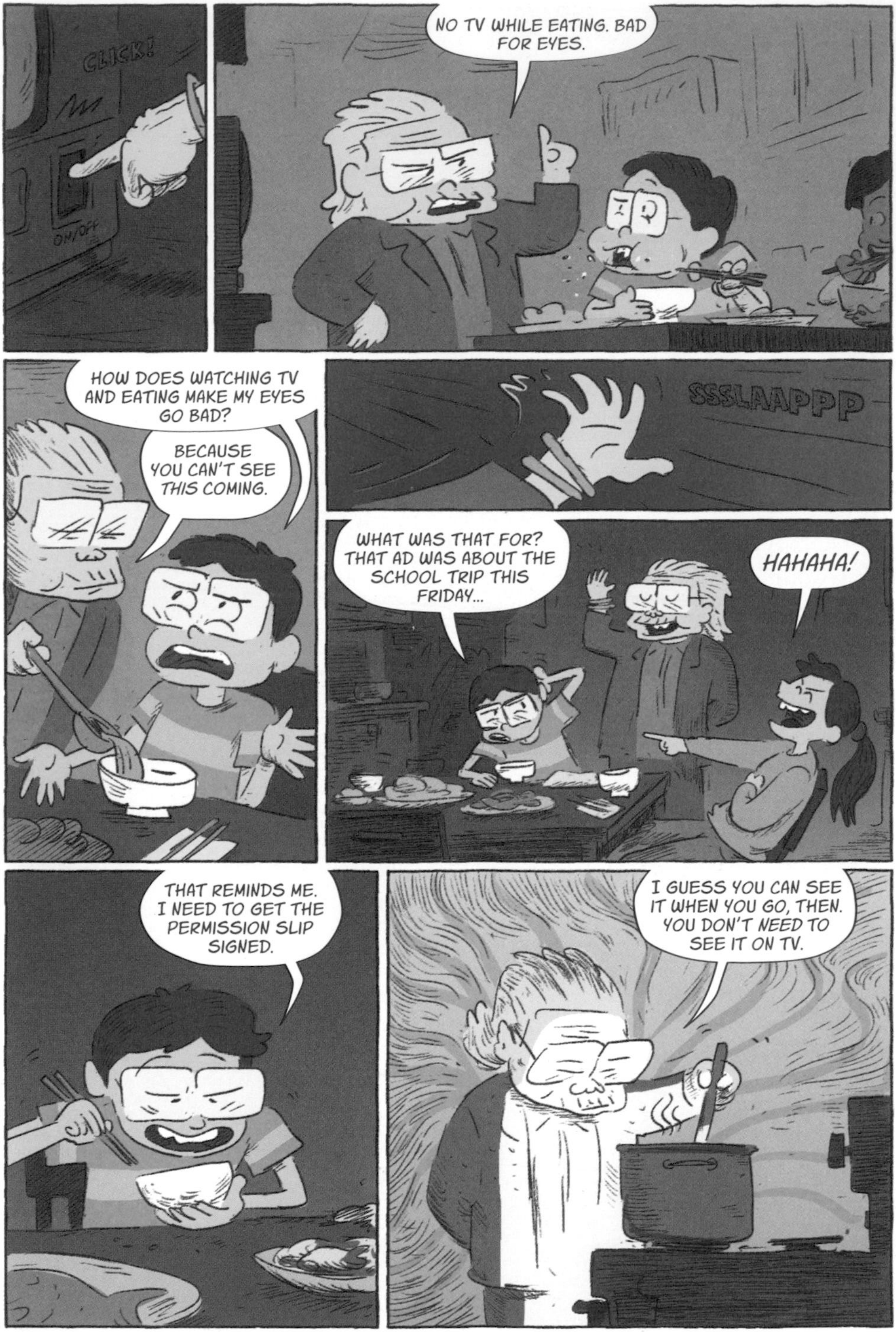
CLICK!
ON/OFF
NO TV WHILE EATING. BAD FOR EYES.
HOW DOES WATCHING TV AND EATING MAKE MY EYES GO BAD?
BECAUSE YOU CAN'T SEE THIS COMING.
SSSLAAPPPP
WHAT WAS THAT FOR? THAT AD WAS ABOUT THE SCHOOL TRIP THIS FRIDAY...
HAHAHA!
THAT REMINDS ME. I NEED TO GET THE PERMISSION SLIP SIGNED.
I GUESS YOU CAN SEE IT WHEN YOU GO, THEN. YOU DON'T NEED TO SEE IT ON TV.

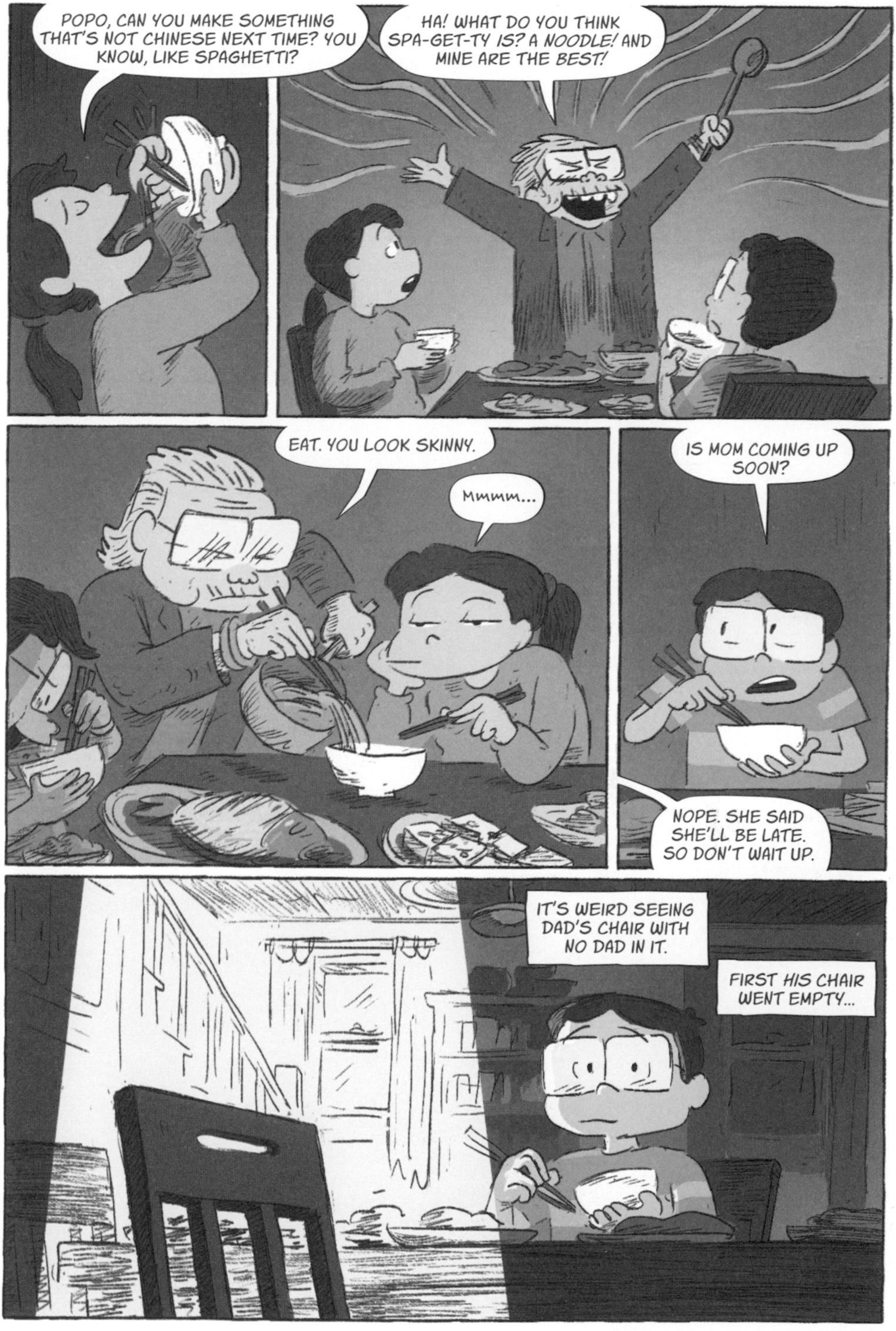
POPO, CAN YOU MAKE SOMETHING THAT'S NOT CHINESE NEXT TIME? YOU KNOW, LIKE SPAGHETTI?
HA! WHAT DO YOU THINK SPA-GET-TY *IS*? A *NOODLE!* AND MINE ARE THE *BEST!*
EAT. YOU LOOK SKINNY.
Mmmm...
IS MOM COMING UP SOON?
NOPE. SHE SAID SHE'LL BE LATE. SO DON'T WAIT UP.
IT'S WEIRD SEEING DAD'S CHAIR WITH NO DAD IN IT.
FIRST *HIS* CHAIR WENT EMPTY...

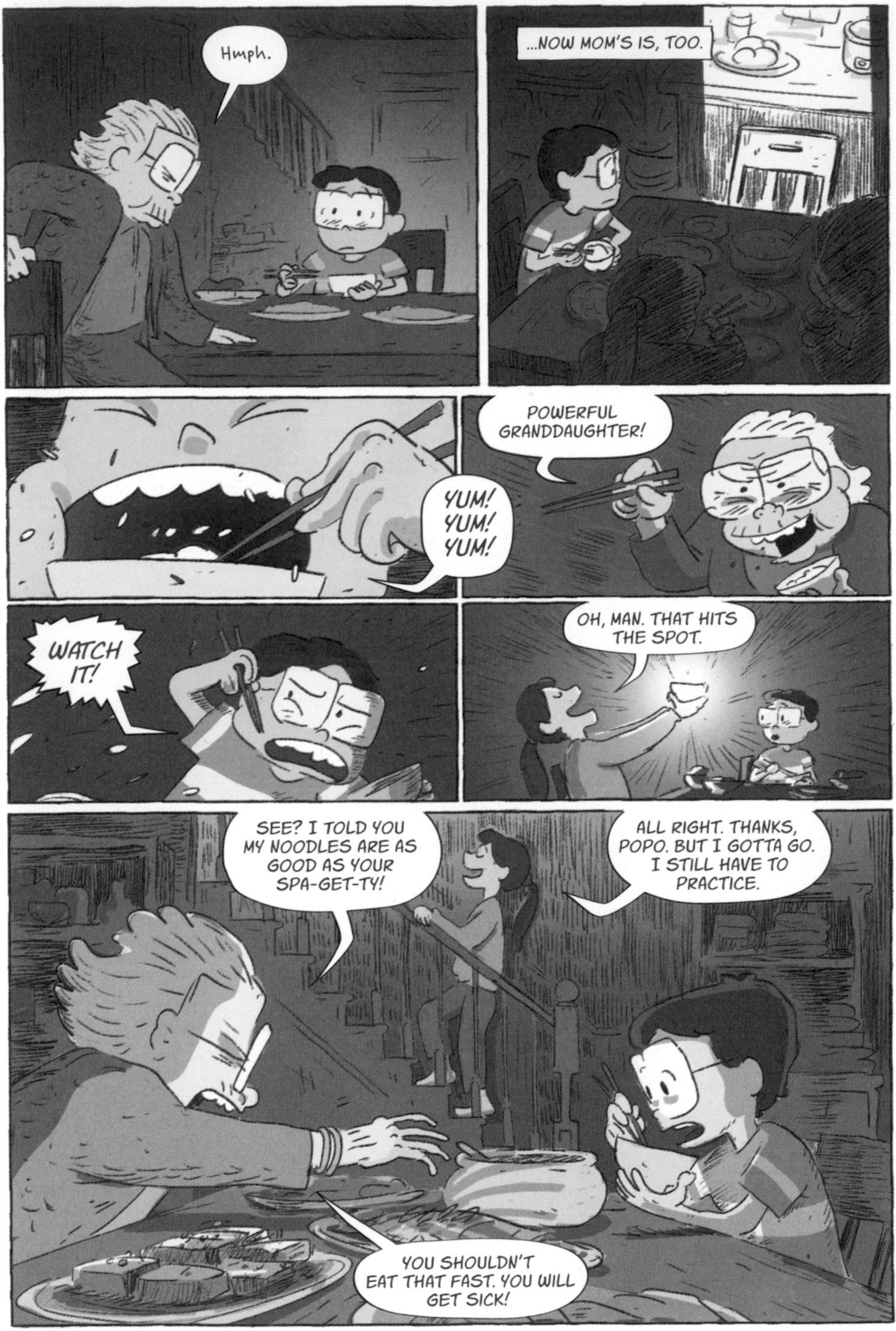
Hmph.
...NOW MOM'S IS, TOO.
YUM! YUM! YUM!
POWERFUL GRANDDAUGHTER!
WATCH IT!
OH, MAN. THAT HITS THE SPOT.
SEE? I TOLD YOU MY NOODLES ARE AS GOOD AS YOUR SPA-GET-TY!
ALL RIGHT. THANKS, POPO. BUT I GOTTA GO. I STILL HAVE TO PRACTICE.
YOU SHOULDN'T EAT THAT FAST. YOU WILL GET SICK!

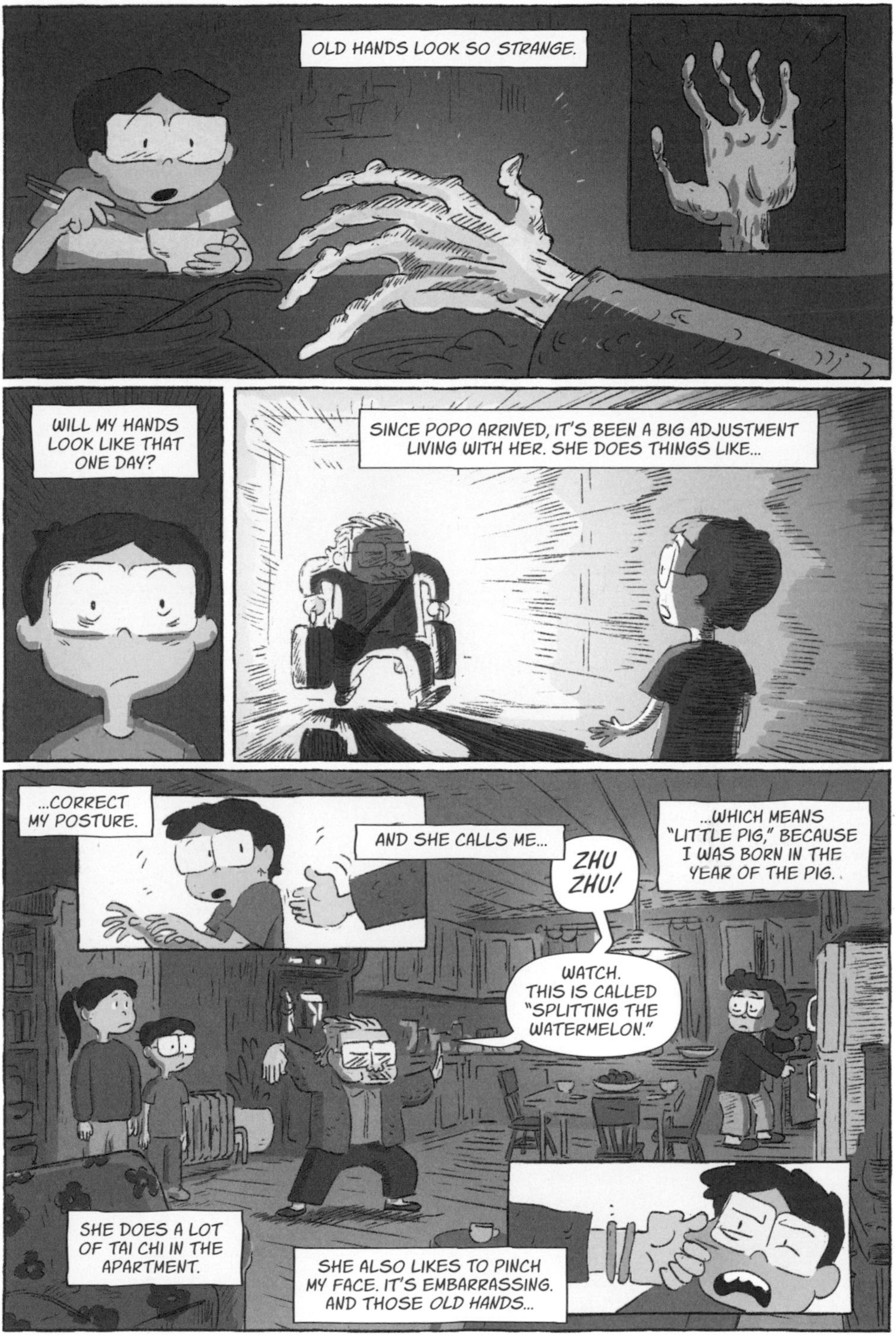
OLD HANDS LOOK SO STRANGE.
WILL MY HANDS LOOK LIKE THAT ONE DAY?
SINCE POPO ARRIVED, IT'S BEEN A BIG ADJUSTMENT LIVING WITH HER. SHE DOES THINGS LIKE...
...CORRECT MY POSTURE.
AND SHE CALLS ME...
ZHU ZHU!
...WHICH MEANS "LITTLE PIG," BECAUSE I WAS BORN IN THE YEAR OF THE PIG.
WATCH. THIS IS CALLED "SPLITTING THE WATERMELON."
SHE DOES A LOT OF TAI CHI IN THE APARTMENT.
SHE ALSO LIKES TO PINCH MY FACE. IT'S EMBARRASSING. AND THOSE OLD HANDS...

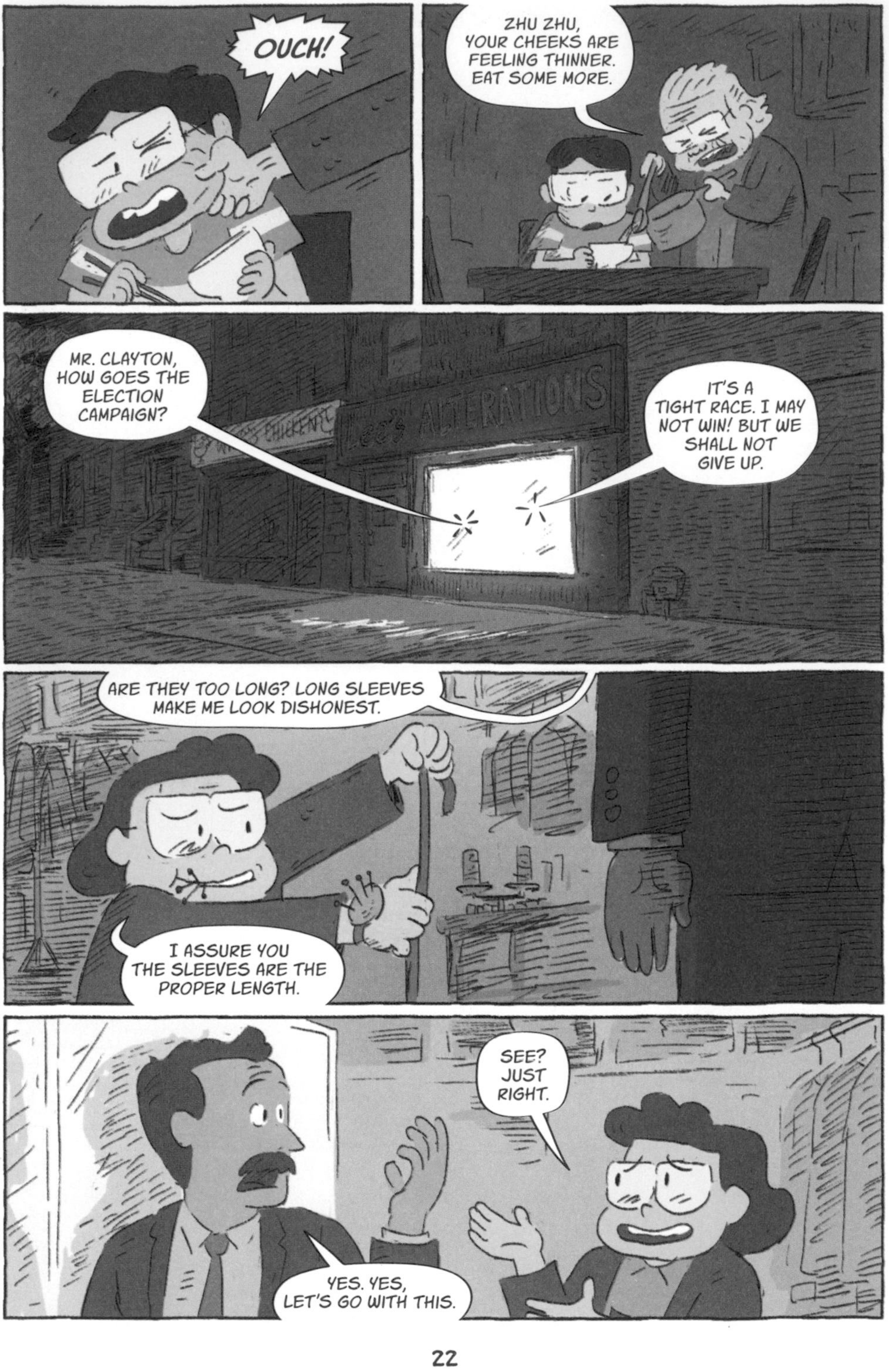
OUCH!
ZHU ZHU, YOUR CHEEKS ARE FEELING THINNER. EAT SOME MORE.
MR. CLAYTON, HOW GOES THE ELECTION CAMPAIGN?
IT'S A TIGHT RACE. I MAY NOT WIN! BUT WE SHALL NOT GIVE UP.
LEE'S ALTERATIONS
ARE THEY TOO LONG? LONG SLEEVES MAKE ME LOOK DISHONEST.
I ASSURE YOU THE SLEEVES ARE THE PROPER LENGTH.
SEE? JUST RIGHT.
YES. YES, LET'S GO WITH THIS.

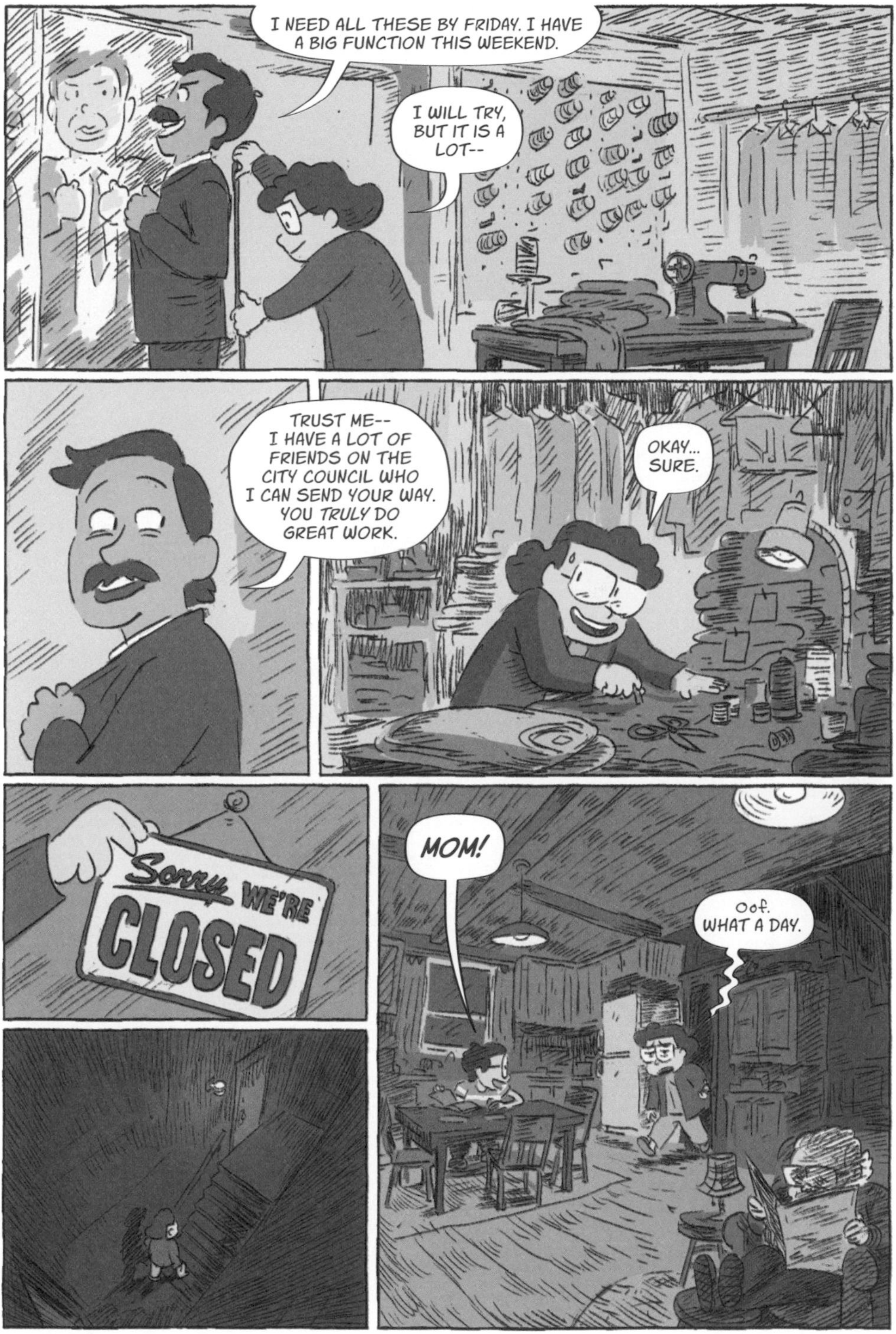
I NEED ALL THESE BY FRIDAY. I HAVE A BIG FUNCTION THIS WEEKEND.
I WILL TRY, BUT IT IS A LOT--
TRUST ME-- I HAVE A LOT OF FRIENDS ON THE CITY COUNCIL WHO I CAN SEND YOUR WAY. YOU *TRULY* DO GREAT WORK.
OKAY... SURE.
Sorry WE'RE CLOSED
MOM!
Oof. WHAT A DAY.

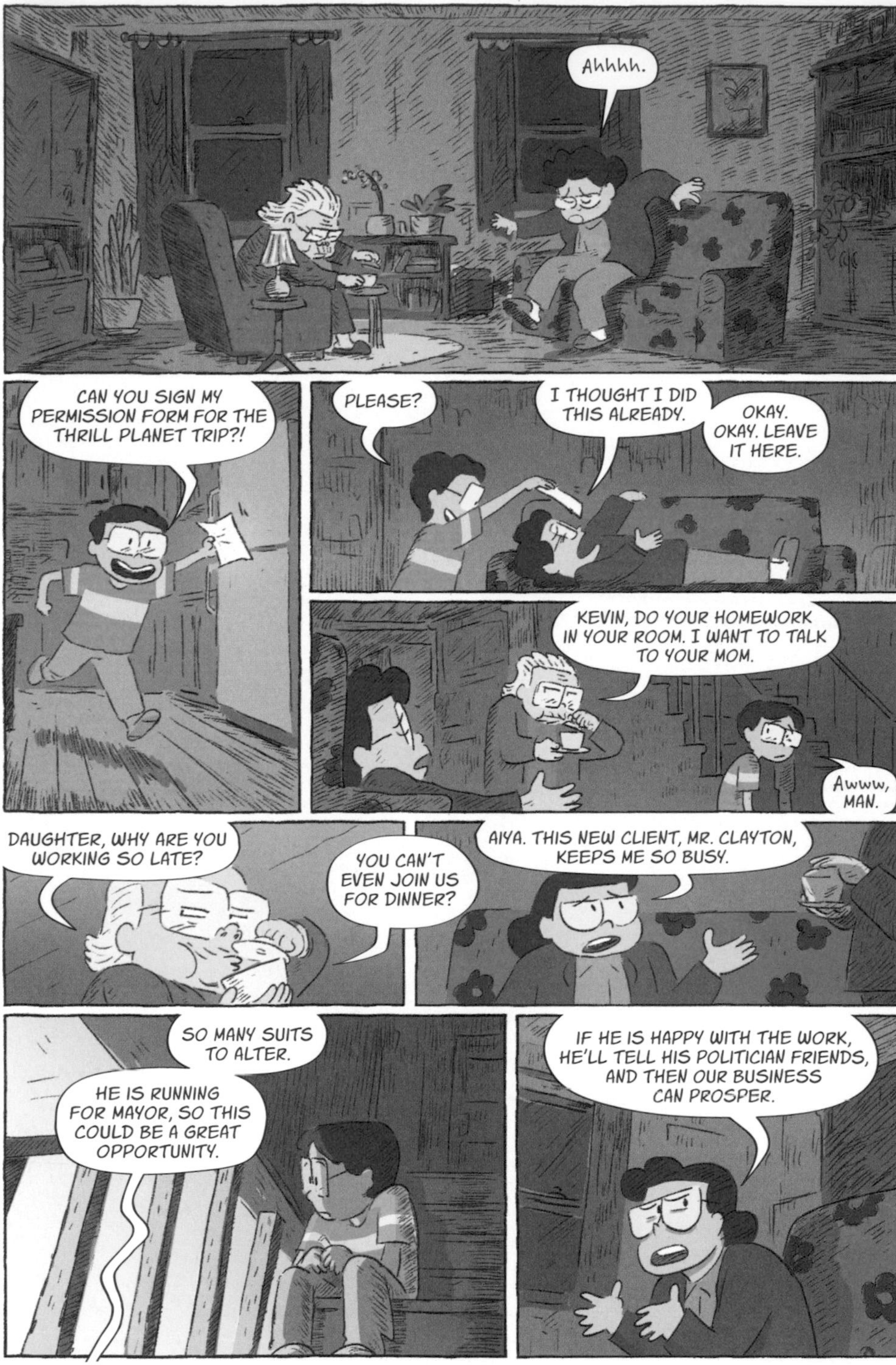
Ahhhh.
CAN YOU SIGN MY PERMISSION FORM FOR THE THRILL PLANET TRIP?!
PLEASE?
I THOUGHT I DID THIS ALREADY.
OKAY. OKAY. LEAVE IT HERE.
KEVIN, DO YOUR HOMEWORK IN YOUR ROOM. I WANT TO TALK TO YOUR MOM.
Awww, MAN.
DAUGHTER, WHY ARE YOU WORKING SO LATE?
YOU CAN'T EVEN JOIN US FOR DINNER?
AIYA. THIS NEW CLIENT, MR. CLAYTON, KEEPS ME SO BUSY.
SO MANY SUITS TO ALTER.
HE IS RUNNING FOR MAYOR, SO THIS COULD BE A GREAT OPPORTUNITY.
IF HE IS HAPPY WITH THE WORK, HE'LL TELL HIS POLITICIAN FRIENDS, AND THEN OUR BUSINESS CAN PROSPER.

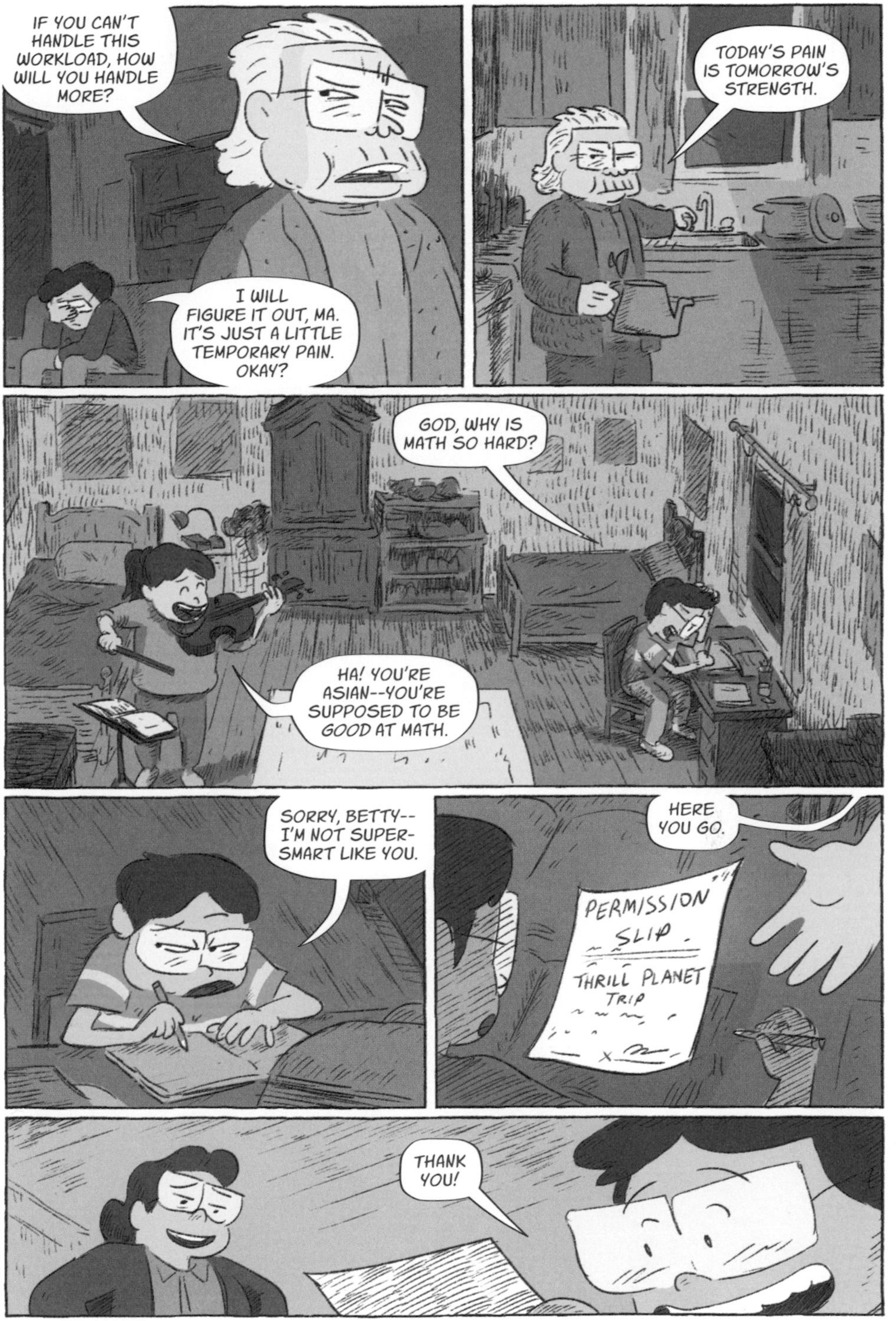
IF YOU CAN'T HANDLE THIS WORKLOAD, HOW WILL YOU HANDLE MORE?
I WILL FIGURE IT OUT, MA. IT'S JUST A LITTLE TEMPORARY PAIN. OKAY?
TODAY'S PAIN IS TOMORROW'S STRENGTH.
GOD, WHY IS MATH SO HARD?
HA! YOU'RE ASIAN--YOU'RE SUPPOSED TO BE GOOD AT MATH.
SORRY, BETTY--I'M NOT SUPER-SMART LIKE YOU.
HERE YOU GO.
PERMISSION SLIP
THRILL PLANET TRIP
THANK YOU!

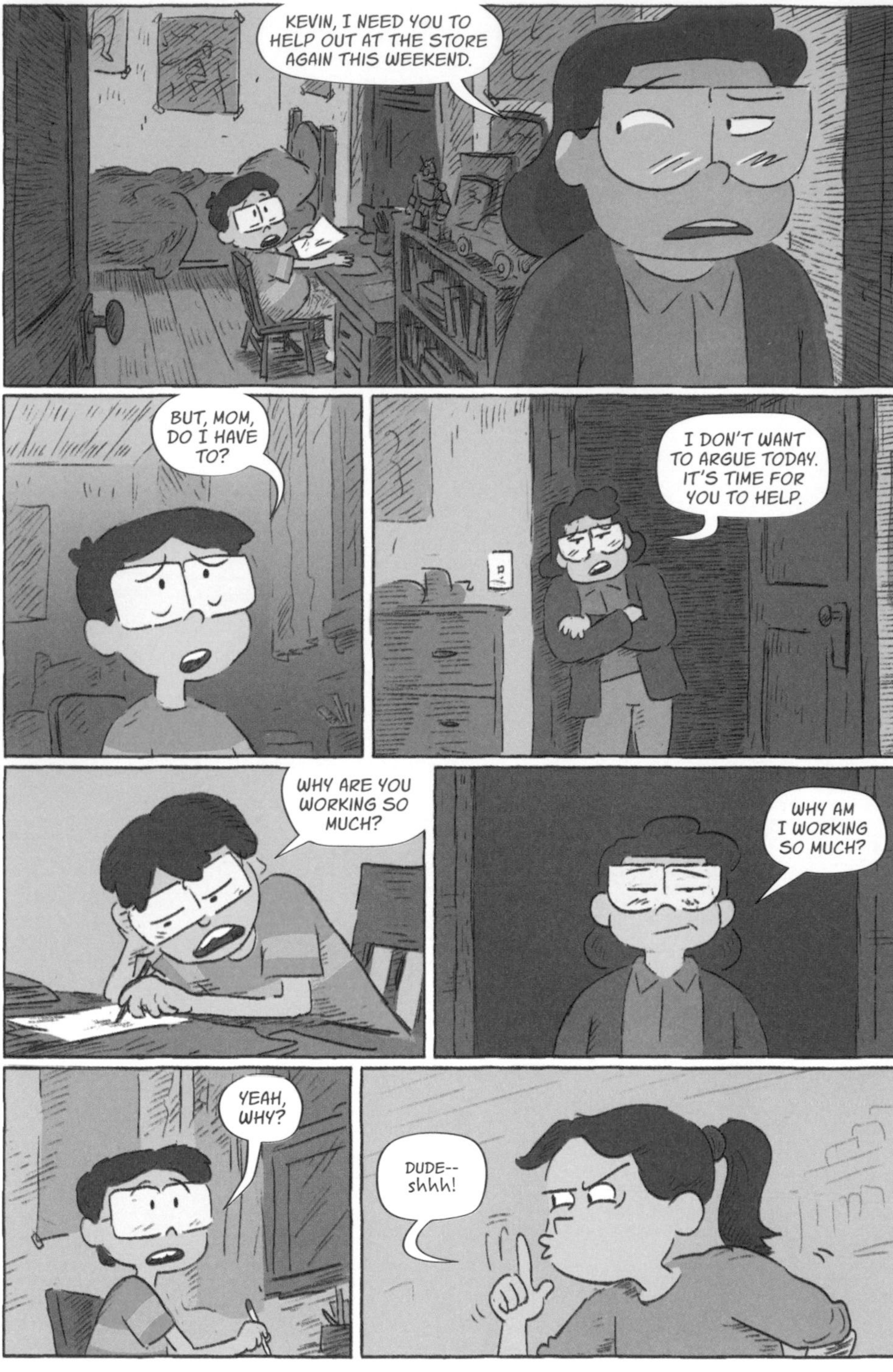
KEVIN, I NEED YOU TO HELP OUT AT THE STORE AGAIN THIS WEEKEND.
BUT, MOM, DO I HAVE TO?
I DON'T WANT TO ARGUE TODAY. IT'S TIME FOR YOU TO HELP.
WHY ARE YOU WORKING SO MUCH?
WHY AM I WORKING SO MUCH?
YEAH, WHY?
DUDE-- shhh!

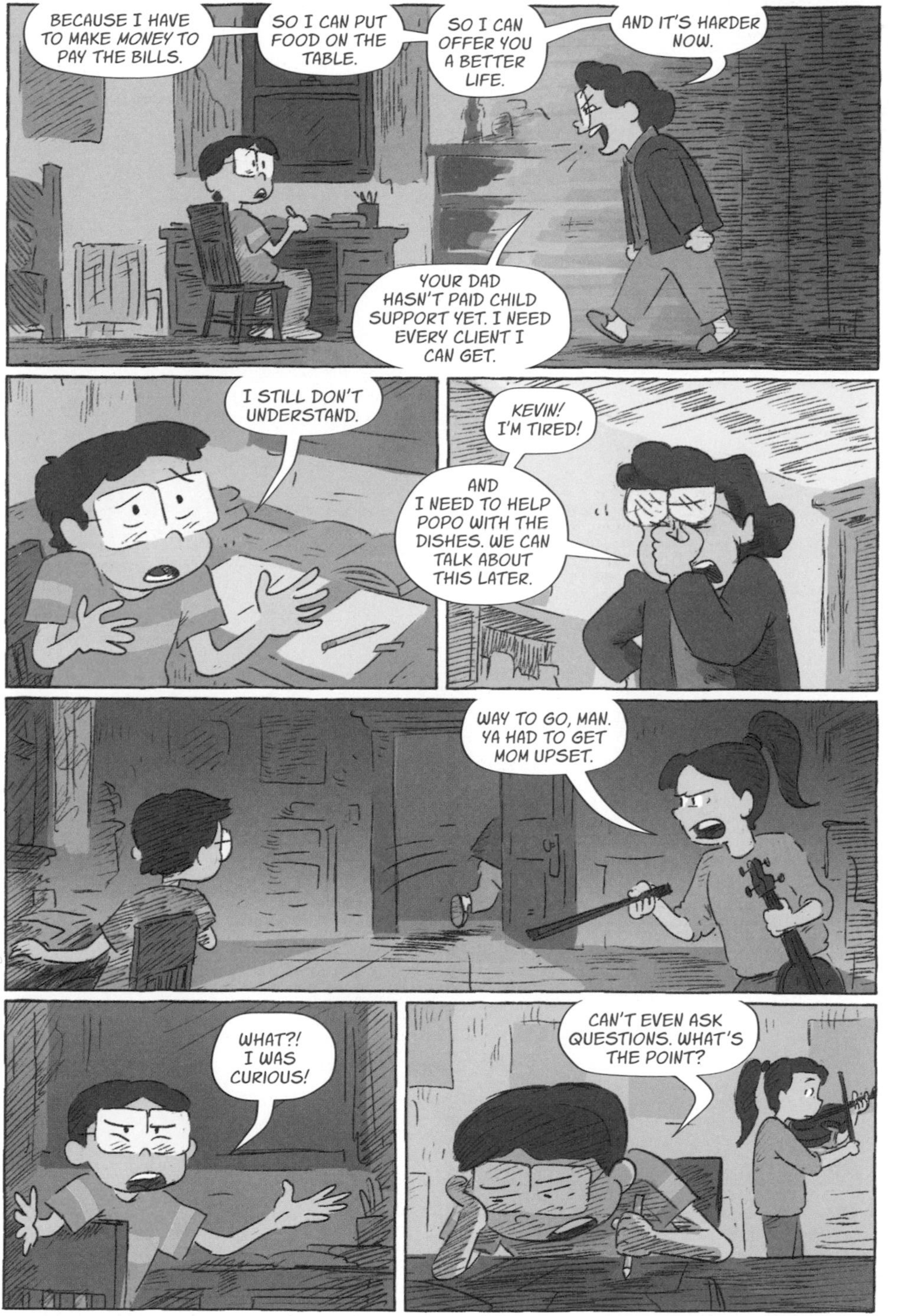

BECAUSE I HAVE TO MAKE MONEY TO PAY THE BILLS.
SO I CAN PUT FOOD ON THE TABLE.
SO I CAN OFFER YOU A BETTER LIFE.
AND IT'S HARDER NOW.
YOUR DAD HASN'T PAID CHILD SUPPORT YET. I NEED EVERY CLIENT I CAN GET.
I STILL DON'T UNDERSTAND.
KEVIN! I'M TIRED!
AND I NEED TO HELP POPO WITH THE DISHES. WE CAN TALK ABOUT THIS LATER.
WAY TO GO, MAN. YA HAD TO GET MOM UPSET.
WHAT?! I WAS CURIOUS!
CAN'T EVEN ASK QUESTIONS. WHAT'S THE POINT?

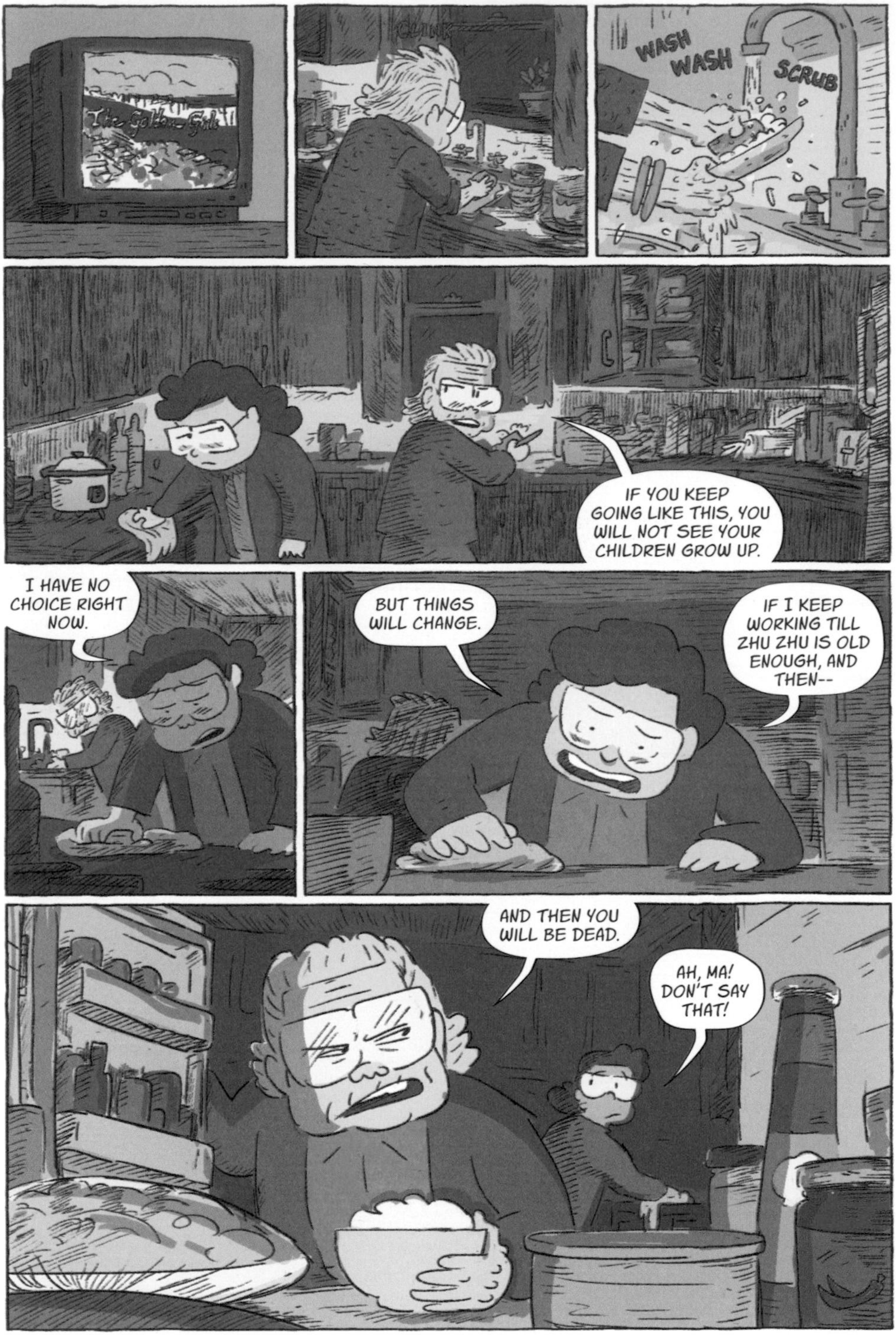
The Golden Girls
CLINK
WASH
WASH
SCRUB
IF YOU KEEP GOING LIKE THIS, YOU WILL NOT SEE YOUR CHILDREN GROW UP.
I HAVE NO CHOICE RIGHT NOW.
BUT THINGS WILL CHANGE.
IF I KEEP WORKING TILL ZHU ZHU IS OLD ENOUGH, AND THEN--
AND THEN YOU WILL BE DEAD.
AH, MA! DON'T SAY THAT!

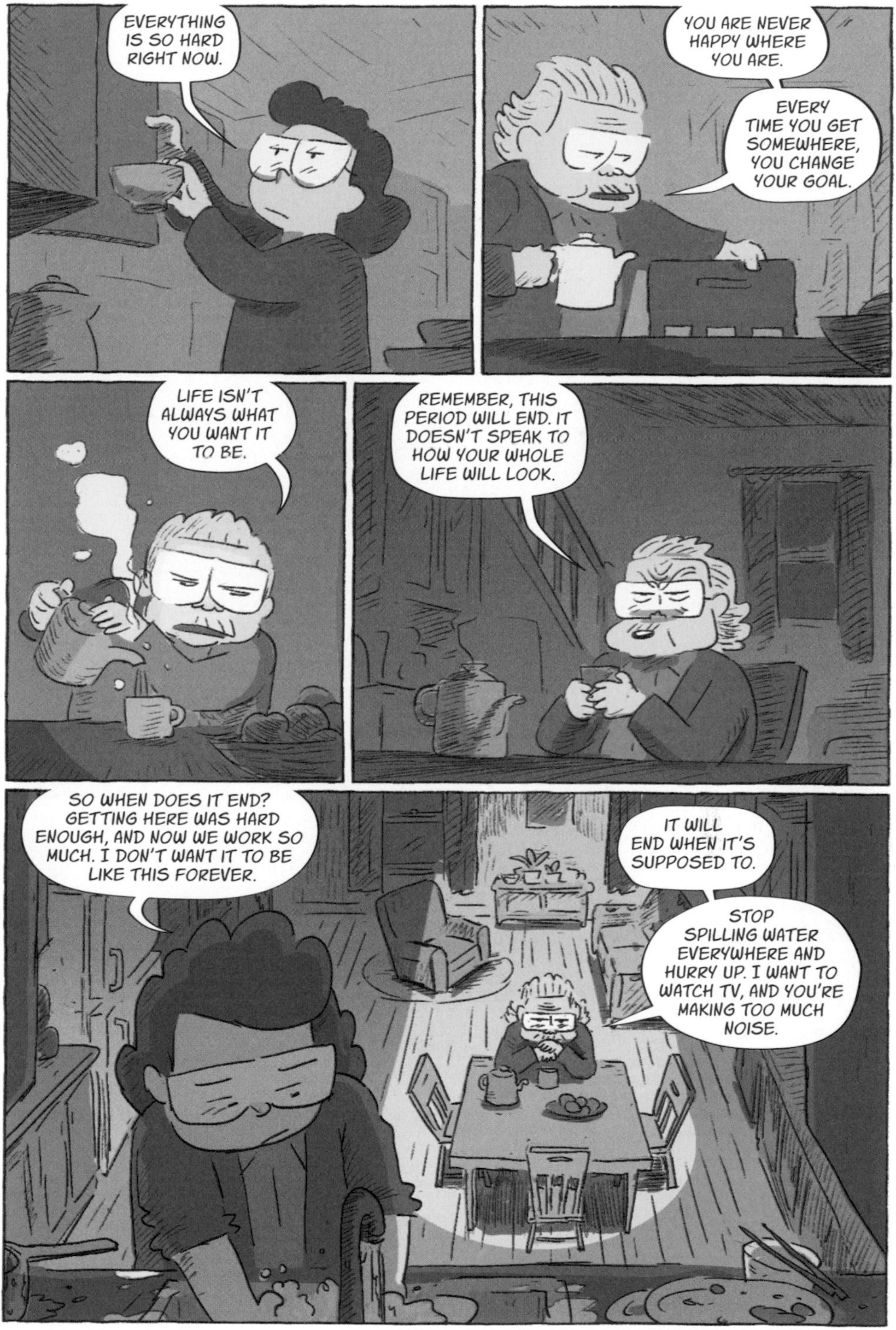
EVERYTHING IS SO HARD RIGHT NOW.
YOU ARE NEVER HAPPY WHERE YOU ARE.
EVERY TIME YOU GET SOMEWHERE, YOU CHANGE YOUR GOAL.
LIFE ISN'T ALWAYS WHAT YOU WANT IT TO BE.
REMEMBER, THIS PERIOD WILL END. IT DOESN'T SPEAK TO HOW YOUR WHOLE LIFE WILL LOOK.
SO WHEN DOES IT END? GETTING HERE WAS HARD ENOUGH, AND NOW WE WORK SO MUCH. I DON'T WANT IT TO BE LIKE THIS FOREVER.
IT WILL END WHEN IT'S SUPPOSED TO.
STOP SPILLING WATER EVERYWHERE AND HURRY UP. I WANT TO WATCH TV, AND YOU'RE MAKING TOO MUCH NOISE.

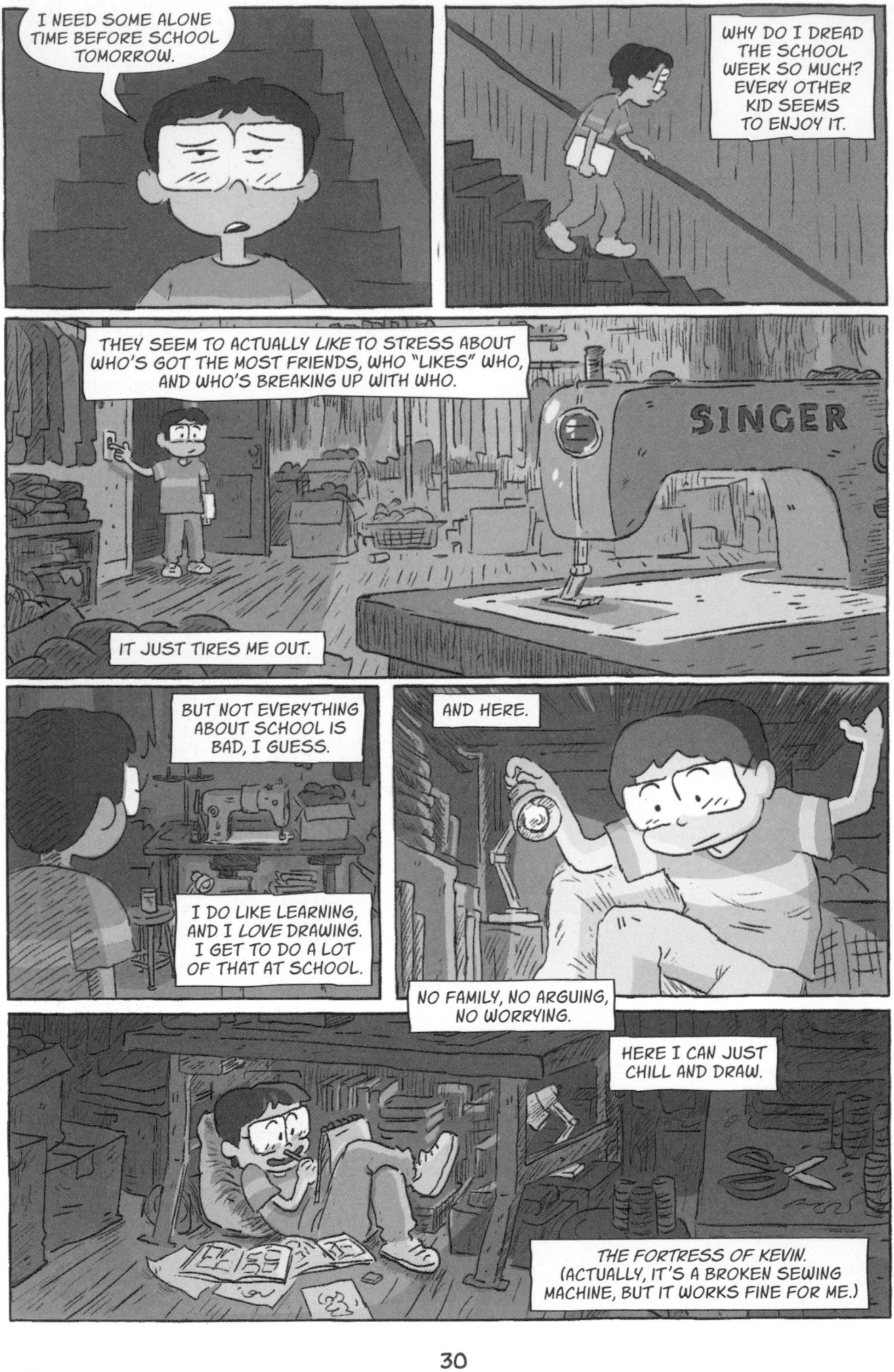

I NEED SOME ALONE TIME BEFORE SCHOOL TOMORROW.
WHY DO I DREAD THE SCHOOL WEEK SO MUCH? EVERY OTHER KID SEEMS TO ENJOY IT.
THEY SEEM TO ACTUALLY *LIKE* TO STRESS ABOUT WHO'S GOT THE MOST FRIENDS, WHO "LIKES" WHO, AND WHO'S BREAKING UP WITH WHO.
SINGER
IT JUST TIRES ME OUT.
BUT NOT EVERYTHING ABOUT SCHOOL IS BAD, I GUESS.
I DO LIKE LEARNING, AND I *LOVE* DRAWING. I GET TO DO A LOT OF THAT AT SCHOOL.
AND HERE.
NO FAMILY, NO ARGUING, NO WORRYING.
HERE I CAN JUST CHILL AND DRAW.
THE FORTRESS OF KEVIN.
(ACTUALLY, IT'S A BROKEN SEWING MACHINE, BUT IT WORKS FINE FOR ME.)

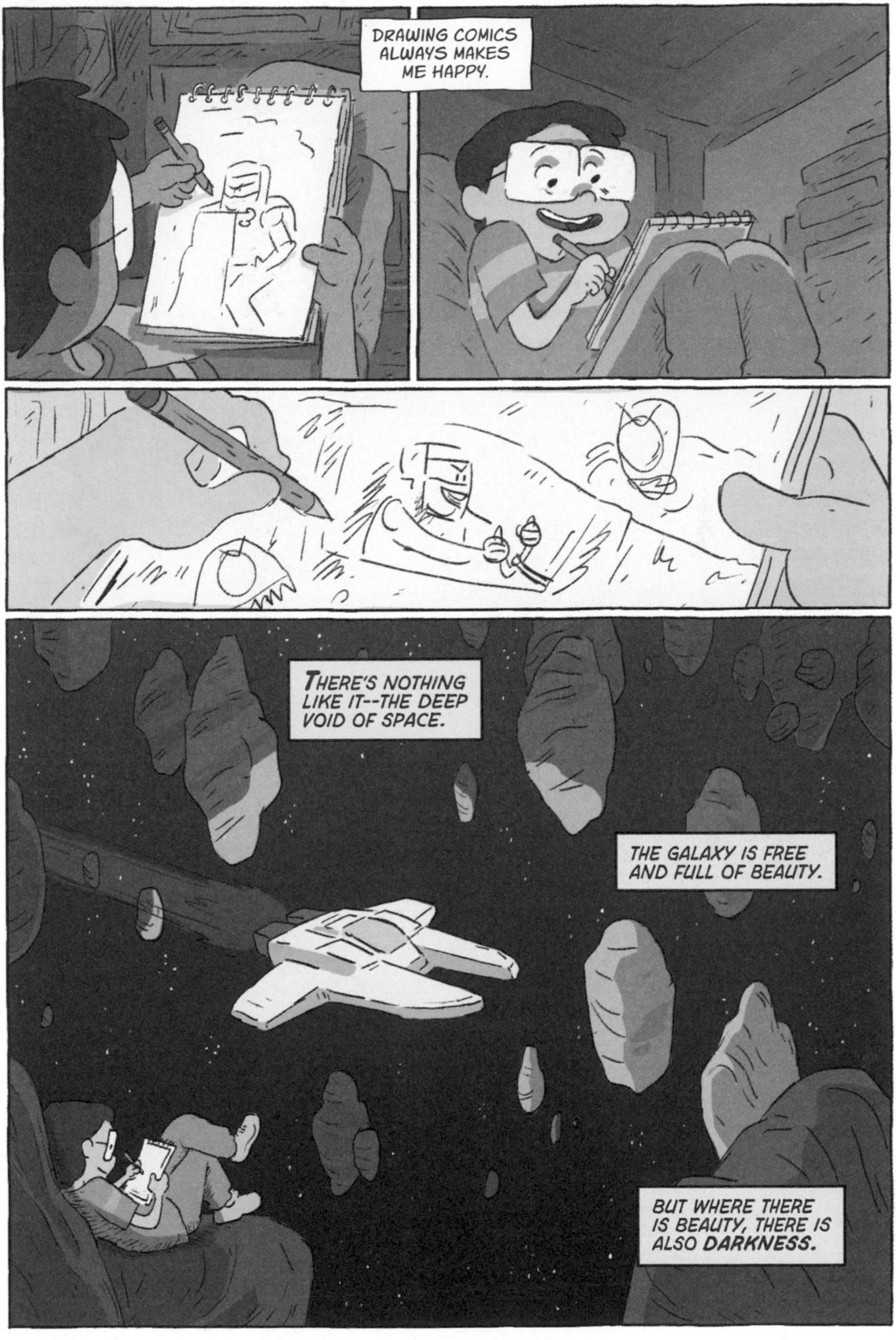
DRAWING COMICS ALWAYS MAKES ME HAPPY.
THERE'S NOTHING LIKE IT--THE DEEP VOID OF SPACE.
THE GALAXY IS FREE AND FULL OF BEAUTY.
BUT WHERE THERE IS BEAUTY, THERE IS ALSO DARKNESS.

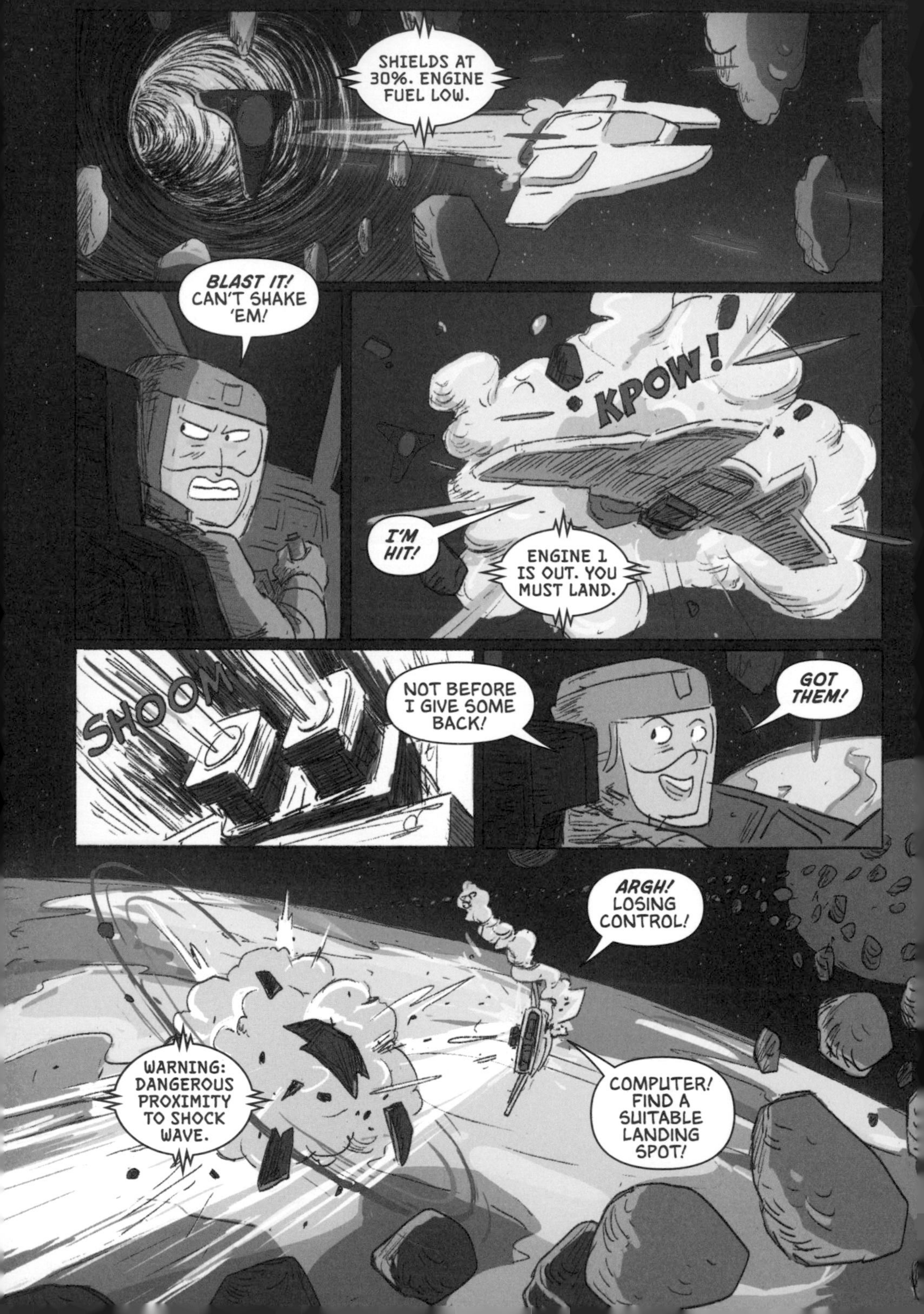

SHIELDS AT 30%. ENGINE FUEL LOW.
BLAST IT! CAN'T SHAKE 'EM!
KPOW!
I'M HIT!
ENGINE 1 IS OUT. YOU MUST LAND.
SHOOM
NOT BEFORE I GIVE SOME BACK!
GOT THEM!
ARGH! LOSING CONTROL!
WARNING: DANGEROUS PROXIMITY TO SHOCK WAVE.
COMPUTER! FIND A SUITABLE LANDING SPOT!

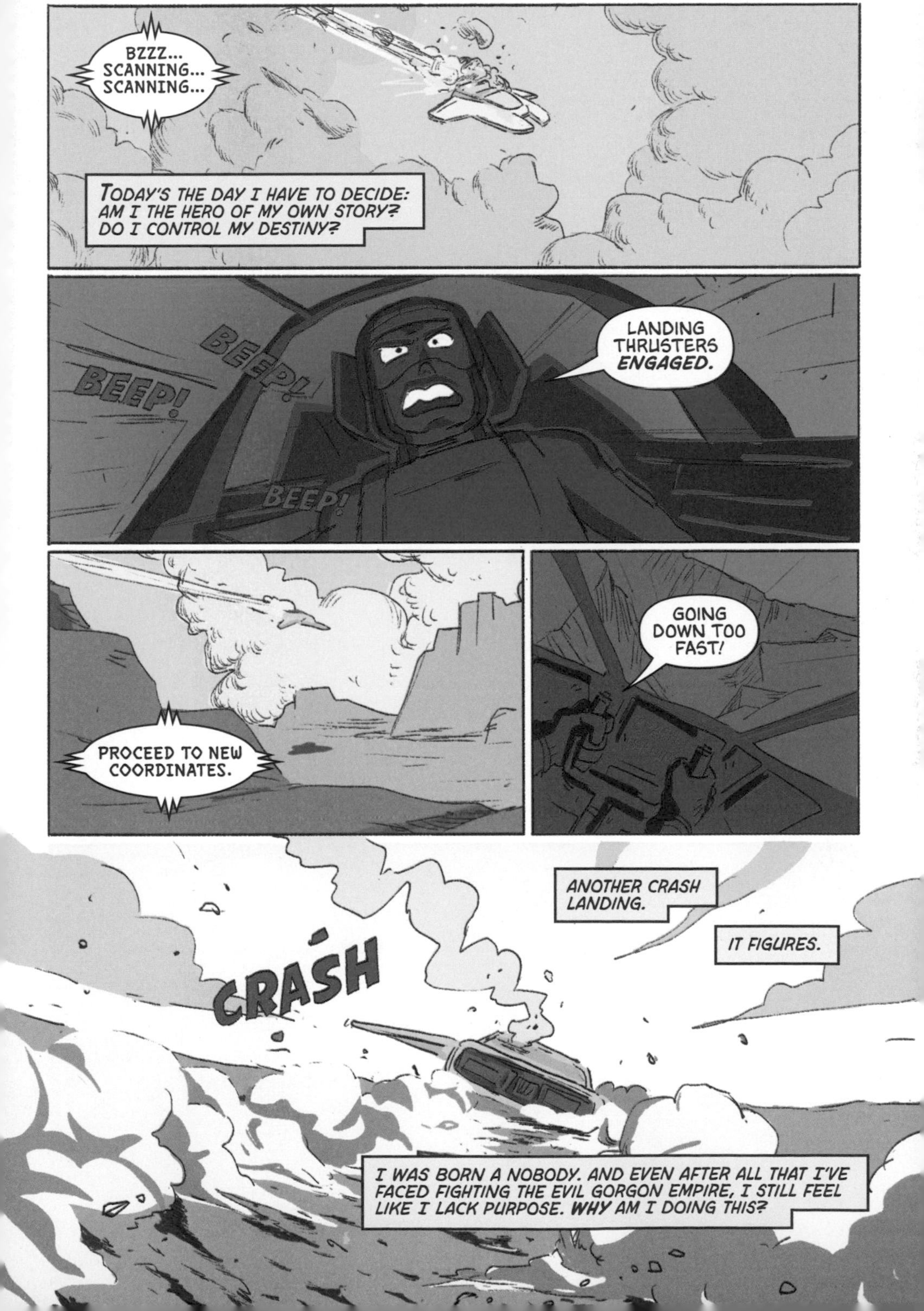
BZZZ... SCANNING... SCANNING...
TODAY'S THE DAY I HAVE TO DECIDE: AM I THE HERO OF MY OWN STORY? DO I CONTROL MY DESTINY?
BEEP!
BEEP!
BEEP!
LANDING THRUSTERS ENGAGED.
PROCEED TO NEW COORDINATES.
GOING DOWN TOO FAST!
ANOTHER CRASH LANDING.
IT FIGURES.
CRASH
I WAS BORN A NOBODY. AND EVEN AFTER ALL THAT I'VE FACED FIGHTING THE EVIL GORGON EMPIRE, I STILL FEEL LIKE I LACK PURPOSE. WHY AM I DOING THIS?

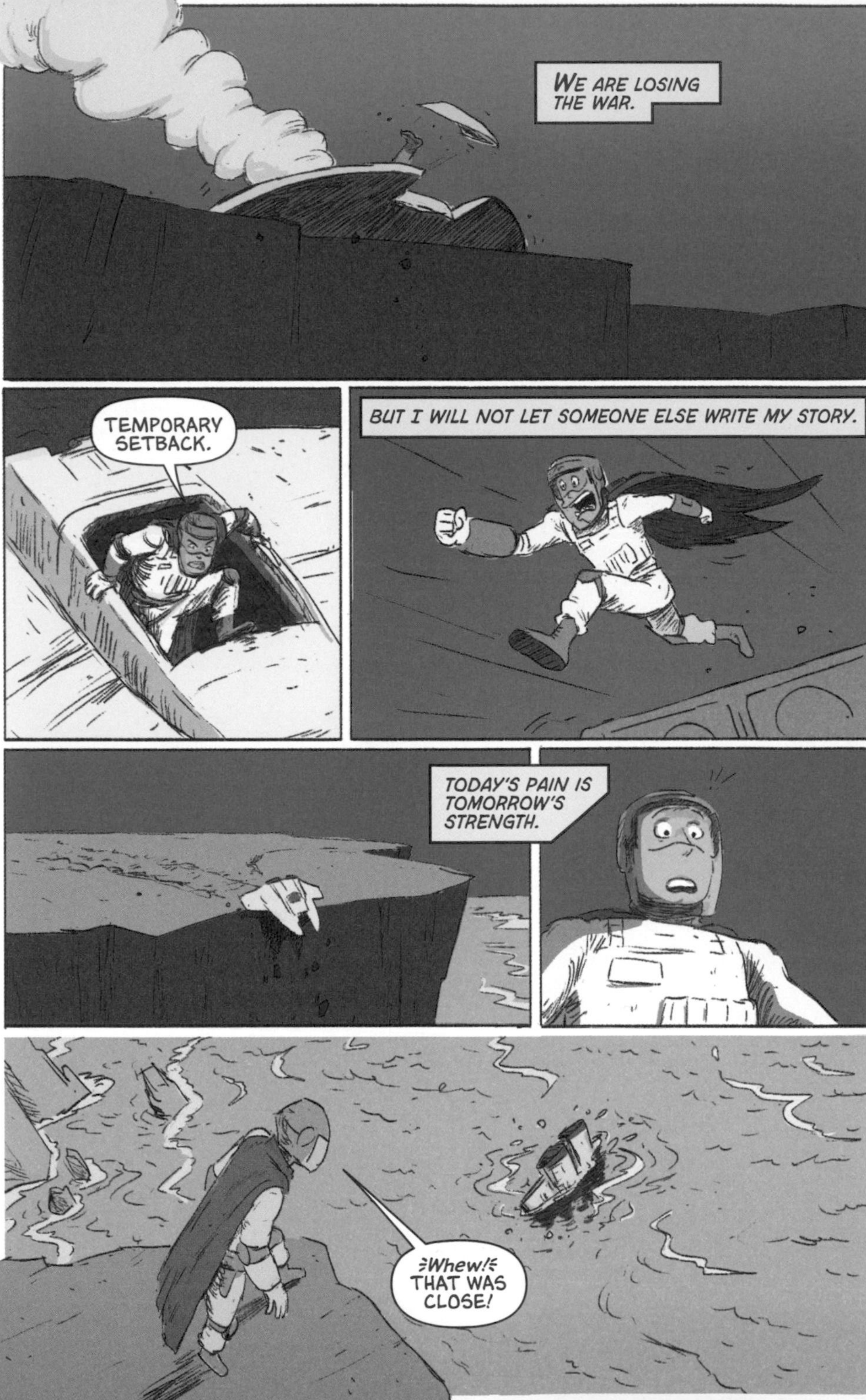
WE ARE LOSING THE WAR.
TEMPORARY SETBACK.
BUT I WILL NOT LET SOMEONE ELSE WRITE MY STORY.
TODAY'S PAIN IS TOMORROW'S STRENGTH.
Whew! THAT WAS CLOSE!

Ugh! POWER REACTOR IS OUT.

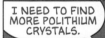

CHALLENGE ACCEPTED.

I NEED TO FIND MORE POLITHIUM CRYSTALS.

ADVANCED LIFE-FORMS DETECTED APPROXIMATELY A HALF DAY'S JOURNEY ON FOOT.

THE RISK IS HIGH, BUT THE REWARD IS WORTH IT. DEFEAT THE ENEMY ONCE AND FOR ALL, AND BALANCE WILL BE RESTORED.

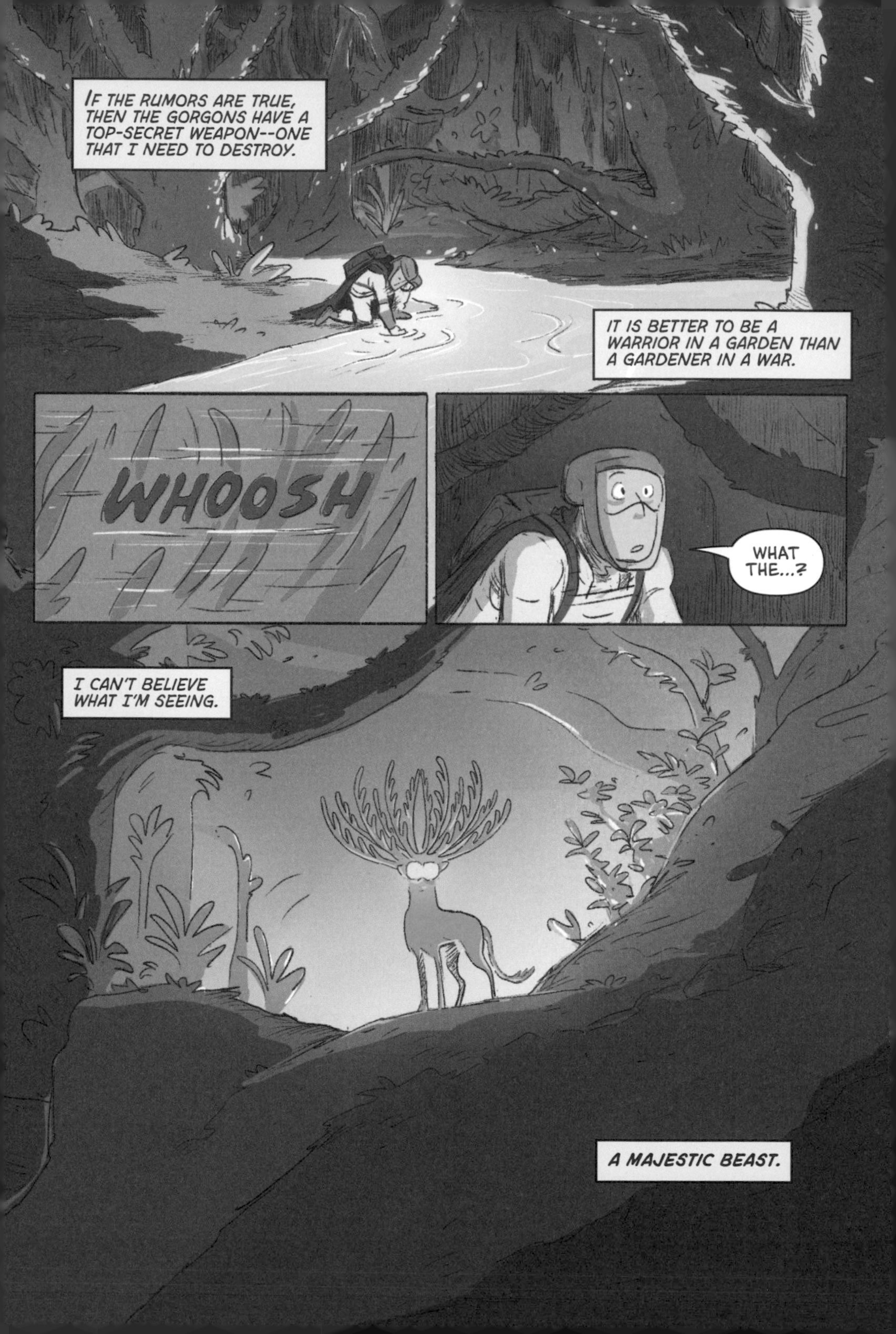
IF THE RUMORS ARE TRUE, THEN THE GORGONS HAVE A TOP-SECRET WEAPON--ONE THAT I NEED TO DESTROY.
IT IS BETTER TO BE A WARRIOR IN A GARDEN THAN A GARDENER IN A WAR.
WHOOSH
WHAT THE...?
I CAN'T BELIEVE WHAT I'M SEEING.
A MAJESTIC BEAST.

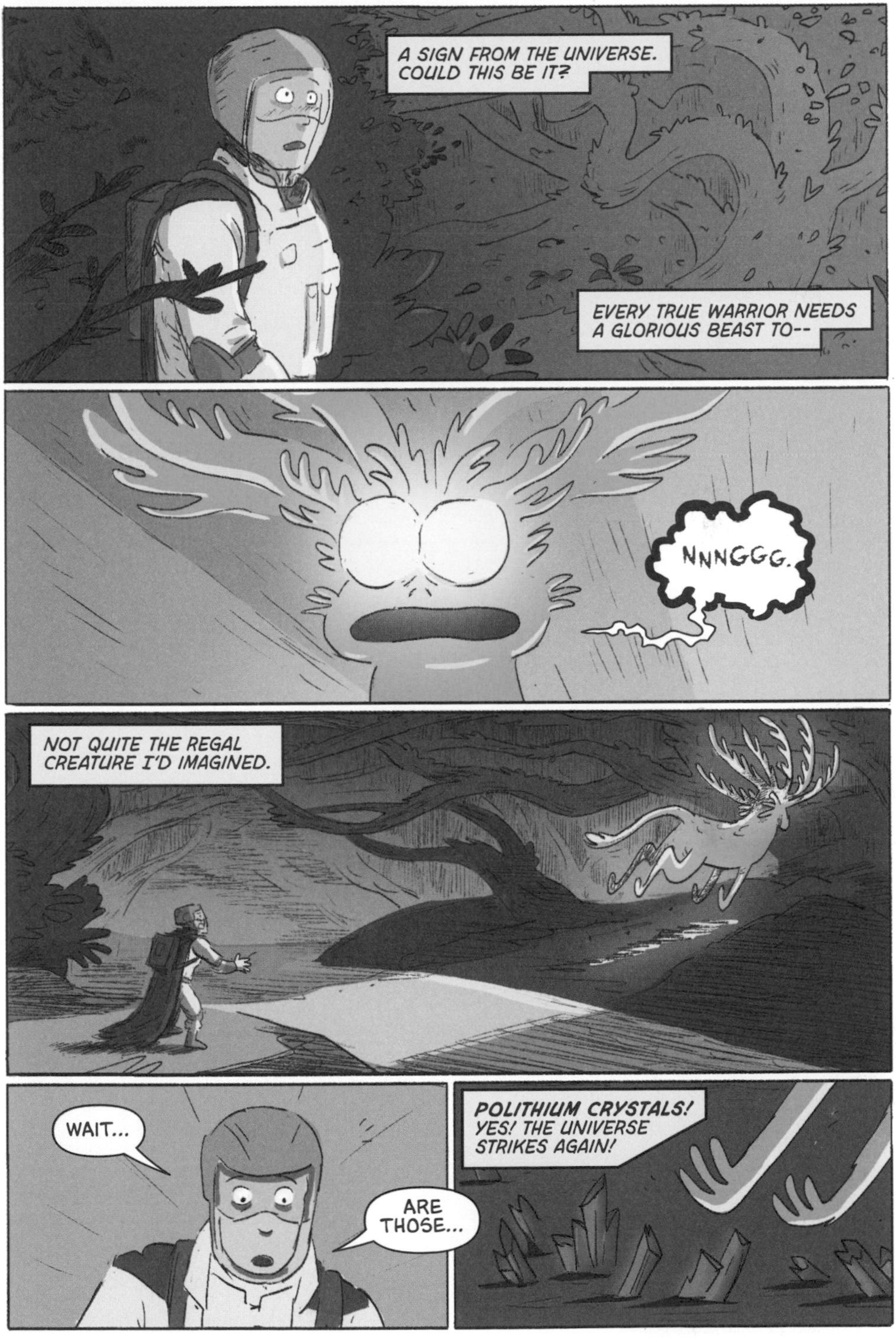
A SIGN FROM THE UNIVERSE. COULD THIS BE IT?
EVERY TRUE WARRIOR NEEDS A GLORIOUS BEAST TO--
NNNGGG.
NOT QUITE THE REGAL CREATURE I'D IMAGINED.
WAIT...
ARE THOSE...
POLITHIUM CRYSTALS! YES! THE UNIVERSE STRIKES AGAIN!

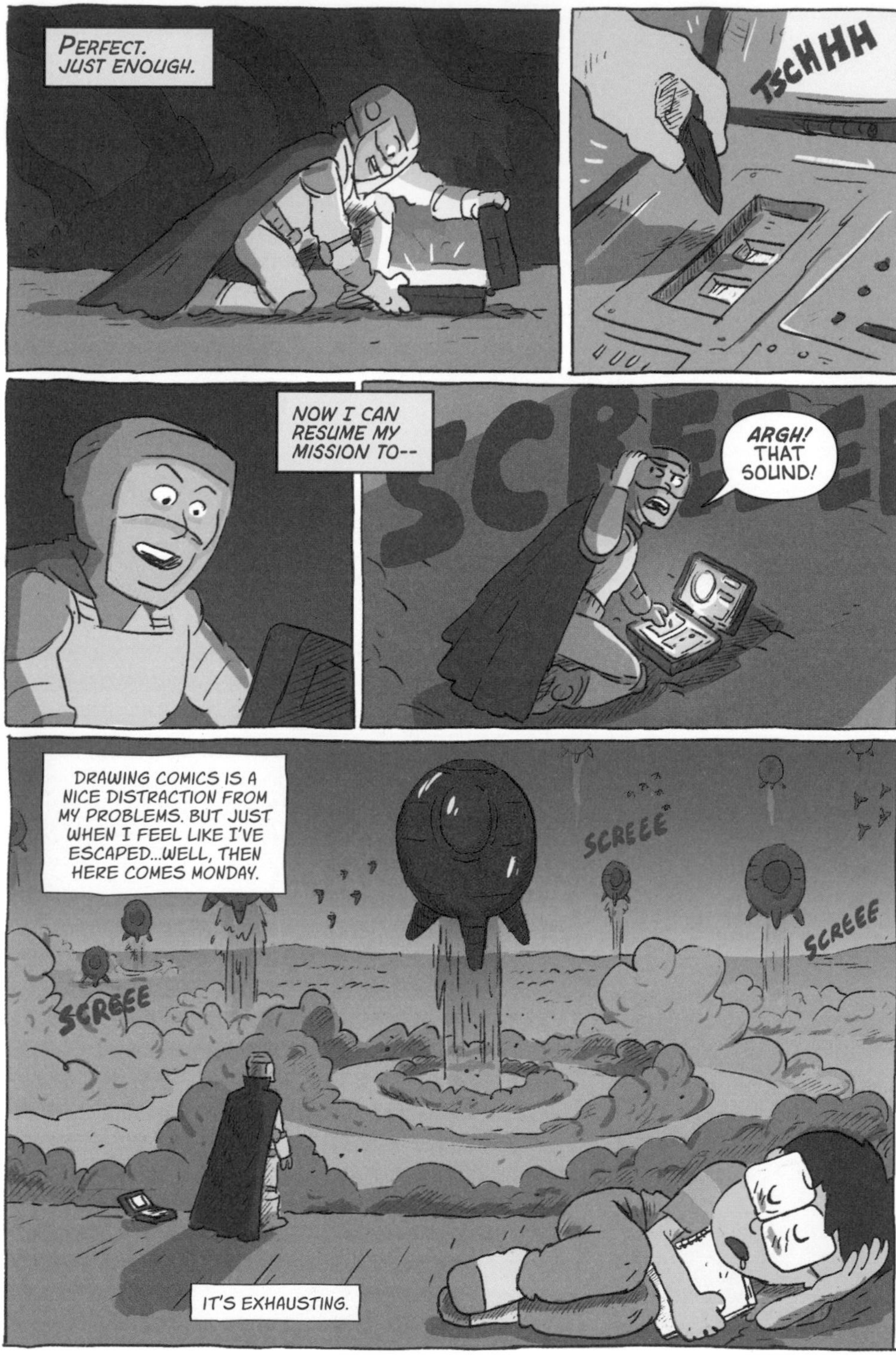
PERFECT. JUST ENOUGH.
TSCHHH
NOW I CAN RESUME MY MISSION TO--
SCREEEE
ARGH! THAT SOUND!
DRAWING COMICS IS A NICE DISTRACTION FROM MY PROBLEMS. BUT JUST WHEN I FEEL LIKE I'VE ESCAPED...WELL, THEN HERE COMES MONDAY.
SCREEE
SCREEE
SCREEE
IT'S EXHAUSTING.

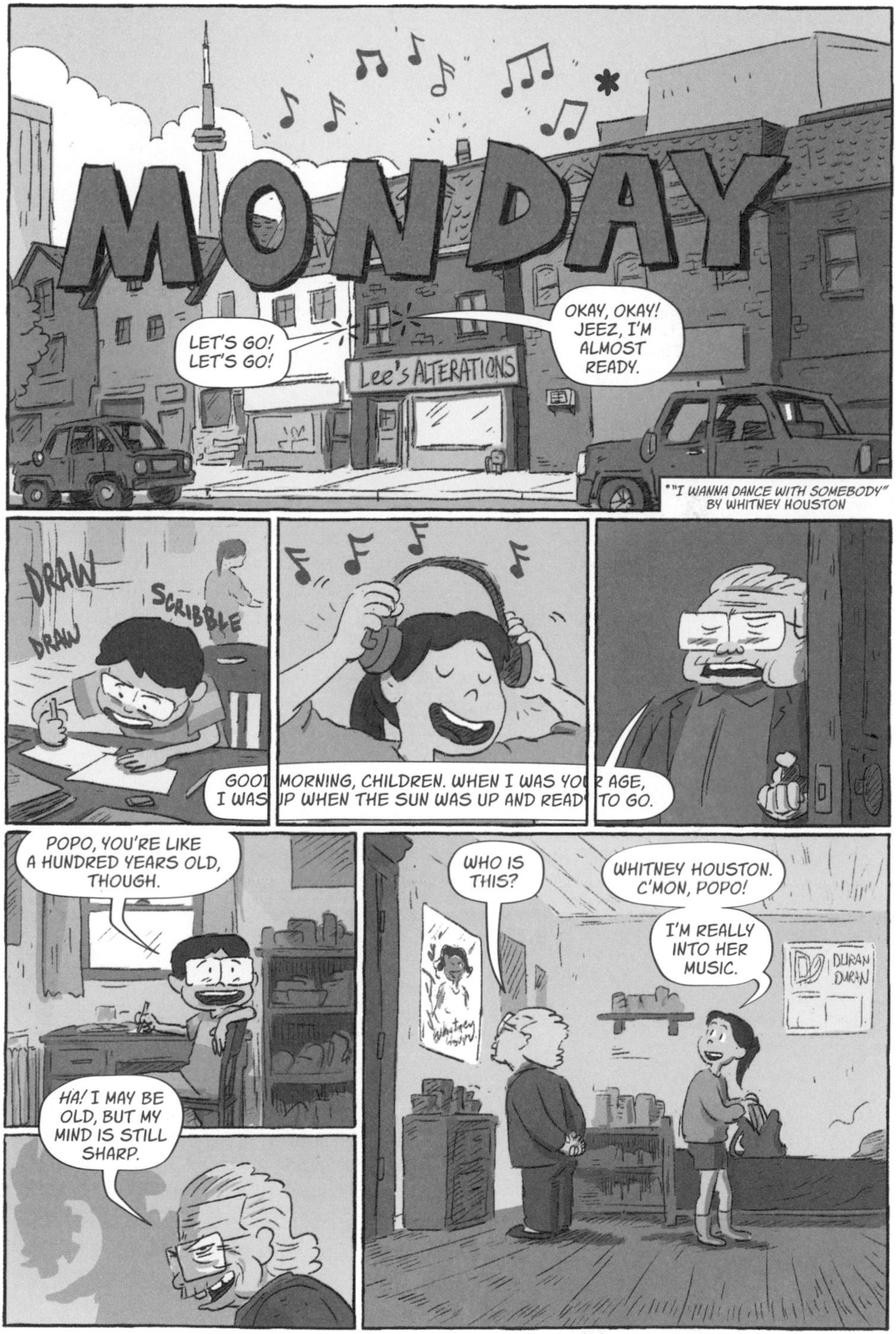
MONDAY
LET'S GO! LET'S GO!
OKAY, OKAY! JEEZ, I'M ALMOST READY.
Lee's ALTERATIONS
*"I WANNA DANCE WITH SOMEBODY" BY WHITNEY HOUSTON
DRAW
SCRIBBLE
DRAW
GOOD MORNING, CHILDREN. WHEN I WAS YOUR AGE, I WAS UP WHEN THE SUN WAS UP AND READY TO GO.
POPO, YOU'RE LIKE A HUNDRED YEARS OLD, THOUGH.
HA! I MAY BE OLD, BUT MY MIND IS STILL SHARP.
WHO IS THIS?
WHITNEY HOUSTON. C'MON, POPO!
I'M REALLY INTO HER MUSIC.
DURAN DURAN

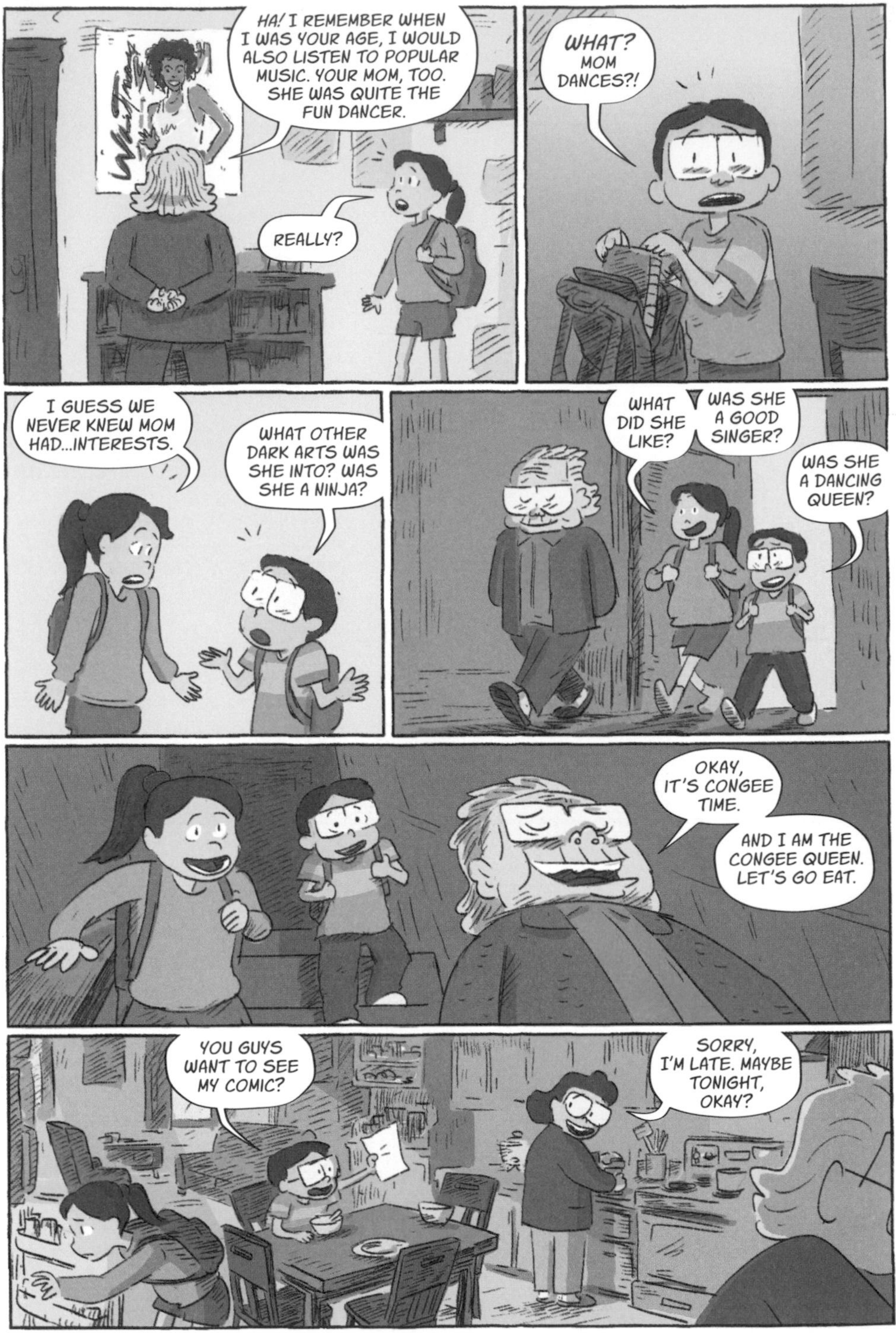
HA! I REMEMBER WHEN I WAS YOUR AGE, I WOULD ALSO LISTEN TO POPULAR MUSIC. YOUR MOM, TOO. SHE WAS QUITE THE FUN DANCER.
REALLY?
WHAT? MOM DANCES?!
I GUESS WE NEVER KNEW MOM HAD...INTERESTS.
WHAT OTHER DARK ARTS WAS SHE INTO? WAS SHE A NINJA?
WHAT DID SHE LIKE?
WAS SHE A GOOD SINGER?
WAS SHE A DANCING QUEEN?
OKAY, IT'S CONGEE TIME.
AND I AM THE CONGEE QUEEN. LET'S GO EAT.
YOU GUYS WANT TO SEE MY COMIC?
SORRY, I'M LATE. MAYBE TONIGHT, OKAY?

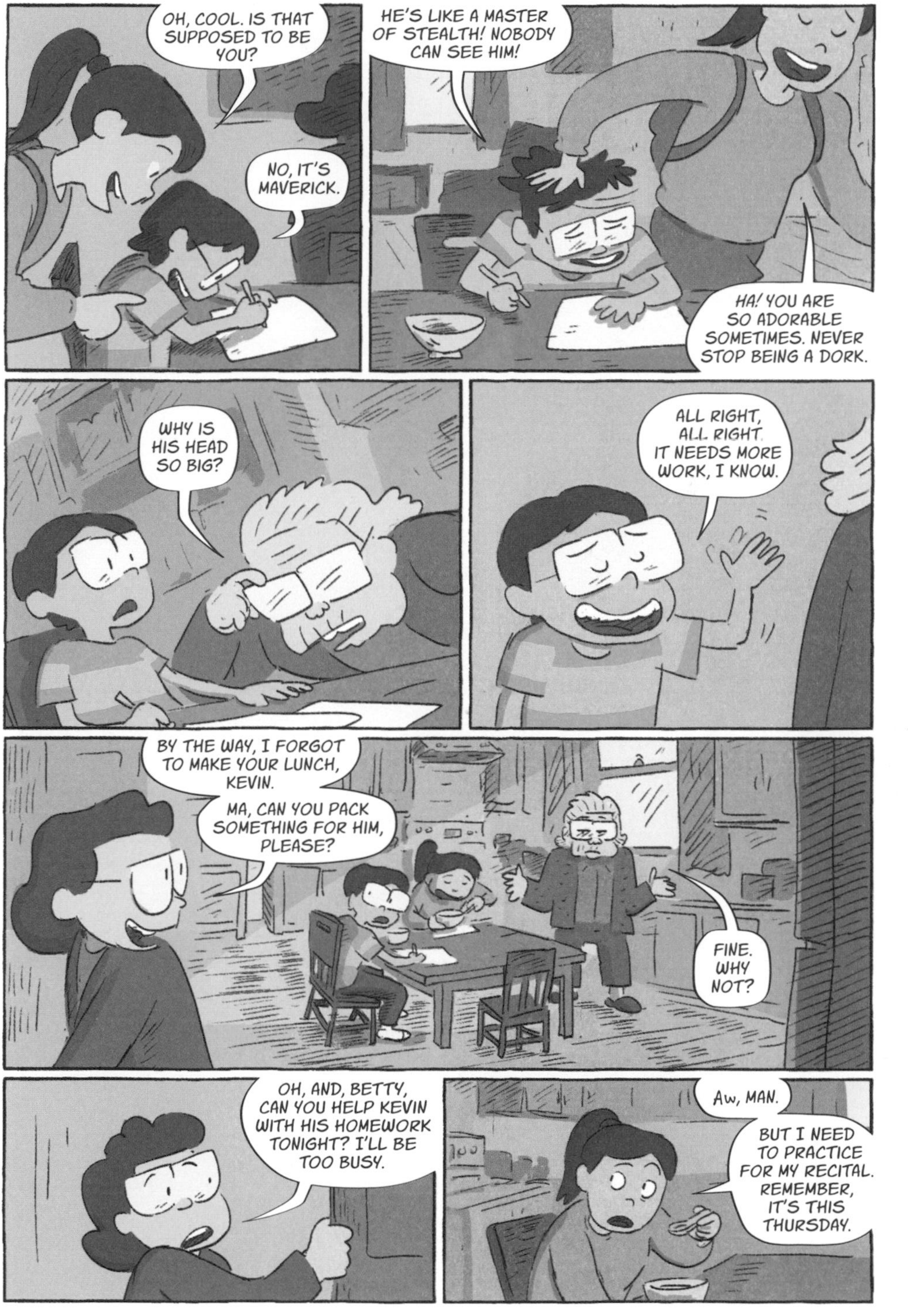
OH, COOL. IS THAT SUPPOSED TO BE YOU?
NO, IT'S MAVERICK.
HE'S LIKE A MASTER OF STEALTH! NOBODY CAN SEE HIM!
HA! YOU ARE SO ADORABLE SOMETIMES. NEVER STOP BEING A DORK.
WHY IS HIS HEAD SO BIG?
ALL RIGHT, ALL RIGHT. IT NEEDS MORE WORK, I KNOW.
BY THE WAY, I FORGOT TO MAKE YOUR LUNCH, KEVIN.
MA, CAN YOU PACK SOMETHING FOR HIM, PLEASE?
FINE. WHY NOT?
OH, AND, BETTY, CAN YOU HELP KEVIN WITH HIS HOMEWORK TONIGHT? I'LL BE TOO BUSY.
Aw, MAN.
BUT I NEED TO PRACTICE FOR MY RECITAL. REMEMBER, IT'S THIS THURSDAY.

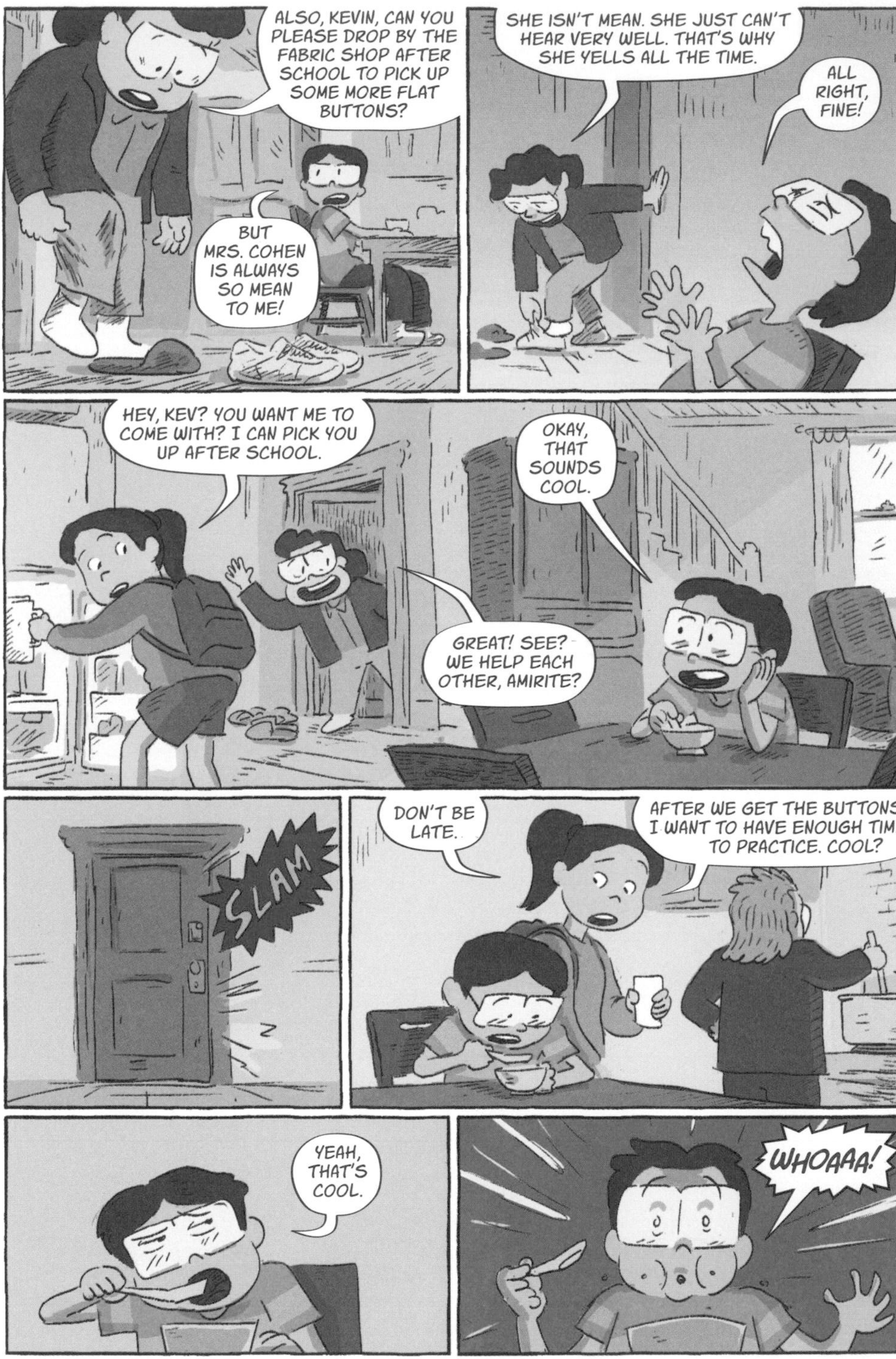
ALSO, KEVIN, CAN YOU PLEASE DROP BY THE FABRIC SHOP AFTER SCHOOL TO PICK UP SOME MORE FLAT BUTTONS?
BUT MRS. COHEN IS ALWAYS SO MEAN TO ME!
SHE ISN'T MEAN. SHE JUST CAN'T HEAR VERY WELL. THAT'S WHY SHE YELLS ALL THE TIME.
ALL RIGHT, FINE!
HEY, KEV? YOU WANT ME TO COME WITH? I CAN PICK YOU UP AFTER SCHOOL.
OKAY, THAT SOUNDS COOL.
GREAT! SEE? WE HELP EACH OTHER, AMIRITE?
SLAM
DON'T BE LATE.
AFTER WE GET THE BUTTONS, I WANT TO HAVE ENOUGH TIME TO PRACTICE. COOL?
YEAH, THAT'S COOL.
WHOAAA!

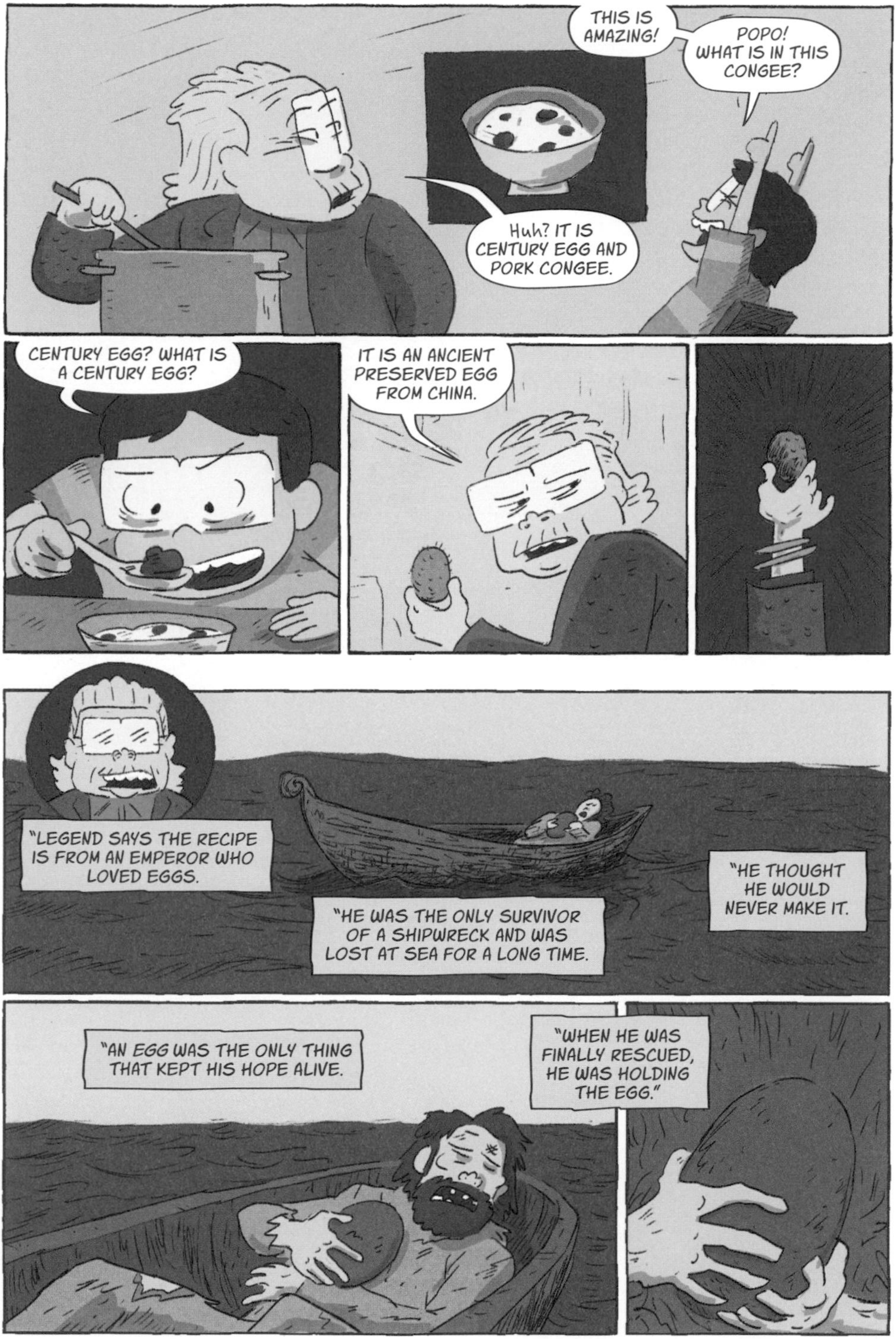
THIS IS AMAZING!
POPO! WHAT IS IN THIS CONGEE?
Huh? IT IS CENTURY EGG AND PORK CONGEE.
CENTURY EGG? WHAT IS A CENTURY EGG?
IT IS AN ANCIENT PRESERVED EGG FROM CHINA.
"LEGEND SAYS THE RECIPE IS FROM AN EMPEROR WHO LOVED EGGS.
"HE WAS THE ONLY SURVIVOR OF A SHIPWRECK AND WAS LOST AT SEA FOR A LONG TIME.
"HE THOUGHT HE WOULD NEVER MAKE IT.
"AN EGG WAS THE ONLY THING THAT KEPT HIS HOPE ALIVE.
"WHEN HE WAS FINALLY RESCUED, HE WAS HOLDING THE EGG."

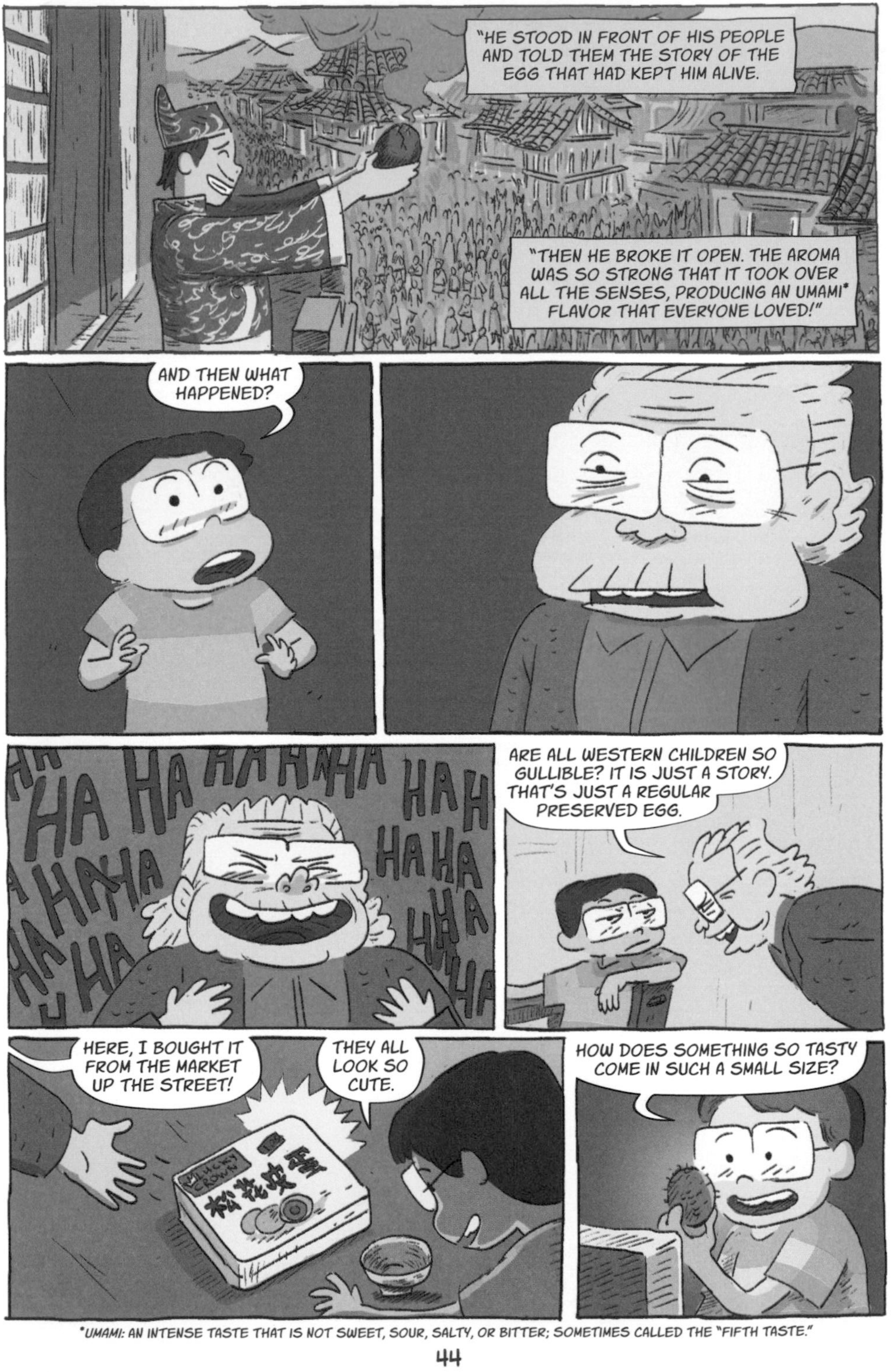

"HE STOOD IN FRONT OF HIS PEOPLE AND TOLD THEM THE STORY OF THE EGG THAT HAD KEPT HIM ALIVE.
"THEN HE BROKE IT OPEN. THE AROMA WAS SO STRONG THAT IT TOOK OVER ALL THE SENSES, PRODUCING AN UMAMI* FLAVOR THAT EVERYONE LOVED!"
AND THEN WHAT HAPPENED?
HA HA HA HA HA HA HA HA HA HA HA HA HA HA HA HA HA
ARE ALL WESTERN CHILDREN SO GULLIBLE? IT IS JUST A STORY. THAT'S JUST A REGULAR PRESERVED EGG.
HERE, I BOUGHT IT FROM THE MARKET UP THE STREET!
THEY ALL LOOK SO CUTE.
LUCKY CROWN
松花皮蛋
HOW DOES SOMETHING SO TASTY COME IN SUCH A SMALL SIZE?

*UMAMI: AN INTENSE TASTE THAT IS NOT SWEET, SOUR, SALTY, OR BITTER; SOMETIMES CALLED THE "FIFTH TASTE."

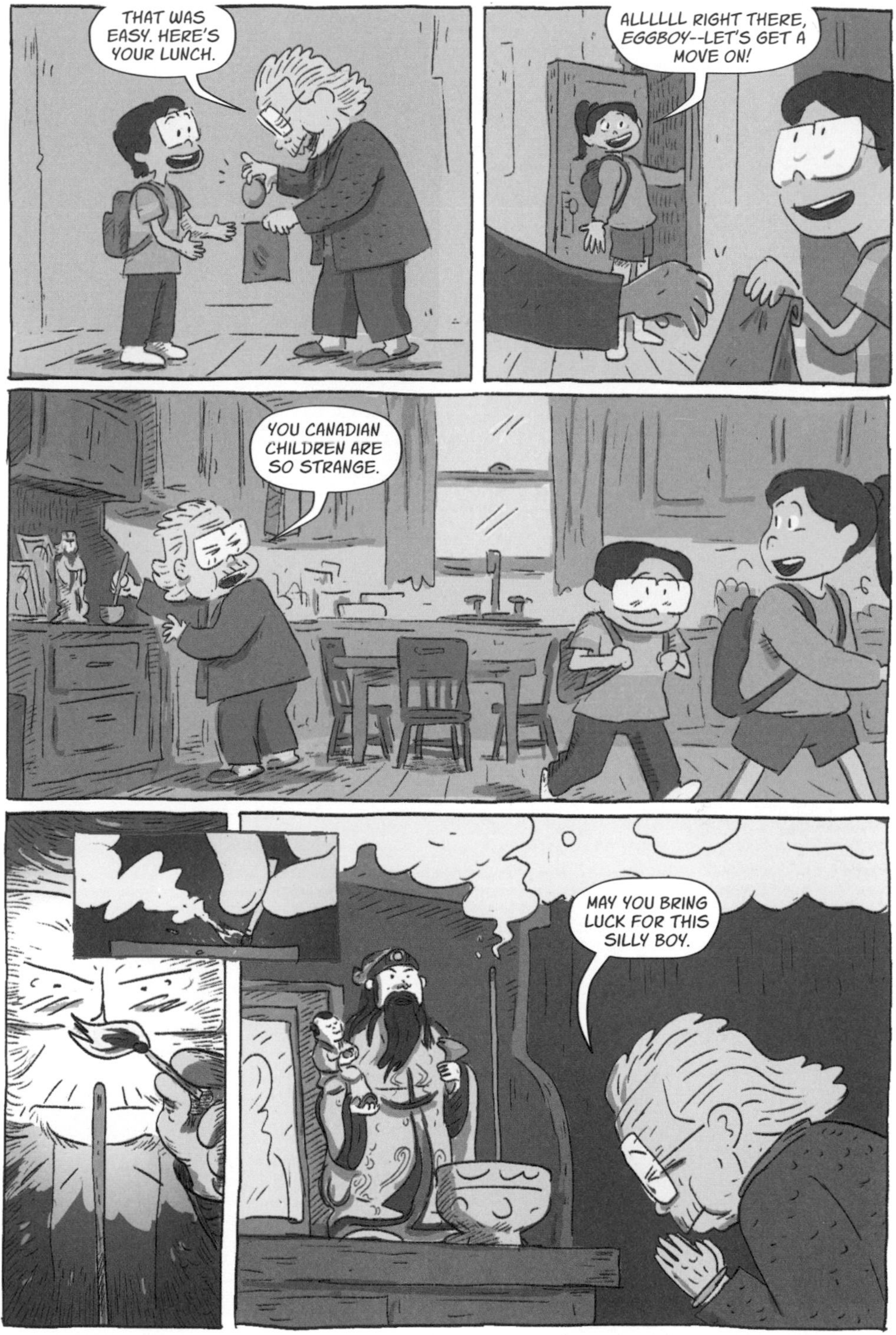
THAT WAS EASY. HERE'S YOUR LUNCH.
ALLLLLL RIGHT THERE, EGGBOY--LET'S GET A MOVE ON!
YOU CANADIAN CHILDREN ARE SO STRANGE.
MAY YOU BRING LUCK FOR THIS SILLY BOY.

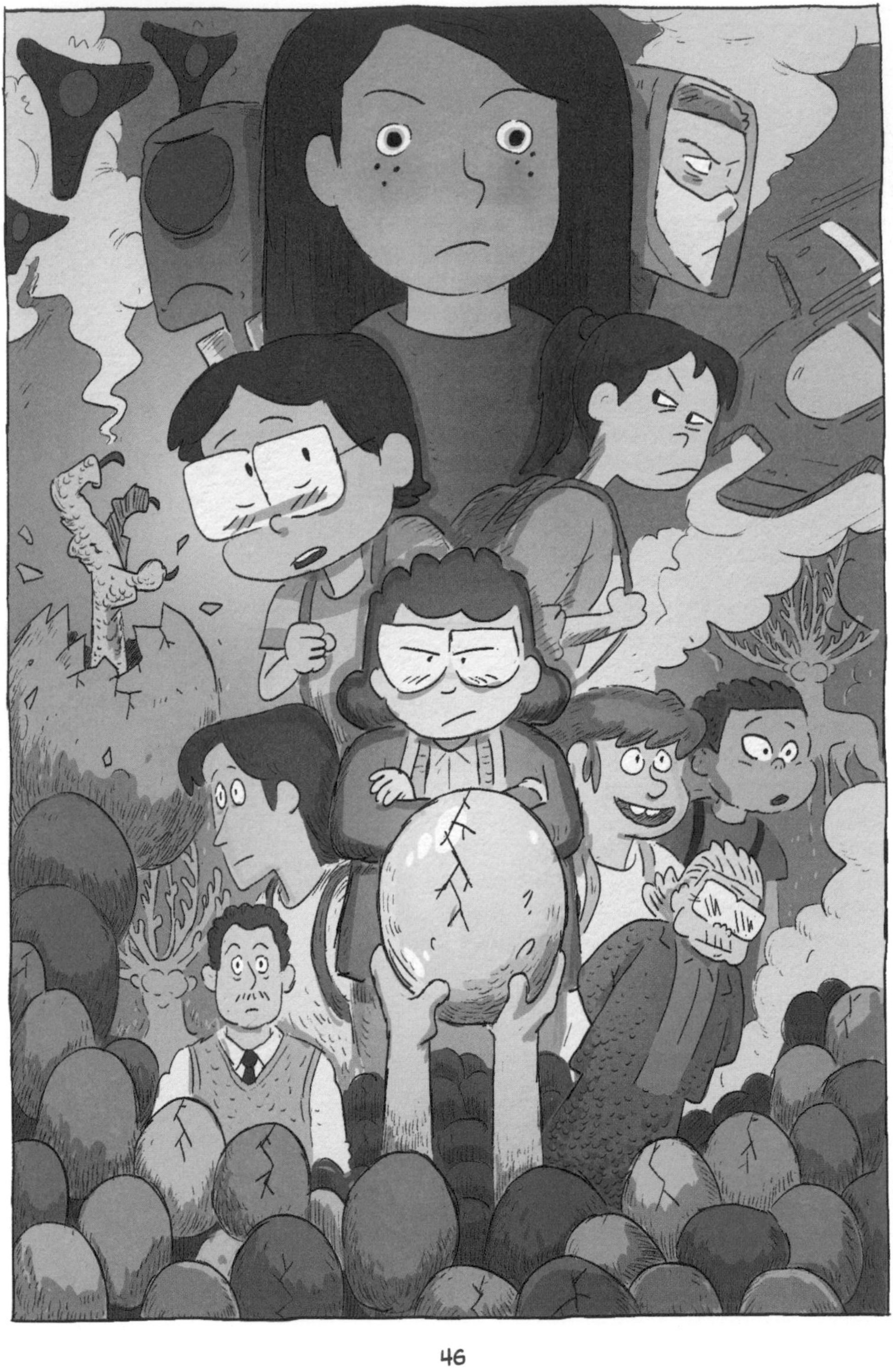

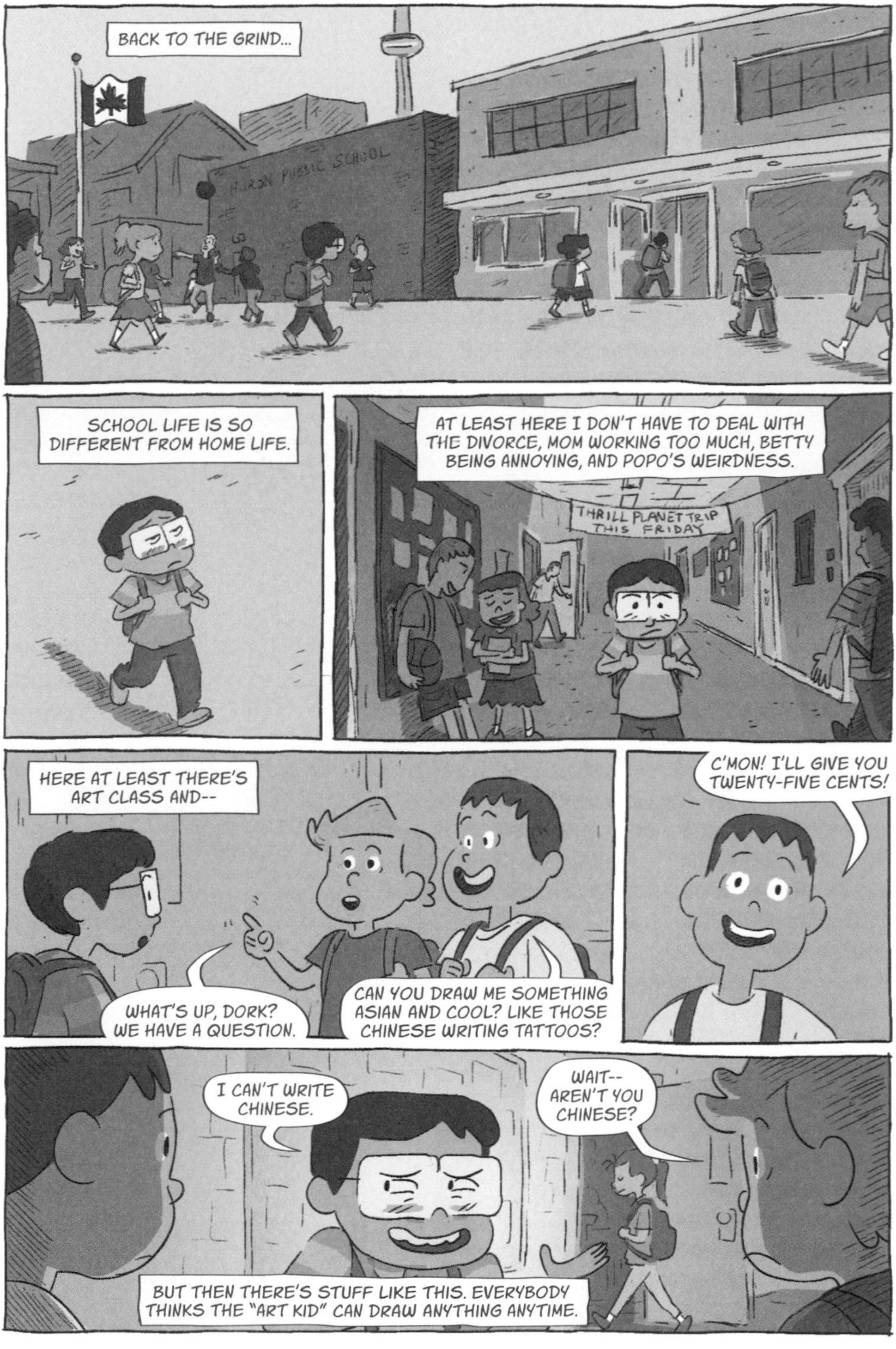
BACK TO THE GRIND...
HURON PUBLIC SCHOOL
SCHOOL LIFE IS SO DIFFERENT FROM HOME LIFE.
AT LEAST HERE I DON'T HAVE TO DEAL WITH THE DIVORCE, MOM WORKING TOO MUCH, BETTY BEING ANNOYING, AND POPO'S WEIRDNESS.
THRILL PLANET TRIP THIS FRIDAY
HERE AT LEAST THERE'S ART CLASS AND--
WHAT'S UP, DORK? WE HAVE A QUESTION.
CAN YOU DRAW ME SOMETHING ASIAN AND COOL? LIKE THOSE CHINESE WRITING TATTOOS?
C'MON! I'LL GIVE YOU TWENTY-FIVE CENTS!
I CAN'T WRITE CHINESE.
WAIT-- AREN'T YOU CHINESE?
BUT THEN THERE'S STUFF LIKE THIS. EVERYBODY THINKS THE "ART KID" CAN DRAW ANYTHING ANYTIME.

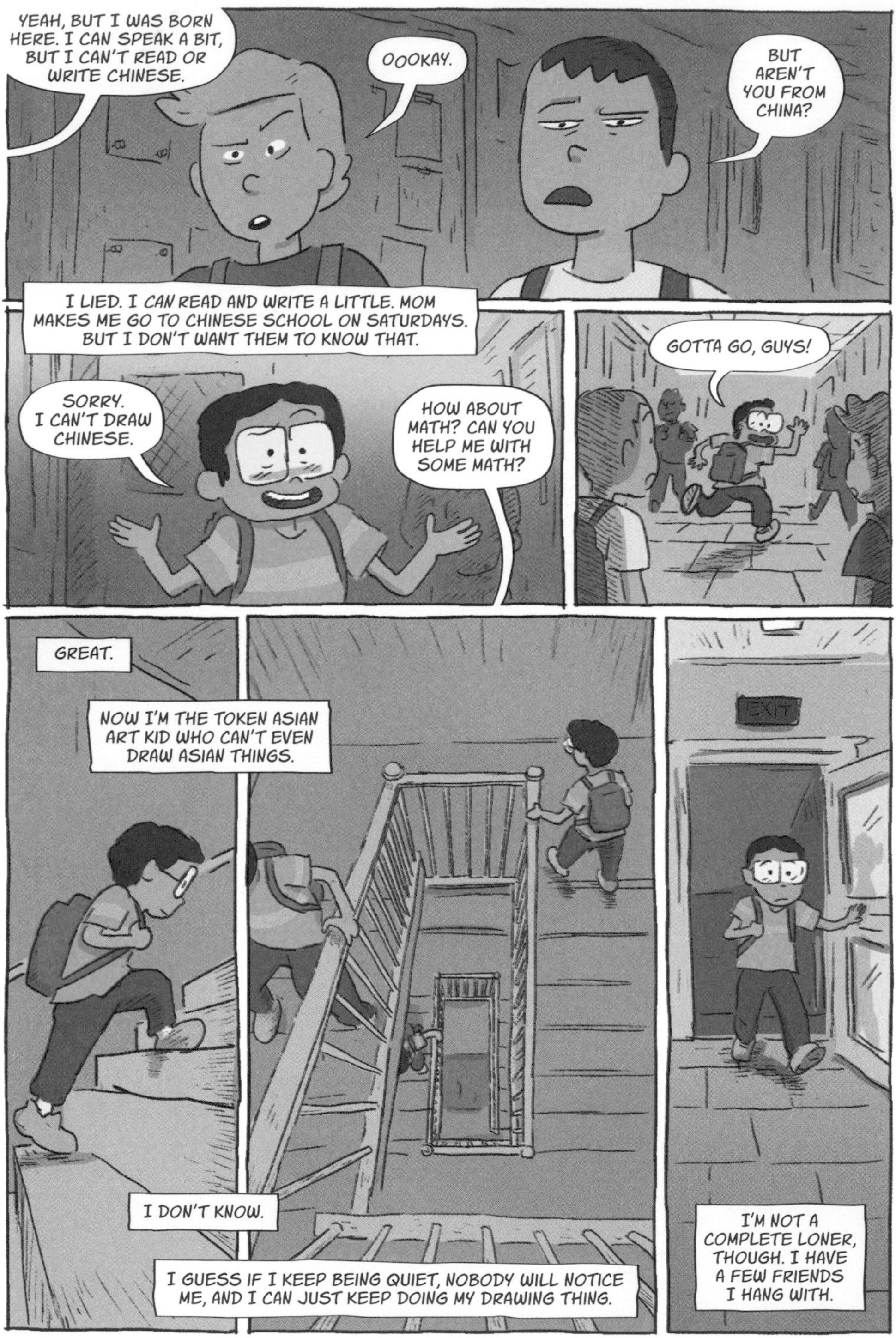

YEAH, BUT I WAS BORN HERE. I CAN SPEAK A BIT, BUT I CAN'T READ OR WRITE CHINESE.
OOOKAY.
BUT AREN'T YOU FROM CHINA?
I LIED. I *CAN* READ AND WRITE A LITTLE. MOM MAKES ME GO TO CHINESE SCHOOL ON SATURDAYS. BUT I DON'T WANT THEM TO KNOW THAT.
SORRY. I CAN'T DRAW CHINESE.
HOW ABOUT MATH? CAN YOU HELP ME WITH SOME MATH?
GOTTA GO, GUYS!
GREAT.
NOW I'M THE TOKEN ASIAN ART KID WHO CAN'T EVEN DRAW ASIAN THINGS.
I DON'T KNOW.
EXIT
I GUESS IF I KEEP BEING QUIET, NOBODY WILL NOTICE ME, AND I CAN JUST KEEP DOING MY DRAWING THING.
I'M NOT A COMPLETE LONER, THOUGH. I HAVE A FEW FRIENDS I HANG WITH.

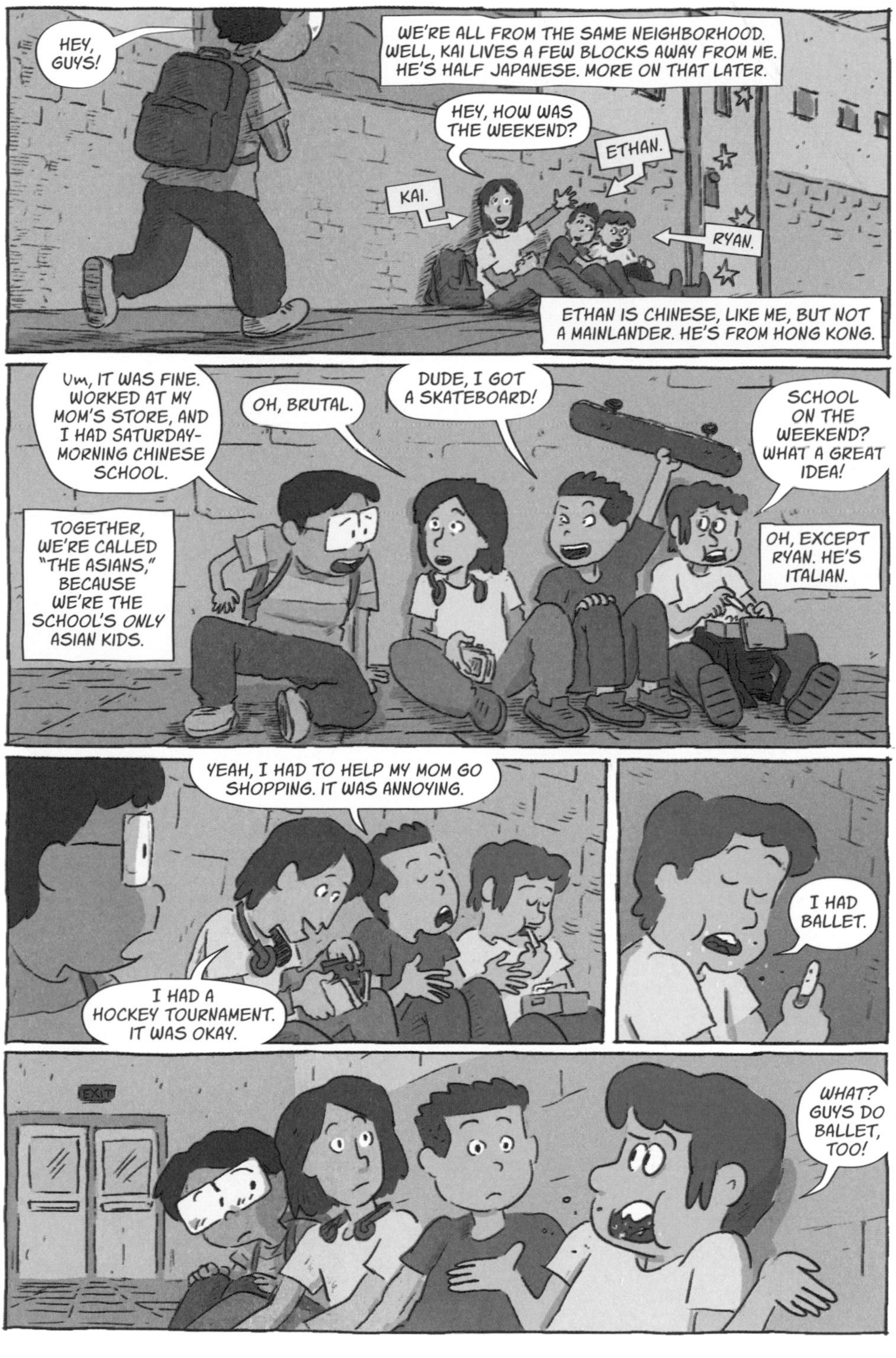

HEY, GUYS!
WE'RE ALL FROM THE SAME NEIGHBORHOOD. WELL, KAI LIVES A FEW BLOCKS AWAY FROM ME. HE'S HALF JAPANESE. MORE ON THAT LATER.
HEY, HOW WAS THE WEEKEND?
ETHAN.
KAI.
RYAN.
ETHAN IS CHINESE, LIKE ME, BUT NOT A MAINLANDER. HE'S FROM HONG KONG.
UM, IT WAS FINE. WORKED AT MY MOM'S STORE, AND I HAD SATURDAY-MORNING CHINESE SCHOOL.
OH, BRUTAL.
DUDE, I GOT A SKATEBOARD!
SCHOOL ON THE WEEKEND? WHAT A GREAT IDEA!
TOGETHER, WE'RE CALLED "THE ASIANS," BECAUSE WE'RE THE SCHOOL'S *ONLY* ASIAN KIDS.
OH, EXCEPT RYAN. HE'S ITALIAN.
YEAH, I HAD TO HELP MY MOM GO SHOPPING. IT WAS ANNOYING.
I HAD A HOCKEY TOURNAMENT. IT WAS OKAY.
I HAD BALLET.
EXIT
WHAT? GUYS DO BALLET, TOO!

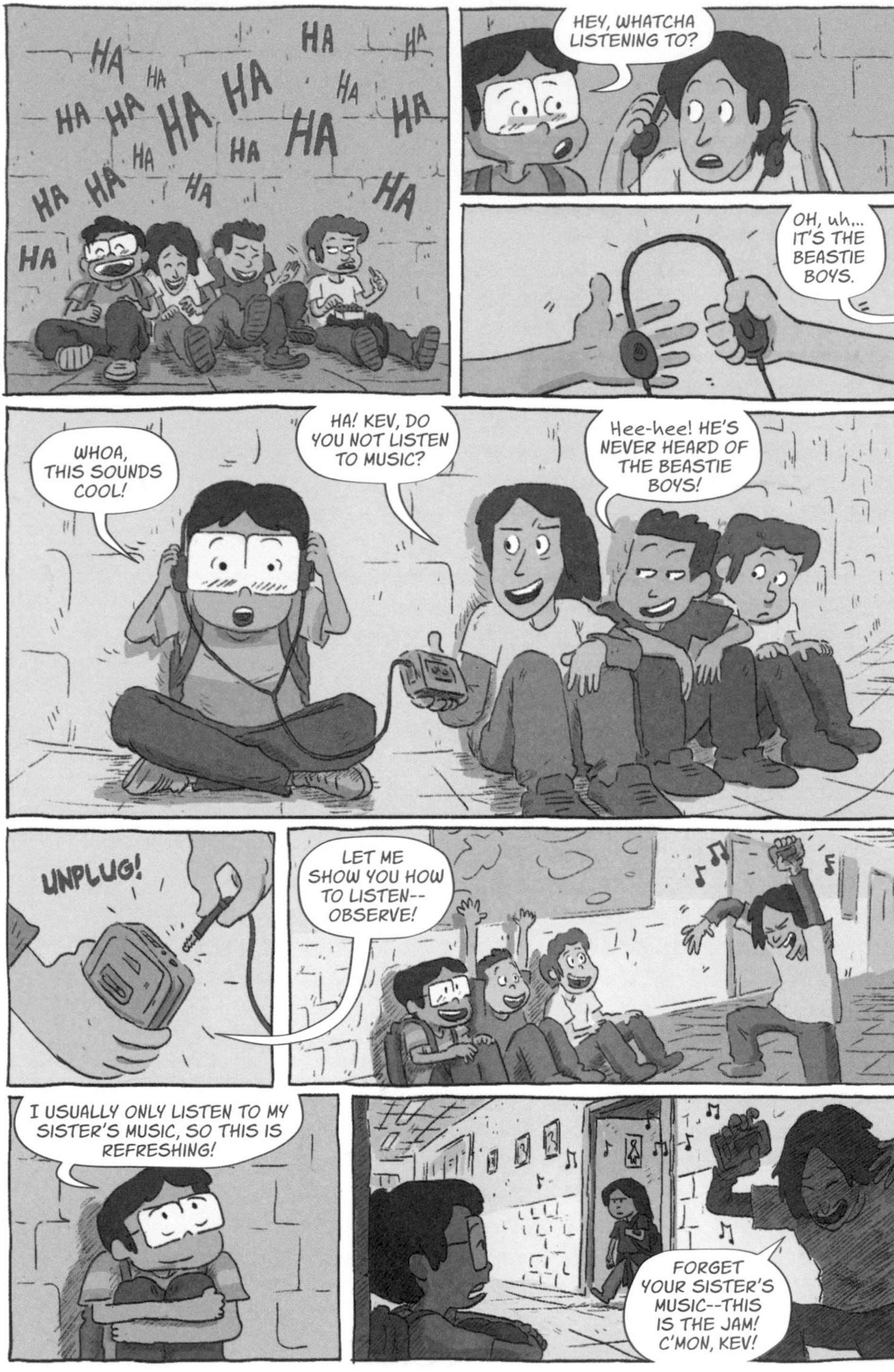
HA HA HA HA HA HA HA HA HA HA HA HA HA HA HA HA HA HA
HEY, WHATCHA LISTENING TO?
OH, uh... IT'S THE BEASTIE BOYS.
WHOA, THIS SOUNDS COOL!
HA! KEV, DO YOU NOT LISTEN TO MUSIC?
Hee-hee! HE'S NEVER HEARD OF THE BEASTIE BOYS!
UNPLUG!
LET ME SHOW YOU HOW TO LISTEN--OBSERVE!
I USUALLY ONLY LISTEN TO MY SISTER'S MUSIC, SO THIS IS REFRESHING!
FORGET YOUR SISTER'S MUSIC--THIS IS THE JAM! C'MON, KEV!

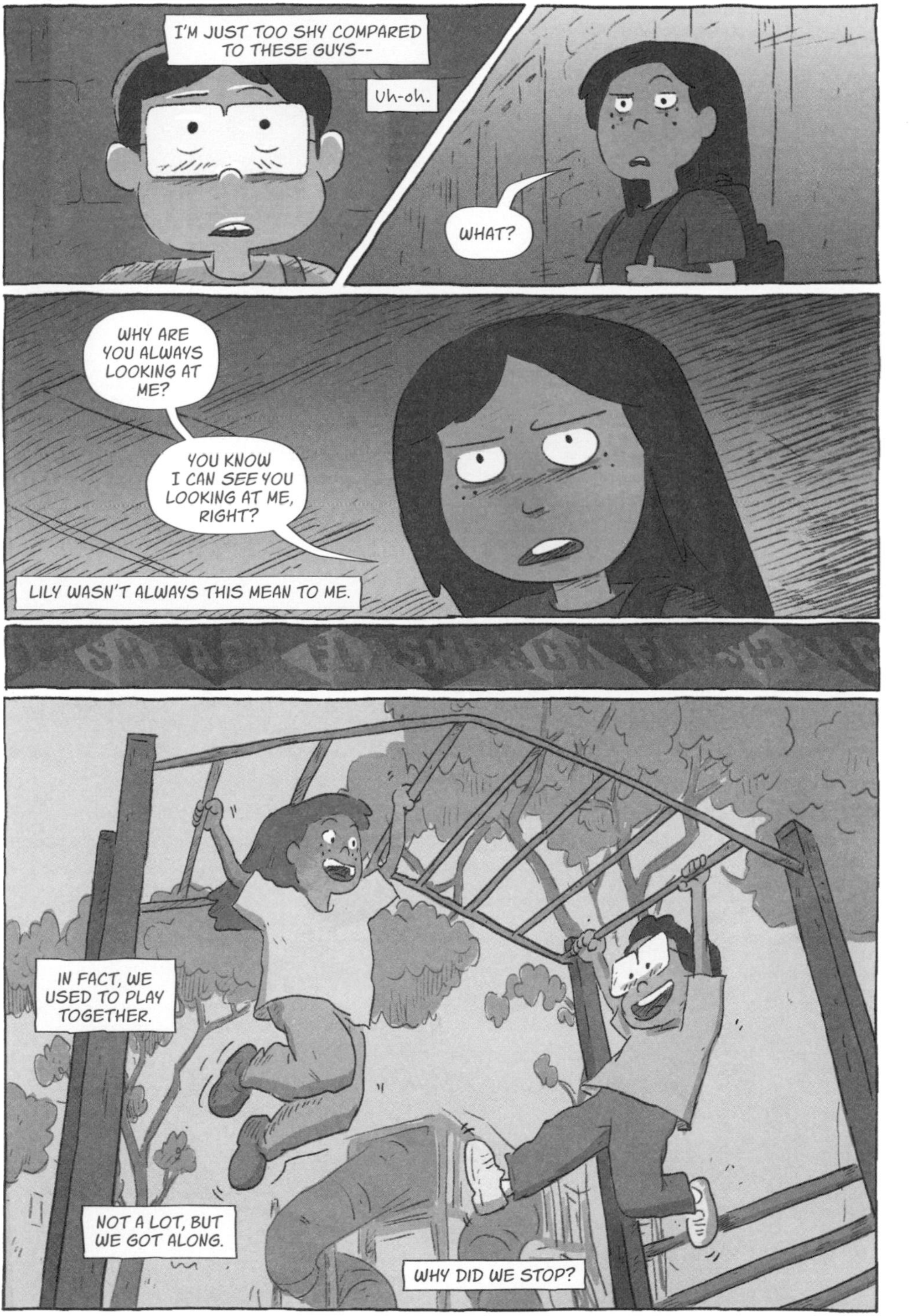
I'M JUST TOO SHY COMPARED TO THESE GUYS--
Uh-oh.
WHAT?
WHY ARE YOU ALWAYS LOOKING AT ME?
YOU KNOW I CAN *SEE* YOU LOOKING AT ME, RIGHT?
LILY WASN'T ALWAYS THIS MEAN TO ME.
IN FACT, WE USED TO PLAY TOGETHER.
NOT A LOT, BUT WE GOT ALONG.
WHY DID WE STOP?

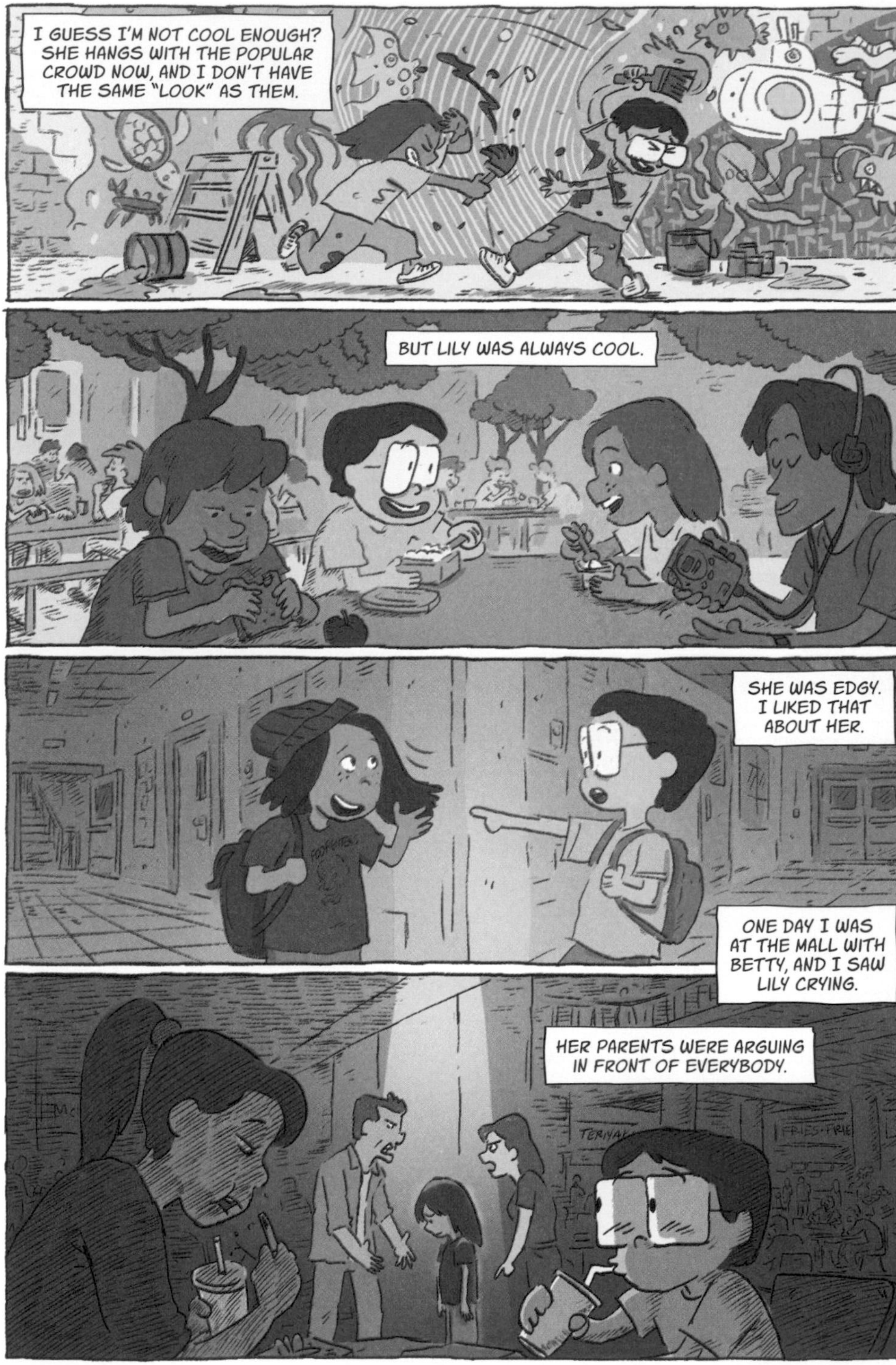
I GUESS I'M NOT COOL ENOUGH? SHE HANGS WITH THE POPULAR CROWD NOW, AND I DON'T HAVE THE SAME "LOOK" AS THEM.
BUT LILY WAS ALWAYS COOL.
SHE WAS EDGY. I LIKED THAT ABOUT HER.
ONE DAY I WAS AT THE MALL WITH BETTY, AND I SAW LILY CRYING.
HER PARENTS WERE ARGUING IN FRONT OF EVERYBODY.

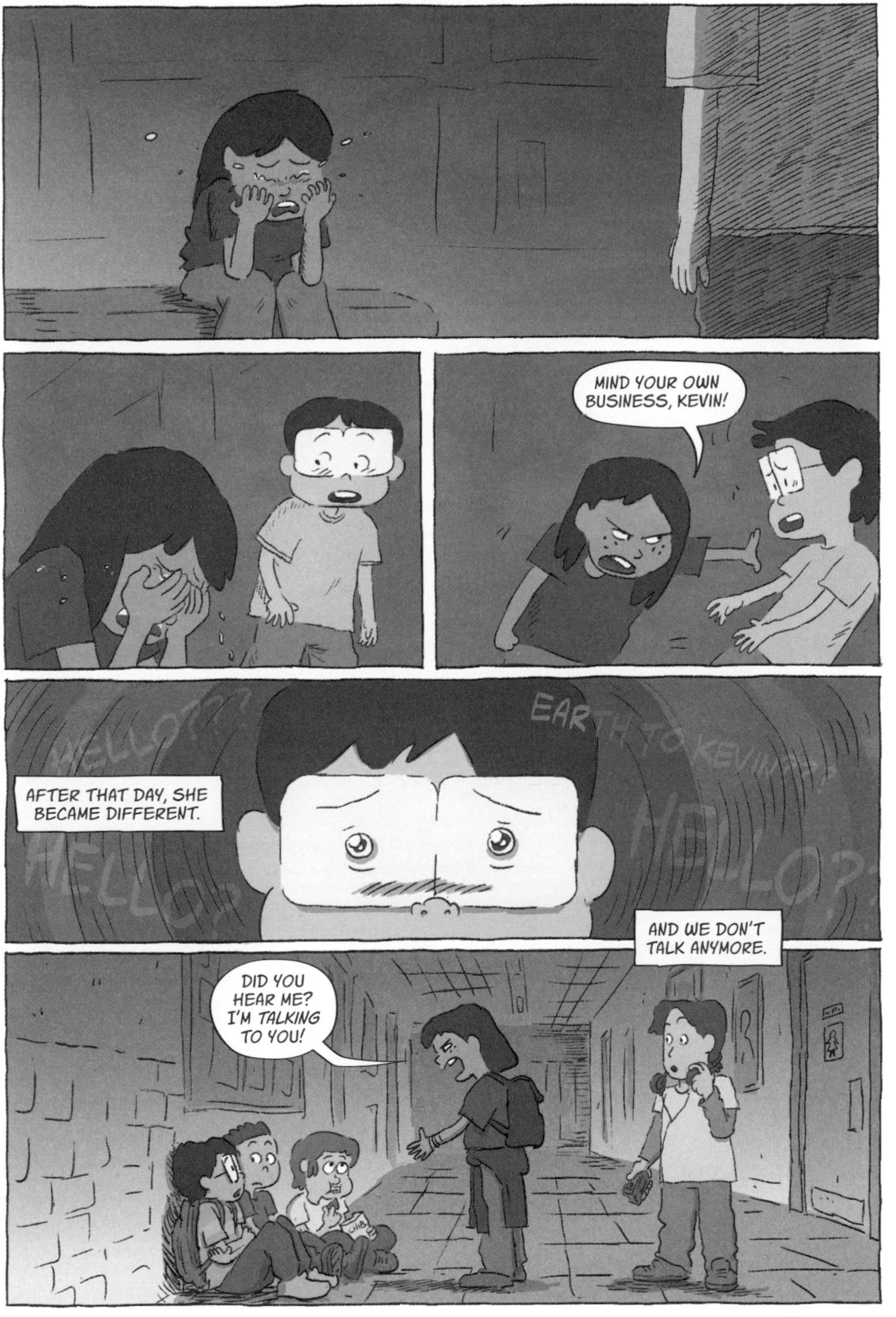
MIND YOUR OWN BUSINESS, KEVIN!
HELLO???
EARTH TO KEVIN???
AFTER THAT DAY, SHE BECAME DIFFERENT.
HELLO???
HELLO??
AND WE DON'T TALK ANYMORE.
DID YOU HEAR ME? I'M TALKING TO YOU!

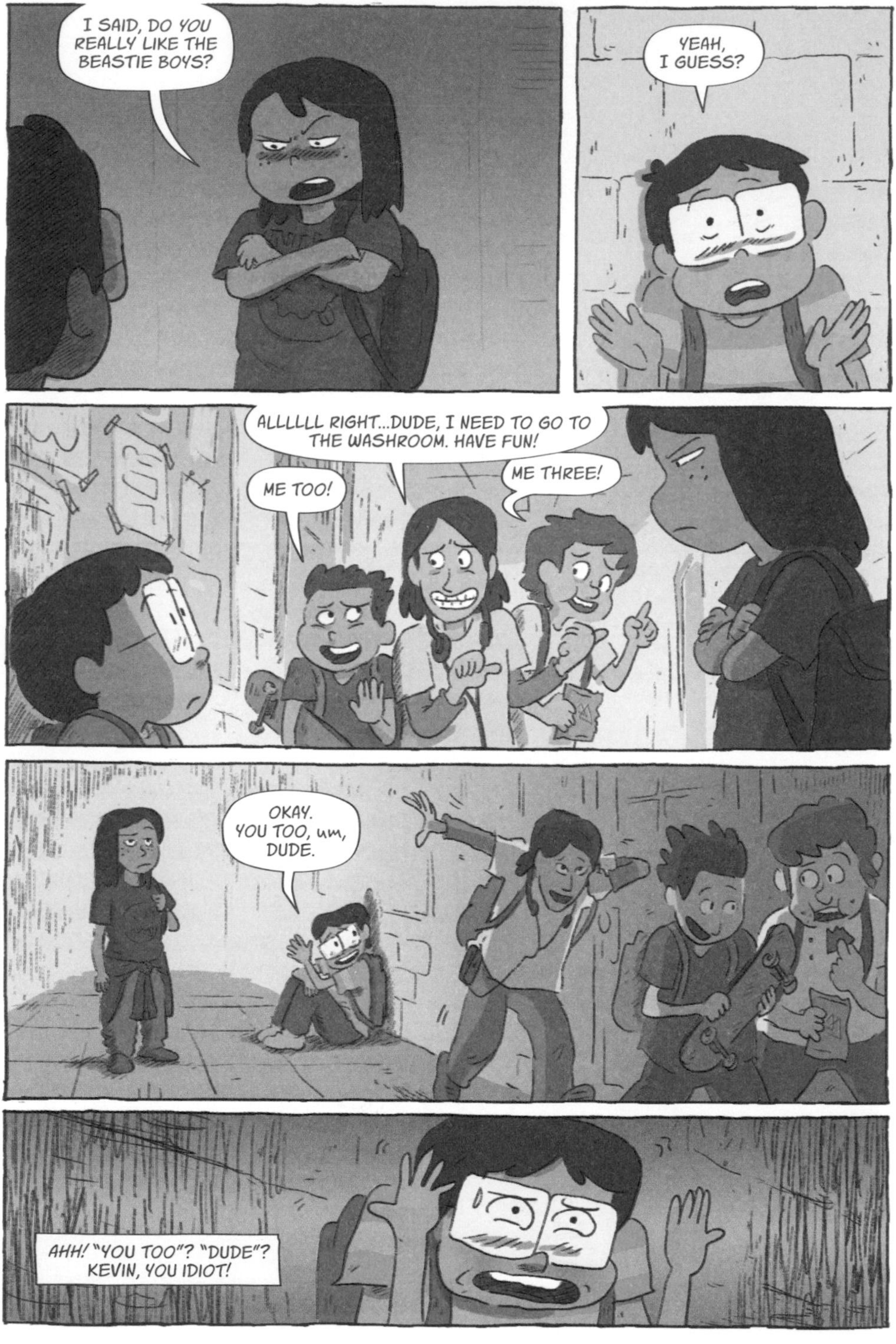
I SAID, DO YOU REALLY LIKE THE BEASTIE BOYS?
YEAH, I GUESS?
ALLLLLL RIGHT...DUDE, I NEED TO GO TO THE WASHROOM. HAVE FUN!
ME TOO!
ME THREE!
OKAY. YOU TOO, um, DUDE.
AHH! "YOU TOO"? "DUDE"? KEVIN, YOU IDIOT!

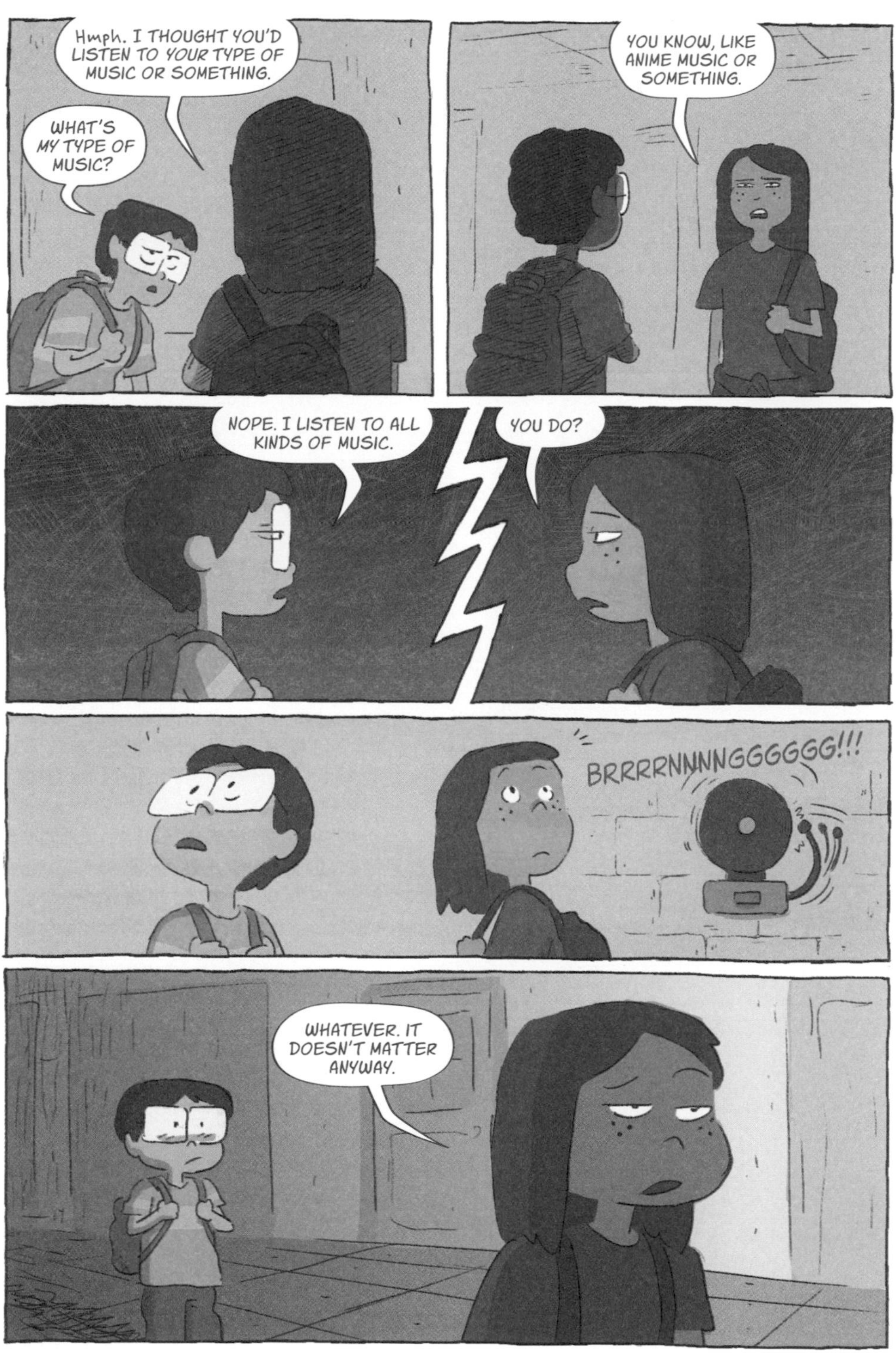
Hmph. I THOUGHT YOU'D LISTEN TO YOUR TYPE OF MUSIC OR SOMETHING.
WHAT'S MY TYPE OF MUSIC?
YOU KNOW, LIKE ANIME MUSIC OR SOMETHING.
NOPE. I LISTEN TO ALL KINDS OF MUSIC.
YOU DO?
BRRRRNNNNGGGGGG!!!
WHATEVER. IT DOESN'T MATTER ANYWAY.

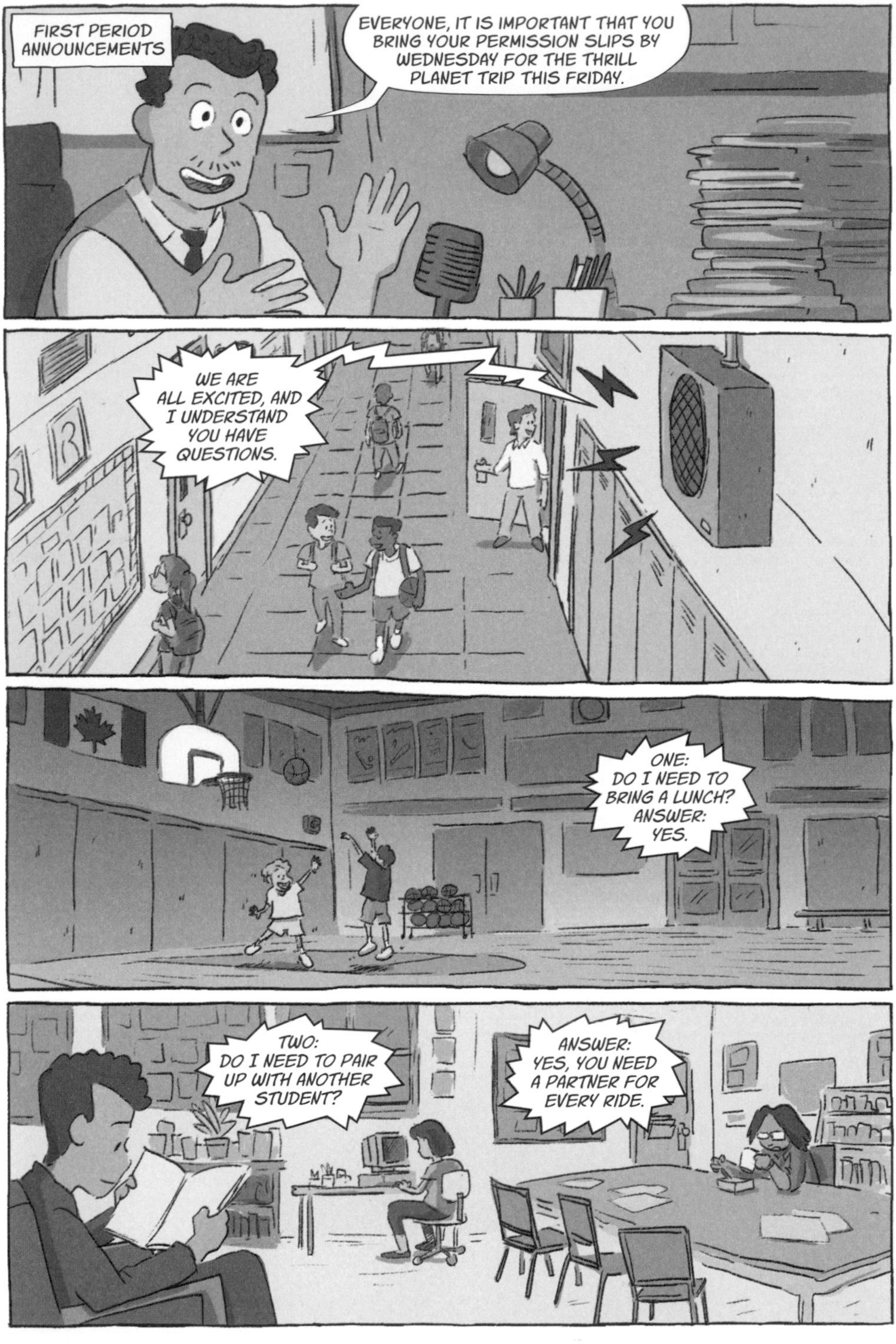
FIRST PERIOD ANNOUNCEMENTS
EVERYONE, IT IS IMPORTANT THAT YOU BRING YOUR PERMISSION SLIPS BY WEDNESDAY FOR THE THRILL PLANET TRIP THIS FRIDAY.
WE ARE ALL EXCITED, AND I UNDERSTAND YOU HAVE QUESTIONS.
ONE: DO I NEED TO BRING A LUNCH? ANSWER: YES.
TWO: DO I NEED TO PAIR UP WITH ANOTHER STUDENT?
ANSWER: YES, YOU NEED A PARTNER FOR EVERY RIDE.

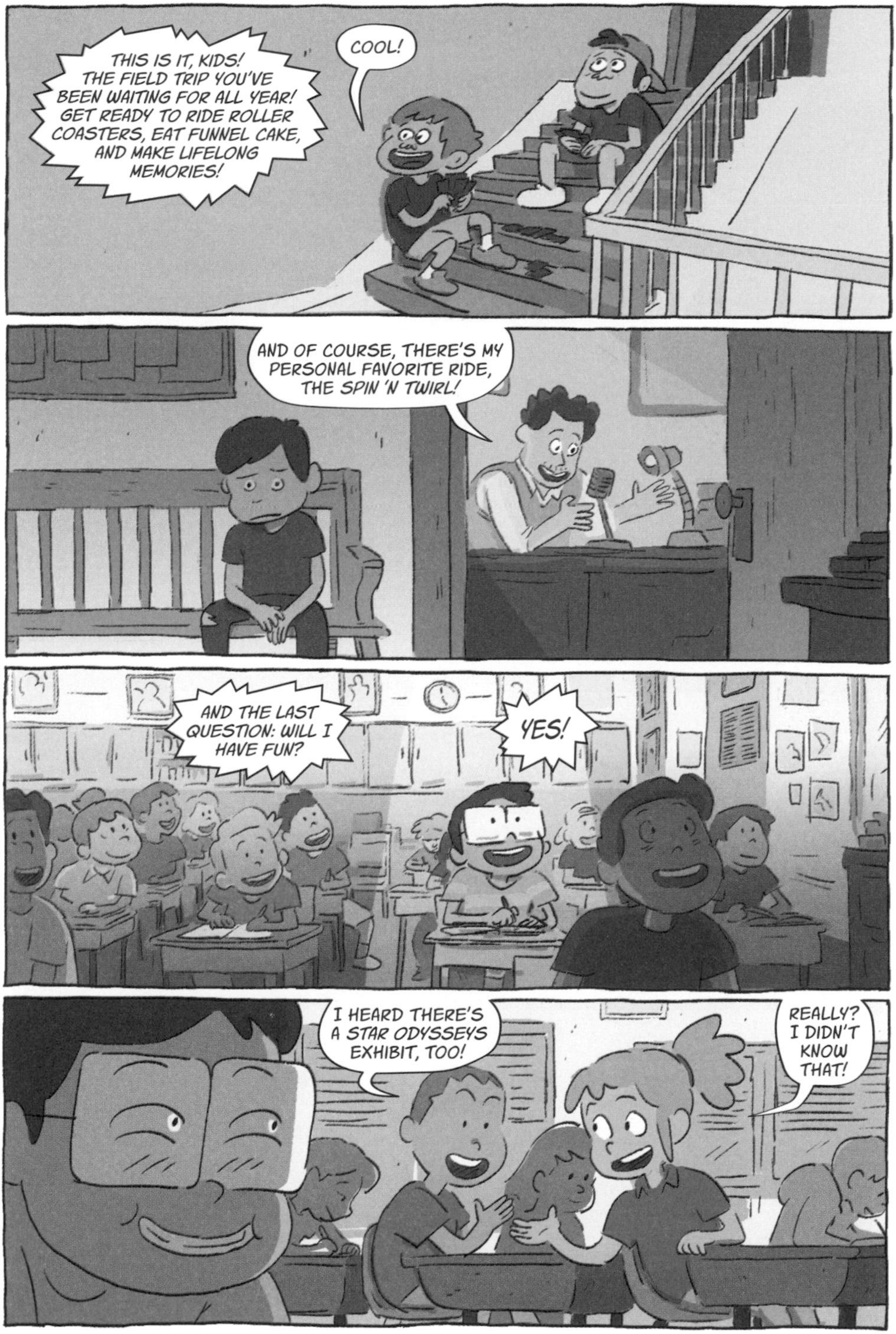
THIS IS IT, KIDS! THE FIELD TRIP YOU'VE BEEN WAITING FOR ALL YEAR! GET READY TO RIDE ROLLER COASTERS, EAT FUNNEL CAKE, AND MAKE LIFELONG MEMORIES!
COOL!
AND OF COURSE, THERE'S MY PERSONAL FAVORITE RIDE, THE SPIN 'N TWIRL!
AND THE LAST QUESTION: WILL I HAVE FUN?
YES!
I HEARD THERE'S A STAR ODYSSEYS EXHIBIT, TOO!
REALLY? I DIDN'T KNOW THAT!

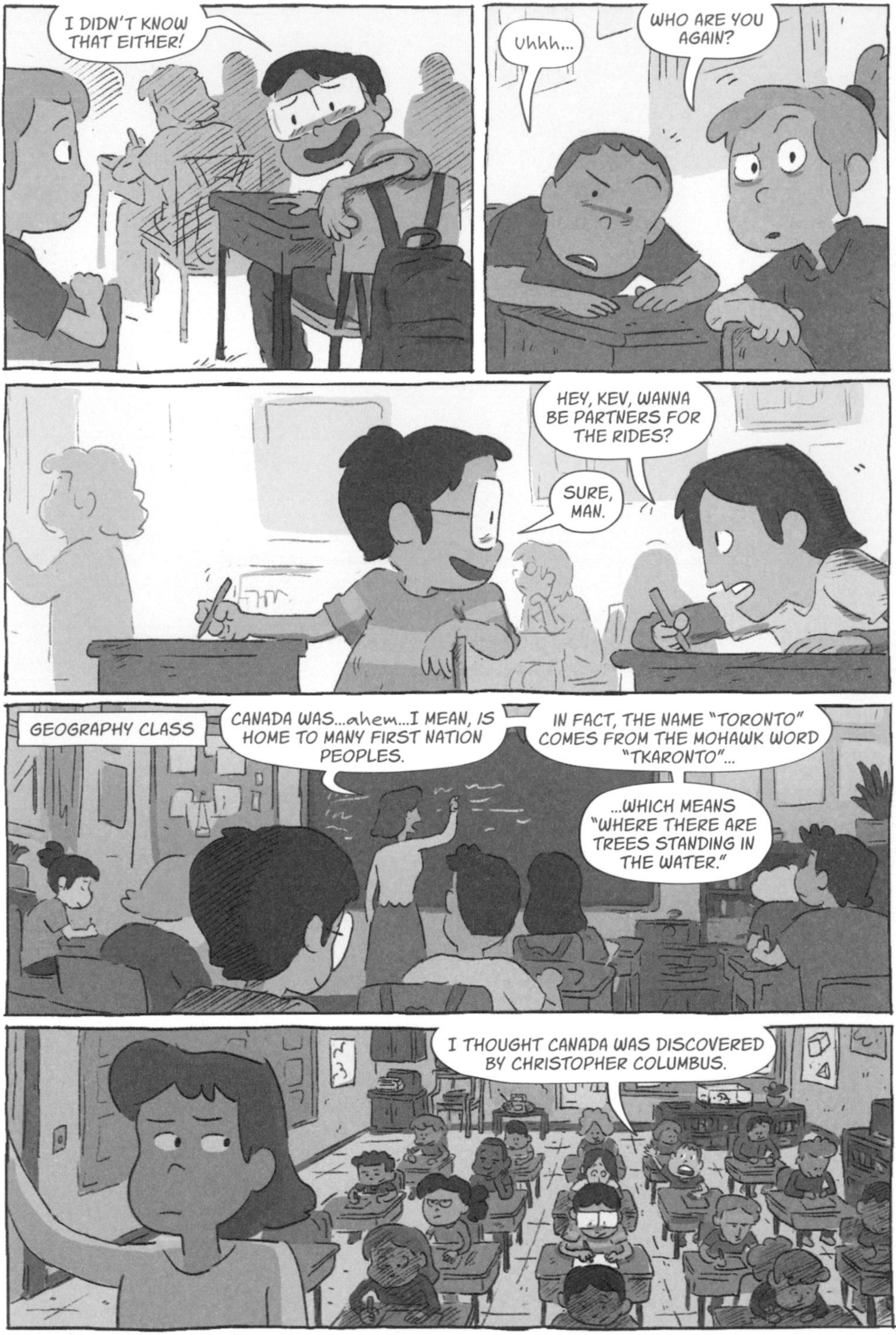
I DIDN'T KNOW THAT EITHER!
Uhhh...
WHO ARE YOU AGAIN?
HEY, KEV, WANNA BE PARTNERS FOR THE RIDES?
SURE, MAN.
GEOGRAPHY CLASS
CANADA WAS...ahem...I MEAN, IS HOME TO MANY FIRST NATION PEOPLES.
IN FACT, THE NAME "TORONTO" COMES FROM THE MOHAWK WORD "TKARONTO"...
...WHICH MEANS "WHERE THERE ARE TREES STANDING IN THE WATER."
I THOUGHT CANADA WAS DISCOVERED BY CHRISTOPHER COLUMBUS.

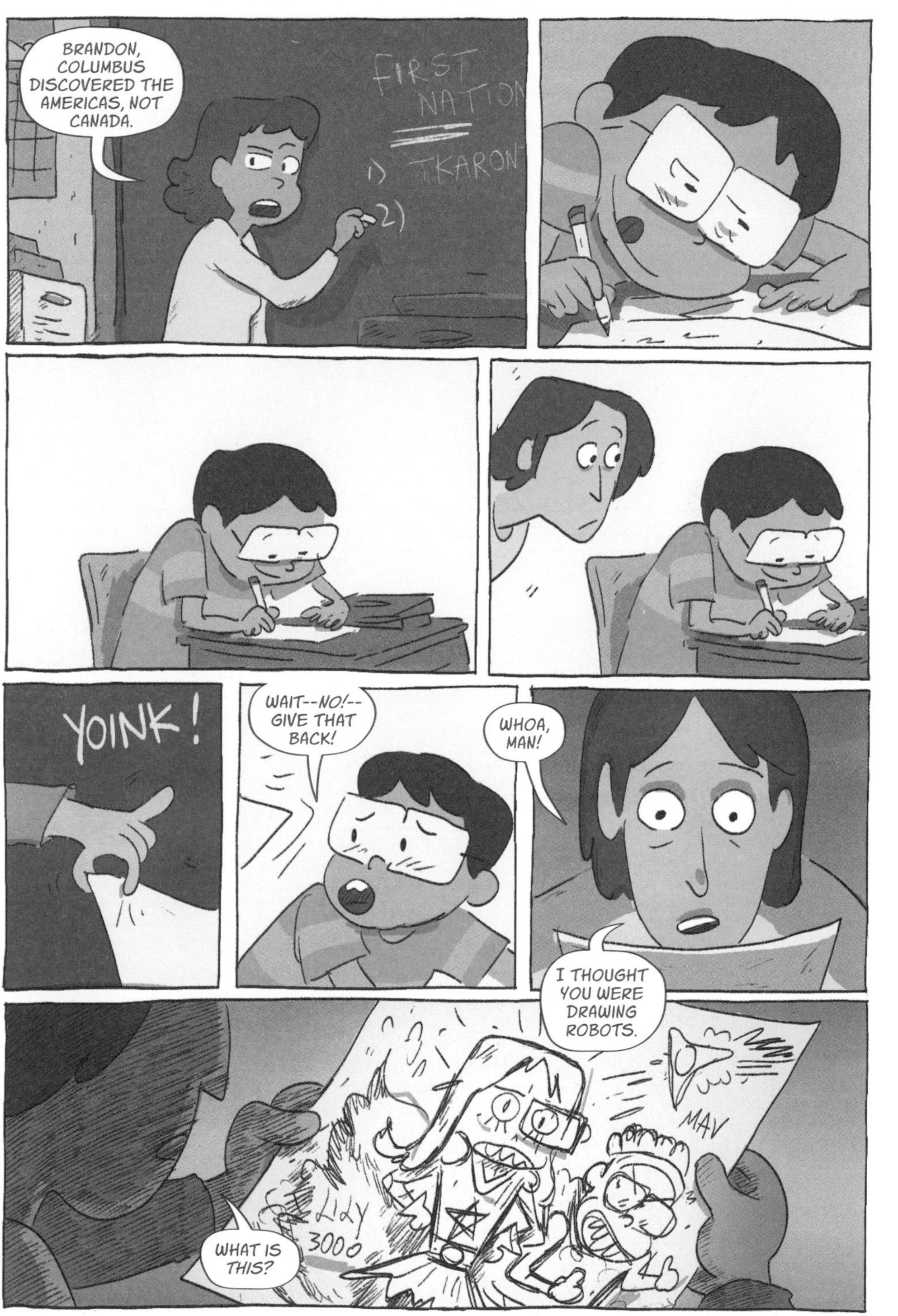
BRANDON, COLUMBUS DISCOVERED THE AMERICAS, NOT CANADA.
FIRST NATION
1) TKARONT
2)
YOINK!
WAIT--NO!-- GIVE THAT BACK!
WHOA, MAN!
I THOUGHT YOU WERE DRAWING ROBOTS.
MAV
LILY 3000
WHAT IS THIS?

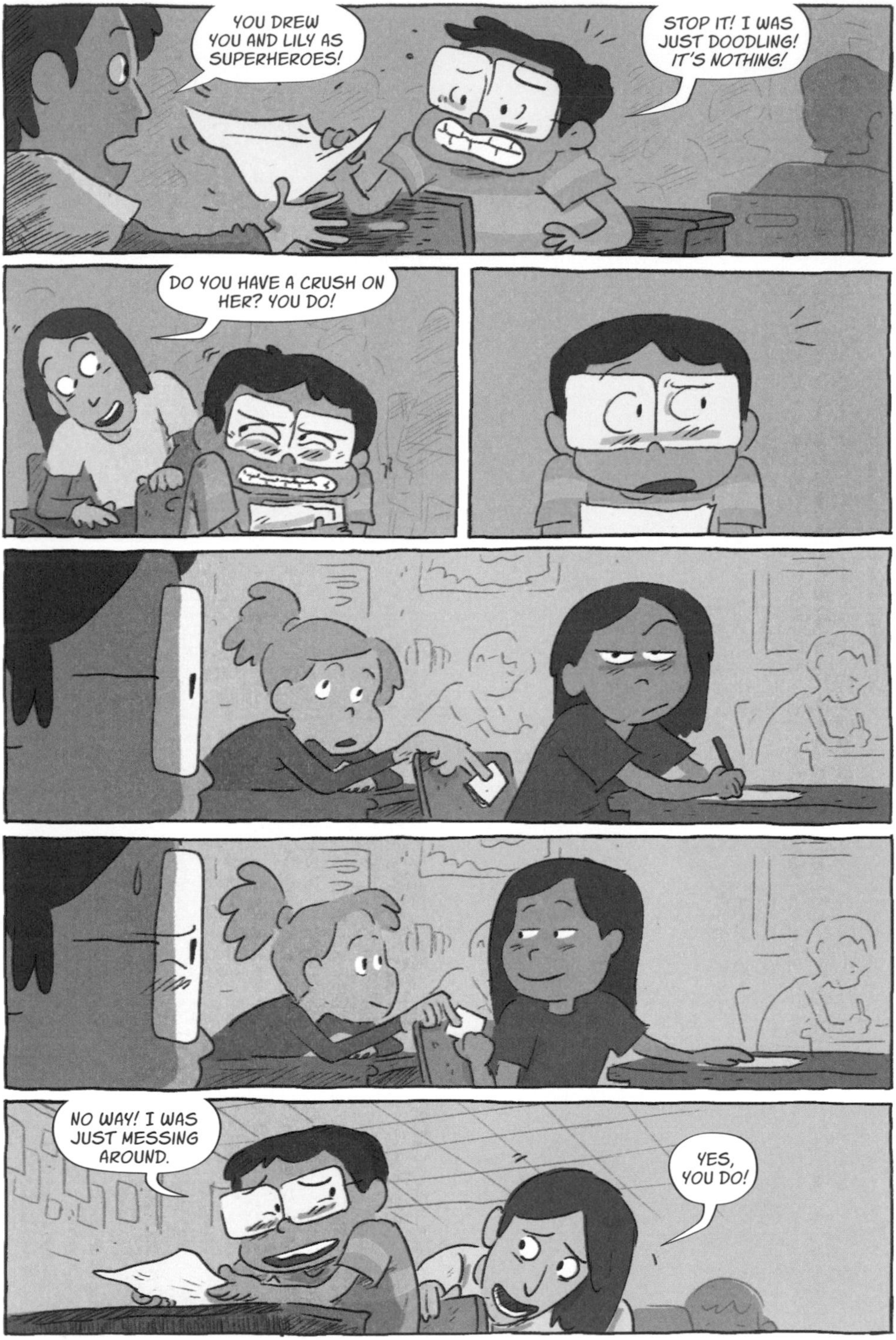
YOU DREW YOU AND LILY AS SUPERHEROES!
STOP IT! I WAS JUST DOODLING! IT'S NOTHING!
DO YOU HAVE A CRUSH ON HER? YOU DO!
NO WAY! I WAS JUST MESSING AROUND.
YES, YOU DO!

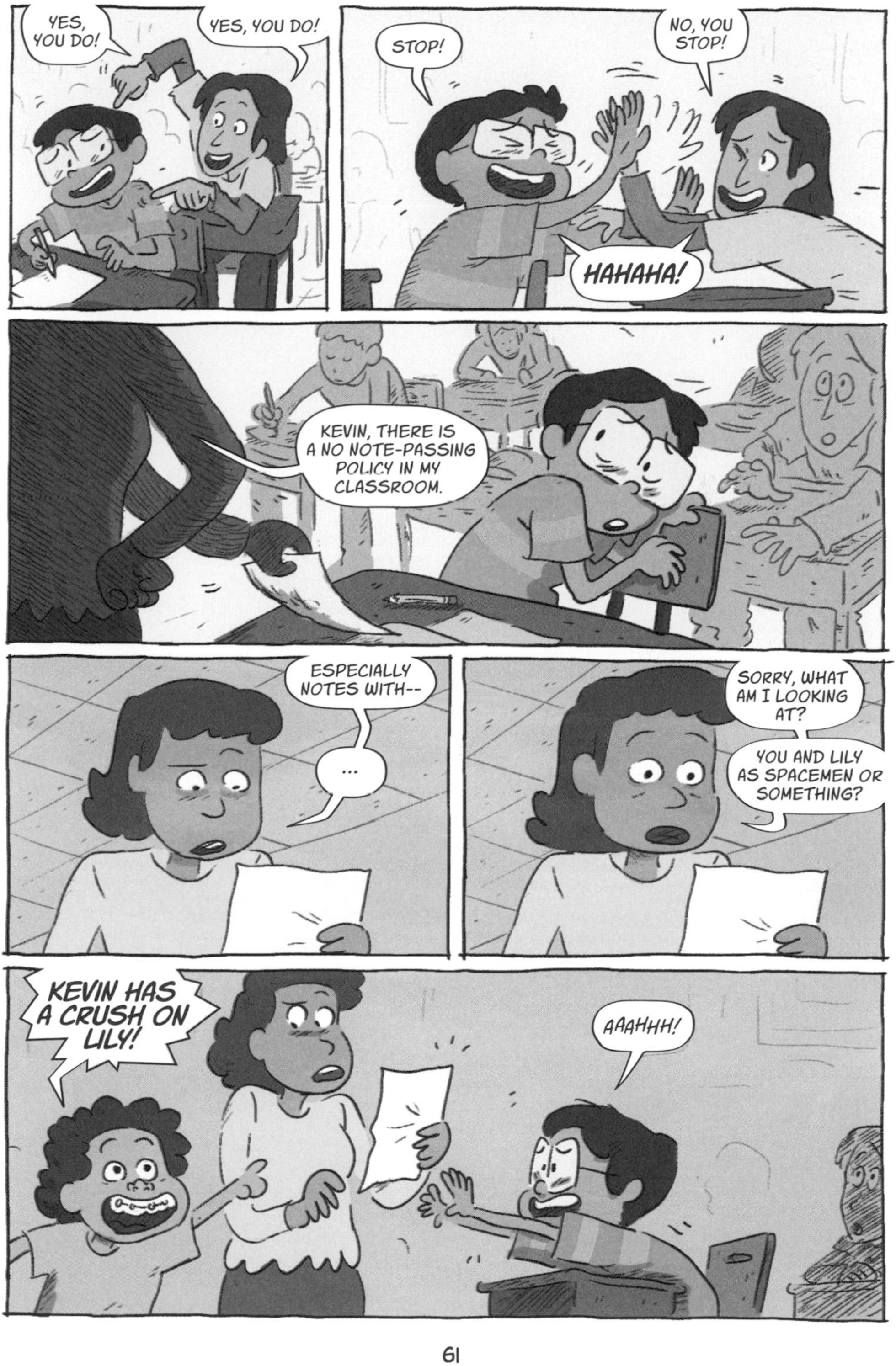
YES, YOU DO!
YES, YOU DO!
STOP!
NO, YOU STOP!
HAHAHA!
KEVIN, THERE IS A NO NOTE-PASSING POLICY IN MY CLASSROOM.
ESPECIALLY NOTES WITH--
...
SORRY, WHAT AM I LOOKING AT?
YOU AND LILY AS SPACEMEN OR SOMETHING?
KEVIN HAS A CRUSH ON LILY!
AAAHHH!

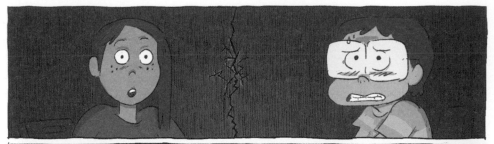

LUNCH BREAK

OH, CRAP. KEEP MOVING.

THANKS FOR LETTING THE WHOLE WORLD KNOW ABOUT LILY, MAN.

SORRY, DUDE. BUT IT'S NOT A BIG DEAL. WHO CARES IF YOU LIKE HER?

SHE IS SUPER MEAN TO YOU, THOUGH.

I KNOW. BUT IT WASN'T ALWAYS THAT WAY.

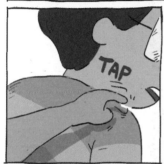

TAP

KEVIN!

I DON'T LIKE YOU, AND YOU CAN'T LIKE ME!

Um, I DON'T KNOW WHAT YOU'RE--

YES, YOU DO! YOU ARE NOT SUPPOSED TO LIKE SOMEONE LIKE ME. GOT IT?

I HAVE A REPUTATION. I AM GOING TO BE VALEDICTORIAN.

I'M SMARTER THAN YOU, AND YOU ARE WEIRD!

WHAT? WHY AM I WEIRD?

YOU STARE AT ME AND DRAW AND DRAW AND DRAW!

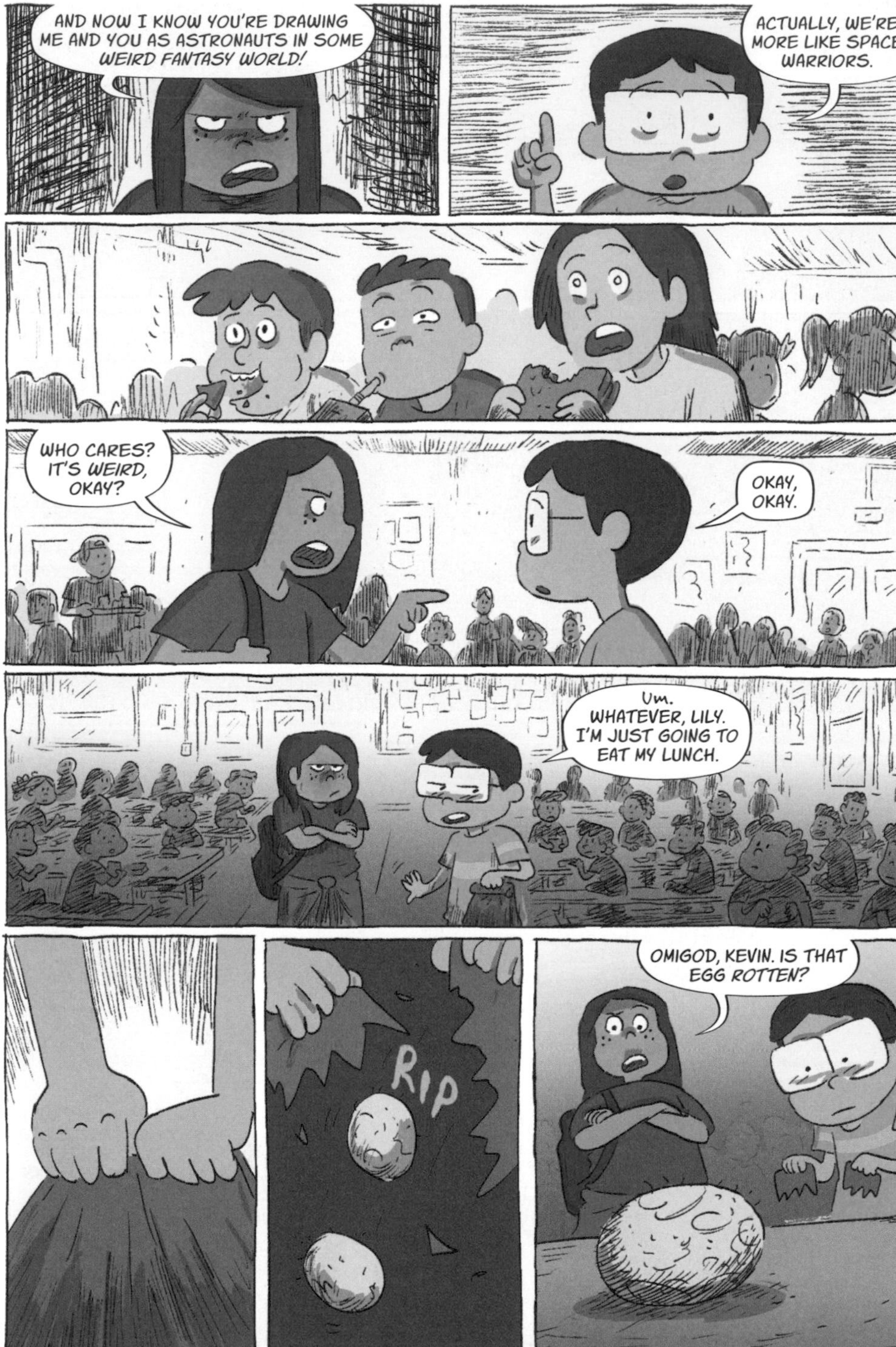
AND NOW I KNOW YOU'RE DRAWING ME AND YOU AS ASTRONAUTS IN SOME WEIRD FANTASY WORLD!
ACTUALLY, WE'RE MORE LIKE SPACE WARRIORS.
WHO CARES? IT'S WEIRD, OKAY?
OKAY, OKAY.
UM. WHATEVER, LILY. I'M JUST GOING TO EAT MY LUNCH.
RIP
OMIGOD, KEVIN. IS THAT EGG ROTTEN?

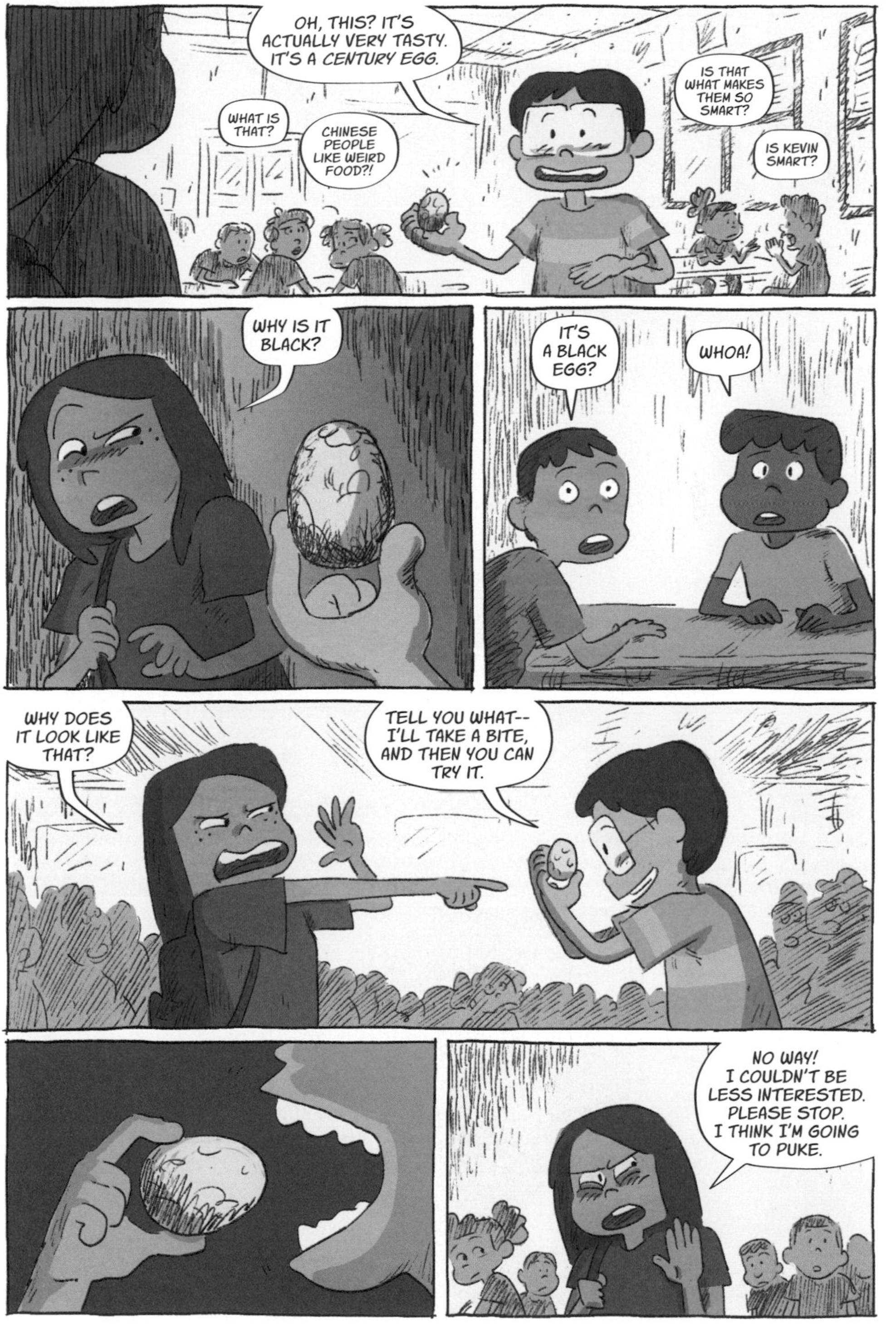
OH, THIS? IT'S ACTUALLY VERY TASTY. IT'S A *CENTURY EGG.*
WHAT IS THAT?
CHINESE PEOPLE LIKE WEIRD FOOD?!
IS THAT WHAT MAKES THEM SO SMART?
IS KEVIN SMART?
WHY IS IT BLACK?
IT'S A BLACK EGG?
WHOA!
WHY DOES IT LOOK LIKE THAT?
TELL YOU WHAT-- I'LL TAKE A BITE, AND THEN YOU CAN TRY IT.
NO WAY! I COULDN'T BE LESS INTERESTED. PLEASE STOP. I THINK I'M GOING TO PUKE.

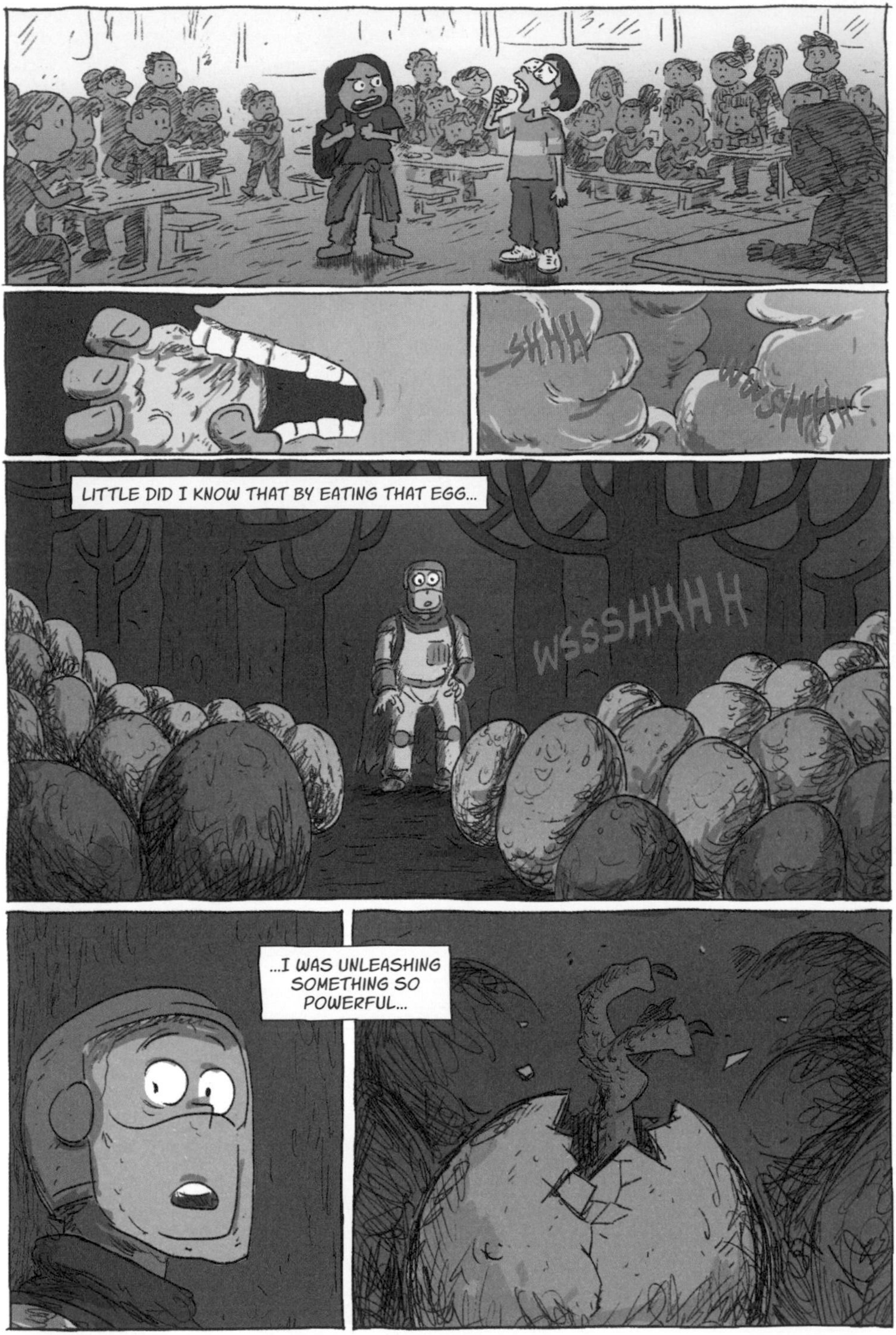
SHHH
LITTLE DID I KNOW THAT BY EATING THAT EGG...
WSSSHHHH
...I WAS UNLEASHING SOMETHING SO POWERFUL...

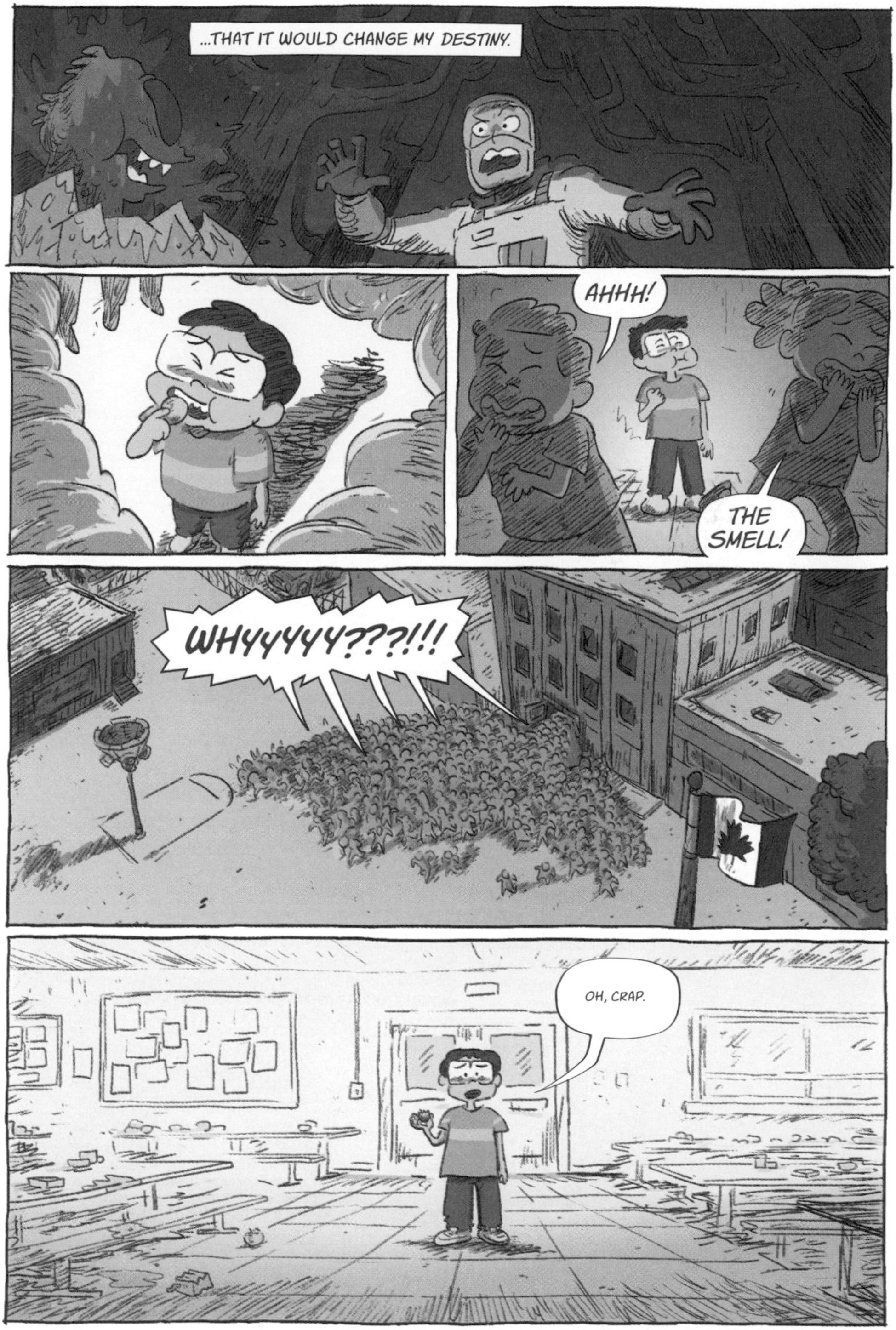
...THAT IT WOULD CHANGE MY DESTINY.
AHHH!
THE SMELL!
WHYYYYY???!!!
OH, CRAP.

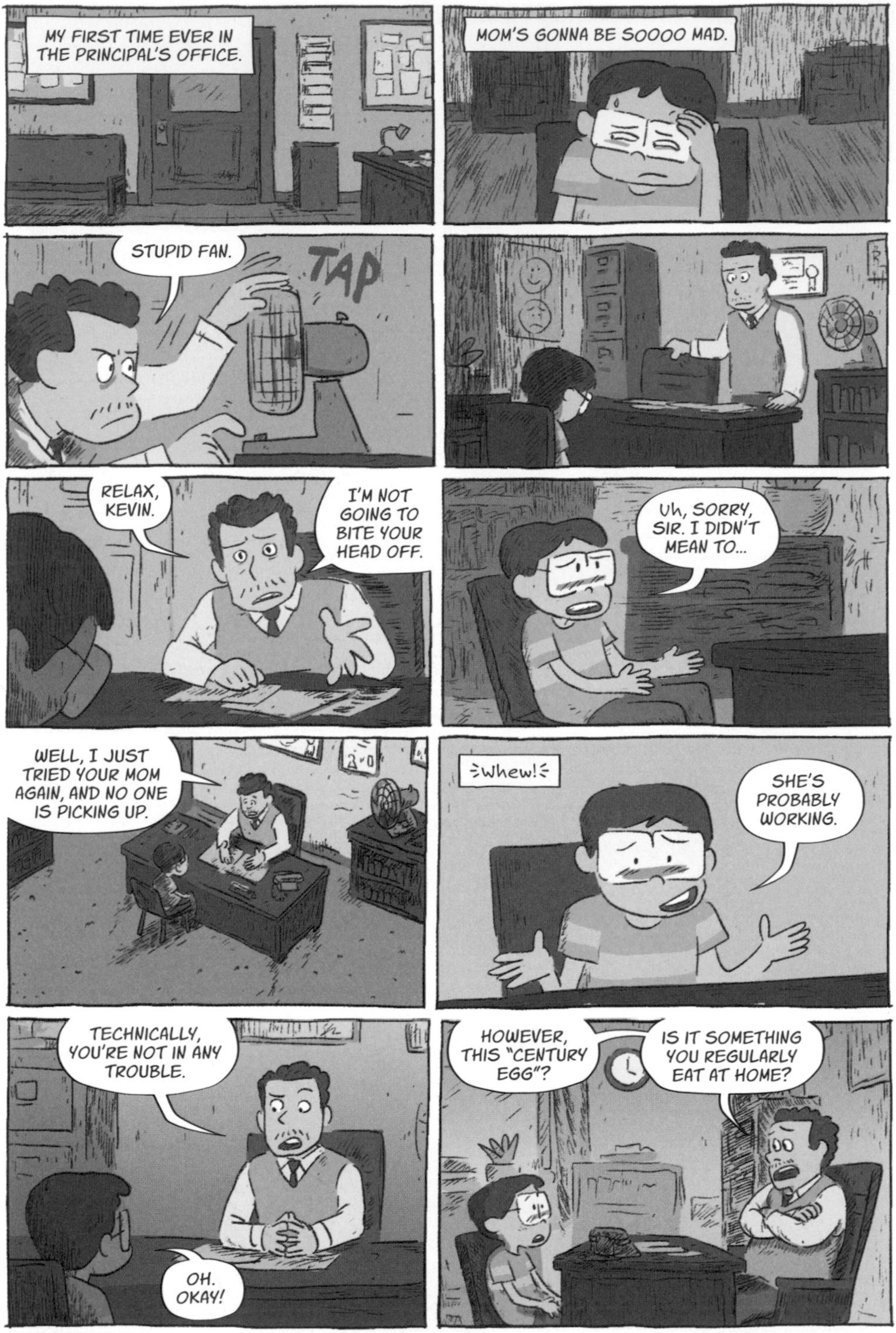
MY FIRST TIME EVER IN THE PRINCIPAL'S OFFICE.
MOM'S GONNA BE SOOOO MAD.
STUPID FAN.
TAP
RELAX, KEVIN.
I'M NOT GOING TO BITE YOUR HEAD OFF.
Uh, SORRY, SIR. I DIDN'T MEAN TO...
WELL, I JUST TRIED YOUR MOM AGAIN, AND NO ONE IS PICKING UP.
Whew!
SHE'S PROBABLY WORKING.
TECHNICALLY, YOU'RE NOT IN ANY TROUBLE.
OH. OKAY!
HOWEVER, THIS "CENTURY EGG"?
IS IT SOMETHING YOU REGULARLY EAT AT HOME?

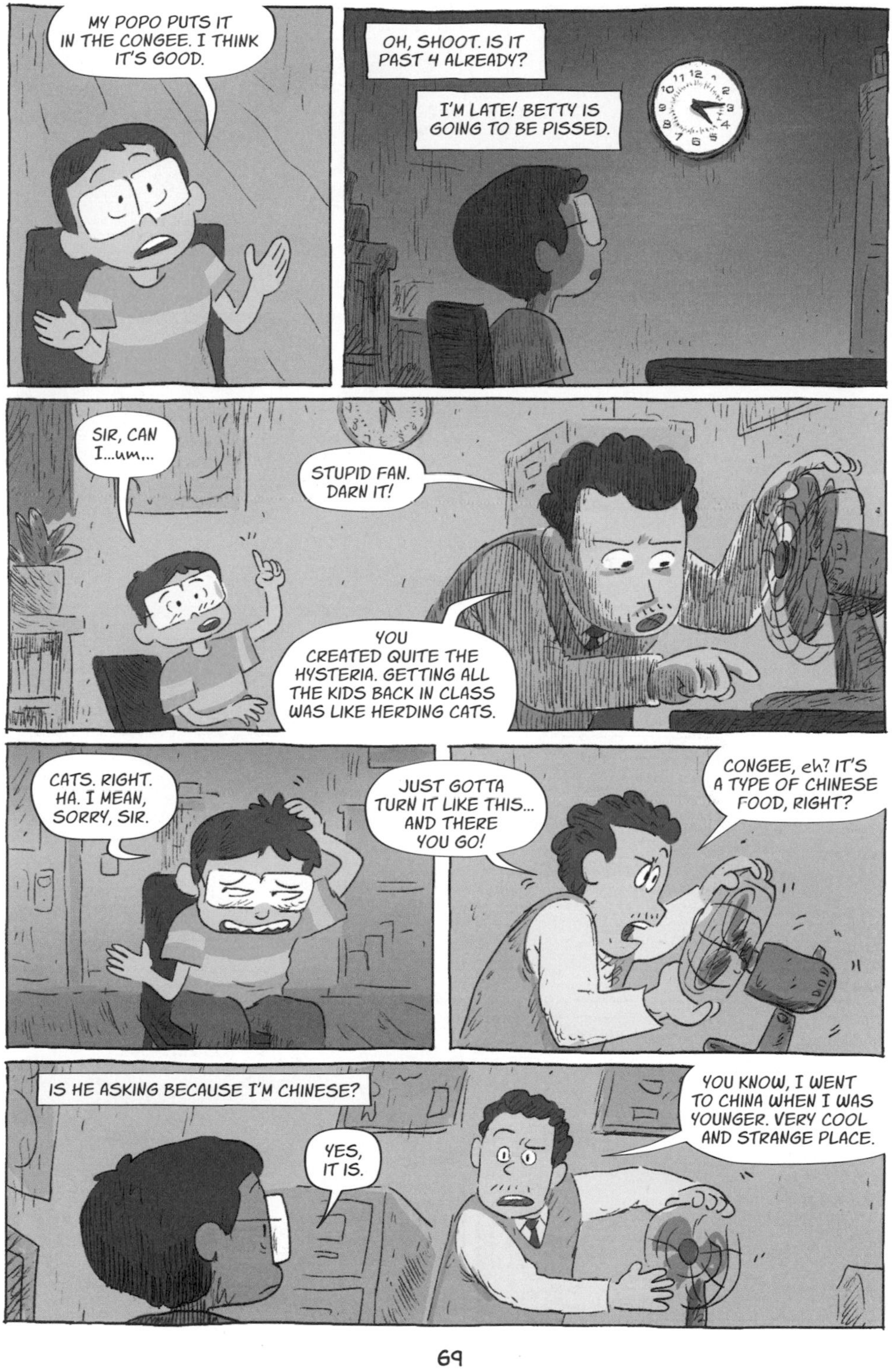
MY POPO PUTS IT IN THE CONGEE. I THINK IT'S GOOD.
OH, SHOOT. IS IT PAST 4 ALREADY?
I'M LATE! BETTY IS GOING TO BE PISSED.
SIR, CAN I...um...
STUPID FAN. DARN IT!
YOU CREATED QUITE THE HYSTERIA. GETTING ALL THE KIDS BACK IN CLASS WAS LIKE HERDING CATS.
CATS. RIGHT. HA. I MEAN, SORRY, SIR.
JUST GOTTA TURN IT LIKE THIS... AND THERE YOU GO!
CONGEE, eh? IT'S A TYPE OF CHINESE FOOD, RIGHT?
IS HE ASKING BECAUSE I'M CHINESE?
YES, IT IS.
YOU KNOW, I WENT TO CHINA WHEN I WAS YOUNGER. VERY COOL AND STRANGE PLACE.

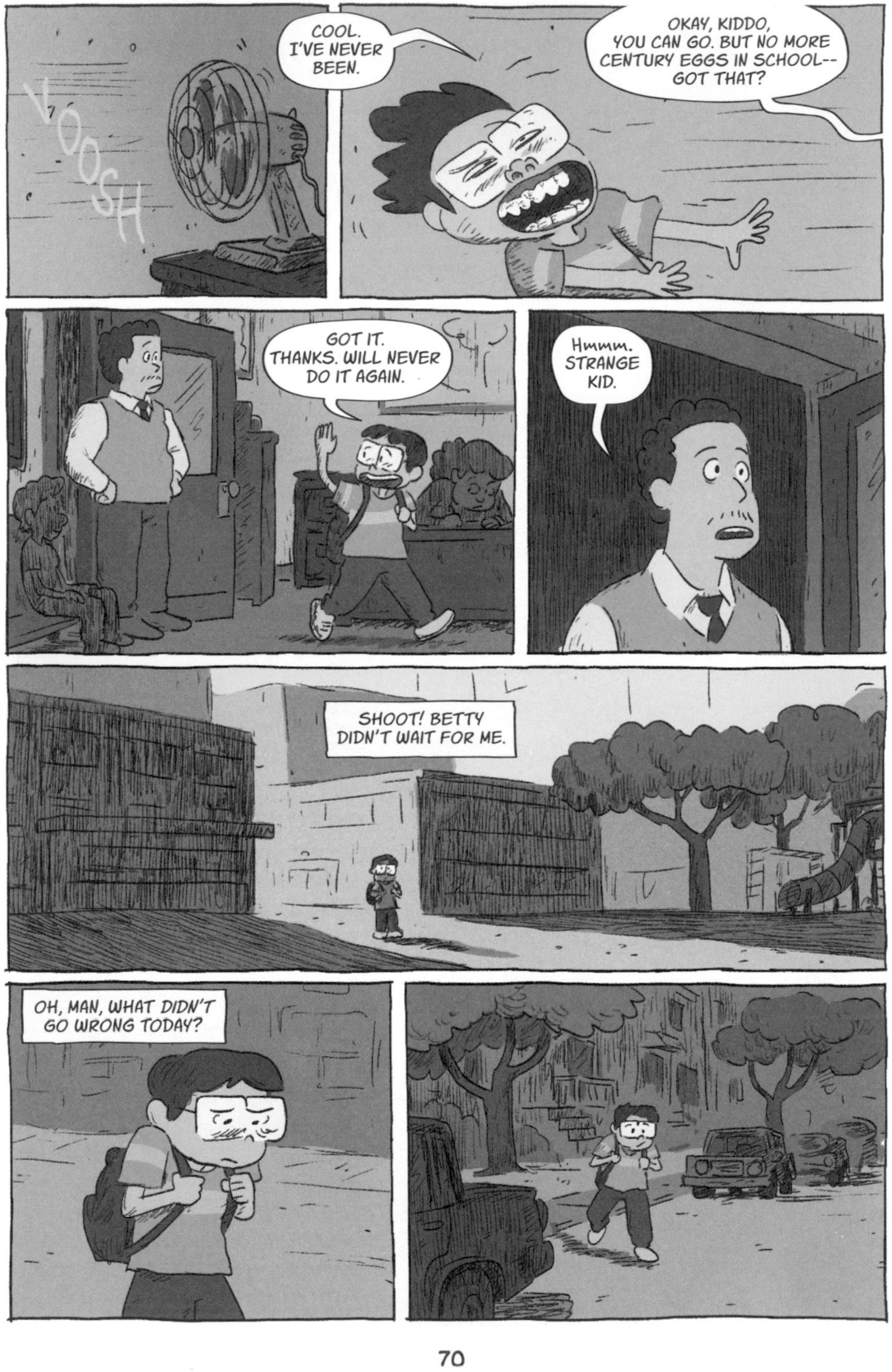
VOOSH
COOL. I'VE NEVER BEEN.
OKAY, KIDDO, YOU CAN GO. BUT NO MORE CENTURY EGGS IN SCHOOL-- GOT THAT?
GOT IT. THANKS. WILL NEVER DO IT AGAIN.
Hmmm. STRANGE KID.
SHOOT! BETTY DIDN'T WAIT FOR ME.
OH, MAN, WHAT DIDN'T GO WRONG TODAY?

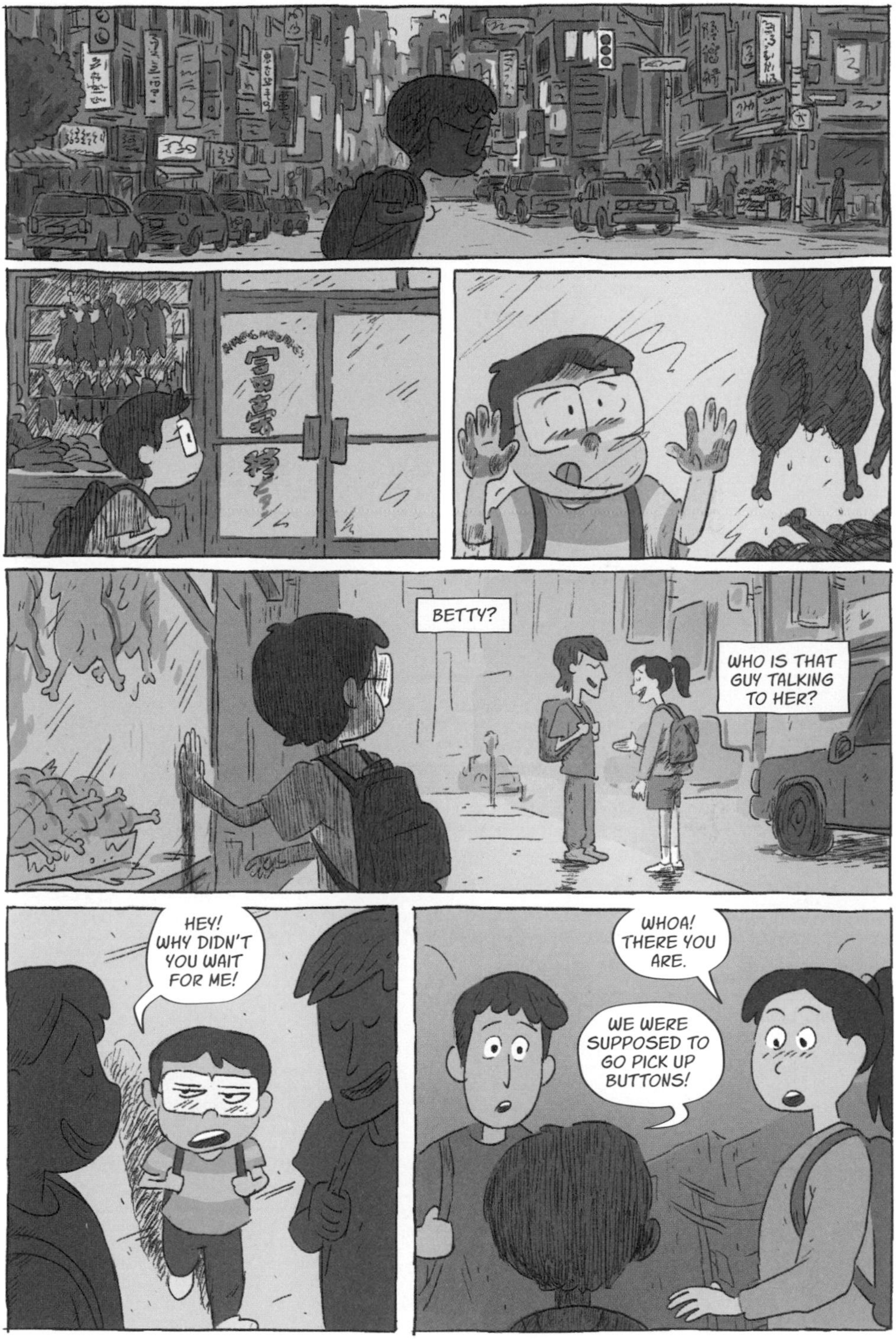
BETTY?
WHO IS THAT GUY TALKING TO HER?
HEY! WHY DIDN'T YOU WAIT FOR ME!
WHOA! THERE YOU ARE.
WE WERE SUPPOSED TO GO PICK UP BUTTONS!

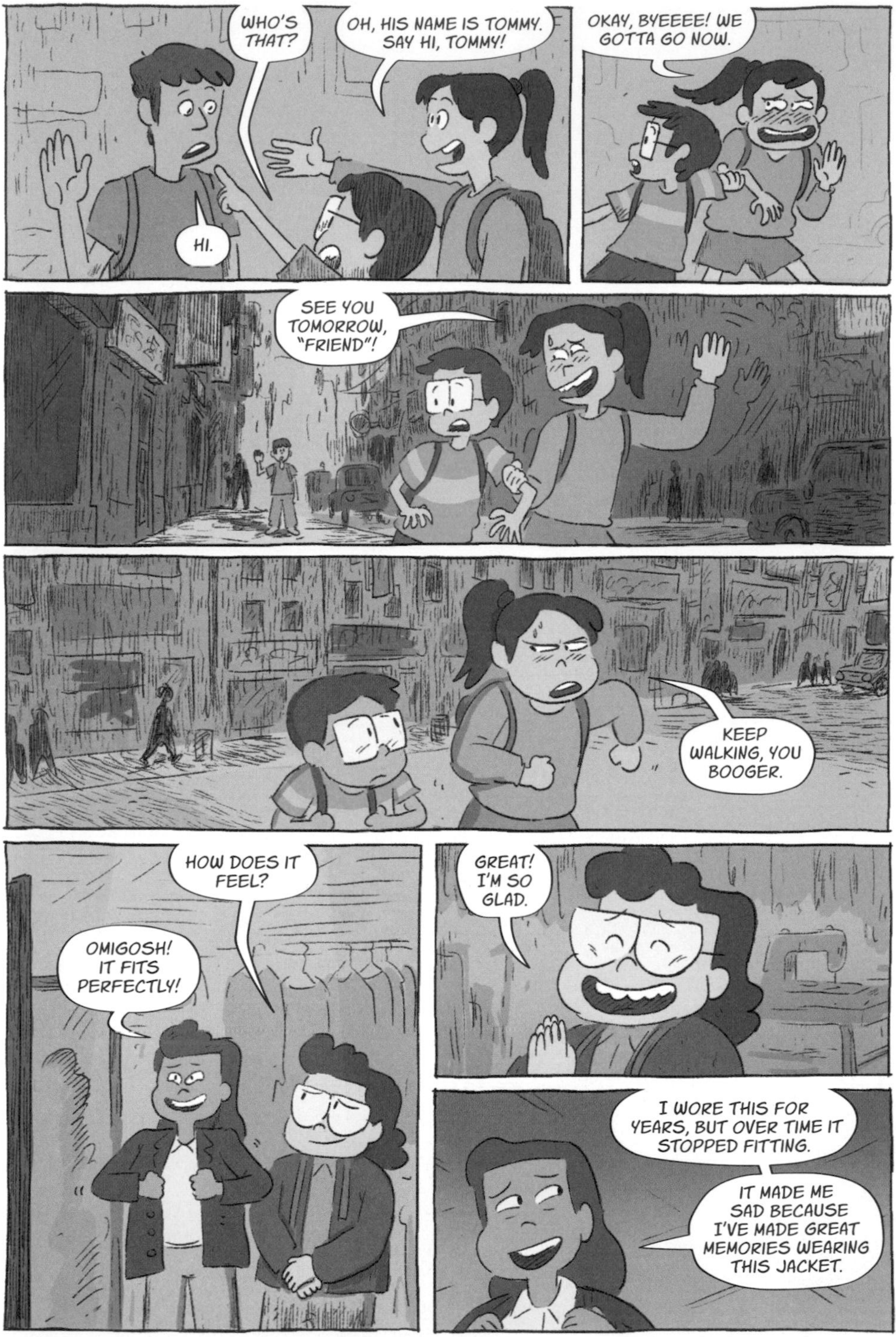
WHO'S THAT?
OH, HIS NAME IS TOMMY. SAY HI, TOMMY!
HI.
OKAY, BYEEEE! WE GOTTA GO NOW.
SEE YOU TOMORROW, "FRIEND"!
KEEP WALKING, YOU BOOGER.
HOW DOES IT FEEL?
OMIGOSH! IT FITS PERFECTLY!
GREAT! I'M SO GLAD.
I WORE THIS FOR YEARS, BUT OVER TIME IT STOPPED FITTING.
IT MADE ME SAD BECAUSE I'VE MADE GREAT MEMORIES WEARING THIS JACKET.

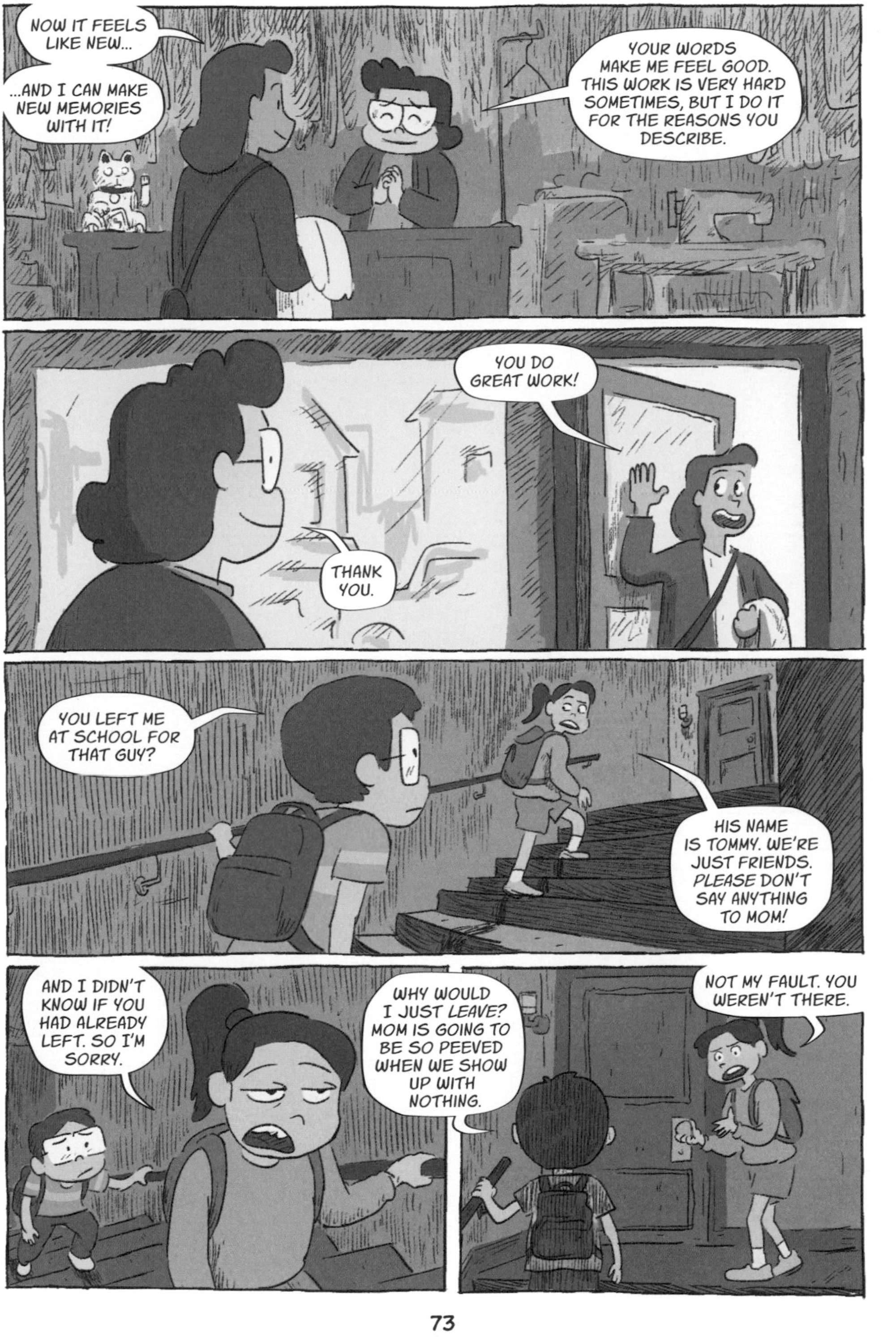
NOW IT FEELS LIKE NEW...
...AND I CAN MAKE NEW MEMORIES WITH IT!
YOUR WORDS MAKE ME FEEL GOOD. THIS WORK IS VERY HARD SOMETIMES, BUT I DO IT FOR THE REASONS YOU DESCRIBE.
YOU DO GREAT WORK!
THANK YOU.
YOU LEFT ME AT SCHOOL FOR THAT GUY?
HIS NAME IS TOMMY. WE'RE JUST FRIENDS. *PLEASE* DON'T SAY ANYTHING TO MOM!
AND I DIDN'T KNOW IF YOU HAD ALREADY LEFT. SO I'M SORRY.
WHY WOULD I JUST *LEAVE*? MOM IS GOING TO BE SO PEEVED WHEN WE SHOW UP WITH NOTHING.
NOT MY FAULT. YOU WEREN'T THERE.

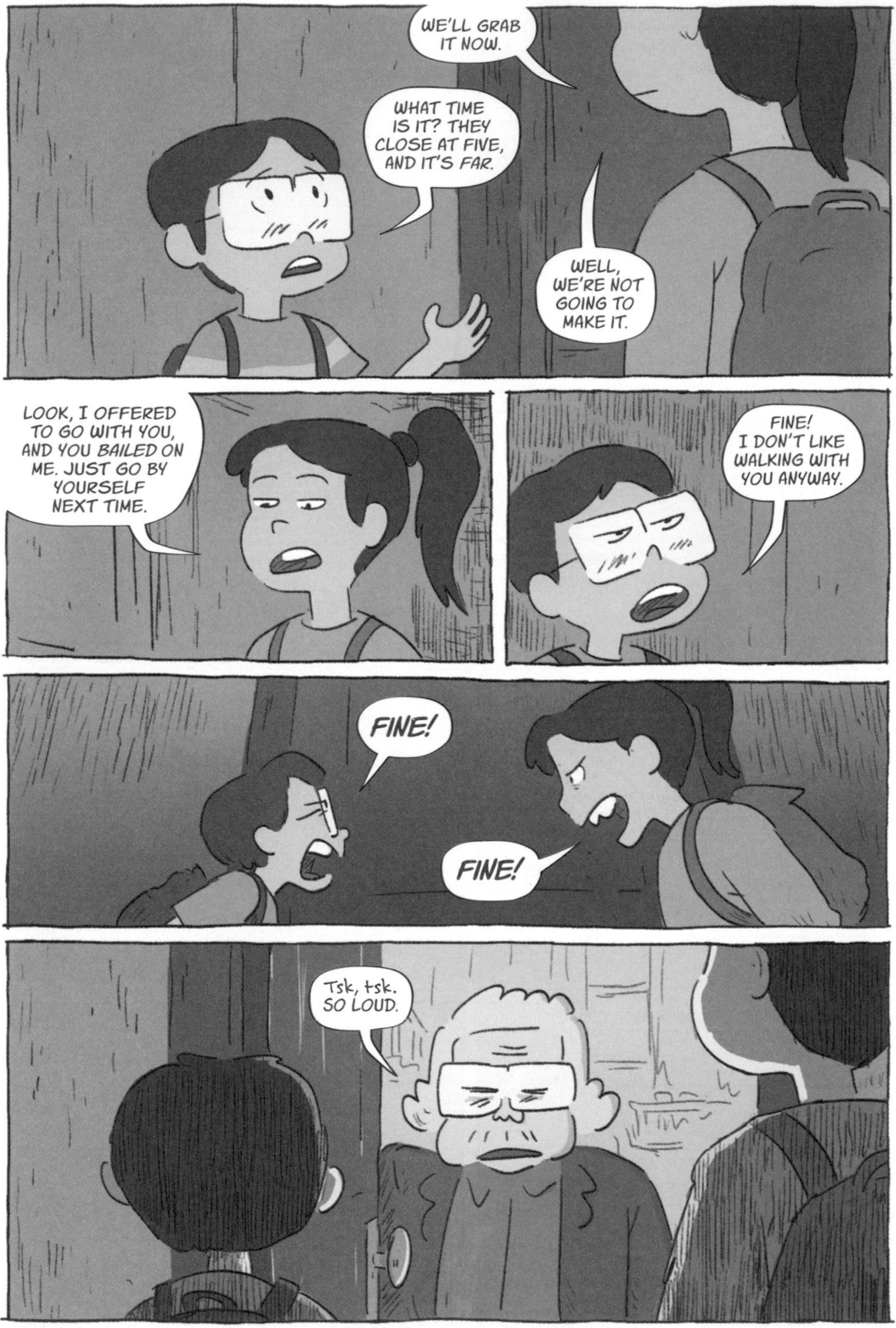
WE'LL GRAB IT NOW.
WHAT TIME IS IT? THEY CLOSE AT FIVE, AND IT'S *FAR*.
WELL, WE'RE NOT GOING TO MAKE IT.
LOOK, I OFFERED TO GO WITH YOU, AND YOU *BAILED* ON ME. JUST GO BY YOURSELF NEXT TIME.
FINE! I DON'T LIKE WALKING WITH YOU ANYWAY.
FINE!
FINE!
Tsk, tsk. SO LOUD.

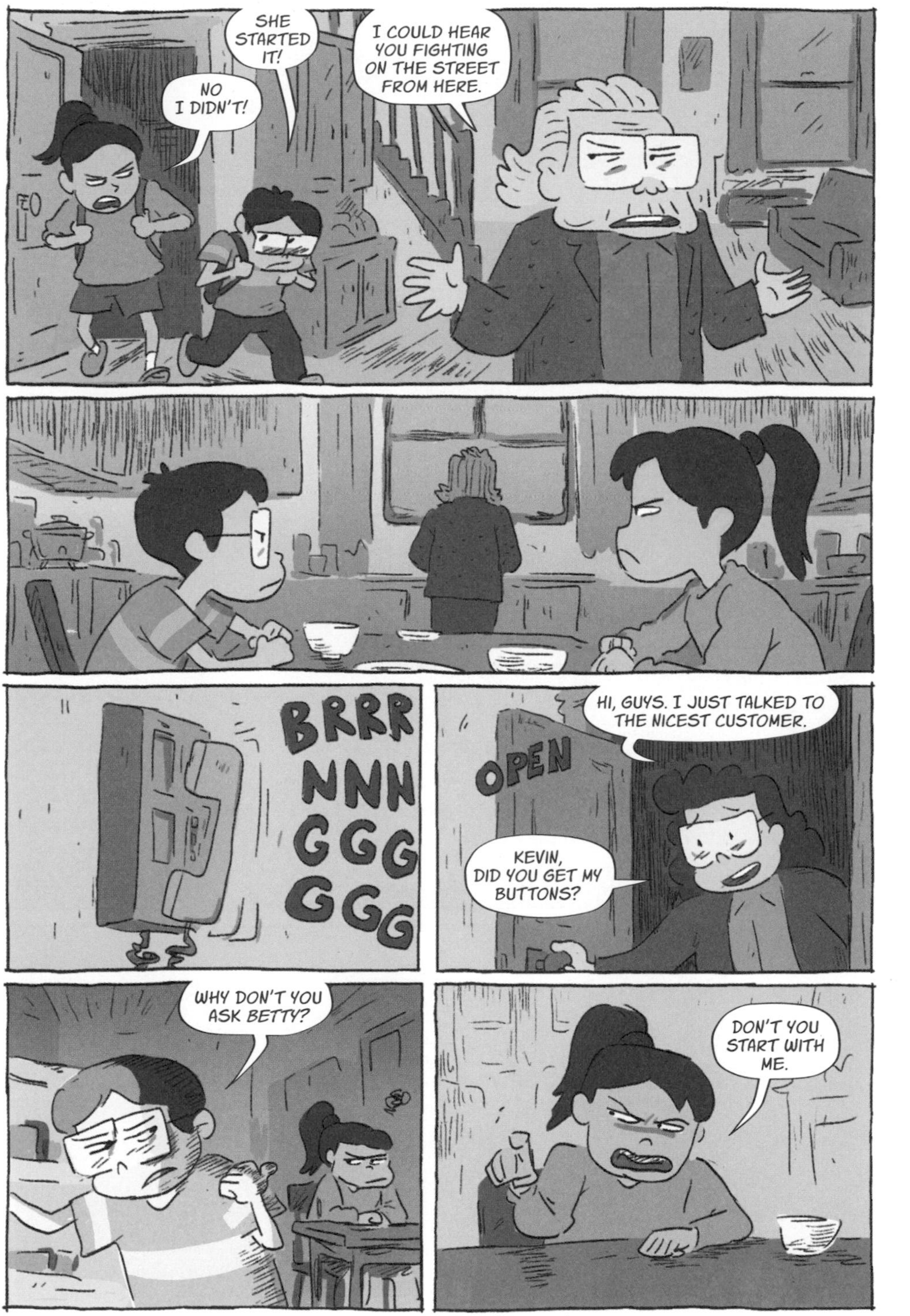
NO I DIDN'T!
SHE STARTED IT!
I COULD HEAR YOU FIGHTING ON THE STREET FROM HERE.
BRRR NNN GGG GGG
HI, GUYS. I JUST TALKED TO THE NICEST CUSTOMER.
OPEN
KEVIN, DID YOU GET MY BUTTONS?
WHY DON'T YOU ASK BETTY?
DON'T YOU START WITH ME.

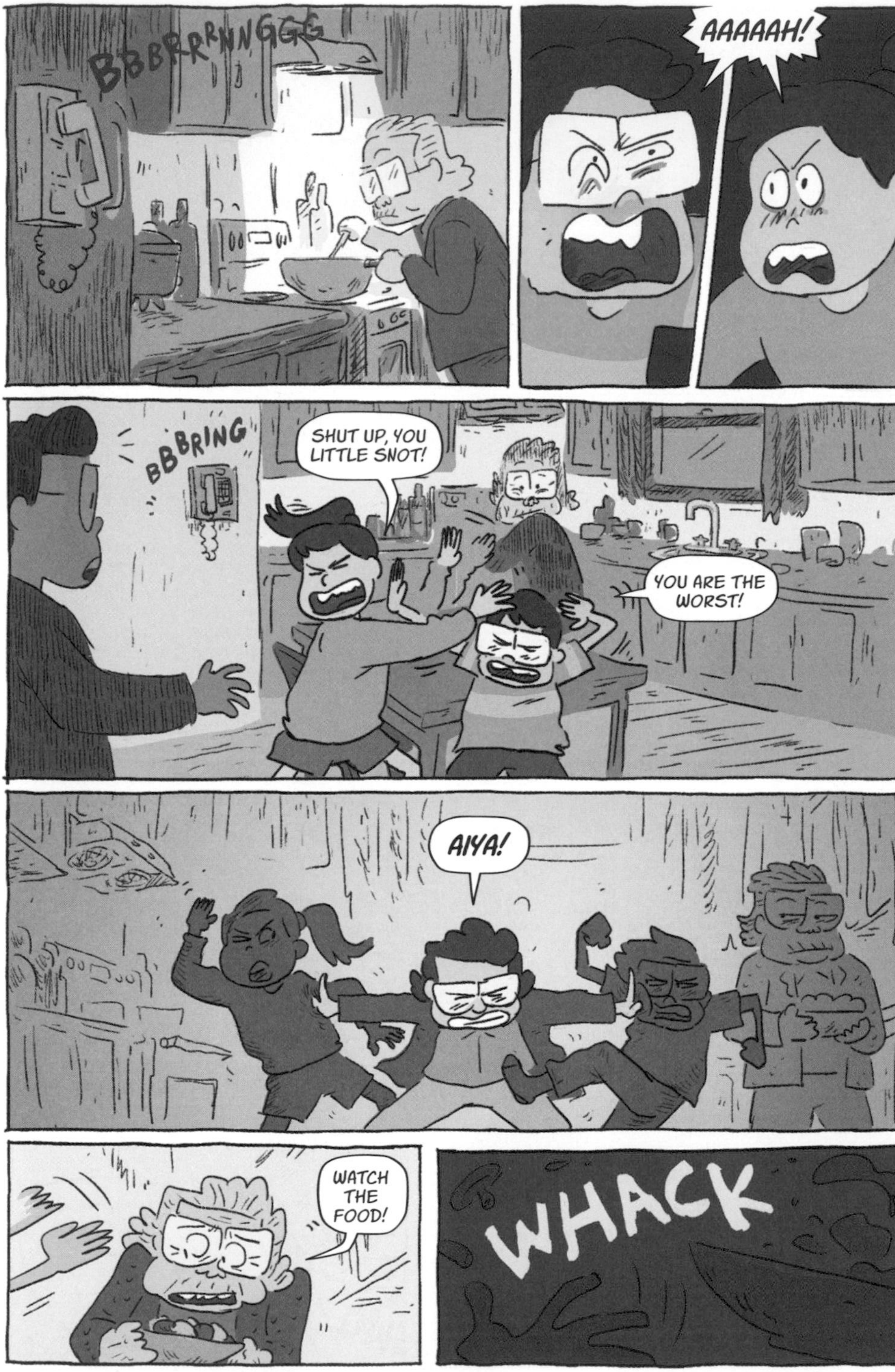
BBBRRRNNGGG
AAAAAH!
BBBRING
SHUT UP, YOU LITTLE SNOT!
YOU ARE THE WORST!
AIYA!
WATCH THE FOOD!
WHACK

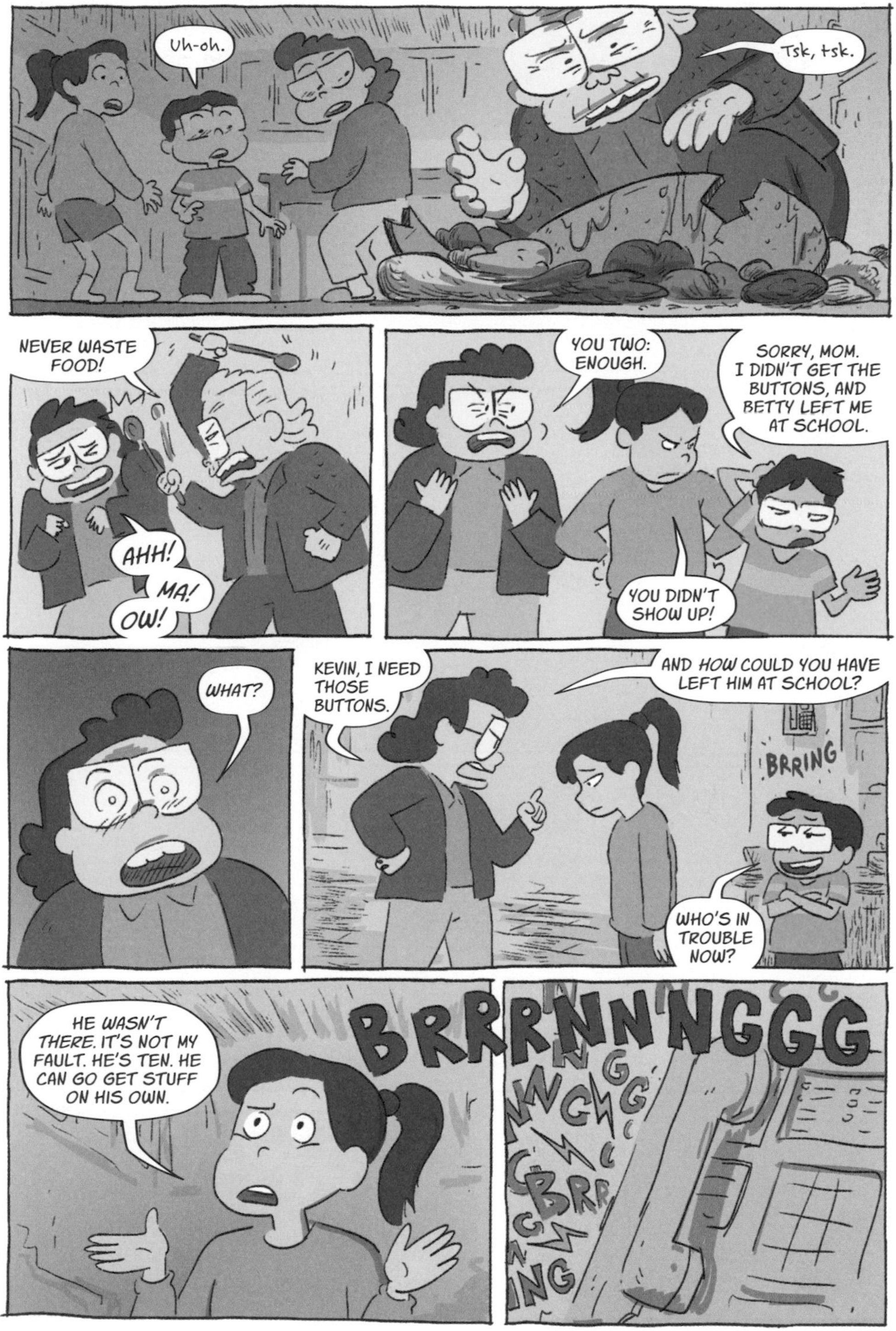
Uh-oh.
Tsk, tsk.
NEVER WASTE FOOD!
AHH!
MA!
OW!
YOU TWO: ENOUGH.
SORRY, MOM. I DIDN'T GET THE BUTTONS, AND BETTY LEFT ME AT SCHOOL.
YOU DIDN'T SHOW UP!
WHAT?
KEVIN, I NEED THOSE BUTTONS.
AND HOW COULD YOU HAVE LEFT HIM AT SCHOOL?
BRRING
WHO'S IN TROUBLE NOW?
HE WASN'T THERE. IT'S NOT MY FAULT. HE'S TEN. HE CAN GO GET STUFF ON HIS OWN.
BRRRNNNGGG

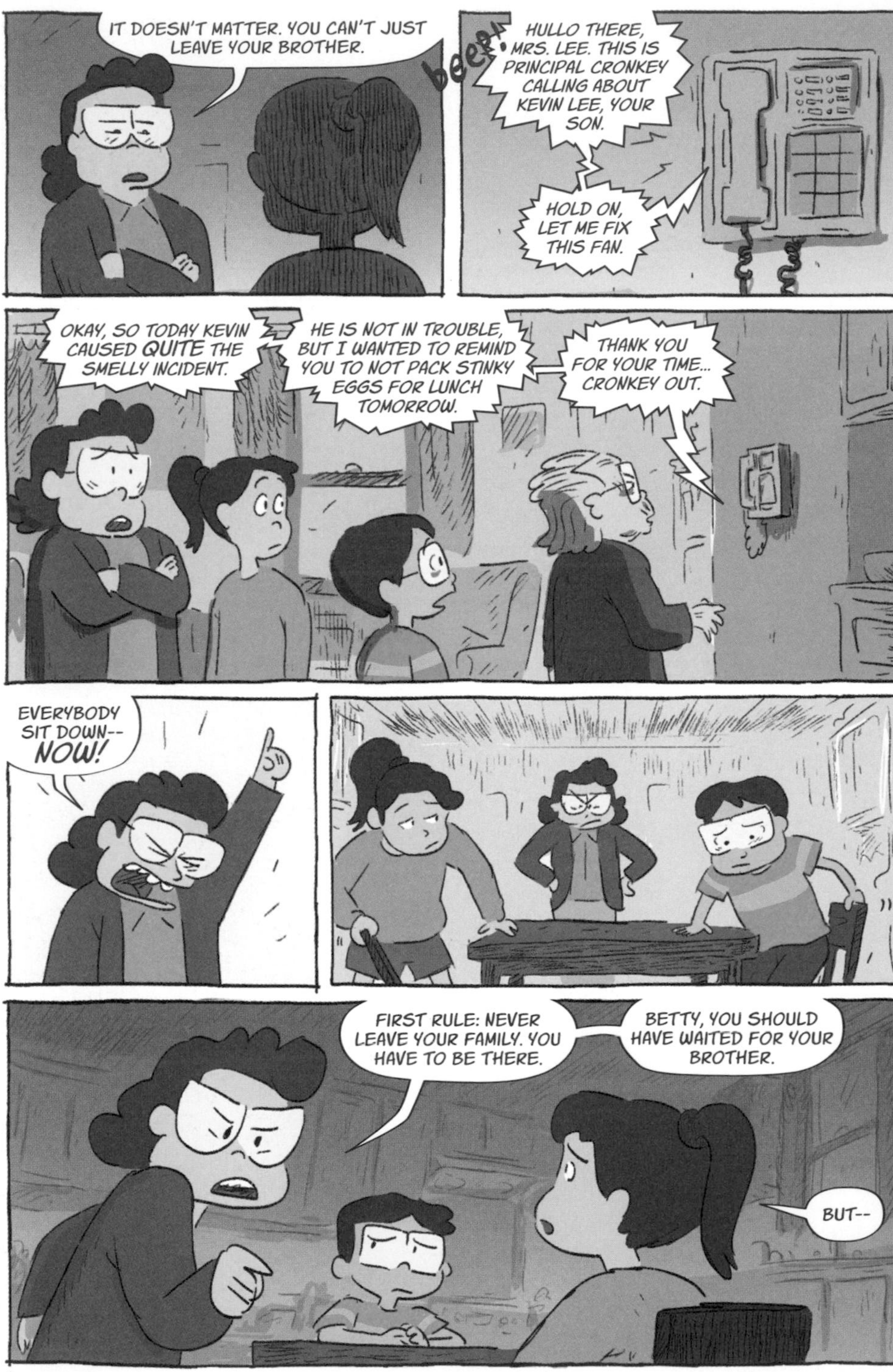
IT DOESN'T MATTER. YOU CAN'T JUST LEAVE YOUR BROTHER.
beep!
HULLO THERE, MRS. LEE. THIS IS PRINCIPAL CRONKEY CALLING ABOUT KEVIN LEE, YOUR SON.
HOLD ON, LET ME FIX THIS FAN.
OKAY, SO TODAY KEVIN CAUSED QUITE THE SMELLY INCIDENT.
HE IS NOT IN TROUBLE, BUT I WANTED TO REMIND YOU TO NOT PACK STINKY EGGS FOR LUNCH TOMORROW.
THANK YOU FOR YOUR TIME... CRONKEY OUT.
EVERYBODY SIT DOWN-- NOW!
FIRST RULE: NEVER LEAVE YOUR FAMILY. YOU HAVE TO BE THERE.
BETTY, YOU SHOULD HAVE WAITED FOR YOUR BROTHER.
BUT--

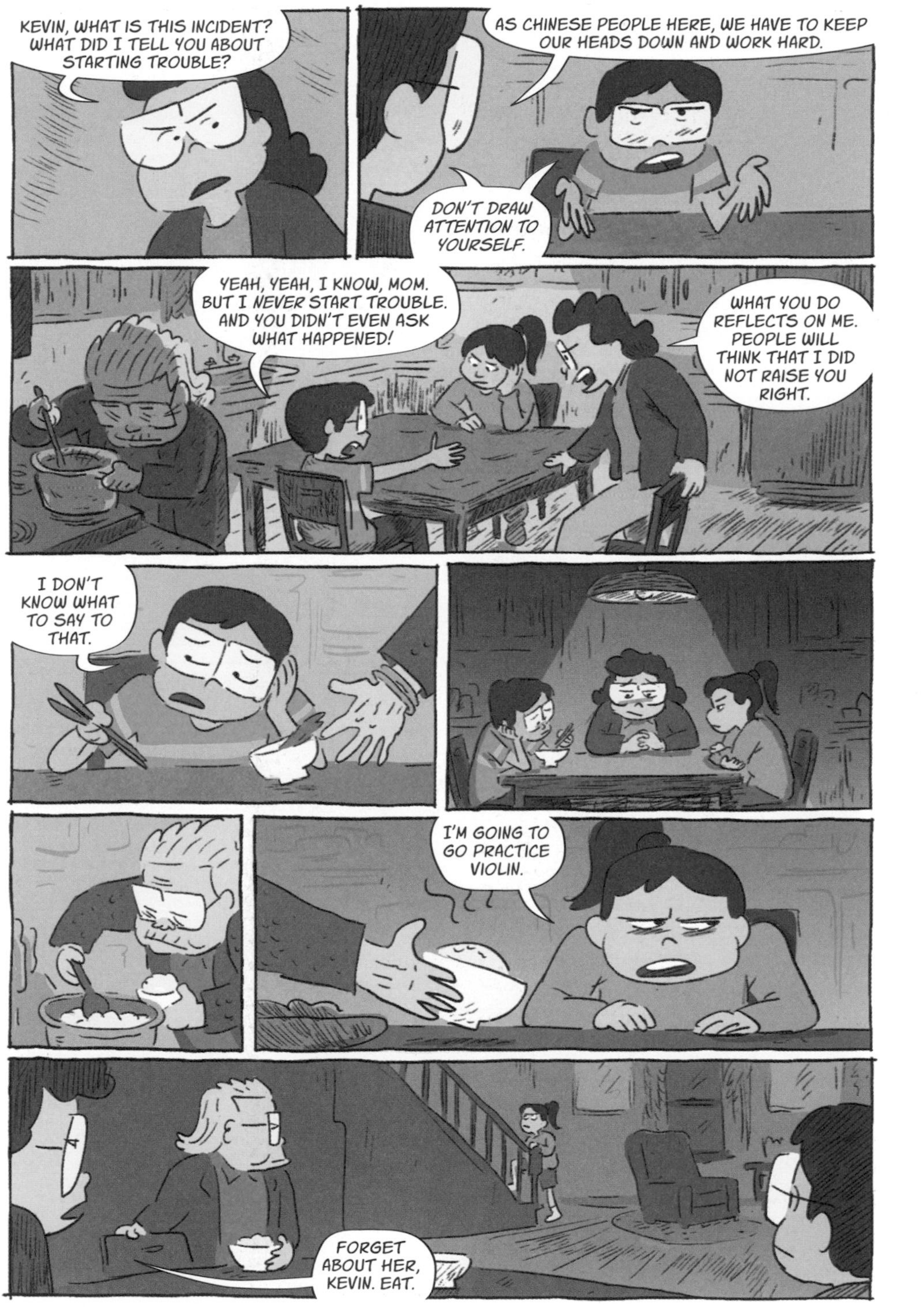
KEVIN, WHAT IS THIS INCIDENT? WHAT DID I TELL YOU ABOUT STARTING TROUBLE?
AS CHINESE PEOPLE HERE, WE HAVE TO KEEP OUR HEADS DOWN AND WORK HARD.
DON'T DRAW ATTENTION TO YOURSELF.
YEAH, YEAH, I KNOW, MOM. BUT I *NEVER* START TROUBLE. AND YOU DIDN'T EVEN ASK WHAT HAPPENED!
WHAT YOU DO REFLECTS ON ME. PEOPLE WILL THINK THAT I DID NOT RAISE YOU RIGHT.
I DON'T KNOW WHAT TO SAY TO THAT.
I'M GOING TO GO PRACTICE VIOLIN.
FORGET ABOUT HER, KEVIN. EAT.

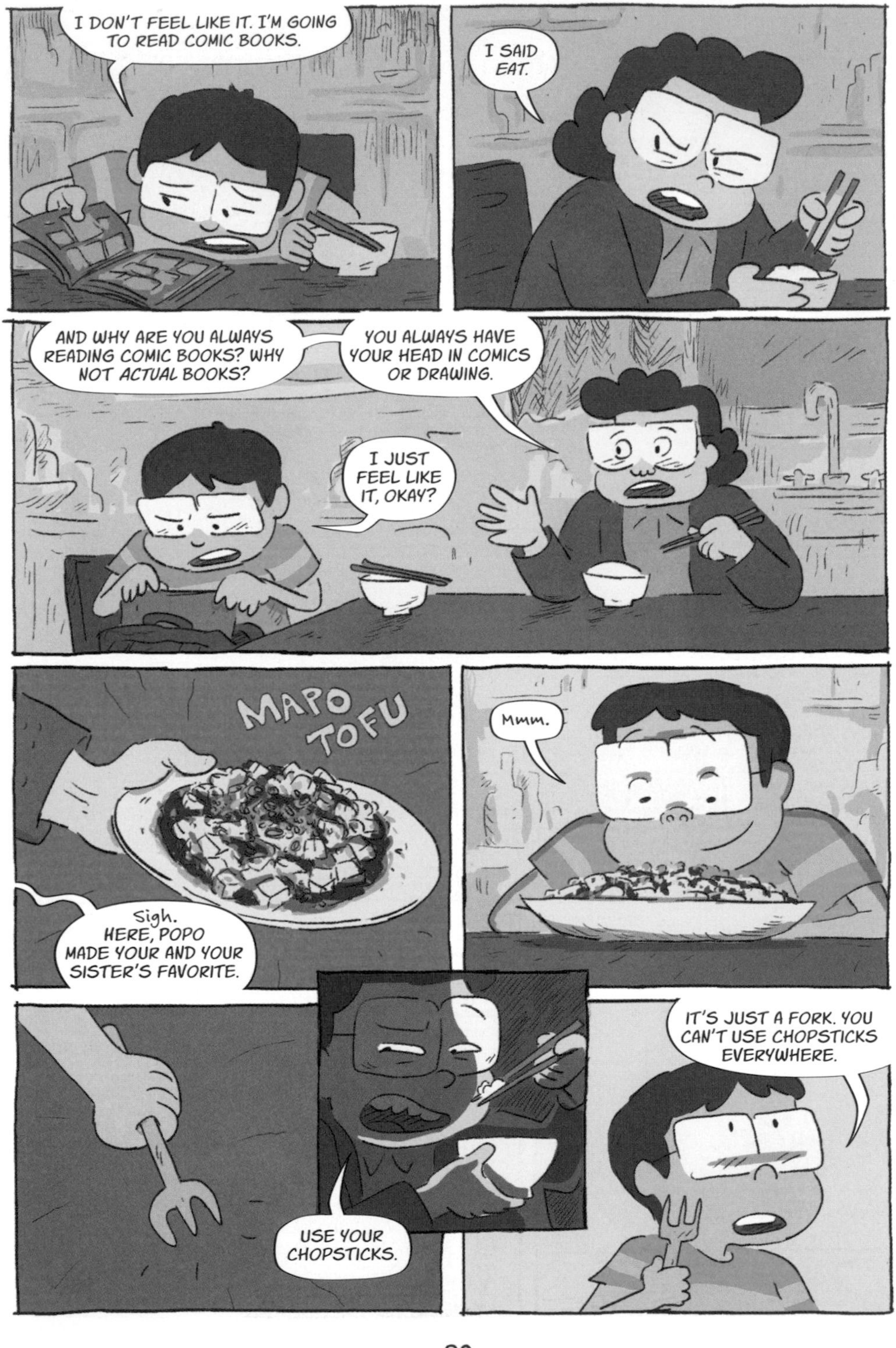
I DON'T FEEL LIKE IT. I'M GOING TO READ COMIC BOOKS.
I SAID EAT.
AND WHY ARE YOU ALWAYS READING COMIC BOOKS? WHY NOT *ACTUAL* BOOKS?
YOU ALWAYS HAVE YOUR HEAD IN COMICS OR DRAWING.
I JUST FEEL LIKE IT, OKAY?
MAPO TOFU
Sigh.
HERE, POPO MADE YOUR AND YOUR SISTER'S FAVORITE.
Mmm.
USE YOUR CHOPSTICKS.
IT'S JUST A FORK. YOU CAN'T USE CHOPSTICKS EVERYWHERE.

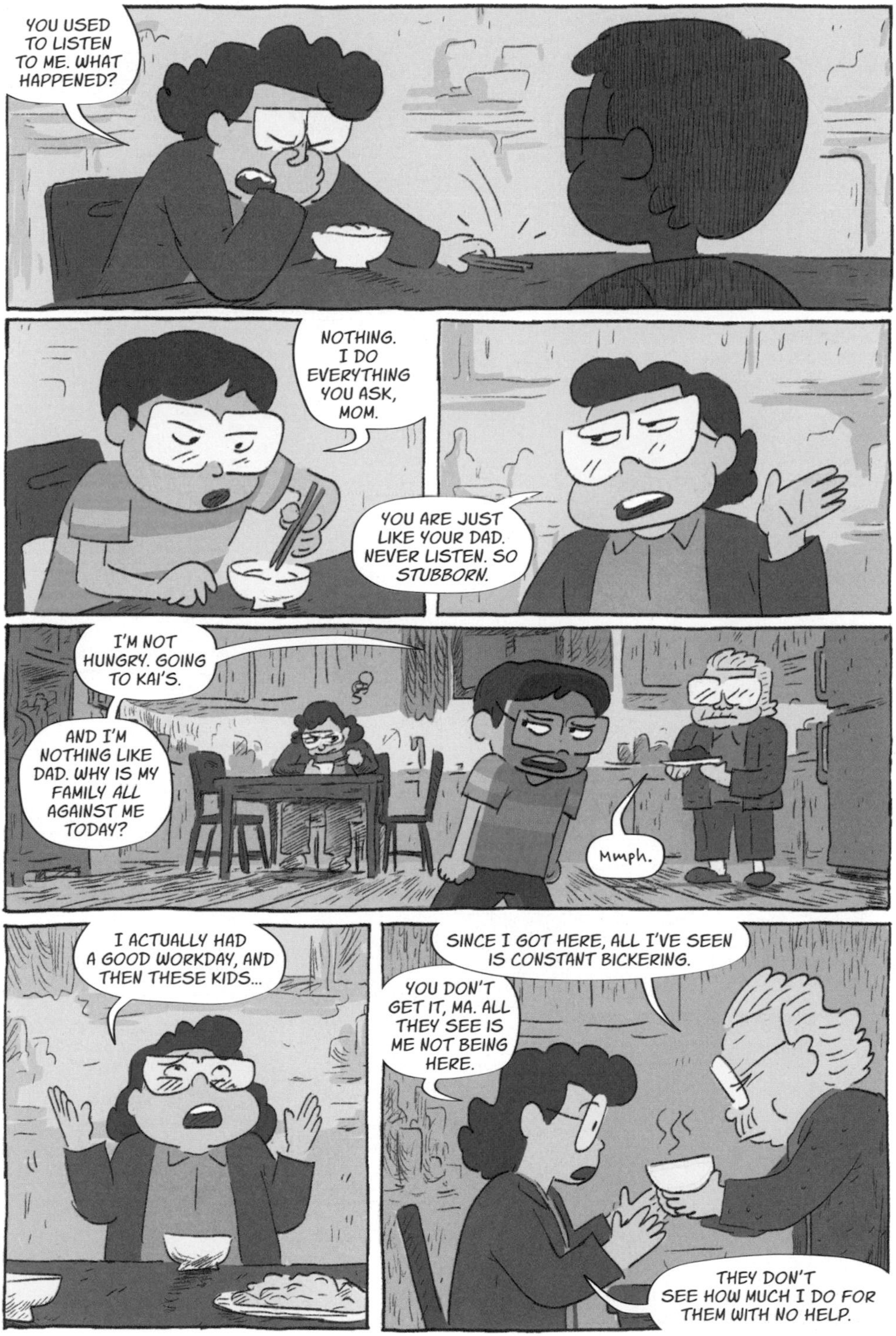
YOU USED TO LISTEN TO ME. WHAT HAPPENED?
NOTHING. I DO EVERYTHING YOU ASK, MOM.
YOU ARE JUST LIKE YOUR DAD. NEVER LISTEN. SO STUBBORN.
I'M NOT HUNGRY. GOING TO KAI'S.
AND I'M NOTHING LIKE DAD. WHY IS MY FAMILY ALL AGAINST ME TODAY?
Mmph.
I ACTUALLY HAD A GOOD WORKDAY, AND THEN THESE KIDS...
SINCE I GOT HERE, ALL I'VE SEEN IS CONSTANT BICKERING.
YOU DON'T GET IT, MA. ALL THEY SEE IS ME NOT BEING HERE.
THEY DON'T SEE HOW MUCH I DO FOR THEM WITH NO HELP.

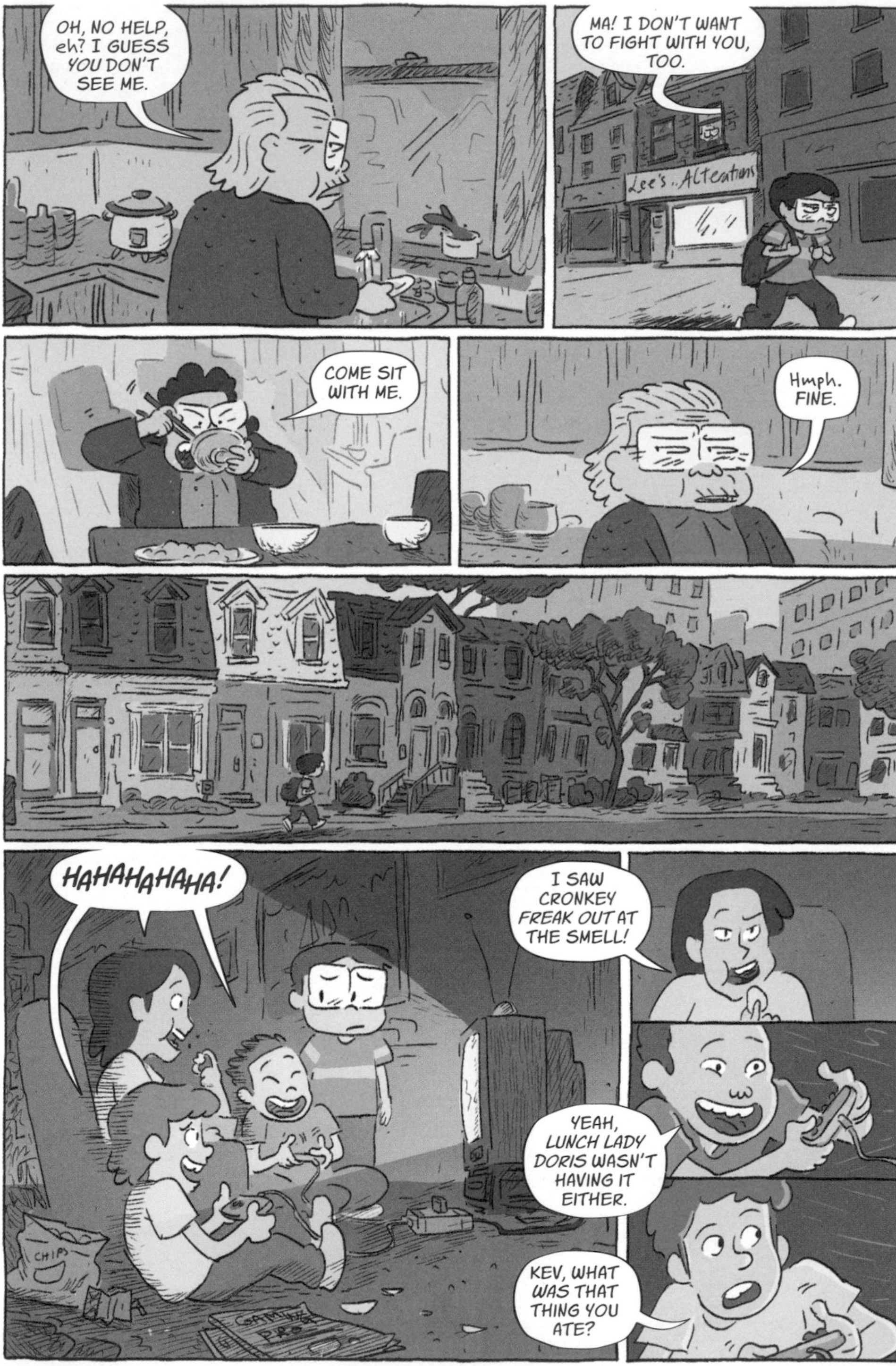
OH, NO HELP, eh? I GUESS YOU DON'T SEE ME.
MA! I DON'T WANT TO FIGHT WITH YOU, TOO.
Lee's ALterations
COME SIT WITH ME.
Hmph. FINE.
HAHAHAHAHA!
I SAW CRONKEY FREAK OUT AT THE SMELL!
YEAH, LUNCH LADY DORIS WASN'T HAVING IT EITHER.
KEV, WHAT WAS THAT THING YOU ATE?
CHIPS

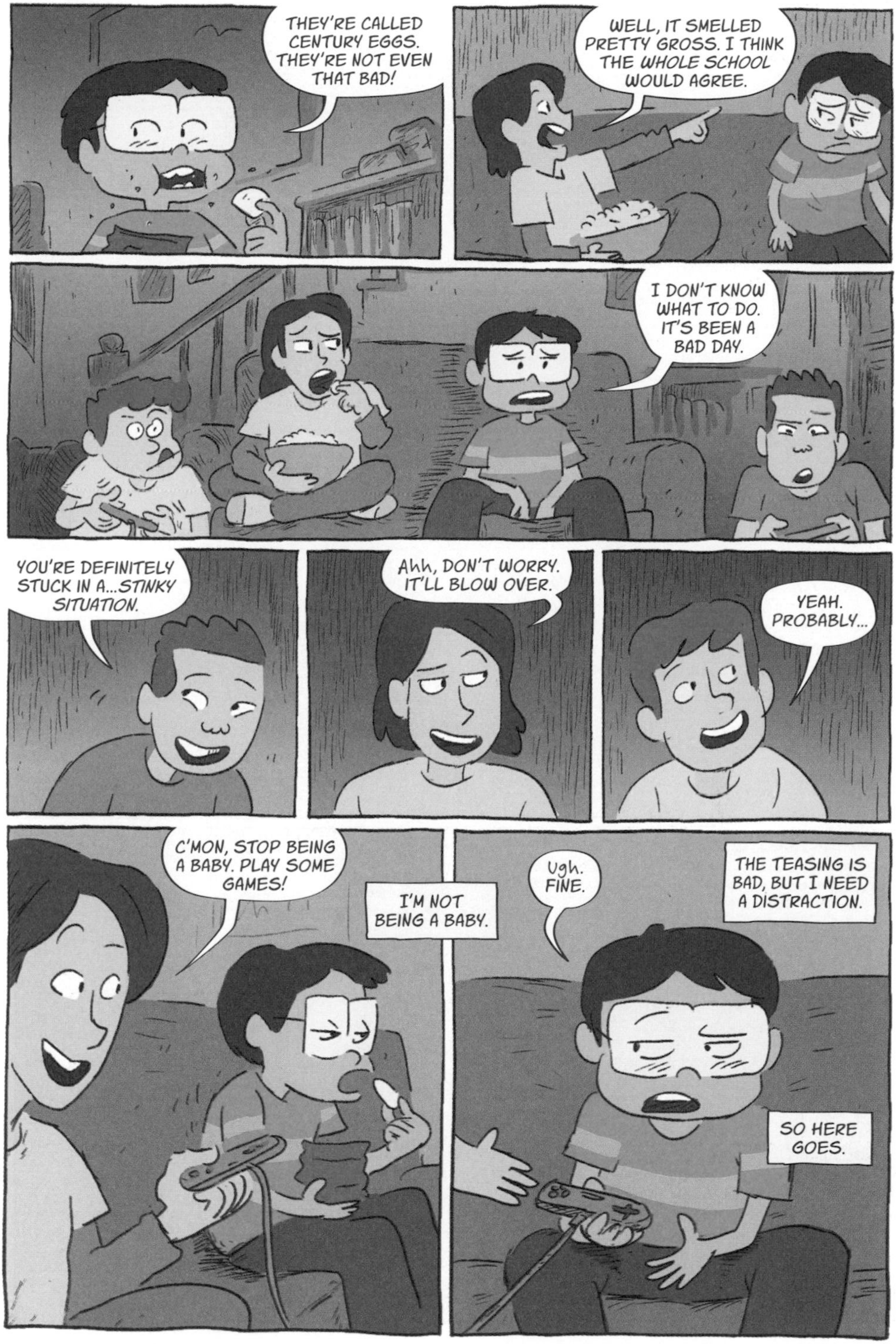
THEY'RE CALLED CENTURY EGGS. THEY'RE NOT EVEN THAT BAD!
WELL, IT SMELLED PRETTY GROSS. I THINK THE *WHOLE SCHOOL* WOULD AGREE.
I DON'T KNOW WHAT TO DO. IT'S BEEN A BAD DAY.
YOU'RE DEFINITELY STUCK IN A...*STINKY SITUATION.*
Ahh, DON'T WORRY. IT'LL BLOW OVER.
YEAH. PROBABLY...
C'MON, STOP BEING A BABY. PLAY SOME GAMES!
I'M NOT BEING A BABY.
Ugh. FINE.
THE TEASING IS BAD, BUT I NEED A DISTRACTION.
SO HERE GOES.

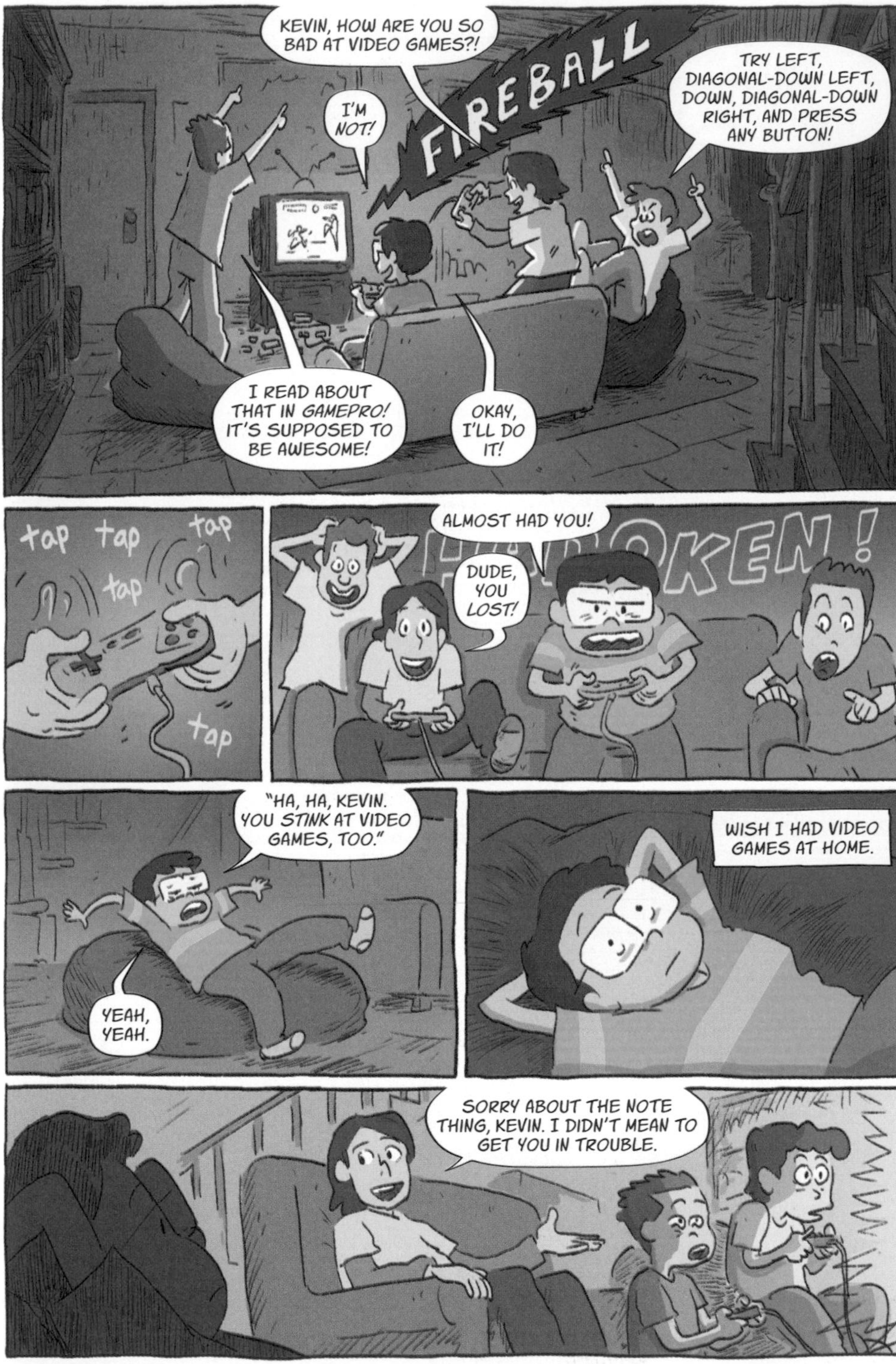
KEVIN, HOW ARE YOU SO BAD AT VIDEO GAMES?!
I'M NOT!
FIREBALL
TRY LEFT, DIAGONAL-DOWN LEFT, DOWN, DIAGONAL-DOWN RIGHT, AND PRESS ANY BUTTON!
I READ ABOUT THAT IN GAMEPRO! IT'S SUPPOSED TO BE AWESOME!
OKAY, I'LL DO IT!
tap tap tap tap tap
ALMOST HAD YOU!
DUDE, YOU LOST!
"HA, HA, KEVIN. YOU STINK AT VIDEO GAMES, TOO."
YEAH, YEAH.
WISH I HAD VIDEO GAMES AT HOME.
SORRY ABOUT THE NOTE THING, KEVIN. I DIDN'T MEAN TO GET YOU IN TROUBLE.

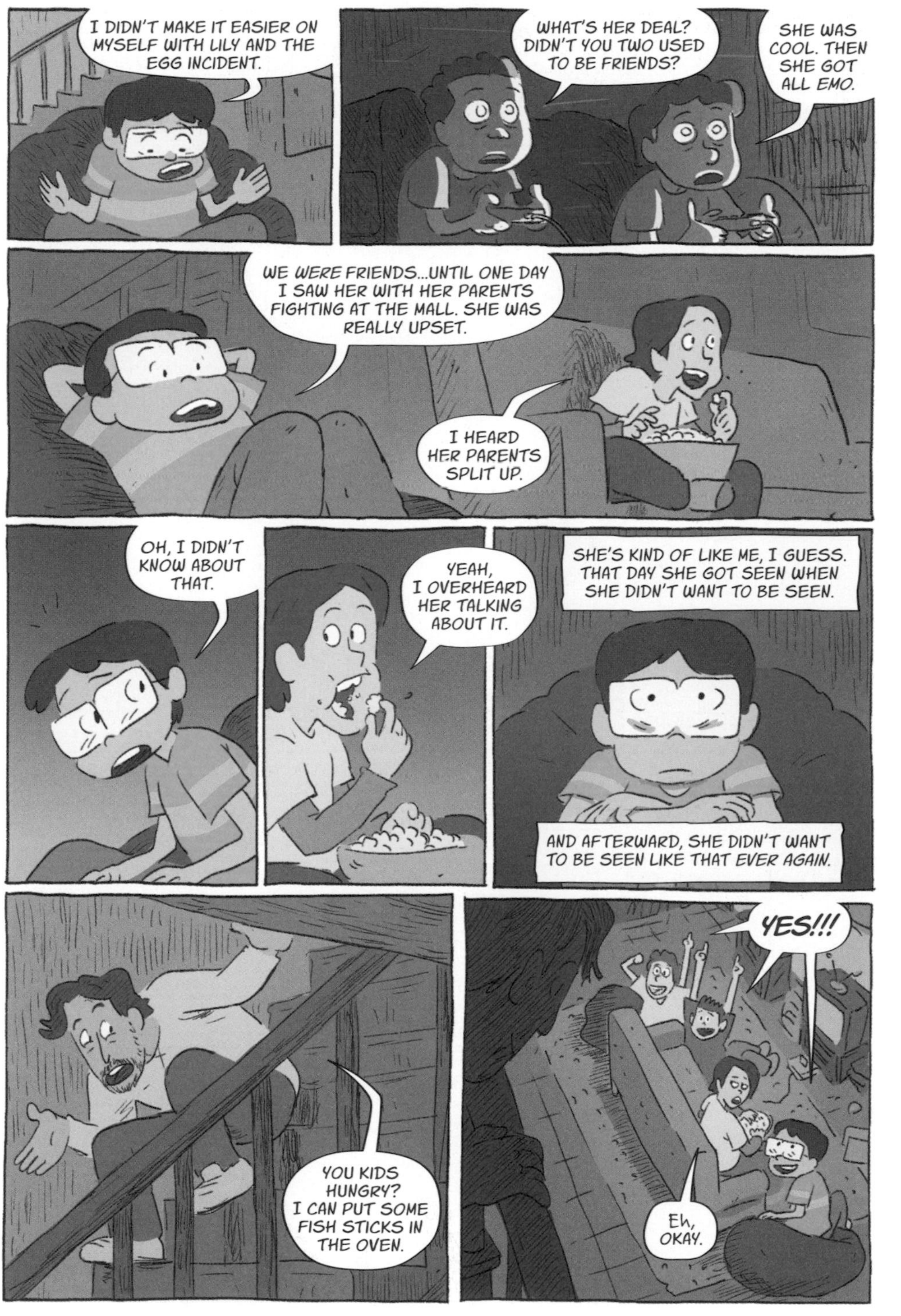
I DIDN'T MAKE IT EASIER ON MYSELF WITH LILY AND THE EGG INCIDENT.
WHAT'S HER DEAL? DIDN'T YOU TWO USED TO BE FRIENDS?
SHE WAS COOL. THEN SHE GOT ALL *EMO*.
WE *WERE* FRIENDS...UNTIL ONE DAY I SAW HER WITH HER PARENTS FIGHTING AT THE MALL. SHE WAS REALLY UPSET.
I HEARD HER PARENTS SPLIT UP.
OH, I DIDN'T KNOW ABOUT THAT.
YEAH, I OVERHEARD HER TALKING ABOUT IT.
SHE'S KIND OF LIKE ME, I GUESS. THAT DAY SHE GOT SEEN WHEN SHE DIDN'T WANT TO BE SEEN.
AND AFTERWARD, SHE DIDN'T WANT TO BE SEEN LIKE THAT EVER AGAIN.
YOU KIDS HUNGRY? I CAN PUT SOME FISH STICKS IN THE OVEN.
YES!!!
Eh, OKAY.

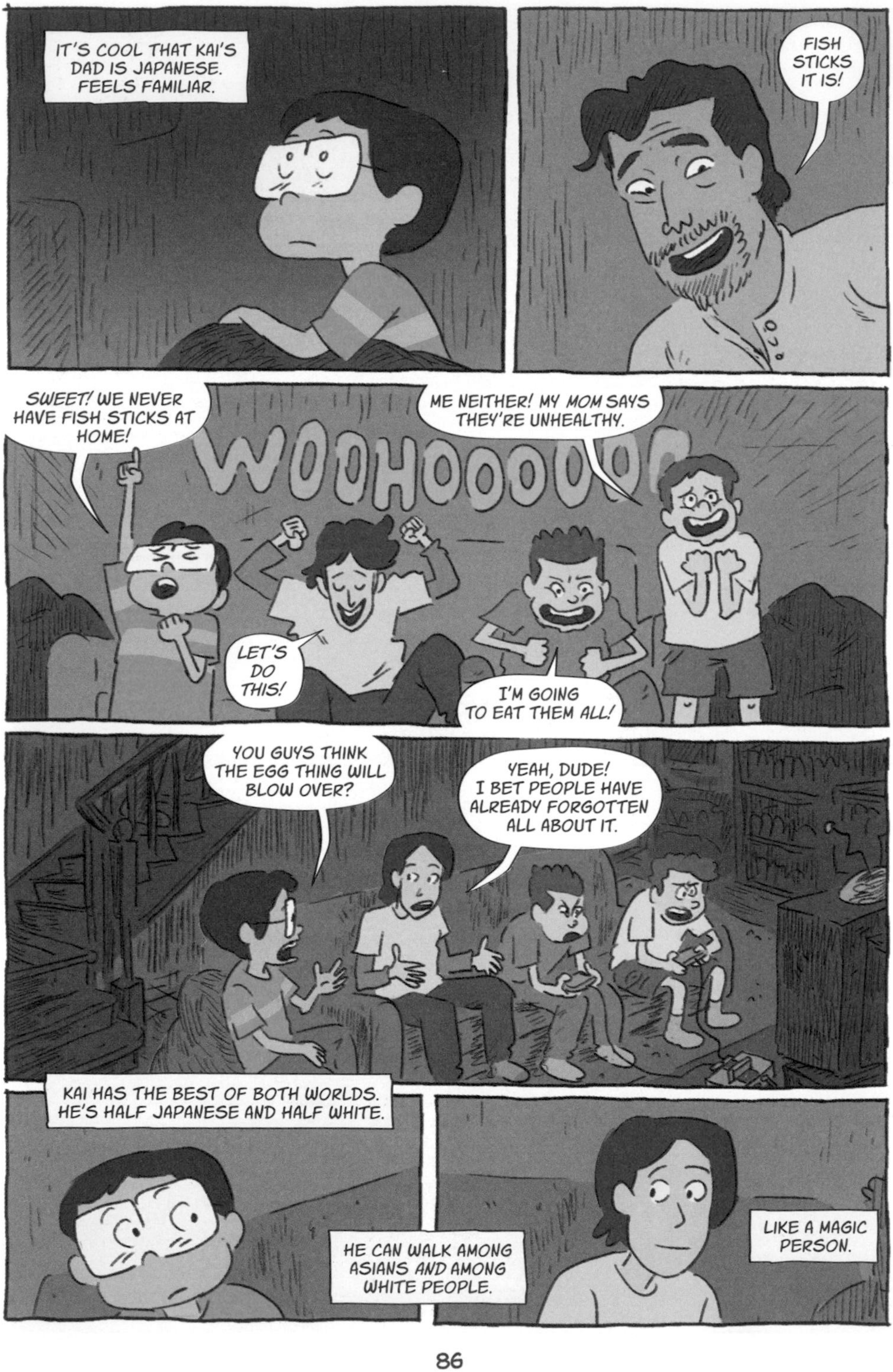
IT'S COOL THAT KAI'S DAD IS JAPANESE. FEELS FAMILIAR.
FISH STICKS IT IS!
SWEET! WE NEVER HAVE FISH STICKS AT HOME!
WOOHOOOOO
ME NEITHER! MY MOM SAYS THEY'RE UNHEALTHY.
LET'S DO THIS!
I'M GOING TO EAT THEM ALL!
YOU GUYS THINK THE EGG THING WILL BLOW OVER?
YEAH, DUDE! I BET PEOPLE HAVE ALREADY FORGOTTEN ALL ABOUT IT.
KAI HAS THE BEST OF BOTH WORLDS. HE'S HALF JAPANESE AND HALF WHITE.
HE CAN WALK AMONG ASIANS AND AMONG WHITE PEOPLE.
LIKE A MAGIC PERSON.

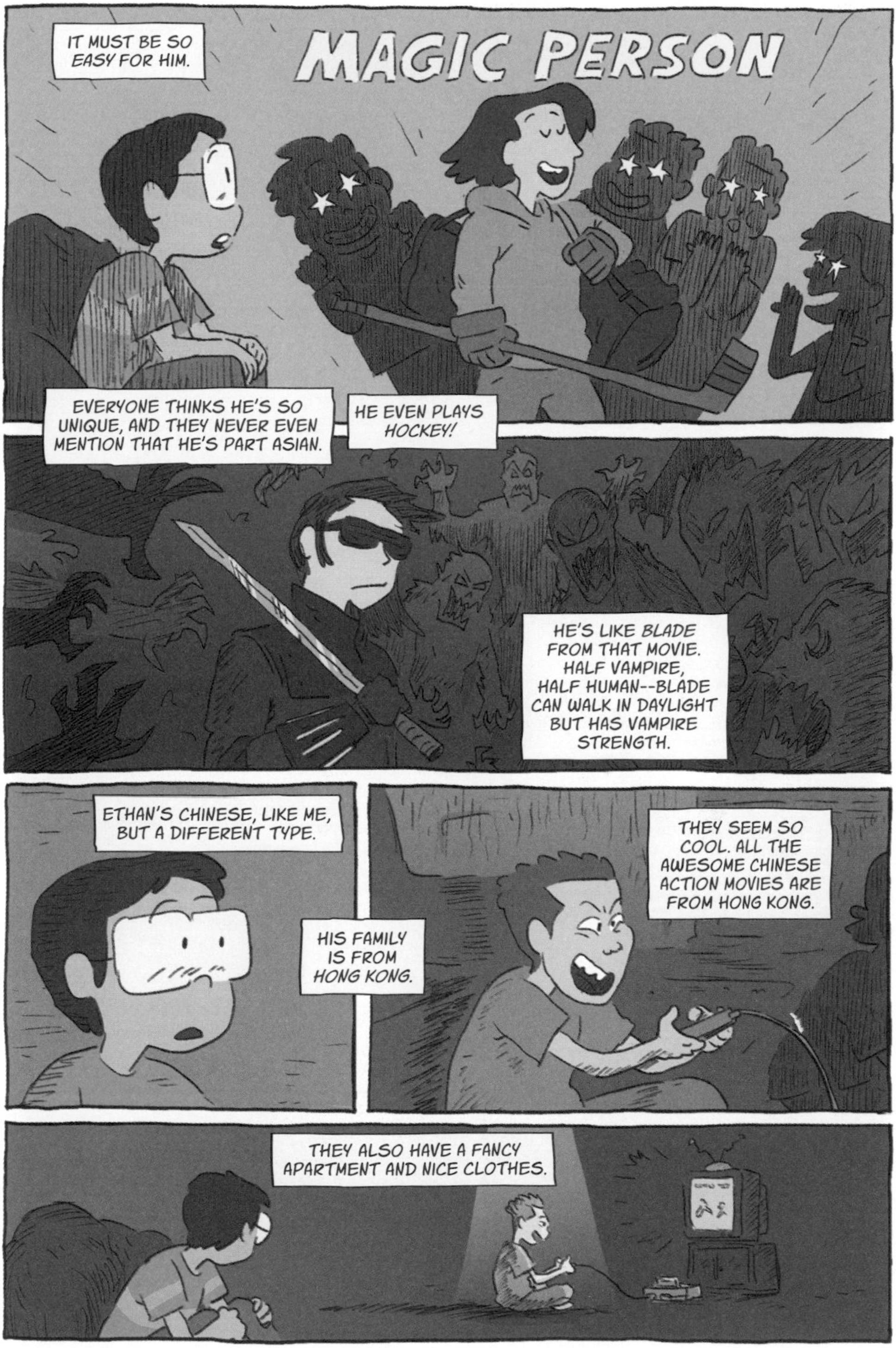
IT MUST BE SO EASY FOR HIM.
MAGIC PERSON
EVERYONE THINKS HE'S SO UNIQUE, AND THEY NEVER EVEN MENTION THAT HE'S PART ASIAN.
HE EVEN PLAYS HOCKEY!
HE'S LIKE BLADE FROM THAT MOVIE. HALF VAMPIRE, HALF HUMAN--BLADE CAN WALK IN DAYLIGHT BUT HAS VAMPIRE STRENGTH.
ETHAN'S CHINESE, LIKE ME, BUT A DIFFERENT TYPE.
HIS FAMILY IS FROM HONG KONG.
THEY SEEM SO COOL. ALL THE AWESOME CHINESE ACTION MOVIES ARE FROM HONG KONG.
THEY ALSO HAVE A FANCY APARTMENT AND NICE CLOTHES.

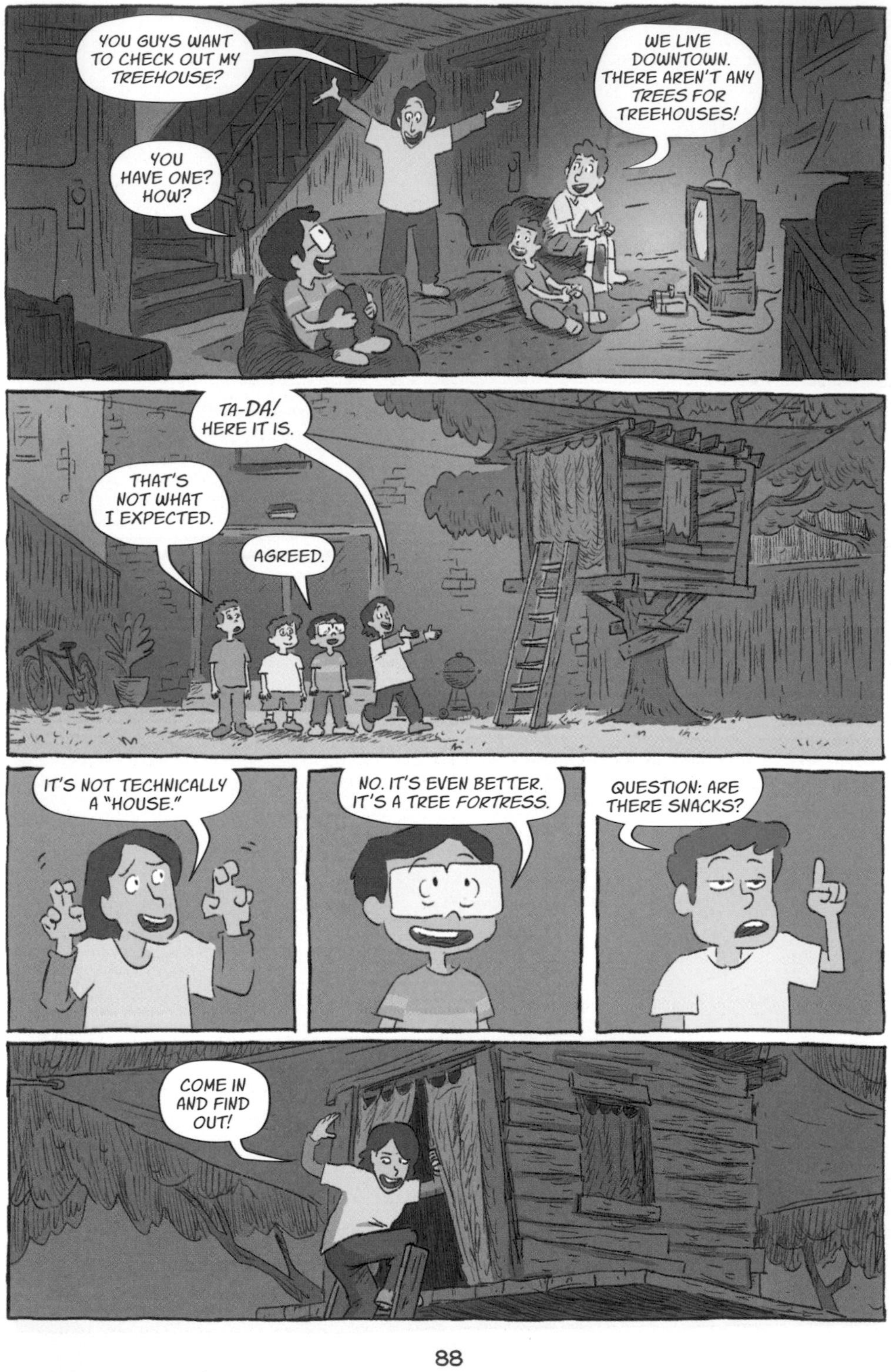
YOU GUYS WANT TO CHECK OUT MY *TREEHOUSE?*
YOU HAVE ONE? HOW?
WE LIVE DOWNTOWN. THERE AREN'T ANY *TREES* FOR TREEHOUSES!
TA-DA! HERE IT IS.
THAT'S NOT WHAT I EXPECTED.
AGREED.
IT'S NOT TECHNICALLY A "HOUSE."
NO. IT'S EVEN BETTER. IT'S A TREE *FORTRESS.*
QUESTION: ARE THERE SNACKS?
COME IN AND FIND OUT!

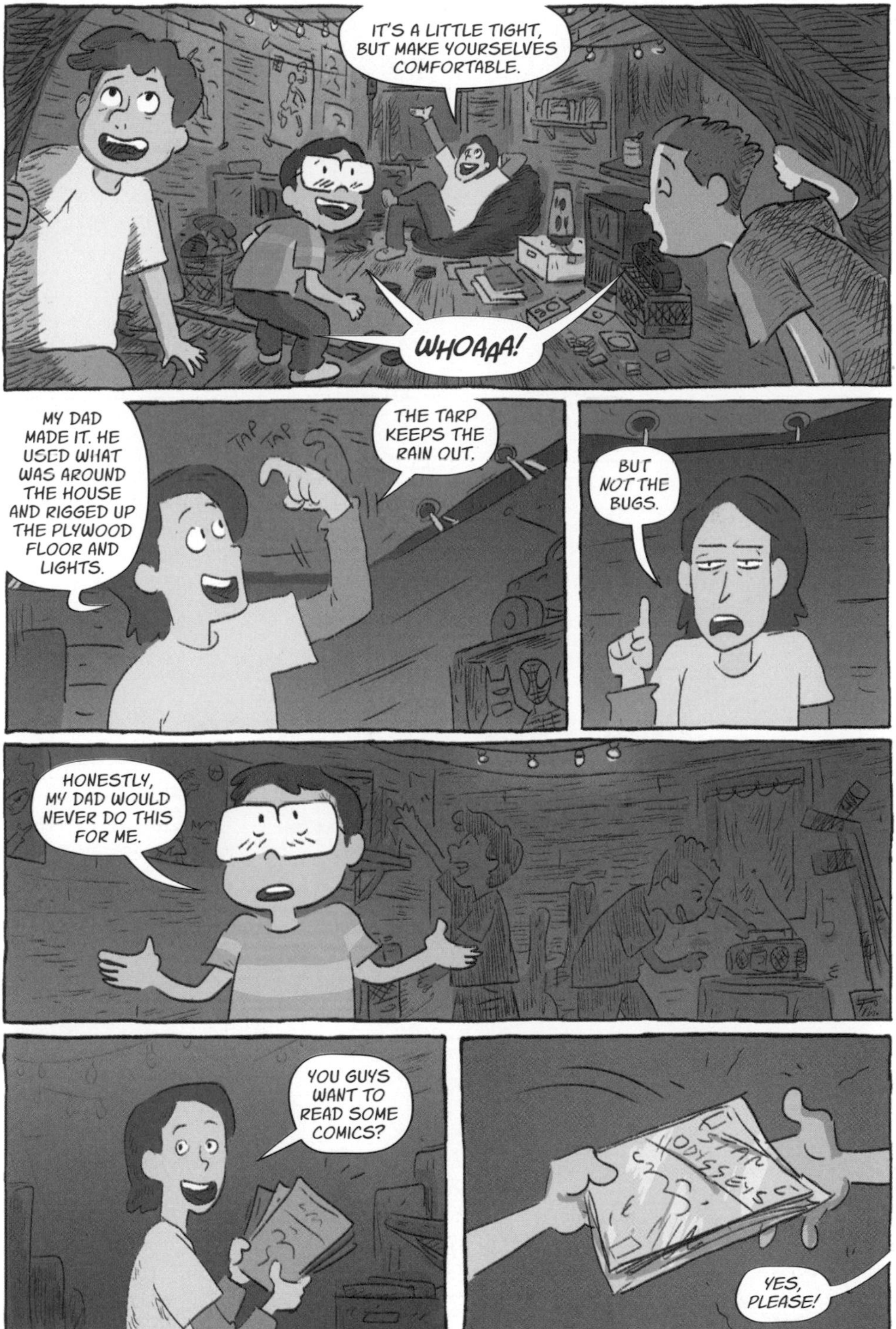
IT'S A LITTLE TIGHT, BUT MAKE YOURSELVES COMFORTABLE.
WHOAAA!
MY DAD MADE IT. HE USED WHAT WAS AROUND THE HOUSE AND RIGGED UP THE PLYWOOD FLOOR AND LIGHTS.
TAP TAP
THE TARP KEEPS THE RAIN OUT.
BUT NOT THE BUGS.
HONESTLY, MY DAD WOULD NEVER DO THIS FOR ME.
YOU GUYS WANT TO READ SOME COMICS?
STAR ODYSSEYS
YES, PLEASE!

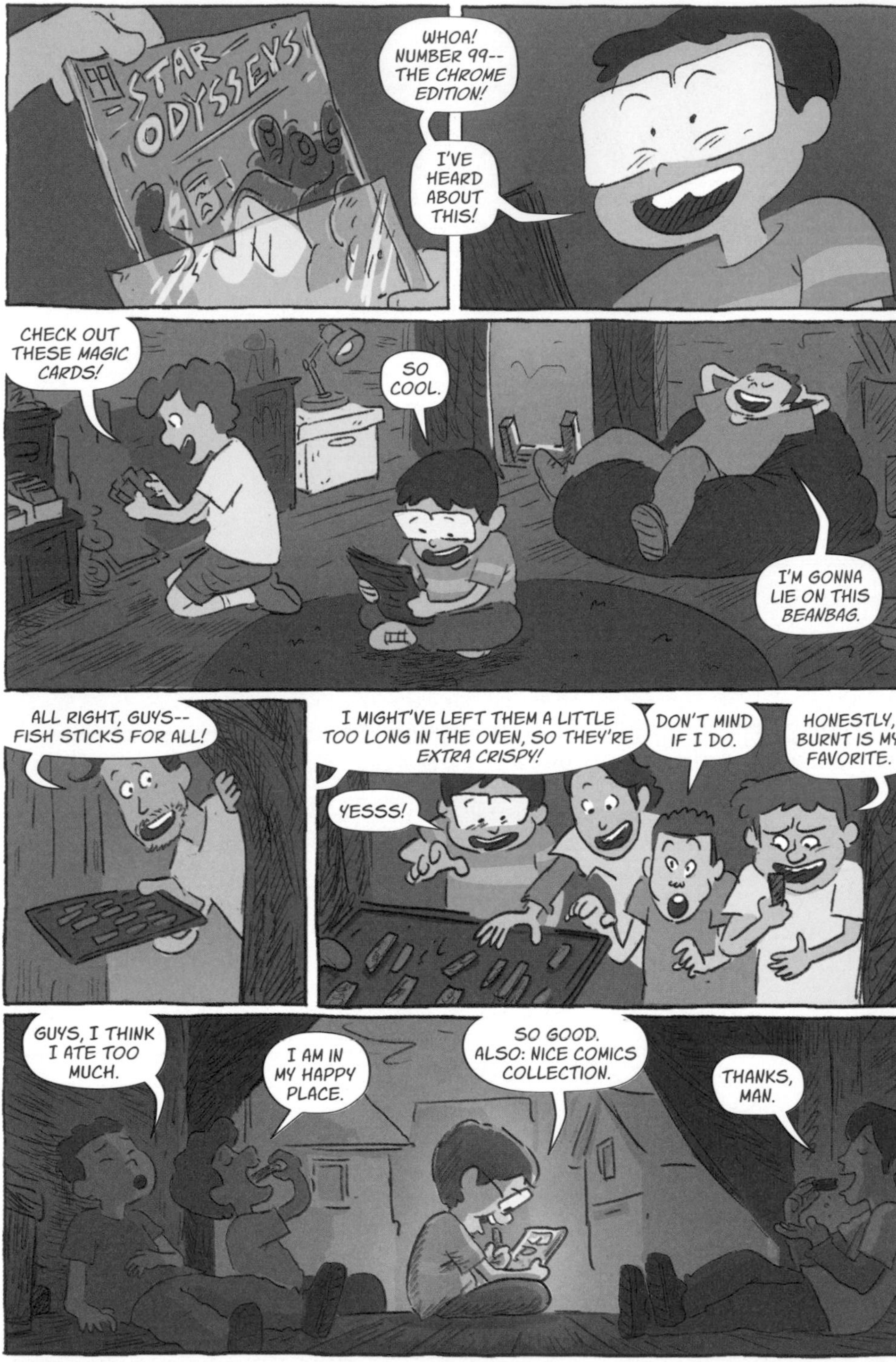
STAR ODYSSEYS
99
WHOA! NUMBER 99-- THE CHROME EDITION!
I'VE HEARD ABOUT THIS!
CHECK OUT THESE MAGIC CARDS!
SO COOL.
I'M GONNA LIE ON THIS BEANBAG.
ALL RIGHT, GUYS-- FISH STICKS FOR ALL!
I MIGHT'VE LEFT THEM A LITTLE TOO LONG IN THE OVEN, SO THEY'RE EXTRA CRISPY!
YESSS!
DON'T MIND IF I DO.
HONESTLY, BURNT IS MY FAVORITE.
GUYS, I THINK I ATE TOO MUCH.
I AM IN MY HAPPY PLACE.
SO GOOD. ALSO: NICE COMICS COLLECTION.
THANKS, MAN.

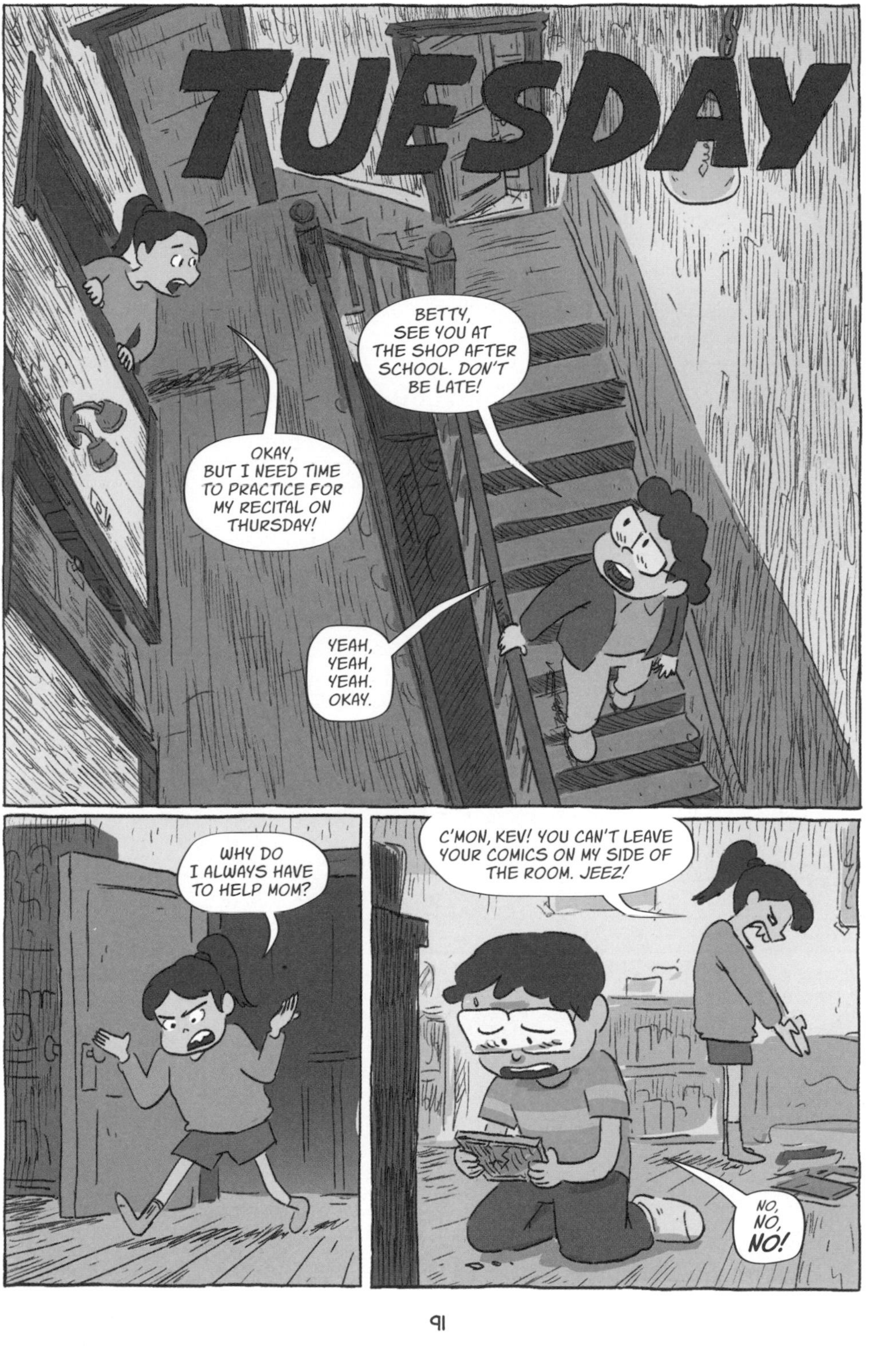
TUESDAY
BETTY, SEE YOU AT THE SHOP AFTER SCHOOL. DON'T BE LATE!
OKAY, BUT I NEED TIME TO PRACTICE FOR MY RECITAL ON THURSDAY!
YEAH, YEAH, YEAH. OKAY.
WHY DO I ALWAYS HAVE TO HELP MOM?
C'MON, KEV! YOU CAN'T LEAVE YOUR COMICS ON MY SIDE OF THE ROOM. JEEZ!
NO, NO, NO!

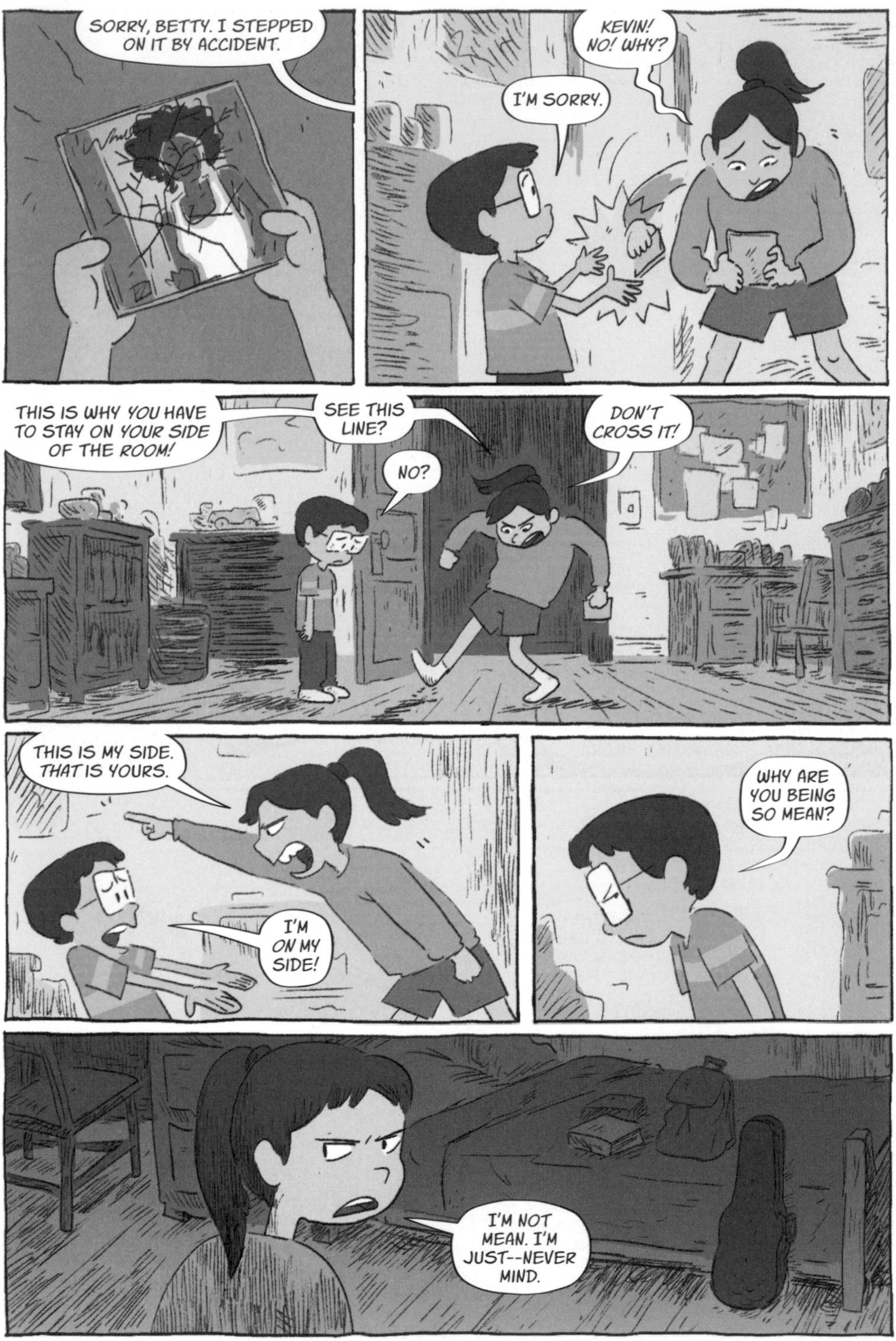
SORRY, BETTY. I STEPPED ON IT BY ACCIDENT.
KEVIN! NO! WHY?
I'M SORRY.
THIS IS WHY YOU HAVE TO STAY ON YOUR SIDE OF THE ROOM!
SEE THIS LINE?
NO?
DON'T CROSS IT!
THIS IS MY SIDE. THAT IS YOURS.
I'M ON MY SIDE!
WHY ARE YOU BEING SO MEAN?
I'M NOT MEAN. I'M JUST--NEVER MIND.

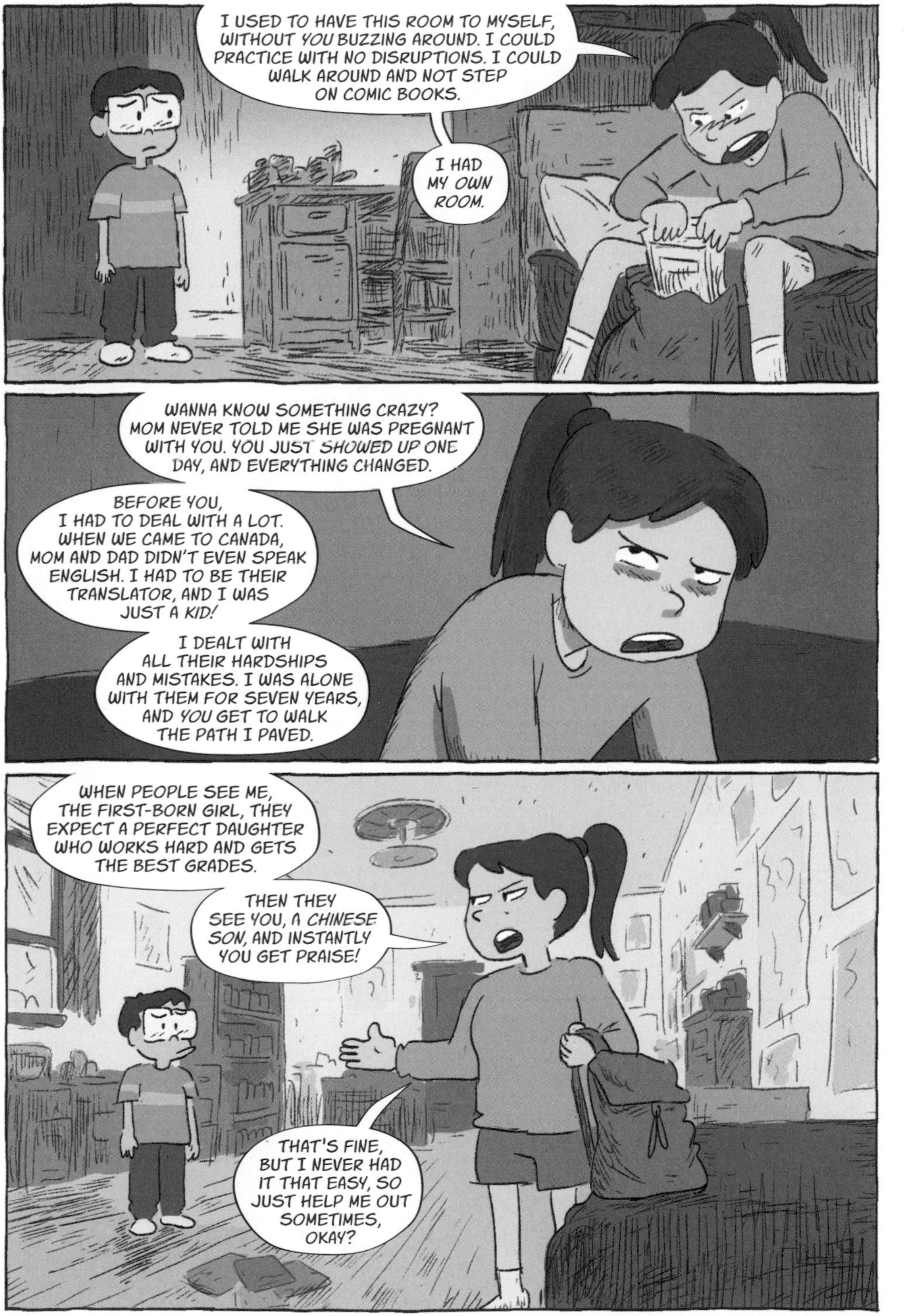
I USED TO HAVE THIS ROOM TO MYSELF, WITHOUT YOU BUZZING AROUND. I COULD PRACTICE WITH NO DISRUPTIONS. I COULD WALK AROUND AND NOT STEP ON COMIC BOOKS.
I HAD MY OWN ROOM.
WANNA KNOW SOMETHING CRAZY? MOM NEVER TOLD ME SHE WAS PREGNANT WITH YOU. YOU JUST SHOWED UP ONE DAY, AND EVERYTHING CHANGED.
BEFORE YOU, I HAD TO DEAL WITH A LOT. WHEN WE CAME TO CANADA, MOM AND DAD DIDN'T EVEN SPEAK ENGLISH. I HAD TO BE THEIR TRANSLATOR, AND I WAS JUST A KID!
I DEALT WITH ALL THEIR HARDSHIPS AND MISTAKES. I WAS ALONE WITH THEM FOR SEVEN YEARS, AND YOU GET TO WALK THE PATH I PAVED.
WHEN PEOPLE SEE ME, THE FIRST-BORN GIRL, THEY EXPECT A PERFECT DAUGHTER WHO WORKS HARD AND GETS THE BEST GRADES.
THEN THEY SEE YOU, A CHINESE SON, AND INSTANTLY YOU GET PRAISE!
THAT'S FINE, BUT I NEVER HAD IT THAT EASY, SO JUST HELP ME OUT SOMETIMES, OKAY?

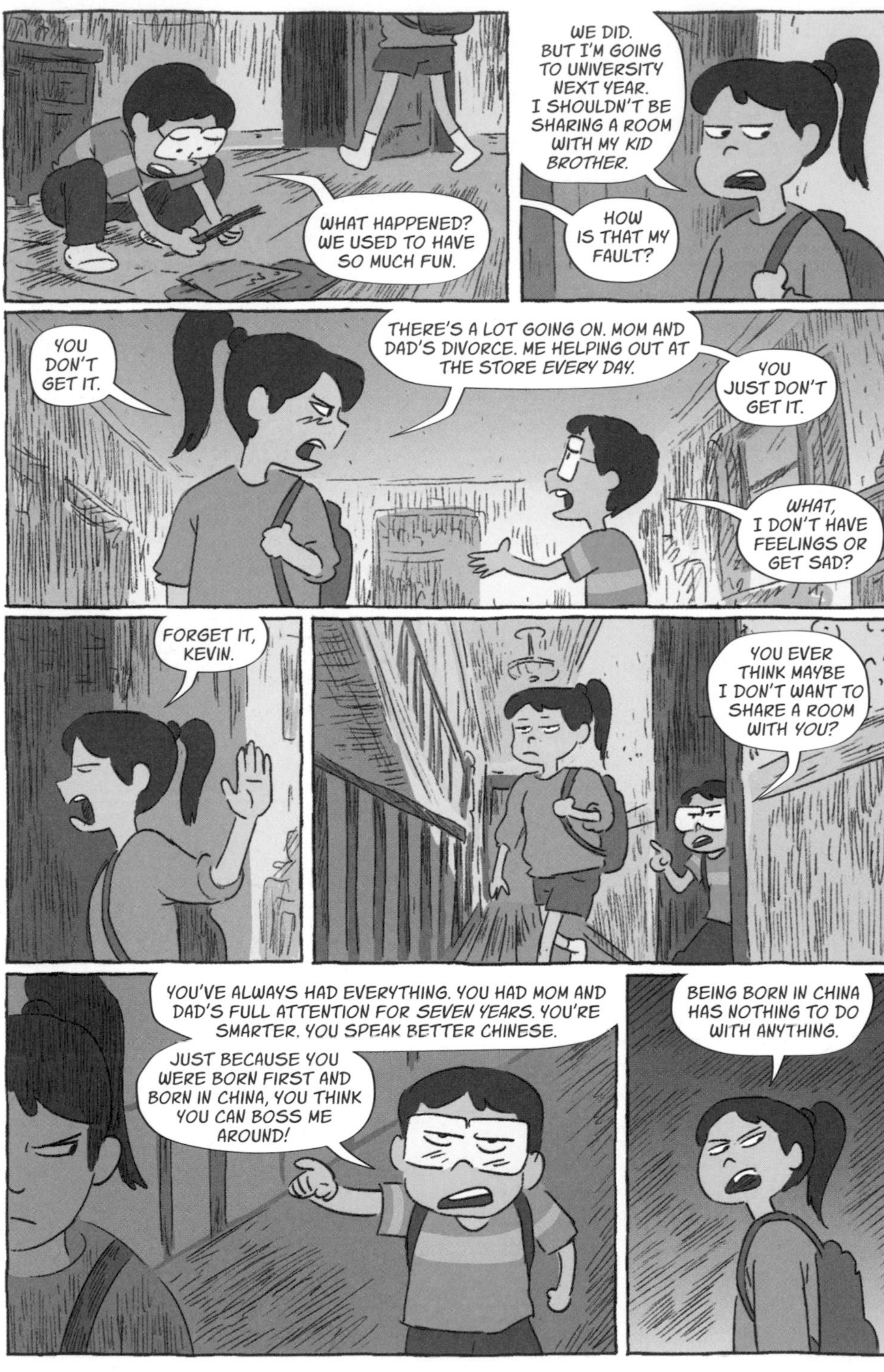
WHAT HAPPENED? WE USED TO HAVE SO MUCH FUN.
WE DID. BUT I'M GOING TO UNIVERSITY NEXT YEAR. I SHOULDN'T BE SHARING A ROOM WITH MY KID BROTHER.
HOW IS THAT MY FAULT?
YOU DON'T GET IT.
THERE'S A LOT GOING ON. MOM AND DAD'S DIVORCE. ME HELPING OUT AT THE STORE *EVERY DAY*.
YOU JUST DON'T GET IT.
WHAT, I DON'T HAVE FEELINGS OR GET SAD?
FORGET IT, KEVIN.
YOU EVER THINK MAYBE I DON'T WANT TO SHARE A ROOM WITH YOU?
JUST BECAUSE YOU WERE BORN FIRST AND BORN IN CHINA, YOU THINK YOU CAN BOSS ME AROUND!
YOU'VE ALWAYS HAD EVERYTHING. YOU HAD MOM AND DAD'S FULL ATTENTION FOR *SEVEN YEARS*. YOU'RE SMARTER. YOU SPEAK BETTER CHINESE.
BEING BORN IN CHINA HAS NOTHING TO DO WITH ANYTHING.

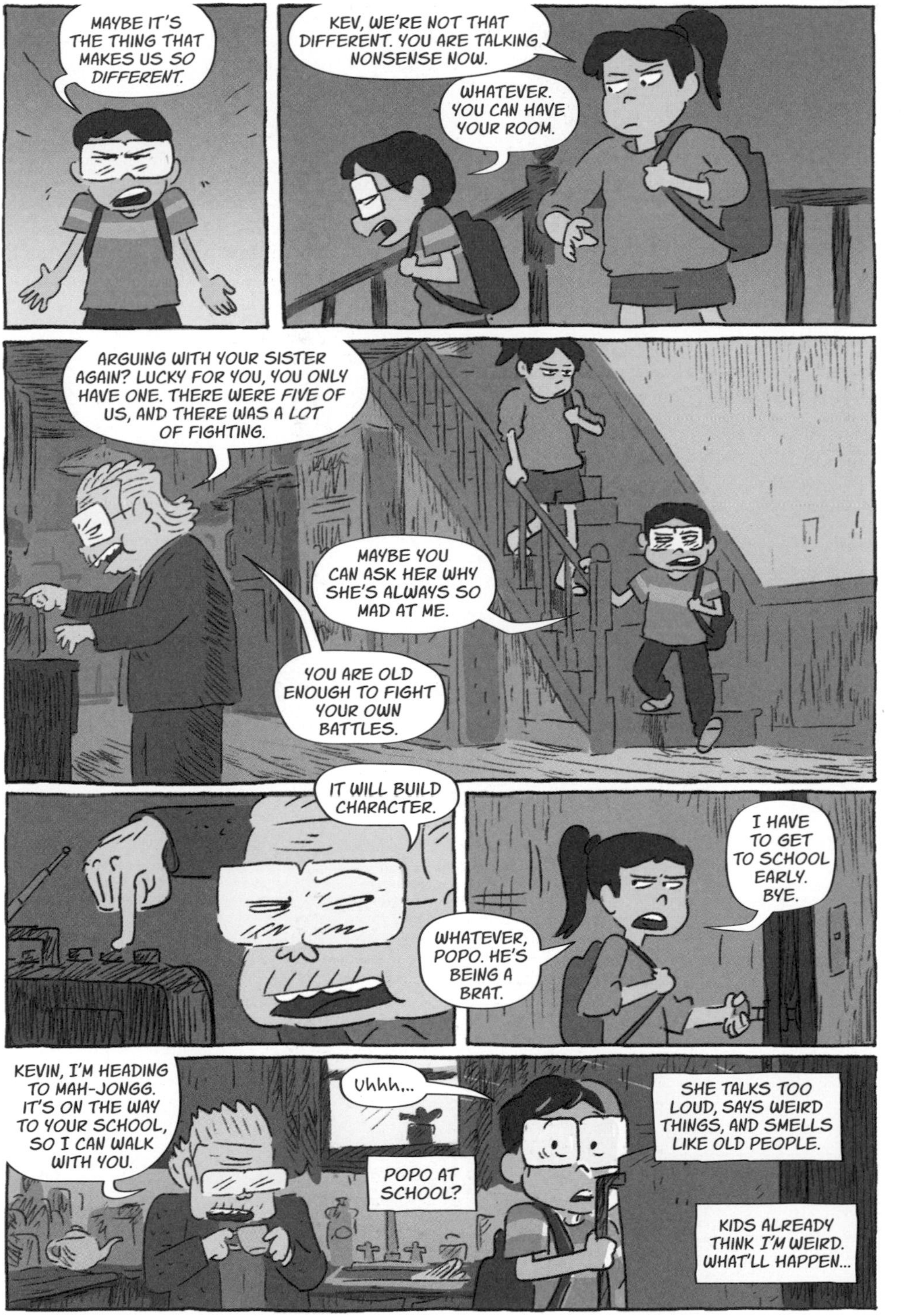

MAYBE IT'S THE THING THAT MAKES US SO *DIFFERENT*.
KEV, WE'RE NOT THAT DIFFERENT. YOU ARE TALKING NONSENSE NOW.
WHATEVER. YOU CAN HAVE YOUR ROOM.
ARGUING WITH YOUR SISTER AGAIN? LUCKY FOR YOU, YOU ONLY HAVE ONE. THERE WERE *FIVE* OF US, AND THERE WAS A *LOT* OF FIGHTING.
MAYBE YOU CAN ASK HER WHY SHE'S ALWAYS SO MAD AT ME.
YOU ARE OLD ENOUGH TO FIGHT YOUR OWN BATTLES.
IT WILL BUILD CHARACTER.
I HAVE TO GET TO SCHOOL EARLY. BYE.
WHATEVER, POPO. HE'S BEING A BRAT.
KEVIN, I'M HEADING TO MAH-JONGG. IT'S ON THE WAY TO YOUR SCHOOL, SO I CAN WALK WITH YOU.
Uhhh...
POPO AT SCHOOL?
SHE TALKS TOO LOUD, SAYS WEIRD THINGS, AND SMELLS LIKE OLD PEOPLE.
KIDS ALREADY THINK I'M WEIRD. WHAT'LL HAPPEN...

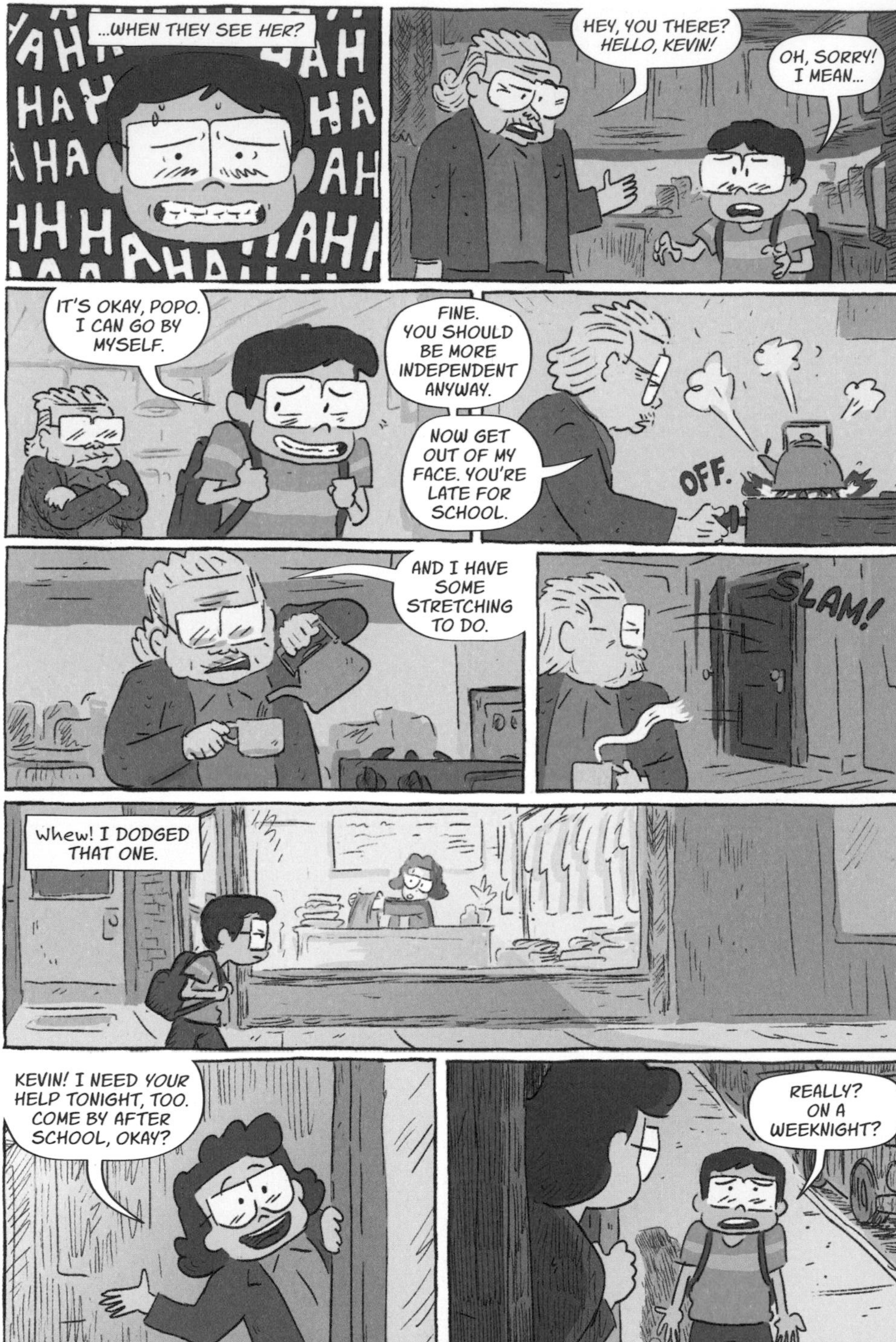

...WHEN THEY SEE HER?
HAHAHAHA
HEY, YOU THERE? HELLO, KEVIN!
OH, SORRY! I MEAN...
IT'S OKAY, POPO. I CAN GO BY MYSELF.
FINE. YOU SHOULD BE MORE INDEPENDENT ANYWAY.
NOW GET OUT OF MY FACE. YOU'RE LATE FOR SCHOOL.
OFF.
AND I HAVE SOME STRETCHING TO DO.
SLAM!
Whew! I DODGED THAT ONE.
KEVIN! I NEED YOUR HELP TONIGHT, TOO. COME BY AFTER SCHOOL, OKAY?
REALLY? ON A WEEKNIGHT?

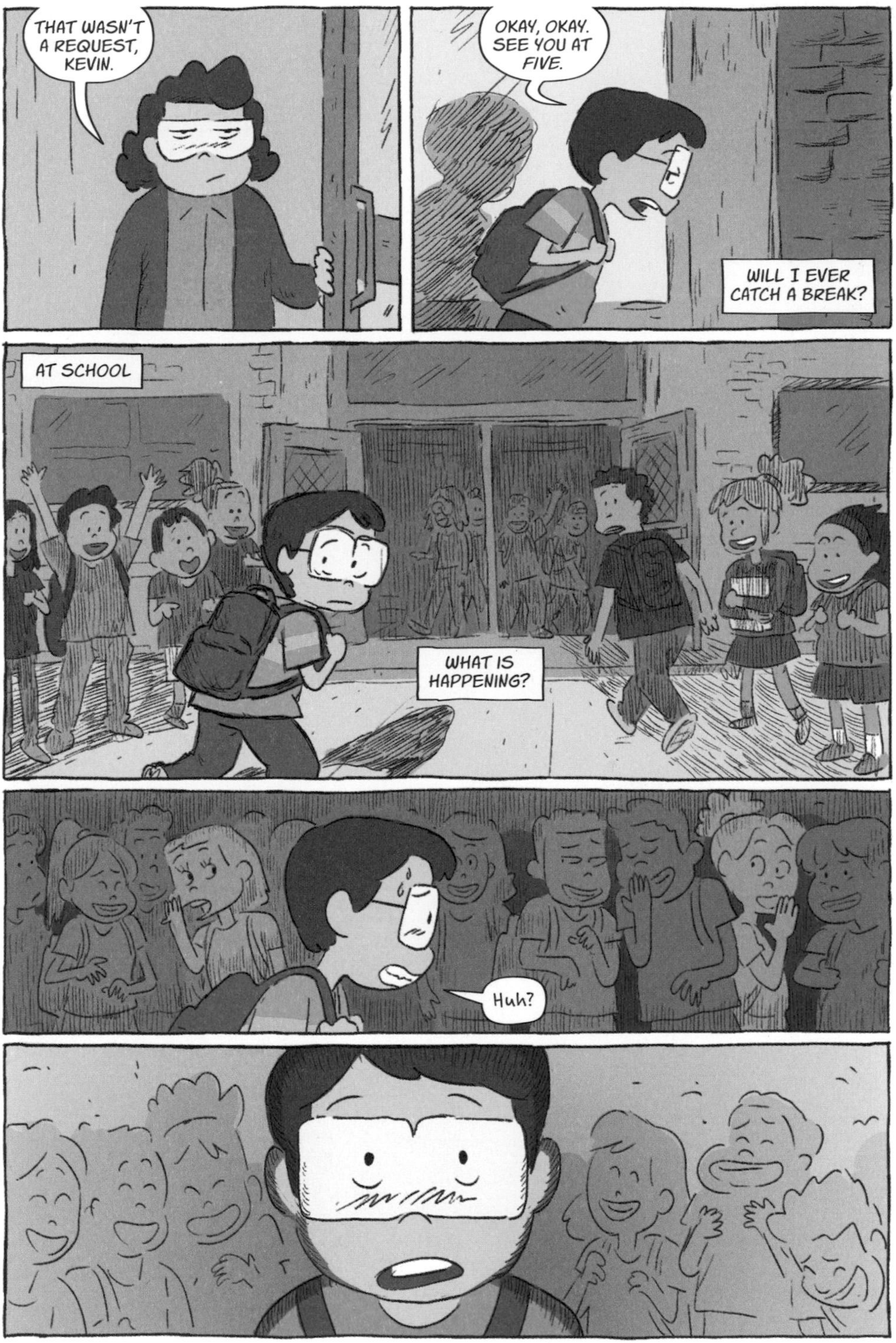
THAT WASN'T A REQUEST, KEVIN.
OKAY, OKAY. SEE YOU AT FIVE.
WILL I EVER CATCH A BREAK?
AT SCHOOL
WHAT IS HAPPENING?
Huh?

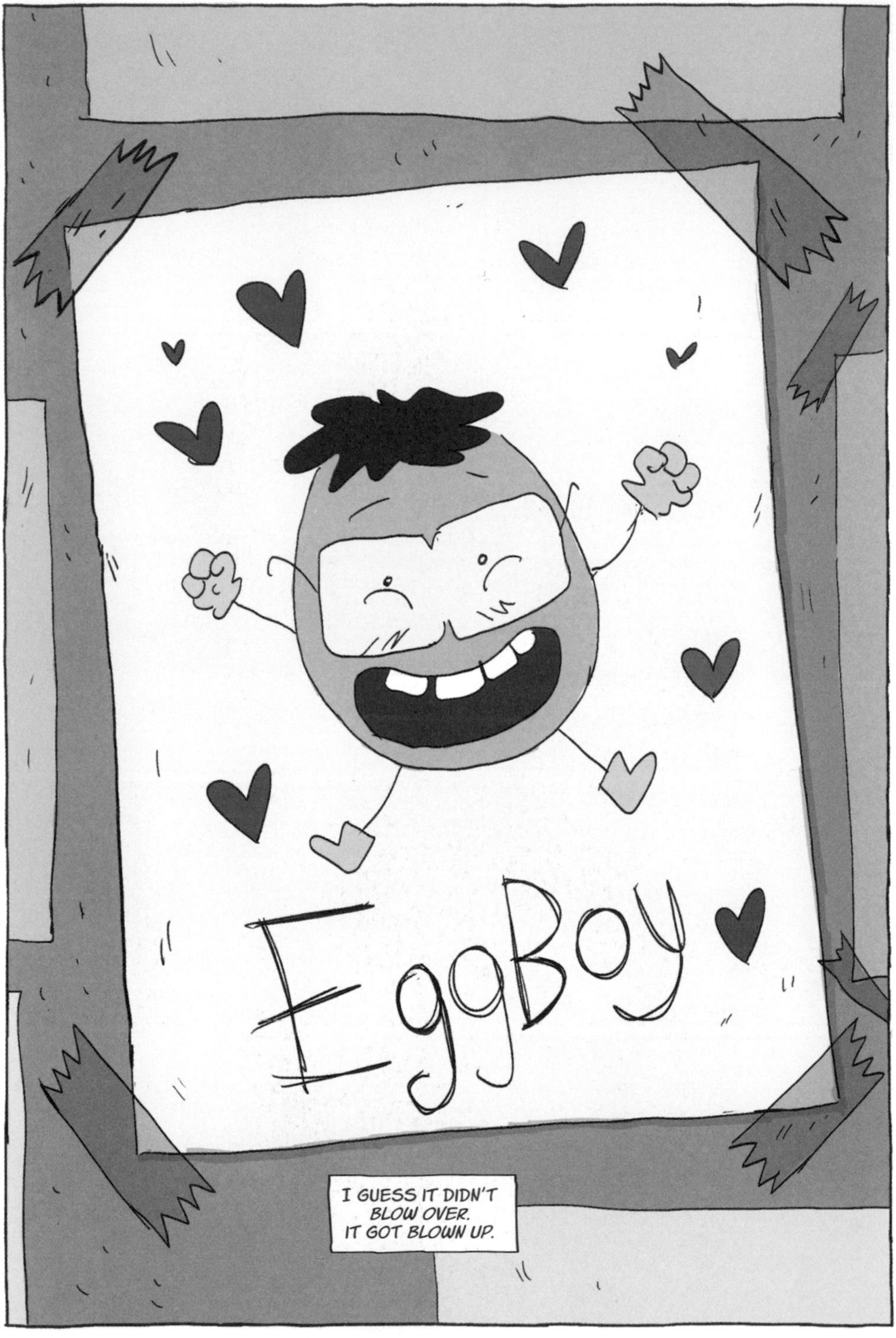
EggBoy
I GUESS IT DIDN'T *BLOW OVER.* IT GOT *BLOWN UP.*

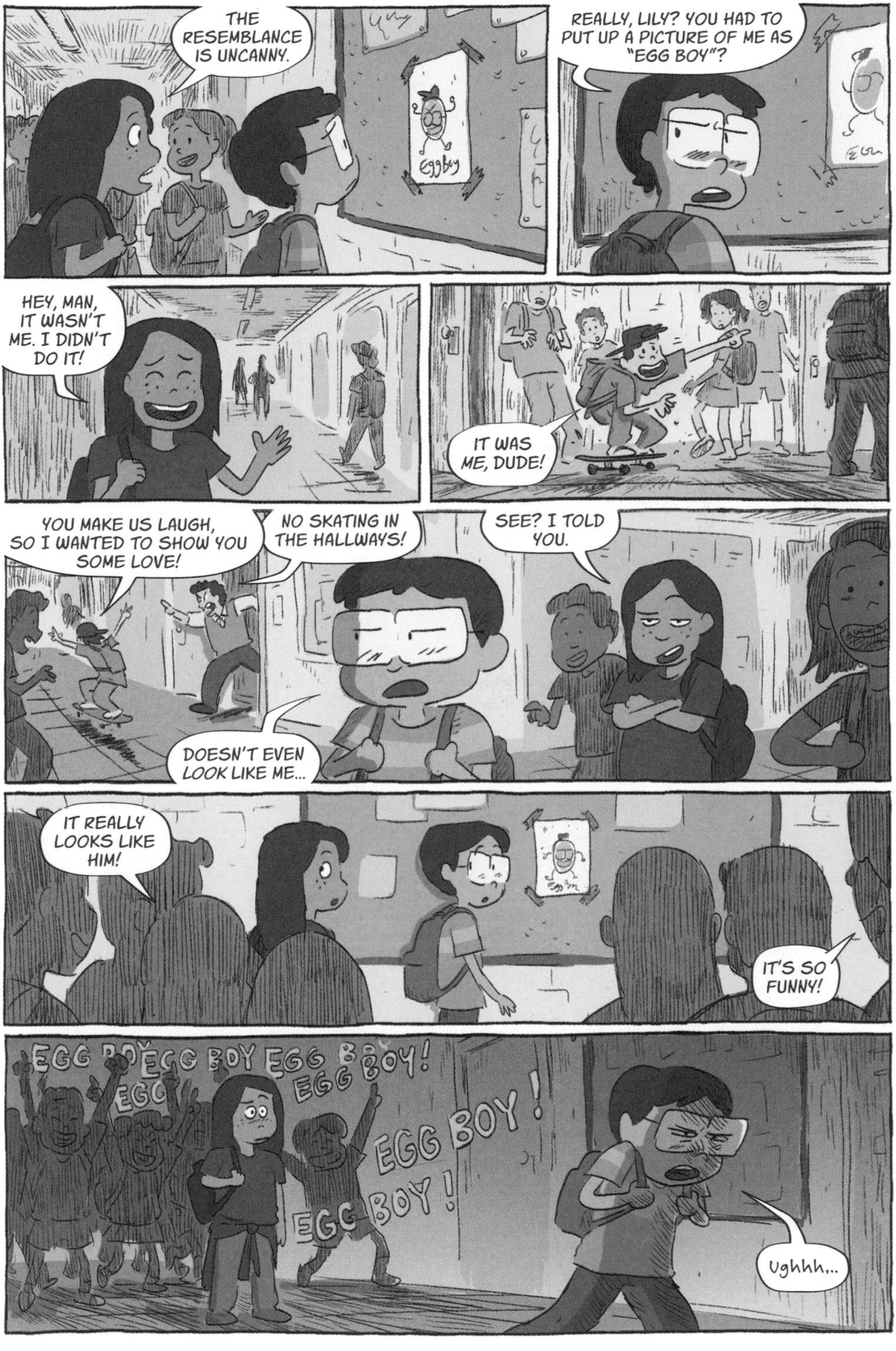
THE RESEMBLANCE IS UNCANNY.
EggBoy
REALLY, LILY? YOU HAD TO PUT UP A PICTURE OF ME AS "EGG BOY"?
HEY, MAN, IT WASN'T ME. I DIDN'T DO IT!
IT WAS ME, DUDE!
YOU MAKE US LAUGH, SO I WANTED TO SHOW YOU SOME LOVE!
NO SKATING IN THE HALLWAYS!
DOESN'T EVEN LOOK LIKE ME...
SEE? I TOLD YOU.
IT REALLY LOOKS LIKE HIM!
IT'S SO FUNNY!
EGG BOY EGG BOY EGG BOY EGG BOY!
EGG
EGG BOY!
EGG BOY!
Ughhh...

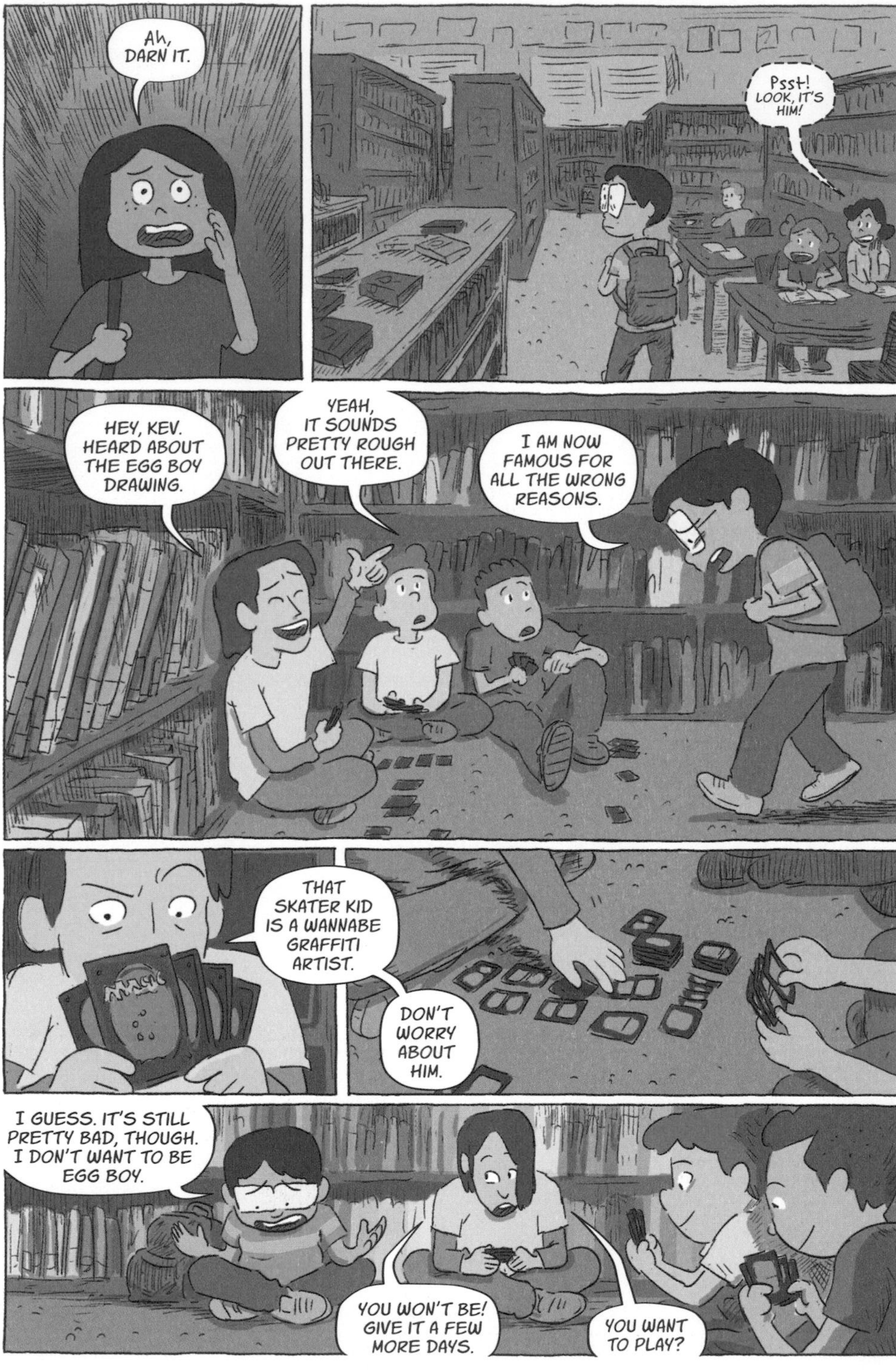
Ah, DARN IT.
Psst! LOOK, IT'S HIM!
HEY, KEV. HEARD ABOUT THE EGG BOY DRAWING.
YEAH, IT SOUNDS PRETTY ROUGH OUT THERE.
I AM NOW FAMOUS FOR ALL THE WRONG REASONS.
THAT SKATER KID IS A WANNABE GRAFFITI ARTIST.
DON'T WORRY ABOUT HIM.
I GUESS. IT'S STILL PRETTY BAD, THOUGH. I DON'T WANT TO BE EGG BOY.
YOU WON'T BE! GIVE IT A FEW MORE DAYS.
YOU WANT TO PLAY?

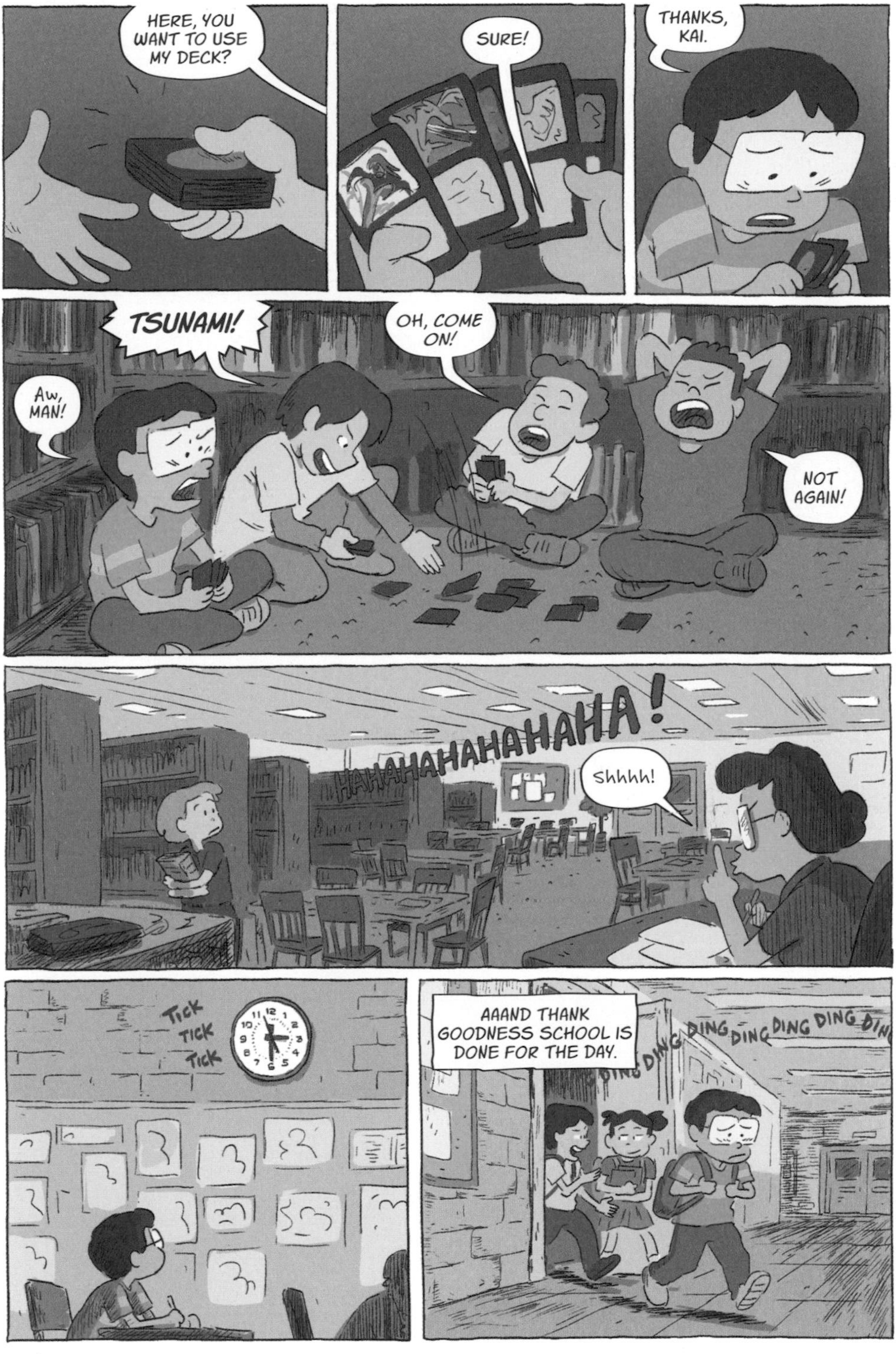
HERE, YOU WANT TO USE MY DECK?
SURE!
THANKS, KAI.
TSUNAMI!
OH, COME ON!
Aw, MAN!
NOT AGAIN!
HAHAHAHAHAHAHA!
Shhhh!
TICK
TICK
TICK
AAAND THANK GOODNESS SCHOOL IS DONE FOR THE DAY.
DING DING DING DING DING DING

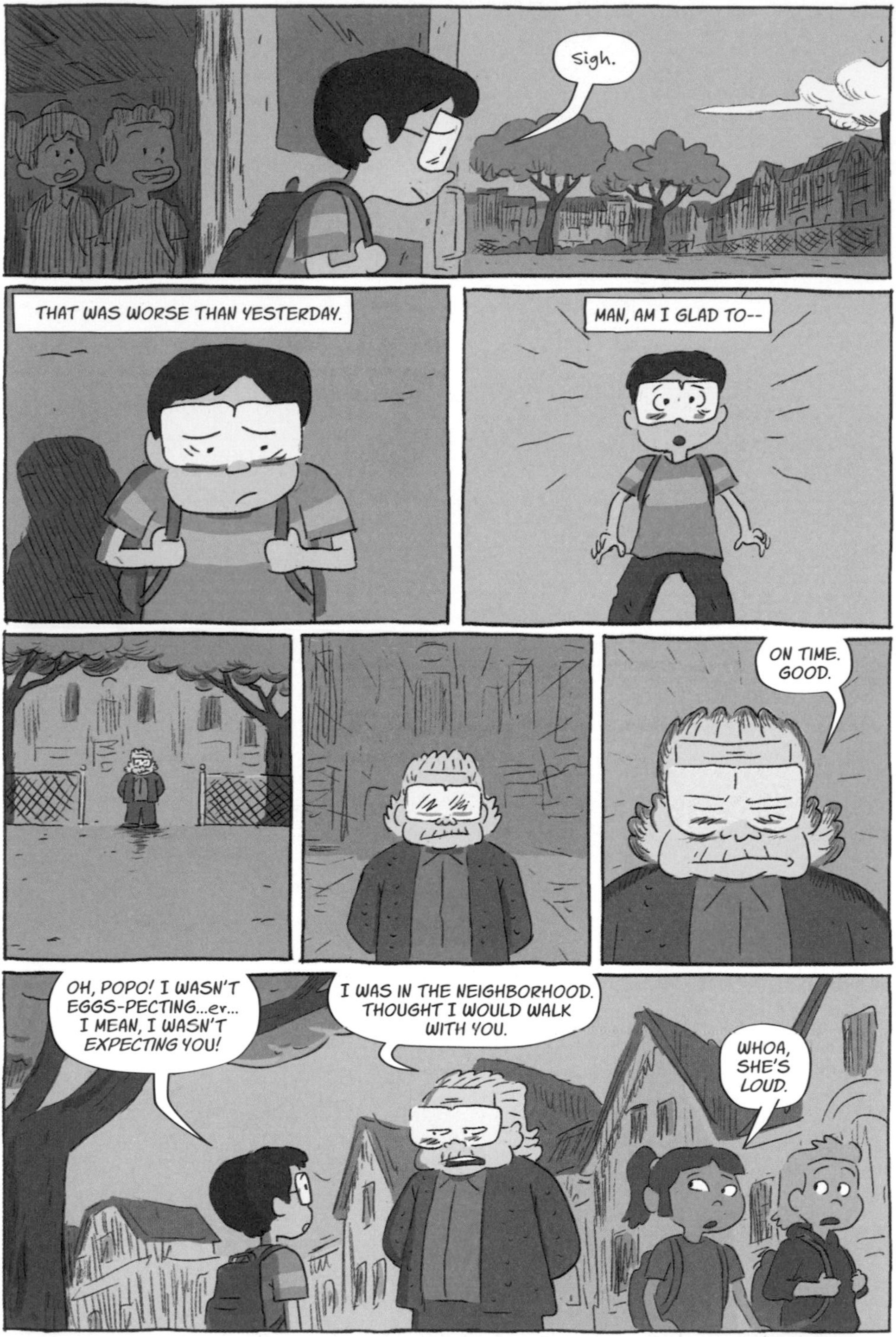
Sigh.
THAT WAS WORSE THAN YESTERDAY.
MAN, AM I GLAD TO--
ON TIME. GOOD.
OH, POPO! I WASN'T EGGS-PECTING...er... I MEAN, I WASN'T *EXPECTING* YOU!
I WAS IN THE NEIGHBORHOOD. THOUGHT I WOULD WALK WITH YOU.
WHOA, SHE'S LOUD.

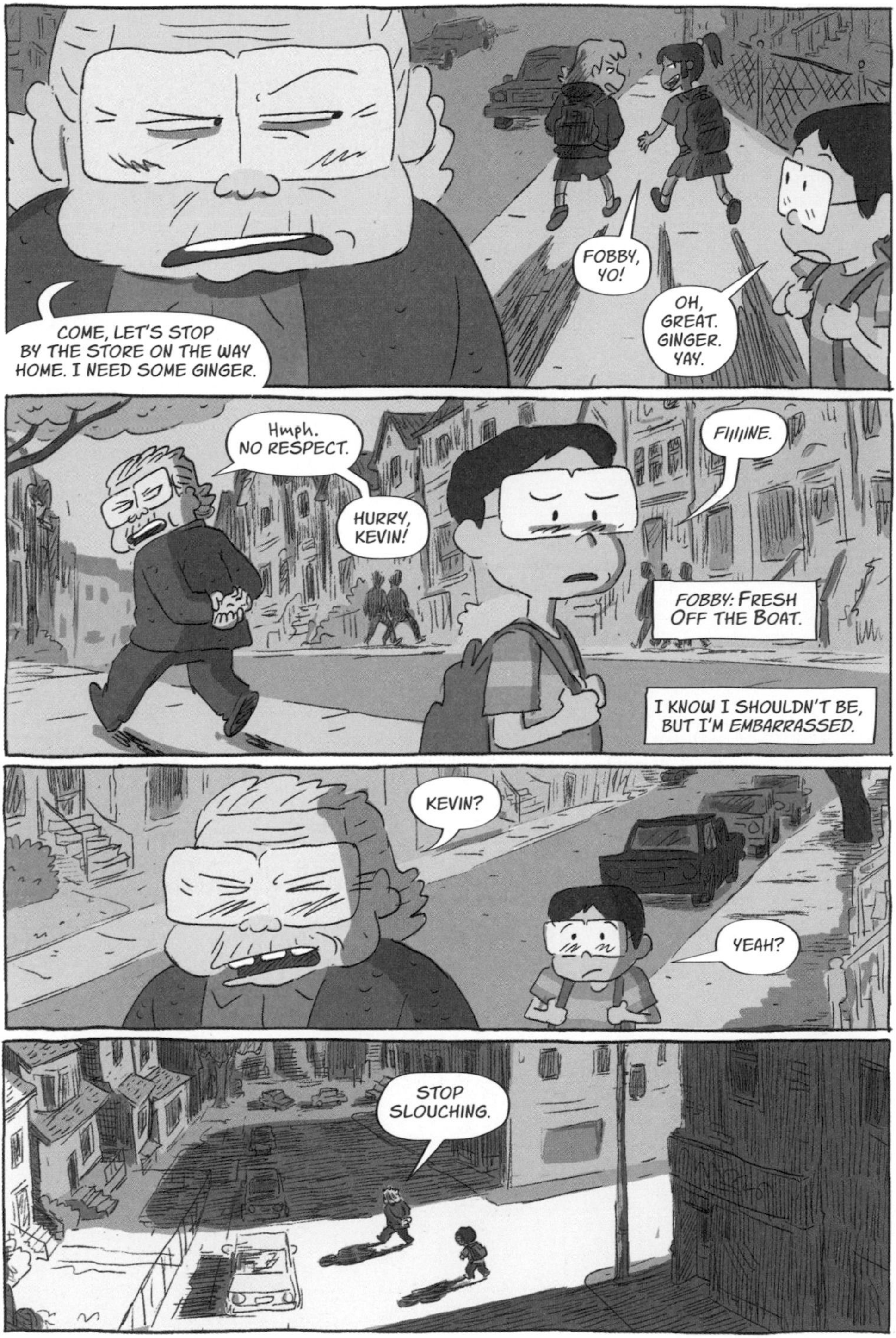
COME, LET'S STOP BY THE STORE ON THE WAY HOME. I NEED SOME GINGER.
FOBBY, YO!
OH, GREAT. GINGER. YAY.
Hmph. NO RESPECT.
HURRY, KEVIN!
FIIIIINE.
FOBBY: FRESH OFF THE BOAT.
I KNOW I SHOULDN'T BE, BUT I'M EMBARRASSED.
KEVIN?
YEAH?
STOP SLOUCHING.

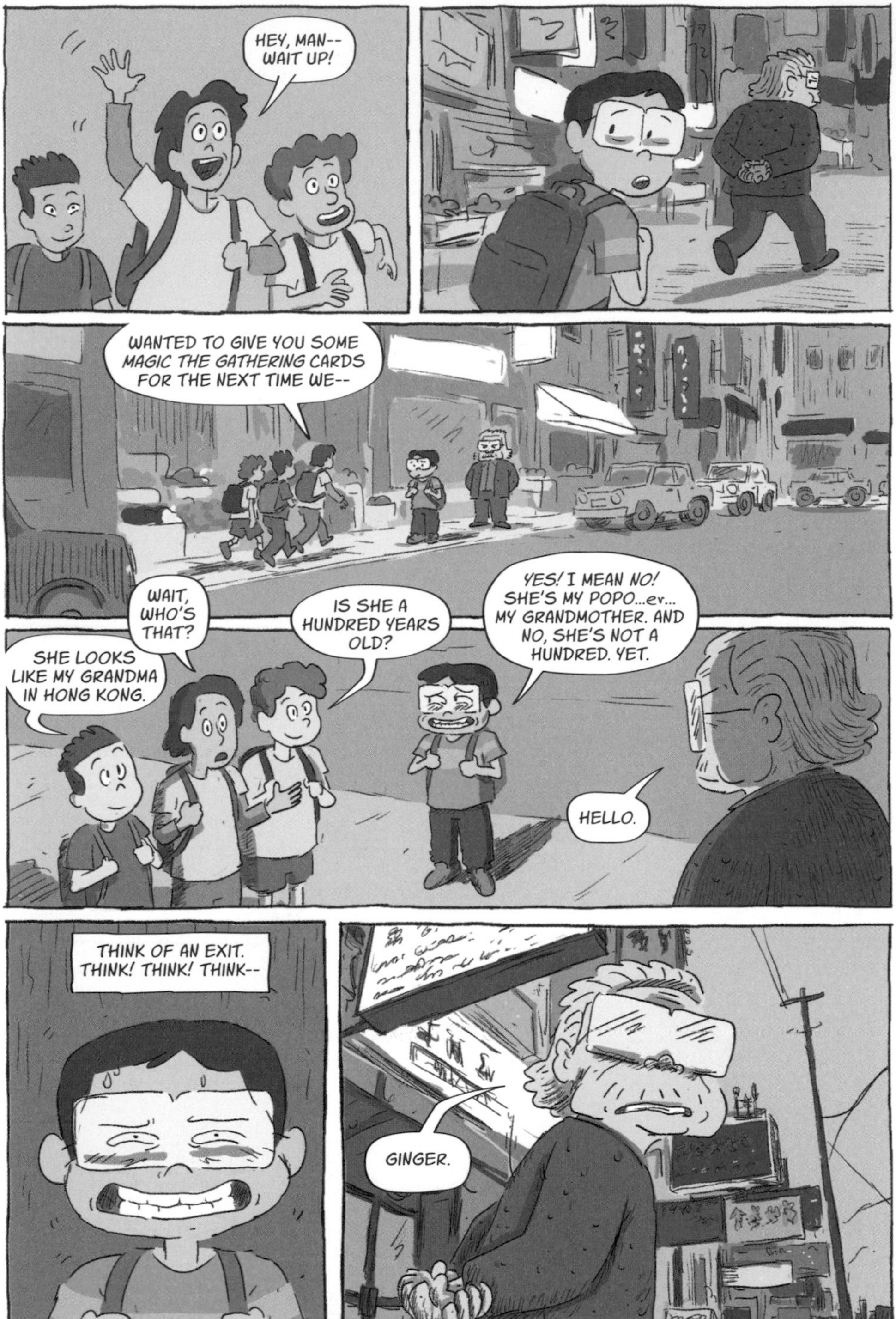
HEY, MAN--
WAIT UP!
WANTED TO GIVE YOU SOME MAGIC THE GATHERING CARDS FOR THE NEXT TIME WE--
SHE LOOKS LIKE MY GRANDMA IN HONG KONG.
WAIT, WHO'S THAT?
IS SHE A HUNDRED YEARS OLD?
YES! I MEAN NO! SHE'S MY POPO...er... MY GRANDMOTHER. AND NO, SHE'S NOT A HUNDRED. YET.
HELLO.
THINK OF AN EXIT. THINK! THINK! THINK--
GINGER.

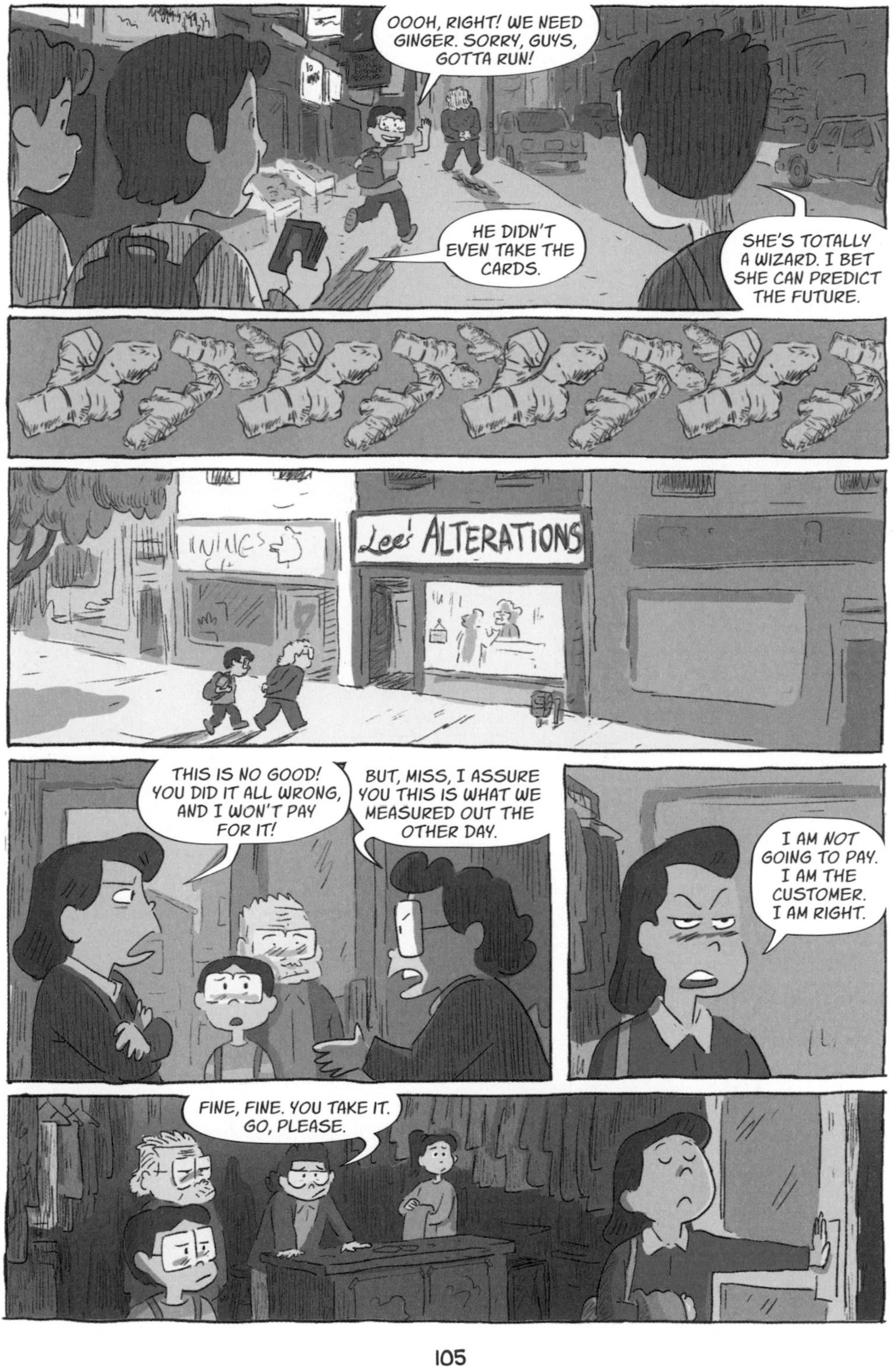
OOOH, RIGHT! WE NEED GINGER. SORRY, GUYS, GOTTA RUN!
HE DIDN'T EVEN TAKE THE CARDS.
SHE'S TOTALLY A WIZARD. I BET SHE CAN PREDICT THE FUTURE.
Lee's ALTERATIONS
THIS IS NO GOOD! YOU DID IT ALL WRONG, AND I WON'T PAY FOR IT!
BUT, MISS, I ASSURE YOU THIS IS WHAT WE MEASURED OUT THE OTHER DAY.
I AM *NOT* GOING TO PAY. I AM THE CUSTOMER. I AM RIGHT.
FINE, FINE. YOU TAKE IT. GO, PLEASE.

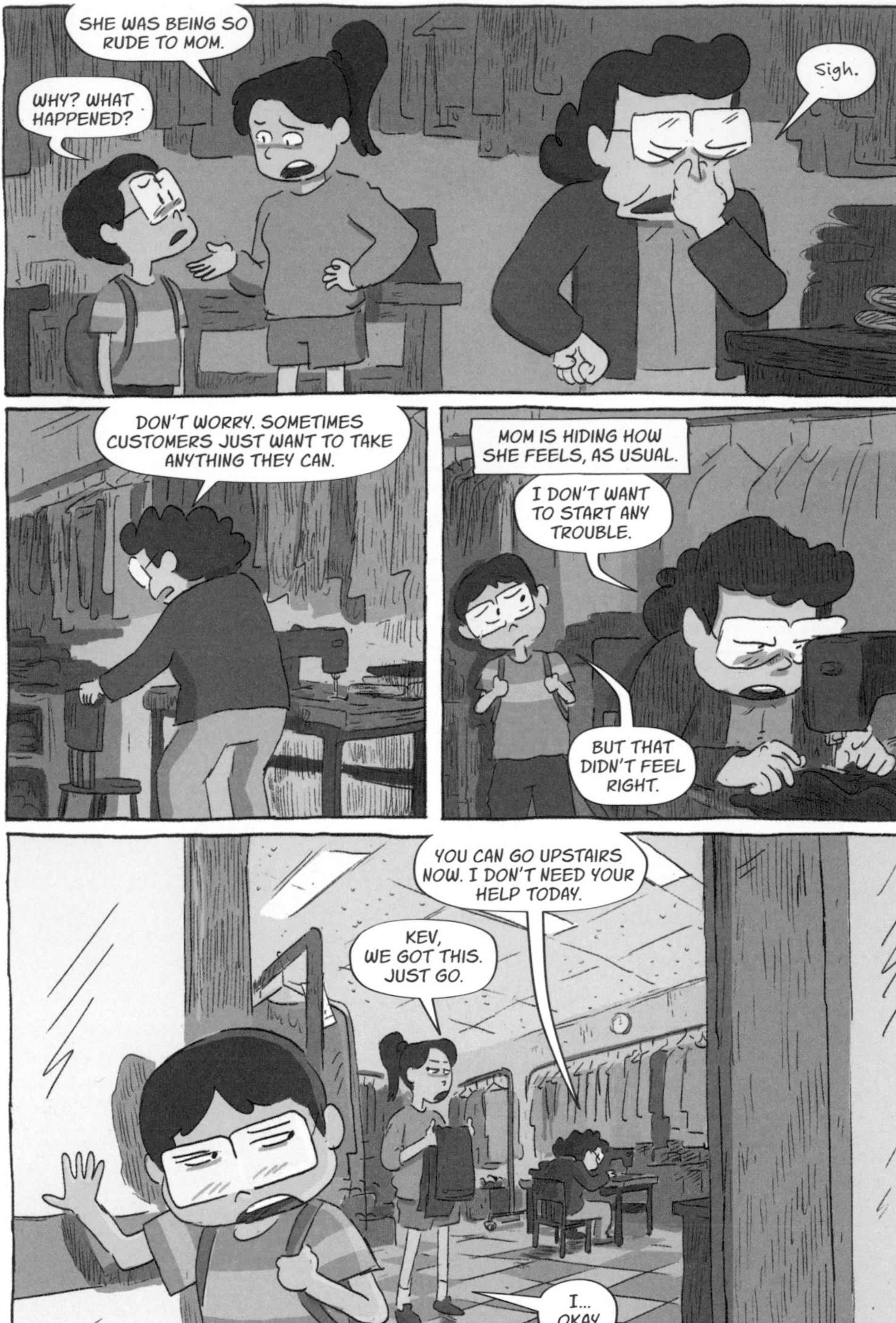
SHE WAS BEING SO RUDE TO MOM.
WHY? WHAT HAPPENED?
Sigh.
DON'T WORRY. SOMETIMES CUSTOMERS JUST WANT TO TAKE ANYTHING THEY CAN.
MOM IS HIDING HOW SHE FEELS, AS USUAL.
I DON'T WANT TO START ANY TROUBLE.
BUT THAT DIDN'T FEEL RIGHT.
YOU CAN GO UPSTAIRS NOW. I DON'T NEED YOUR HELP TODAY.
KEV, WE GOT THIS. JUST GO.
I... OKAY.

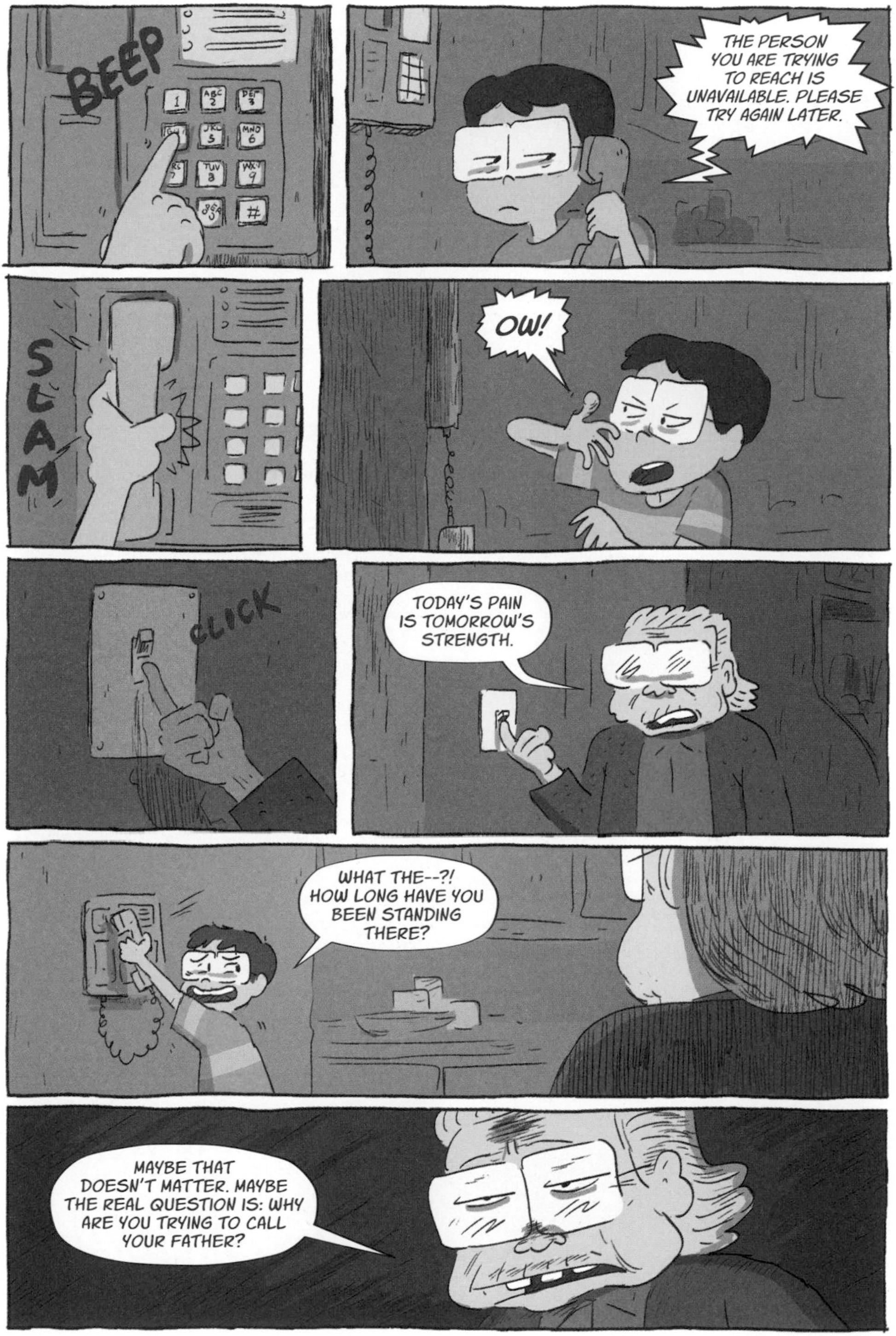
BEEP
THE PERSON YOU ARE TRYING TO REACH IS UNAVAILABLE. PLEASE TRY AGAIN LATER.
SLAM
OW!
CLICK
TODAY'S PAIN IS TOMORROW'S STRENGTH.
WHAT THE--?! HOW LONG HAVE YOU BEEN STANDING THERE?
MAYBE THAT DOESN'T MATTER. MAYBE THE REAL QUESTION IS: WHY ARE YOU TRYING TO CALL YOUR FATHER?

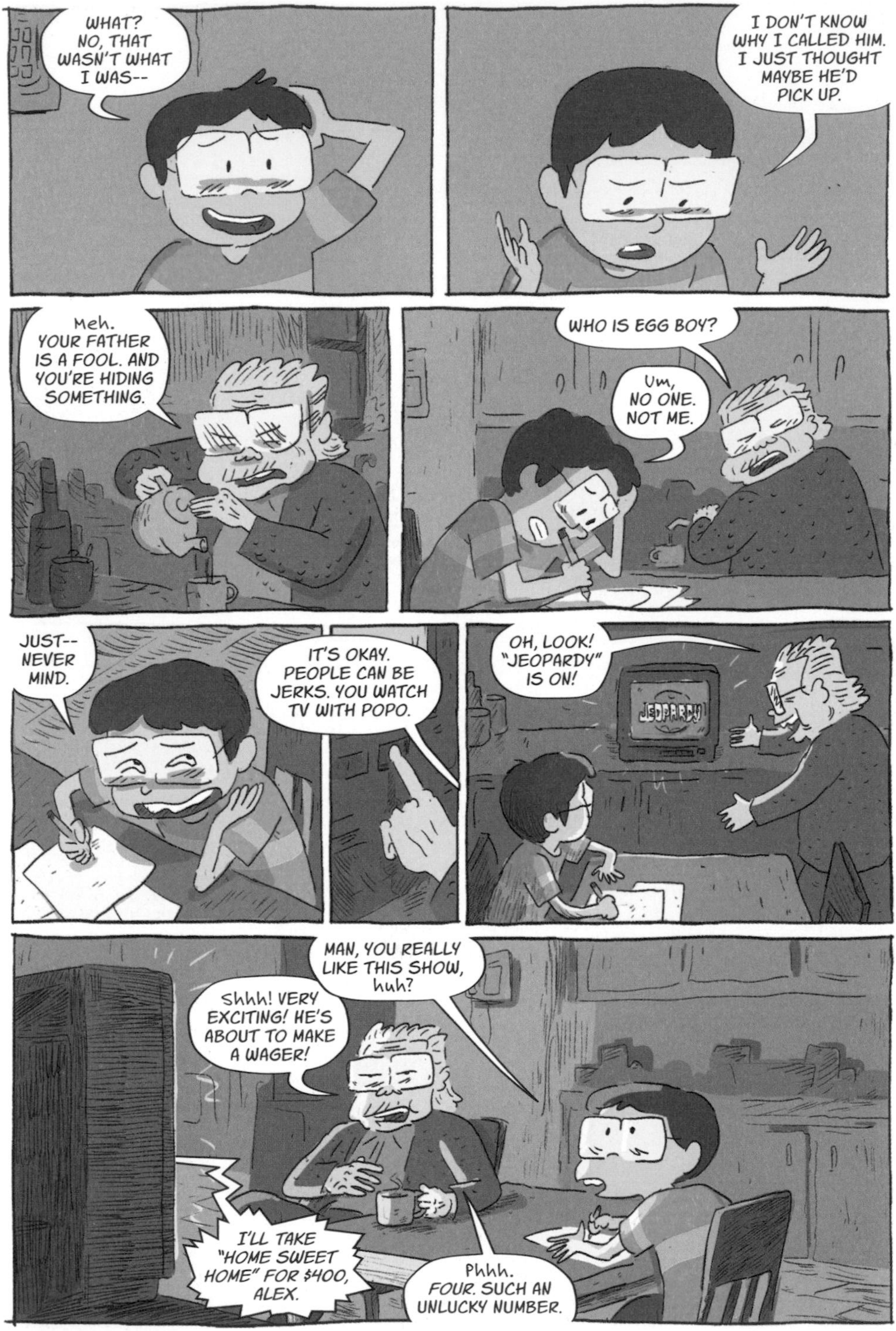
WHAT? NO, THAT WASN'T WHAT I WAS--
I DON'T KNOW WHY I CALLED HIM. I JUST THOUGHT MAYBE HE'D PICK UP.
Meh. YOUR FATHER IS A FOOL. AND YOU'RE HIDING SOMETHING.
WHO IS EGG BOY?
Um, NO ONE. NOT ME.
JUST-- NEVER MIND.
IT'S OKAY. PEOPLE CAN BE JERKS. YOU WATCH TV WITH POPO.
OH, LOOK! "JEOPARDY" IS ON!
JEOPARDY!
MAN, YOU REALLY LIKE THIS SHOW, huh?
Shhh! VERY EXCITING! HE'S ABOUT TO MAKE A WAGER!
I'LL TAKE "HOME SWEET HOME" FOR $400, ALEX.
Phhh. FOUR. SUCH AN UNLUCKY NUMBER.

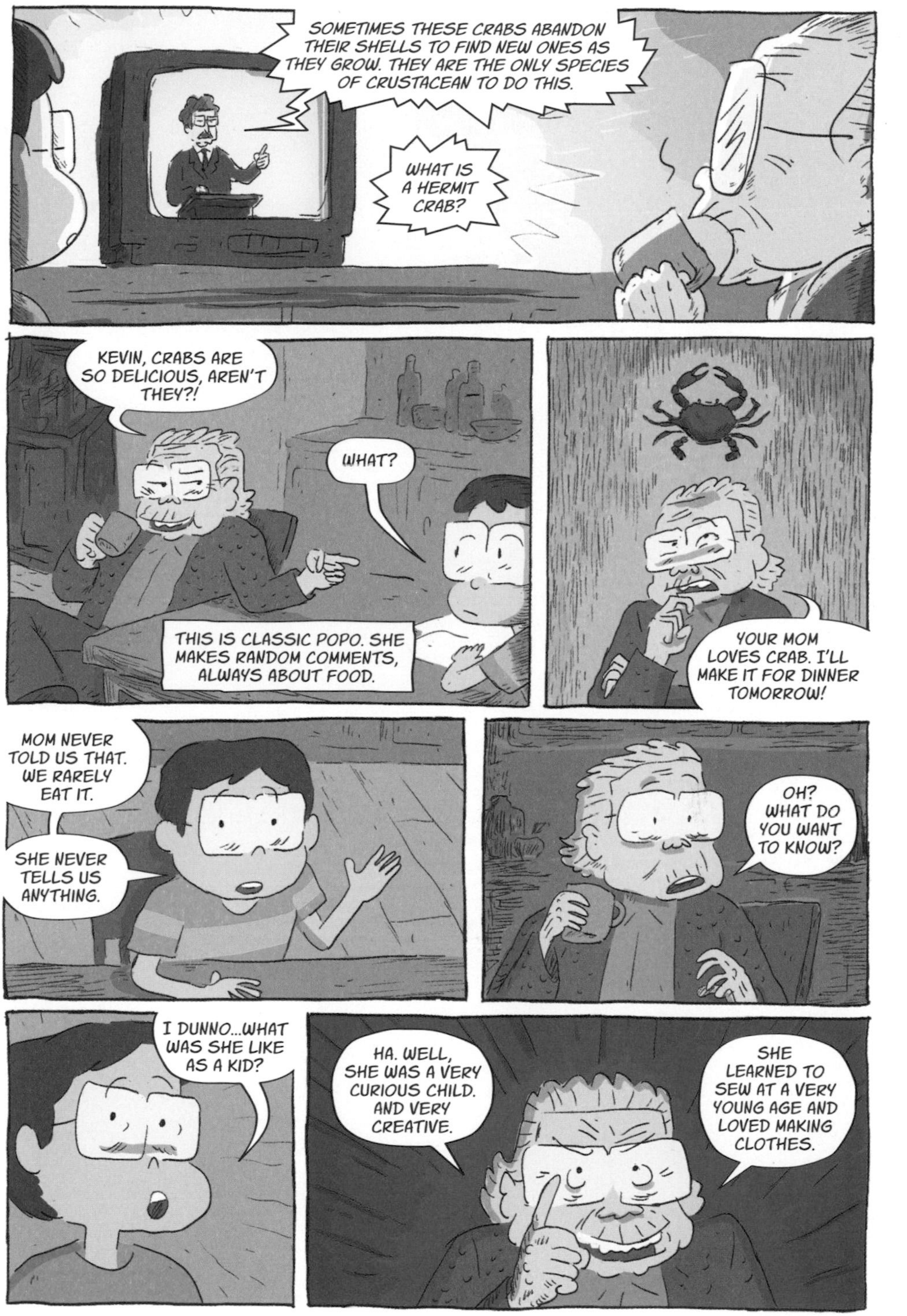

SOMETIMES THESE CRABS ABANDON THEIR SHELLS TO FIND NEW ONES AS THEY GROW. THEY ARE THE ONLY SPECIES OF CRUSTACEAN TO DO THIS.
WHAT IS A HERMIT CRAB?
KEVIN, CRABS ARE SO DELICIOUS, AREN'T THEY?!
WHAT?
THIS IS CLASSIC POPO. SHE MAKES RANDOM COMMENTS, ALWAYS ABOUT FOOD.
YOUR MOM LOVES CRAB. I'LL MAKE IT FOR DINNER TOMORROW!
MOM NEVER TOLD US THAT. WE RARELY EAT IT.
SHE NEVER TELLS US ANYTHING.
OH? WHAT DO YOU WANT TO KNOW?
I DUNNO...WHAT WAS SHE LIKE AS A KID?
HA. WELL, SHE WAS A VERY CURIOUS CHILD. AND VERY CREATIVE.
SHE LEARNED TO SEW AT A VERY YOUNG AGE AND LOVED MAKING CLOTHES.

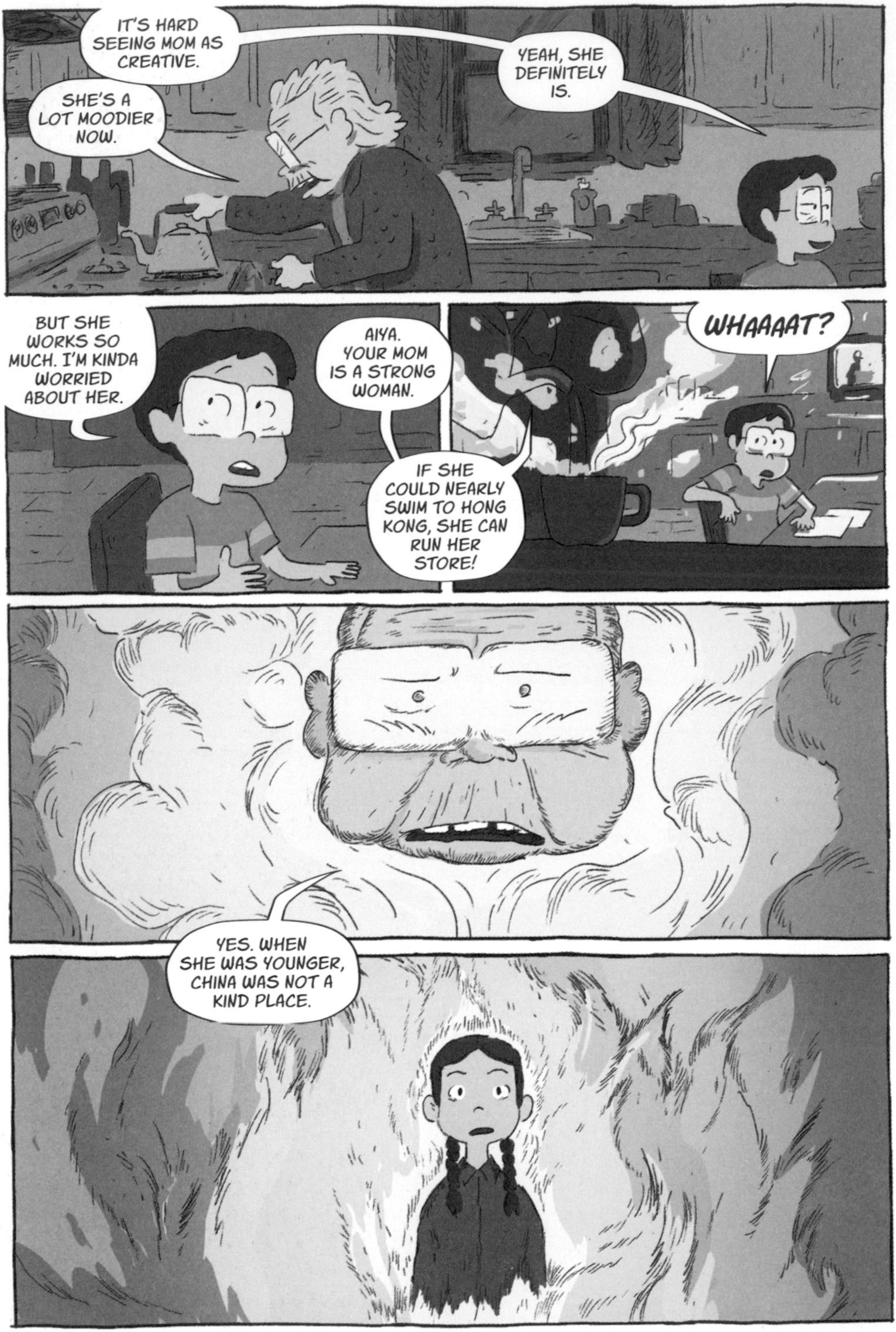
IT'S HARD SEEING MOM AS CREATIVE.
YEAH, SHE DEFINITELY IS.
SHE'S A LOT MOODIER NOW.
BUT SHE WORKS SO MUCH. I'M KINDA WORRIED ABOUT HER.
AIYA. YOUR MOM IS A STRONG WOMAN.
IF SHE COULD NEARLY SWIM TO HONG KONG, SHE CAN RUN HER STORE!
WHAAAAT?
YES. WHEN SHE WAS YOUNGER, CHINA WAS NOT A KIND PLACE.

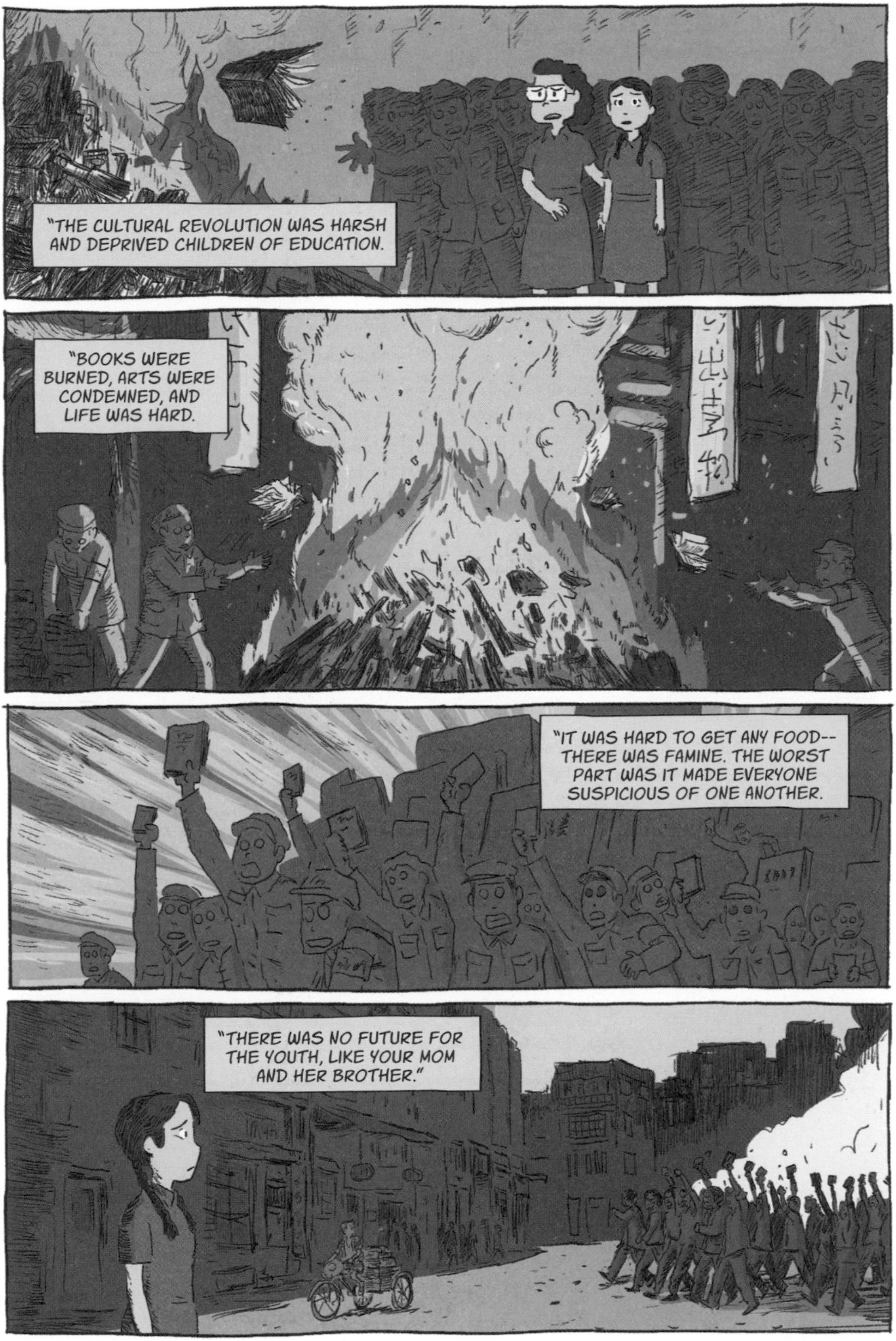
"THE CULTURAL REVOLUTION WAS HARSH AND DEPRIVED CHILDREN OF EDUCATION.
"BOOKS WERE BURNED, ARTS WERE CONDEMNED, AND LIFE WAS HARD.
"IT WAS HARD TO GET ANY FOOD-- THERE WAS FAMINE. THE WORST PART WAS IT MADE EVERYONE SUSPICIOUS OF ONE ANOTHER.
"THERE WAS NO FUTURE FOR THE YOUTH, LIKE YOUR MOM AND HER BROTHER."

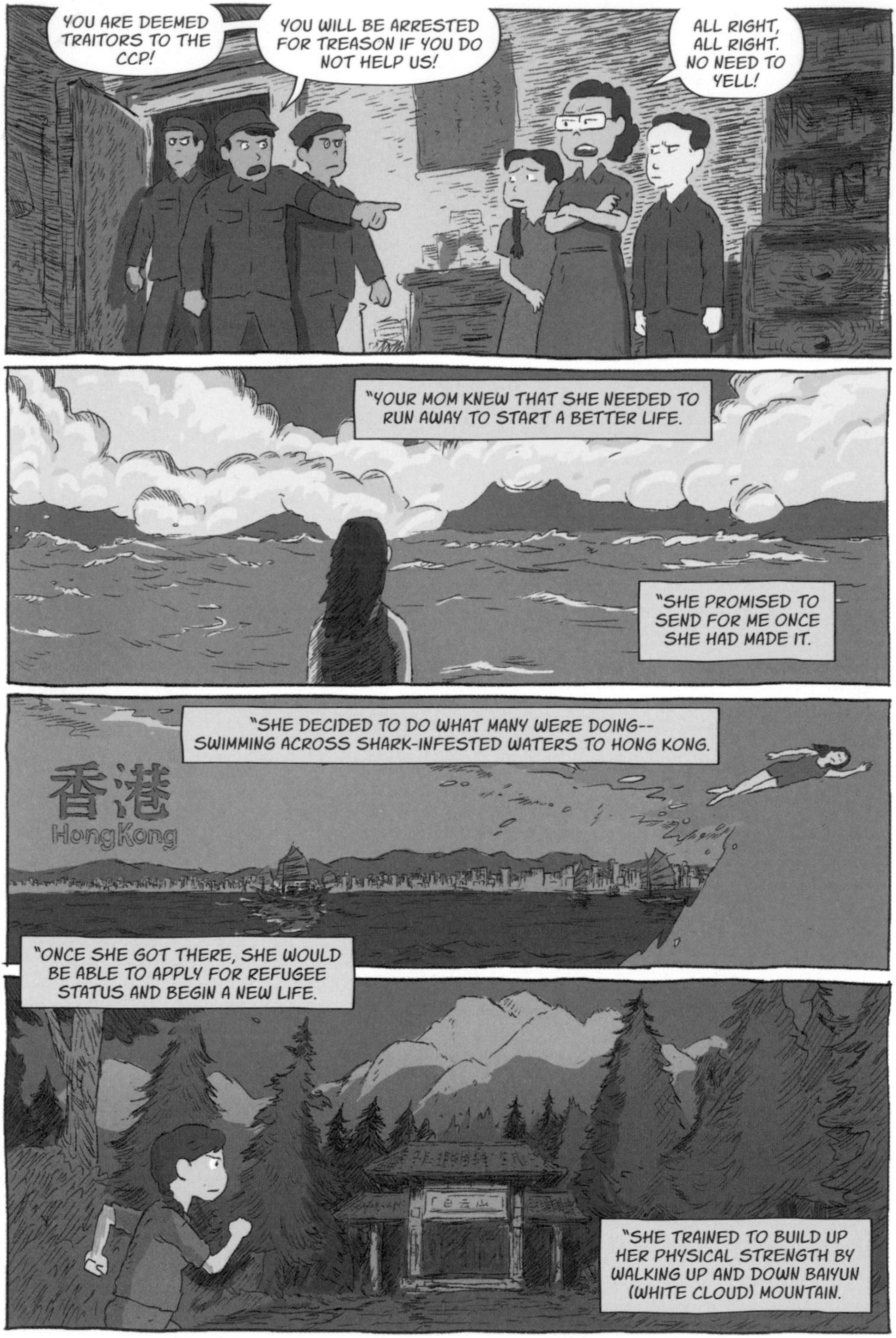

YOU ARE DEEMED TRAITORS TO THE CCP!
YOU WILL BE ARRESTED FOR TREASON IF YOU DO NOT HELP US!
ALL RIGHT, ALL RIGHT. NO NEED TO YELL!
"YOUR MOM KNEW THAT SHE NEEDED TO RUN AWAY TO START A BETTER LIFE.
"SHE PROMISED TO SEND FOR ME ONCE SHE HAD MADE IT.
"SHE DECIDED TO DO WHAT MANY WERE DOING-- SWIMMING ACROSS SHARK-INFESTED WATERS TO HONG KONG.
香港
HongKong
"ONCE SHE GOT THERE, SHE WOULD BE ABLE TO APPLY FOR REFUGEE STATUS AND BEGIN A NEW LIFE.
"SHE TRAINED TO BUILD UP HER PHYSICAL STRENGTH BY WALKING UP AND DOWN BAIYUN (WHITE CLOUD) MOUNTAIN.

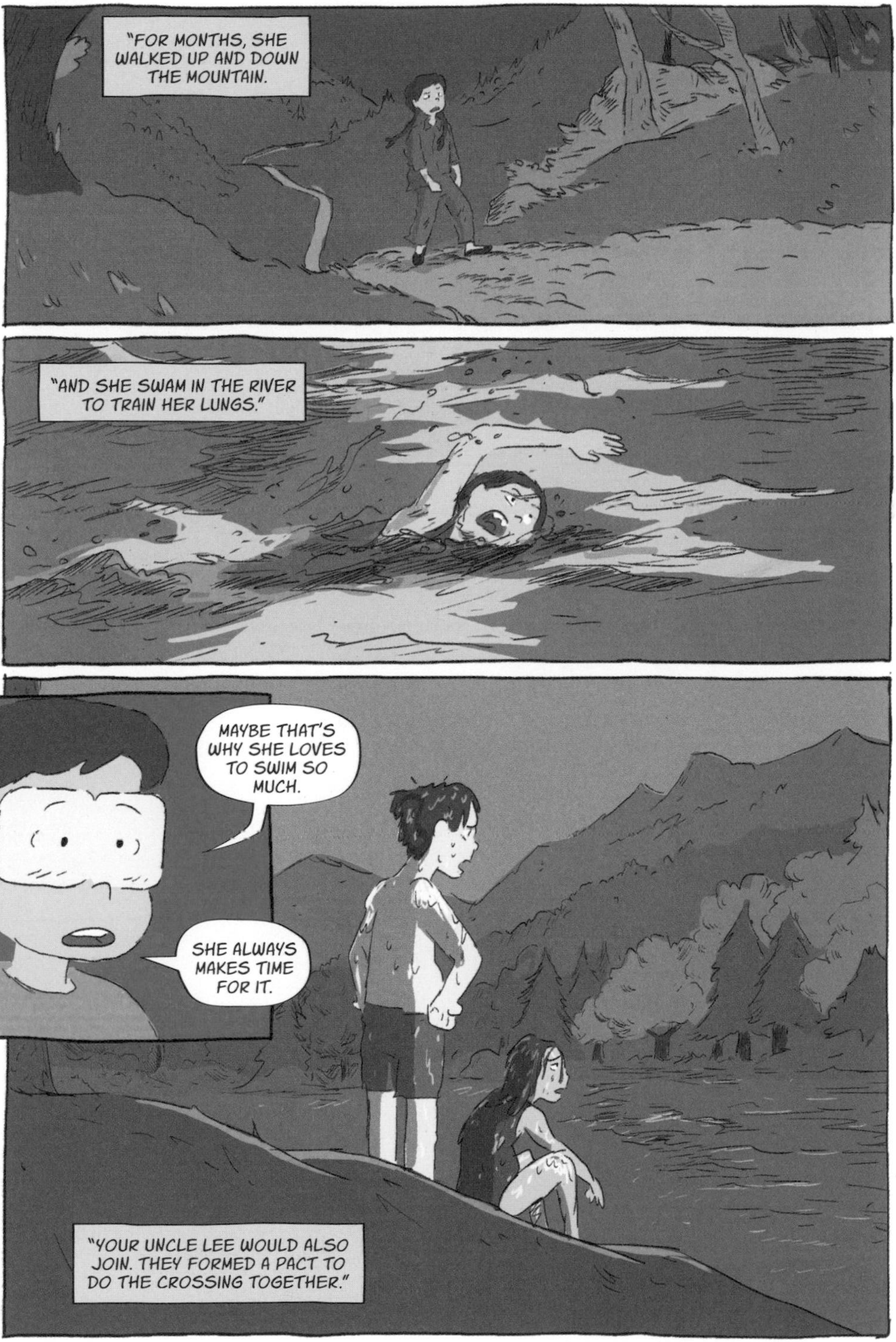
"FOR MONTHS, SHE WALKED UP AND DOWN THE MOUNTAIN.
"AND SHE SWAM IN THE RIVER TO TRAIN HER LUNGS."
MAYBE THAT'S WHY SHE LOVES TO SWIM SO MUCH.
SHE ALWAYS MAKES TIME FOR IT.
"YOUR UNCLE LEE WOULD ALSO JOIN. THEY FORMED A PACT TO DO THE CROSSING TOGETHER."

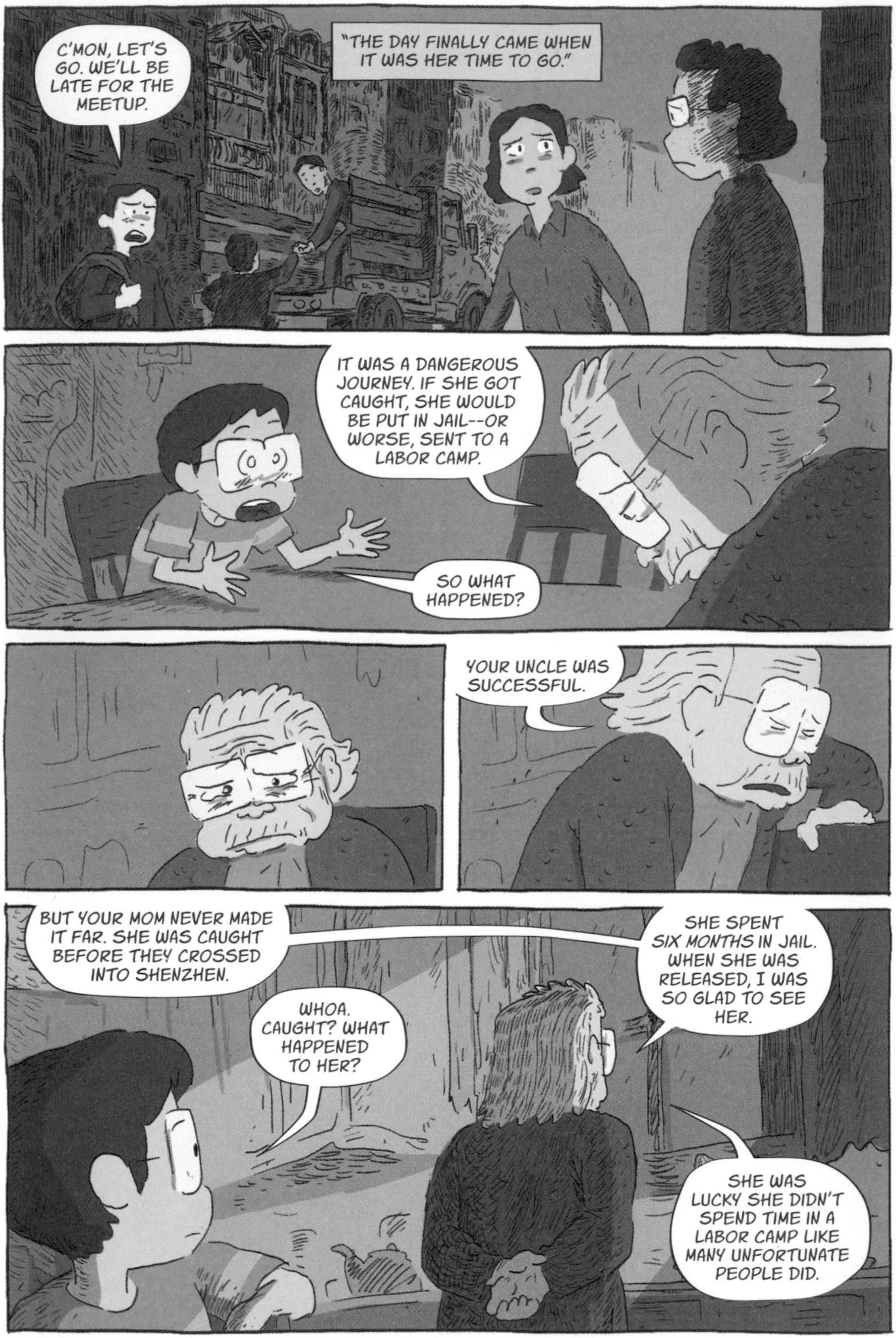
C'MON, LET'S GO. WE'LL BE LATE FOR THE MEETUP.
"THE DAY FINALLY CAME WHEN IT WAS HER TIME TO GO."
IT WAS A DANGEROUS JOURNEY. IF SHE GOT CAUGHT, SHE WOULD BE PUT IN JAIL--OR WORSE, SENT TO A LABOR CAMP.
SO WHAT HAPPENED?
YOUR UNCLE WAS SUCCESSFUL.
BUT YOUR MOM NEVER MADE IT FAR. SHE WAS CAUGHT BEFORE THEY CROSSED INTO SHENZHEN.
WHOA. CAUGHT? WHAT HAPPENED TO HER?
SHE SPENT SIX MONTHS IN JAIL. WHEN SHE WAS RELEASED, I WAS SO GLAD TO SEE HER.
SHE WAS LUCKY SHE DIDN'T SPEND TIME IN A LABOR CAMP LIKE MANY UNFORTUNATE PEOPLE DID.

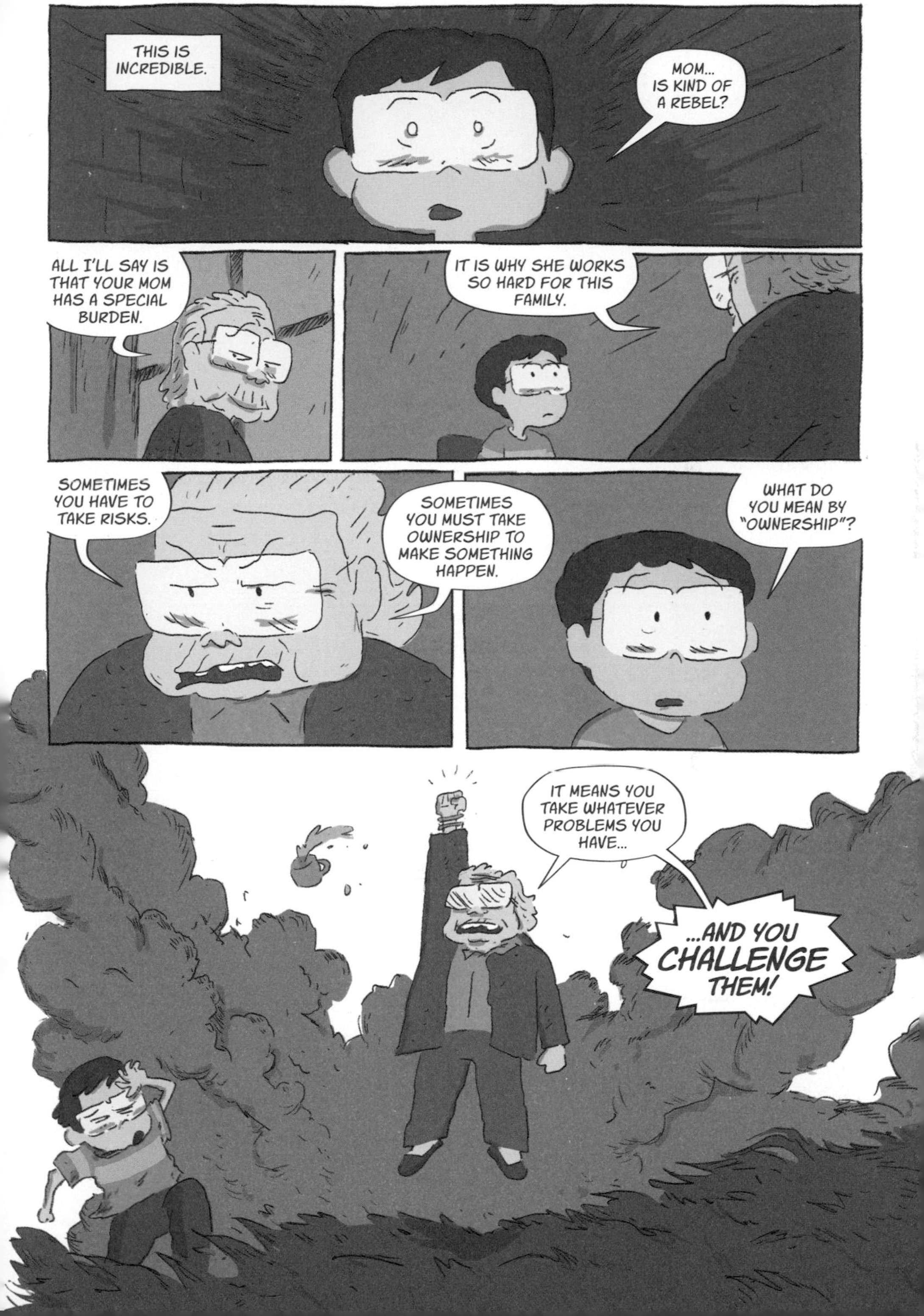
THIS IS INCREDIBLE.
MOM... IS KIND OF A REBEL?
ALL I'LL SAY IS THAT YOUR MOM HAS A SPECIAL BURDEN.
IT IS WHY SHE WORKS SO HARD FOR THIS FAMILY.
SOMETIMES YOU HAVE TO TAKE RISKS.
SOMETIMES YOU MUST TAKE OWNERSHIP TO MAKE SOMETHING HAPPEN.
WHAT DO YOU MEAN BY "OWNERSHIP"?
IT MEANS YOU TAKE WHATEVER PROBLEMS YOU HAVE...
...AND YOU CHALLENGE THEM!

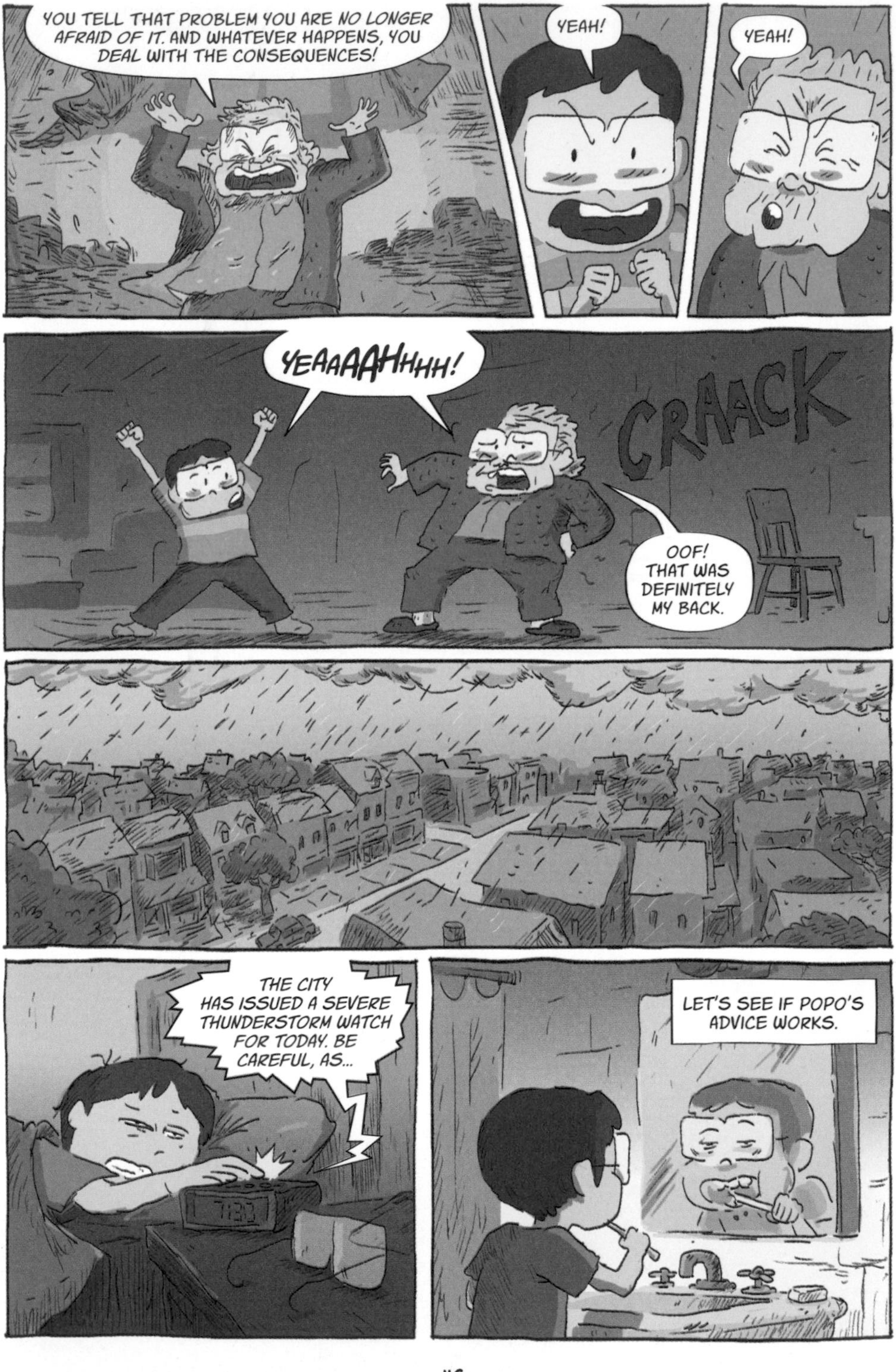
YOU TELL THAT PROBLEM YOU ARE NO LONGER AFRAID OF IT. AND WHATEVER HAPPENS, YOU DEAL WITH THE CONSEQUENCES!
YEAH!
YEAH!
YEAAAAHHHH!
CRAACK
OOF! THAT WAS DEFINITELY MY BACK.
THE CITY HAS ISSUED A SEVERE THUNDERSTORM WATCH FOR TODAY. BE CAREFUL, AS...
LET'S SEE IF POPO'S ADVICE WORKS.

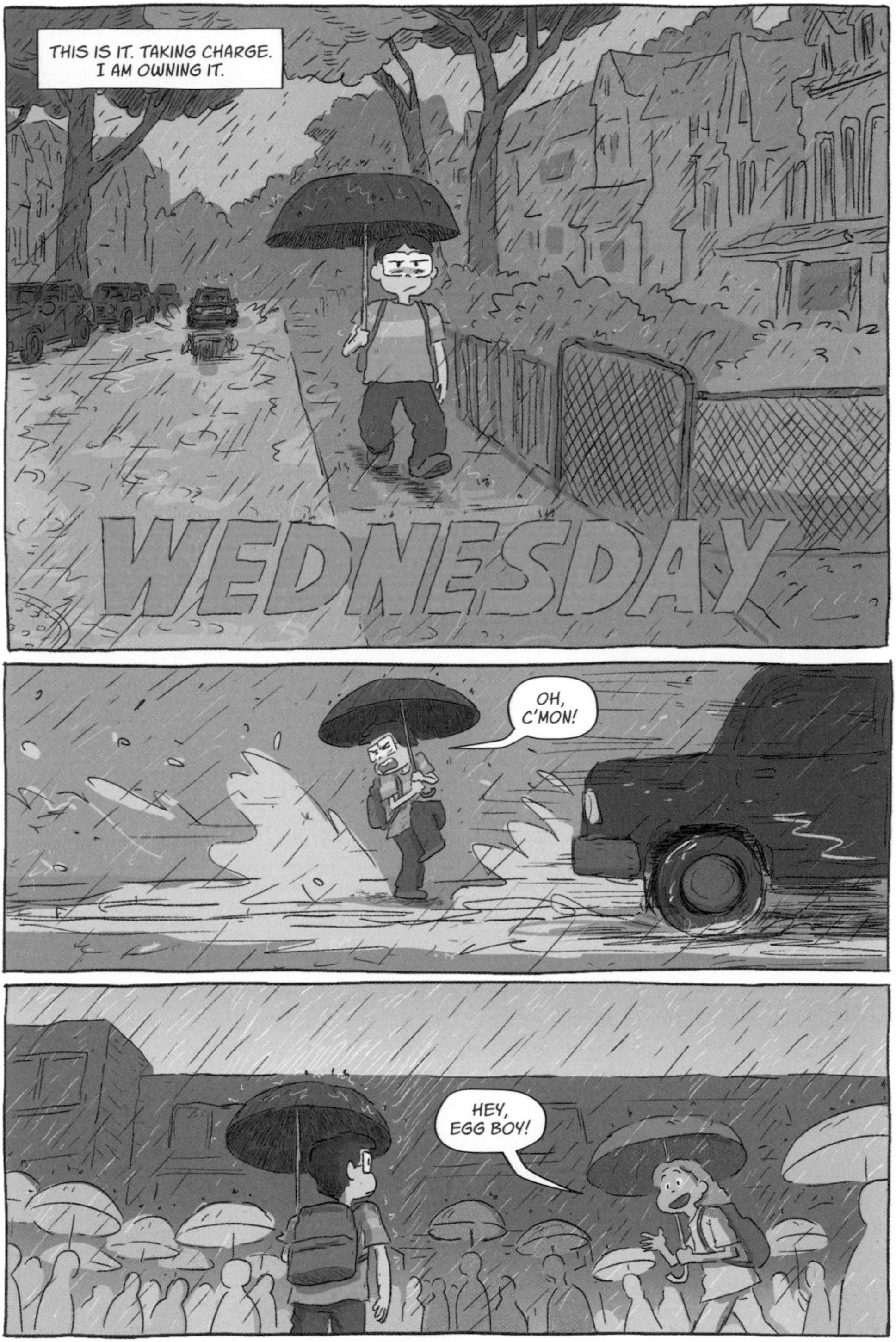

THIS IS IT. TAKING CHARGE. I AM OWNING IT.
WEDNESDAY
OH, C'MON!
HEY, EGG BOY!

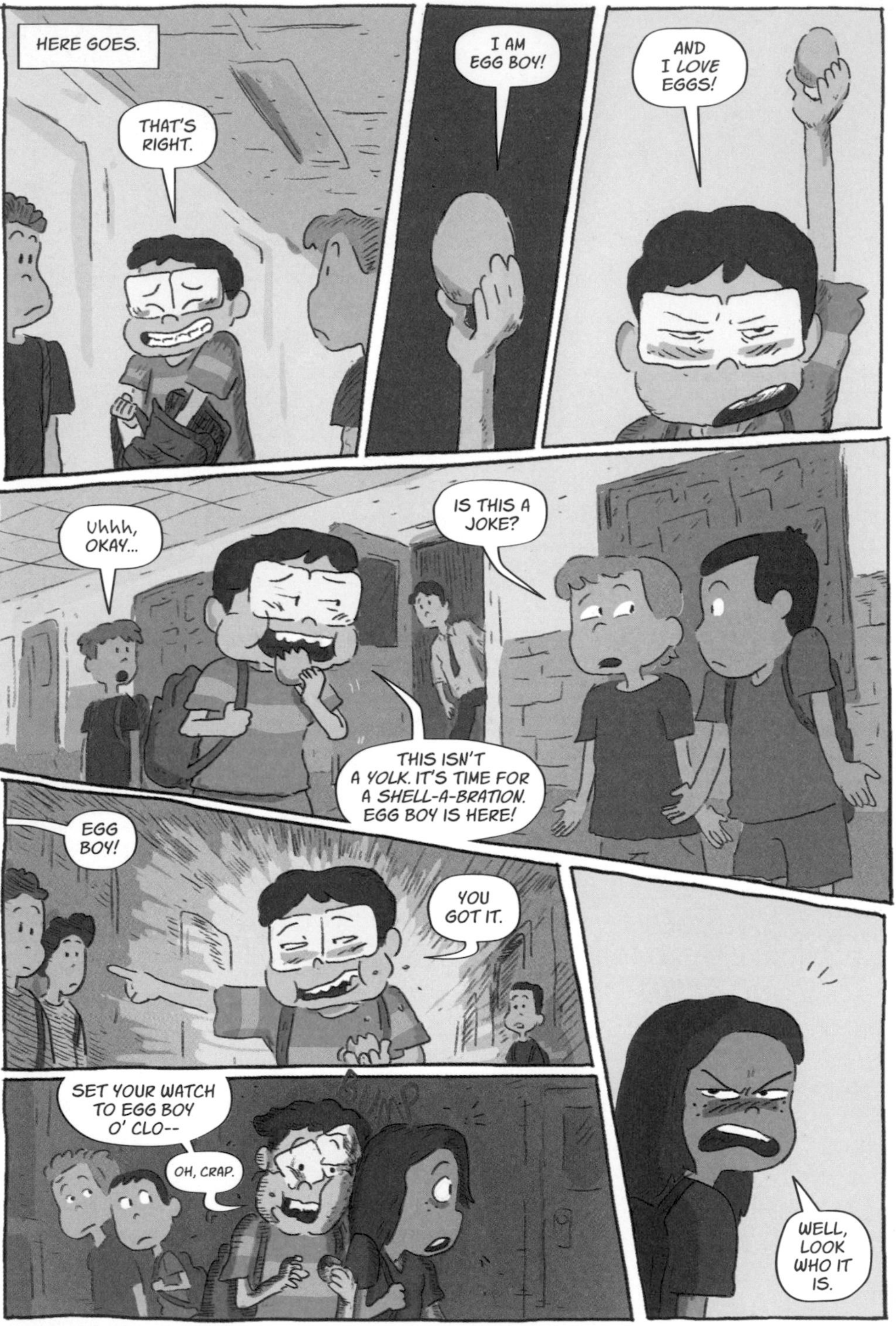
HERE GOES.
THAT'S RIGHT.
I AM EGG BOY!
AND I *LOVE* EGGS!
Uhhh, OKAY...
IS THIS A JOKE?
THIS ISN'T A *YOLK*. IT'S TIME FOR A *SHELL-A-BRATION*. EGG BOY IS HERE!
EGG BOY!
YOU GOT IT.
SET YOUR WATCH TO EGG BOY O' CLO--
OH, CRAP.
BUMP
WELL, LOOK WHO IT IS.

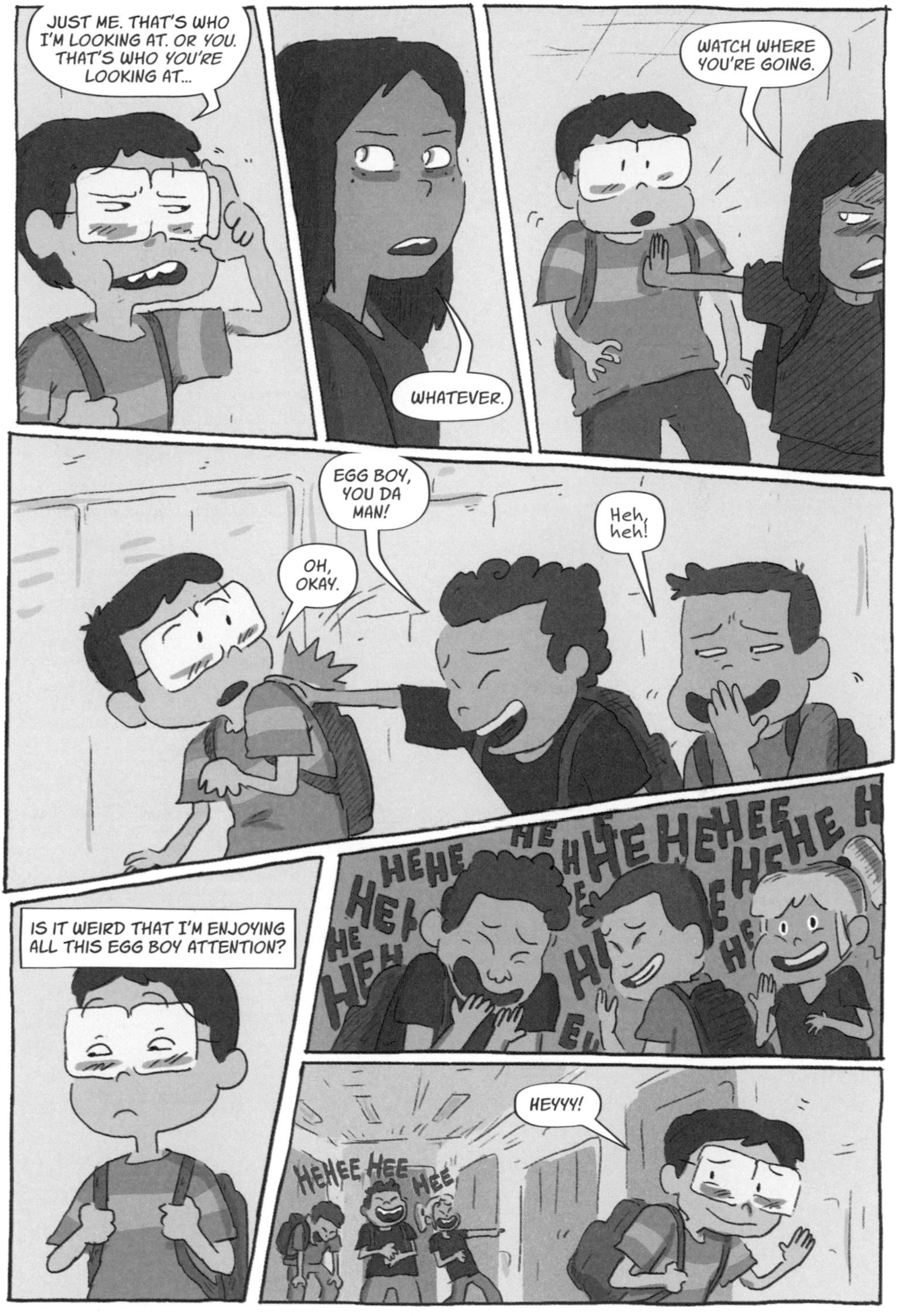

JUST ME. THAT'S WHO I'M LOOKING AT. OR YOU. THAT'S WHO YOU'RE LOOKING AT...
WHATEVER.
WATCH WHERE YOU'RE GOING.
EGG BOY, YOU DA MAN!
OH, OKAY.
Heh, heh!
IS IT WEIRD THAT I'M ENJOYING ALL THIS EGG BOY ATTENTION?
HEYYY!
HEHEE HEE HEE

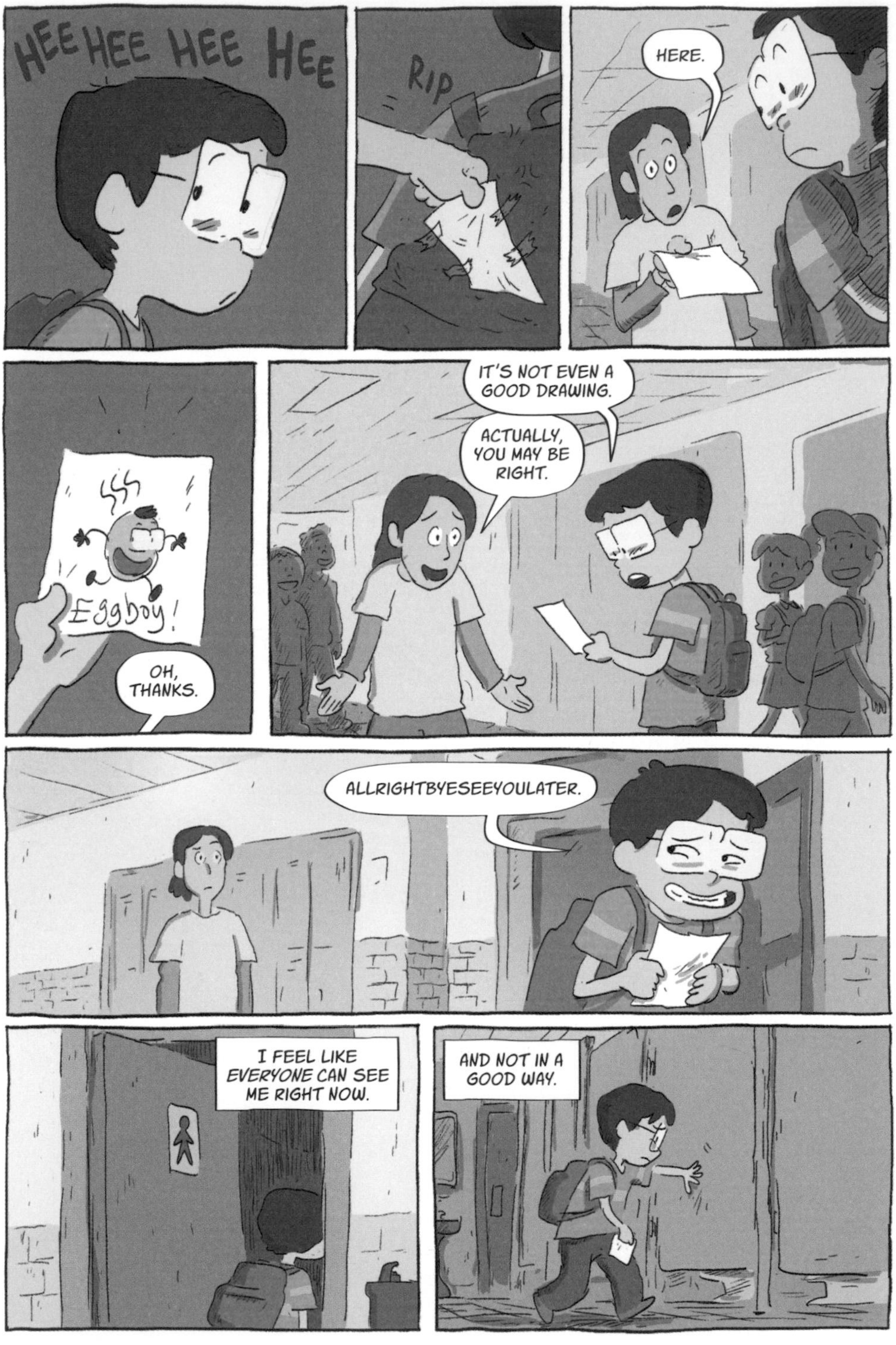
HEE HEE HEE HEE
RIP
HERE.
Eggboy!
OH, THANKS.
IT'S NOT EVEN A GOOD DRAWING.
ACTUALLY, YOU MAY BE RIGHT.
ALLRIGHTBYESEEYOULATER.
I FEEL LIKE *EVERYONE* CAN SEE ME RIGHT NOW.
AND NOT IN A GOOD WAY.

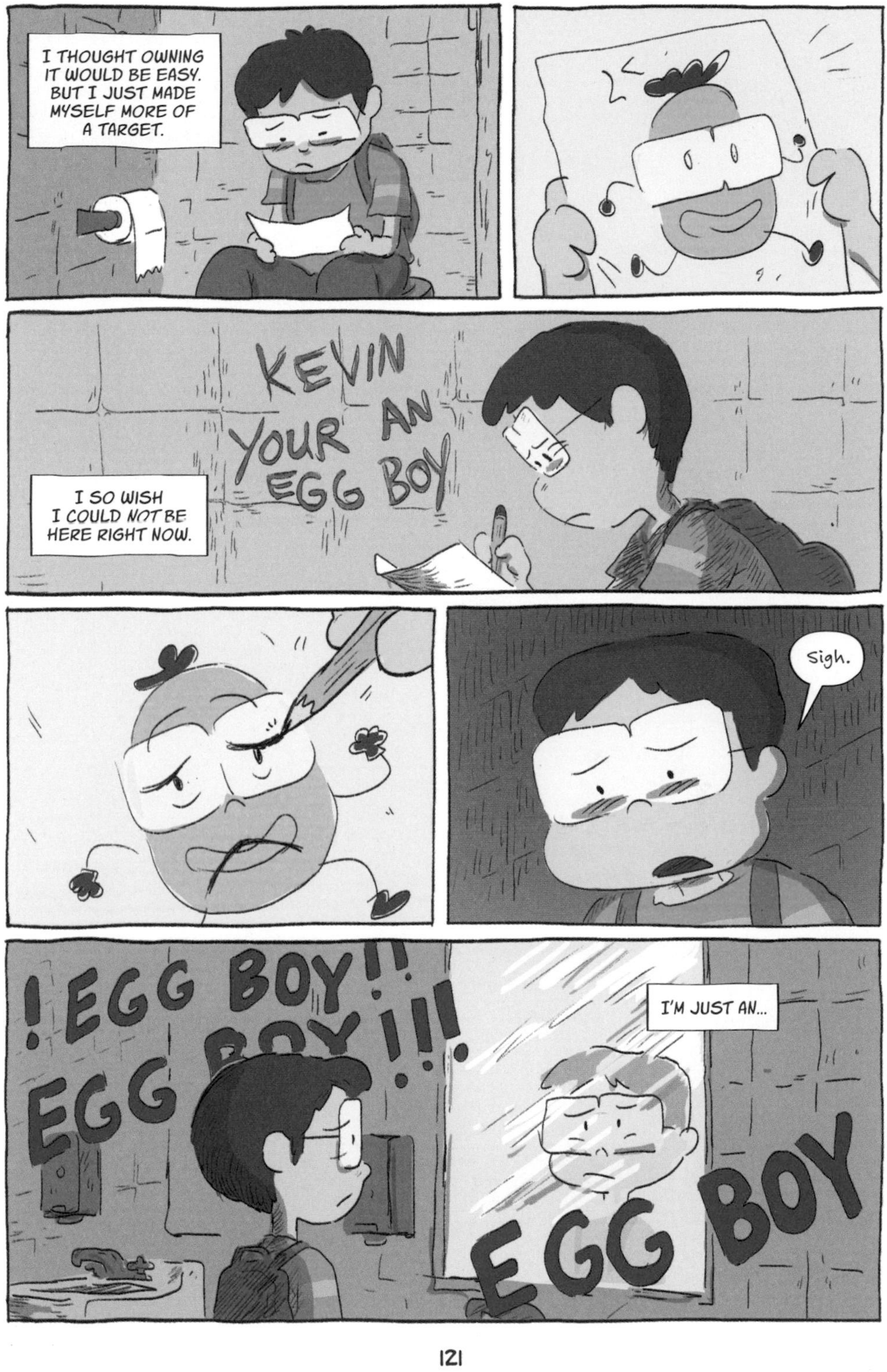
I THOUGHT OWNING IT WOULD BE EASY. BUT I JUST MADE MYSELF MORE OF A TARGET.
KEVIN YOUR AN EGG BOY
I SO WISH I COULD NOT BE HERE RIGHT NOW.
Sigh.
!EGG BOY!!
EGG BOY!!!
I'M JUST AN...
EGG BOY

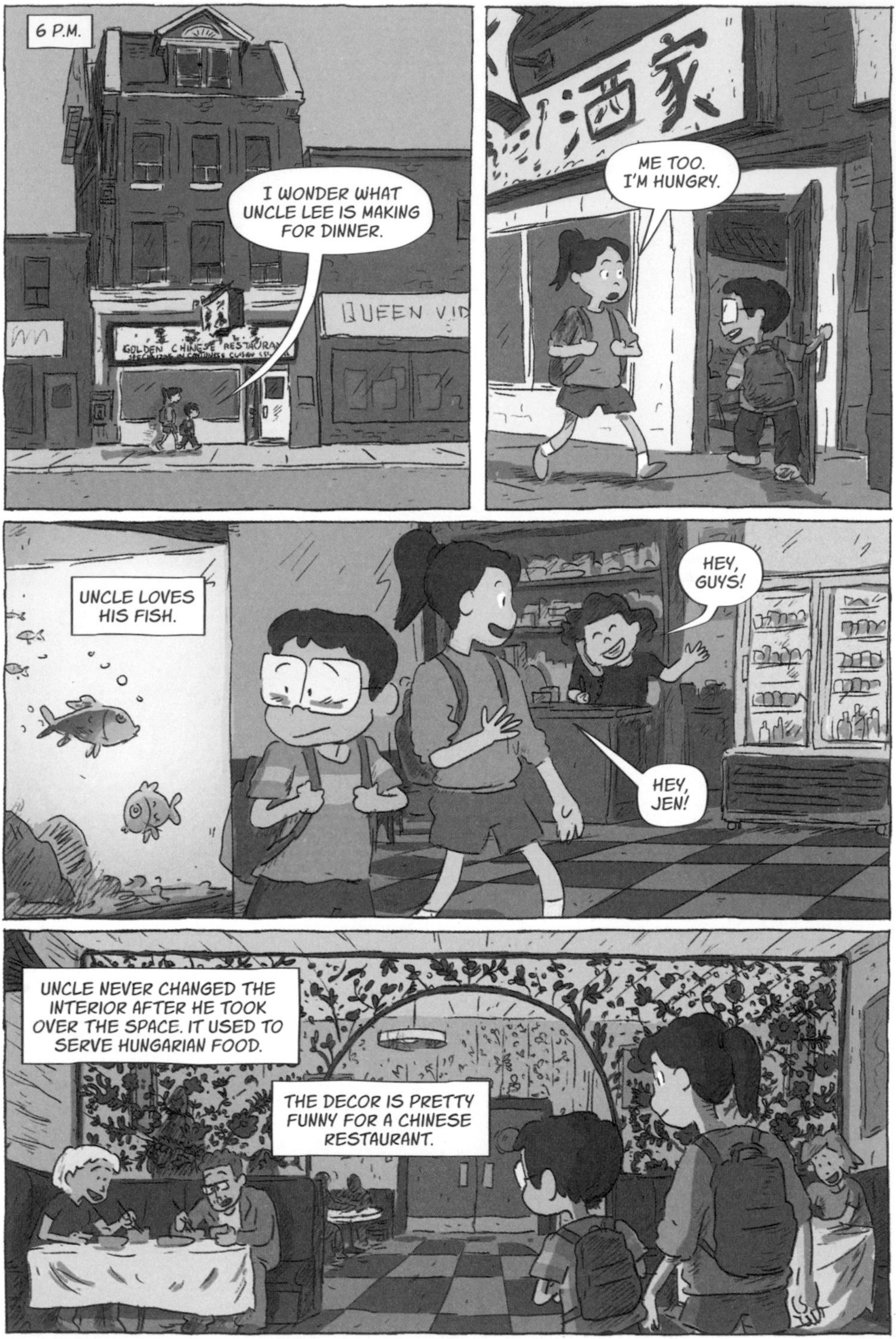
6 P.M.
I WONDER WHAT UNCLE LEE IS MAKING FOR DINNER.
酒家
ME TOO. I'M HUNGRY.
UNCLE LOVES HIS FISH.
HEY, GUYS!
HEY, JEN!
UNCLE NEVER CHANGED THE INTERIOR AFTER HE TOOK OVER THE SPACE. IT USED TO SERVE HUNGARIAN FOOD.
THE DECOR IS PRETTY FUNNY FOR A CHINESE RESTAURANT.

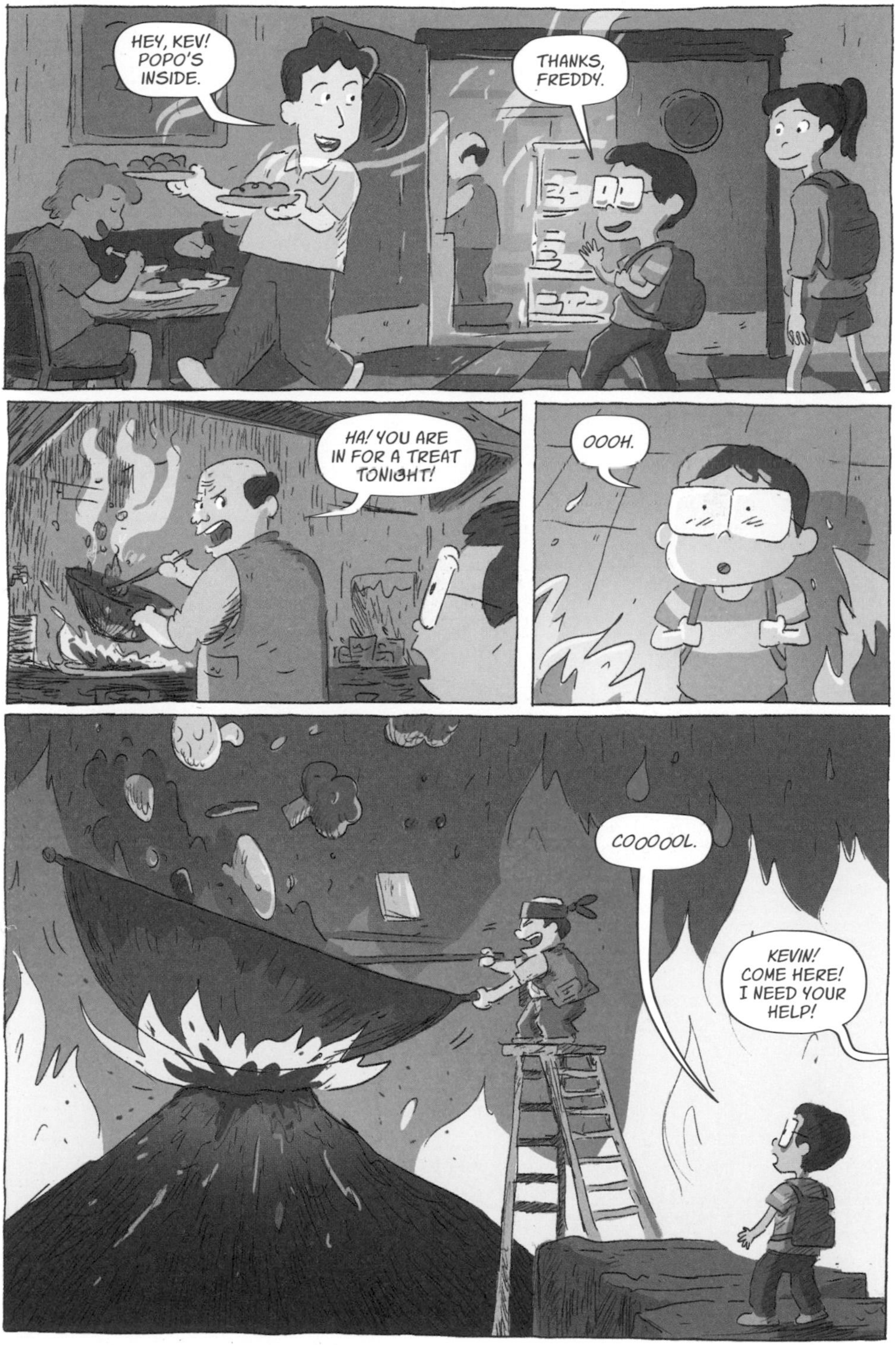
HEY, KEV! POPO'S INSIDE.
THANKS, FREDDY.
HA! YOU ARE IN FOR A TREAT TONIGHT!
OOOH.
COOOOOL.
KEVIN! COME HERE! I NEED YOUR HELP!

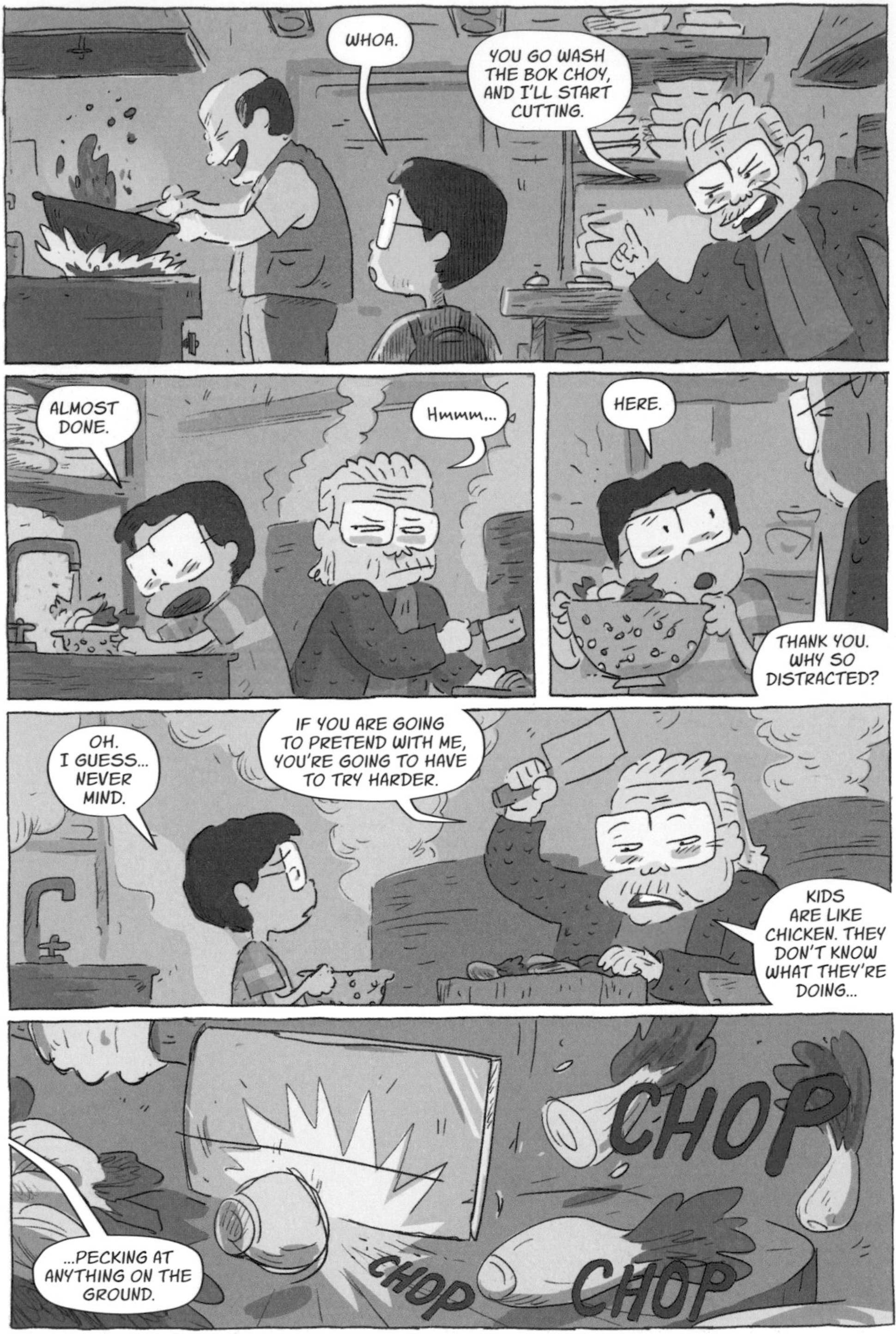
WHOA.
YOU GO WASH THE BOK CHOY, AND I'LL START CUTTING.
ALMOST DONE.
Hmmm...
HERE.
THANK YOU. WHY SO DISTRACTED?
OH. I GUESS... NEVER MIND.
IF YOU ARE GOING TO PRETEND WITH ME, YOU'RE GOING TO HAVE TO TRY HARDER.
KIDS ARE LIKE CHICKEN. THEY DON'T KNOW WHAT THEY'RE DOING...
CHOP
...PECKING AT ANYTHING ON THE GROUND.
CHOP
CHOP

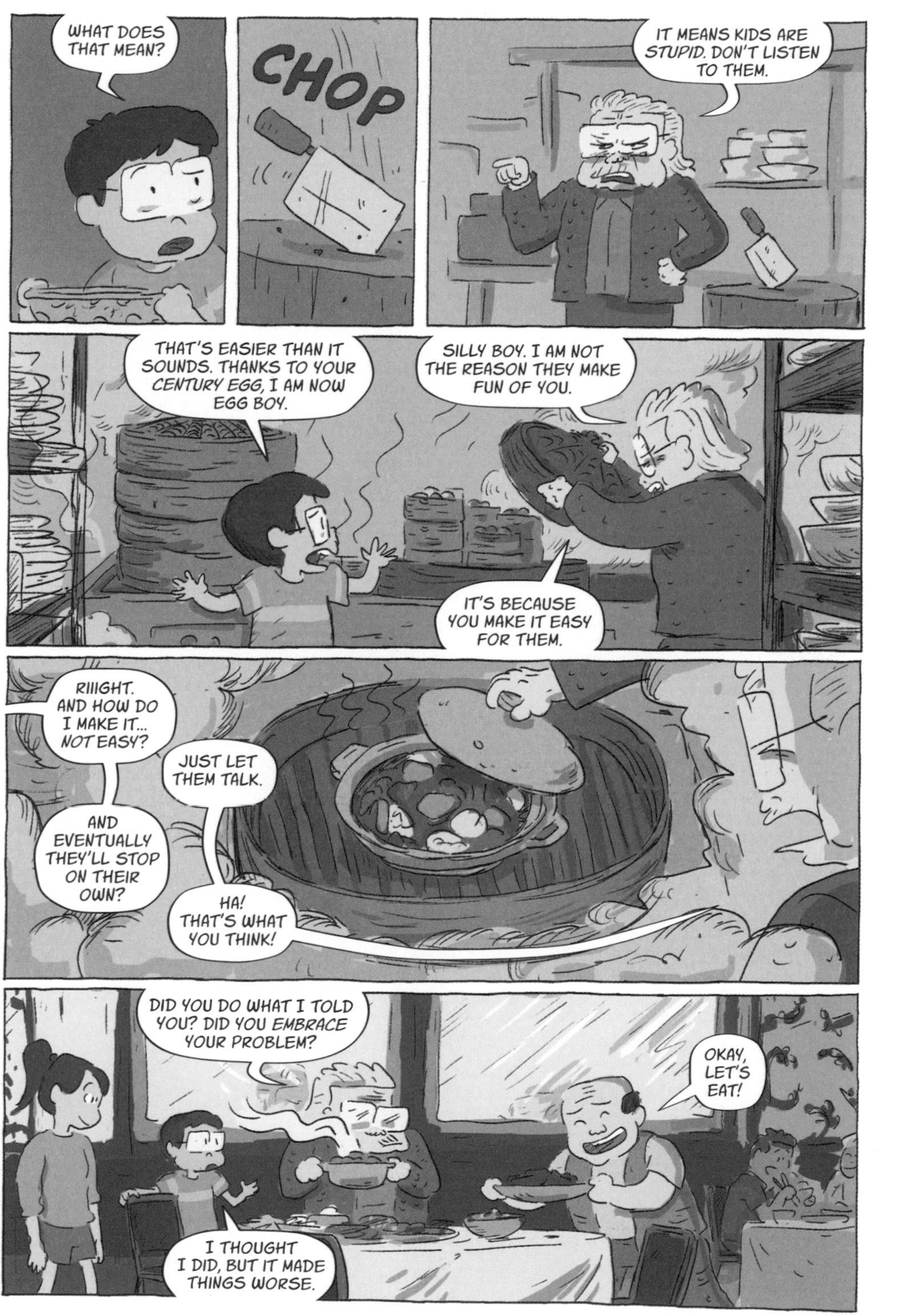
WHAT DOES THAT MEAN?
CHOP
IT MEANS KIDS ARE STUPID. DON'T LISTEN TO THEM.
THAT'S EASIER THAN IT SOUNDS. THANKS TO YOUR CENTURY EGG, I AM NOW EGG BOY.
SILLY BOY. I AM NOT THE REASON THEY MAKE FUN OF YOU.
IT'S BECAUSE YOU MAKE IT EASY FOR THEM.
RIIIGHT. AND HOW DO I MAKE IT... NOT EASY?
JUST LET THEM TALK.
AND EVENTUALLY THEY'LL STOP ON THEIR OWN?
HA! THAT'S WHAT YOU THINK!
DID YOU DO WHAT I TOLD YOU? DID YOU EMBRACE YOUR PROBLEM?
OKAY, LET'S EAT!
I THOUGHT I DID, BUT IT MADE THINGS WORSE.

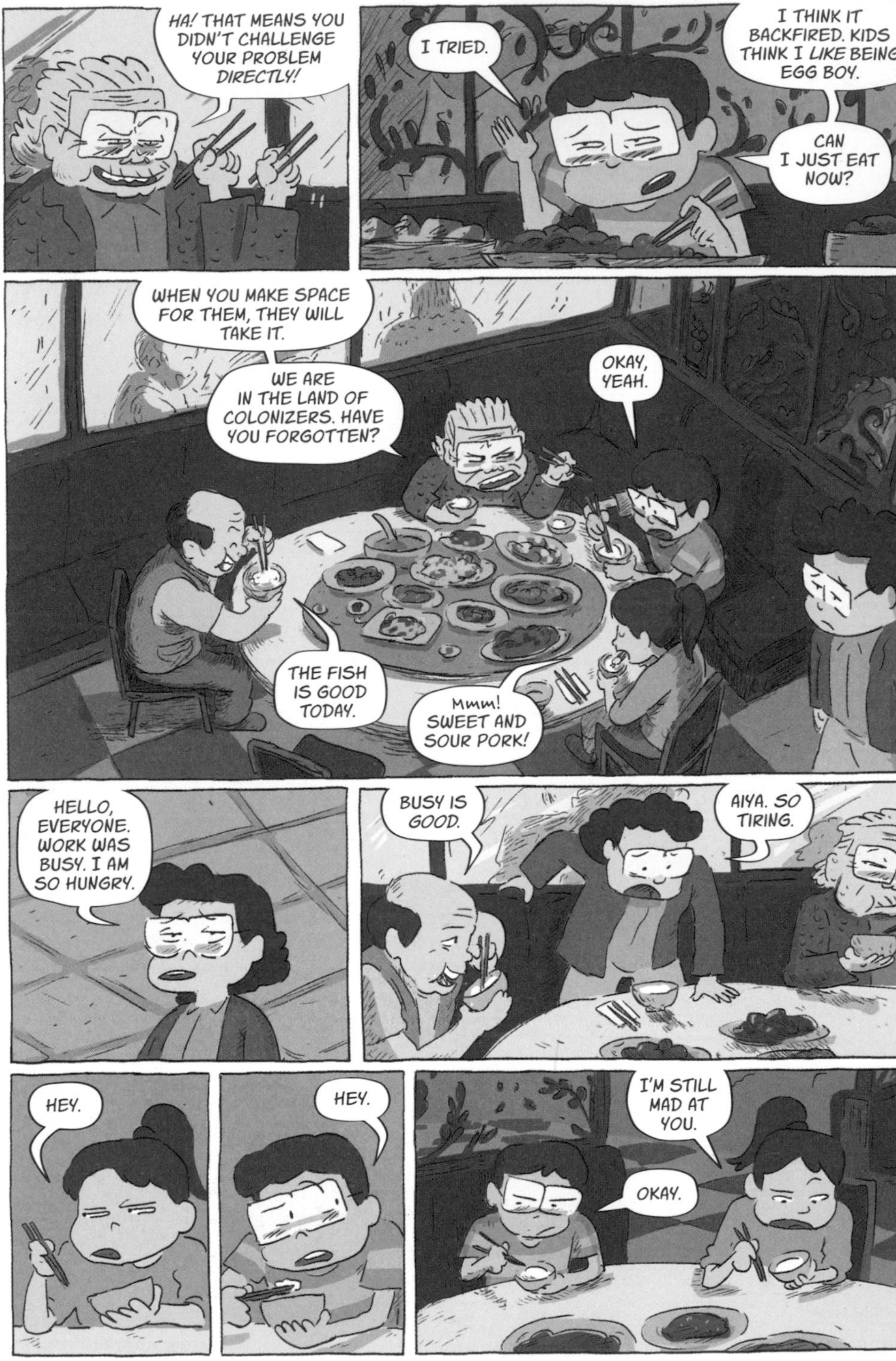
HA! THAT MEANS YOU DIDN'T CHALLENGE YOUR PROBLEM DIRECTLY!
I TRIED.
I THINK IT BACKFIRED. KIDS THINK I LIKE BEING EGG BOY.
CAN I JUST EAT NOW?
WHEN YOU MAKE SPACE FOR THEM, THEY WILL TAKE IT.
WE ARE IN THE LAND OF COLONIZERS. HAVE YOU FORGOTTEN?
OKAY, YEAH.
THE FISH IS GOOD TODAY.
Mmm! SWEET AND SOUR PORK!
HELLO, EVERYONE. WORK WAS BUSY. I AM SO HUNGRY.
BUSY IS GOOD.
AIYA. SO TIRING.
HEY.
HEY.
I'M STILL MAD AT YOU.
OKAY.

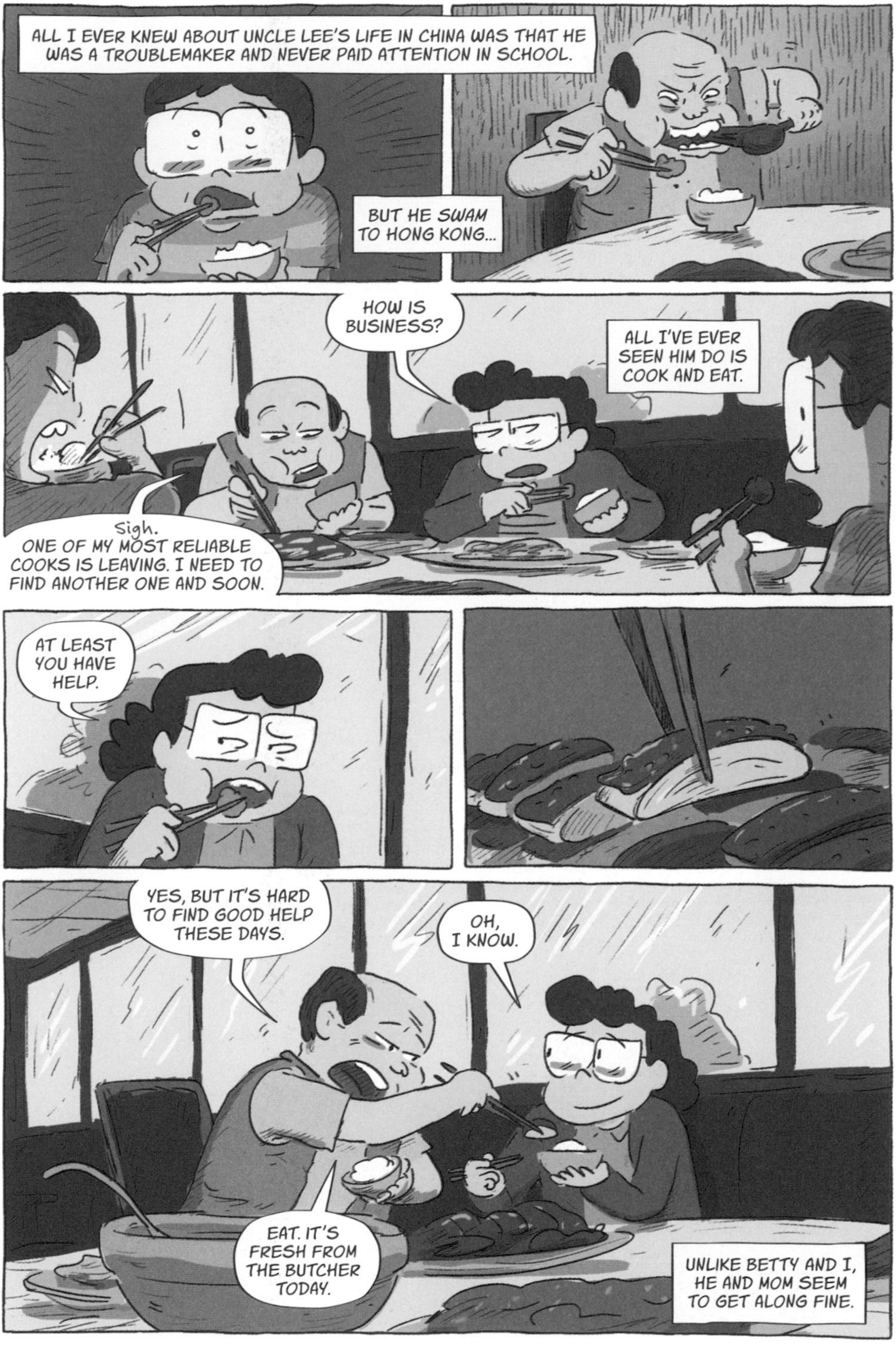
ALL I EVER KNEW ABOUT UNCLE LEE'S LIFE IN CHINA WAS THAT HE WAS A TROUBLEMAKER AND NEVER PAID ATTENTION IN SCHOOL.
BUT HE SWAM TO HONG KONG...
HOW IS BUSINESS?
ALL I'VE EVER SEEN HIM DO IS COOK AND EAT.
Sigh.
ONE OF MY MOST RELIABLE COOKS IS LEAVING. I NEED TO FIND ANOTHER ONE AND SOON.
AT LEAST YOU HAVE HELP.
YES, BUT IT'S HARD TO FIND GOOD HELP THESE DAYS.
OH, I KNOW.
EAT. IT'S FRESH FROM THE BUTCHER TODAY.
UNLIKE BETTY AND I, HE AND MOM SEEM TO GET ALONG FINE.

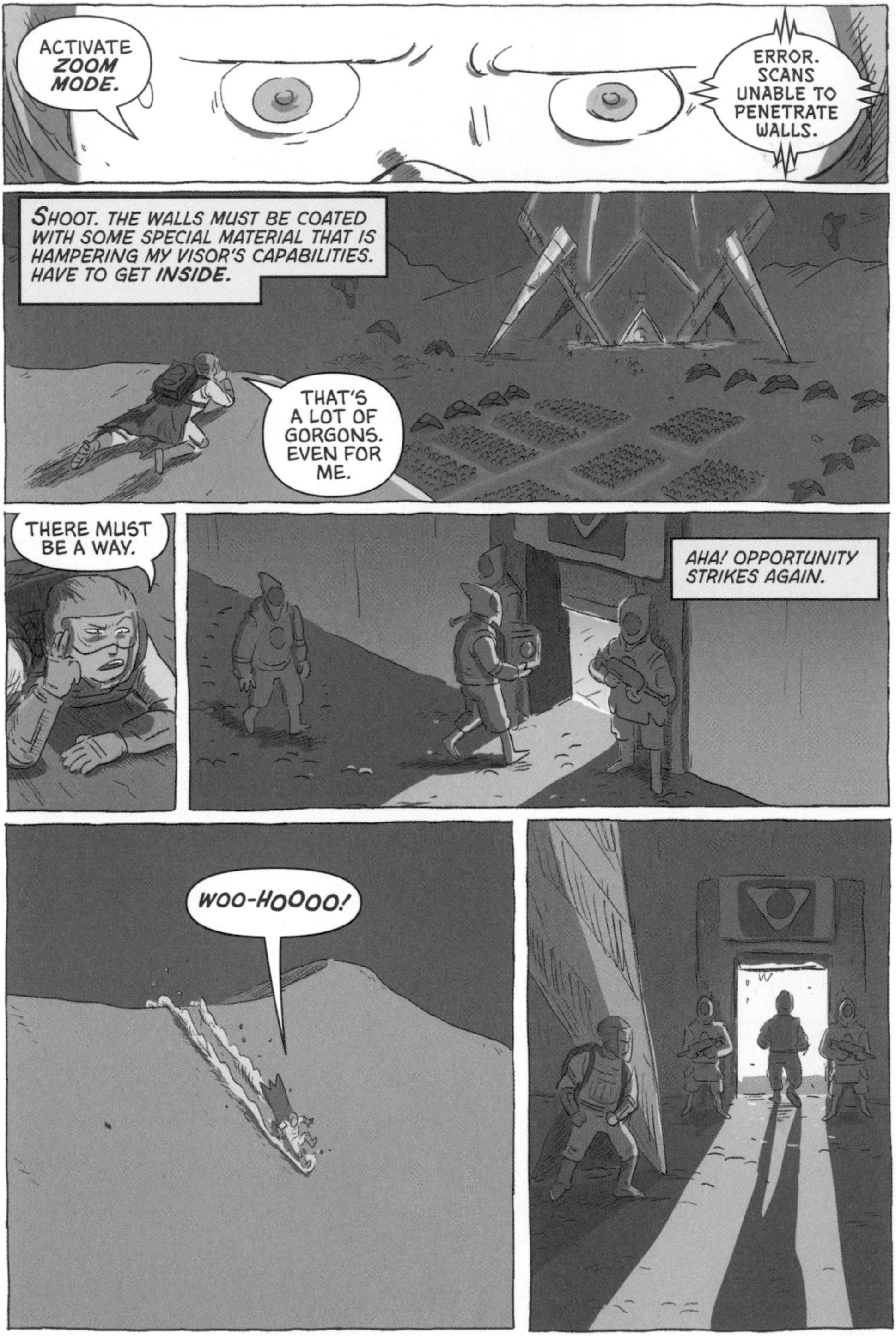
ACTIVATE ZOOM MODE.
ERROR. SCANS UNABLE TO PENETRATE WALLS.
SHOOT. THE WALLS MUST BE COATED WITH SOME SPECIAL MATERIAL THAT IS HAMPERING MY VISOR'S CAPABILITIES. HAVE TO GET INSIDE.
THAT'S A LOT OF GORGONS. EVEN FOR ME.
THERE MUST BE A WAY.
AHA! OPPORTUNITY STRIKES AGAIN.
WOO-HOOOO!

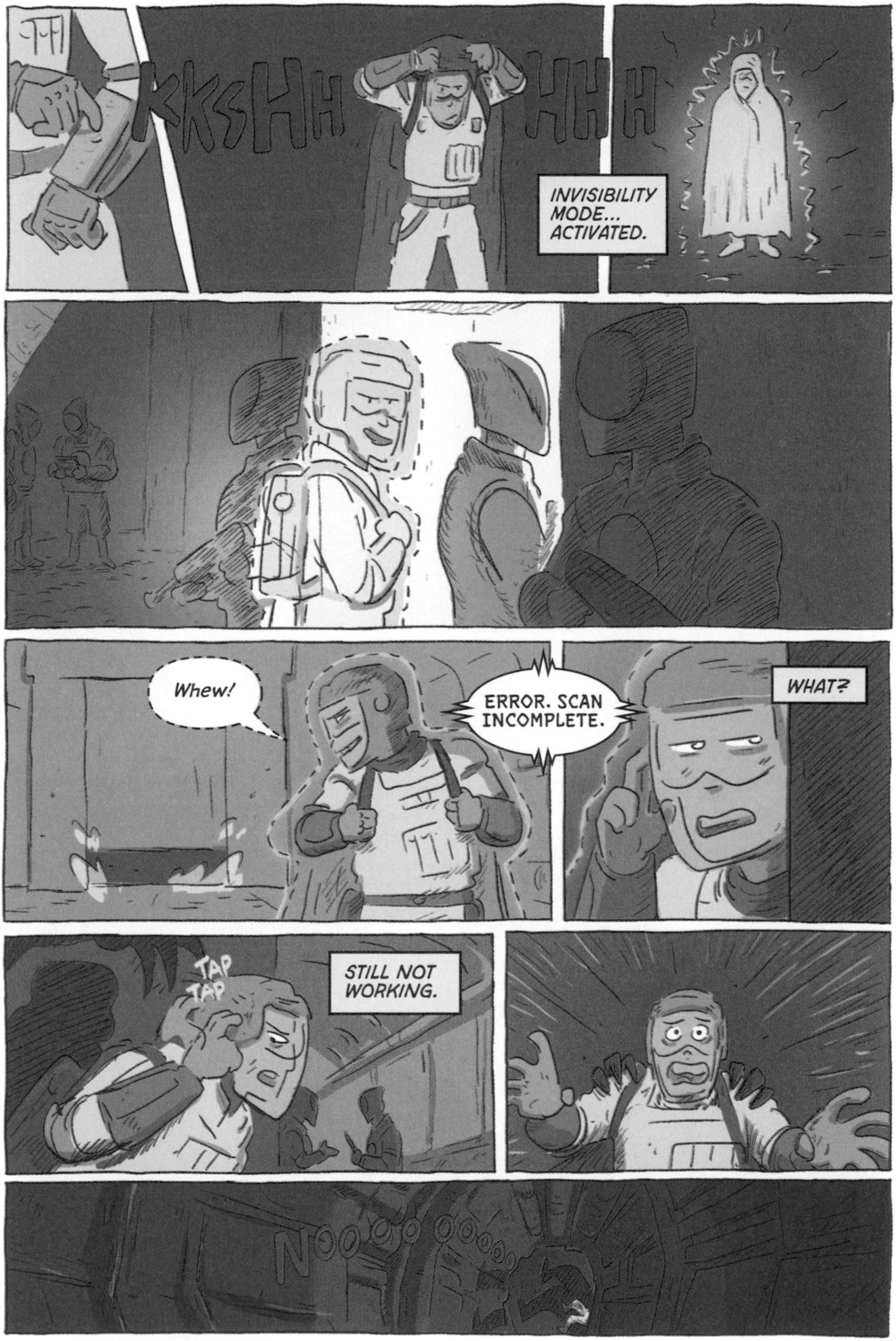
KKSHHHHH
INVISIBILITY MODE... ACTIVATED.
Whew!
ERROR. SCAN INCOMPLETE.
WHAT?
TAP TAP
STILL NOT WORKING.
NOOOOOOOOO

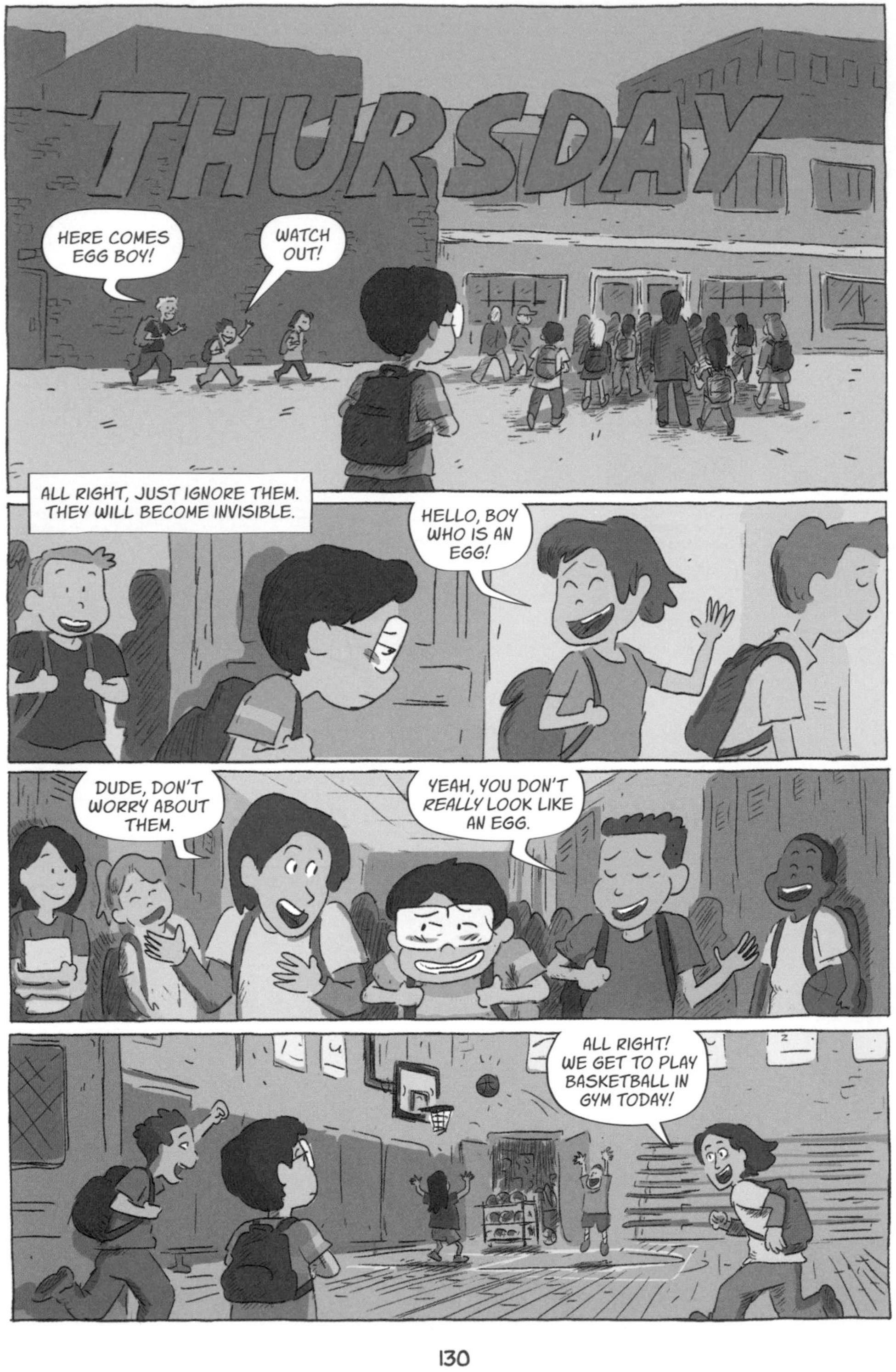
THURSDAY
HERE COMES EGG BOY!
WATCH OUT!
ALL RIGHT, JUST IGNORE THEM. THEY WILL BECOME INVISIBLE.
HELLO, BOY WHO IS AN EGG!
DUDE, DON'T WORRY ABOUT THEM.
YEAH, YOU DON'T REALLY LOOK LIKE AN EGG.
ALL RIGHT! WE GET TO PLAY BASKETBALL IN GYM TODAY!

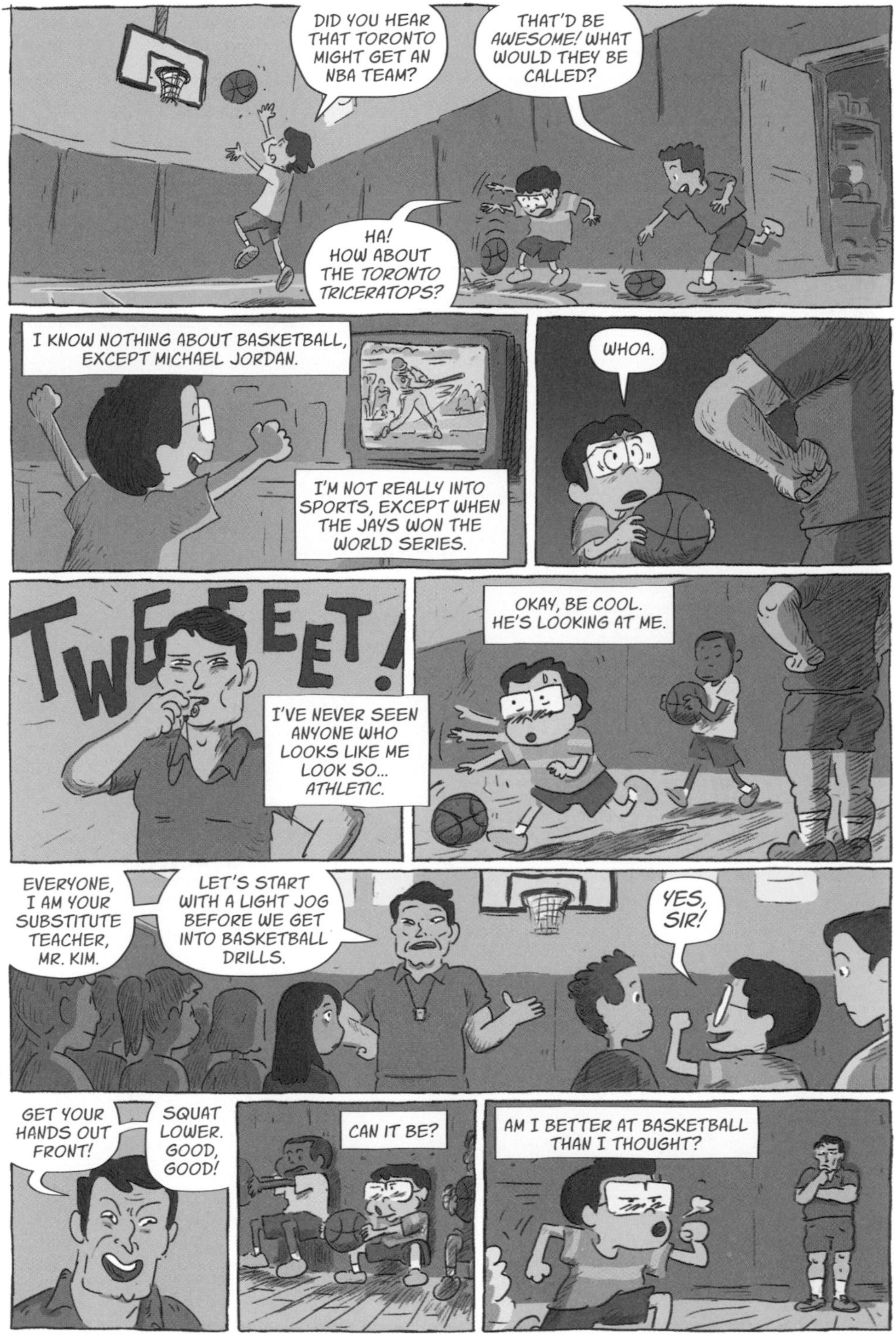

DID YOU HEAR THAT TORONTO MIGHT GET AN NBA TEAM?
THAT'D BE AWESOME! WHAT WOULD THEY BE CALLED?
HA! HOW ABOUT THE TORONTO TRICERATOPS?
I KNOW NOTHING ABOUT BASKETBALL, EXCEPT MICHAEL JORDAN.
I'M NOT REALLY INTO SPORTS, EXCEPT WHEN THE JAYS WON THE WORLD SERIES.
WHOA.
TWEEEET!
I'VE NEVER SEEN ANYONE WHO LOOKS LIKE ME LOOK SO... ATHLETIC.
OKAY, BE COOL. HE'S LOOKING AT ME.
EVERYONE, I AM YOUR SUBSTITUTE TEACHER, MR. KIM.
LET'S START WITH A LIGHT JOG BEFORE WE GET INTO BASKETBALL DRILLS.
YES, SIR!
GET YOUR HANDS OUT FRONT!
SQUAT LOWER. GOOD, GOOD!
CAN IT BE?
AM I BETTER AT BASKETBALL THAN I THOUGHT?

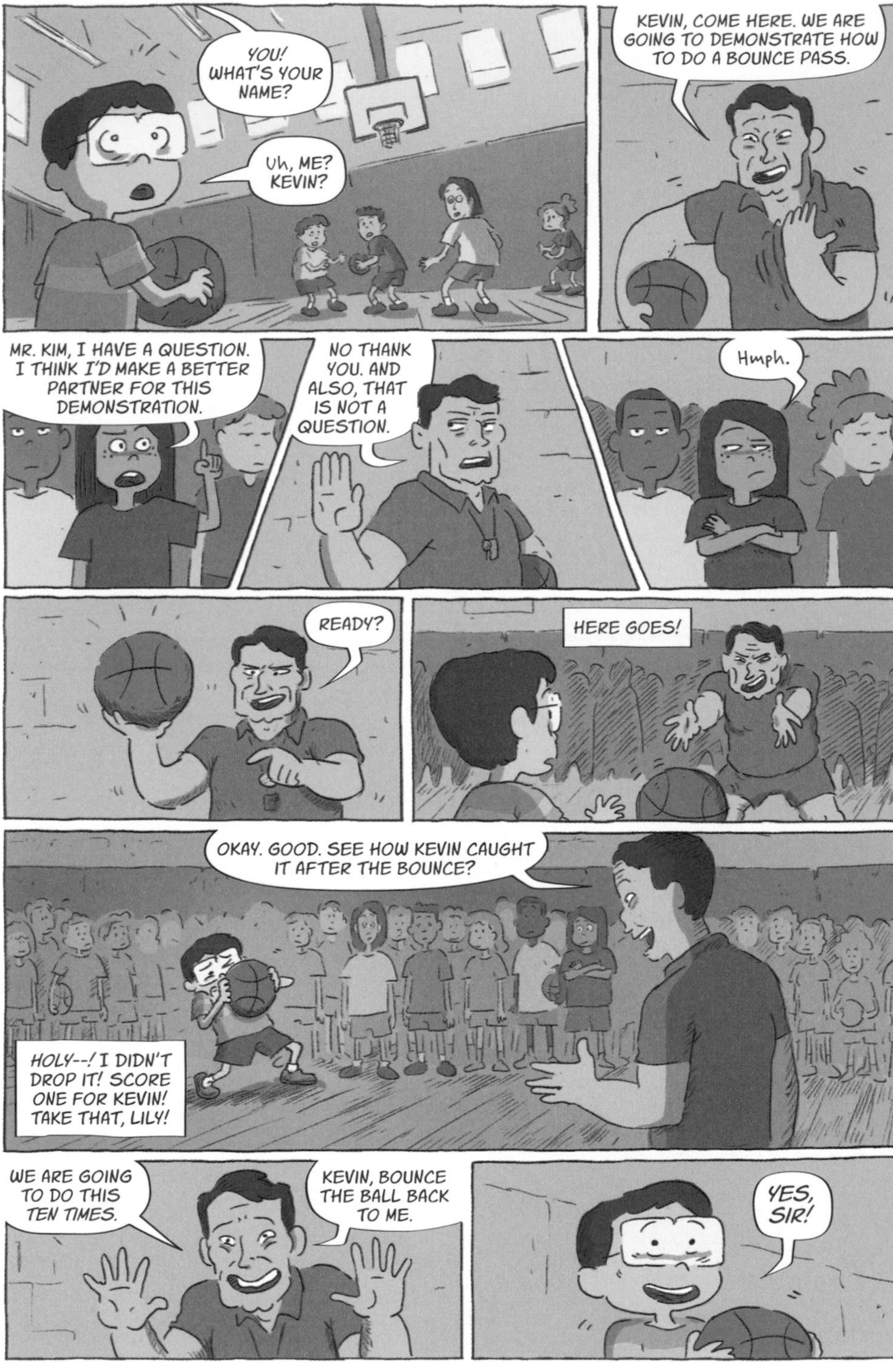
YOU! WHAT'S YOUR NAME?
Uh, ME? KEVIN?
KEVIN, COME HERE. WE ARE GOING TO DEMONSTRATE HOW TO DO A BOUNCE PASS.
MR. KIM, I HAVE A QUESTION. I THINK I'D MAKE A BETTER PARTNER FOR THIS DEMONSTRATION.
NO THANK YOU. AND ALSO, THAT IS NOT A QUESTION.
Hmph.
READY?
HERE GOES!
OKAY. GOOD. SEE HOW KEVIN CAUGHT IT AFTER THE BOUNCE?
HOLY--! I DIDN'T DROP IT! SCORE ONE FOR KEVIN! TAKE THAT, LILY!
WE ARE GOING TO DO THIS TEN TIMES.
KEVIN, BOUNCE THE BALL BACK TO ME.
YES, SIR!

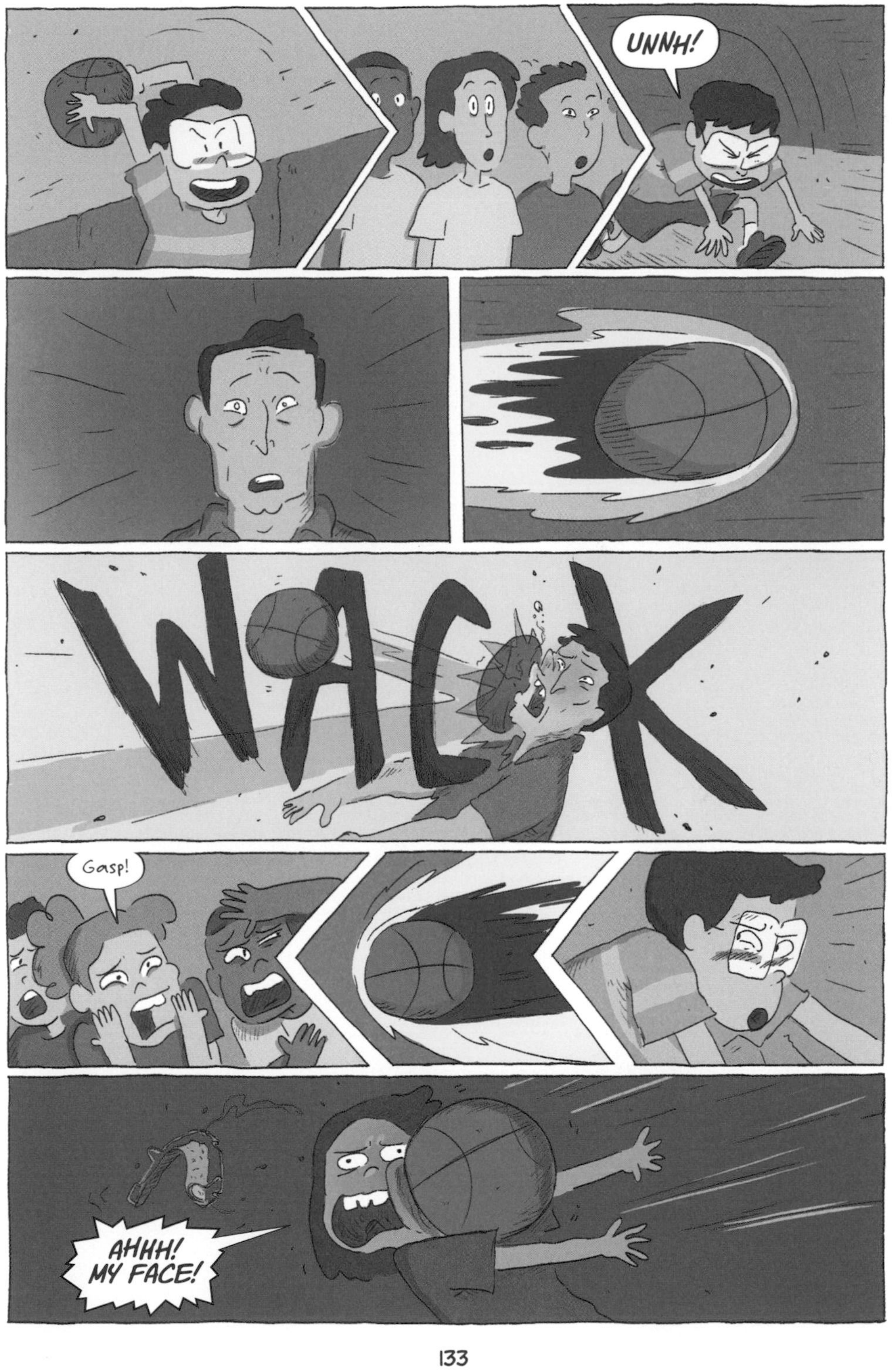
UNNH!
WACK
Gasp!
AHHH! MY FACE!

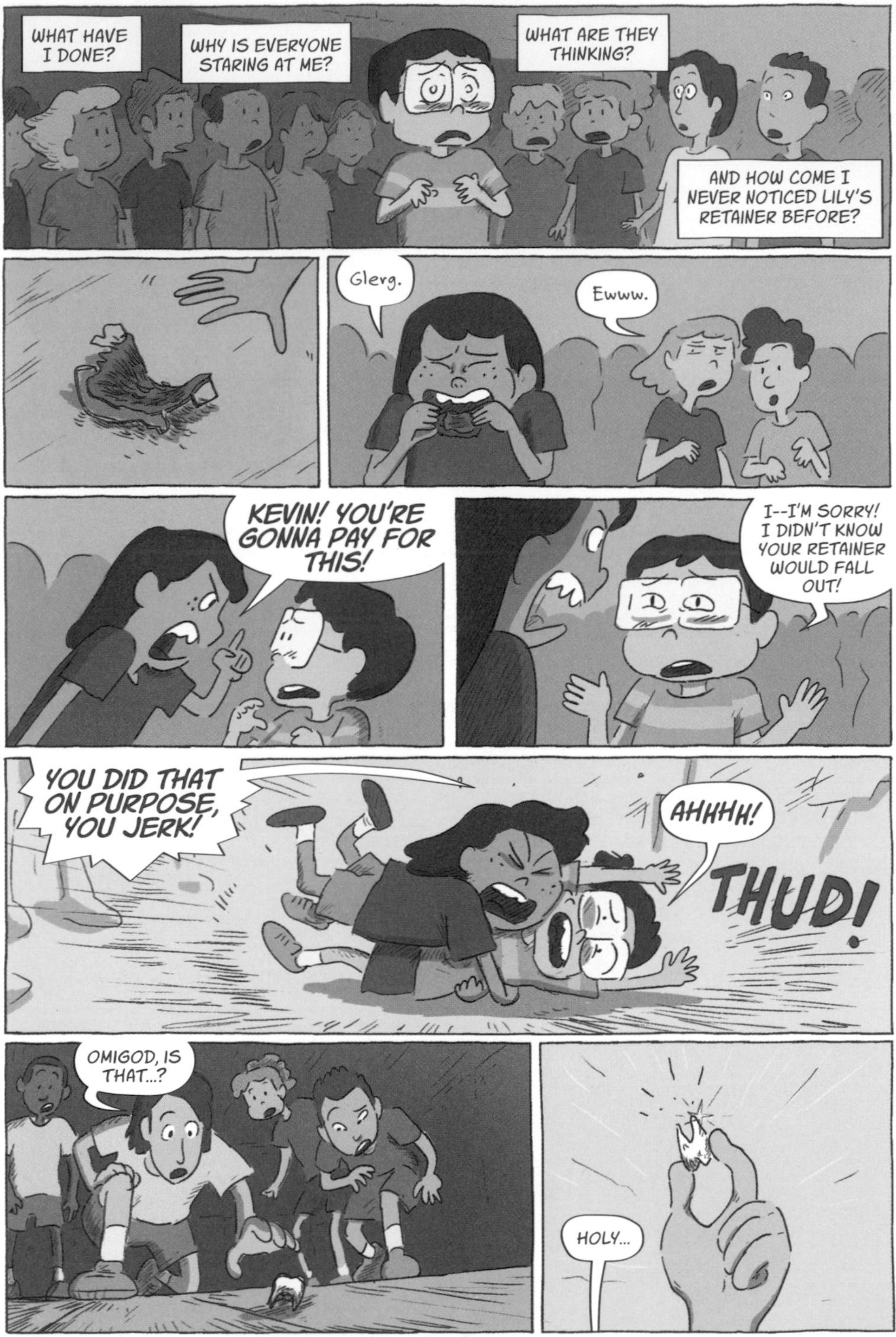
WHAT HAVE I DONE?
WHY IS EVERYONE STARING AT ME?
WHAT ARE THEY THINKING?
AND HOW COME I NEVER NOTICED LILY'S RETAINER BEFORE?
Glerg.
Ewww.
KEVIN! YOU'RE GONNA PAY FOR THIS!
I--I'M SORRY! I DIDN'T KNOW YOUR RETAINER WOULD FALL OUT!
YOU DID THAT ON PURPOSE, YOU JERK!
AHHHH!
THUD!
OMIGOD, IS THAT...?
HOLY...

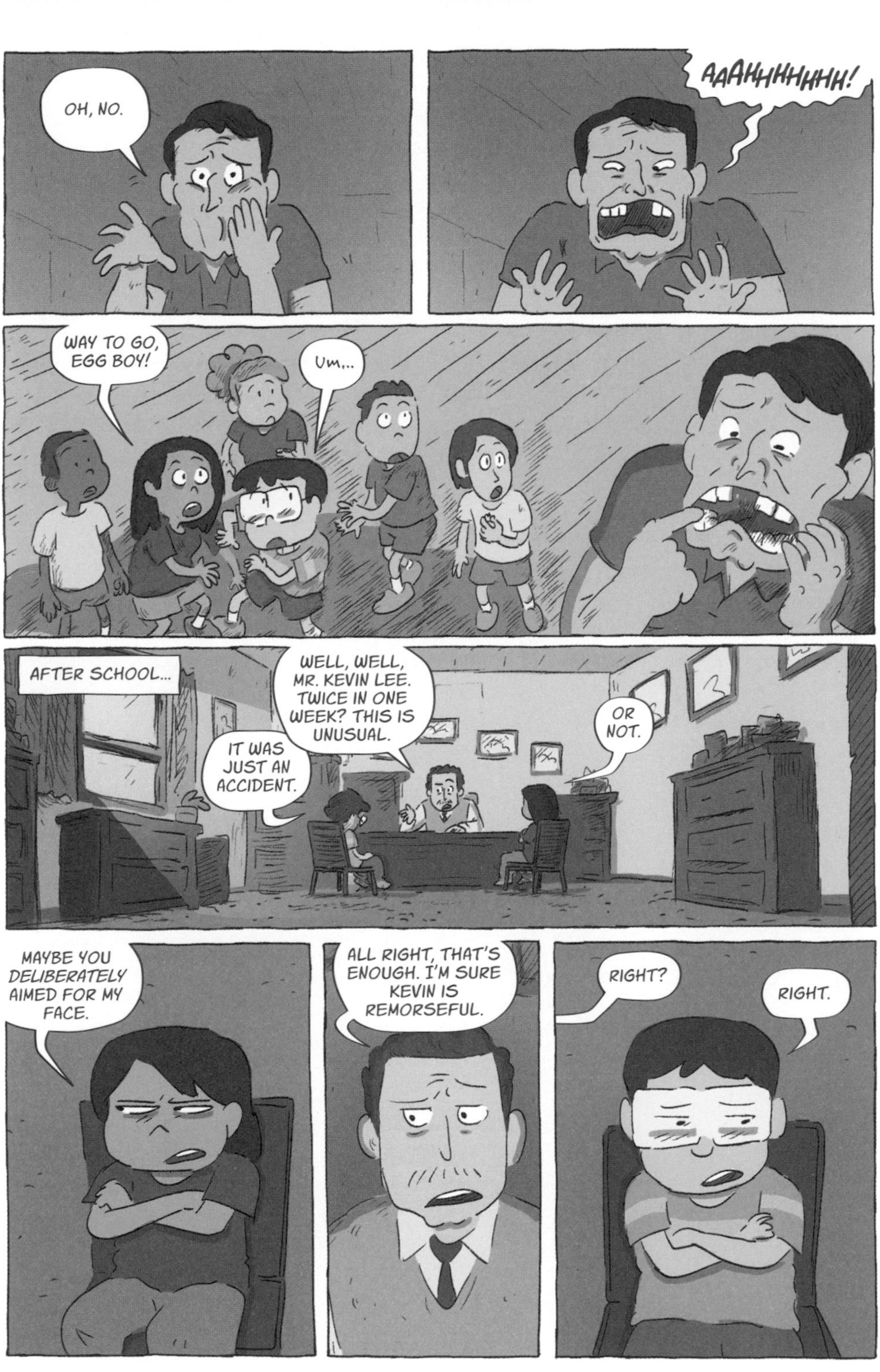
OH, NO.
AAAHHHHHHH!
WAY TO GO, EGG BOY!
Um...
AFTER SCHOOL...
WELL, WELL, MR. KEVIN LEE. TWICE IN ONE WEEK? THIS IS UNUSUAL.
IT WAS JUST AN ACCIDENT.
OR NOT.
MAYBE YOU DELIBERATELY AIMED FOR MY FACE.
ALL RIGHT, THAT'S ENOUGH. I'M SURE KEVIN IS REMORSEFUL.
RIGHT?
RIGHT.

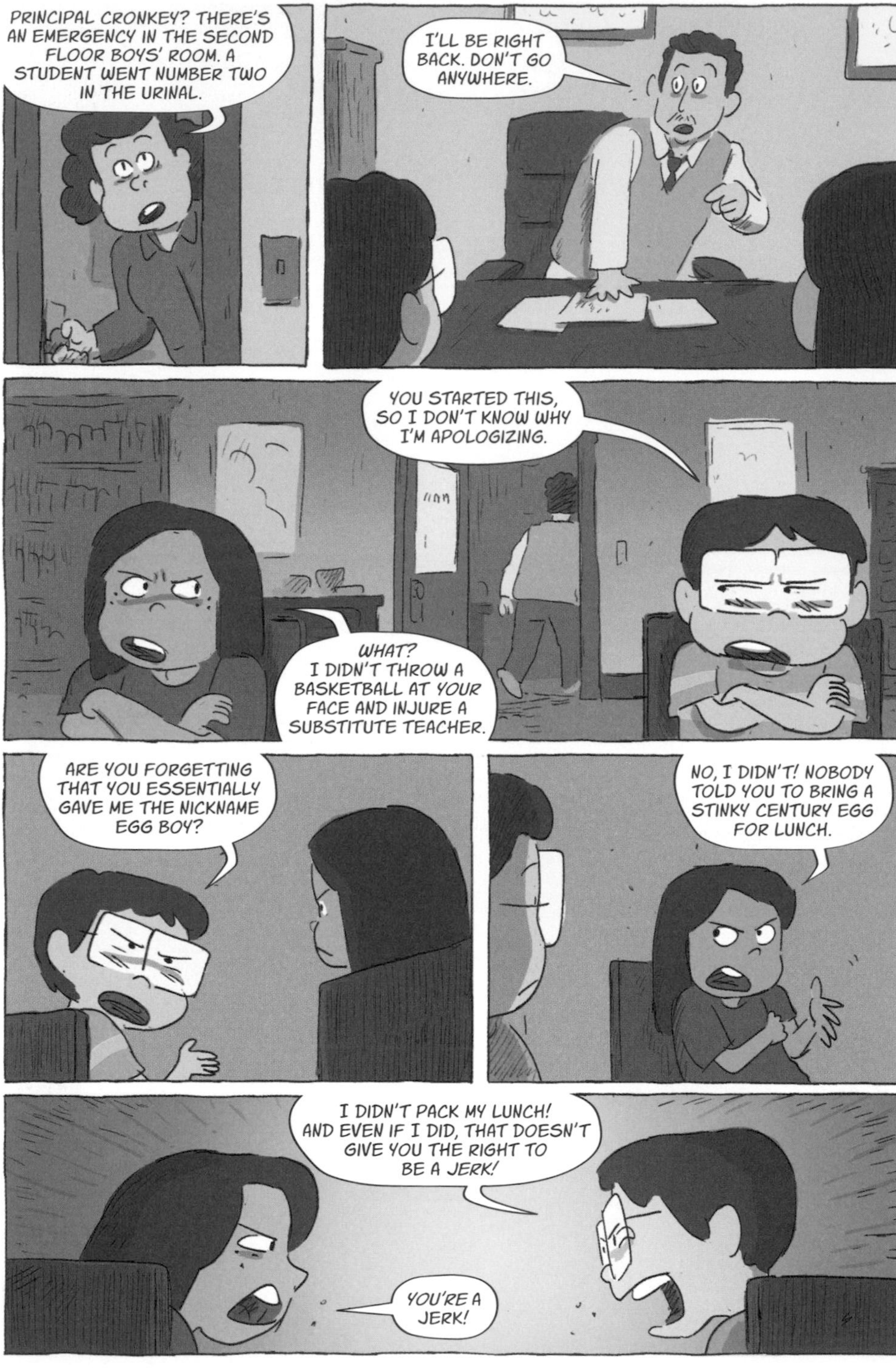
PRINCIPAL CRONKEY? THERE'S AN EMERGENCY IN THE SECOND FLOOR BOYS' ROOM. A STUDENT WENT NUMBER TWO IN THE URINAL.
I'LL BE RIGHT BACK. DON'T GO ANYWHERE.
YOU STARTED THIS, SO I DON'T KNOW WHY I'M APOLOGIZING.
WHAT? I DIDN'T THROW A BASKETBALL AT YOUR FACE AND INJURE A SUBSTITUTE TEACHER.
ARE YOU FORGETTING THAT YOU ESSENTIALLY GAVE ME THE NICKNAME EGG BOY?
NO, I DIDN'T! NOBODY TOLD YOU TO BRING A STINKY CENTURY EGG FOR LUNCH.
I DIDN'T PACK MY LUNCH! AND EVEN IF I DID, THAT DOESN'T GIVE YOU THE RIGHT TO BE A JERK!
YOU'RE A JERK!

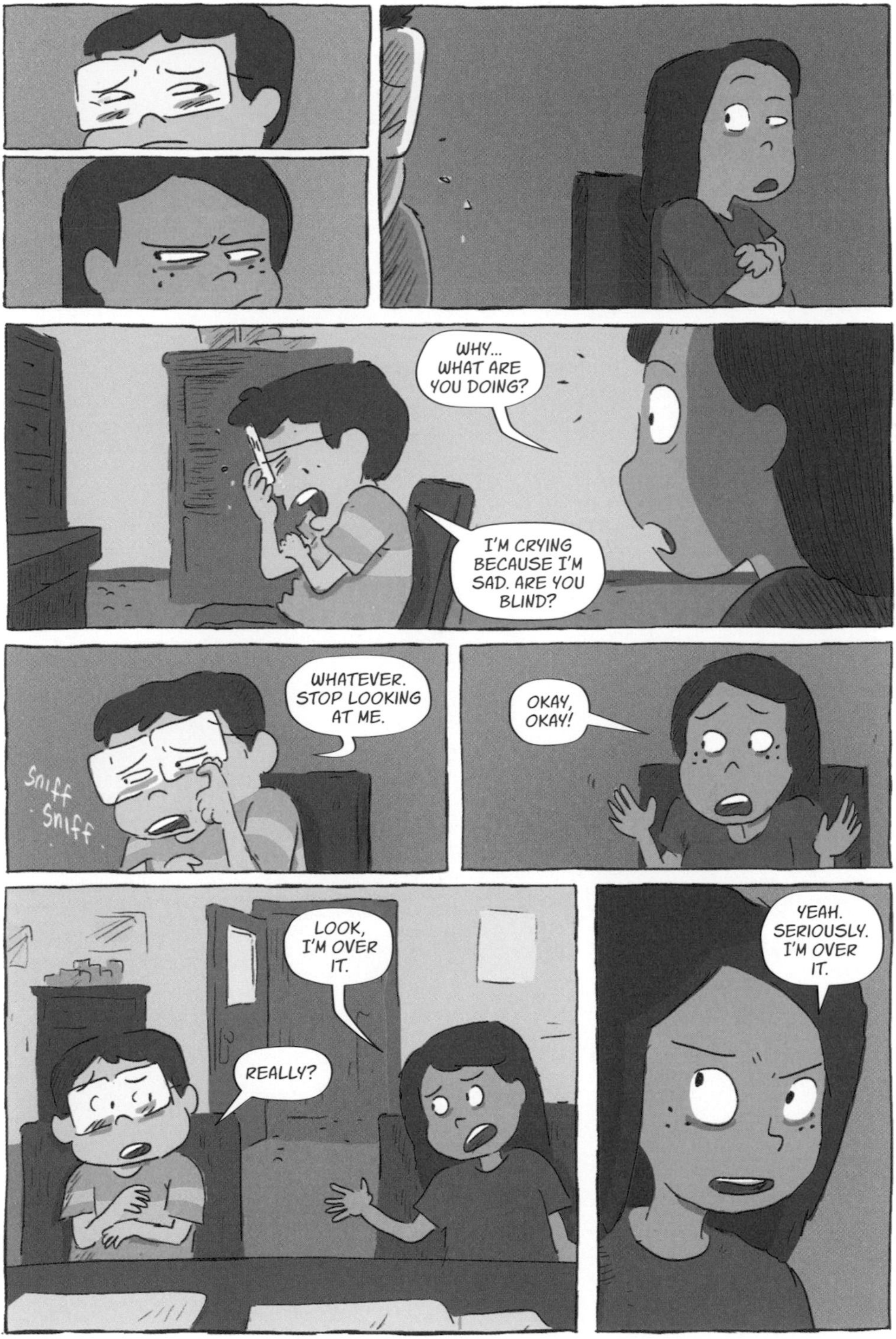
WHY... WHAT ARE YOU DOING?
I'M CRYING BECAUSE I'M SAD. ARE YOU BLIND?
WHATEVER. STOP LOOKING AT ME.
Sniff Sniff
OKAY, OKAY!
LOOK, I'M OVER IT.
REALLY?
YEAH. SERIOUSLY. I'M OVER IT.

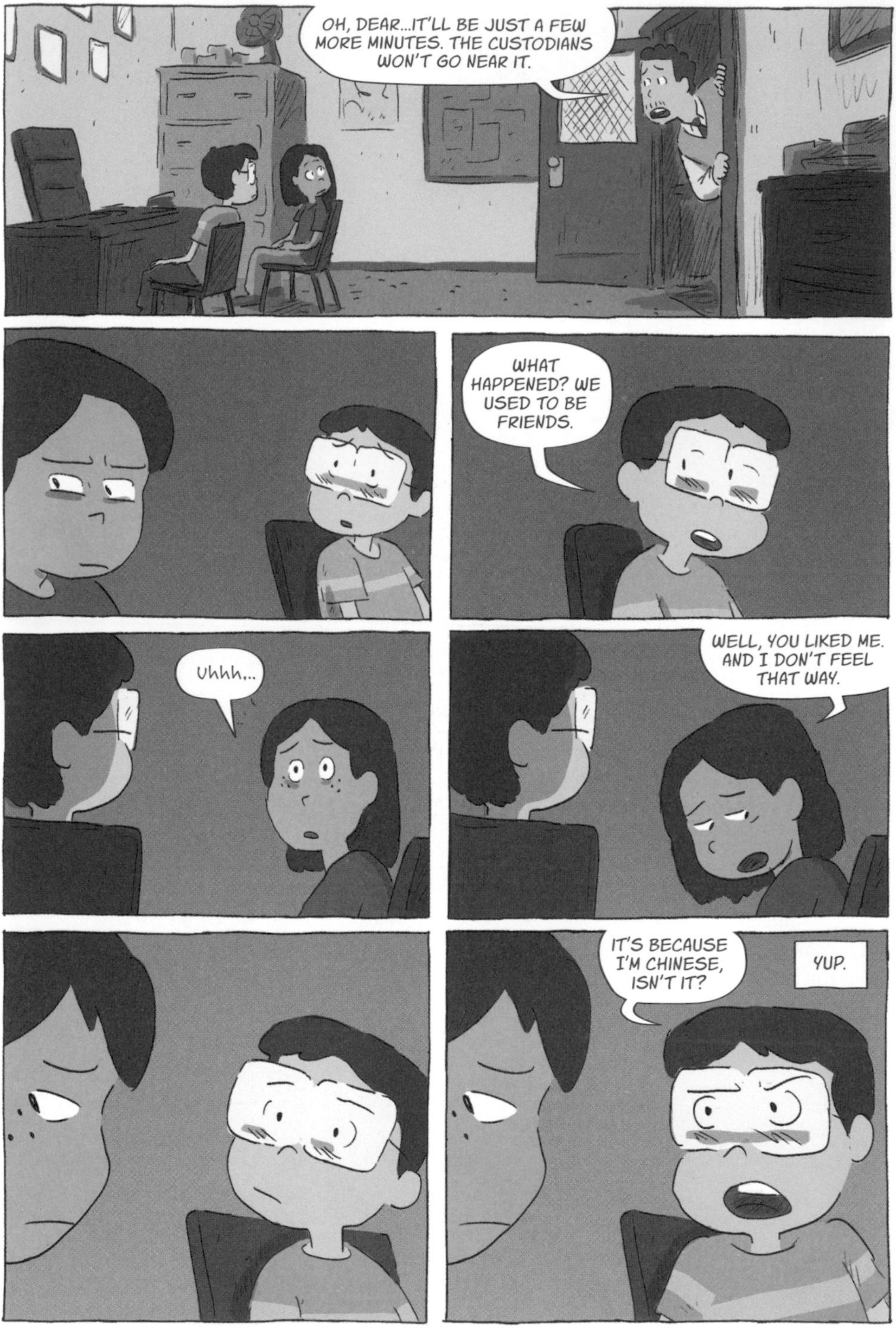
OH, DEAR...IT'LL BE JUST A FEW MORE MINUTES. THE CUSTODIANS WON'T GO NEAR IT.
WHAT HAPPENED? WE USED TO BE FRIENDS.
Uhhh...
WELL, YOU LIKED ME. AND I DON'T FEEL THAT WAY.
IT'S BECAUSE I'M CHINESE, ISN'T IT?
YUP.

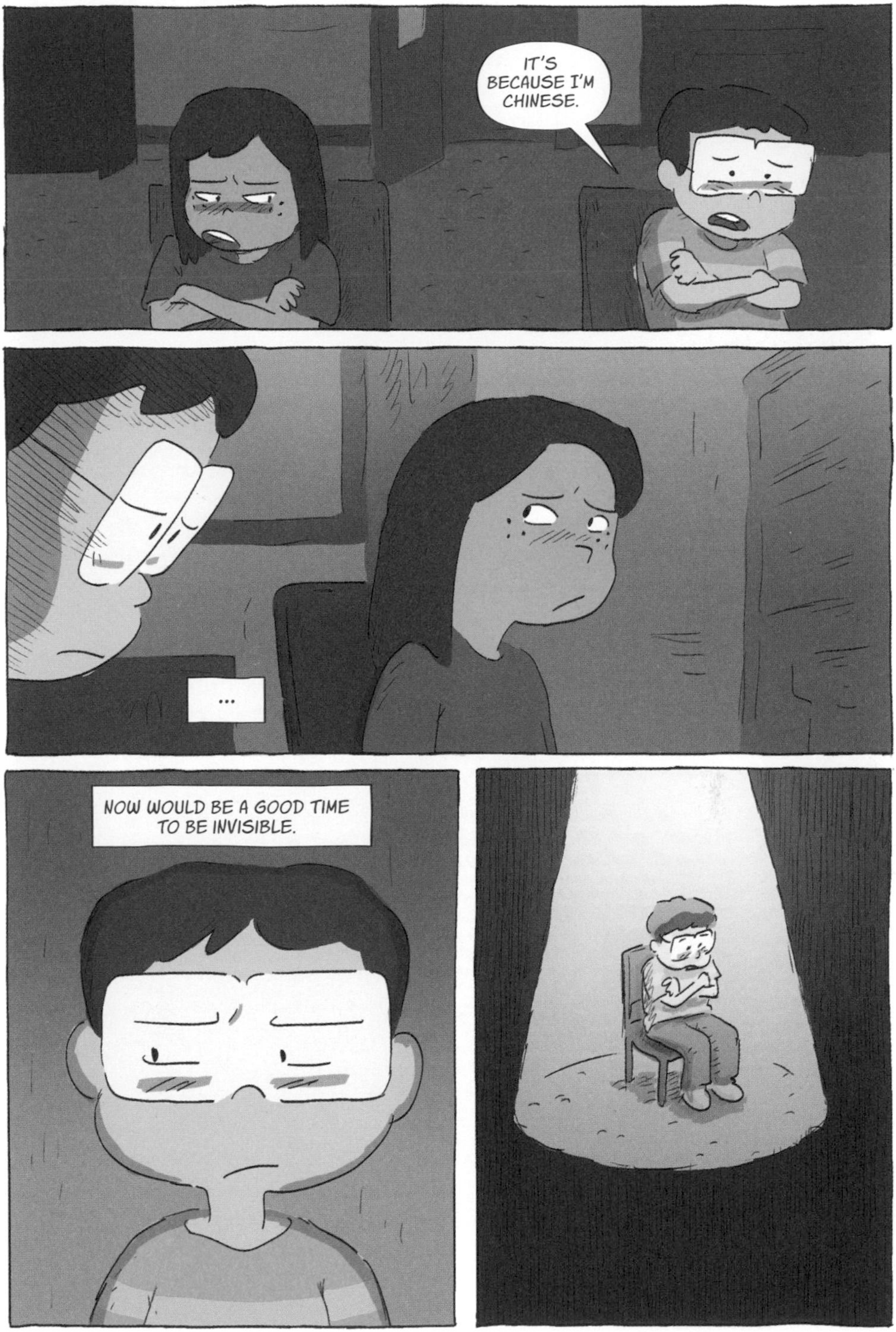
IT'S BECAUSE I'M CHINESE.
...
NOW WOULD BE A GOOD TIME TO BE INVISIBLE.

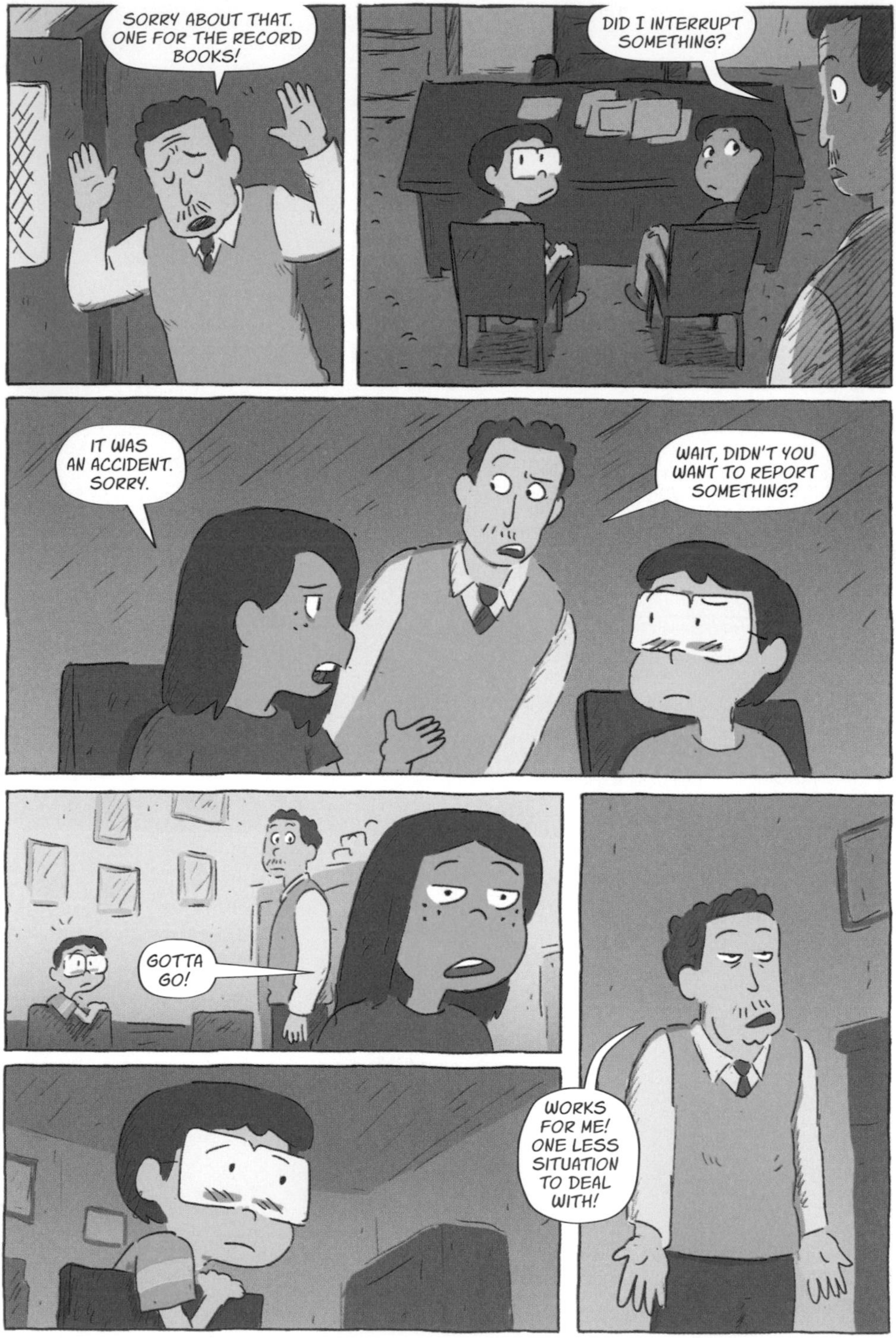
SORRY ABOUT THAT. ONE FOR THE RECORD BOOKS!
DID I INTERRUPT SOMETHING?
IT WAS AN ACCIDENT. SORRY.
WAIT, DIDN'T YOU WANT TO REPORT SOMETHING?
GOTTA GO!
WORKS FOR ME! ONE LESS SITUATION TO DEAL WITH!

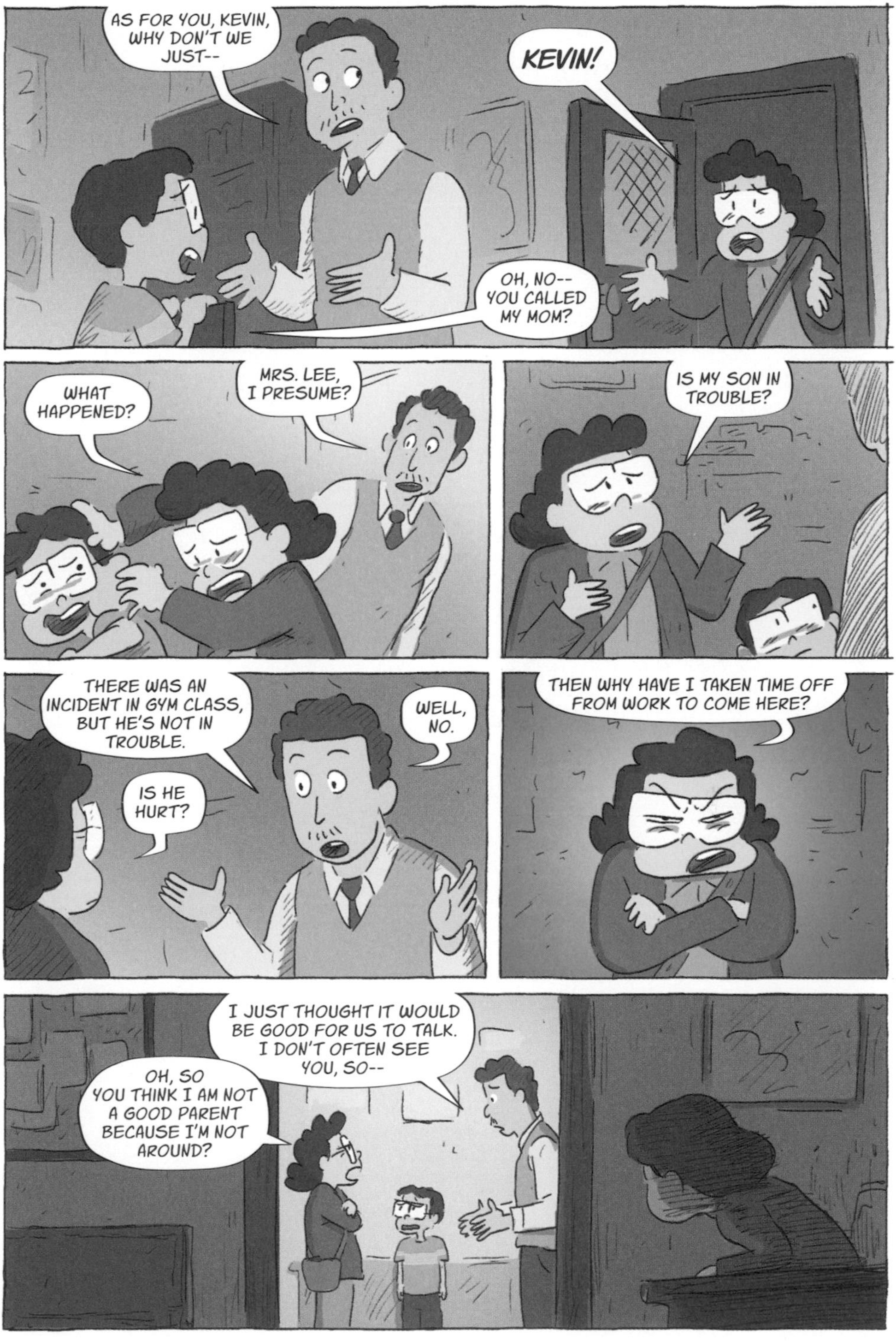
AS FOR YOU, KEVIN, WHY DON'T WE JUST--
KEVIN!
OH, NO-- YOU CALLED MY MOM?
WHAT HAPPENED?
MRS. LEE, I PRESUME?
IS MY SON IN TROUBLE?
THERE WAS AN INCIDENT IN GYM CLASS, BUT HE'S NOT IN TROUBLE.
IS HE HURT?
WELL, NO.
THEN WHY HAVE I TAKEN TIME OFF FROM WORK TO COME HERE?
I JUST THOUGHT IT WOULD BE GOOD FOR US TO TALK. I DON'T OFTEN SEE YOU, SO--
OH, SO YOU THINK I AM NOT A GOOD PARENT BECAUSE I'M NOT AROUND?

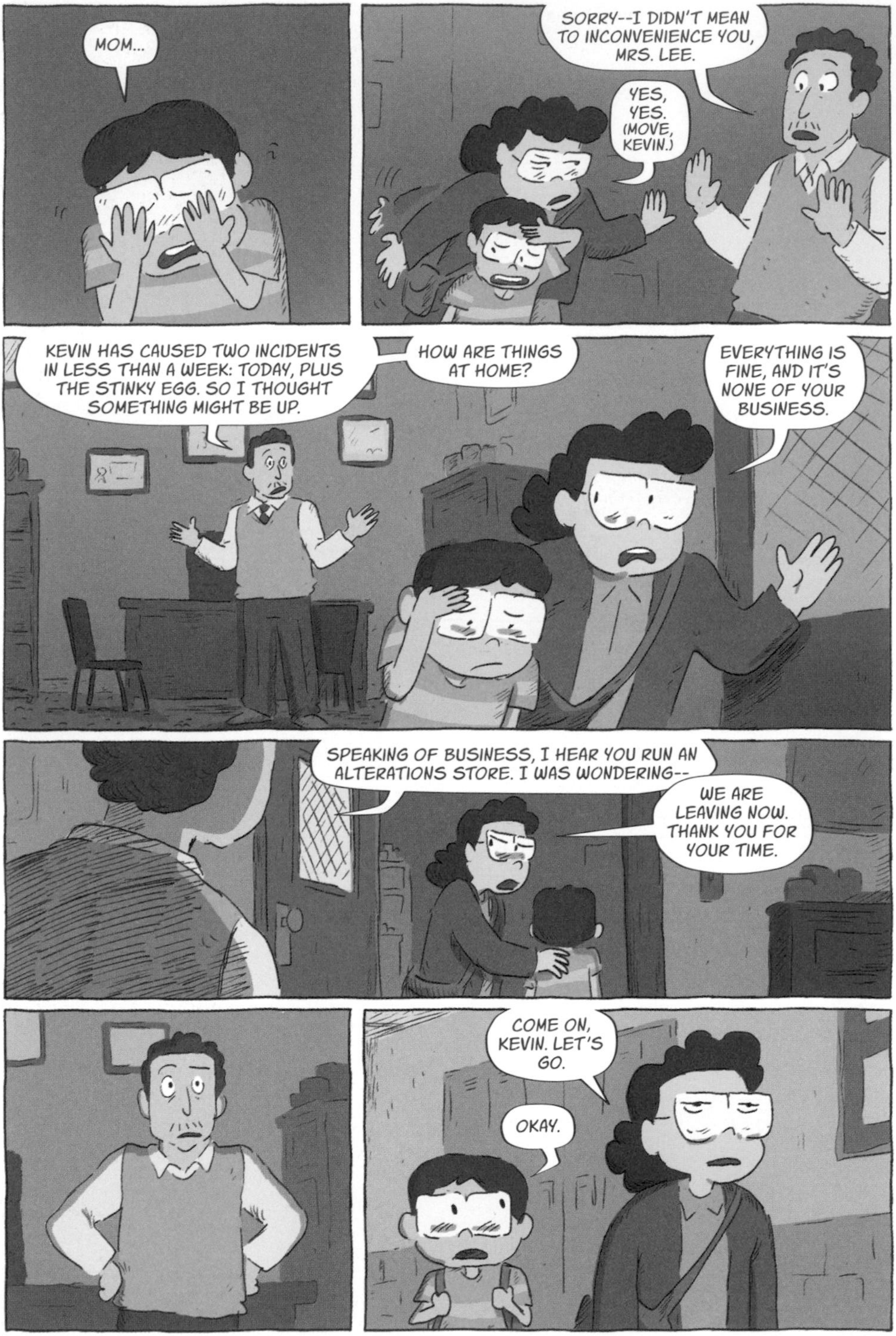
MOM...
SORRY--I DIDN'T MEAN TO INCONVENIENCE YOU, MRS. LEE.
YES, YES. (MOVE, KEVIN.)
KEVIN HAS CAUSED TWO INCIDENTS IN LESS THAN A WEEK: TODAY, PLUS THE STINKY EGG. SO I THOUGHT SOMETHING MIGHT BE UP.
HOW ARE THINGS AT HOME?
EVERYTHING IS FINE, AND IT'S NONE OF YOUR BUSINESS.
SPEAKING OF BUSINESS, I HEAR YOU RUN AN ALTERATIONS STORE. I WAS WONDERING--
WE ARE LEAVING NOW. THANK YOU FOR YOUR TIME.
COME ON, KEVIN. LET'S GO.
OKAY.

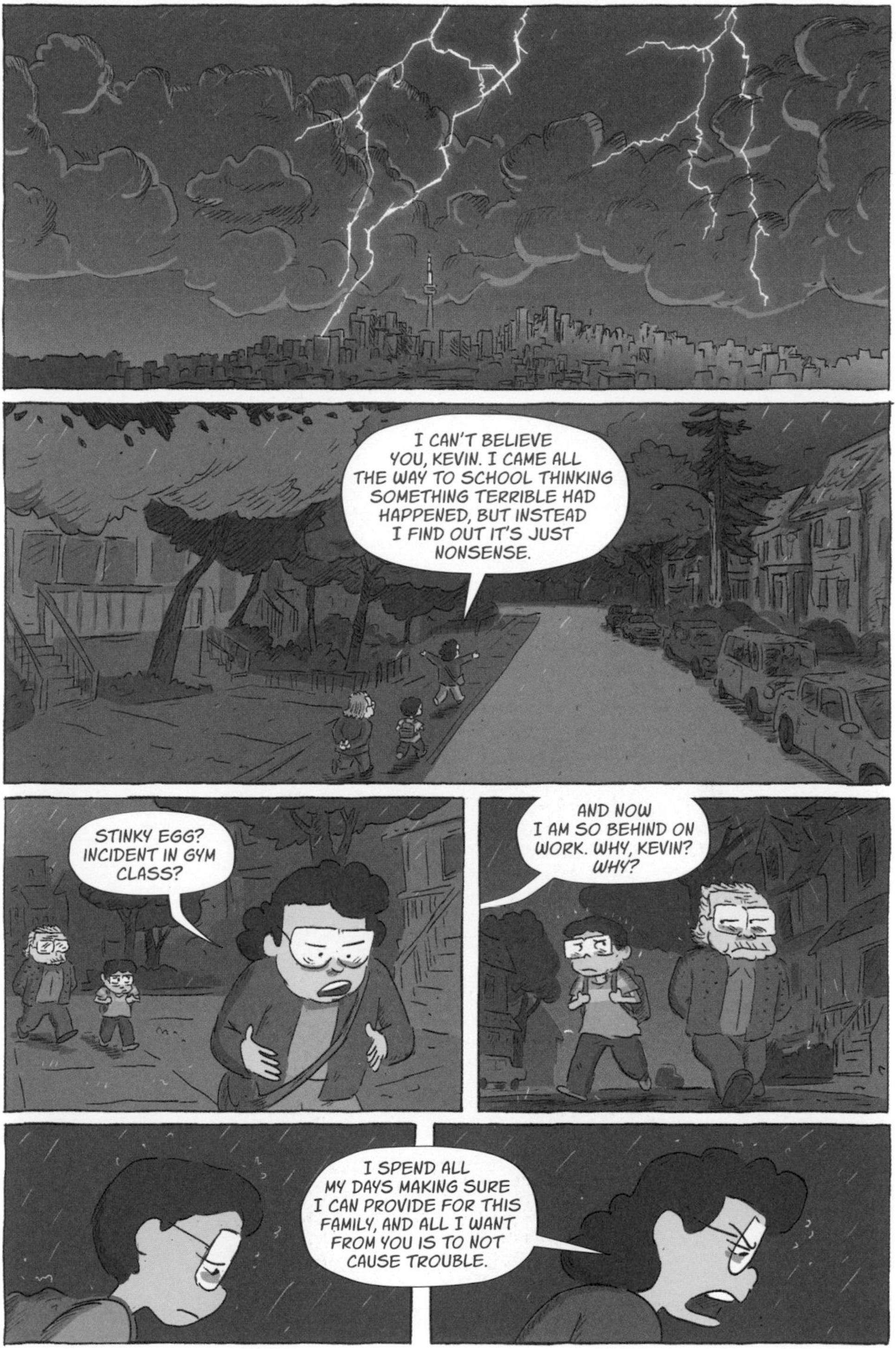
I CAN'T BELIEVE YOU, KEVIN. I CAME ALL THE WAY TO SCHOOL THINKING SOMETHING TERRIBLE HAD HAPPENED, BUT INSTEAD I FIND OUT IT'S JUST NONSENSE.
STINKY EGG? INCIDENT IN GYM CLASS?
AND NOW I AM SO BEHIND ON WORK. WHY, KEVIN? *WHY?*
I SPEND ALL MY DAYS MAKING SURE I CAN PROVIDE FOR THIS FAMILY, AND ALL I WANT FROM YOU IS TO NOT CAUSE TROUBLE.

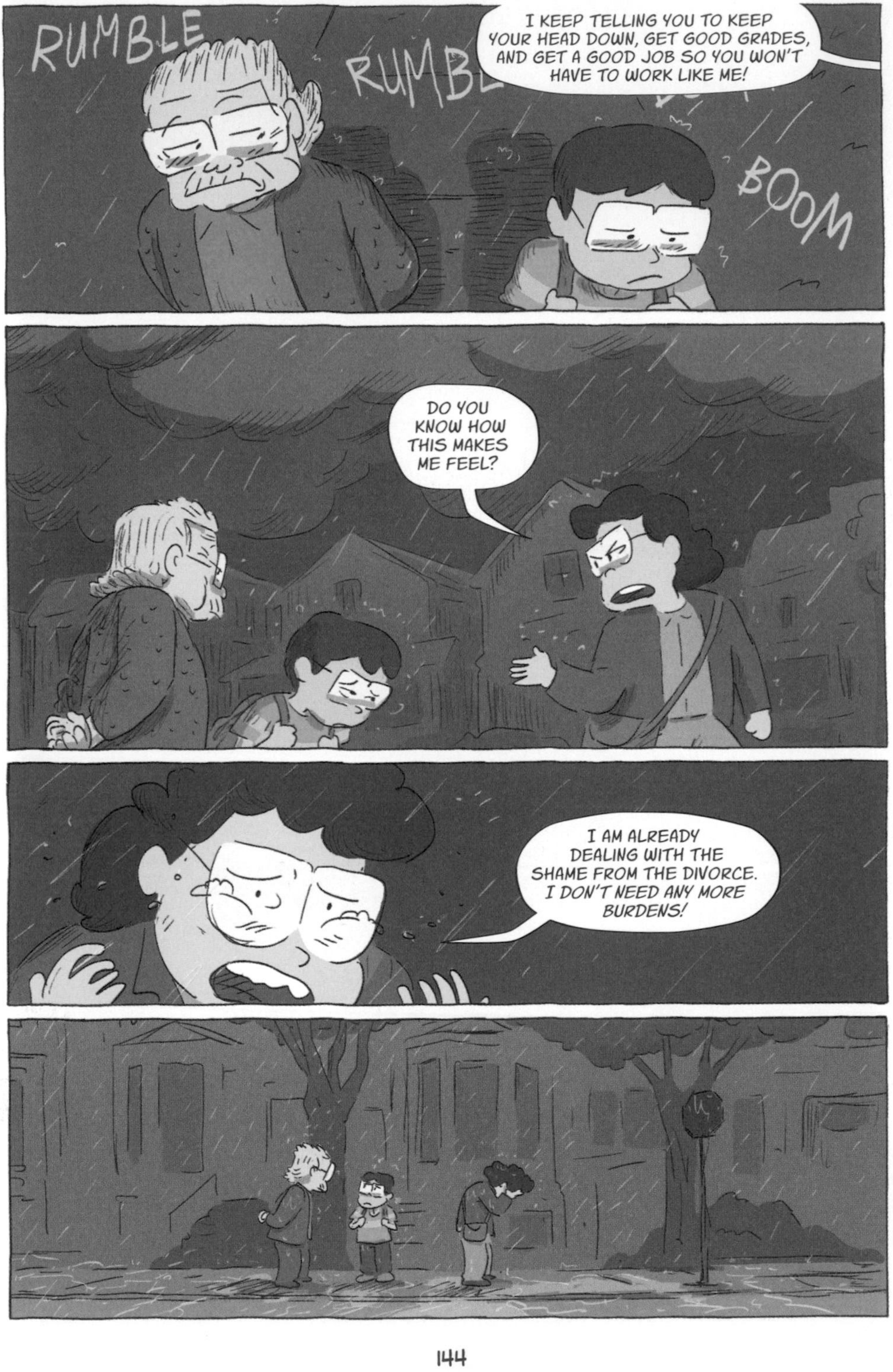
RUMBLE
I KEEP TELLING YOU TO KEEP YOUR HEAD DOWN, GET GOOD GRADES, AND GET A GOOD JOB SO YOU WON'T HAVE TO WORK LIKE ME!
BOOM
DO YOU KNOW HOW THIS MAKES ME FEEL?
I AM ALREADY DEALING WITH THE SHAME FROM THE DIVORCE. I DON'T NEED ANY MORE BURDENS!

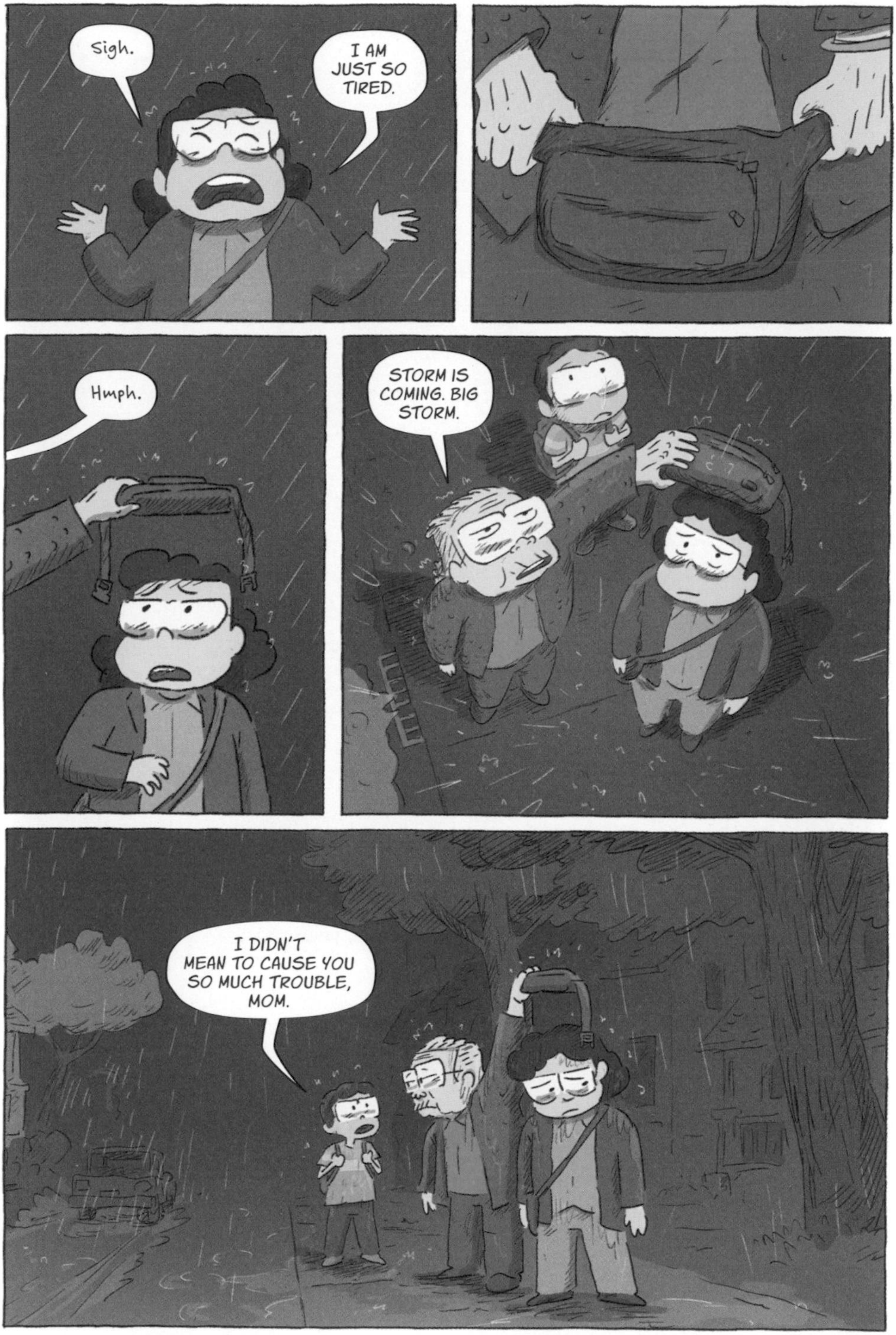
Sigh.
I AM JUST SO TIRED.
Hmph.
STORM IS COMING. BIG STORM.
I DIDN'T MEAN TO CAUSE YOU SO MUCH TROUBLE, MOM.

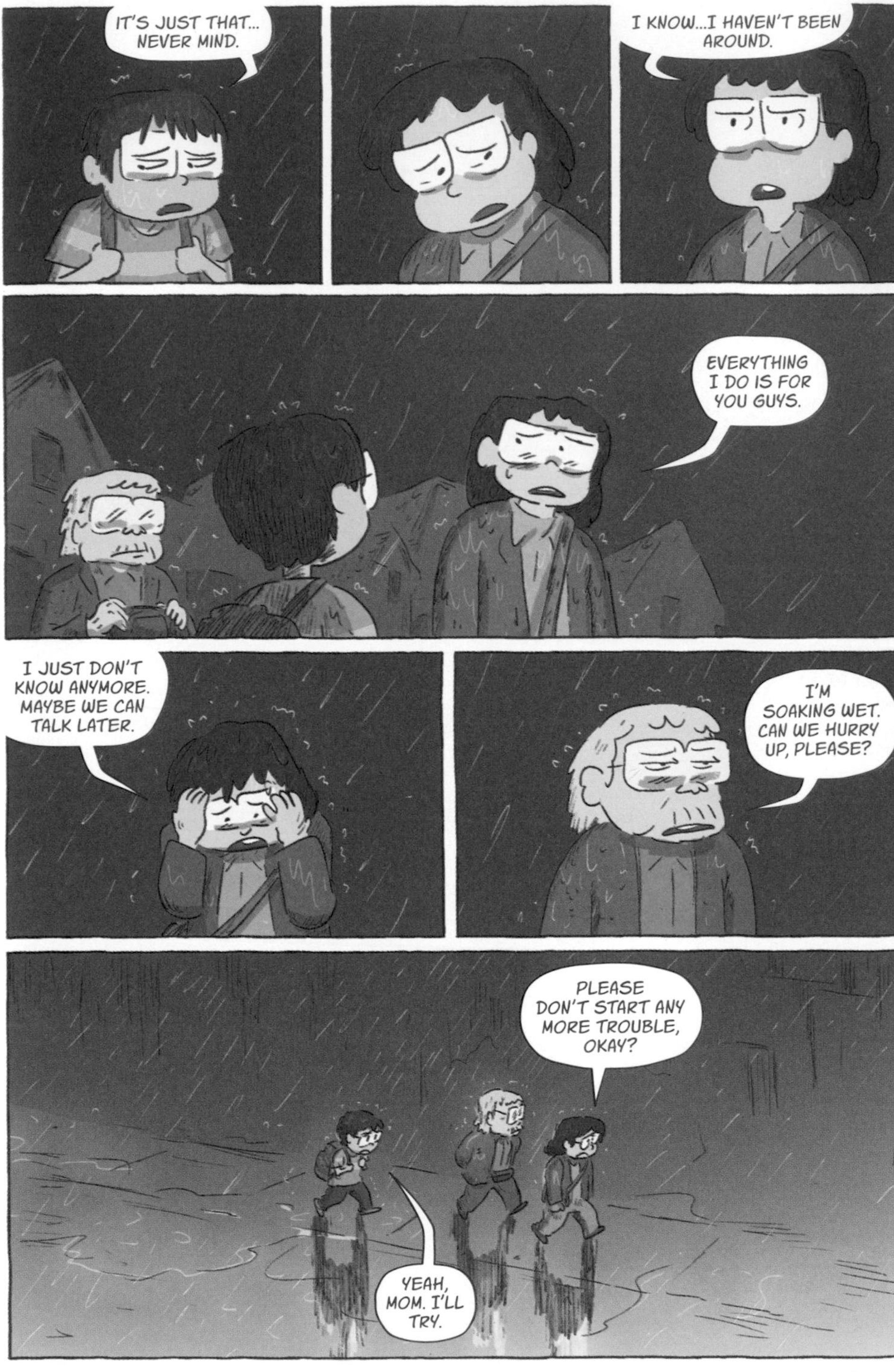
IT'S JUST THAT... NEVER MIND.
I KNOW...I HAVEN'T BEEN AROUND.
EVERYTHING I DO IS FOR YOU GUYS.
I JUST DON'T KNOW ANYMORE. MAYBE WE CAN TALK LATER.
I'M SOAKING WET. CAN WE HURRY UP, PLEASE?
PLEASE DON'T START ANY MORE TROUBLE, OKAY?
YEAH, MOM. I'LL TRY.

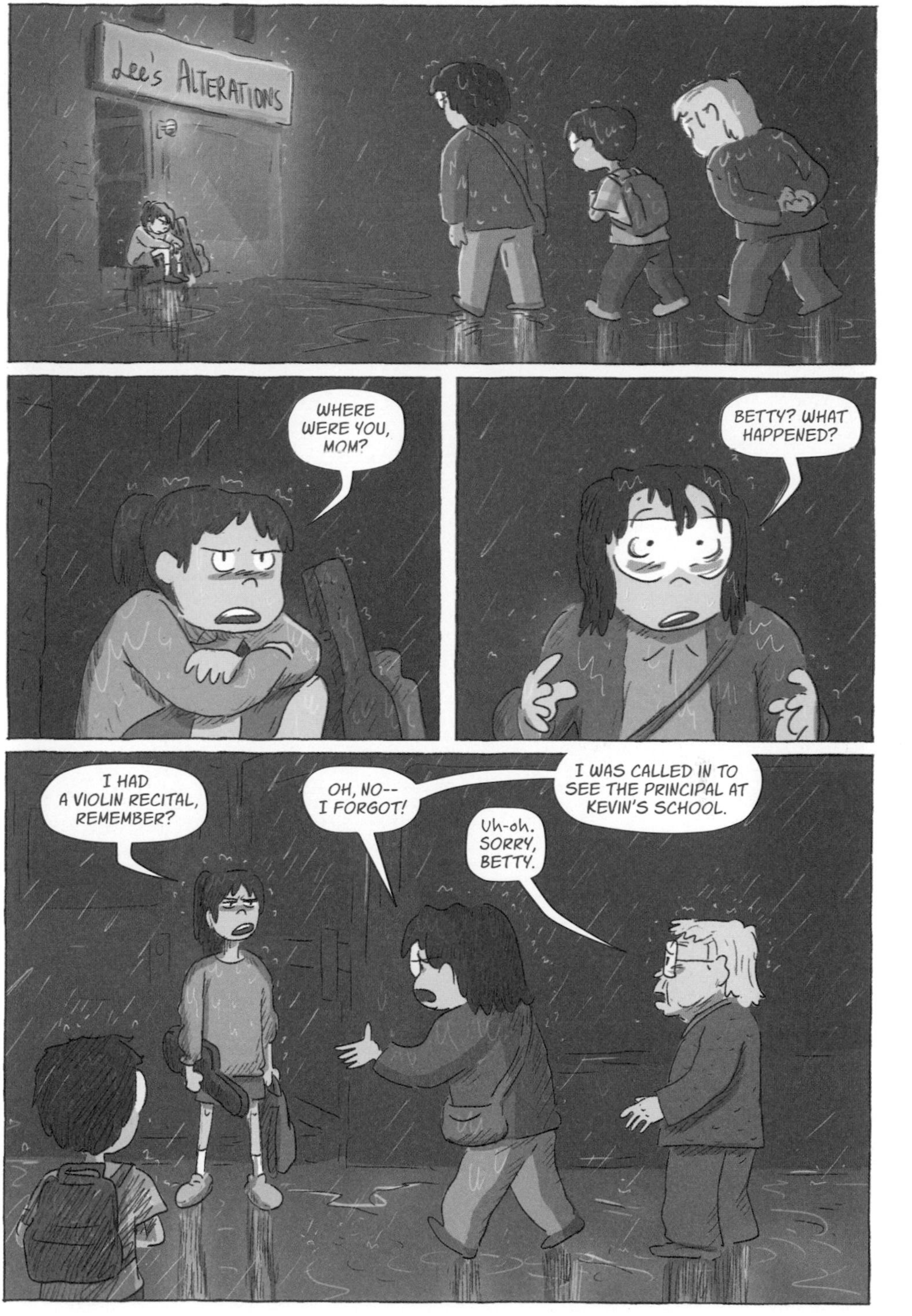
Lee's ALTERATIONS
WHERE WERE YOU, MOM?
BETTY? WHAT HAPPENED?
I HAD A VIOLIN RECITAL, REMEMBER?
OH, NO-- I FORGOT!
I WAS CALLED IN TO SEE THE PRINCIPAL AT KEVIN'S SCHOOL.
Uh-oh. SORRY, BETTY.

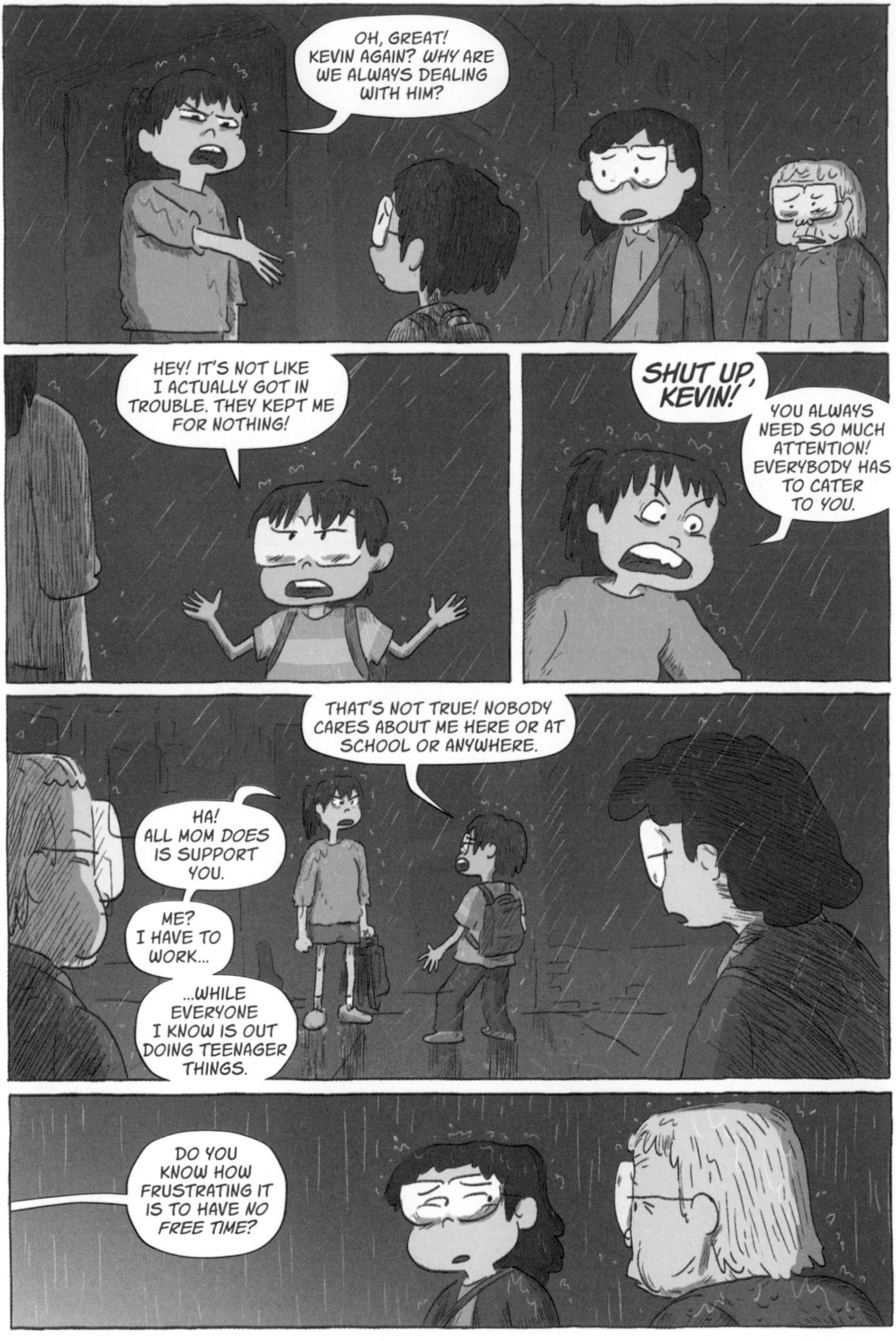
OH, GREAT! KEVIN AGAIN? WHY ARE WE ALWAYS DEALING WITH HIM?
HEY! IT'S NOT LIKE I ACTUALLY GOT IN TROUBLE. THEY KEPT ME FOR NOTHING!
SHUT UP, KEVIN!
YOU ALWAYS NEED SO MUCH ATTENTION! EVERYBODY HAS TO CATER TO YOU.
THAT'S NOT TRUE! NOBODY CARES ABOUT ME HERE OR AT SCHOOL OR ANYWHERE.
HA! ALL MOM DOES IS SUPPORT YOU.
ME? I HAVE TO WORK...
...WHILE EVERYONE I KNOW IS OUT DOING TEENAGER THINGS.
DO YOU KNOW HOW FRUSTRATING IT IS TO HAVE NO FREE TIME?

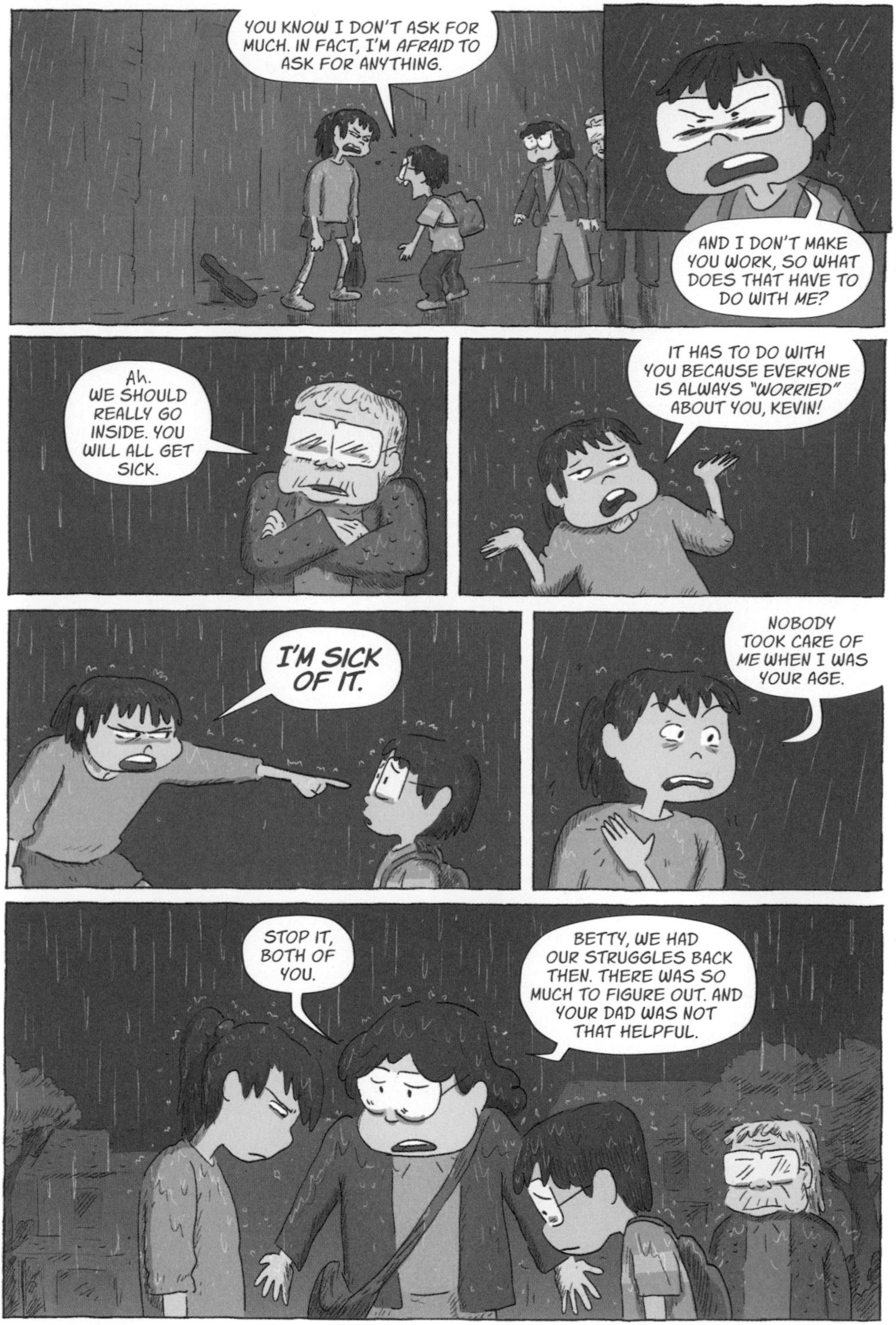
YOU KNOW I DON'T ASK FOR MUCH. IN FACT, I'M *AFRAID* TO ASK FOR ANYTHING.
AND I DON'T MAKE YOU WORK, SO WHAT DOES THAT HAVE TO DO WITH *ME*?
Ah. WE SHOULD REALLY GO INSIDE. YOU WILL ALL GET SICK.
IT HAS TO DO WITH YOU BECAUSE EVERYONE IS ALWAYS "*WORRIED*" ABOUT YOU, KEVIN!
I'M SICK OF IT.
NOBODY TOOK CARE OF *ME* WHEN I WAS YOUR AGE.
STOP IT, BOTH OF YOU.
BETTY, WE HAD OUR STRUGGLES BACK THEN. THERE WAS SO MUCH TO FIGURE OUT. AND YOUR DAD WAS NOT THAT HELPFUL.

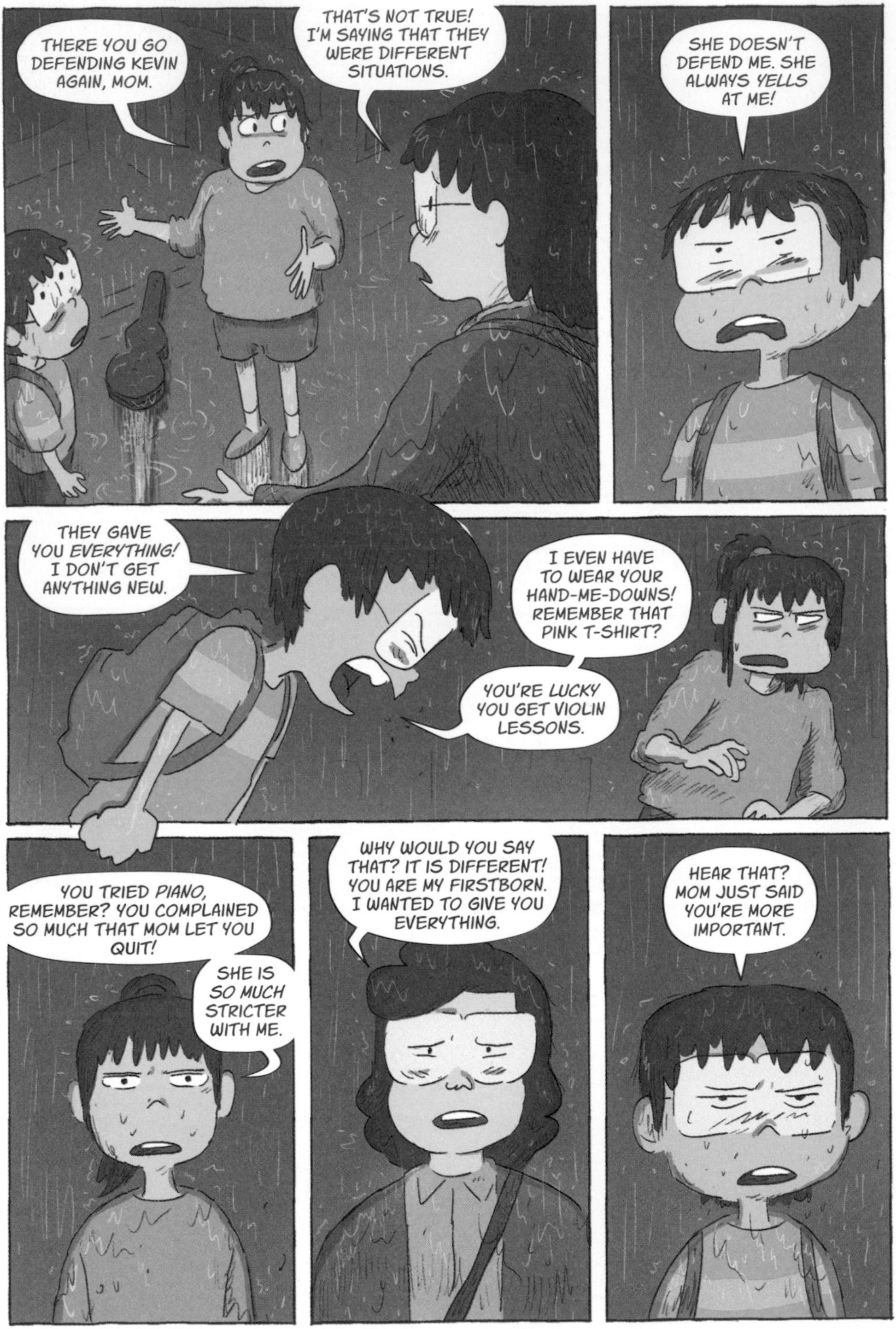

THERE YOU GO DEFENDING KEVIN AGAIN, MOM.
THAT'S NOT TRUE! I'M SAYING THAT THEY WERE DIFFERENT SITUATIONS.
SHE DOESN'T DEFEND ME. SHE ALWAYS *YELLS* AT ME!
THEY GAVE YOU *EVERYTHING*! I DON'T GET ANYTHING NEW.
I EVEN HAVE TO WEAR YOUR HAND-ME-DOWNS! REMEMBER THAT PINK T-SHIRT?
YOU'RE LUCKY YOU GET VIOLIN LESSONS.
YOU TRIED *PIANO*, REMEMBER? YOU COMPLAINED SO MUCH THAT MOM LET YOU QUIT!
SHE IS SO MUCH STRICTER WITH ME.
WHY WOULD YOU SAY THAT? IT IS DIFFERENT! YOU ARE MY FIRSTBORN. I WANTED TO GIVE YOU EVERYTHING.
HEAR THAT? MOM JUST SAID YOU'RE MORE IMPORTANT.

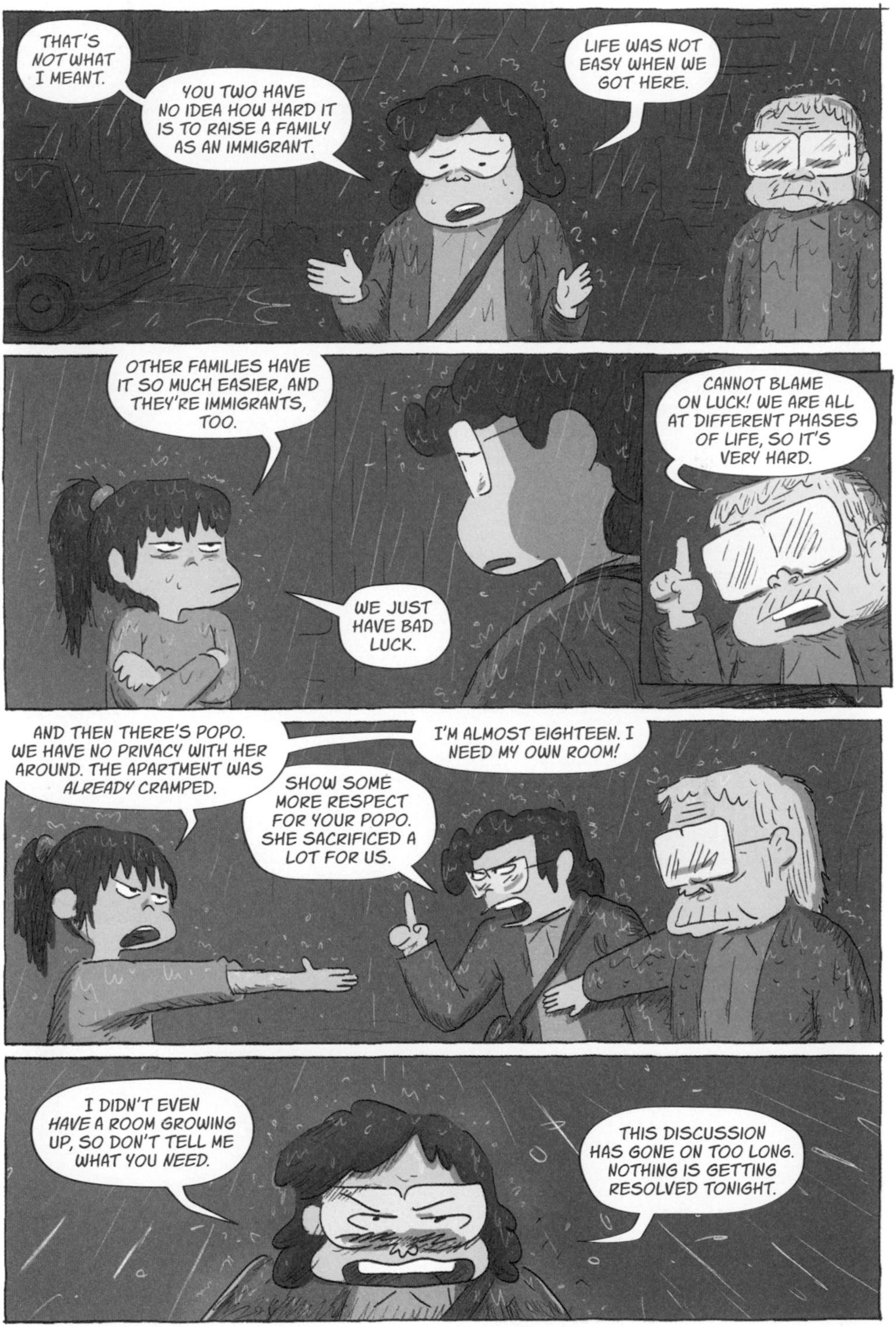
THAT'S NOT WHAT I MEANT.
YOU TWO HAVE NO IDEA HOW HARD IT IS TO RAISE A FAMILY AS AN IMMIGRANT.
LIFE WAS NOT EASY WHEN WE GOT HERE.
OTHER FAMILIES HAVE IT SO MUCH EASIER, AND THEY'RE IMMIGRANTS, TOO.
WE JUST HAVE BAD LUCK.
CANNOT BLAME ON LUCK! WE ARE ALL AT DIFFERENT PHASES OF LIFE, SO IT'S VERY HARD.
AND THEN THERE'S POPO. WE HAVE NO PRIVACY WITH HER AROUND. THE APARTMENT WAS ALREADY CRAMPED.
I'M ALMOST EIGHTEEN. I NEED MY OWN ROOM!
SHOW SOME MORE RESPECT FOR YOUR POPO. SHE SACRIFICED A LOT FOR US.
I DIDN'T EVEN HAVE A ROOM GROWING UP, SO DON'T TELL ME WHAT YOU NEED.
THIS DISCUSSION HAS GONE ON TOO LONG. NOTHING IS GETTING RESOLVED TONIGHT.

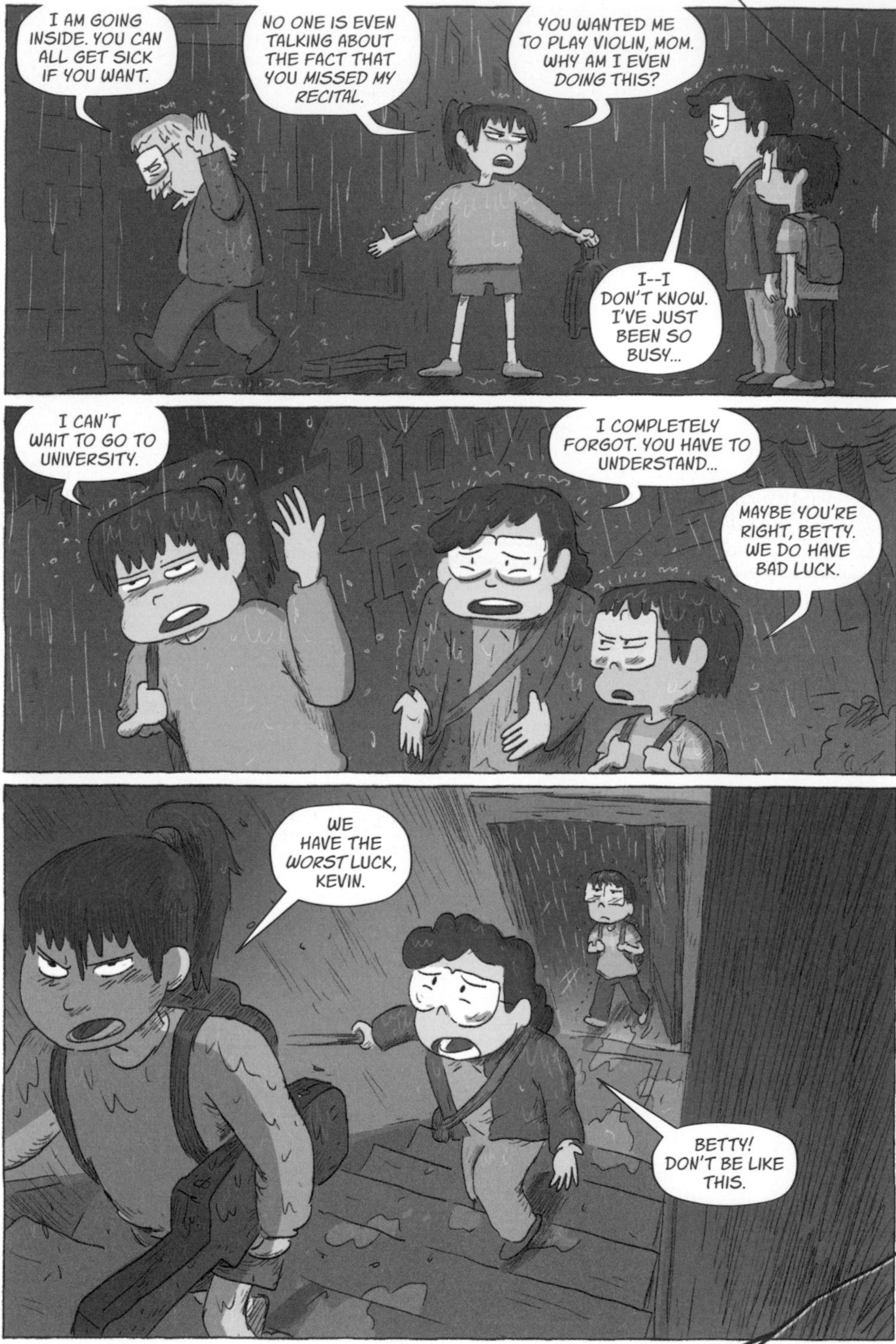
I AM GOING INSIDE. YOU CAN ALL GET SICK IF YOU WANT.
NO ONE IS EVEN TALKING ABOUT THE FACT THAT YOU MISSED MY RECITAL.
YOU WANTED ME TO PLAY VIOLIN, MOM. WHY AM I EVEN DOING THIS?
I--I DON'T KNOW. I'VE JUST BEEN SO BUSY...
I CAN'T WAIT TO GO TO UNIVERSITY.
I COMPLETELY FORGOT. YOU HAVE TO UNDERSTAND...
MAYBE YOU'RE RIGHT, BETTY. WE DO HAVE BAD LUCK.
WE HAVE THE WORST LUCK, KEVIN.
BETTY! DON'T BE LIKE THIS.

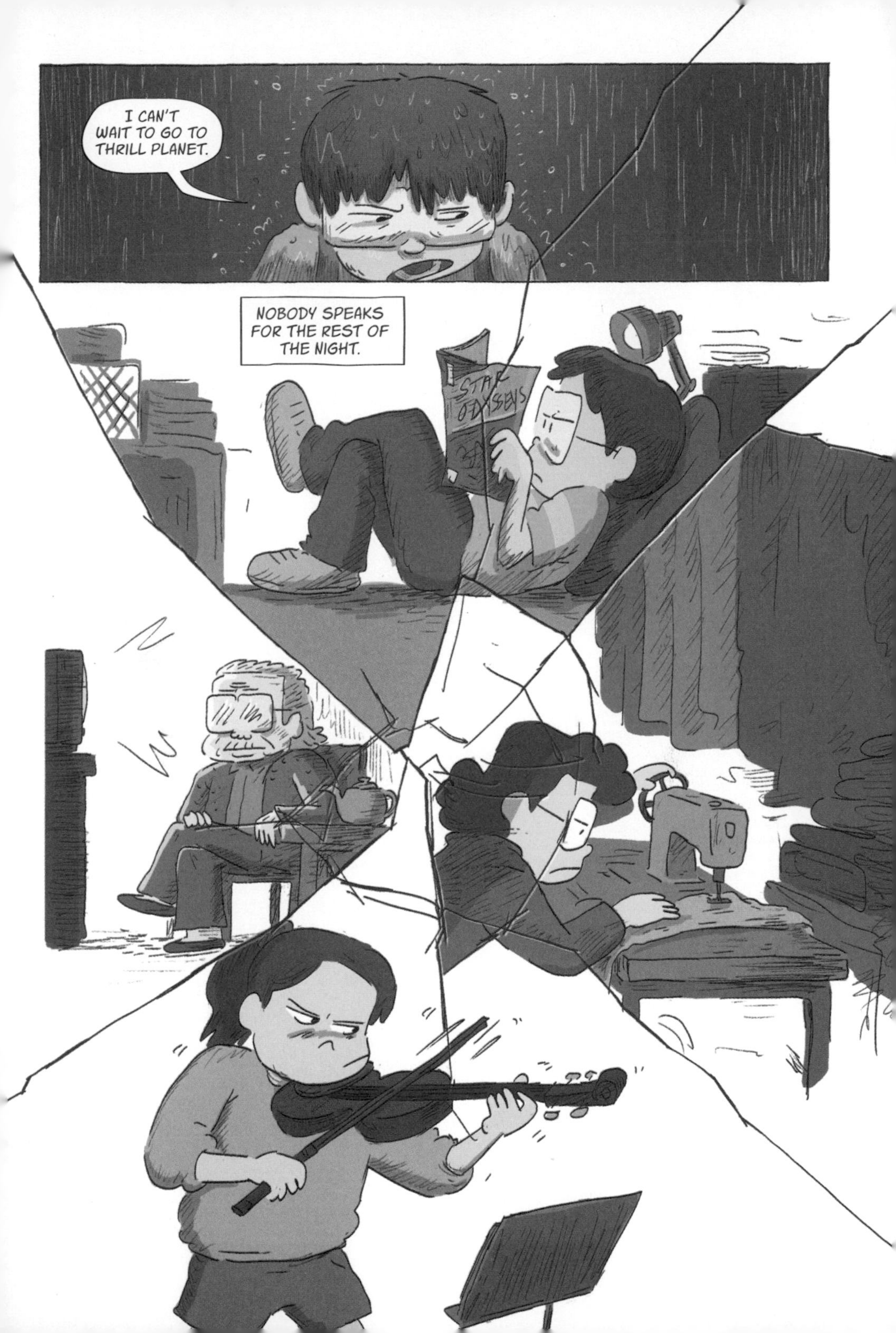
I CAN'T WAIT TO GO TO THRILL PLANET.
NOBODY SPEAKS FOR THE REST OF THE NIGHT.
STAR ODYSSEYS

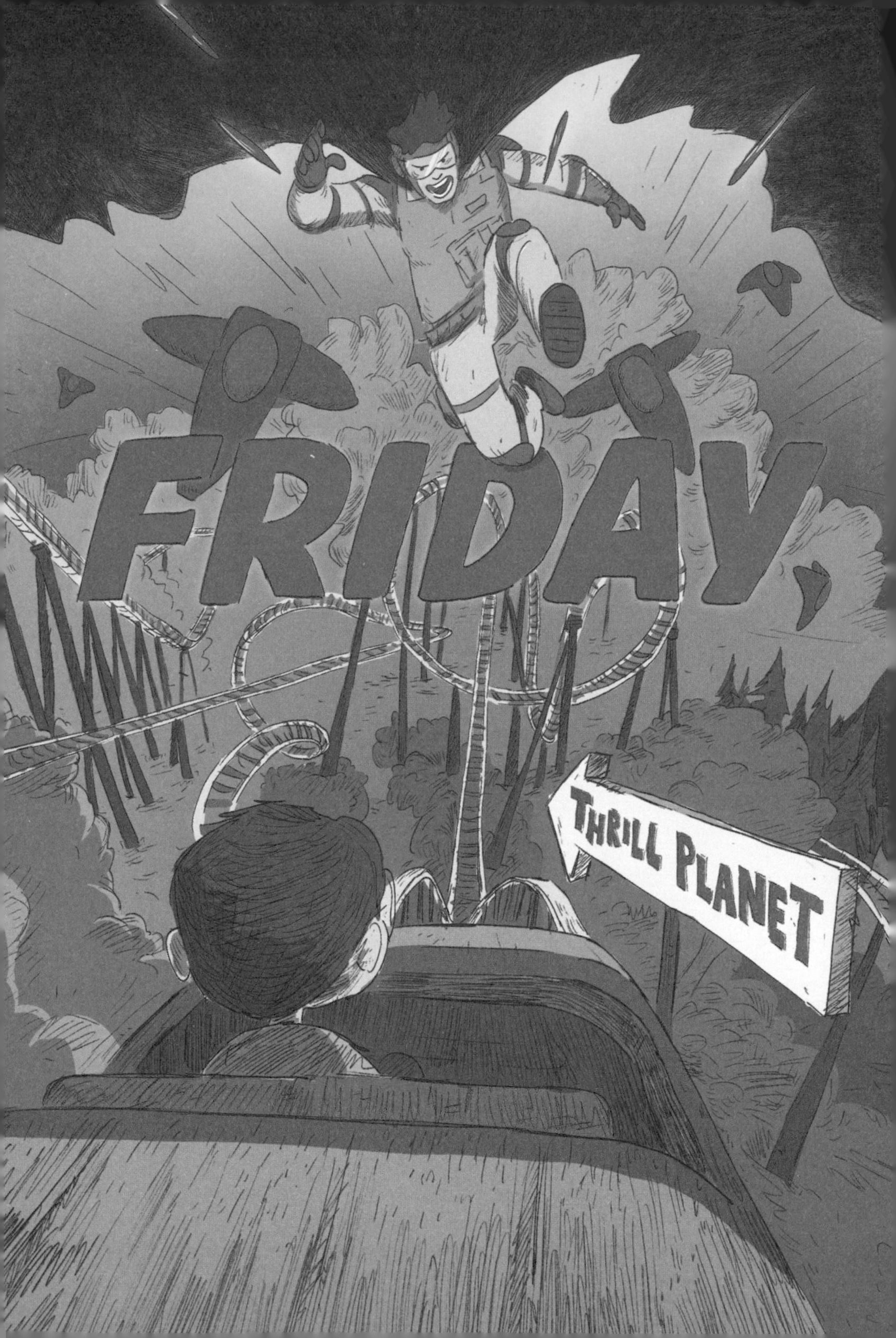
FRIDAY
THRILL PLANET

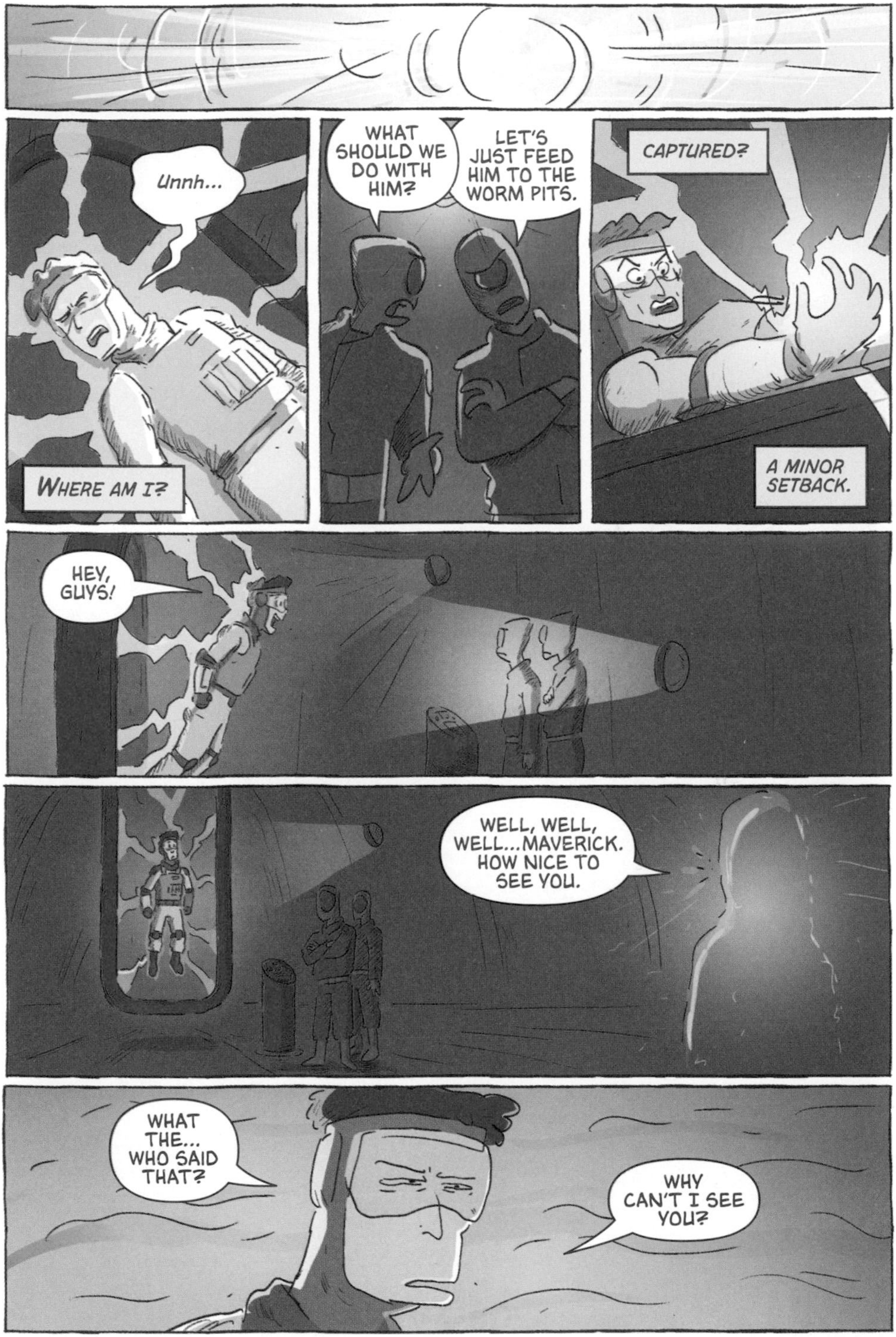
Unnh...
WHERE AM I?
WHAT SHOULD WE DO WITH HIM?
LET'S JUST FEED HIM TO THE WORM PITS.
CAPTURED?
A MINOR SETBACK.
HEY, GUYS!
WELL, WELL, WELL...MAVERICK. HOW NICE TO SEE YOU.
WHAT THE... WHO SAID THAT?
WHY CAN'T I SEE YOU?

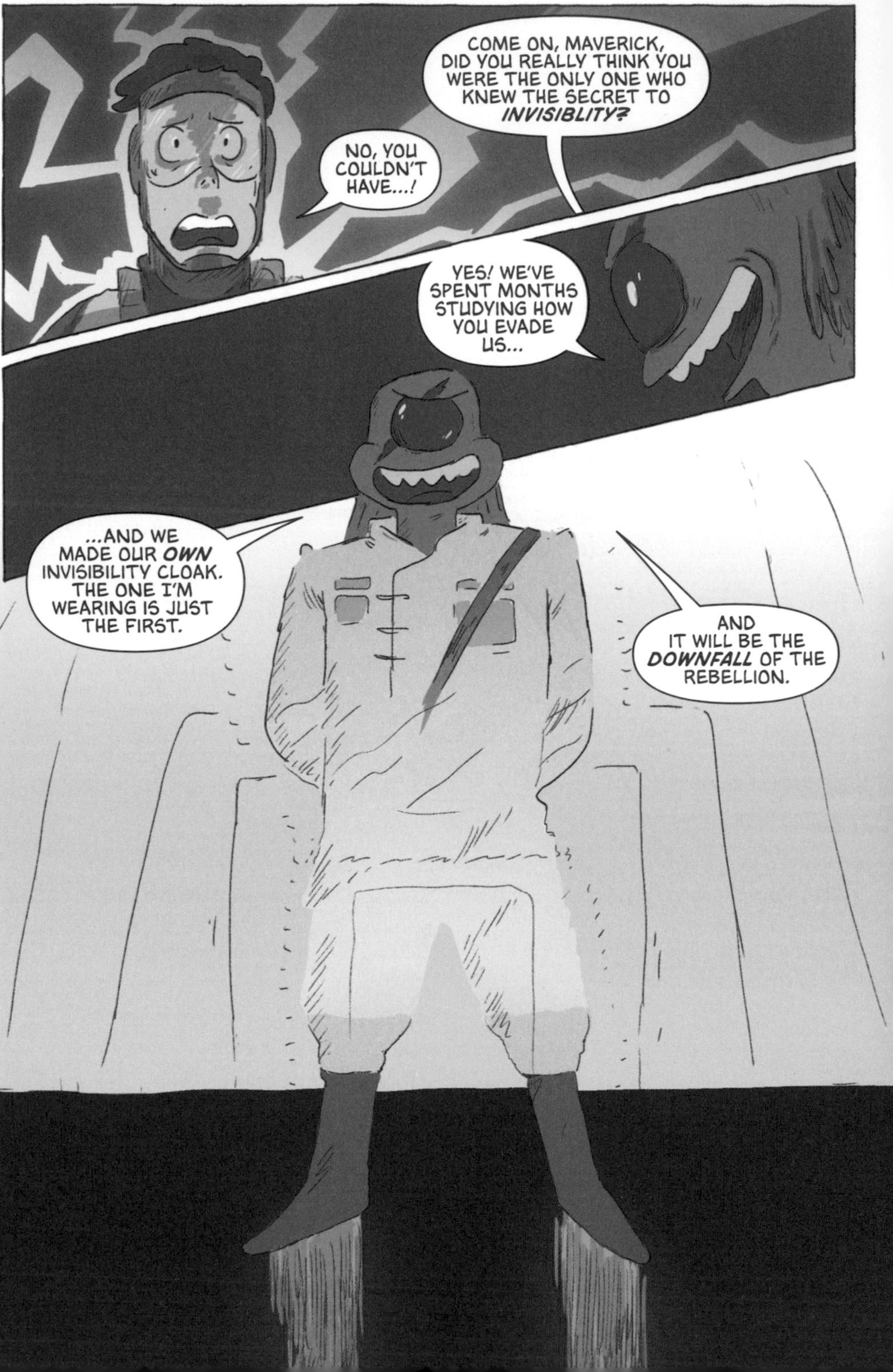
COME ON, MAVERICK, DID YOU REALLY THINK YOU WERE THE ONLY ONE WHO KNEW THE SECRET TO *INVISIBLITY?*
NO, YOU COULDN'T HAVE...!
YES! WE'VE SPENT MONTHS STUDYING HOW YOU EVADE US...
...AND WE MADE OUR *OWN* INVISIBILITY CLOAK. THE ONE I'M WEARING IS JUST THE FIRST.
AND IT WILL BE THE *DOWNFALL* OF THE REBELLION.

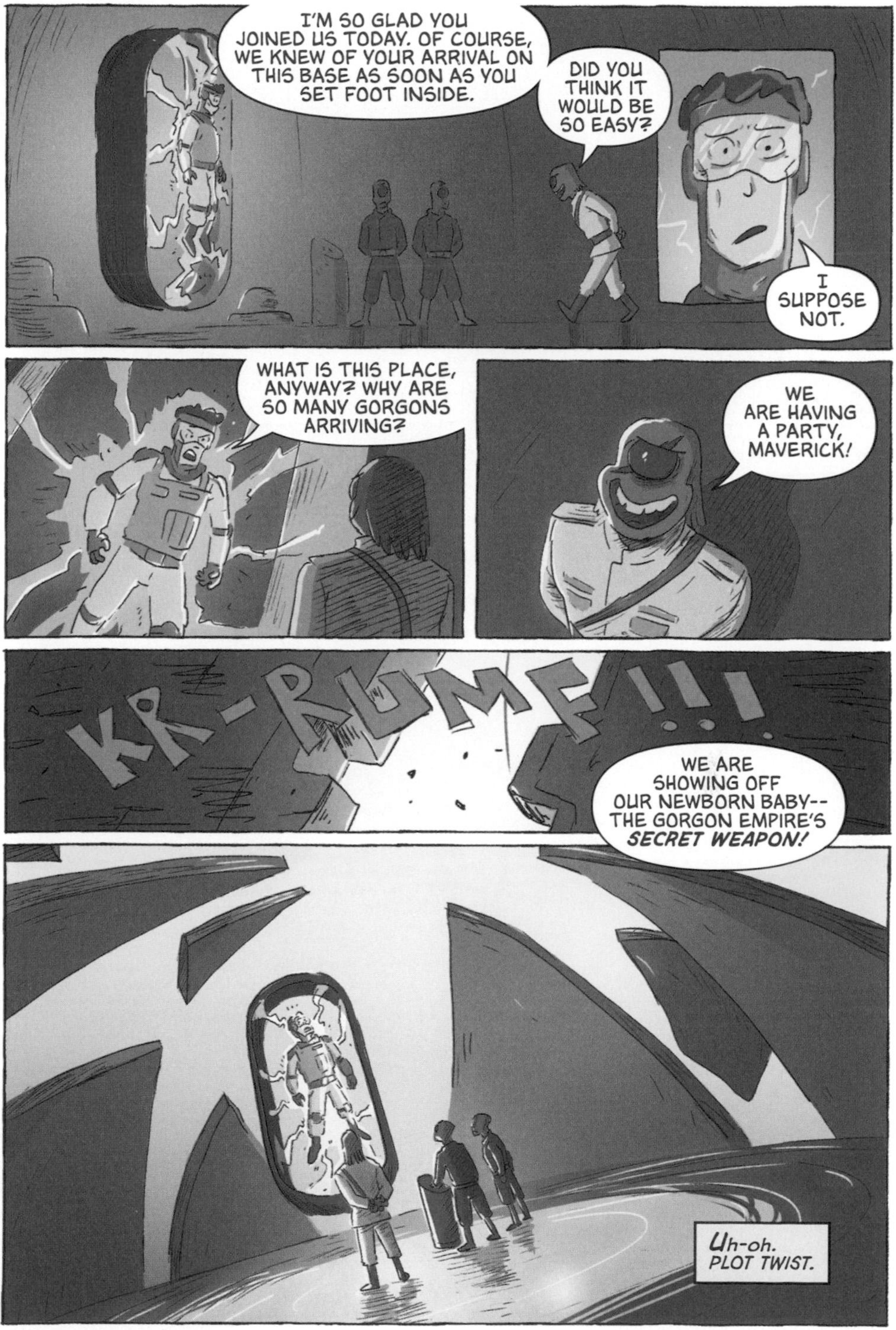
I'M SO GLAD YOU JOINED US TODAY. OF COURSE, WE KNEW OF YOUR ARRIVAL ON THIS BASE AS SOON AS YOU SET FOOT INSIDE.
DID YOU THINK IT WOULD BE SO EASY?
I SUPPOSE NOT.
WHAT IS THIS PLACE, ANYWAY? WHY ARE SO MANY GORGONS ARRIVING?
WE ARE HAVING A PARTY, MAVERICK!
KR-RUMF!!!
WE ARE SHOWING OFF OUR NEWBORN BABY--THE GORGON EMPIRE'S SECRET WEAPON!
Uh-oh. PLOT TWIST.

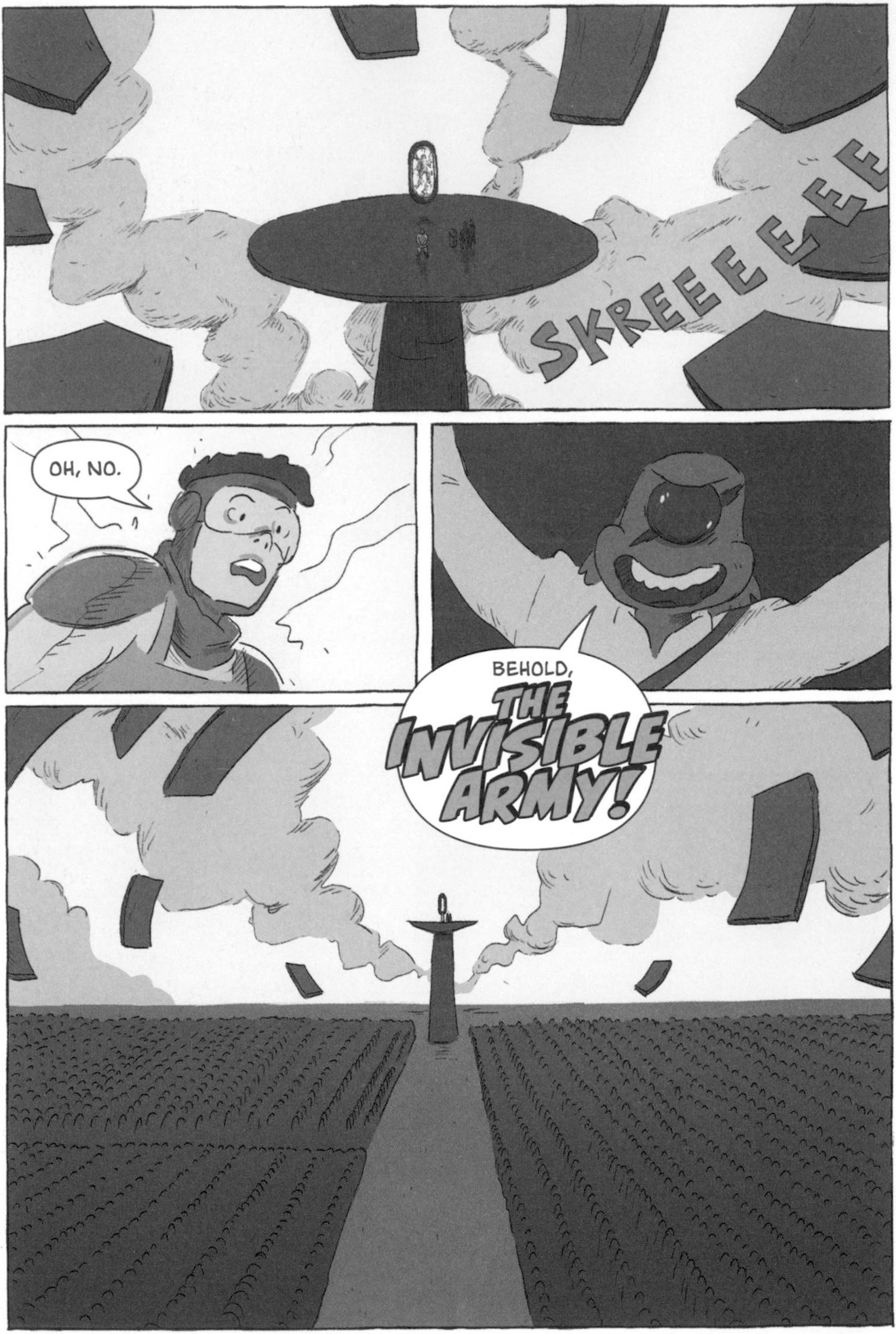
SKREEEEEEE
OH, NO.
BEHOLD, THE INVISIBLE ARMY!

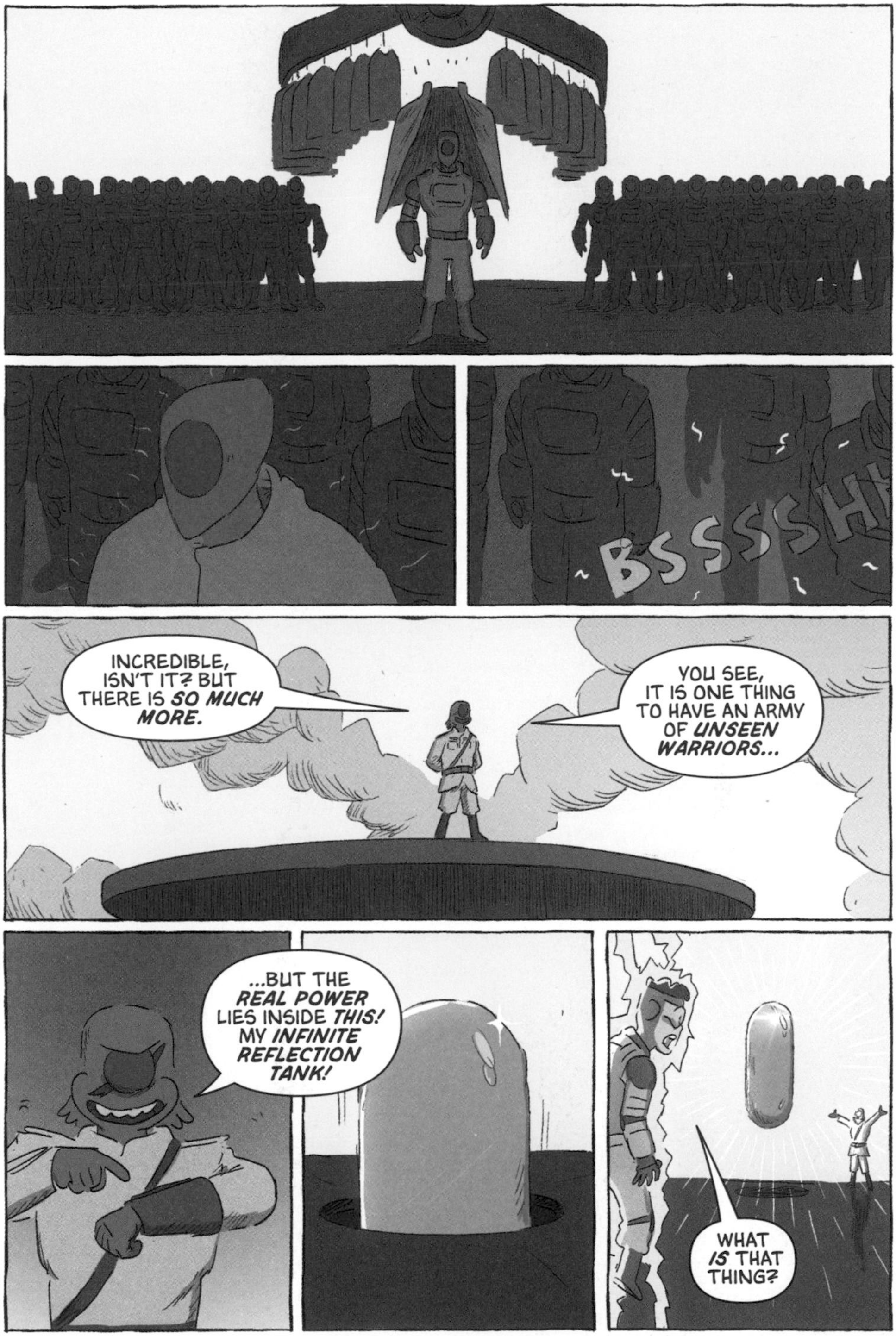
BSSSSH
INCREDIBLE, ISN'T IT? BUT THERE IS *SO MUCH MORE.*
YOU SEE, IT IS ONE THING TO HAVE AN ARMY OF *UNSEEN WARRIORS...*
...BUT THE *REAL POWER* LIES INSIDE *THIS!* MY *INFINITE REFLECTION TANK!*
WHAT *IS* THAT THING?

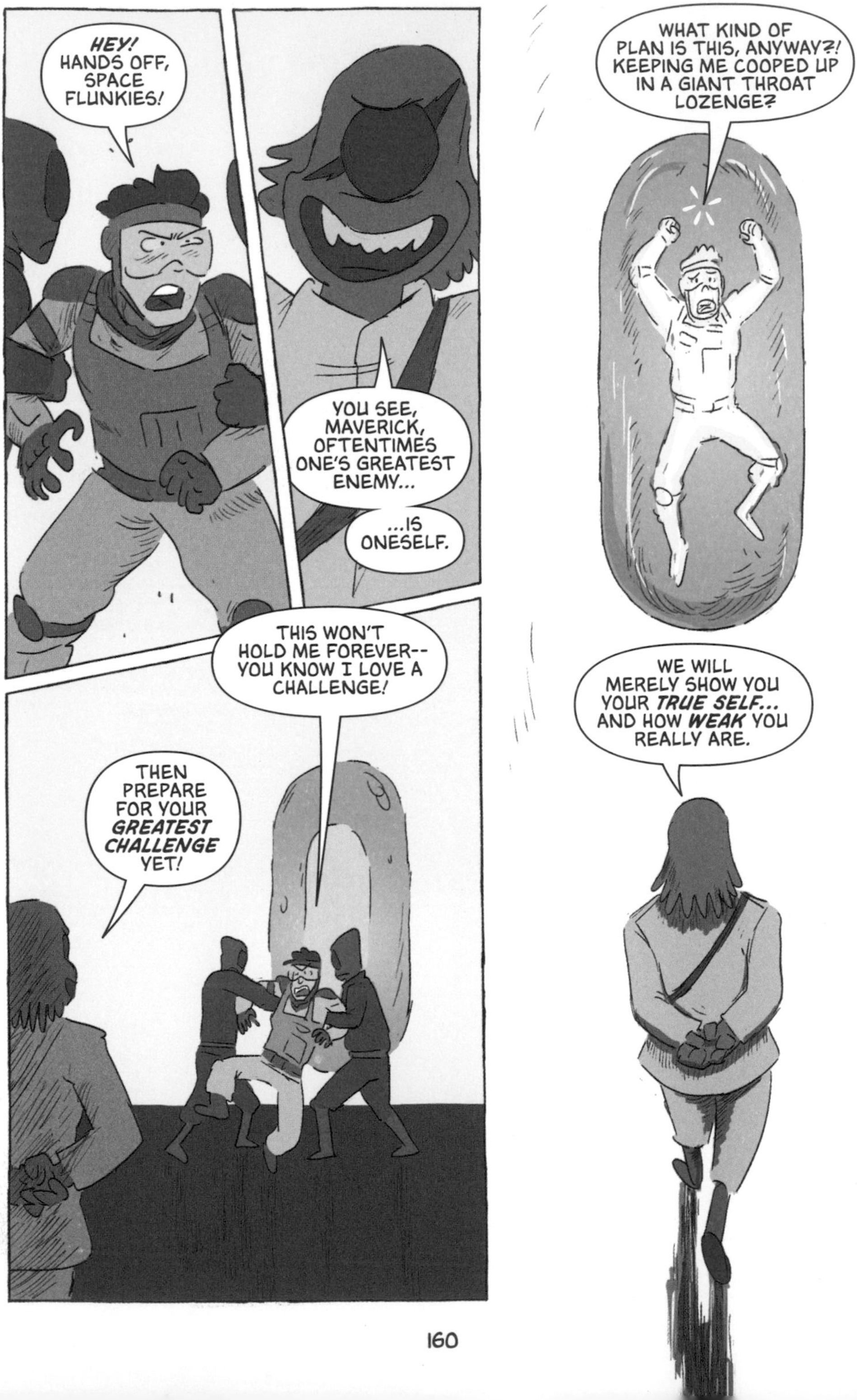
HEY! HANDS OFF, SPACE FLUNKIES!
YOU SEE, MAVERICK, OFTENTIMES ONE'S GREATEST ENEMY...
...IS ONESELF.
THIS WON'T HOLD ME FOREVER-- YOU KNOW I LOVE A CHALLENGE!
THEN PREPARE FOR YOUR GREATEST CHALLENGE YET!
WHAT KIND OF PLAN IS THIS, ANYWAY?! KEEPING ME COOPED UP IN A GIANT THROAT LOZENGE?
WE WILL MERELY SHOW YOU YOUR TRUE SELF... AND HOW WEAK YOU REALLY ARE.

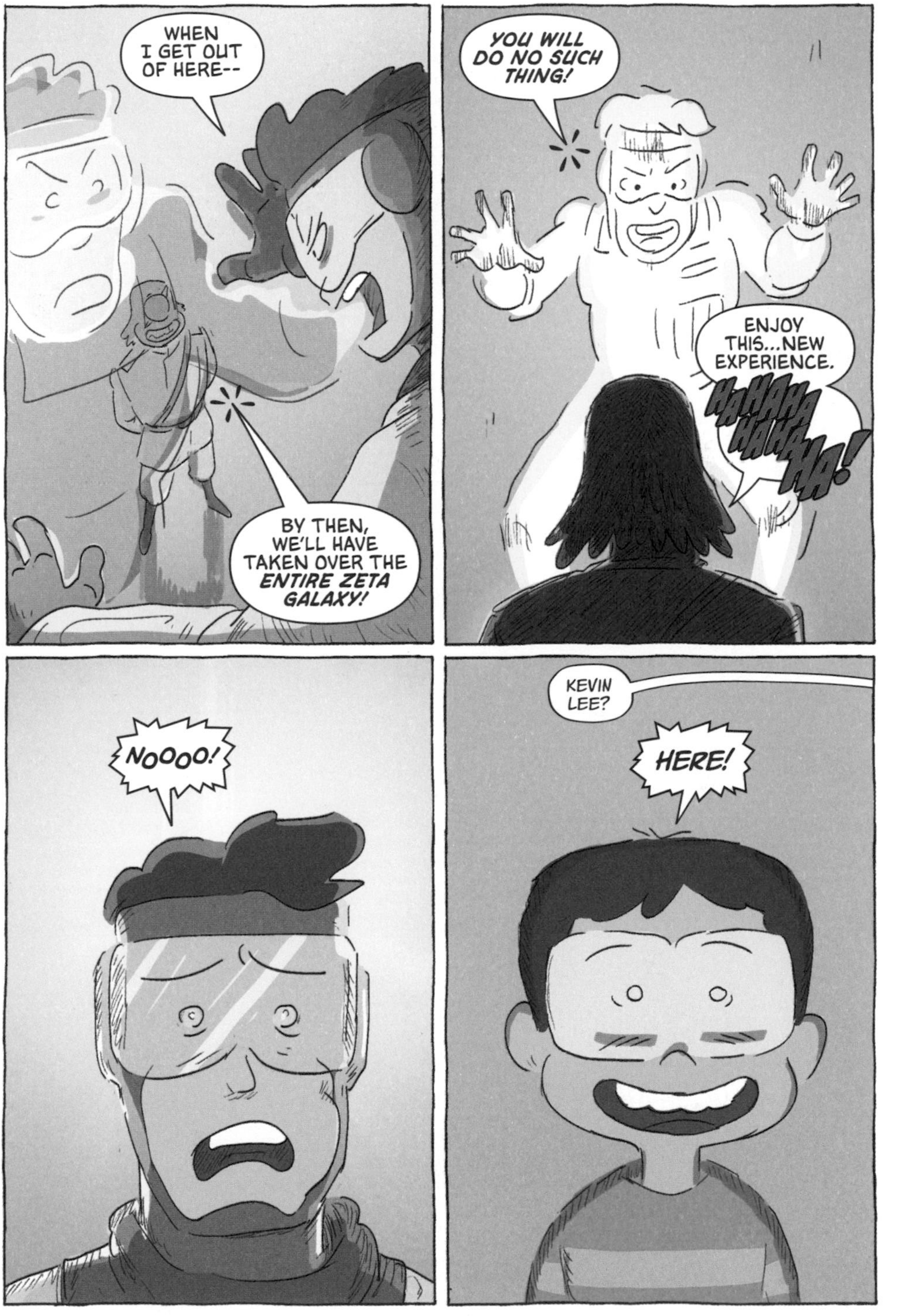
WHEN I GET OUT OF HERE--
BY THEN, WE'LL HAVE TAKEN OVER THE ENTIRE ZETA GALAXY!
YOU WILL DO NO SUCH THING!
ENJOY THIS...NEW EXPERIENCE.
HAHAHAHAHAHA!
NOOOO!
KEVIN LEE?
HERE!

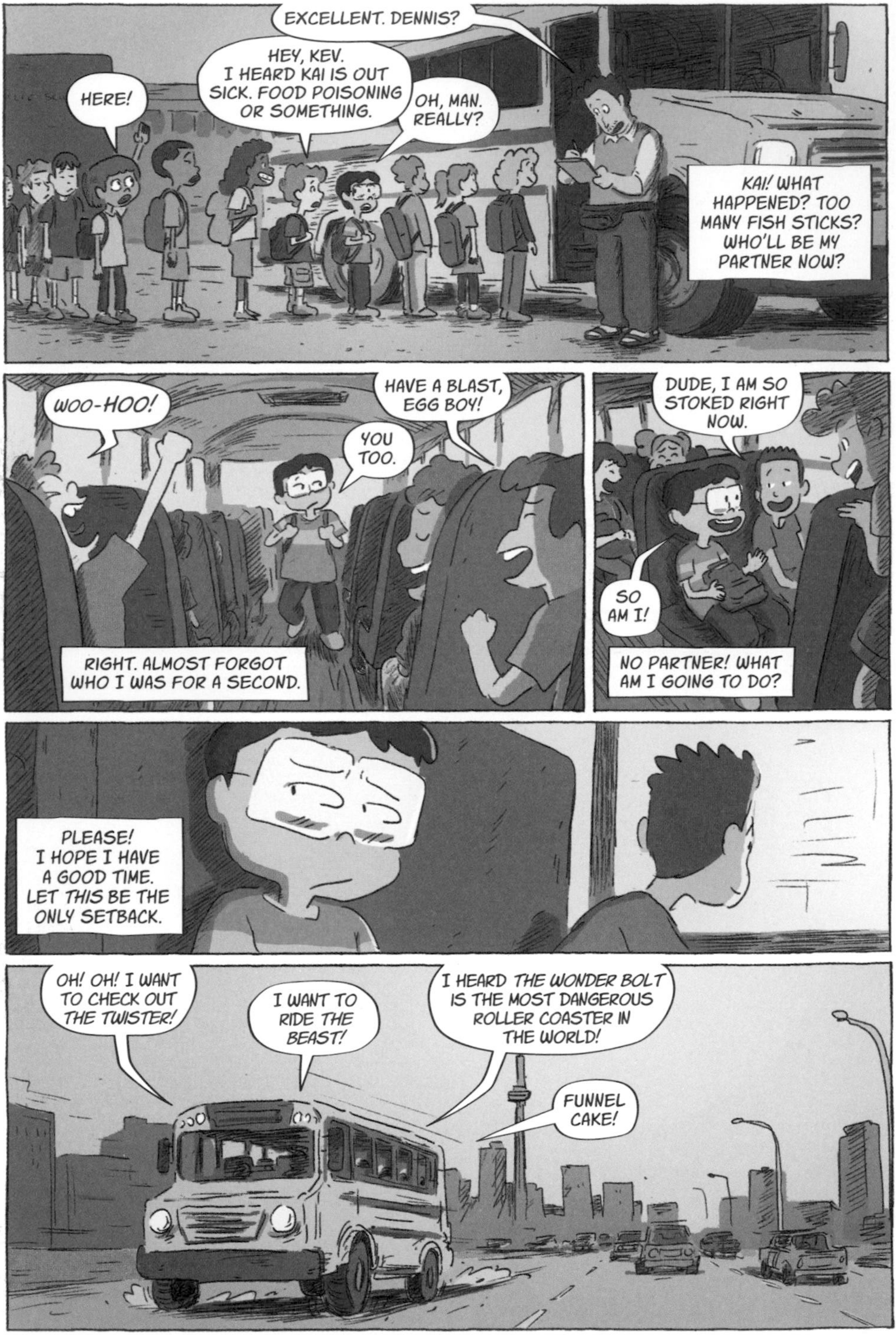
EXCELLENT. DENNIS?
HERE!
HEY, KEV. I HEARD KAI IS OUT SICK. FOOD POISONING OR SOMETHING.
OH, MAN. REALLY?
KAI! WHAT HAPPENED? TOO MANY FISH STICKS? WHO'LL BE MY PARTNER NOW?
WOO-HOO!
HAVE A BLAST, EGG BOY!
YOU TOO.
RIGHT. ALMOST FORGOT WHO I WAS FOR A SECOND.
DUDE, I AM SO STOKED RIGHT NOW.
SO AM I!
NO PARTNER! WHAT AM I GOING TO DO?
PLEASE! I HOPE I HAVE A GOOD TIME. LET THIS BE THE ONLY SETBACK.
OH! OH! I WANT TO CHECK OUT THE TWISTER!
I WANT TO RIDE THE BEAST!
I HEARD THE WONDER BOLT IS THE MOST DANGEROUS ROLLER COASTER IN THE WORLD!
FUNNEL CAKE!

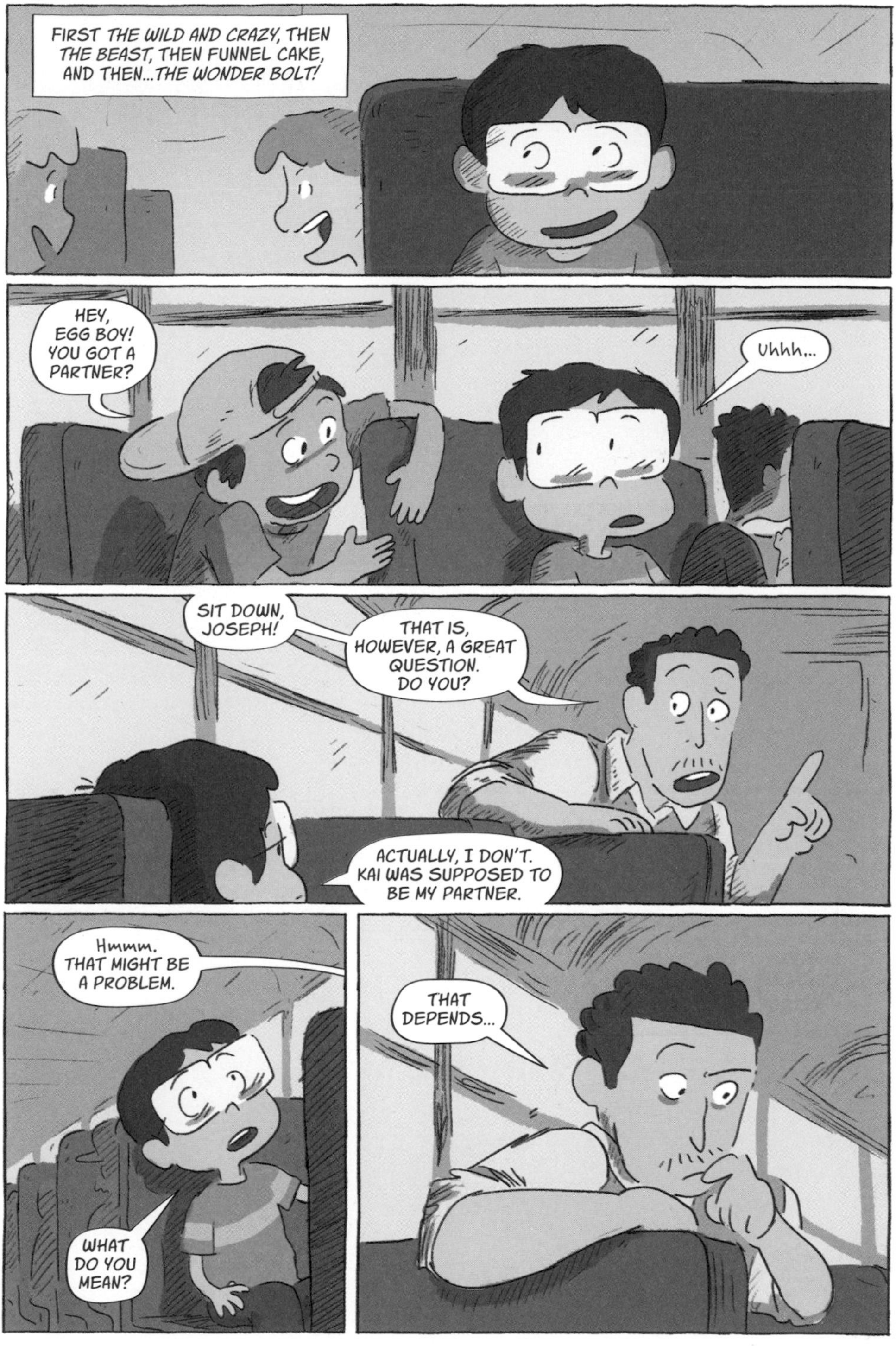
FIRST THE WILD AND CRAZY, THEN THE BEAST, THEN FUNNEL CAKE, AND THEN...THE WONDER BOLT!
HEY, EGG BOY! YOU GOT A PARTNER?
Uhhh...
SIT DOWN, JOSEPH!
THAT IS, HOWEVER, A GREAT QUESTION. DO YOU?
ACTUALLY, I DON'T. KAI WAS SUPPOSED TO BE MY PARTNER.
Hmmm. THAT MIGHT BE A PROBLEM.
WHAT DO YOU MEAN?
THAT DEPENDS...

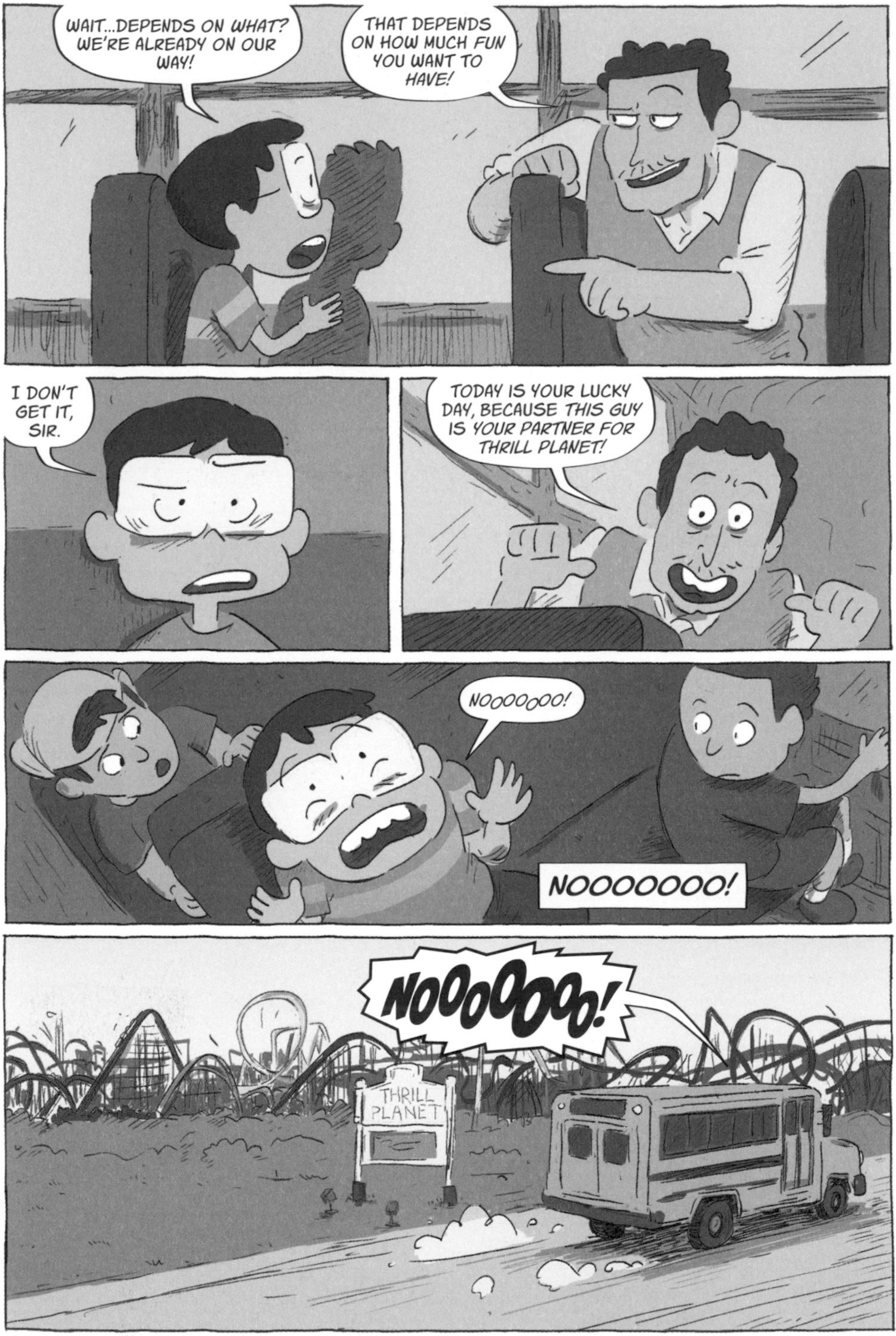
WAIT...DEPENDS ON WHAT? WE'RE ALREADY ON OUR WAY!
THAT DEPENDS ON HOW MUCH FUN YOU WANT TO HAVE!
I DON'T GET IT, SIR.
TODAY IS YOUR LUCKY DAY, BECAUSE THIS GUY IS YOUR PARTNER FOR THRILL PLANET!
NOOOOOOO!
NOOOOOOO!
NOOOOOOO!
THRILL PLANET

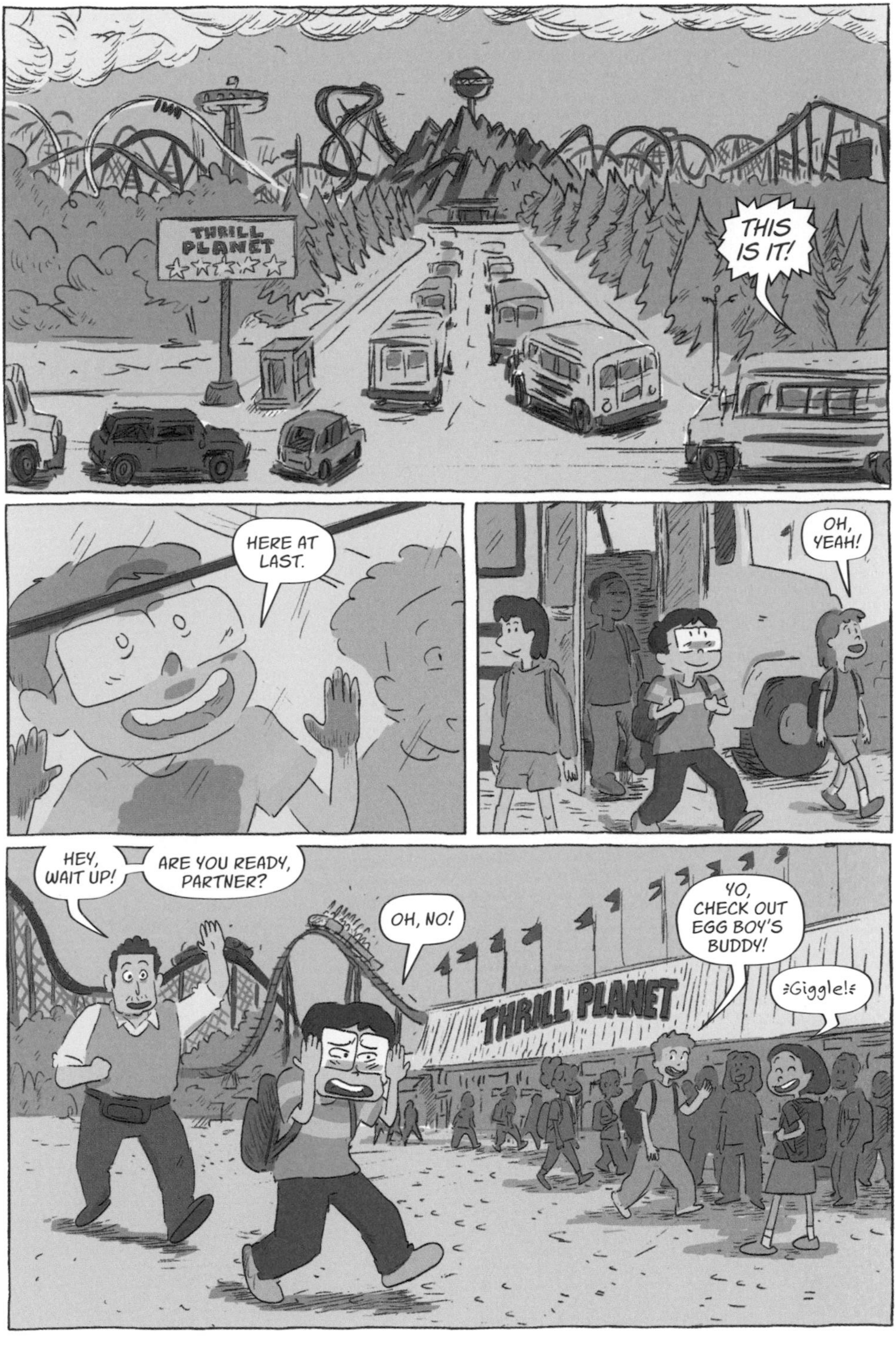
THRILL PLANET
THIS IS IT!
HERE AT LAST.
OH, YEAH!
HEY, WAIT UP!
ARE YOU READY, PARTNER?
OH, NO!
YO, CHECK OUT EGG BOY'S BUDDY!
THRILL PLANET
Giggle!

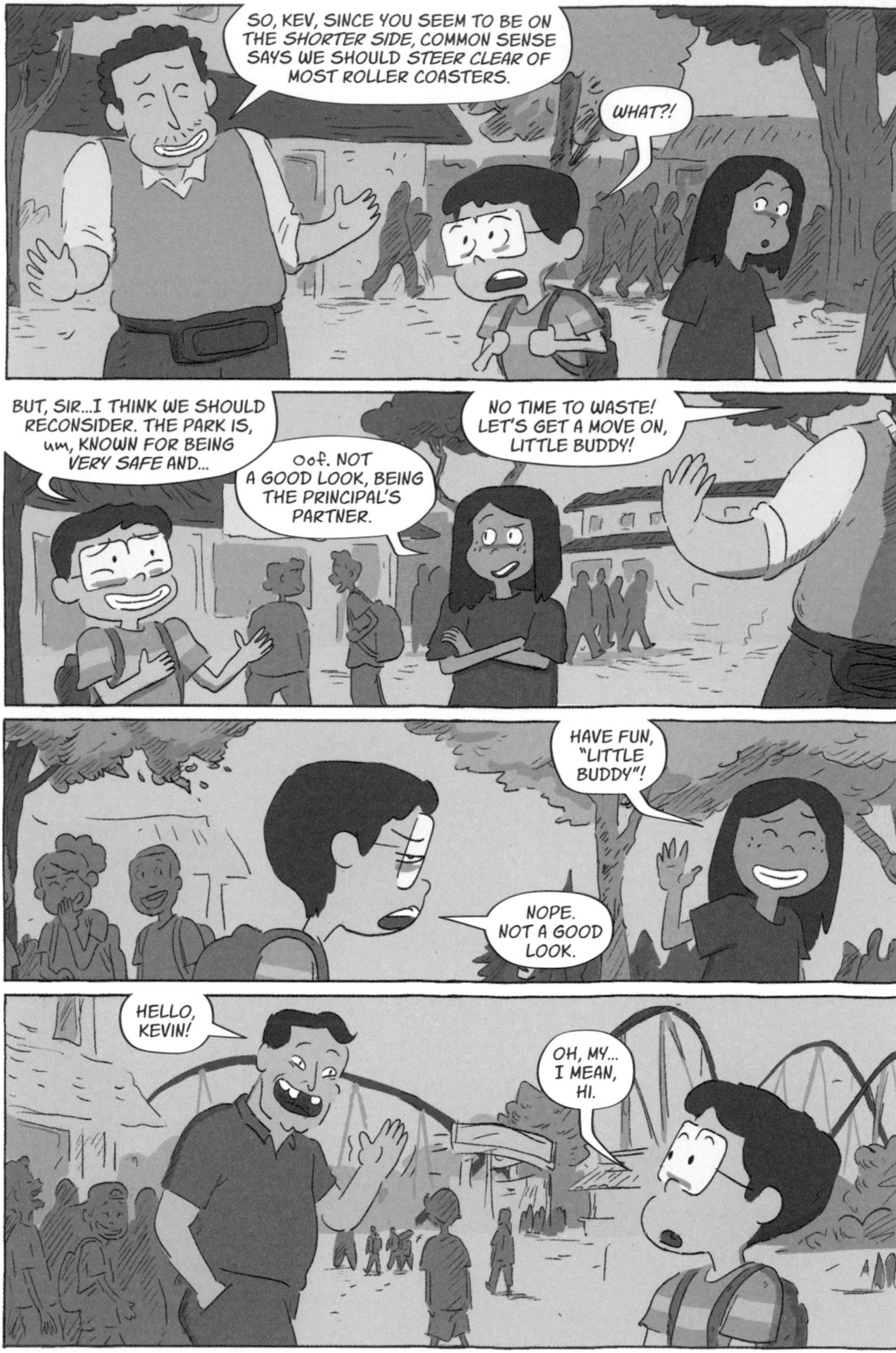
SO, KEV, SINCE YOU SEEM TO BE ON THE SHORTER SIDE, COMMON SENSE SAYS WE SHOULD STEER CLEAR OF MOST ROLLER COASTERS.
WHAT?!
BUT, SIR...I THINK WE SHOULD RECONSIDER. THE PARK IS, um, KNOWN FOR BEING VERY SAFE AND...
Oof. NOT A GOOD LOOK, BEING THE PRINCIPAL'S PARTNER.
NO TIME TO WASTE! LET'S GET A MOVE ON, LITTLE BUDDY!
HAVE FUN, "LITTLE BUDDY"!
NOPE. NOT A GOOD LOOK.
HELLO, KEVIN!
OH, MY... I MEAN, HI.

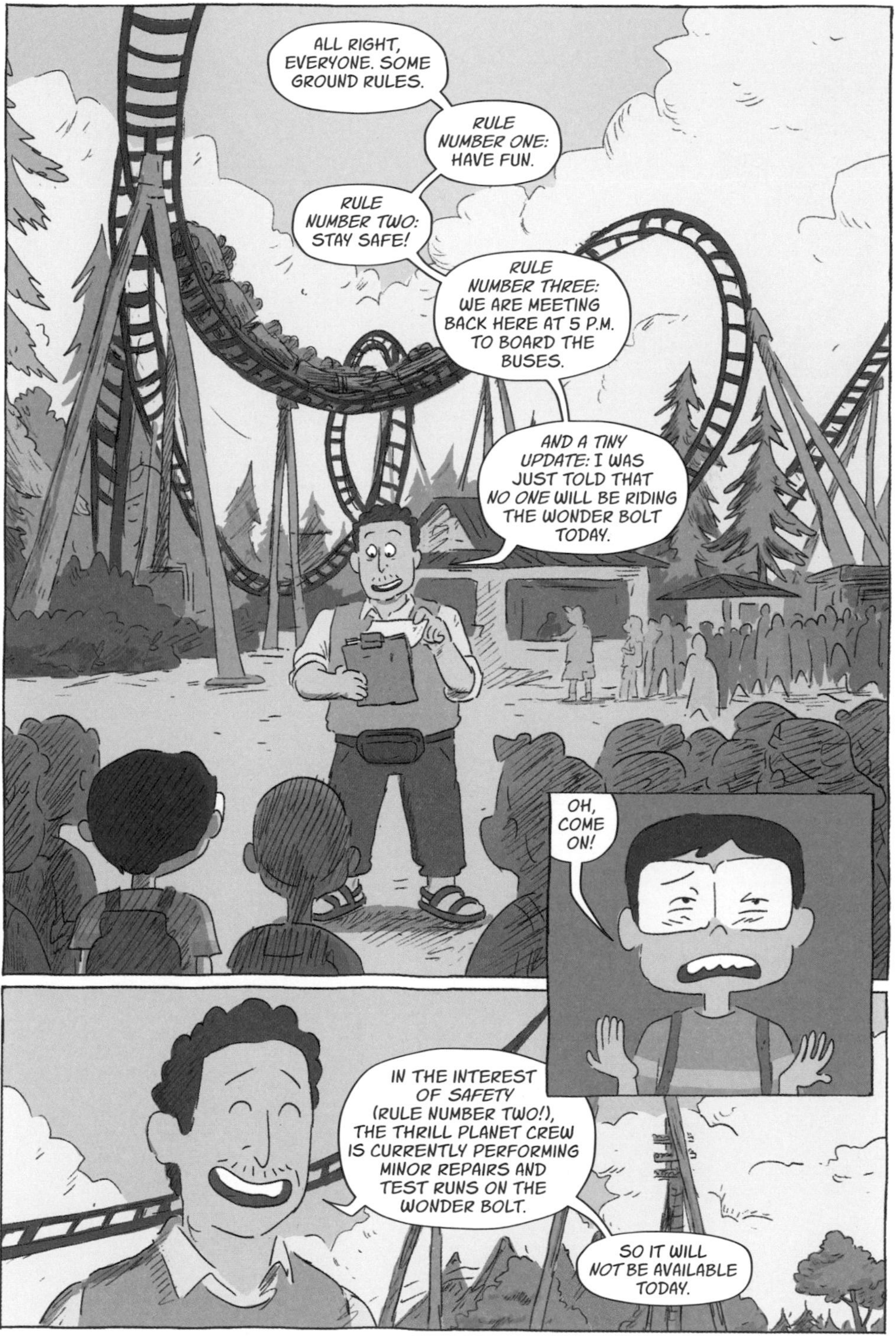
ALL RIGHT, EVERYONE. SOME GROUND RULES.
RULE NUMBER ONE: HAVE FUN.
RULE NUMBER TWO: STAY SAFE!
RULE NUMBER THREE: WE ARE MEETING BACK HERE AT 5 P.M. TO BOARD THE BUSES.
AND A TINY UPDATE: I WAS JUST TOLD THAT NO ONE WILL BE RIDING THE WONDER BOLT TODAY.
OH, COME ON!
IN THE INTEREST OF SAFETY (RULE NUMBER TWO!), THE THRILL PLANET CREW IS CURRENTLY PERFORMING MINOR REPAIRS AND TEST RUNS ON THE WONDER BOLT.
SO IT WILL NOT BE AVAILABLE TODAY.

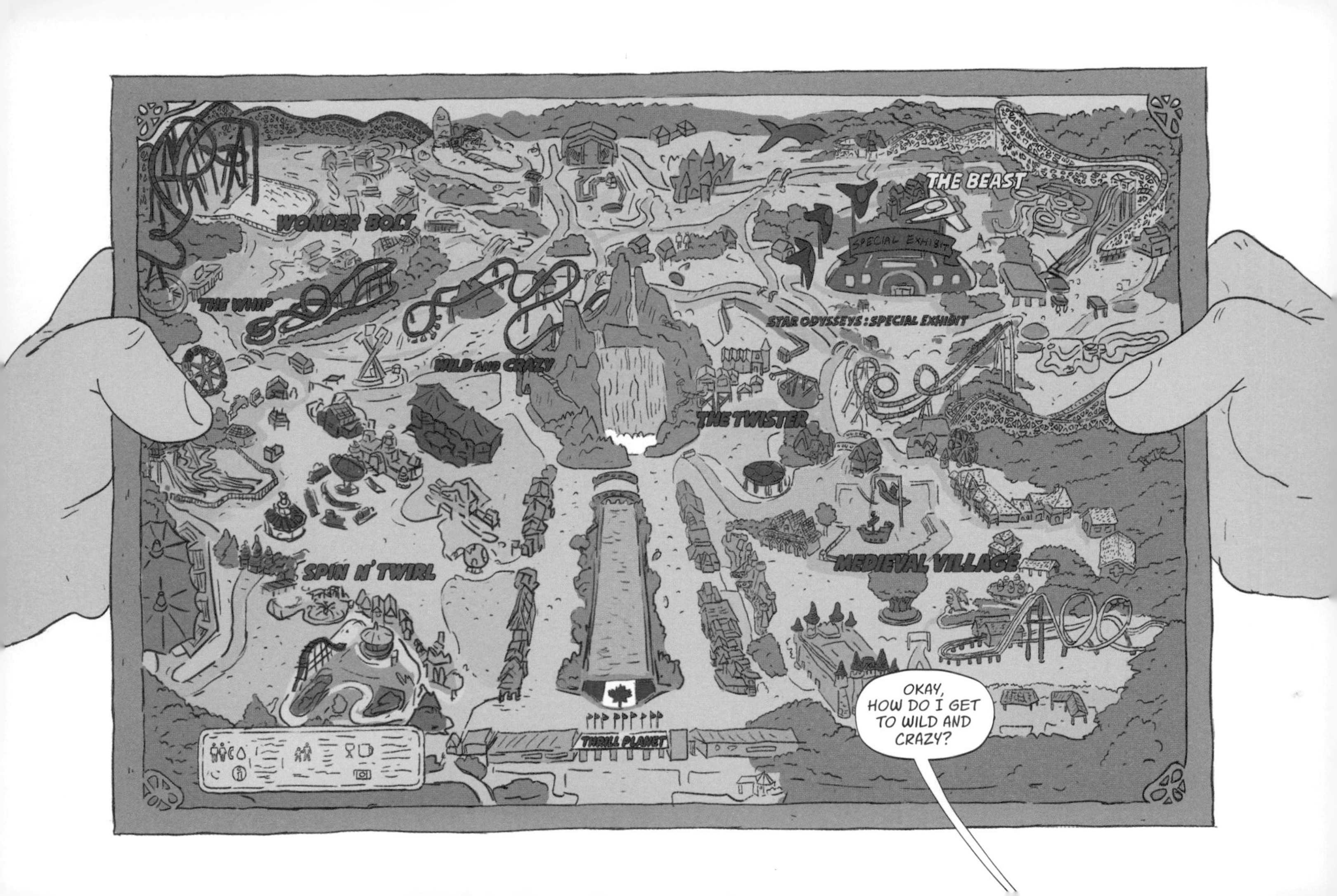
WONDER BOLT
THE BEAST
SPECIAL EXHIBIT
THE WHIP
STAR ODYSSEYS : SPECIAL EXHIBIT
WILD AND CRAZY
THE TWISTER
SPIN N' TWIRL
MEDIEVAL VILLAGE
THRILL PLANET
OKAY, HOW DO I GET TO WILD AND CRAZY?

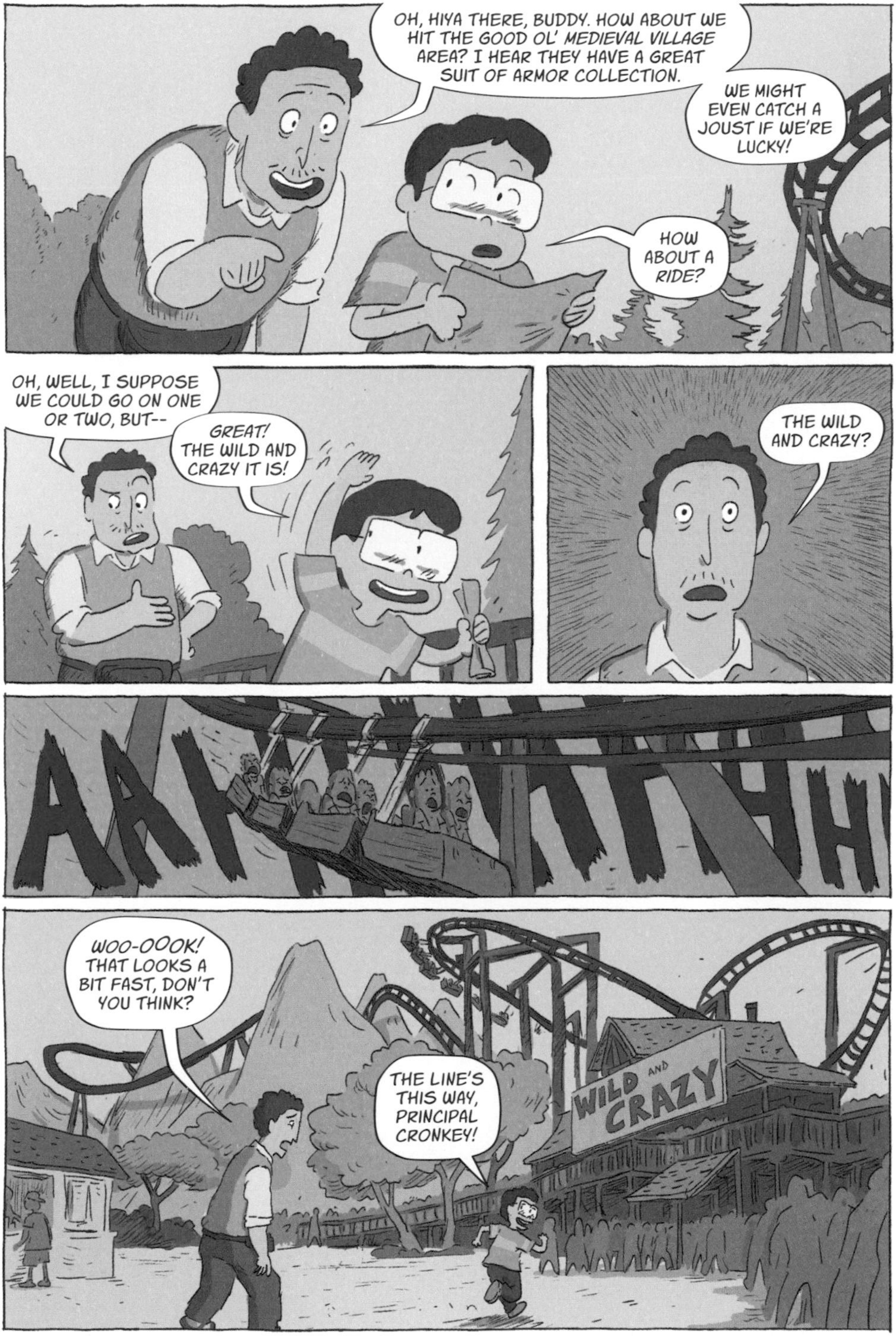
OH, HIYA THERE, BUDDY. HOW ABOUT WE HIT THE GOOD OL' MEDIEVAL VILLAGE AREA? I HEAR THEY HAVE A GREAT SUIT OF ARMOR COLLECTION.
WE MIGHT EVEN CATCH A JOUST IF WE'RE LUCKY!
HOW ABOUT A RIDE?
OH, WELL, I SUPPOSE WE COULD GO ON ONE OR TWO, BUT--
GREAT! THE WILD AND CRAZY IT IS!
THE WILD AND CRAZY?
AAHHHHHH
WOO-OOOK! THAT LOOKS A BIT FAST, DON'T YOU THINK?
THE LINE'S THIS WAY, PRINCIPAL CRONKEY!
WILD AND CRAZY

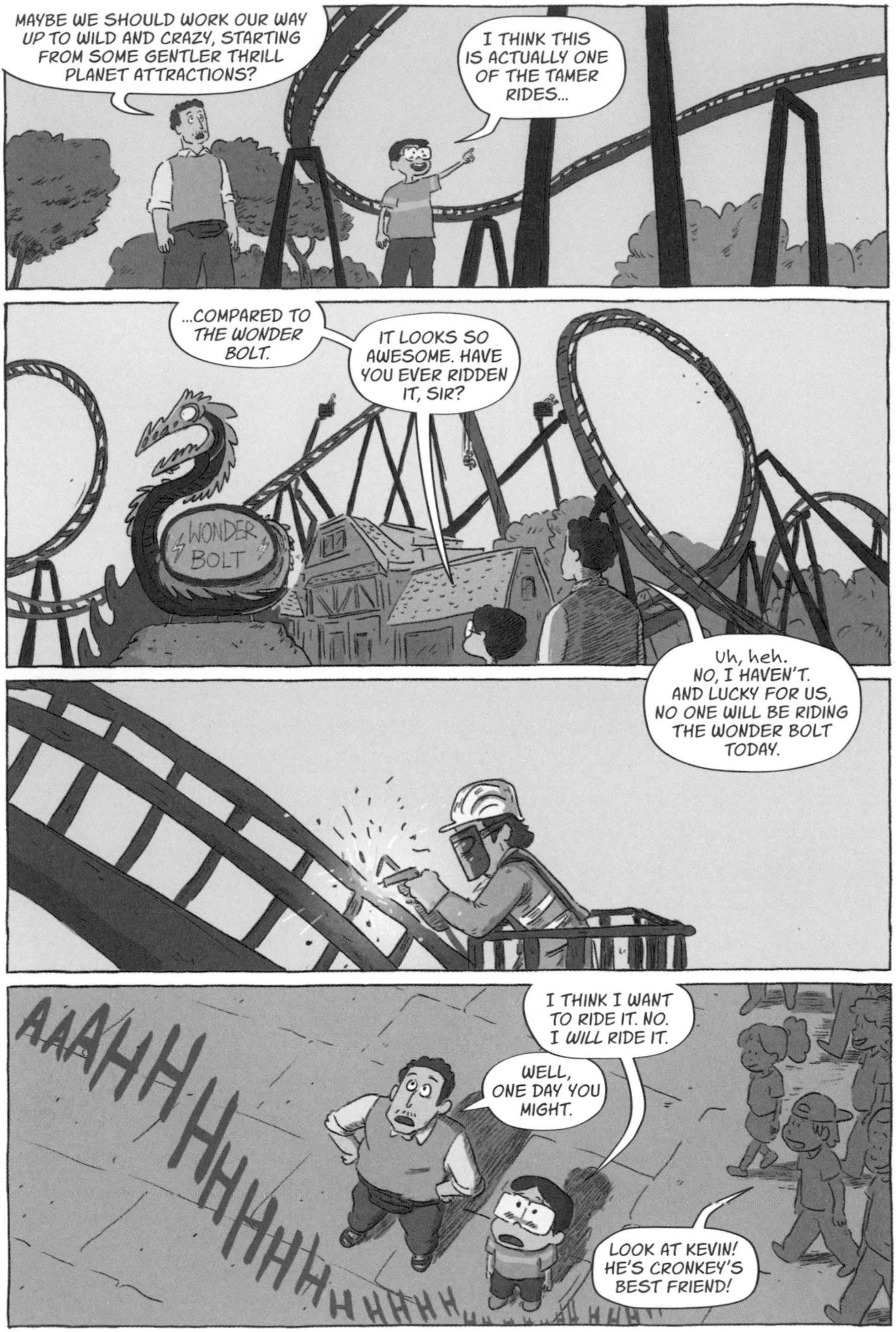
MAYBE WE SHOULD WORK OUR WAY UP TO WILD AND CRAZY, STARTING FROM SOME GENTLER THRILL PLANET ATTRACTIONS?
I THINK THIS IS ACTUALLY ONE OF THE TAMER RIDES...
...COMPARED TO THE WONDER BOLT.
IT LOOKS SO AWESOME. HAVE YOU EVER RIDDEN IT, SIR?
WONDER BOLT
Uh, heh. NO, I HAVEN'T. AND LUCKY FOR US, NO ONE WILL BE RIDING THE WONDER BOLT TODAY.
AAAHHHHHHHHHHHHHHHHHHH
I THINK I WANT TO RIDE IT. NO. I WILL RIDE IT.
WELL, ONE DAY YOU MIGHT.
LOOK AT KEVIN! HE'S CRONKEY'S BEST FRIEND!

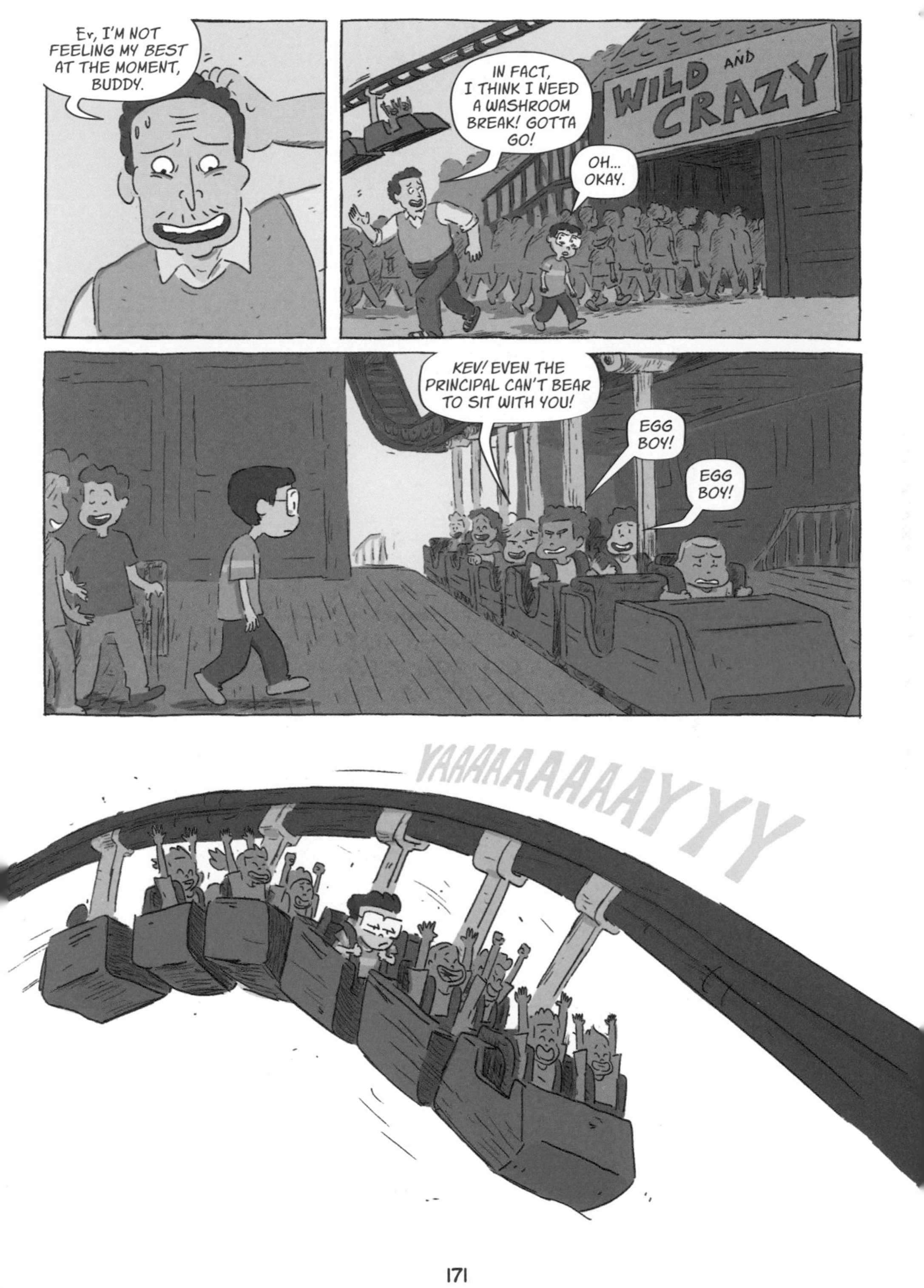
Er, I'M NOT FEELING MY BEST AT THE MOMENT, BUDDY.
IN FACT, I THINK I NEED A WASHROOM BREAK! GOTTA GO!
WILD AND CRAZY
OH... OKAY.
KEV! EVEN THE PRINCIPAL CAN'T BEAR TO SIT WITH YOU!
EGG BOY!
EGG BOY!
YAAAAAAAAAYYY

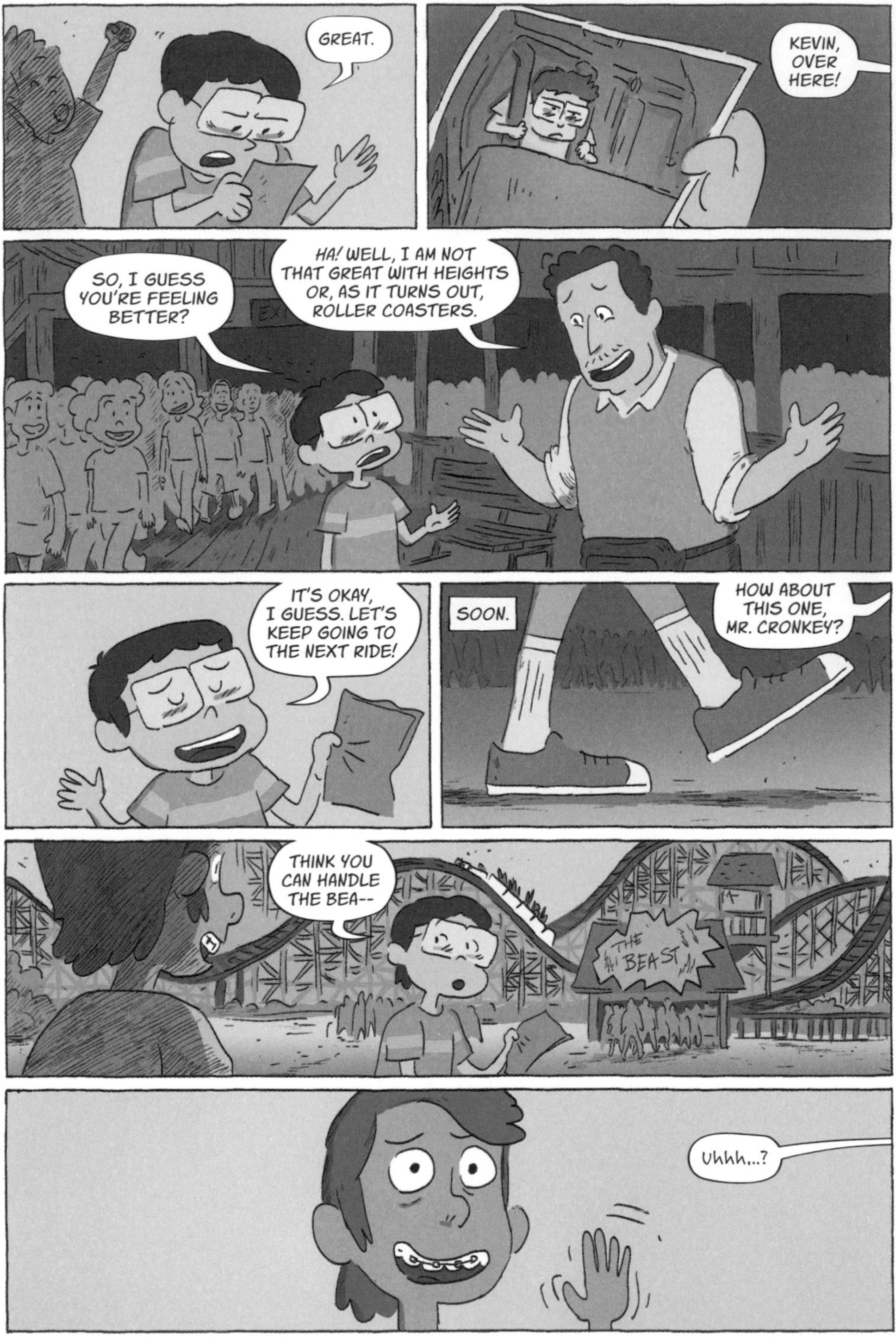
GREAT.
KEVIN, OVER HERE!
SO, I GUESS YOU'RE FEELING BETTER?
HA! WELL, I AM NOT THAT GREAT WITH HEIGHTS OR, AS IT TURNS OUT, ROLLER COASTERS.
EXIT
IT'S OKAY, I GUESS. LET'S KEEP GOING TO THE NEXT RIDE!
SOON.
HOW ABOUT THIS ONE, MR. CRONKEY?
THINK YOU CAN HANDLE THE BEA--
THE BEAST
Uhhh...?

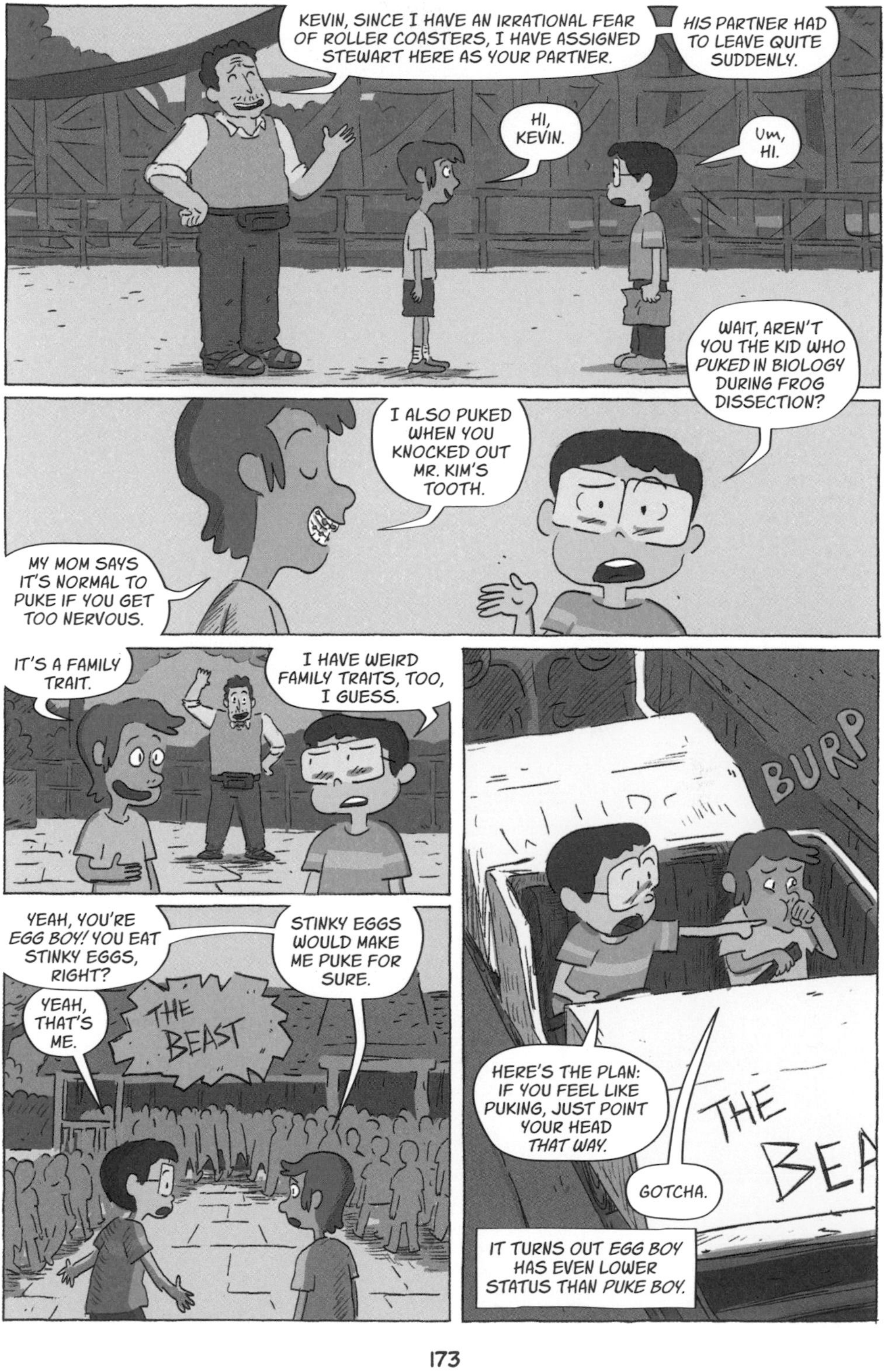
KEVIN, SINCE I HAVE AN IRRATIONAL FEAR OF ROLLER COASTERS, I HAVE ASSIGNED STEWART HERE AS YOUR PARTNER.
HIS PARTNER HAD TO LEAVE QUITE SUDDENLY.
HI, KEVIN.
UM, HI.
WAIT, AREN'T YOU THE KID WHO PUKED IN BIOLOGY DURING FROG DISSECTION?
I ALSO PUKED WHEN YOU KNOCKED OUT MR. KIM'S TOOTH.
MY MOM SAYS IT'S NORMAL TO PUKE IF YOU GET TOO NERVOUS.
IT'S A FAMILY TRAIT.
I HAVE WEIRD FAMILY TRAITS, TOO, I GUESS.
YEAH, YOU'RE EGG BOY! YOU EAT STINKY EGGS, RIGHT?
STINKY EGGS WOULD MAKE ME PUKE FOR SURE.
YEAH, THAT'S ME.
THE BEAST
BURP
HERE'S THE PLAN: IF YOU FEEL LIKE PUKING, JUST POINT YOUR HEAD THAT WAY.
GOTCHA.
THE BEA
IT TURNS OUT EGG BOY HAS EVEN LOWER STATUS THAN PUKE BOY.

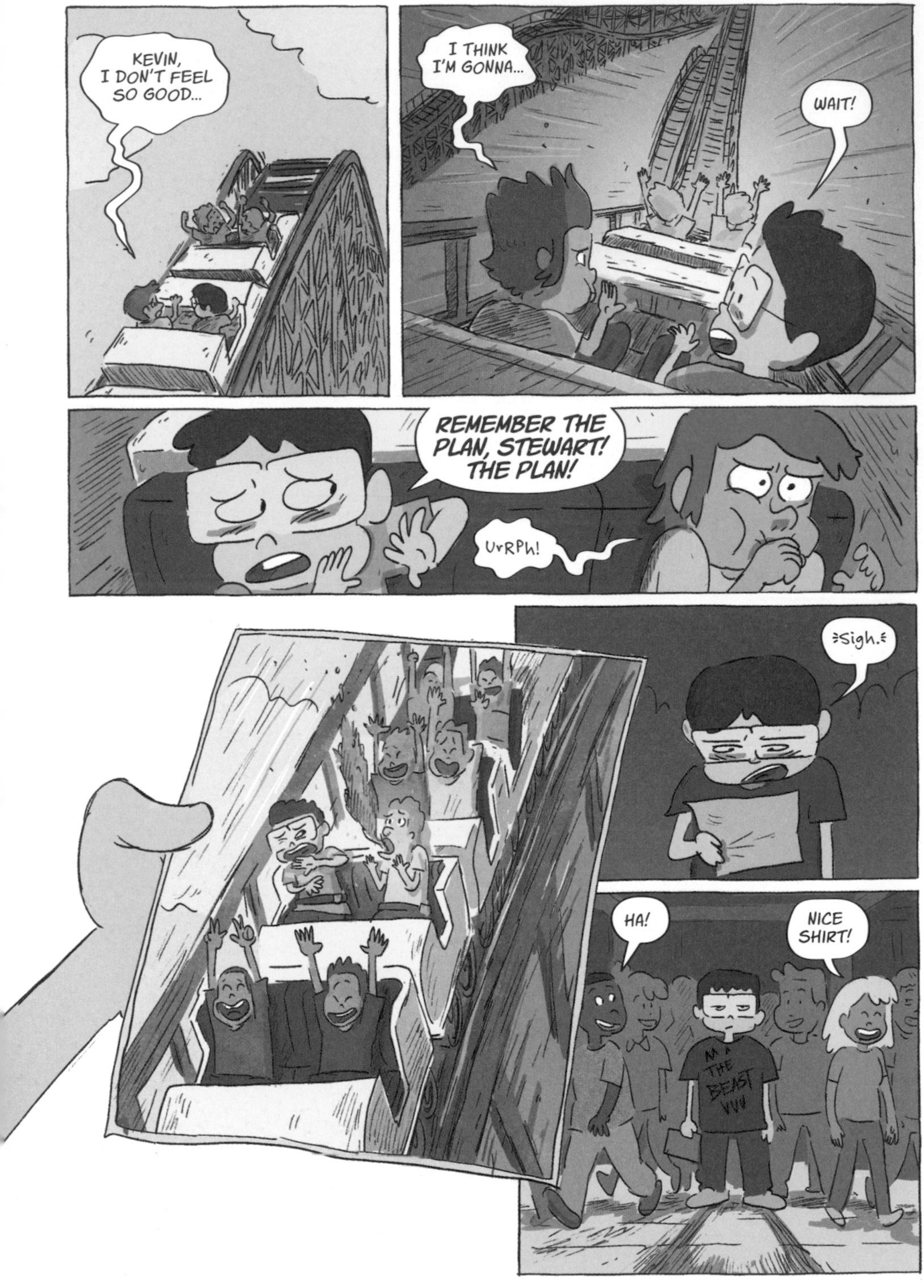
KEVIN, I DON'T FEEL SO GOOD...
I THINK I'M GONNA...
WAIT!
REMEMBER THE PLAN, STEWART! THE PLAN!
UrRPh!
Sigh.
HA!
NICE SHIRT!
THE BEAST

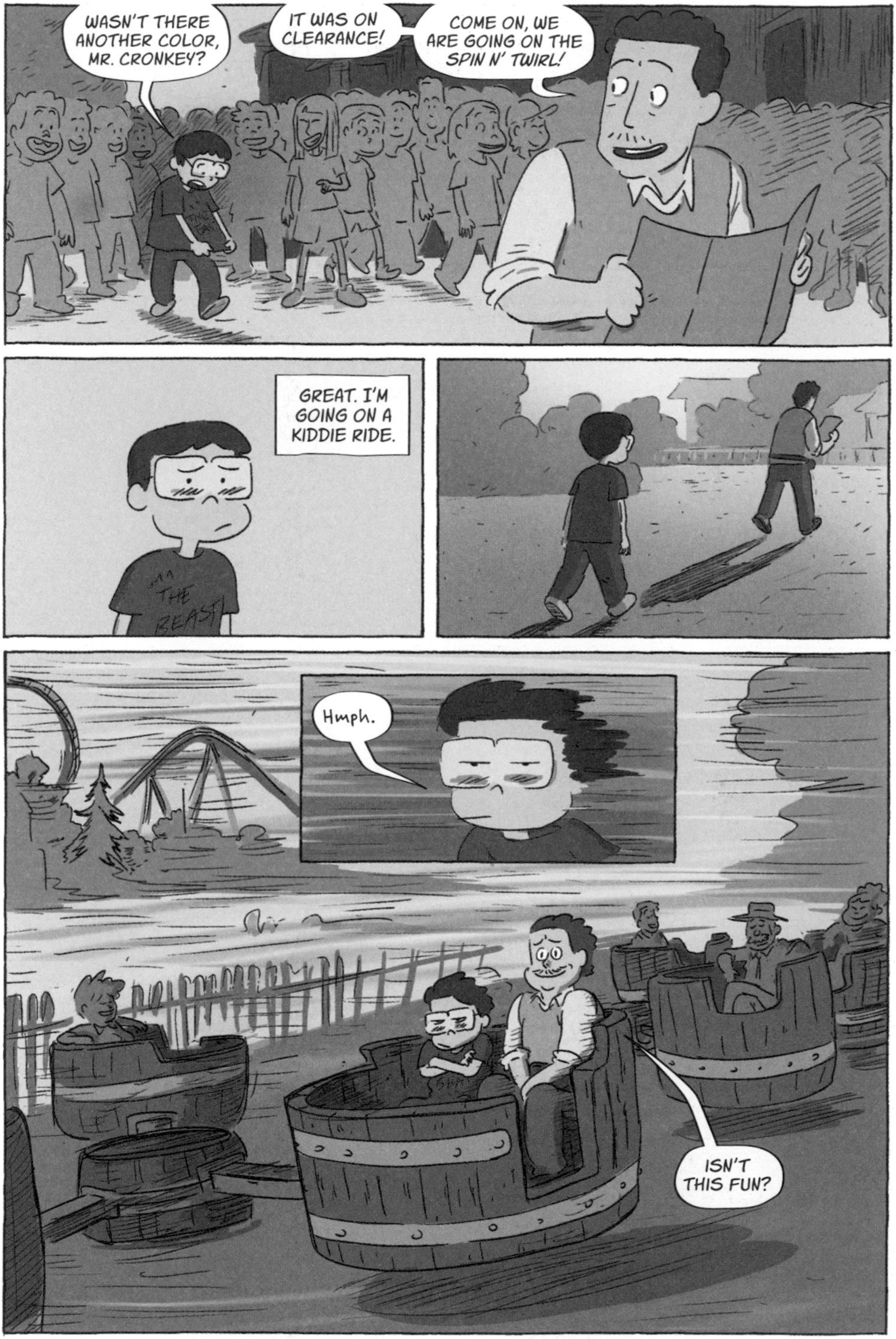
WASN'T THERE ANOTHER COLOR, MR. CRONKEY?
IT WAS ON CLEARANCE!
COME ON, WE ARE GOING ON THE SPIN N' TWIRL!
GREAT. I'M GOING ON A KIDDIE RIDE.
Hmph.
ISN'T THIS FUN?

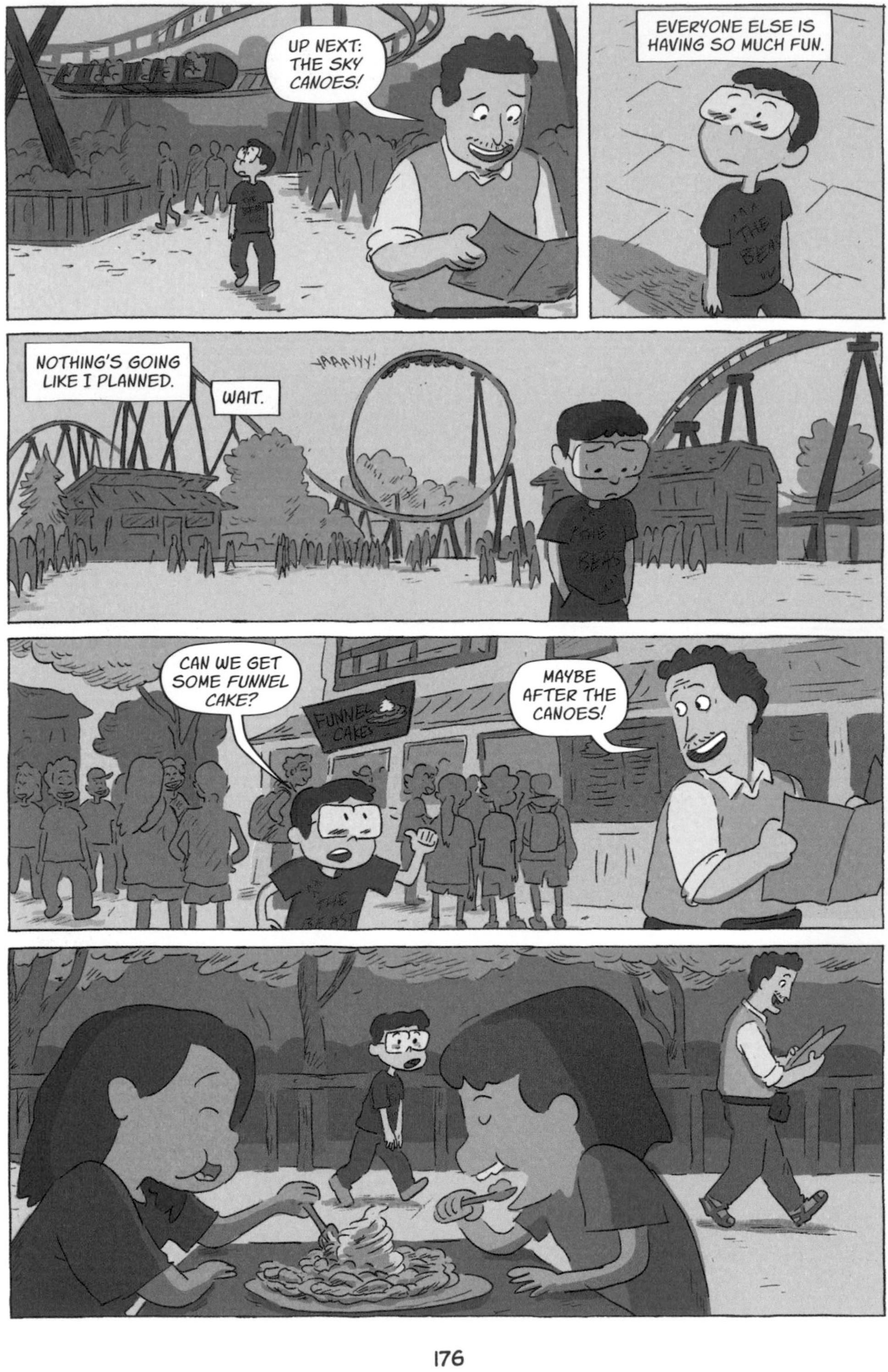
UP NEXT: THE SKY CANOES!
EVERYONE ELSE IS HAVING SO MUCH FUN.
NOTHING'S GOING LIKE I PLANNED.
WAIT.
CAN WE GET SOME FUNNEL CAKE?
FUNNEL CAKES
MAYBE AFTER THE CANOES!

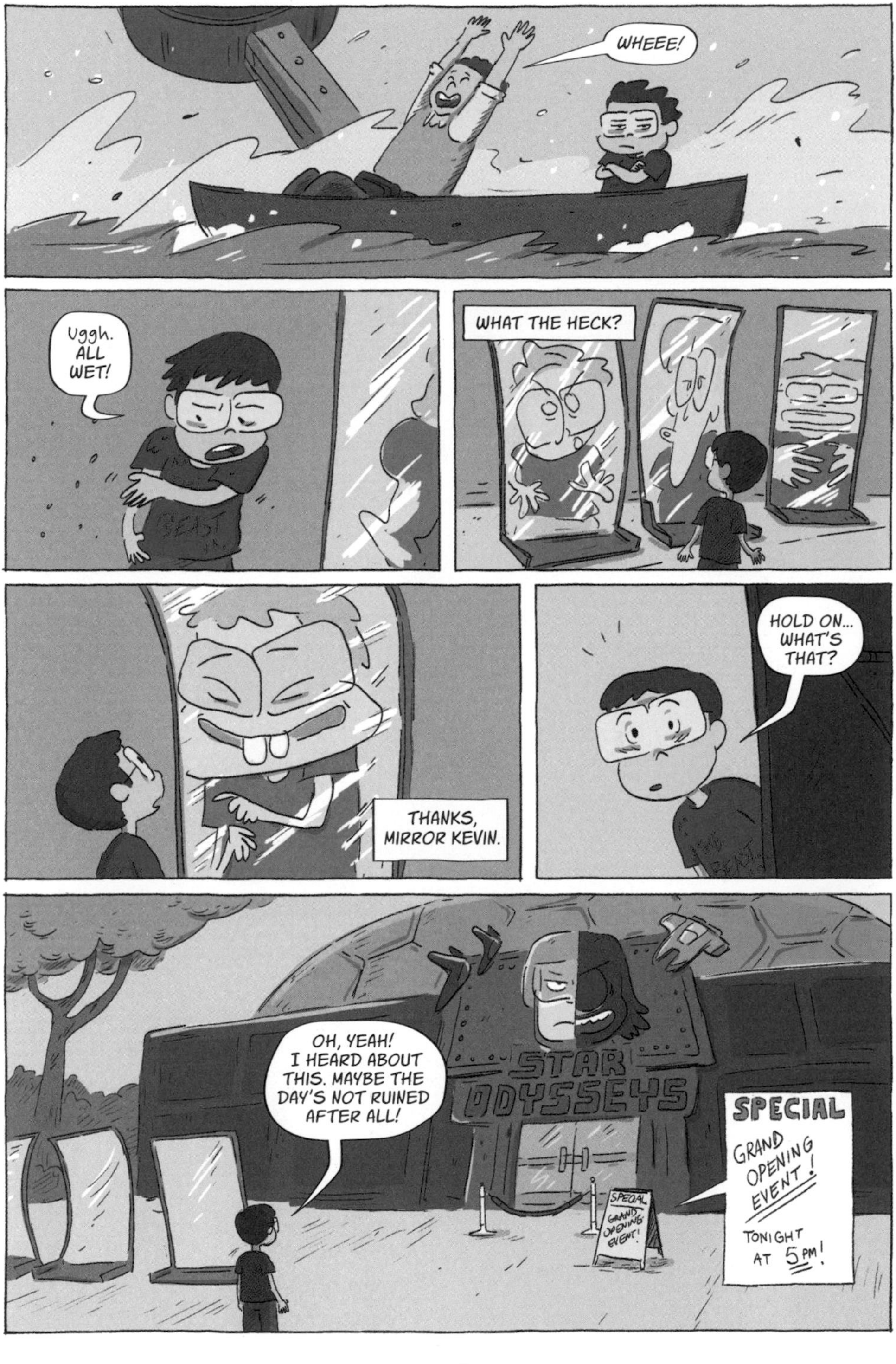
WHEEE!
Uggh. ALL WET!
WHAT THE HECK?
THANKS, MIRROR KEVIN.
HOLD ON... WHAT'S THAT?
OH, YEAH! I HEARD ABOUT THIS. MAYBE THE DAY'S NOT RUINED AFTER ALL!
STAR ODYSSEYS
SPECIAL GRAND OPENING EVENT!
SPECIAL GRAND OPENING EVENT! TONIGHT AT 5PM!

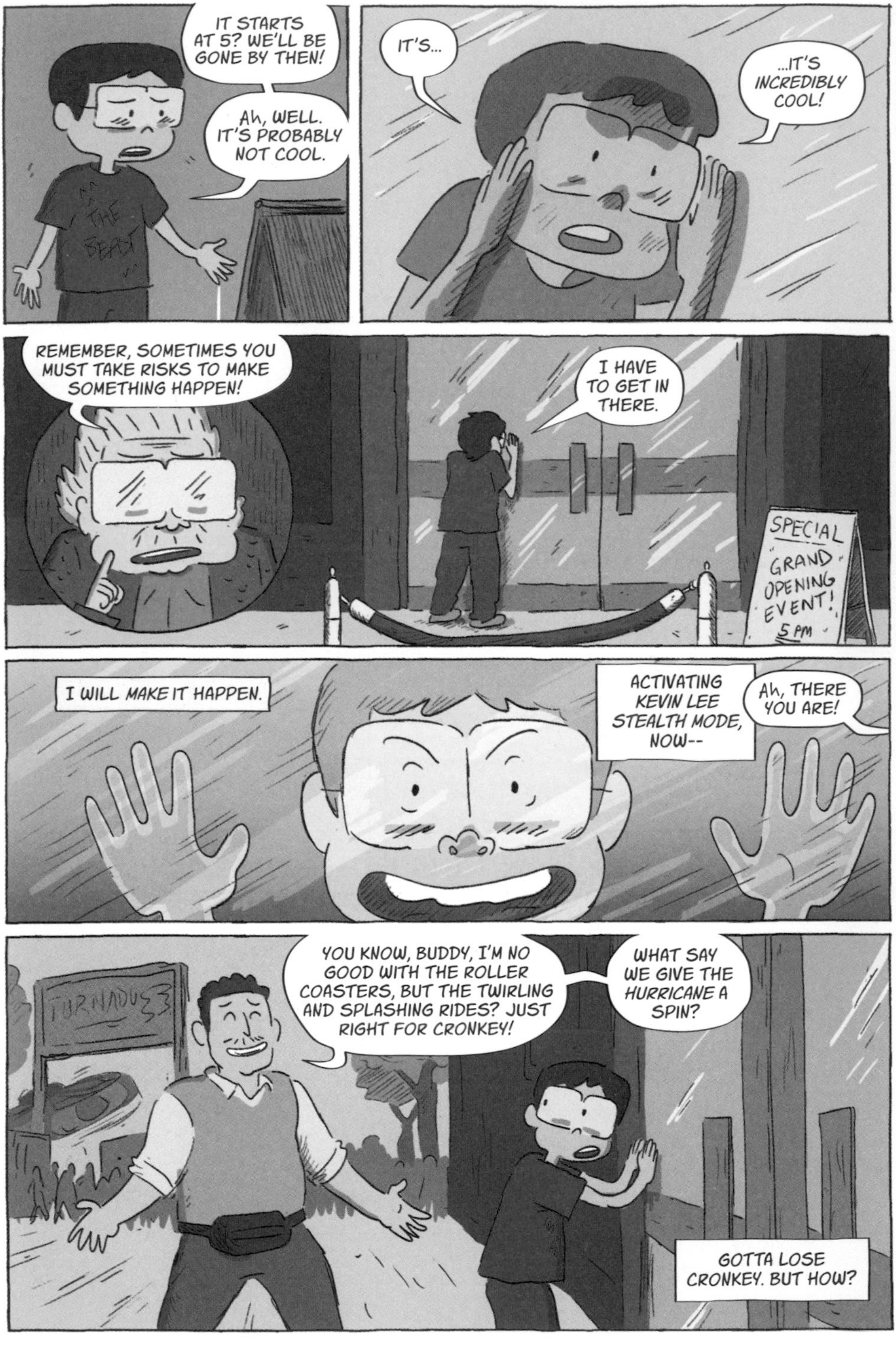
IT STARTS AT 5? WE'LL BE GONE BY THEN!
Ah, WELL. IT'S PROBABLY NOT COOL.
IT'S...
...IT'S INCREDIBLY COOL!
REMEMBER, SOMETIMES YOU MUST TAKE RISKS TO MAKE SOMETHING HAPPEN!
I HAVE TO GET IN THERE.
SPECIAL "GRAND OPENING" EVENT! 5 PM
I WILL MAKE IT HAPPEN.
ACTIVATING KEVIN LEE STEALTH MODE, NOW--
Ah, THERE YOU ARE!
YOU KNOW, BUDDY, I'M NO GOOD WITH THE ROLLER COASTERS, BUT THE TWIRLING AND SPLASHING RIDES? JUST RIGHT FOR CRONKEY!
WHAT SAY WE GIVE THE HURRICANE A SPIN?
GOTTA LOSE CRONKEY. BUT HOW?

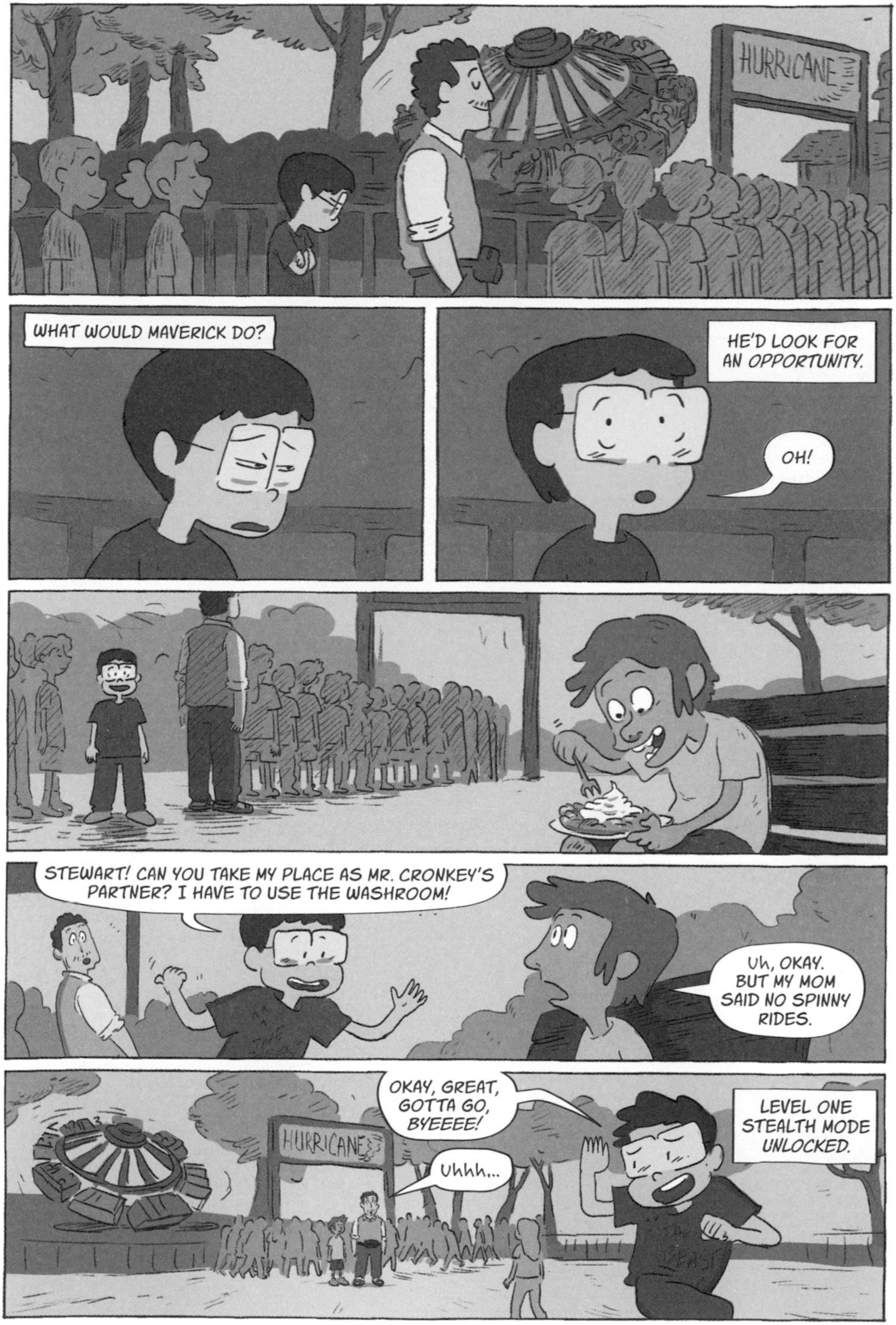
HURRICANE
WHAT WOULD MAVERICK DO?
HE'D LOOK FOR AN OPPORTUNITY.
OH!
STEWART! CAN YOU TAKE MY PLACE AS MR. CRONKEY'S PARTNER? I HAVE TO USE THE WASHROOM!
Uh, OKAY. BUT MY MOM SAID NO SPINNY RIDES.
HURRICANE
OKAY, GREAT, GOTTA GO, BYEEEE!
Uhhh...
LEVEL ONE STEALTH MODE UNLOCKED.

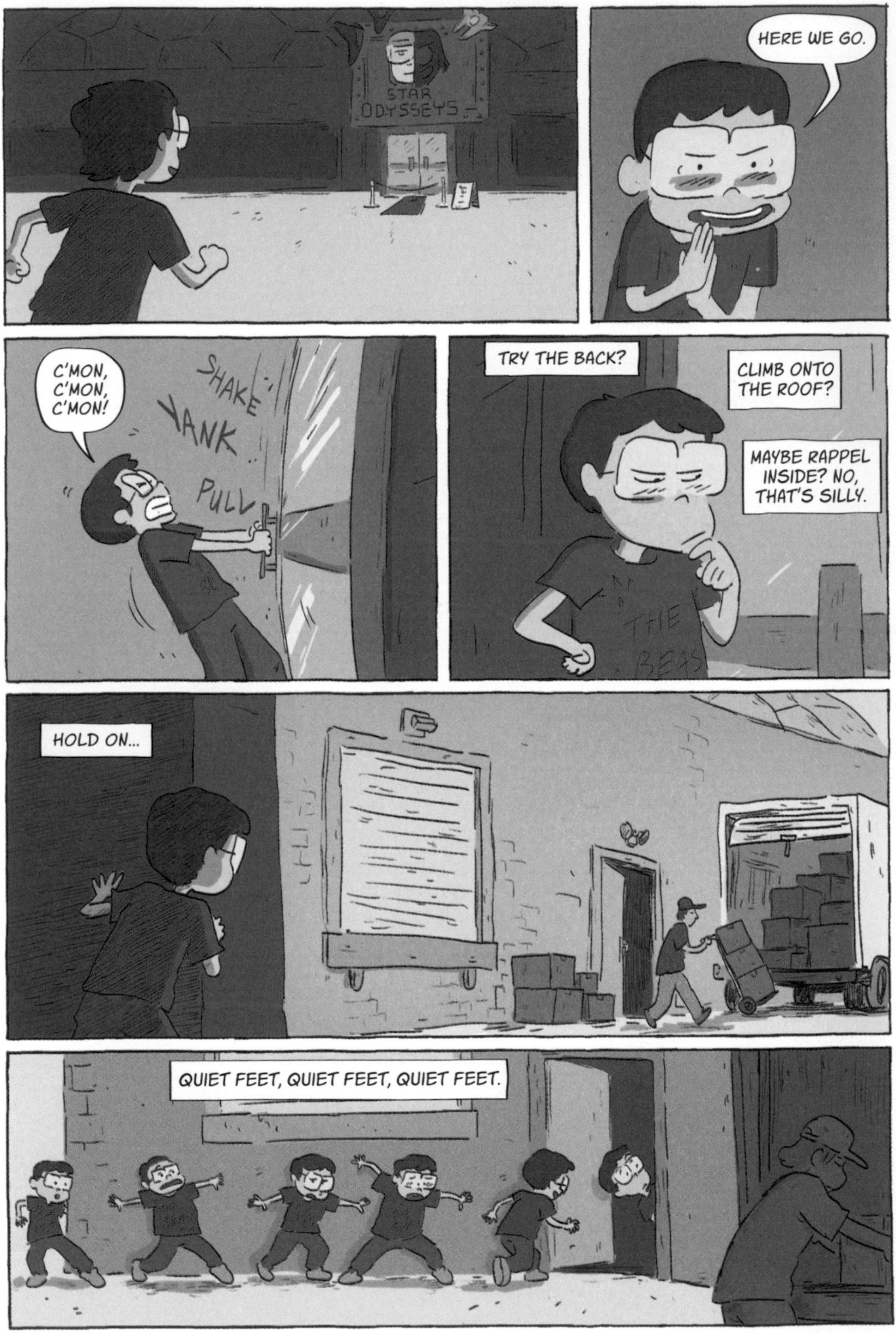
STAR ODYSSEYS
HERE WE GO.
C'MON, C'MON, C'MON!
SHAKE
YANK
PULL
TRY THE BACK?
CLIMB ONTO THE ROOF?
MAYBE RAPPEL INSIDE? NO, THAT'S SILLY.
HOLD ON...
QUIET FEET, QUIET FEET, QUIET FEET.

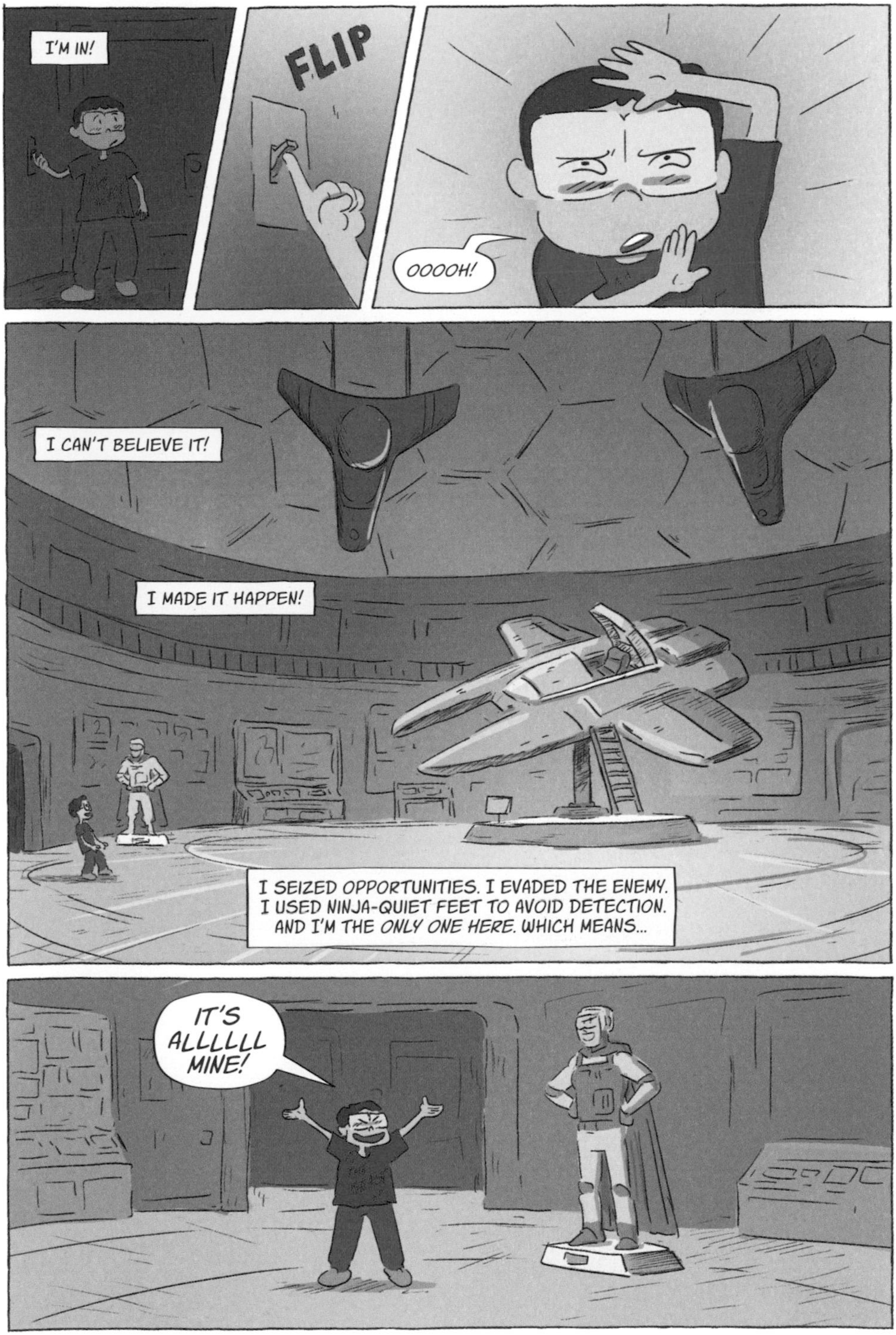
I'M IN!
FLIP
OOOOH!
I CAN'T BELIEVE IT!
I MADE IT HAPPEN!
I SEIZED OPPORTUNITIES. I EVADED THE ENEMY. I USED NINJA-QUIET FEET TO AVOID DETECTION. AND I'M THE ONLY ONE HERE. WHICH MEANS...
IT'S ALLLLLL MINE!

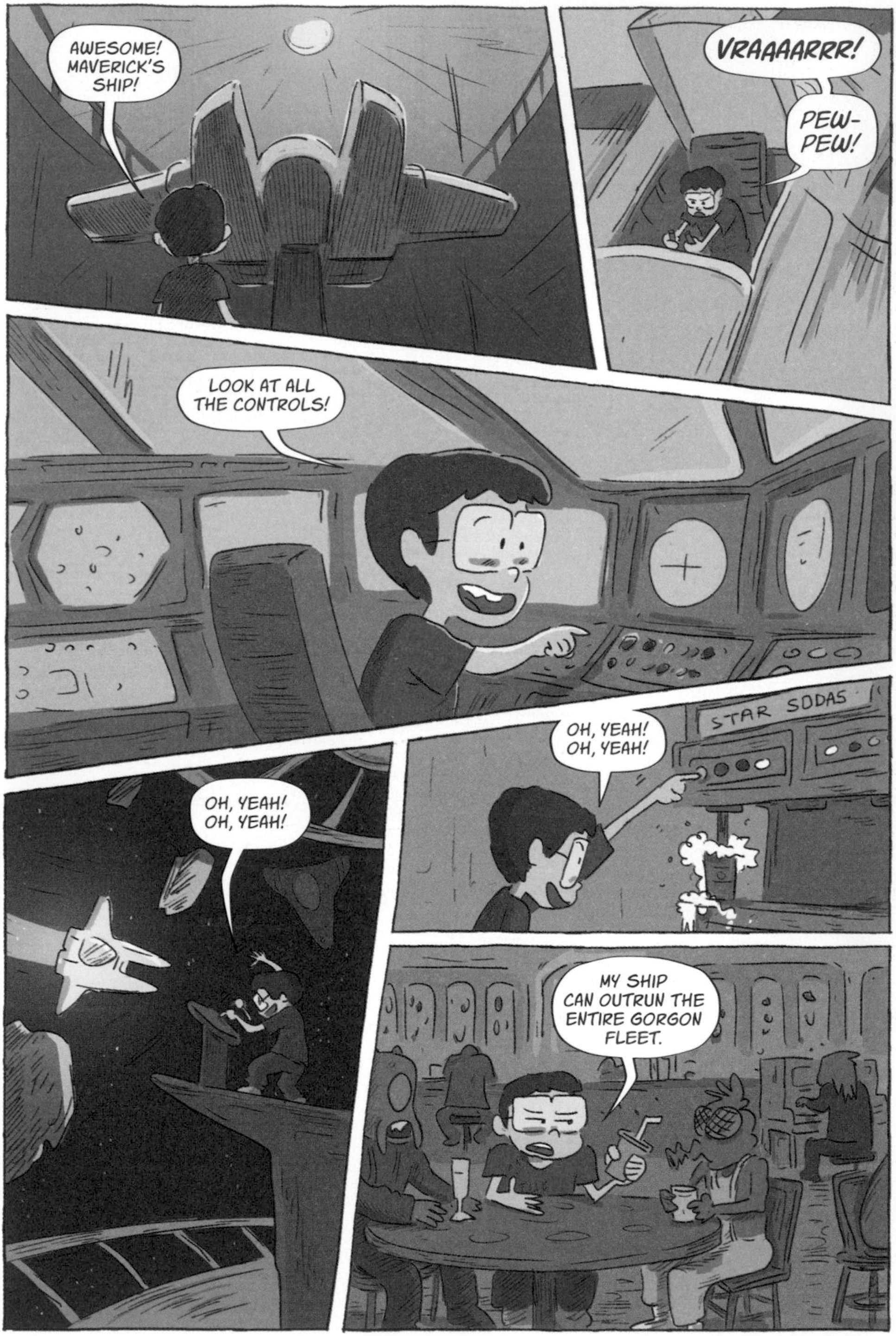
AWESOME! MAVERICK'S SHIP!
VRAAAARRR!
PEW-PEW!
LOOK AT ALL THE CONTROLS!
STAR SODAS
OH, YEAH! OH, YEAH!
OH, YEAH! OH, YEAH!
MY SHIP CAN OUTRUN THE ENTIRE GORGON FLEET.

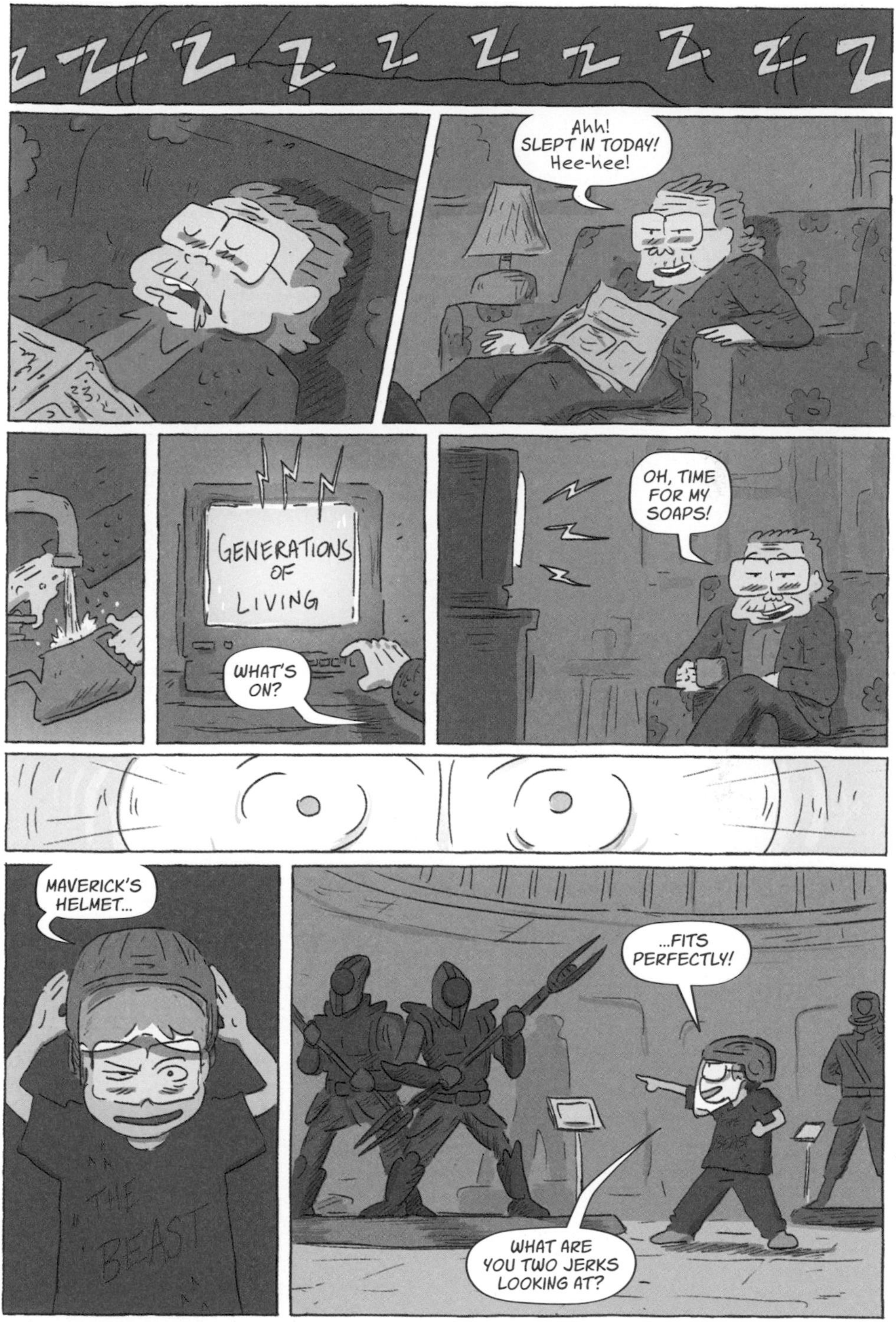
Z Z Z Z Z Z Z Z Z Z
Ahh! SLEPT IN TODAY! Hee-hee!
GENERATIONS OF LIVING
WHAT'S ON?
OH, TIME FOR MY SOAPS!
MAVERICK'S HELMET...
THE BEAST
...FITS PERFECTLY!
WHAT ARE YOU TWO JERKS LOOKING AT?

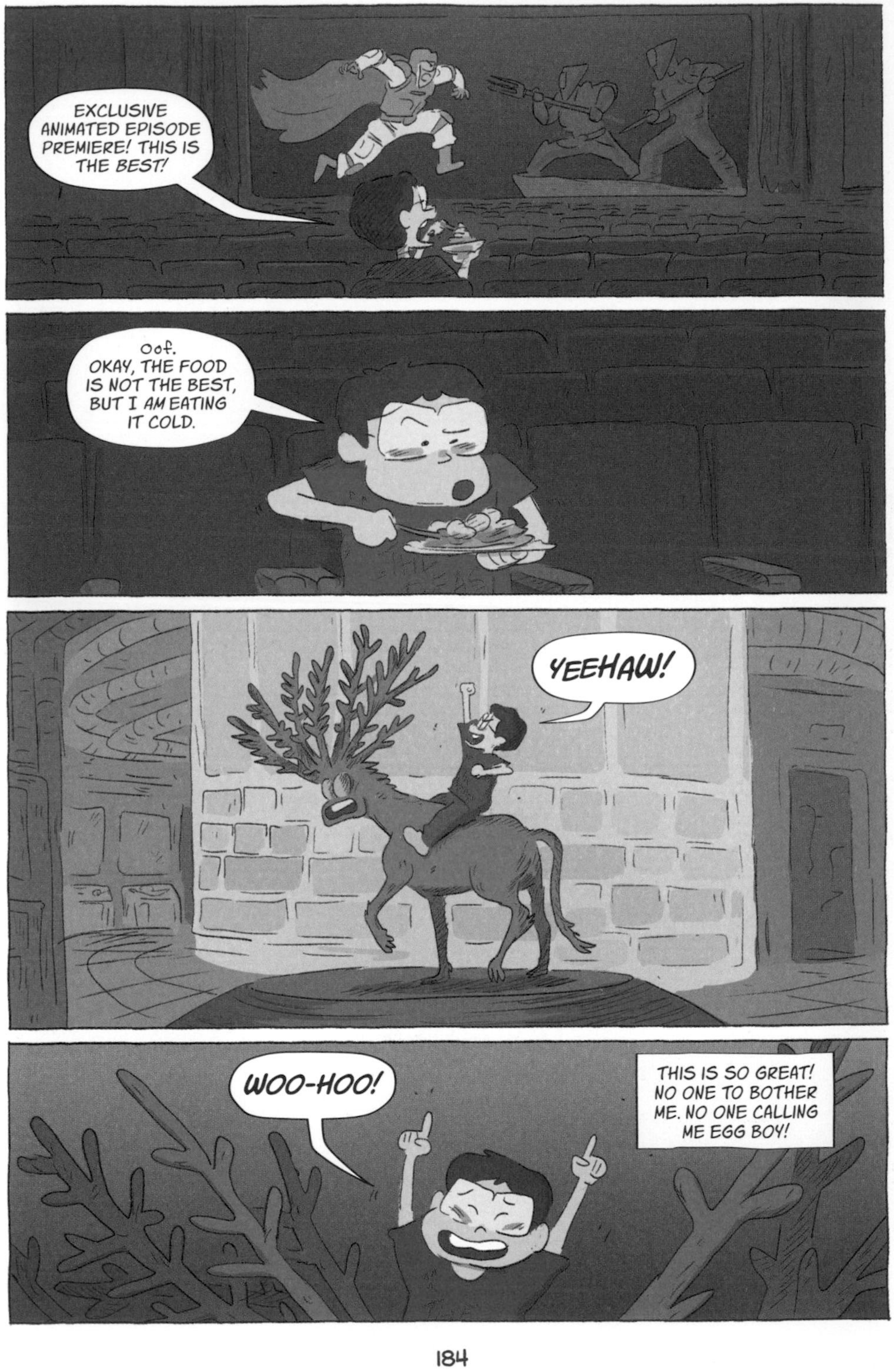
EXCLUSIVE ANIMATED EPISODE PREMIERE! THIS IS THE *BEST!*
Oof.
OKAY, THE FOOD IS NOT THE BEST, BUT I *AM* EATING IT COLD.
YEEHAW!
WOO-HOO!
THIS IS SO GREAT! NO ONE TO BOTHER ME. NO ONE CALLING ME EGG BOY!

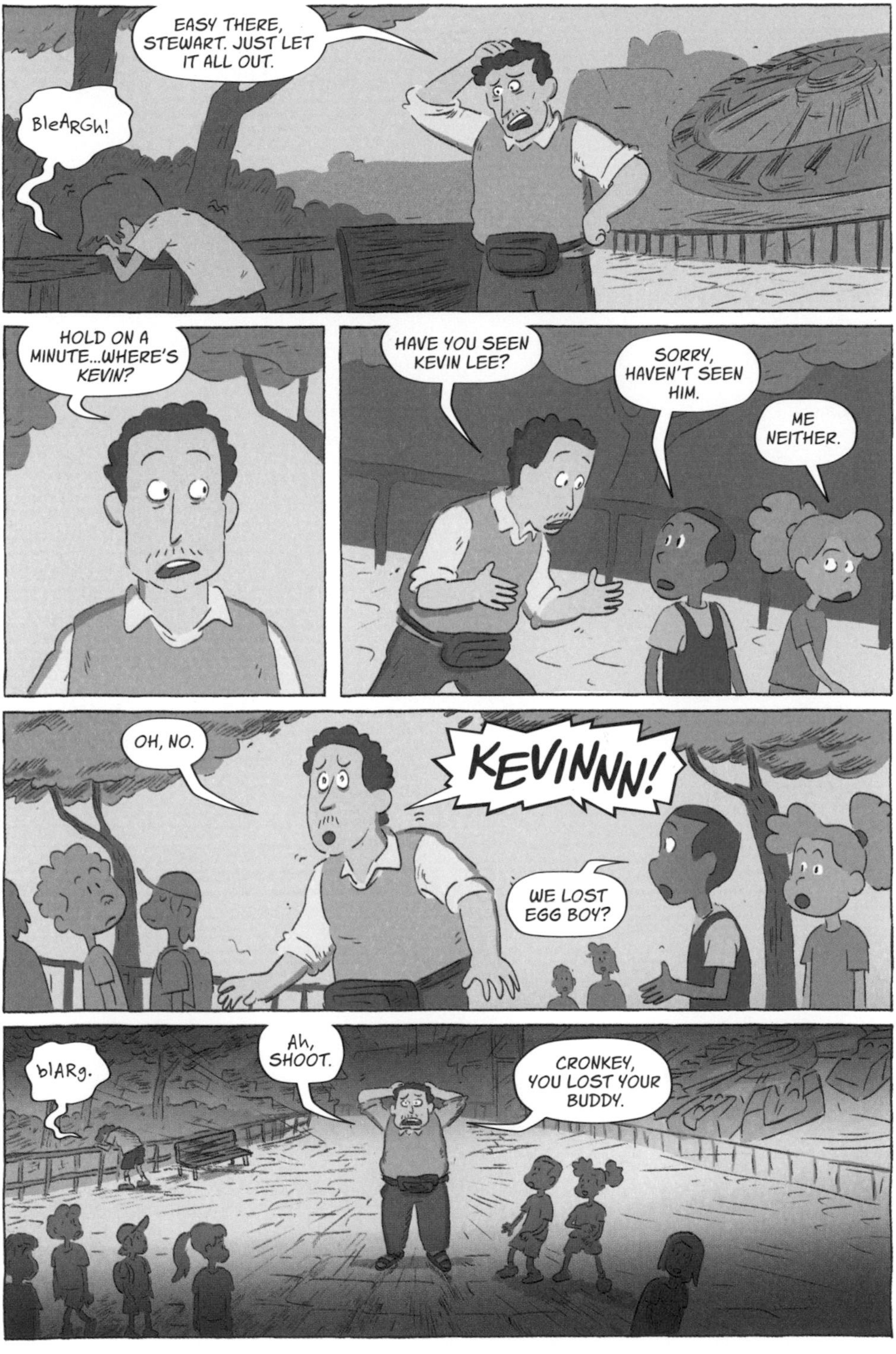
EASY THERE, STEWART. JUST LET IT ALL OUT.
BleARGh!
HOLD ON A MINUTE...WHERE'S KEVIN?
HAVE YOU SEEN KEVIN LEE?
SORRY, HAVEN'T SEEN HIM.
ME NEITHER.
OH, NO.
KEVINNN!
WE LOST EGG BOY?
blARg.
Ah, SHOOT.
CRONKEY, YOU LOST YOUR BUDDY.

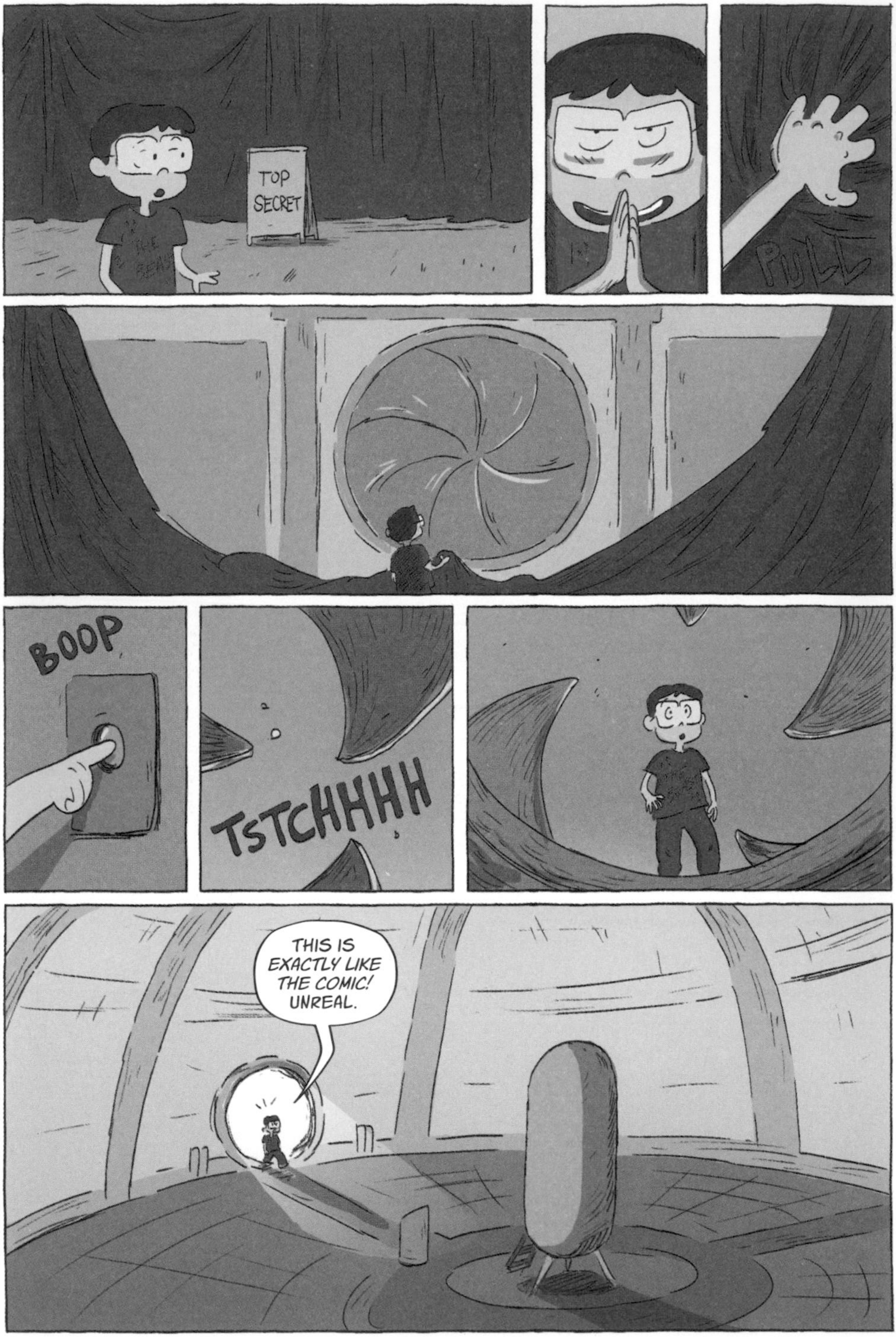
TOP SECRET
PULL
BOOP
TSTCHHHH
THIS IS EXACTLY LIKE THE COMIC! UNREAL.

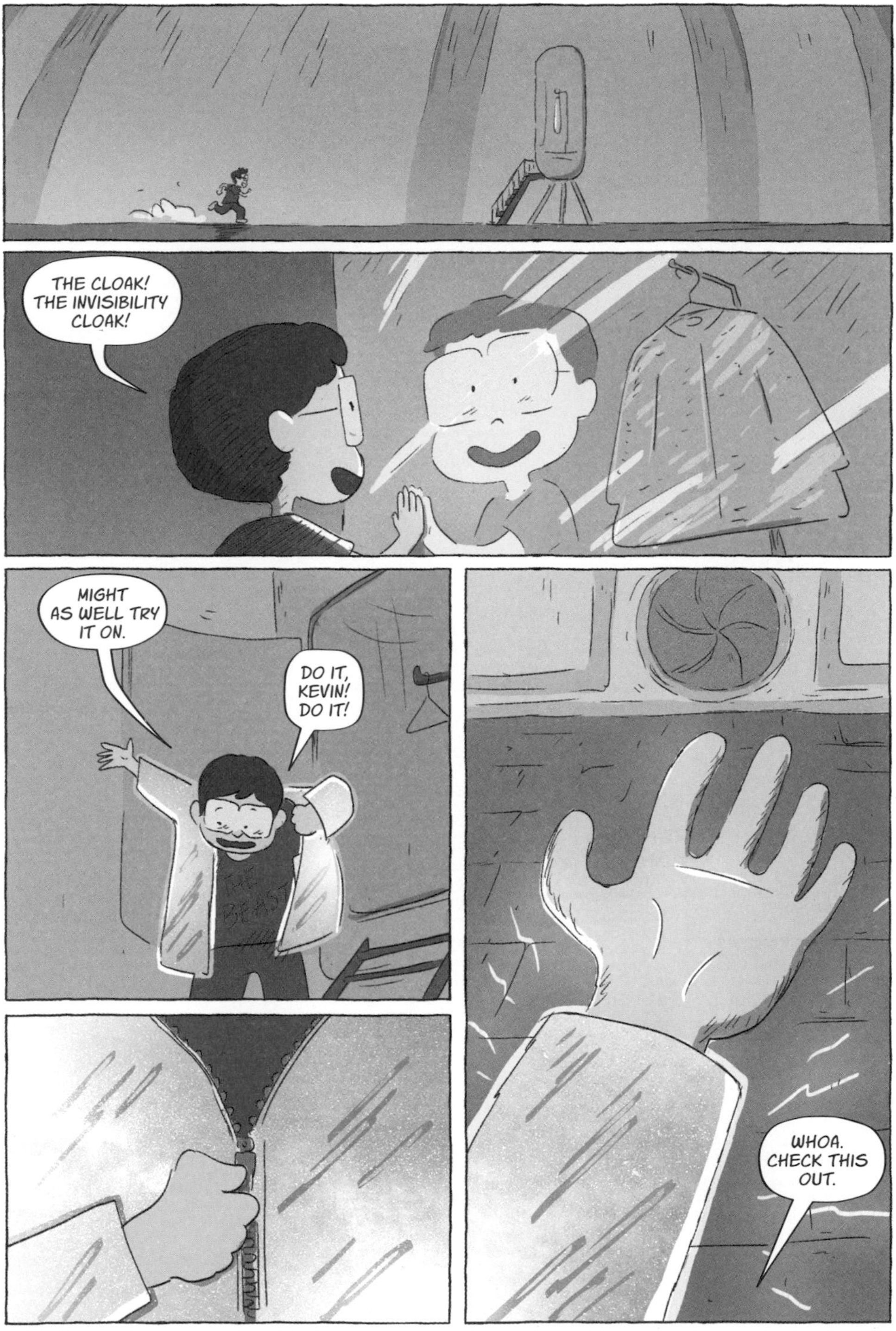
THE CLOAK! THE INVISIBILITY CLOAK!
MIGHT AS WELL TRY IT ON.
DO IT, KEVIN! DO IT!
THE BEAST
WHOA. CHECK THIS OUT.

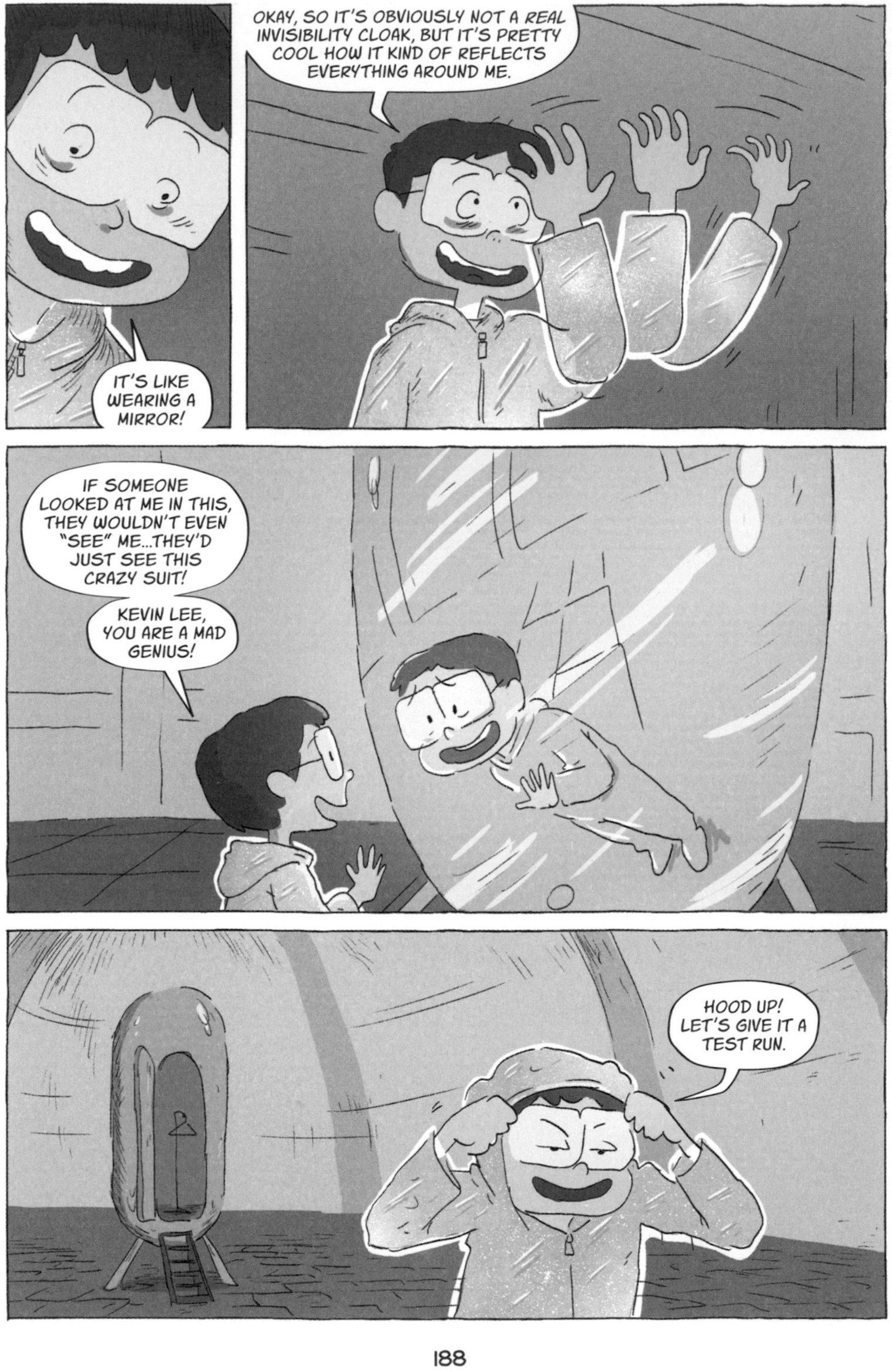
OKAY, SO IT'S OBVIOUSLY NOT A REAL INVISIBILITY CLOAK, BUT IT'S PRETTY COOL HOW IT KIND OF REFLECTS EVERYTHING AROUND ME.
IT'S LIKE WEARING A MIRROR!
IF SOMEONE LOOKED AT ME IN THIS, THEY WOULDN'T EVEN "SEE" ME...THEY'D JUST SEE THIS CRAZY SUIT!
KEVIN LEE, YOU ARE A MAD GENIUS!
HOOD UP! LET'S GIVE IT A TEST RUN.

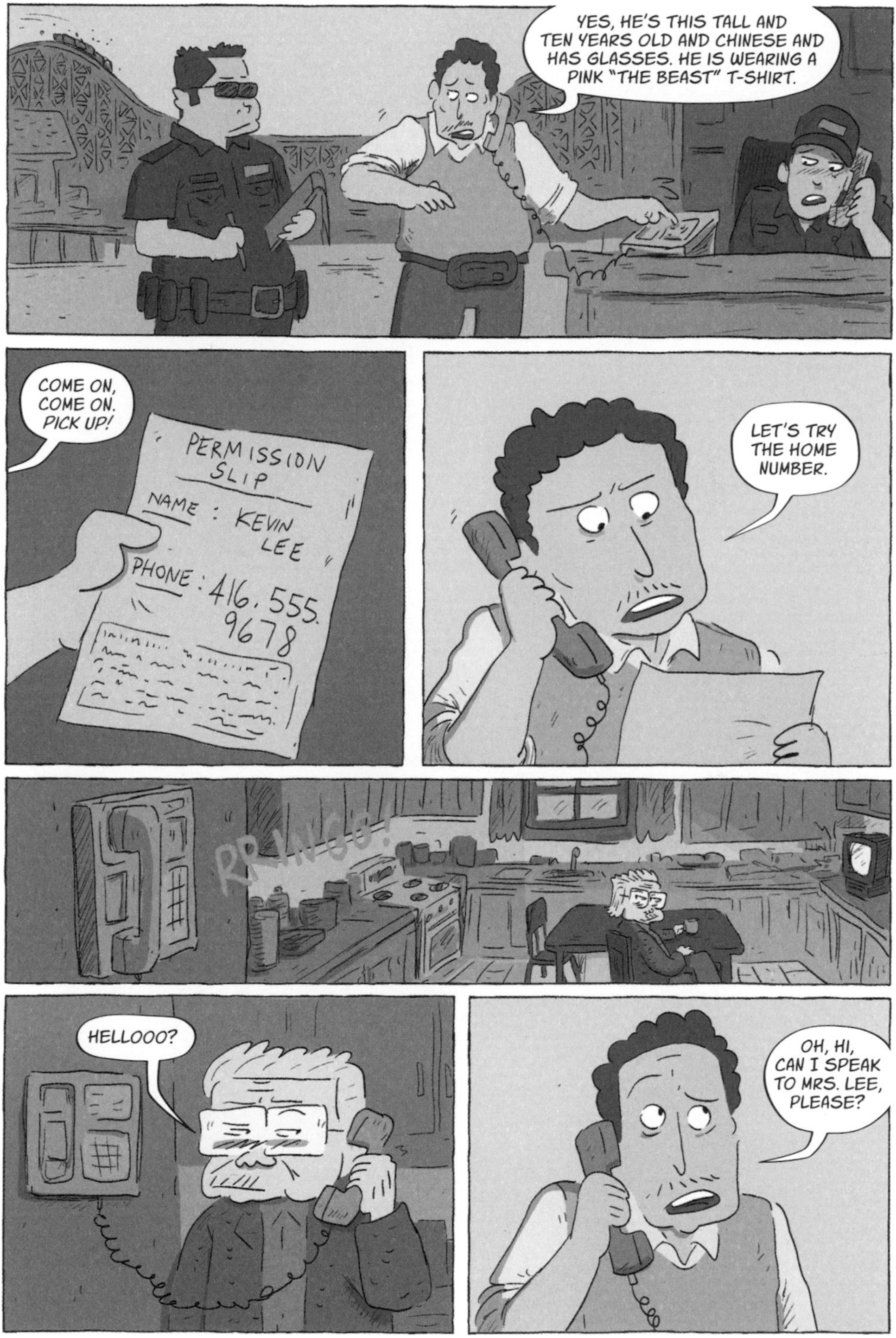
YES, HE'S THIS TALL AND TEN YEARS OLD AND CHINESE AND HAS GLASSES. HE IS WEARING A PINK "THE BEAST" T-SHIRT.
COME ON, COME ON. PICK UP!
PERMISSION SLIP
NAME : KEVIN LEE
PHONE : 416.555.9678
LET'S TRY THE HOME NUMBER.
RRINGG!
HELLOOO?
OH, HI, CAN I SPEAK TO MRS. LEE, PLEASE?

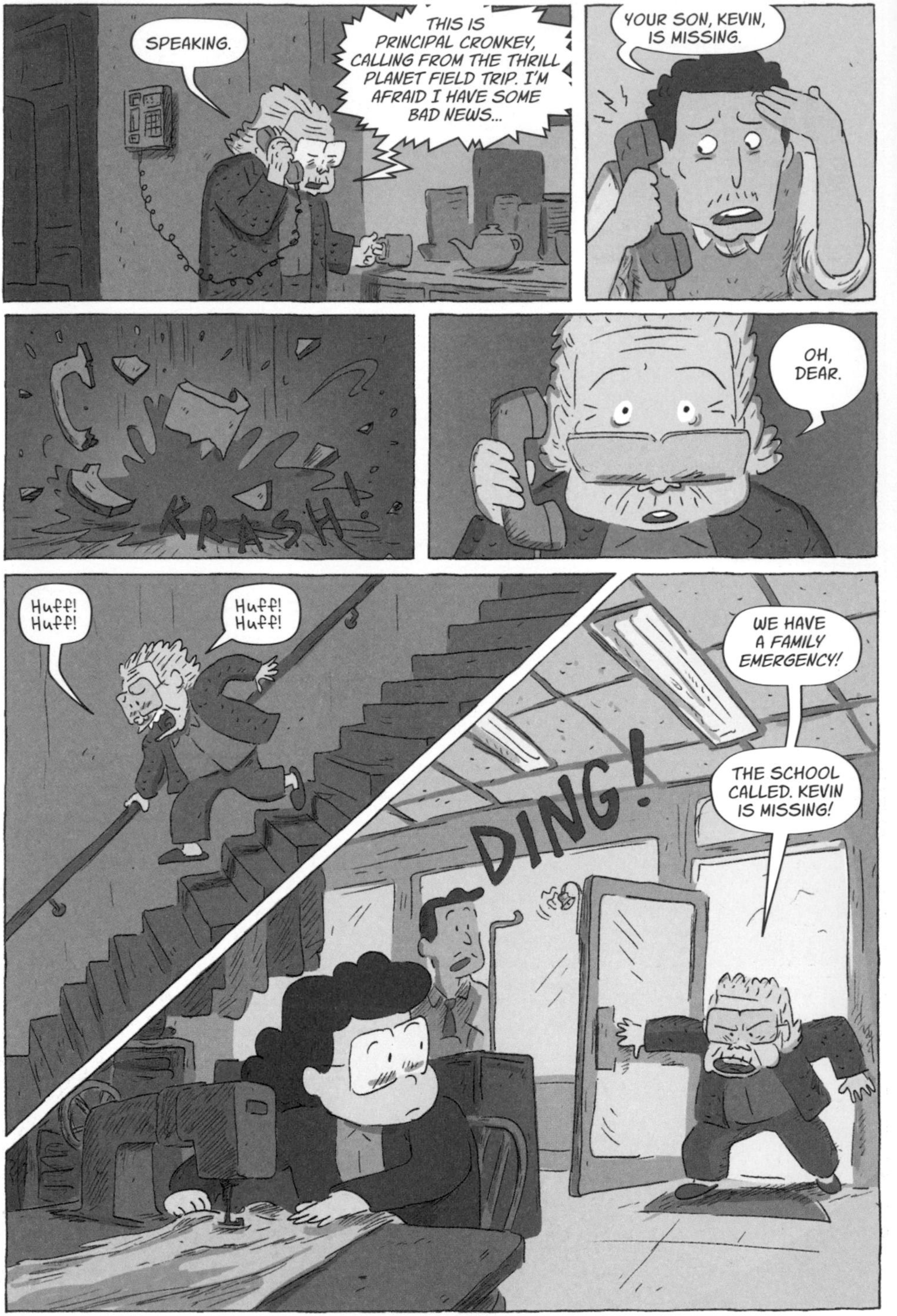
SPEAKING.
THIS IS PRINCIPAL CRONKEY, CALLING FROM THE THRILL PLANET FIELD TRIP. I'M AFRAID I HAVE SOME BAD NEWS...
YOUR SON, KEVIN, IS MISSING.
KRASH!
OH, DEAR.
Huff! Huff!
Huff! Huff!
DING!
WE HAVE A FAMILY EMERGENCY!
THE SCHOOL CALLED. KEVIN IS MISSING!

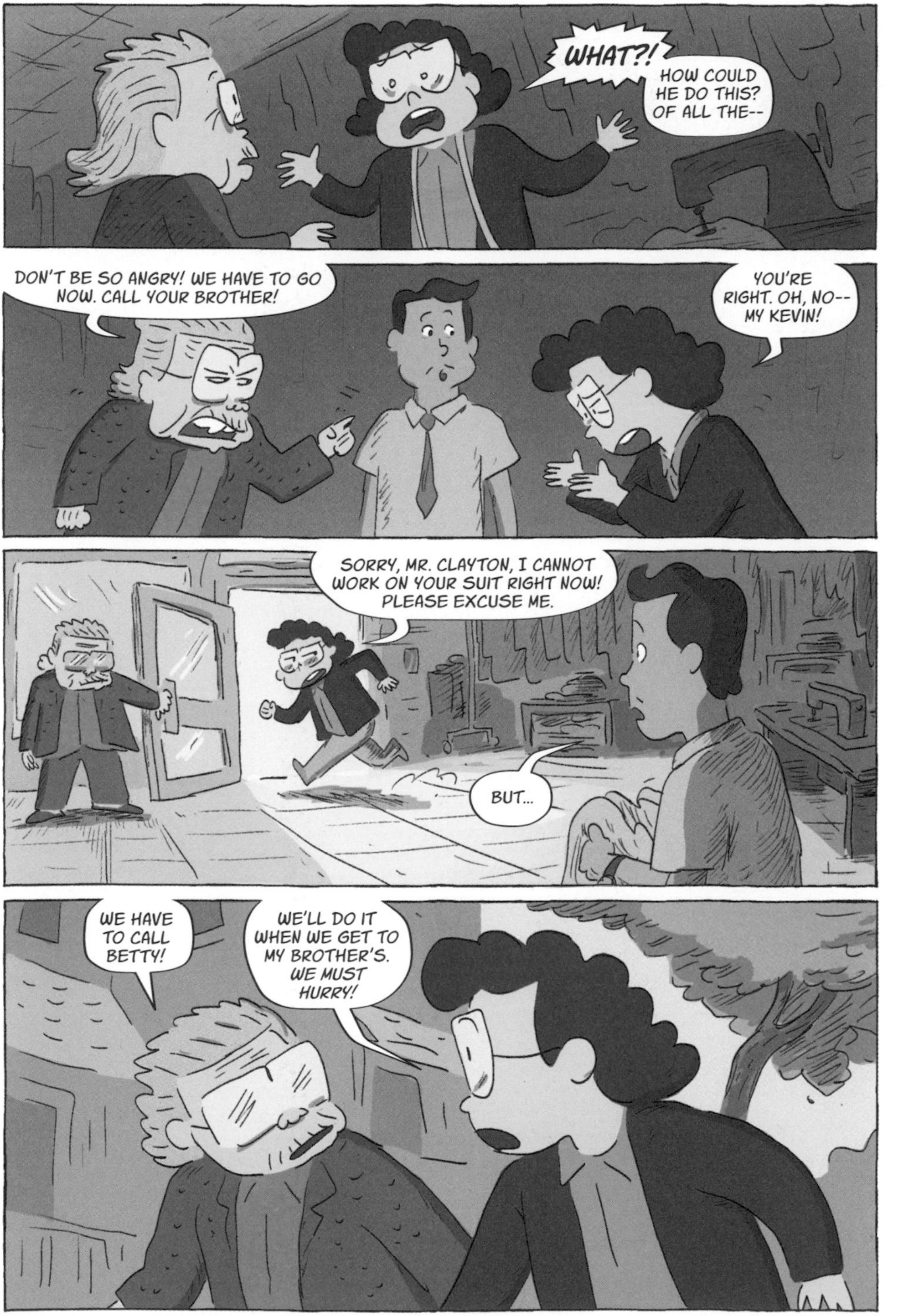
WHAT?!
HOW COULD HE DO THIS? OF ALL THE--
DON'T BE SO ANGRY! WE HAVE TO GO NOW. CALL YOUR BROTHER!
YOU'RE RIGHT. OH, NO-- MY KEVIN!
SORRY, MR. CLAYTON, I CANNOT WORK ON YOUR SUIT RIGHT NOW! PLEASE EXCUSE ME.
BUT...
WE HAVE TO CALL BETTY!
WE'LL DO IT WHEN WE GET TO MY BROTHER'S. WE MUST HURRY!

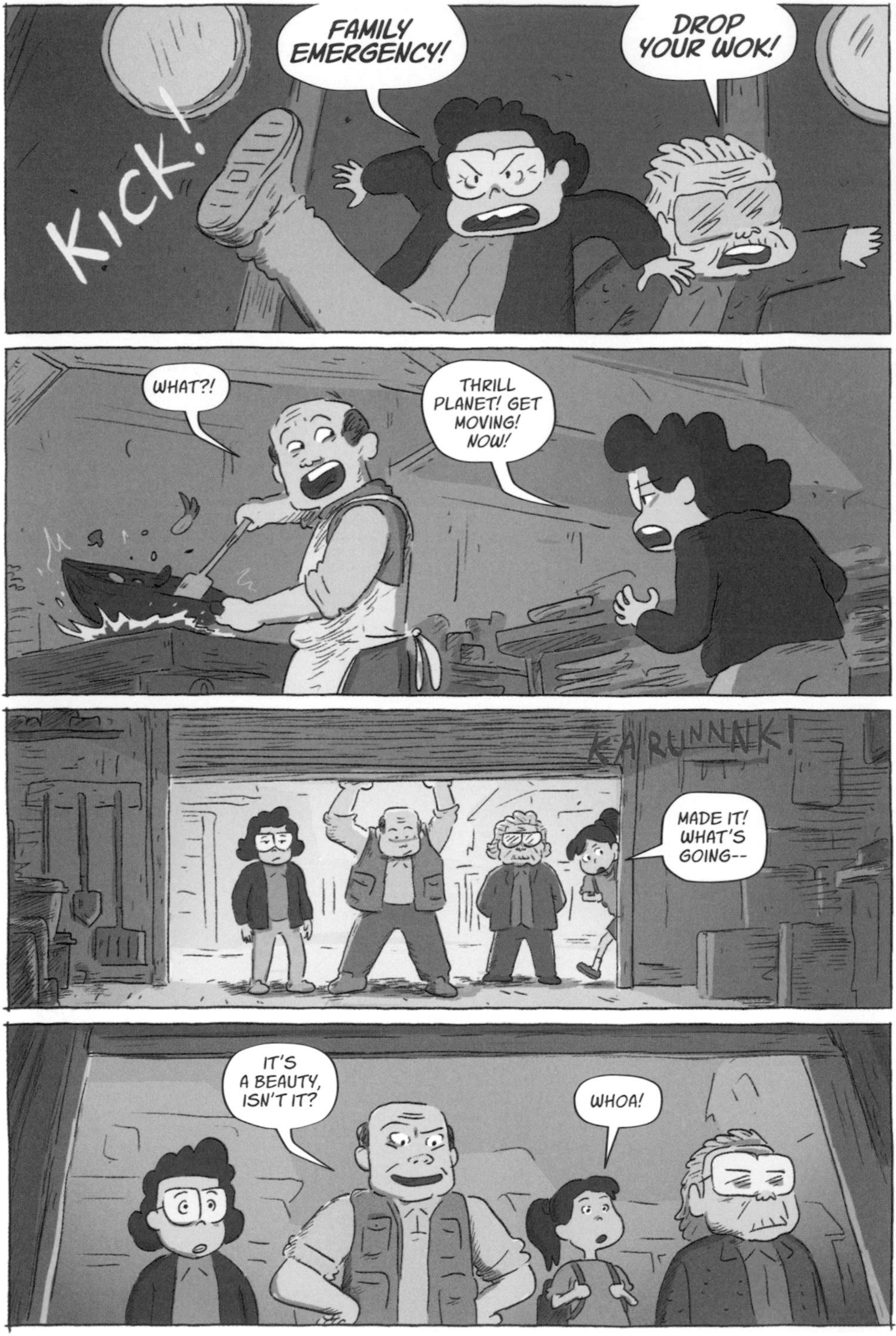
KICK!
FAMILY EMERGENCY!
DROP YOUR WOK!
WHAT?!
THRILL PLANET! GET MOVING! NOW!
KARUNNAK!
MADE IT! WHAT'S GOING--
IT'S A BEAUTY, ISN'T IT?
WHOA!

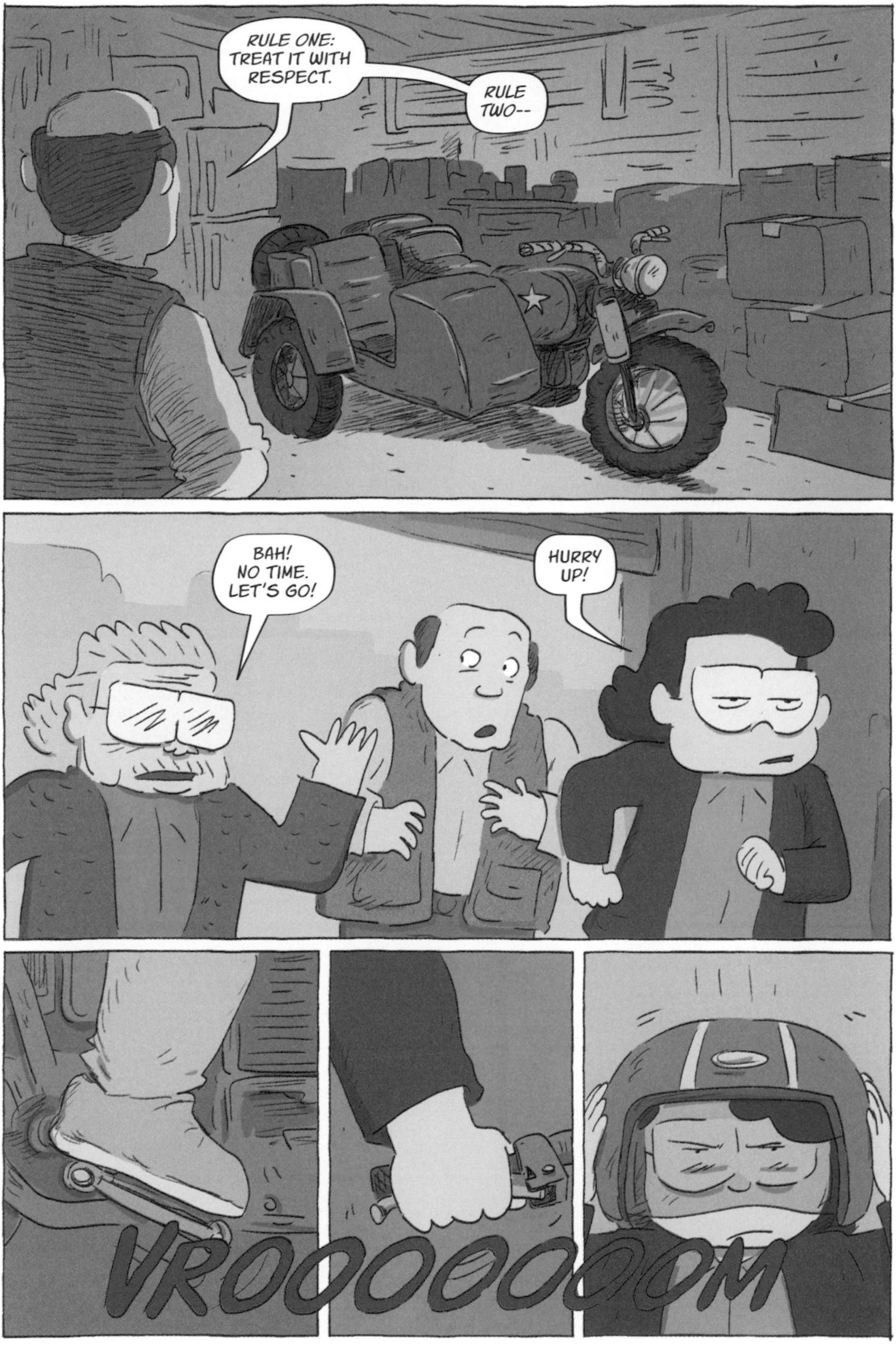
RULE ONE: TREAT IT WITH RESPECT.
RULE TWO--
BAH! NO TIME. LET'S GO!
HURRY UP!
VROOOOOOOM

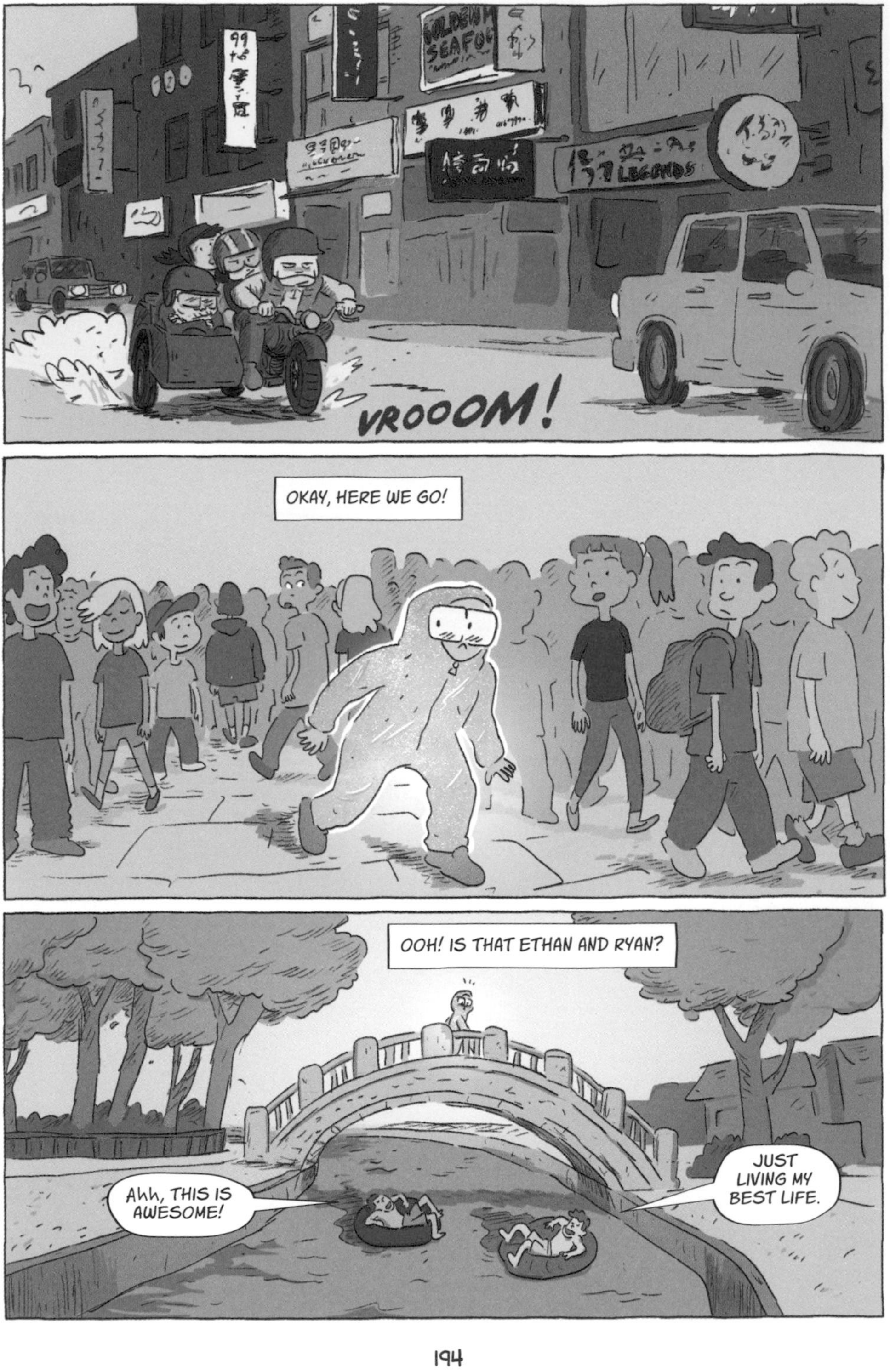
VROOOM!
OKAY, HERE WE GO!
OOH! IS THAT ETHAN AND RYAN?
Ahh, THIS IS AWESOME!
JUST LIVING MY BEST LIFE.

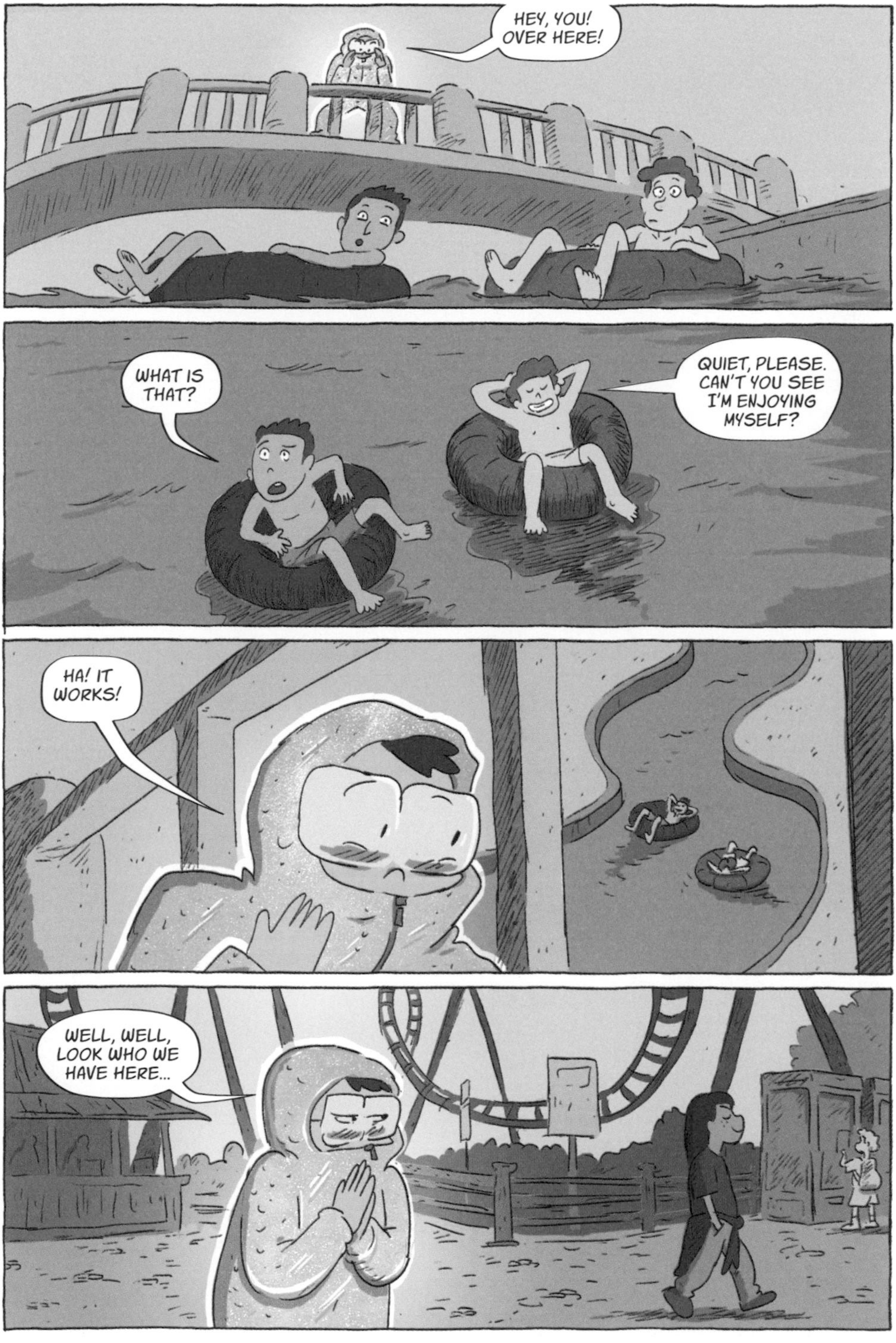
HEY, YOU! OVER HERE!
WHAT IS THAT?
QUIET, PLEASE. CAN'T YOU SEE I'M ENJOYING MYSELF?
HA! IT WORKS!
WELL, WELL, LOOK WHO WE HAVE HERE...

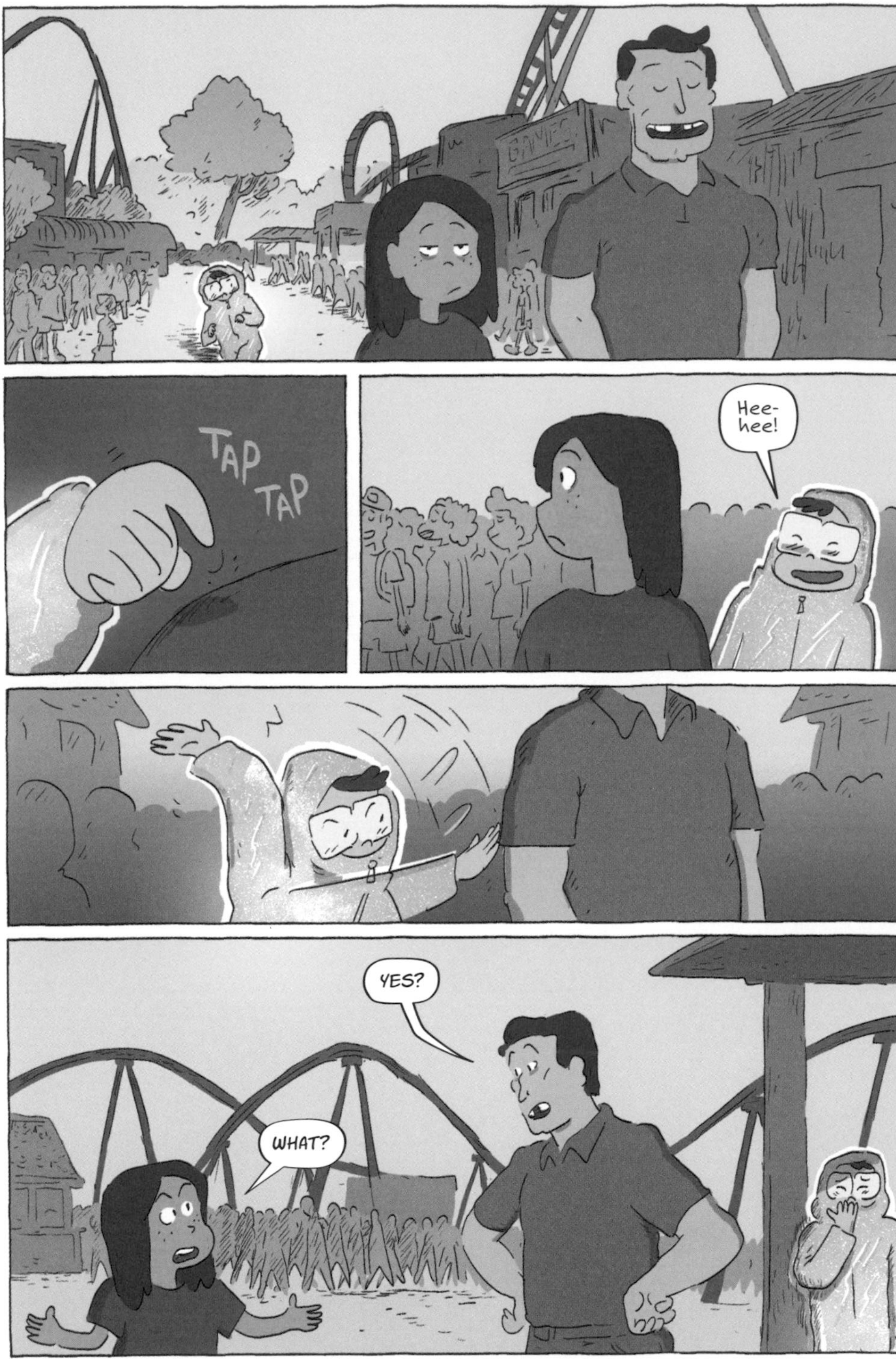
TAP
TAP
Hee-hee!
YES?
WHAT?

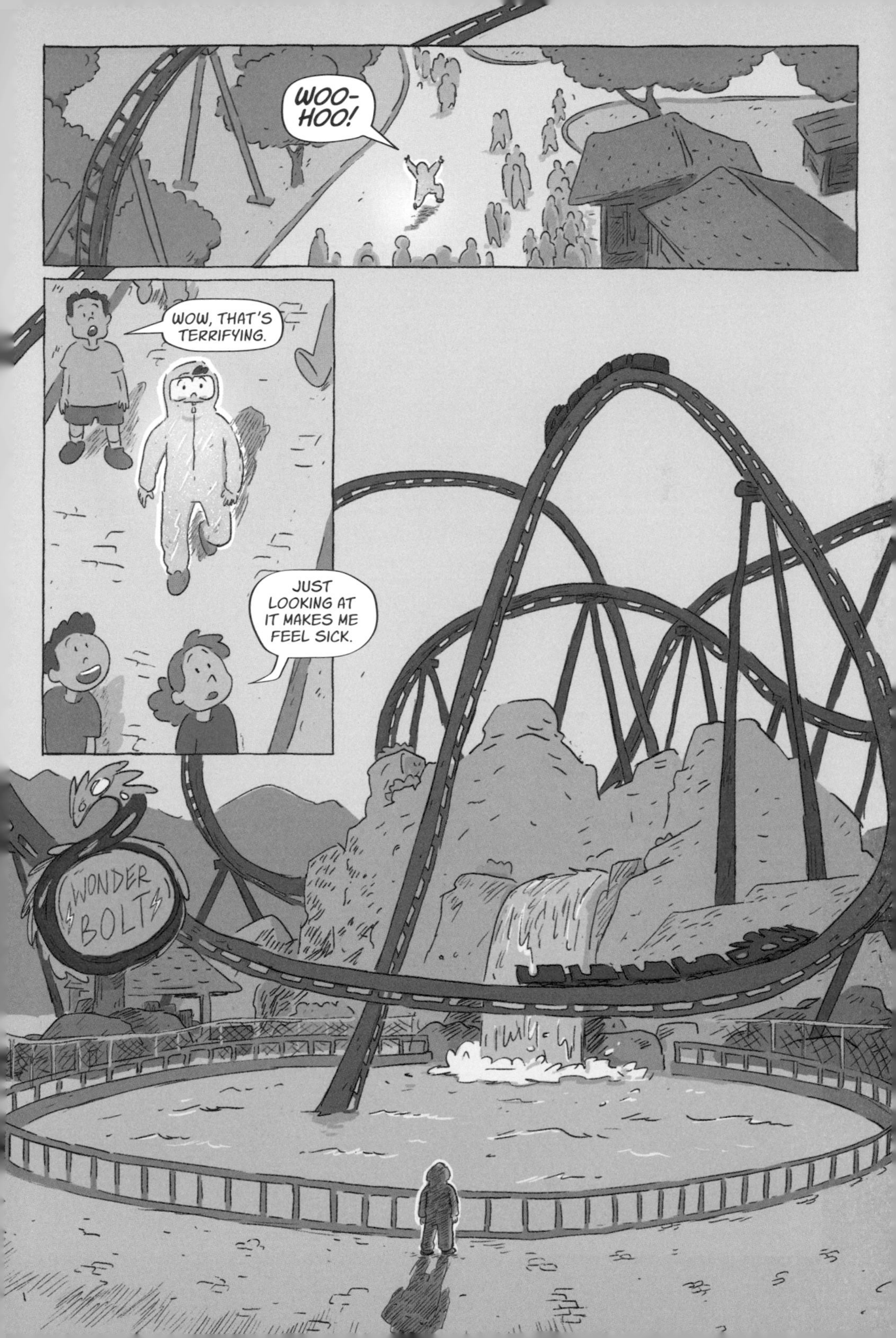
WOO-HOO!
WOW, THAT'S TERRIFYING.
JUST LOOKING AT IT MAKES ME FEEL SICK.
WONDER BOLT

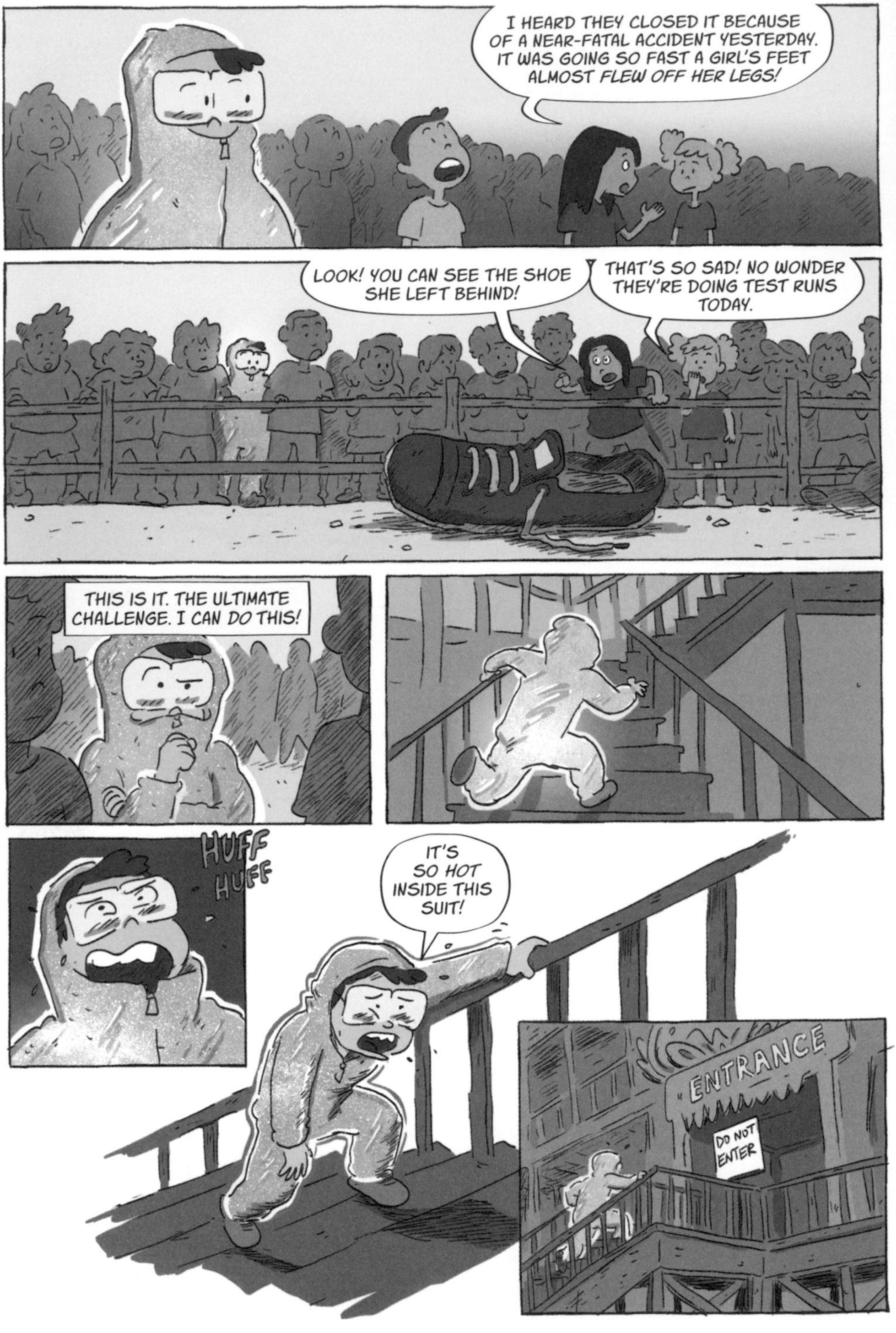
I HEARD THEY CLOSED IT BECAUSE OF A NEAR-FATAL ACCIDENT YESTERDAY. IT WAS GOING SO FAST A GIRL'S FEET ALMOST FLEW OFF HER LEGS!
LOOK! YOU CAN SEE THE SHOE SHE LEFT BEHIND!
THAT'S SO SAD! NO WONDER THEY'RE DOING TEST RUNS TODAY.
THIS IS IT. THE ULTIMATE CHALLENGE. I CAN DO THIS!
HUFF HUFF
IT'S SO HOT INSIDE THIS SUIT!
ENTRANCE
DO NOT ENTER

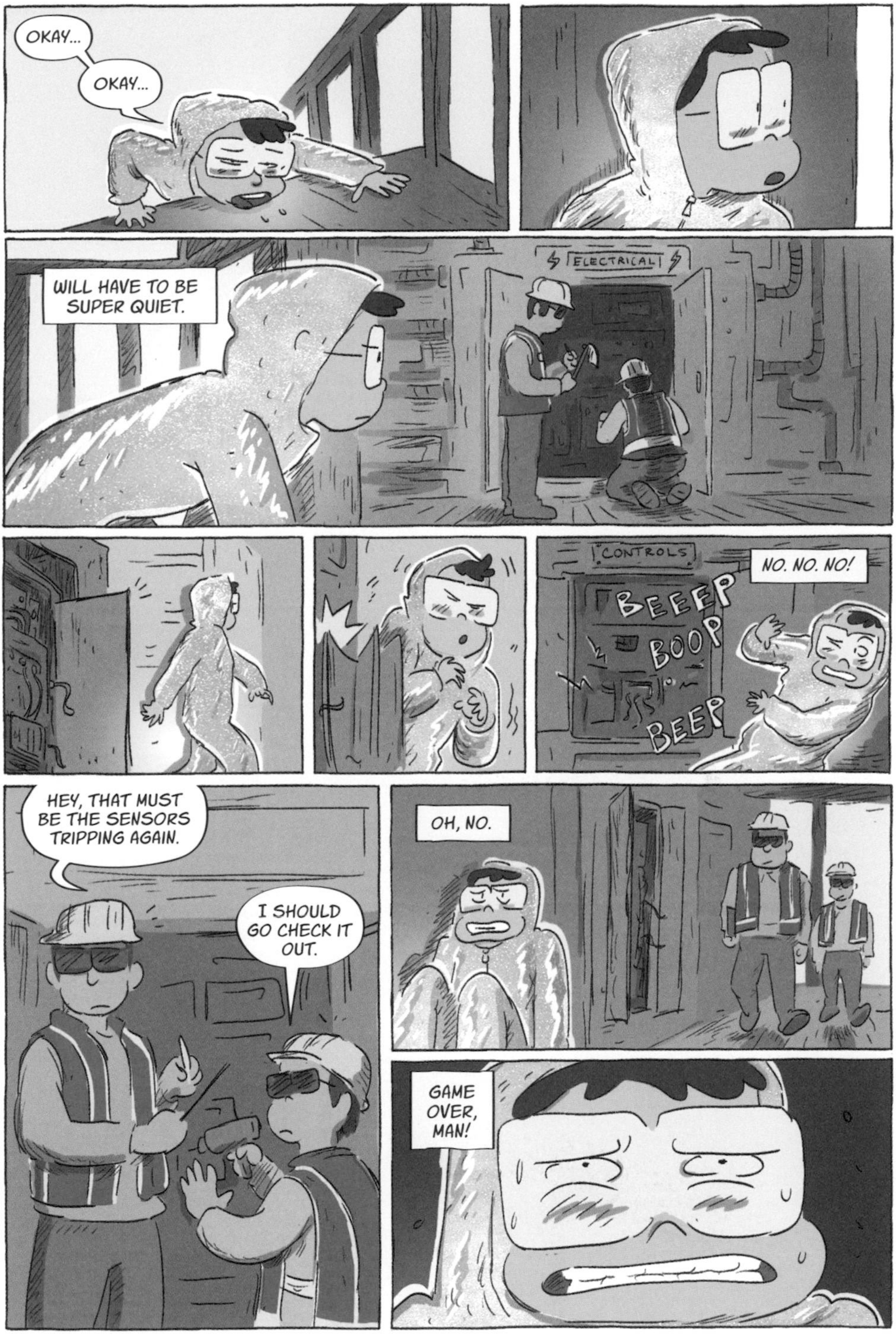
OKAY...
OKAY...
WILL HAVE TO BE SUPER QUIET.
ELECTRICAL
CONTROLS
NO. NO. NO!
BEEEP
BOOP
BEEP
HEY, THAT MUST BE THE SENSORS TRIPPING AGAIN.
I SHOULD GO CHECK IT OUT.
OH, NO.
GAME OVER, MAN!

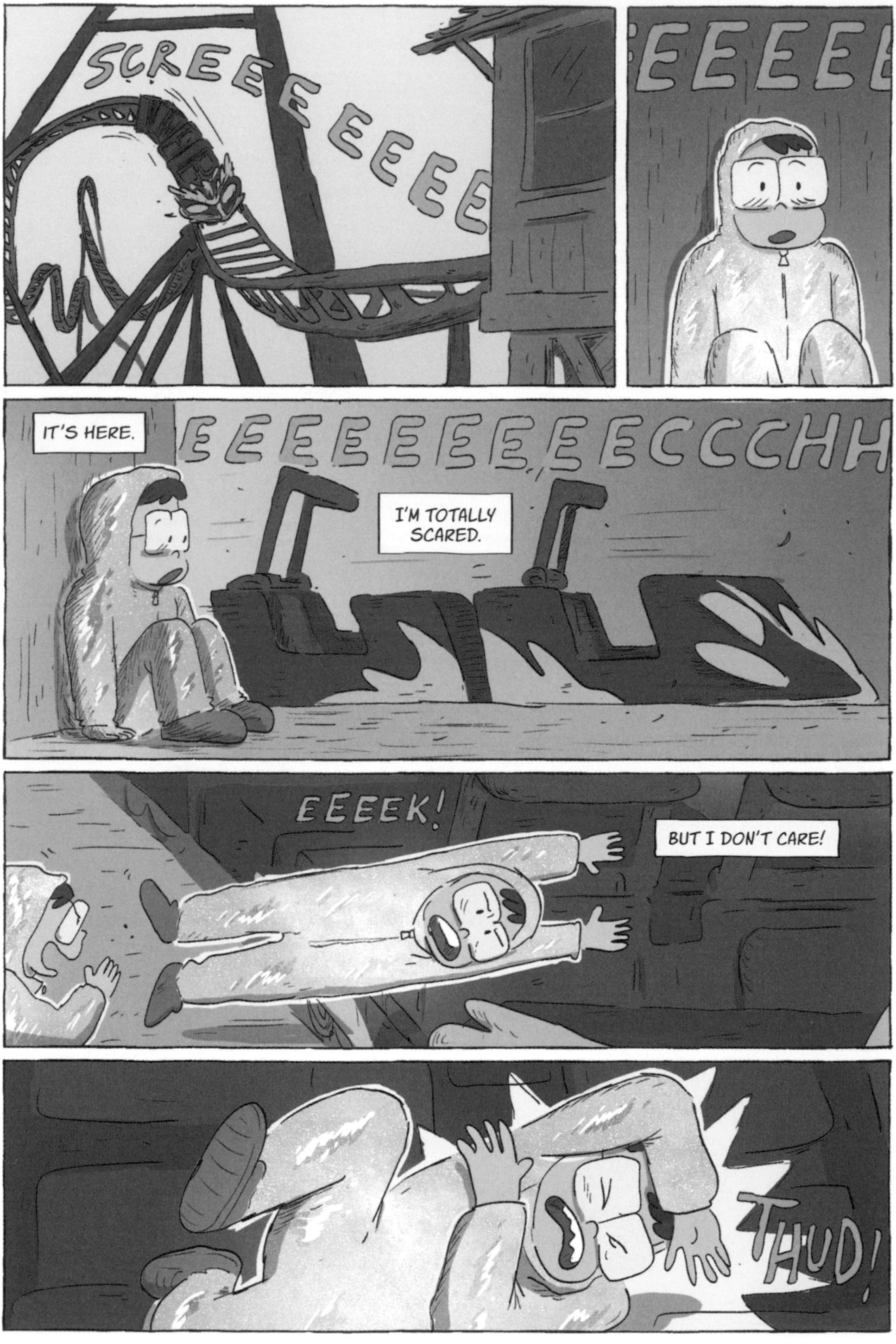
SCREEEEEEEEE
EEEEE
IT'S HERE.
EEEEEEEEECCCHH
I'M TOTALLY SCARED.
EEEEK!
BUT I DON'T CARE!
THUD!

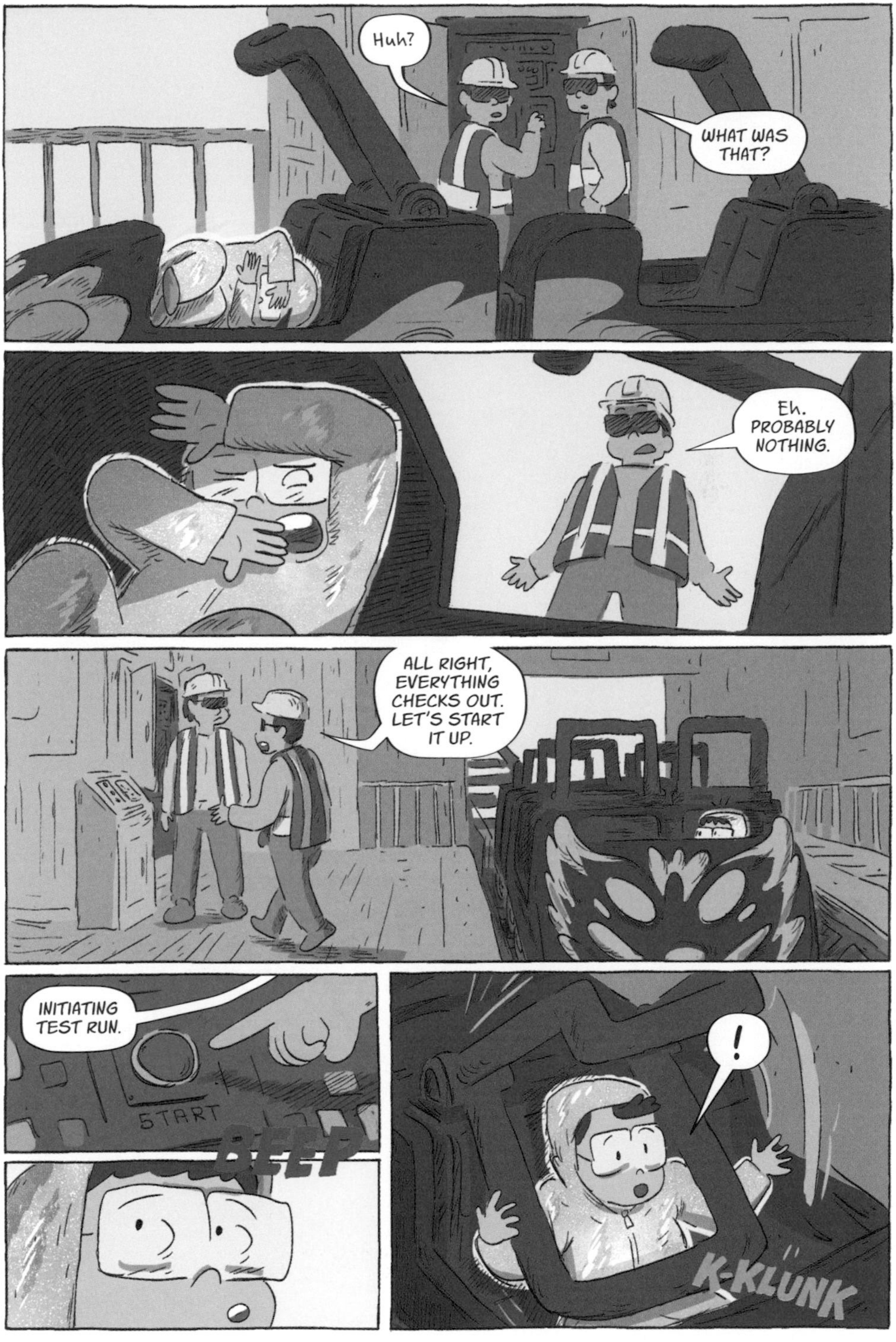
Huh?
WHAT WAS THAT?
Eh. PROBABLY NOTHING.
ALL RIGHT, EVERYTHING CHECKS OUT. LET'S START IT UP.
INITIATING TEST RUN.
START
BEEP
!
K-KLUNK

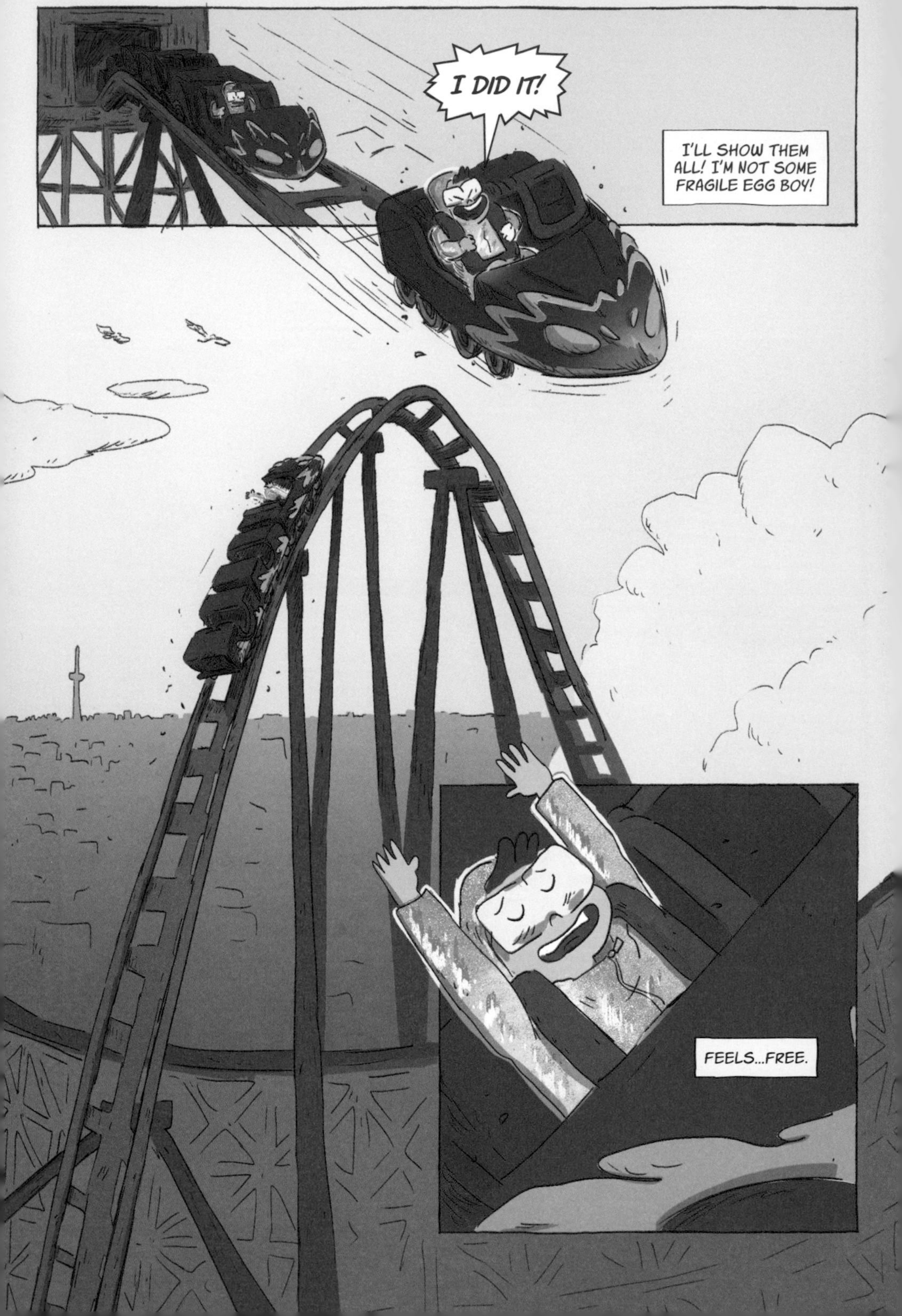
I DID IT!
I'LL SHOW THEM ALL! I'M NOT SOME FRAGILE EGG BOY!
FEELS...FREE.

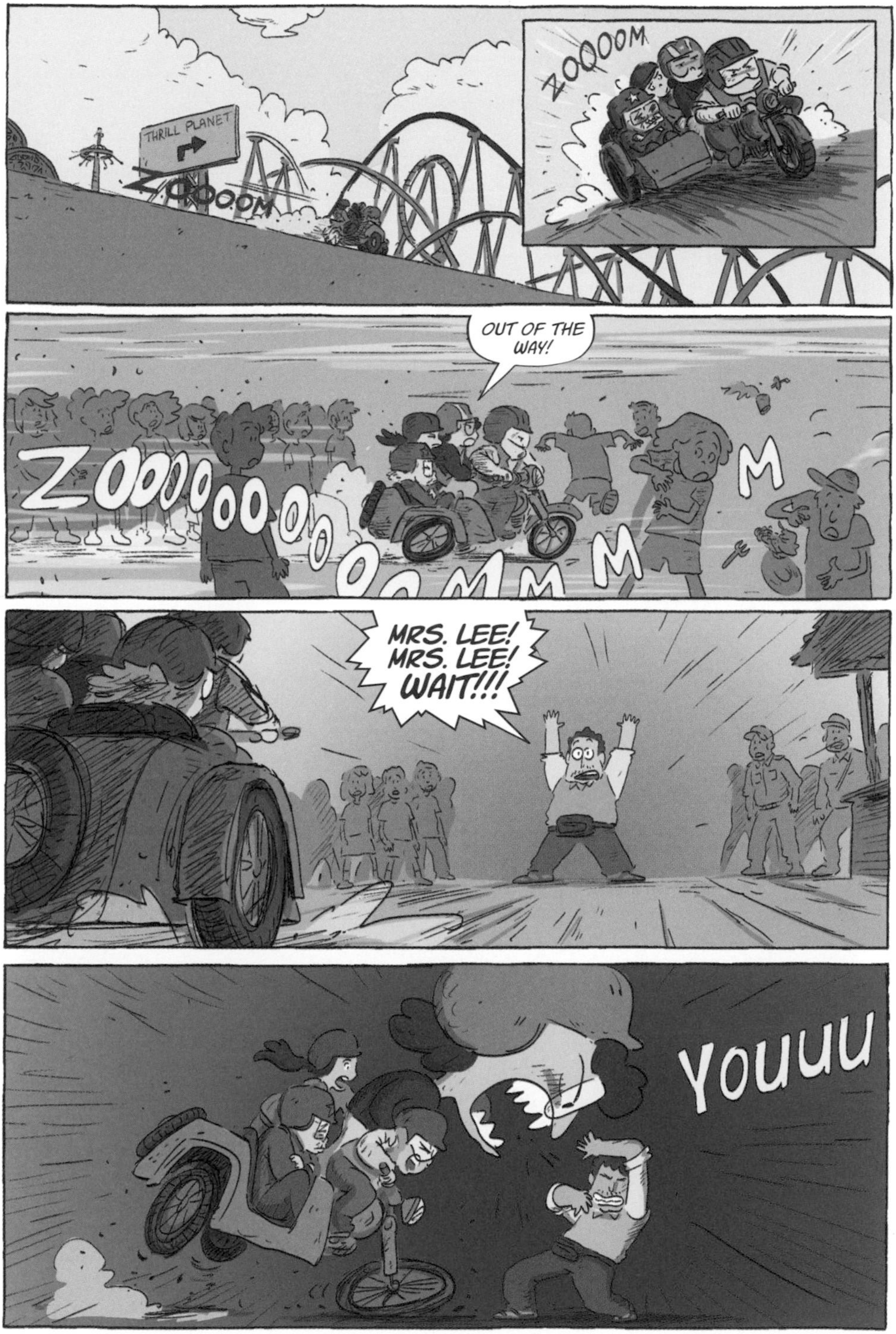
THRILL PLANET
ZOOOOM
ZOOOOM
OUT OF THE WAY!
ZOOOOOOOOOOMMMMM
MRS. LEE! MRS. LEE! WAIT!!!
YOUUU

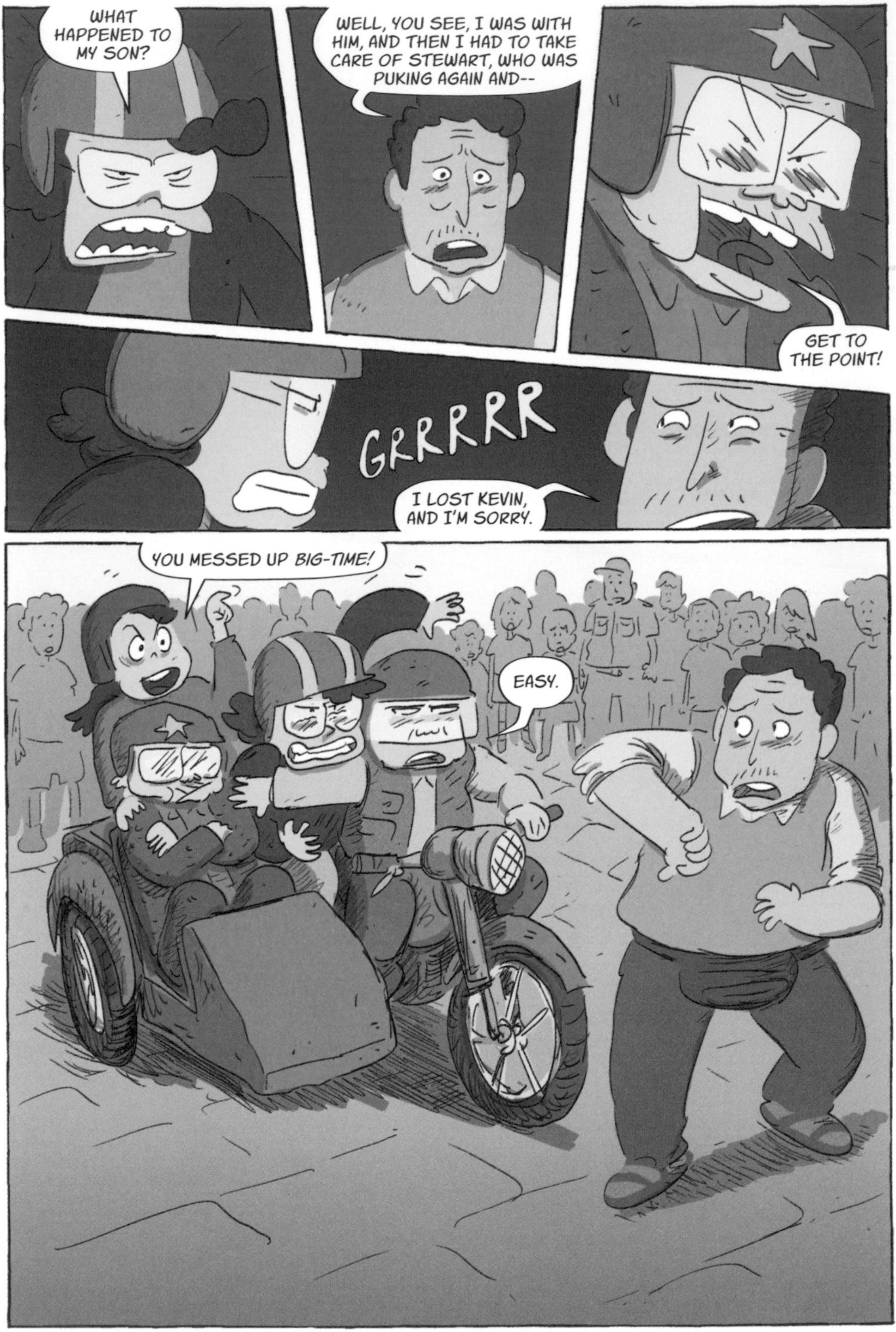
WHAT HAPPENED TO MY SON?
WELL, YOU SEE, I WAS WITH HIM, AND THEN I HAD TO TAKE CARE OF STEWART, WHO WAS PUKING AGAIN AND--
GET TO THE POINT!
GRRRRR
I LOST KEVIN, AND I'M SORRY.
YOU MESSED UP BIG-TIME!
EASY.

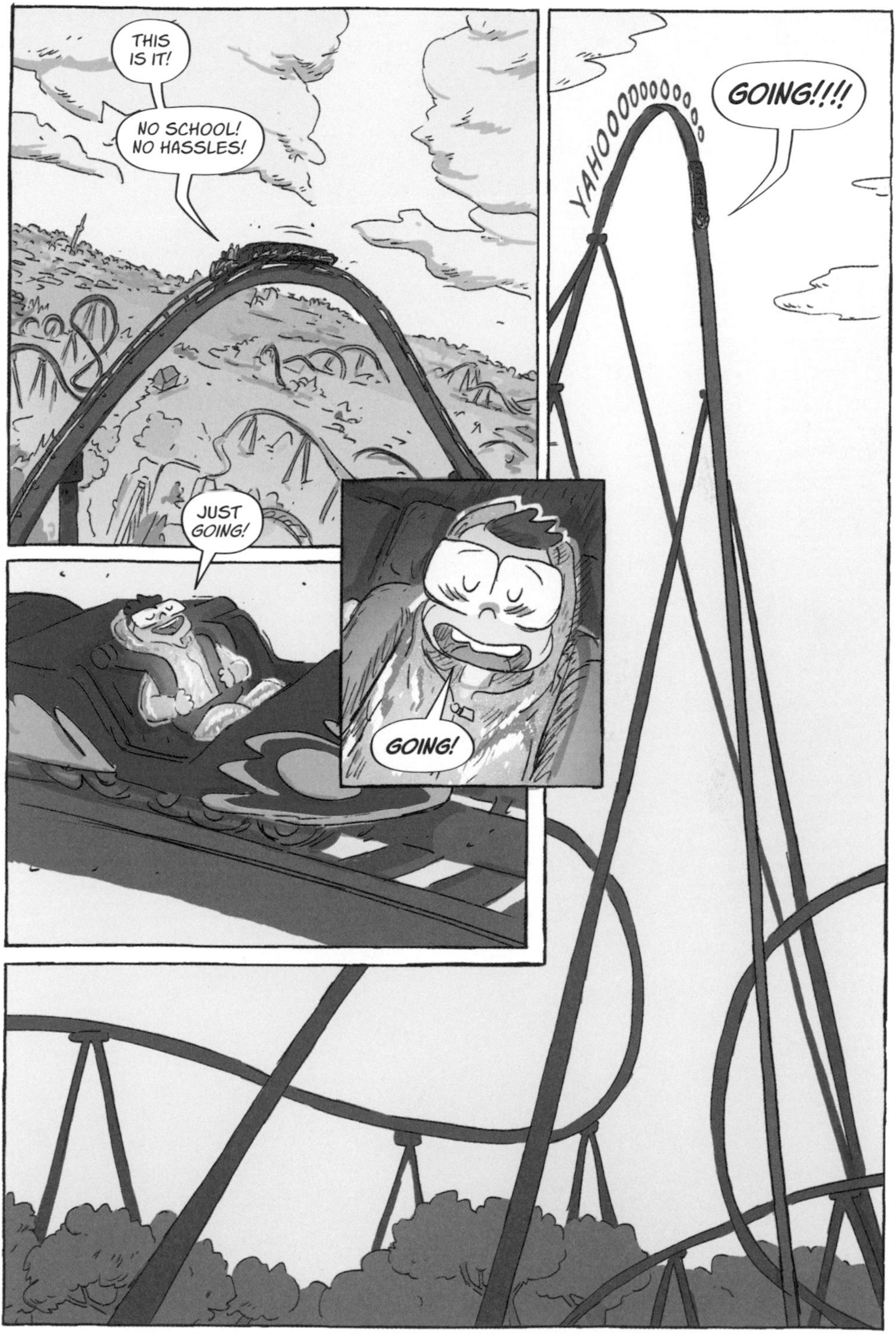
THIS IS IT!
NO SCHOOL! NO HASSLES!
JUST GOING!
GOING!
YAHOOOOOOOOOOO
GOING!!!!

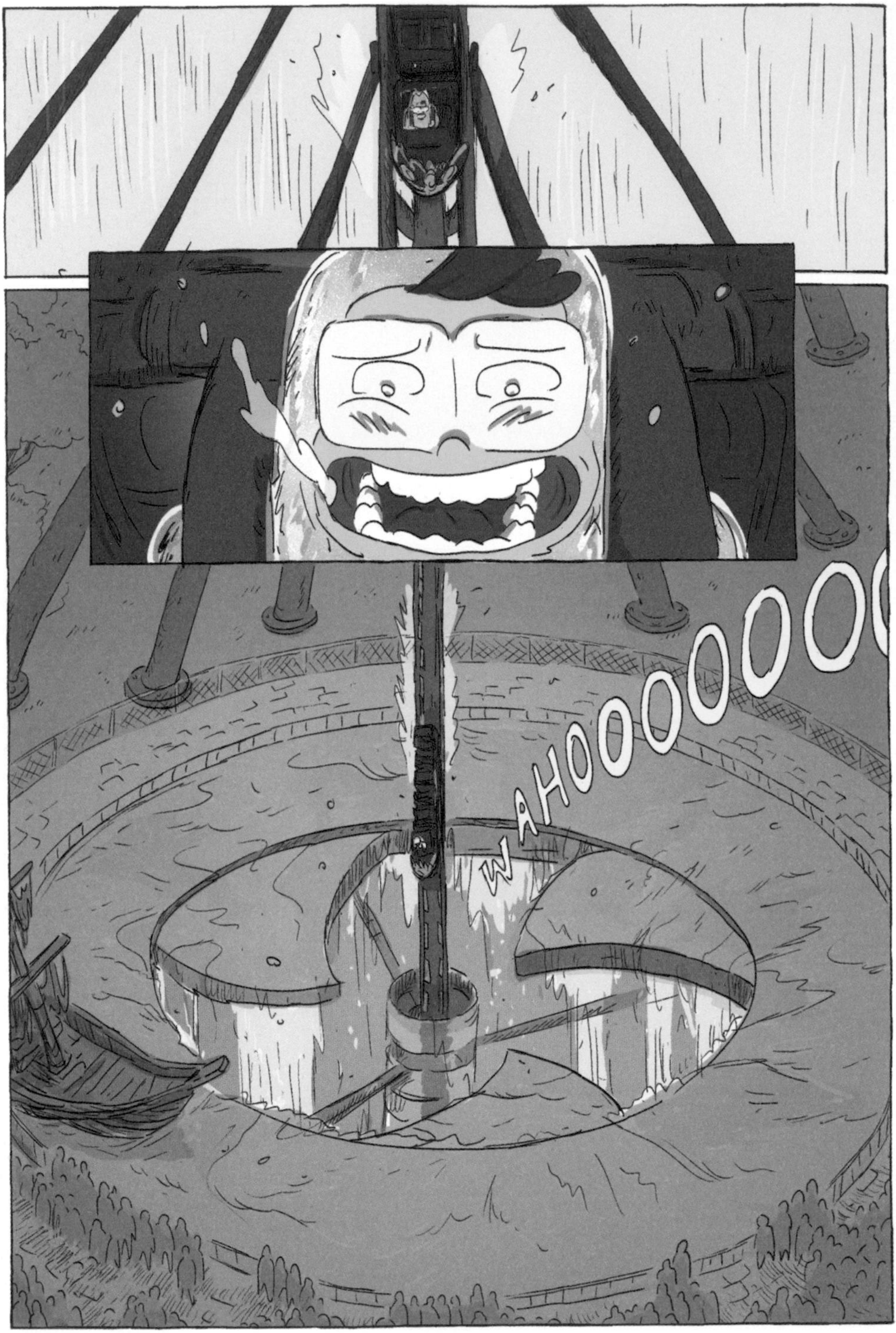
WAHOOOOOOOO

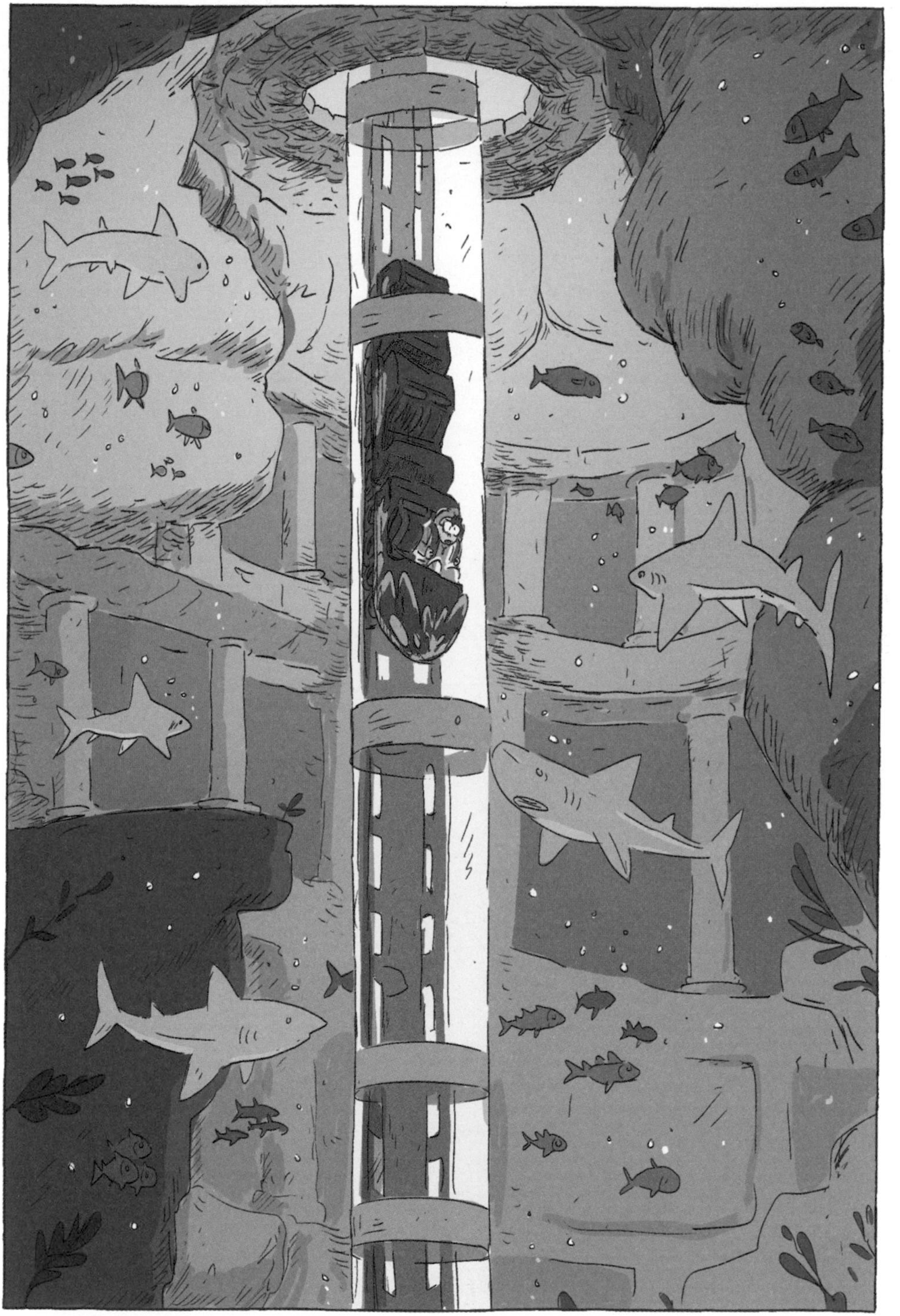

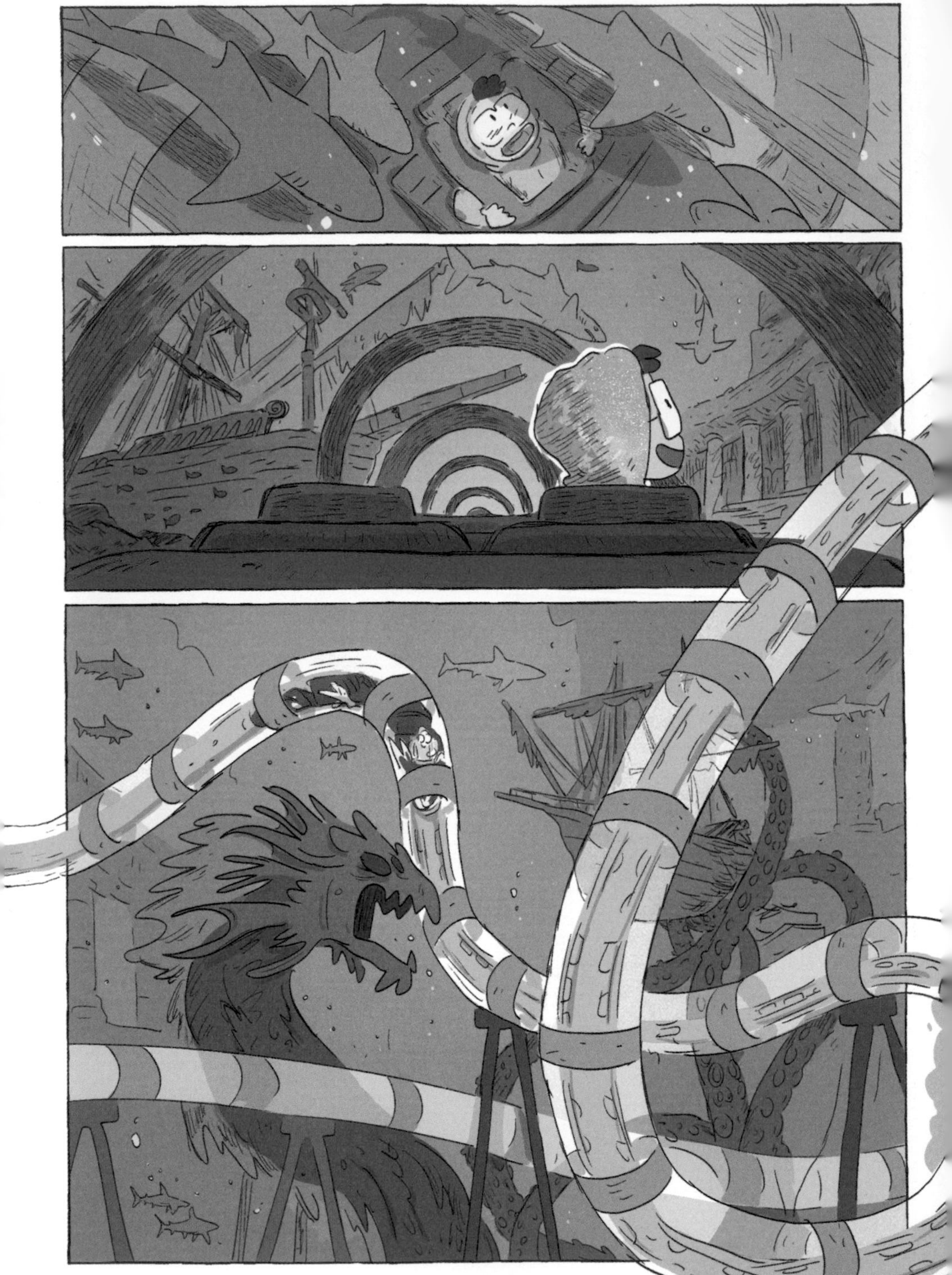

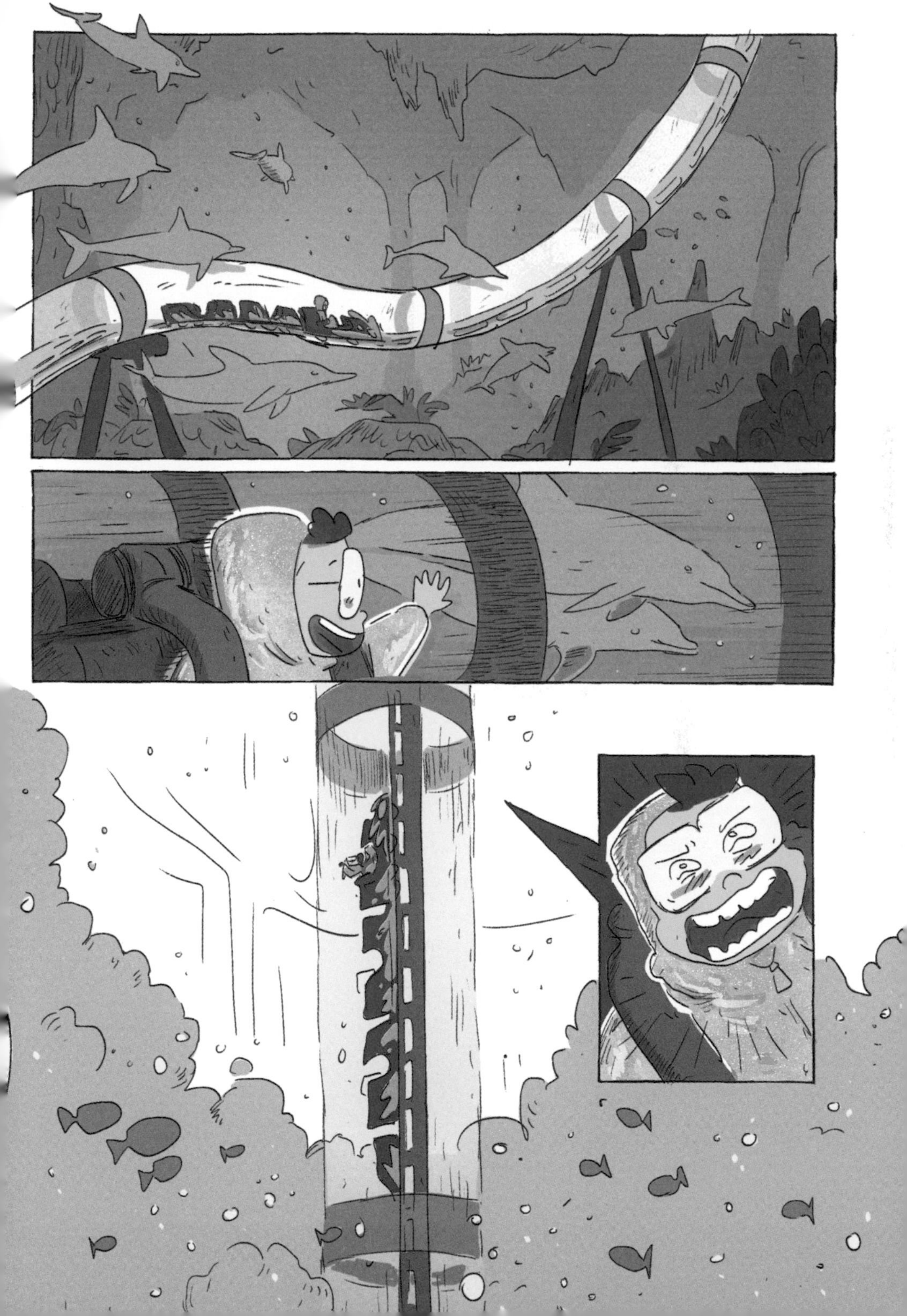

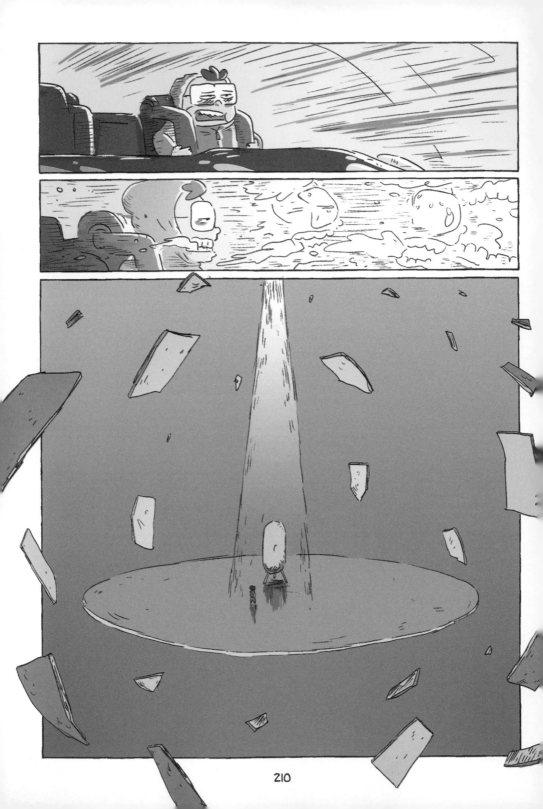

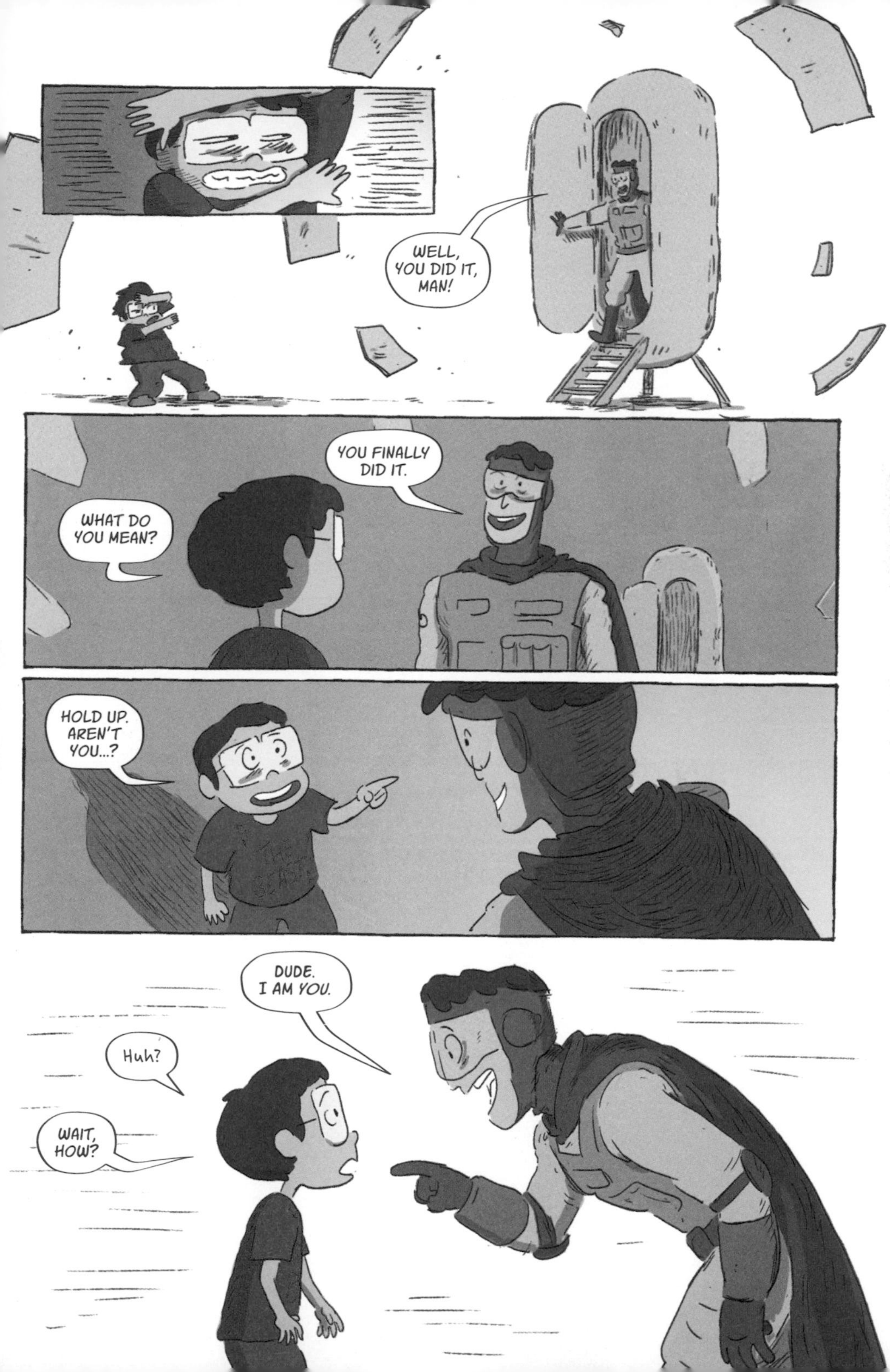
WELL, YOU DID IT, MAN!
YOU FINALLY DID IT.
WHAT DO YOU MEAN?
HOLD UP. AREN'T YOU...?
DUDE. I AM YOU.
Huh?
WAIT, HOW?

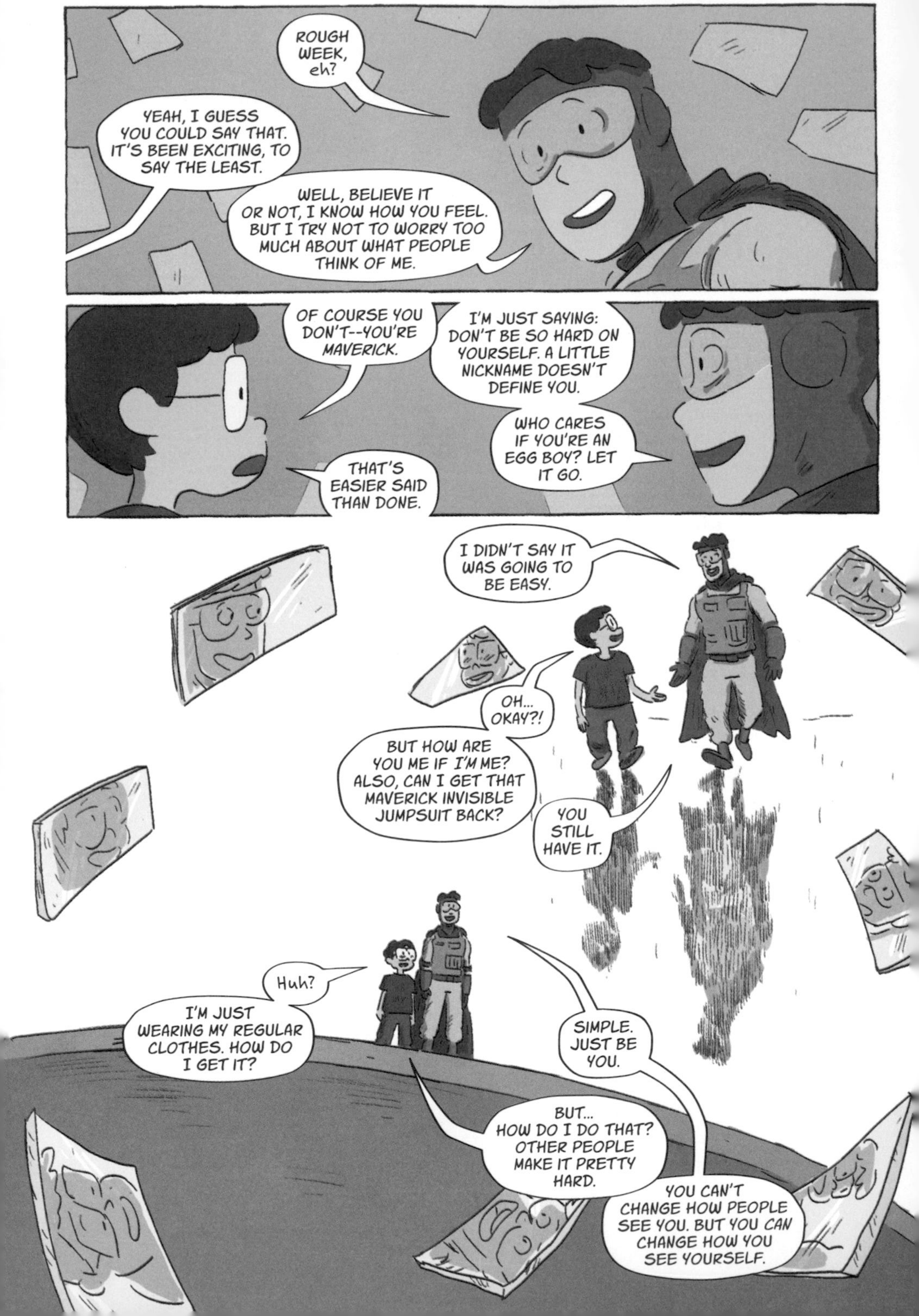

ROUGH WEEK, eh?
YEAH, I GUESS YOU COULD SAY THAT. IT'S BEEN EXCITING, TO SAY THE LEAST.
WELL, BELIEVE IT OR NOT, I KNOW HOW YOU FEEL. BUT I TRY NOT TO WORRY TOO MUCH ABOUT WHAT PEOPLE THINK OF ME.
OF COURSE YOU DON'T--YOU'RE MAVERICK.
I'M JUST SAYING: DON'T BE SO HARD ON YOURSELF. A LITTLE NICKNAME DOESN'T DEFINE YOU.
WHO CARES IF YOU'RE AN EGG BOY? LET IT GO.
THAT'S EASIER SAID THAN DONE.
I DIDN'T SAY IT WAS GOING TO BE EASY.
OH... OKAY?!
BUT HOW ARE YOU ME IF I'M ME? ALSO, CAN I GET THAT MAVERICK INVISIBLE JUMPSUIT BACK?
YOU STILL HAVE IT.
Huh?
I'M JUST WEARING MY REGULAR CLOTHES. HOW DO I GET IT?
SIMPLE. JUST BE YOU.
BUT... HOW DO I DO THAT? OTHER PEOPLE MAKE IT PRETTY HARD.
YOU CAN'T CHANGE HOW PEOPLE SEE YOU. BUT YOU CAN CHANGE HOW YOU SEE YOURSELF.

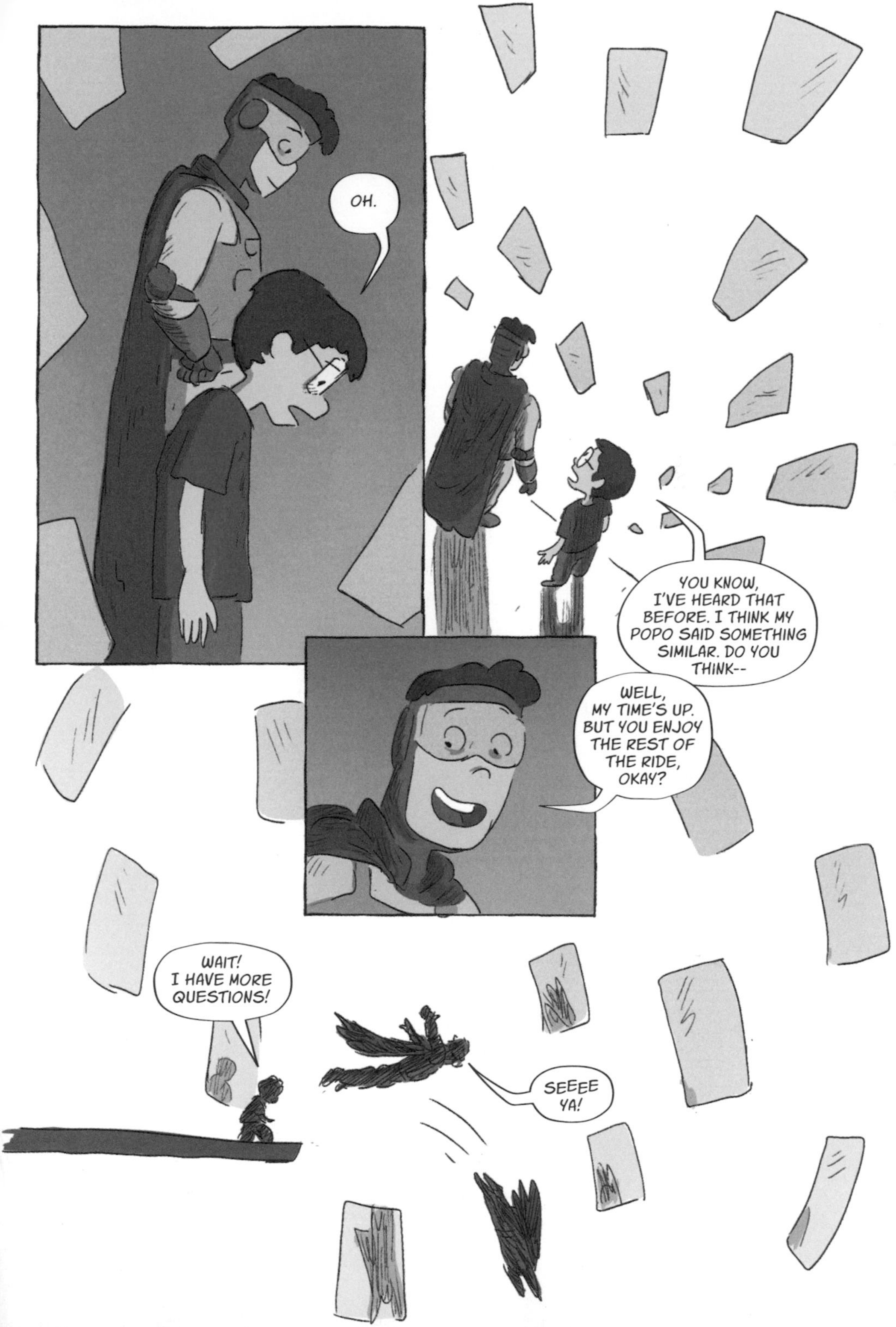
OH.
YOU KNOW, I'VE HEARD THAT BEFORE. I THINK MY POPO SAID SOMETHING SIMILAR. DO YOU THINK--
WELL, MY TIME'S UP. BUT YOU ENJOY THE REST OF THE RIDE, OKAY?
WAIT! I HAVE MORE QUESTIONS!
SEEEE YA!

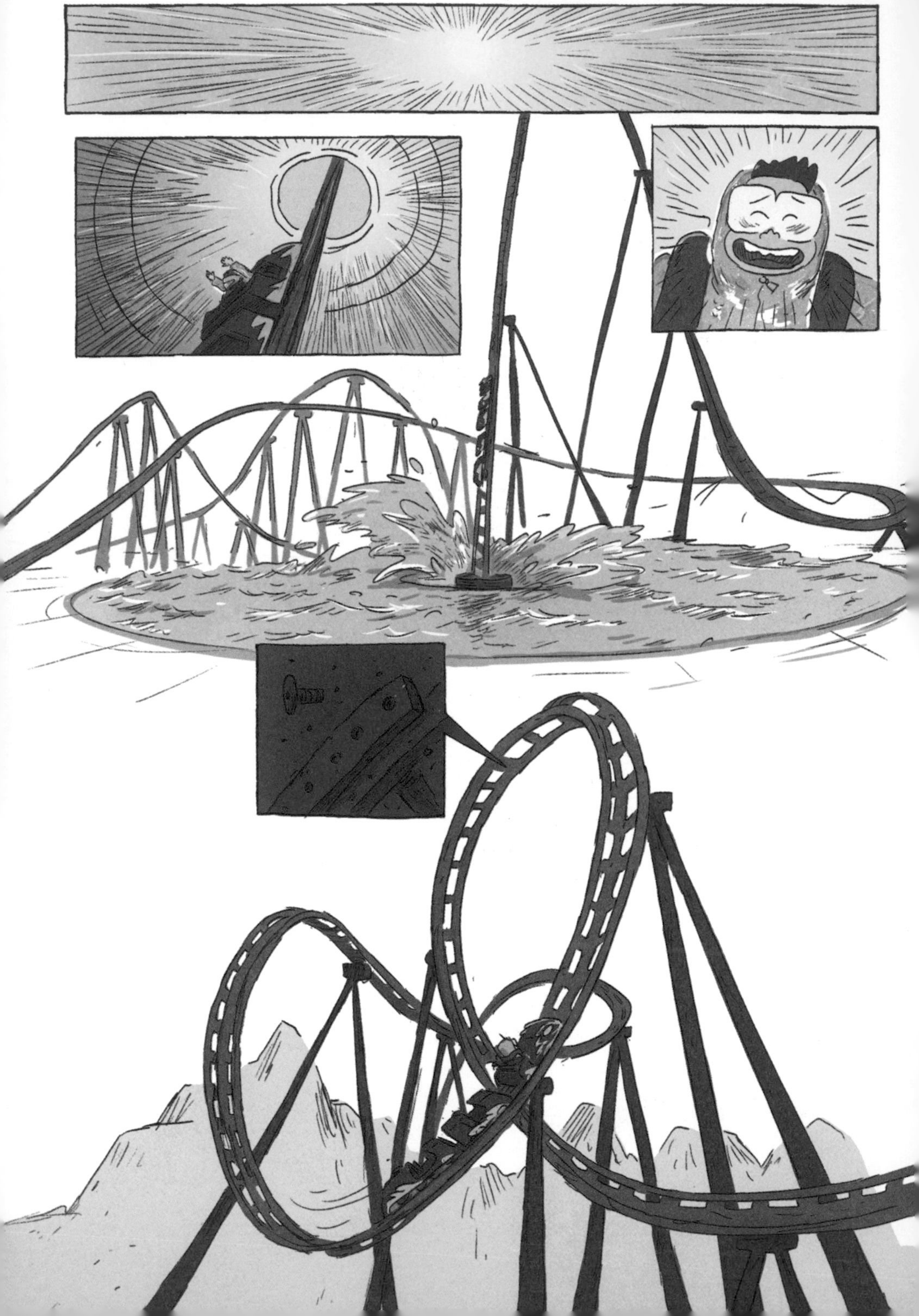

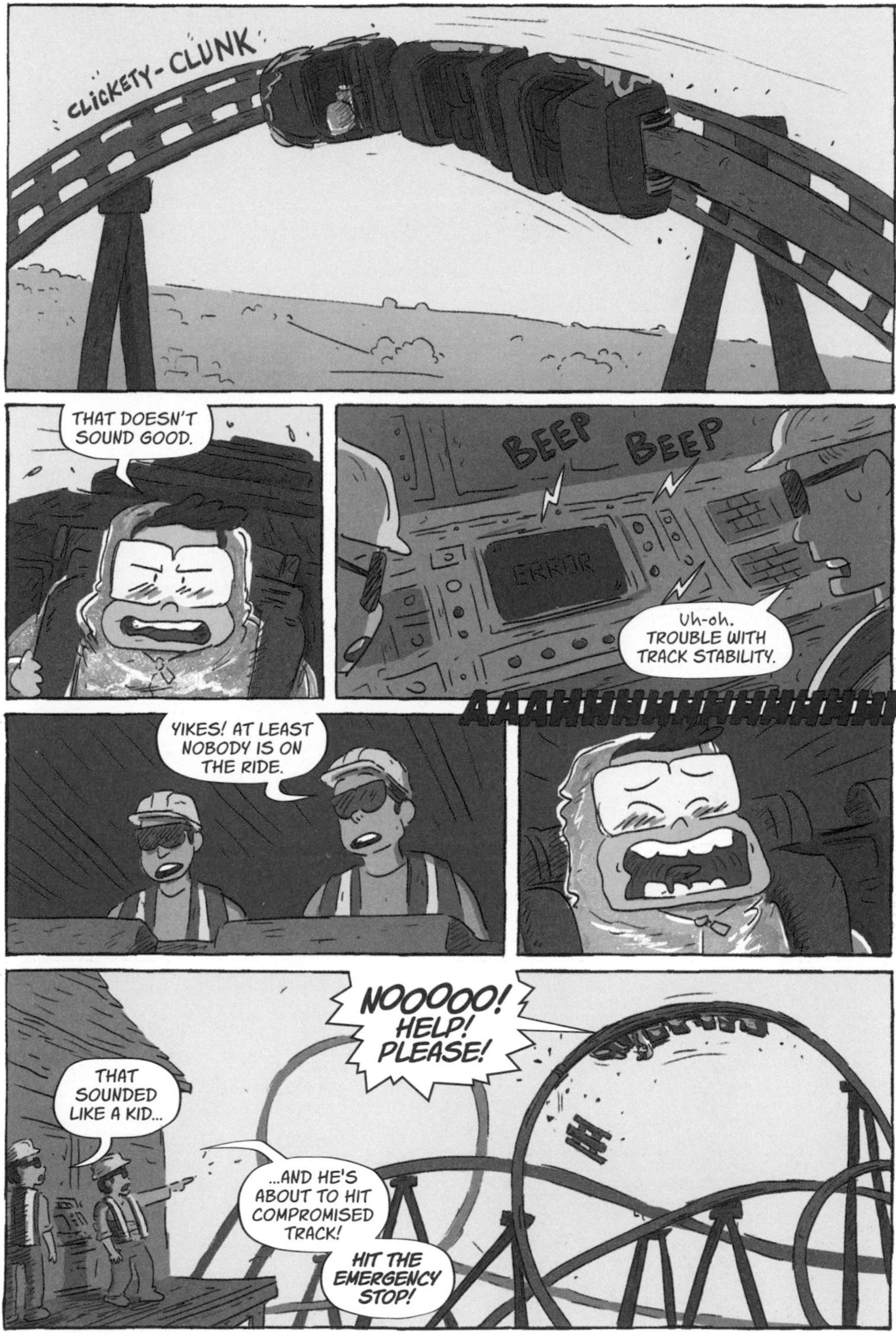

CLICKETY-CLUNK
THAT DOESN'T SOUND GOOD.
BEEP BEEP
ERROR
Uh-oh. TROUBLE WITH TRACK STABILITY.
YIKES! AT LEAST NOBODY IS ON THE RIDE.
AAAHHHHHHHHHHHHH
NOOOOO! HELP! PLEASE!
THAT SOUNDED LIKE A KID...
...AND HE'S ABOUT TO HIT COMPROMISED TRACK!
HIT THE EMERGENCY STOP!

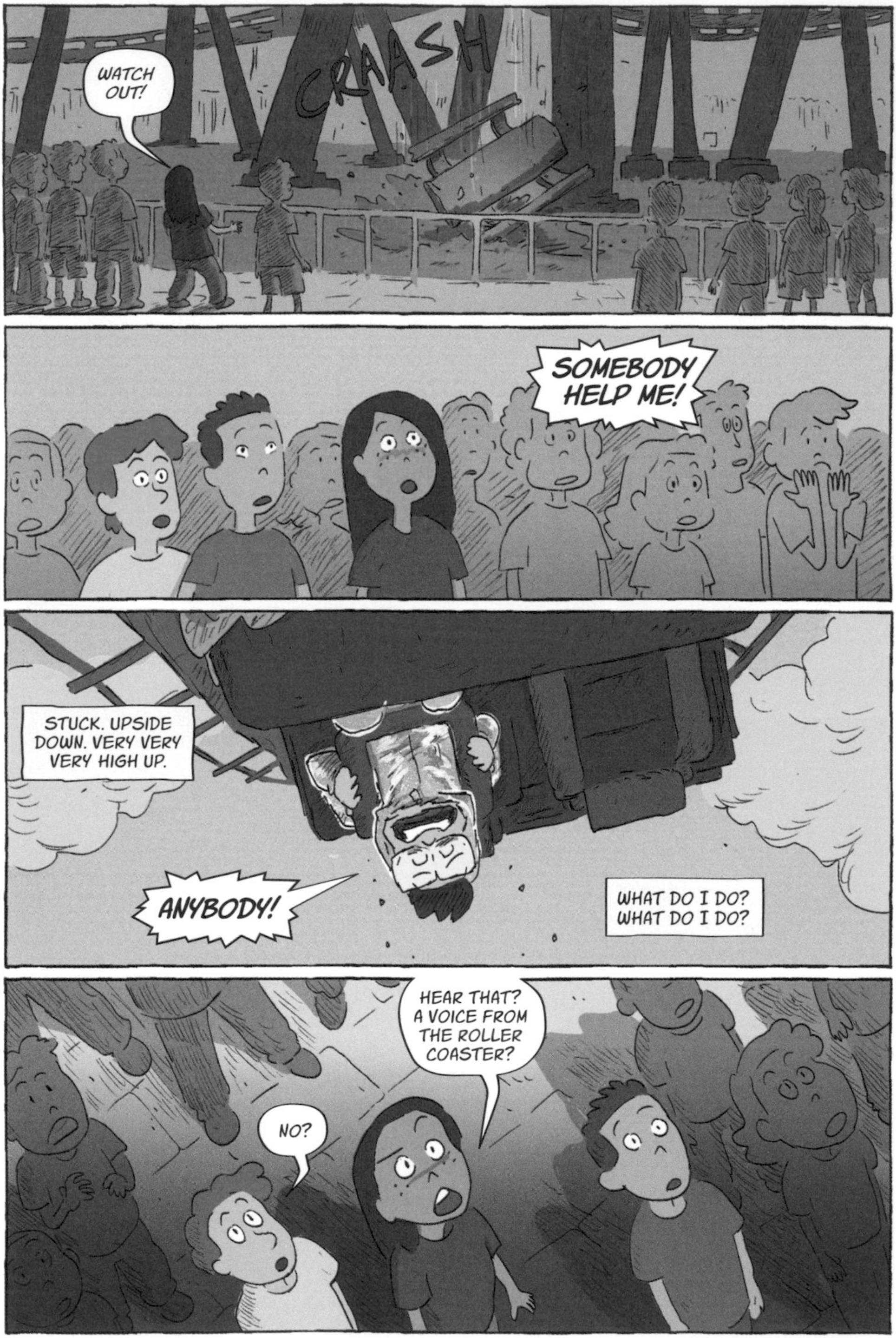
WATCH OUT!
CRAASH
SOMEBODY HELP ME!
STUCK. UPSIDE DOWN. VERY VERY VERY HIGH UP.
ANYBODY!
WHAT DO I DO? WHAT DO I DO?
HEAR THAT? A VOICE FROM THE ROLLER COASTER?
NO?

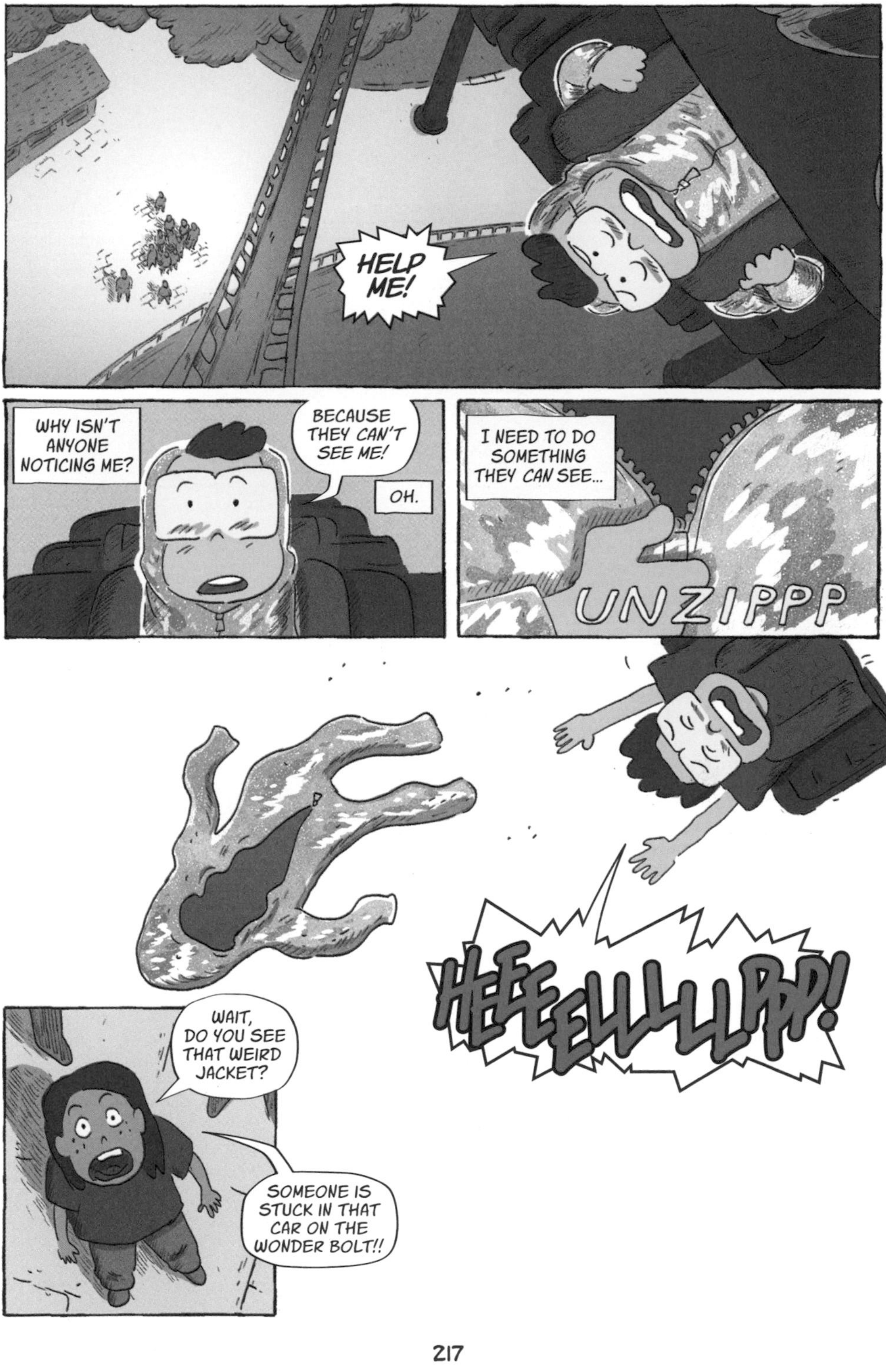
HELP ME!
WHY ISN'T ANYONE NOTICING ME?
BECAUSE THEY CAN'T SEE ME!
OH.
I NEED TO DO SOMETHING THEY CAN SEE...
UNZIPPP
HEEEELLLLLPP!
WAIT, DO YOU SEE THAT WEIRD JACKET?
SOMEONE IS STUCK IN THAT CAR ON THE WONDER BOLT!!

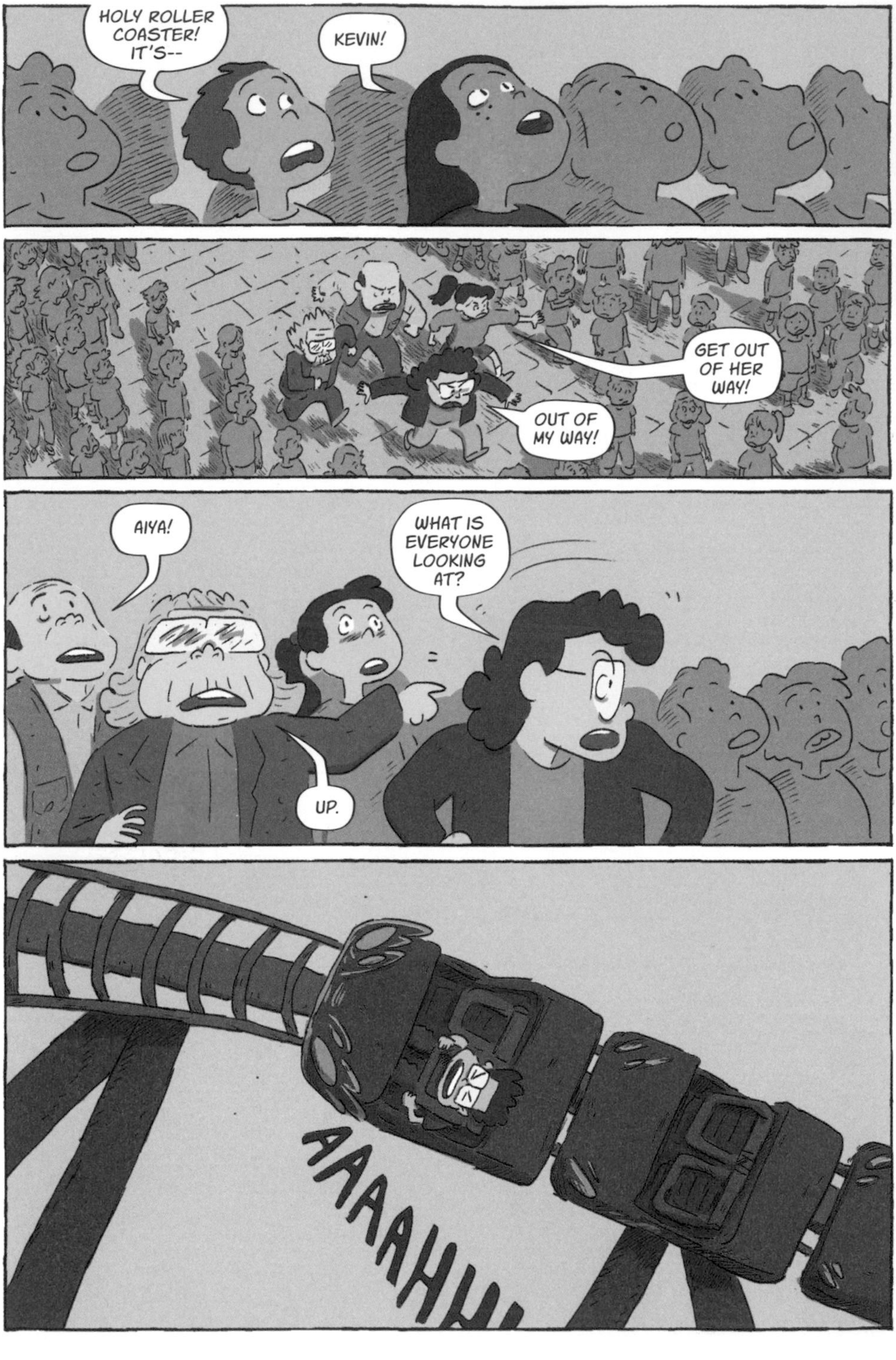
HOLY ROLLER COASTER! IT'S--
KEVIN!
GET OUT OF HER WAY!
OUT OF MY WAY!
AIYA!
WHAT IS EVERYONE LOOKING AT?
UP.
AAAAHH

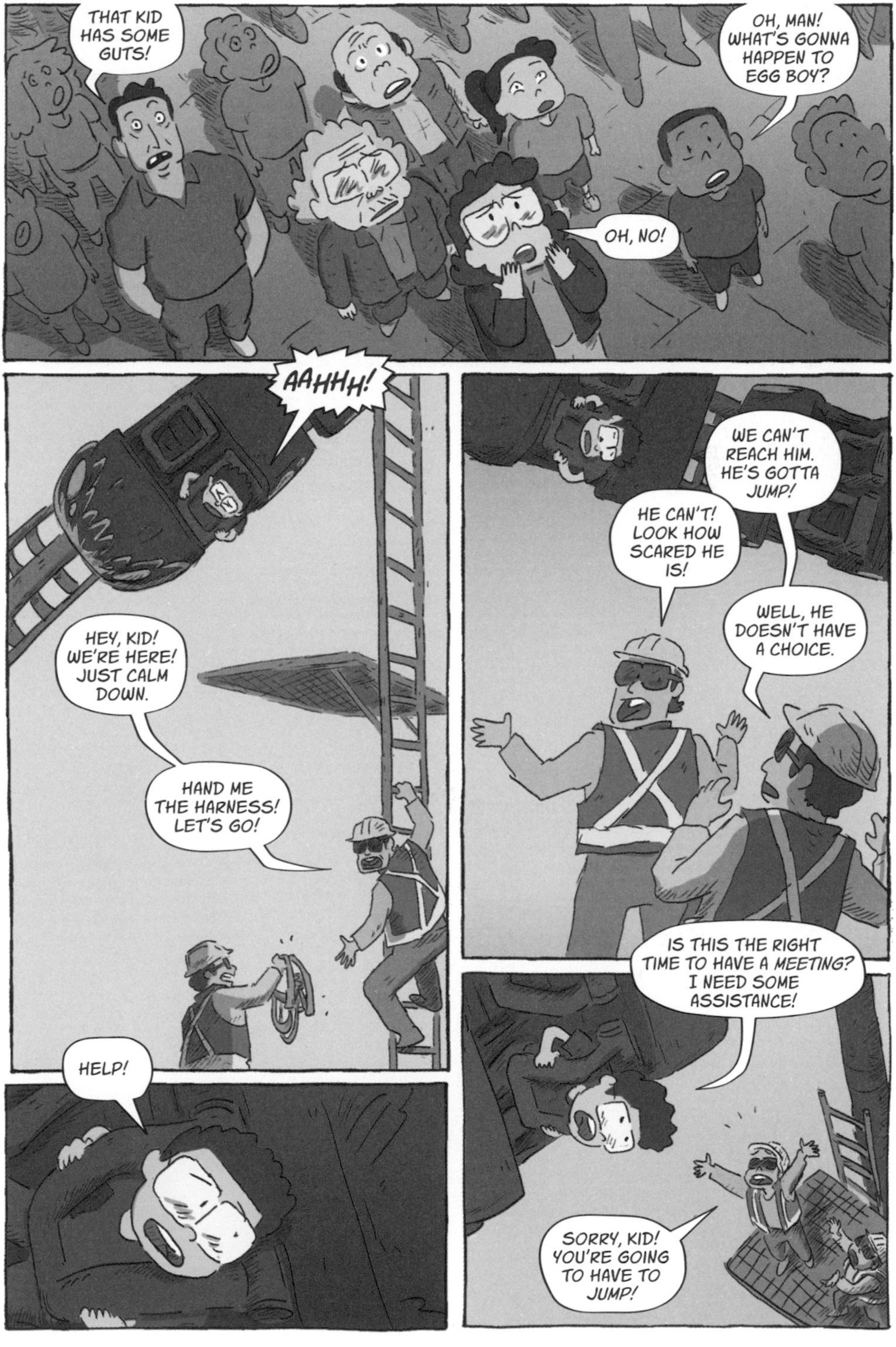
THAT KID HAS SOME GUTS!
OH, MAN! WHAT'S GONNA HAPPEN TO EGG BOY?
OH, NO!
AAHHH!
HEY, KID! WE'RE HERE! JUST CALM DOWN.
HAND ME THE HARNESS! LET'S GO!
WE CAN'T REACH HIM. HE'S GOTTA JUMP!
HE CAN'T! LOOK HOW SCARED HE IS!
WELL, HE DOESN'T HAVE A CHOICE.
HELP!
IS THIS THE RIGHT TIME TO HAVE A *MEETING*? I NEED SOME ASSISTANCE!
SORRY, KID! YOU'RE GOING TO HAVE TO JUMP!

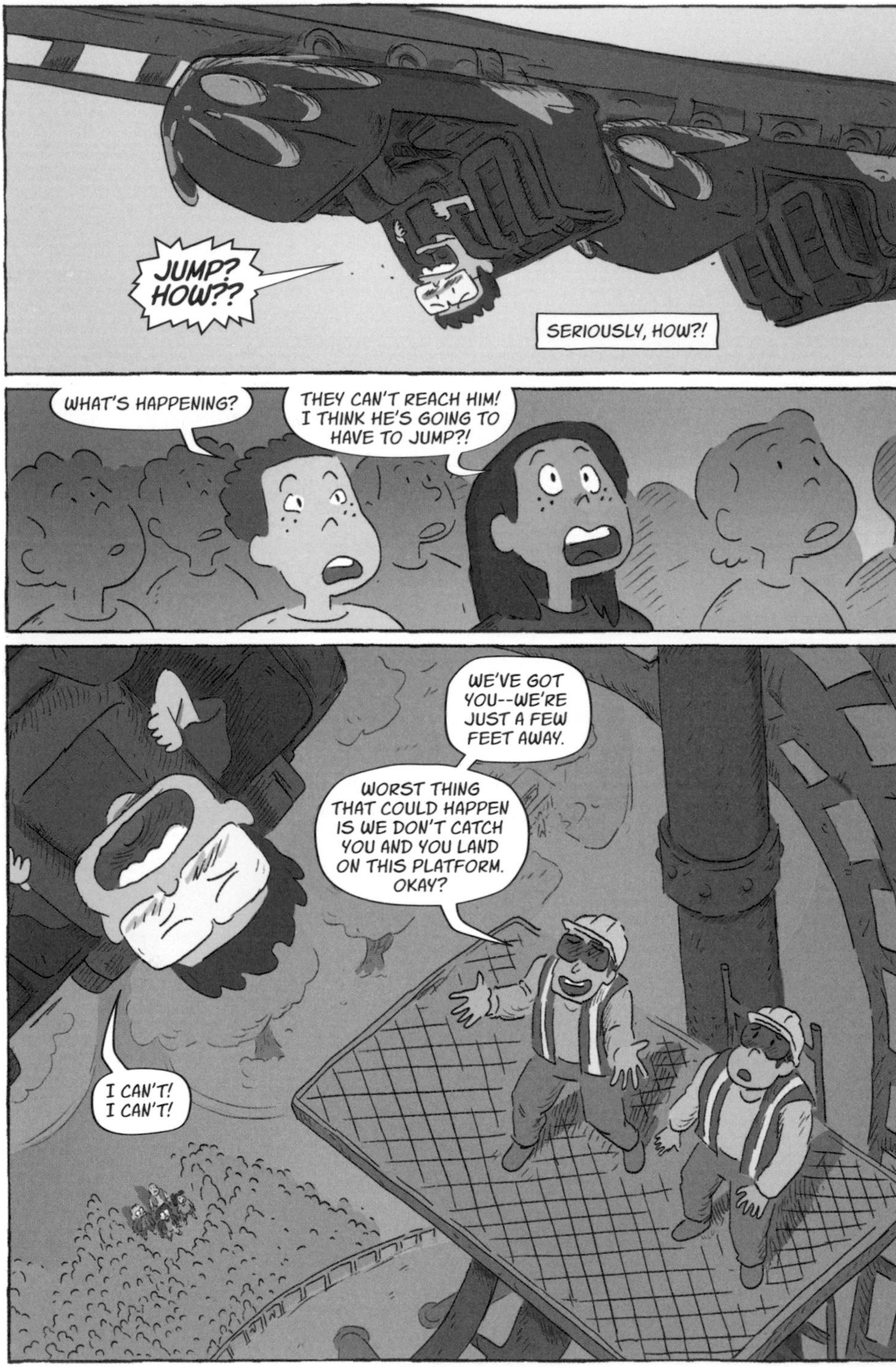
JUMP? HOW??
SERIOUSLY, HOW?!
WHAT'S HAPPENING?
THEY CAN'T REACH HIM! I THINK HE'S GOING TO HAVE TO JUMP?!
WE'VE GOT YOU--WE'RE JUST A FEW FEET AWAY.
WORST THING THAT COULD HAPPEN IS WE DON'T CATCH YOU AND YOU LAND ON THIS PLATFORM. OKAY?
I CAN'T! I CAN'T!

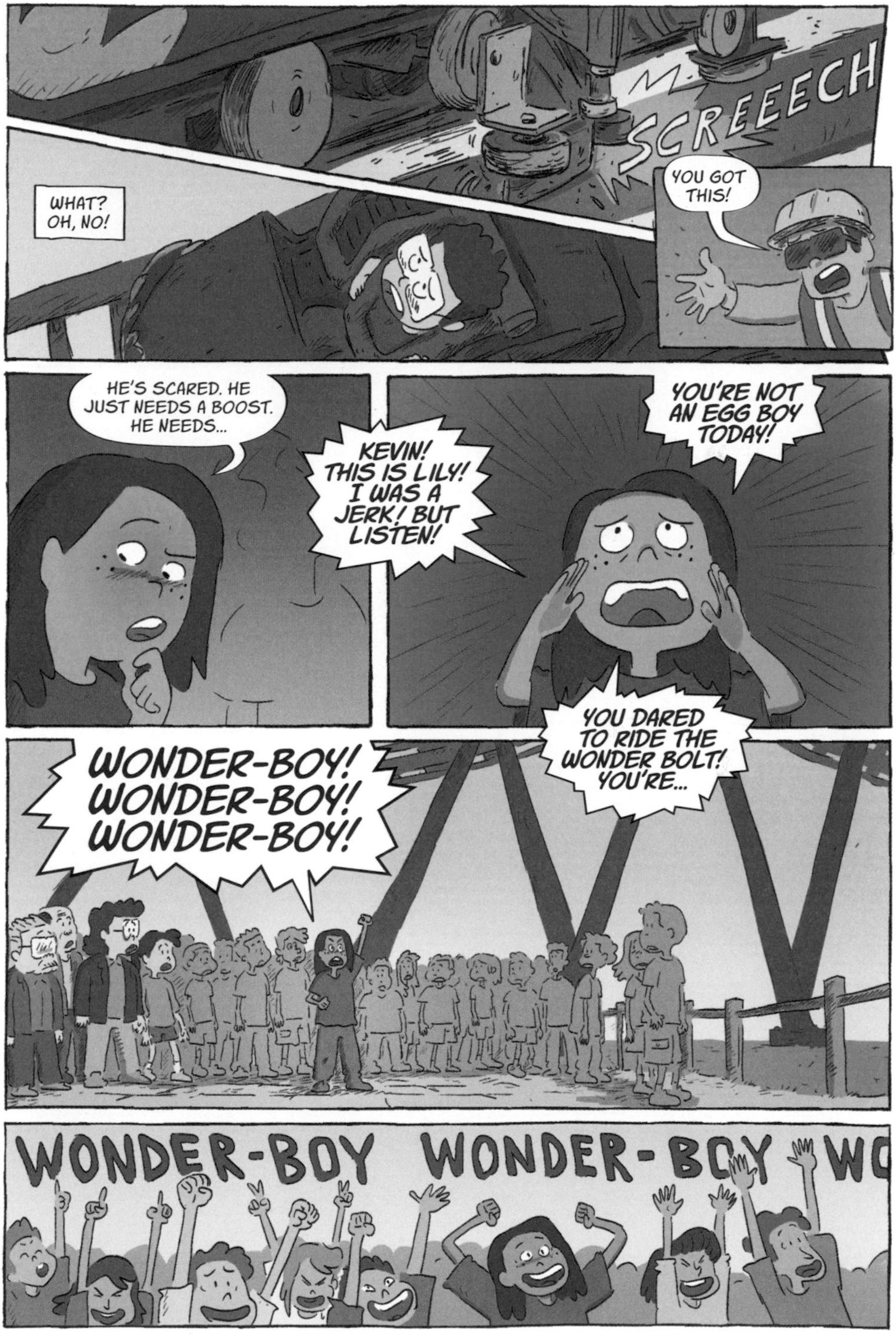
SCREEECH
WHAT? OH, NO!
YOU GOT THIS!
HE'S SCARED. HE JUST NEEDS A BOOST. HE NEEDS...
KEVIN! THIS IS LILY! I WAS A JERK! BUT LISTEN!
YOU'RE NOT AN EGG BOY TODAY!
YOU DARED TO RIDE THE WONDER BOLT! YOU'RE...
WONDER-BOY! WONDER-BOY! WONDER-BOY!
WONDER-BOY WONDER-BOY WO

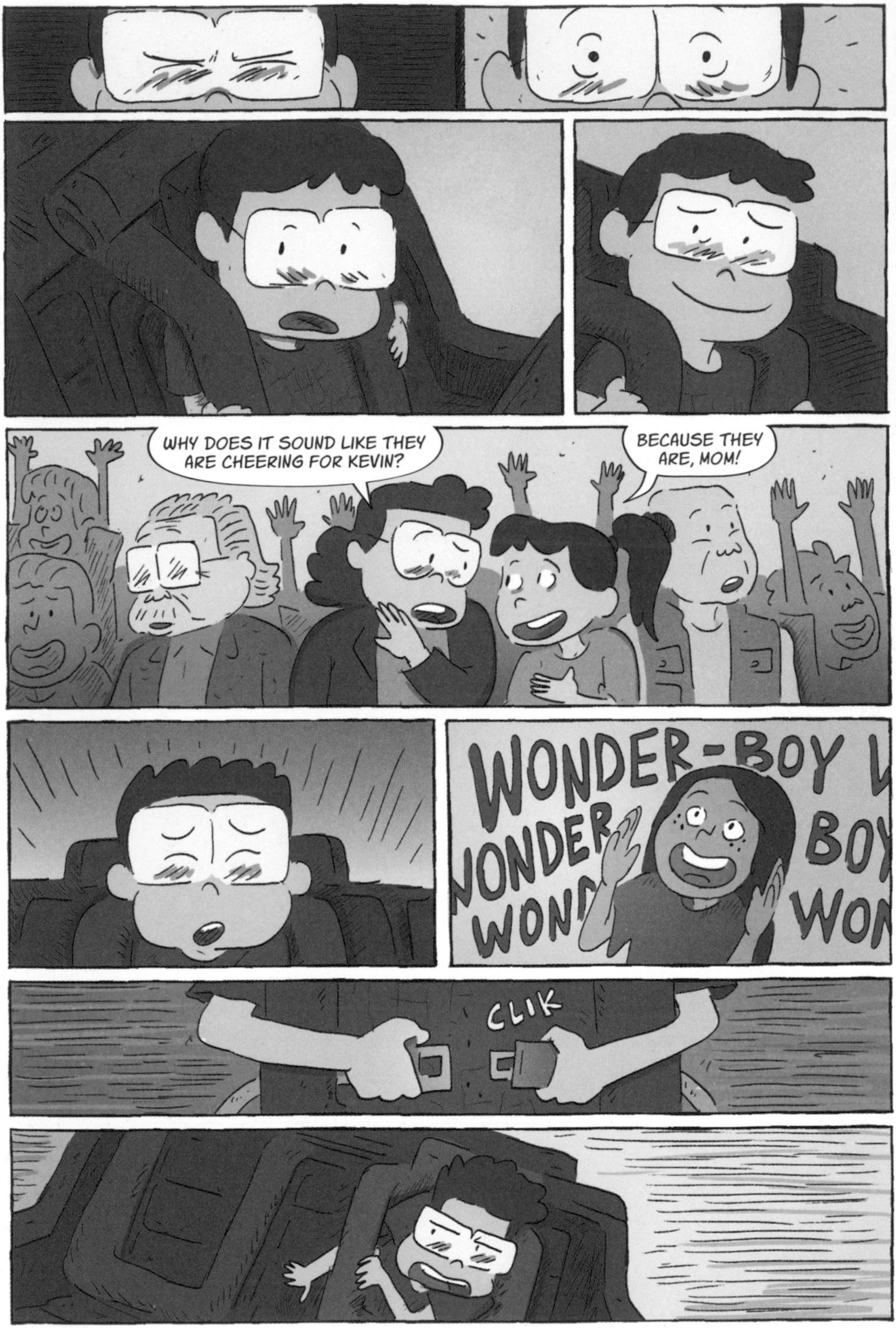
WHY DOES IT SOUND LIKE THEY ARE CHEERING FOR KEVIN?
BECAUSE THEY ARE, MOM!
WONDER-BOY
WONDER
BOY
CLIK

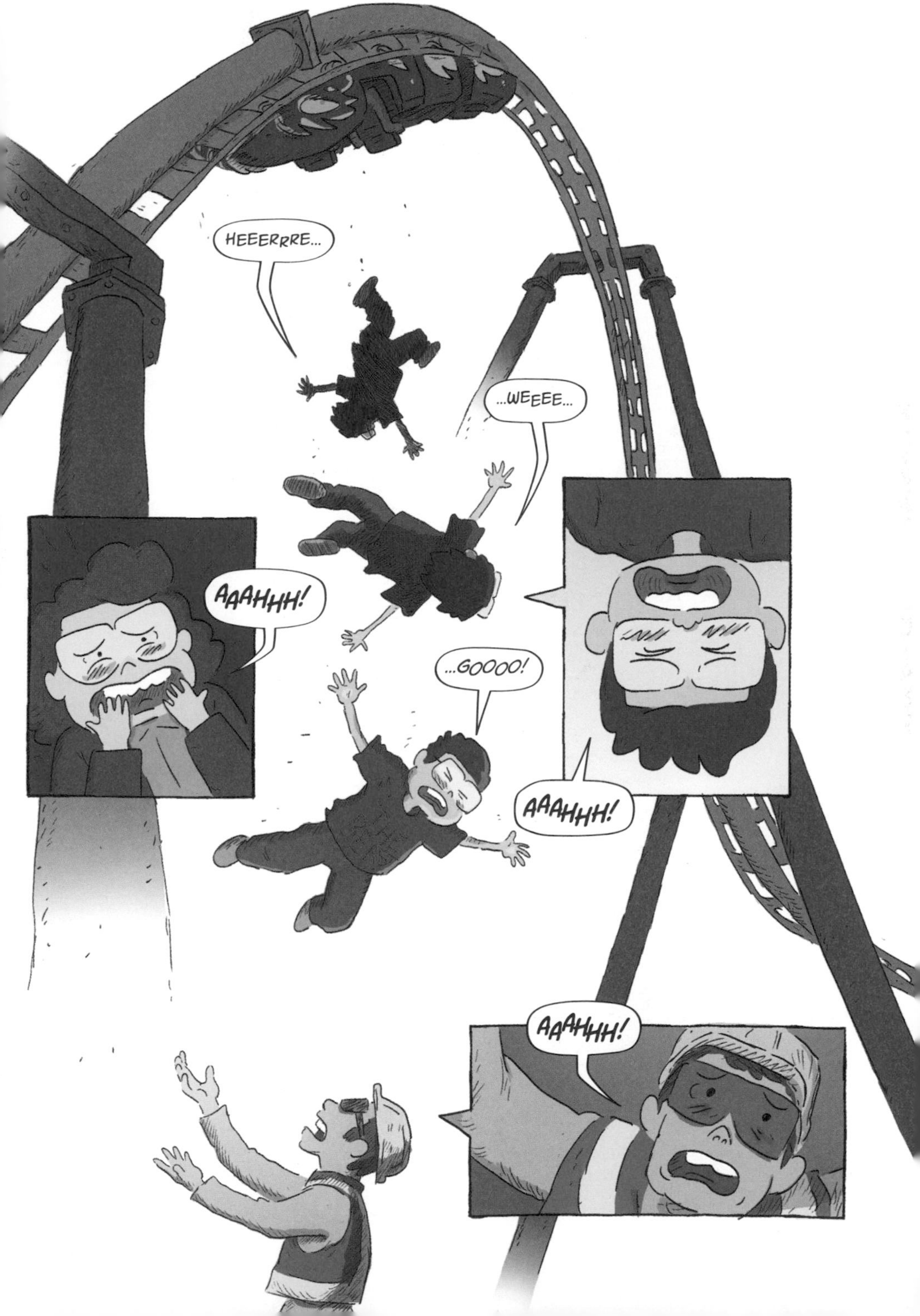
HEEERRRE...
...WEEEE...
AAAHHH!
...GOOOO!
AAAHHH!
AAAHHH!

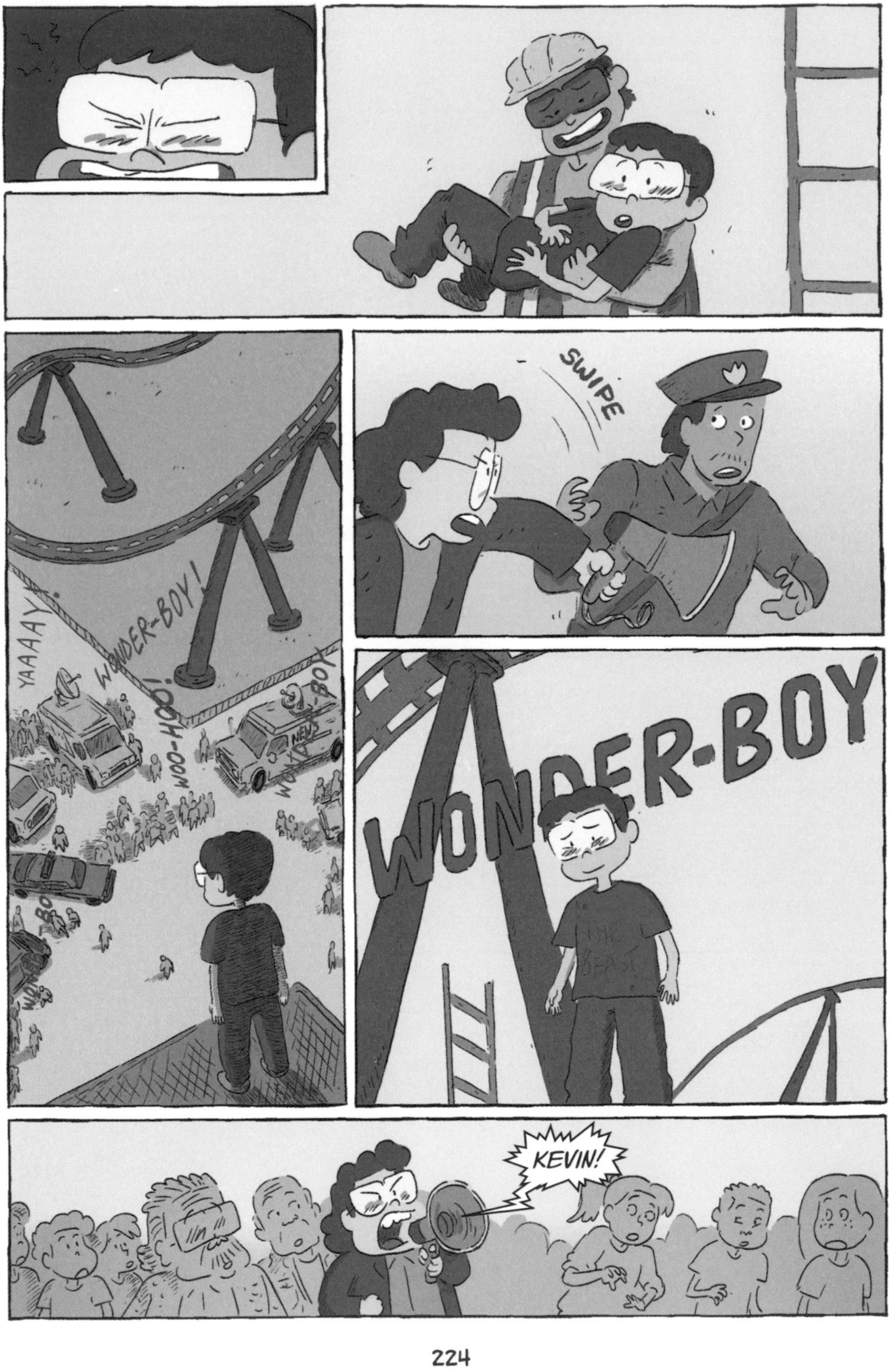
YAAAAAY!
WONDER-BOY!
WOO-HOO!
SWIPE
WONDER-BOY
KEVIN!

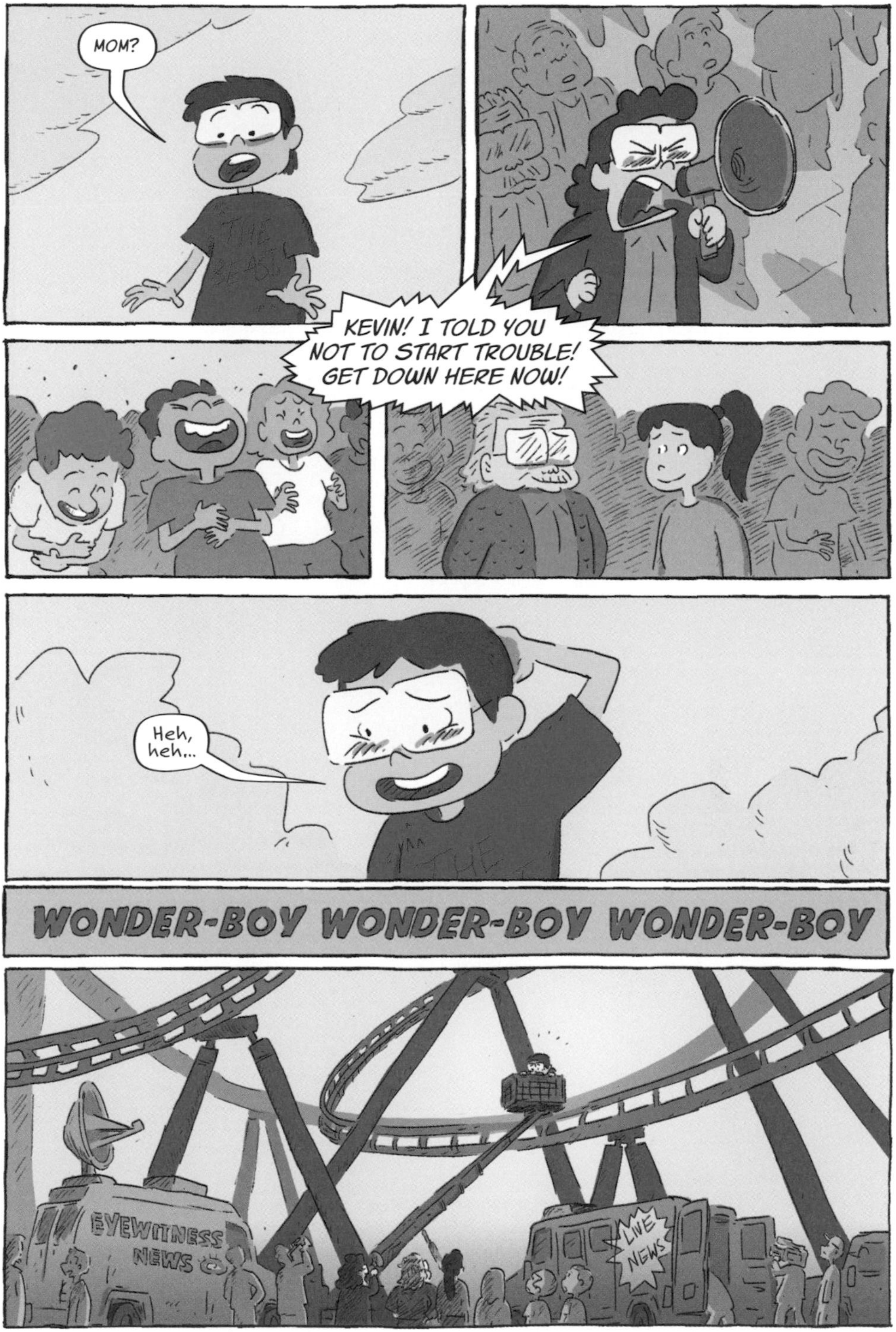
MOM?
KEVIN! I TOLD YOU NOT TO START TROUBLE! GET DOWN HERE NOW!
Heh, heh...
WONDER-BOY WONDER-BOY WONDER-BOY
EYEWITNESS NEWS
LIVE NEWS

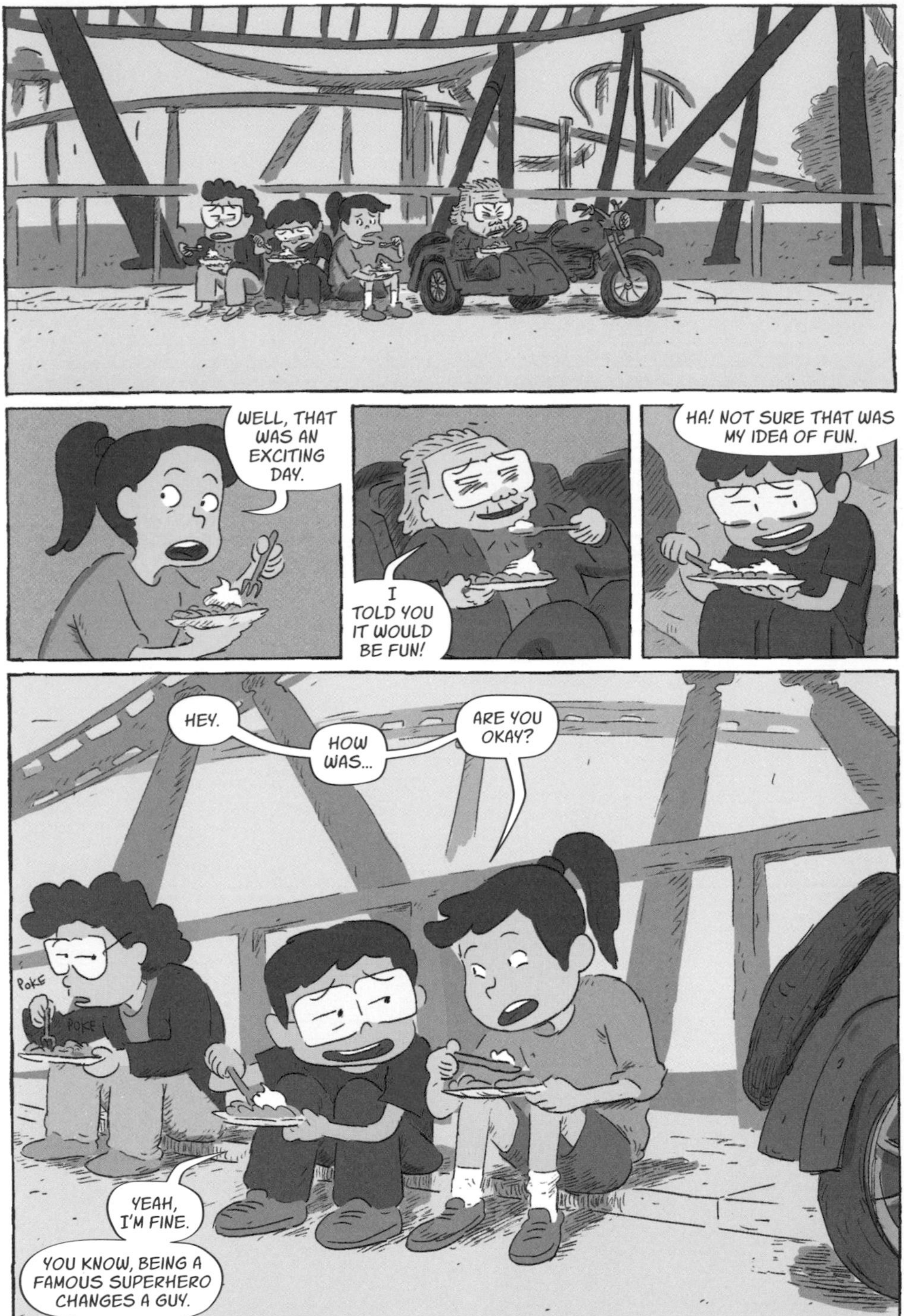
WELL, THAT WAS AN EXCITING DAY.
I TOLD YOU IT WOULD BE FUN!
HA! NOT SURE THAT WAS MY IDEA OF FUN.
HEY.
HOW WAS...
ARE YOU OKAY?
POKE
POKE
YEAH, I'M FINE.
YOU KNOW, BEING A FAMOUS SUPERHERO CHANGES A GUY.

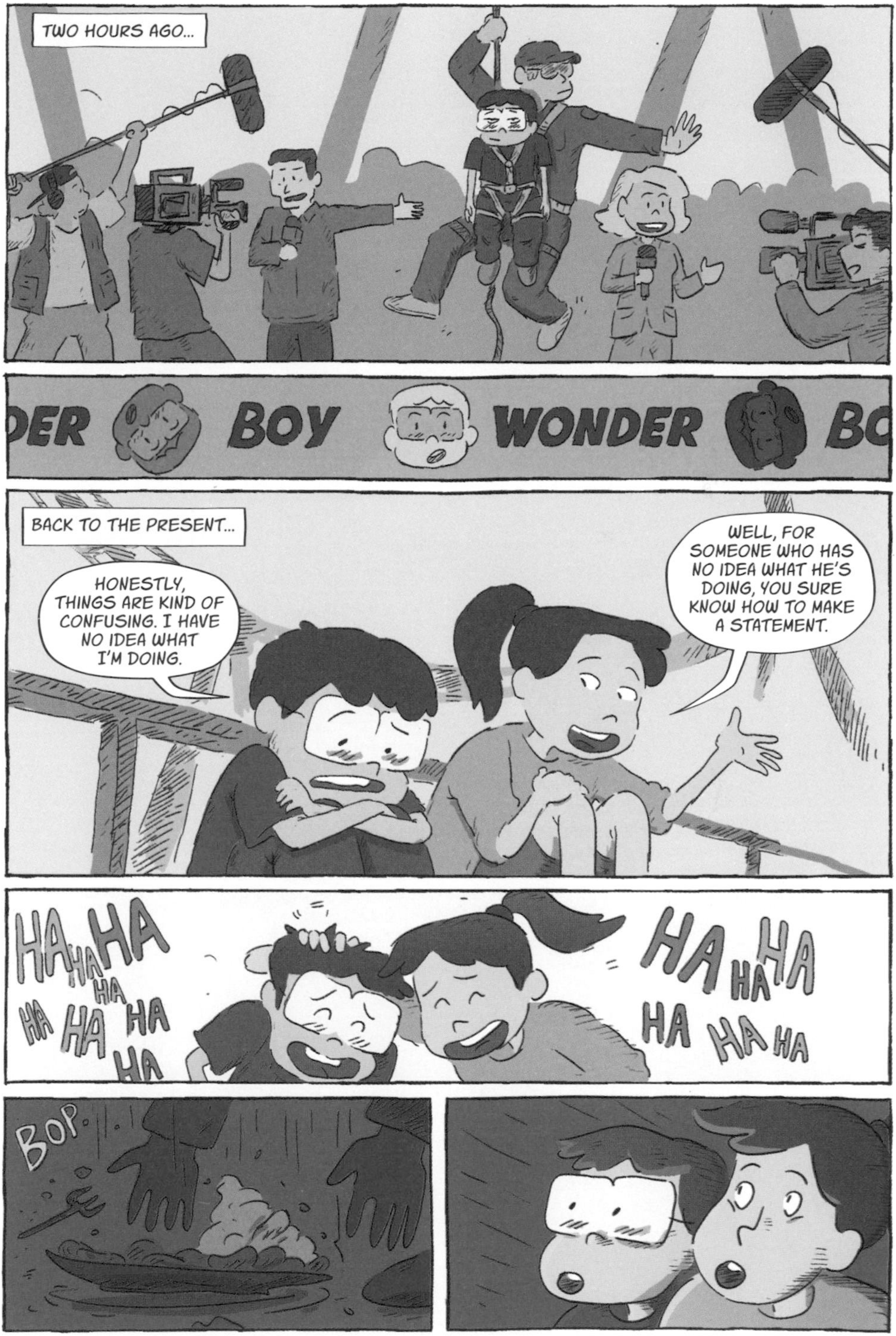

TWO HOURS AGO...
DER BOY WONDER BO
BACK TO THE PRESENT...
HONESTLY, THINGS ARE KIND OF CONFUSING. I HAVE NO IDEA WHAT I'M DOING.
WELL, FOR SOMEONE WHO HAS NO IDEA WHAT HE'S DOING, YOU SURE KNOW HOW TO MAKE A STATEMENT.
HA HA HA HA HA HA HA HA HA
HA HA HA HA HA HA HA HA
BOP.

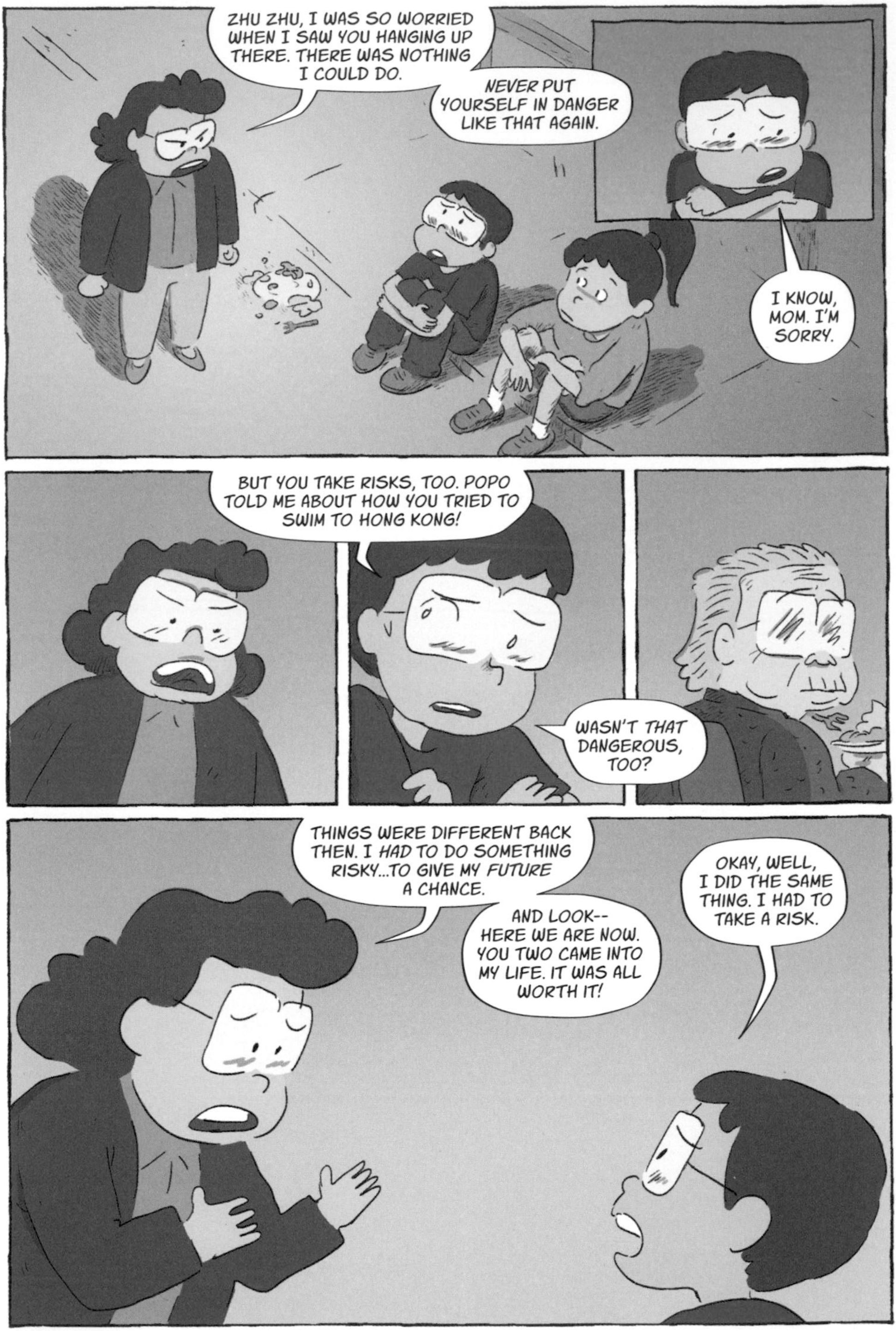
ZHU ZHU, I WAS SO WORRIED WHEN I SAW YOU HANGING UP THERE. THERE WAS NOTHING I COULD DO.
NEVER PUT YOURSELF IN DANGER LIKE THAT AGAIN.
I KNOW, MOM. I'M SORRY.
BUT YOU TAKE RISKS, TOO. POPO TOLD ME ABOUT HOW YOU TRIED TO SWIM TO HONG KONG!
WASN'T THAT DANGEROUS, TOO?
THINGS WERE DIFFERENT BACK THEN. I *HAD* TO DO SOMETHING RISKY...TO GIVE MY *FUTURE* A CHANCE.
AND LOOK-- HERE WE ARE NOW. YOU TWO CAME INTO MY LIFE. IT WAS ALL WORTH IT!
OKAY, WELL, I DID THE SAME THING. I HAD TO TAKE A RISK.

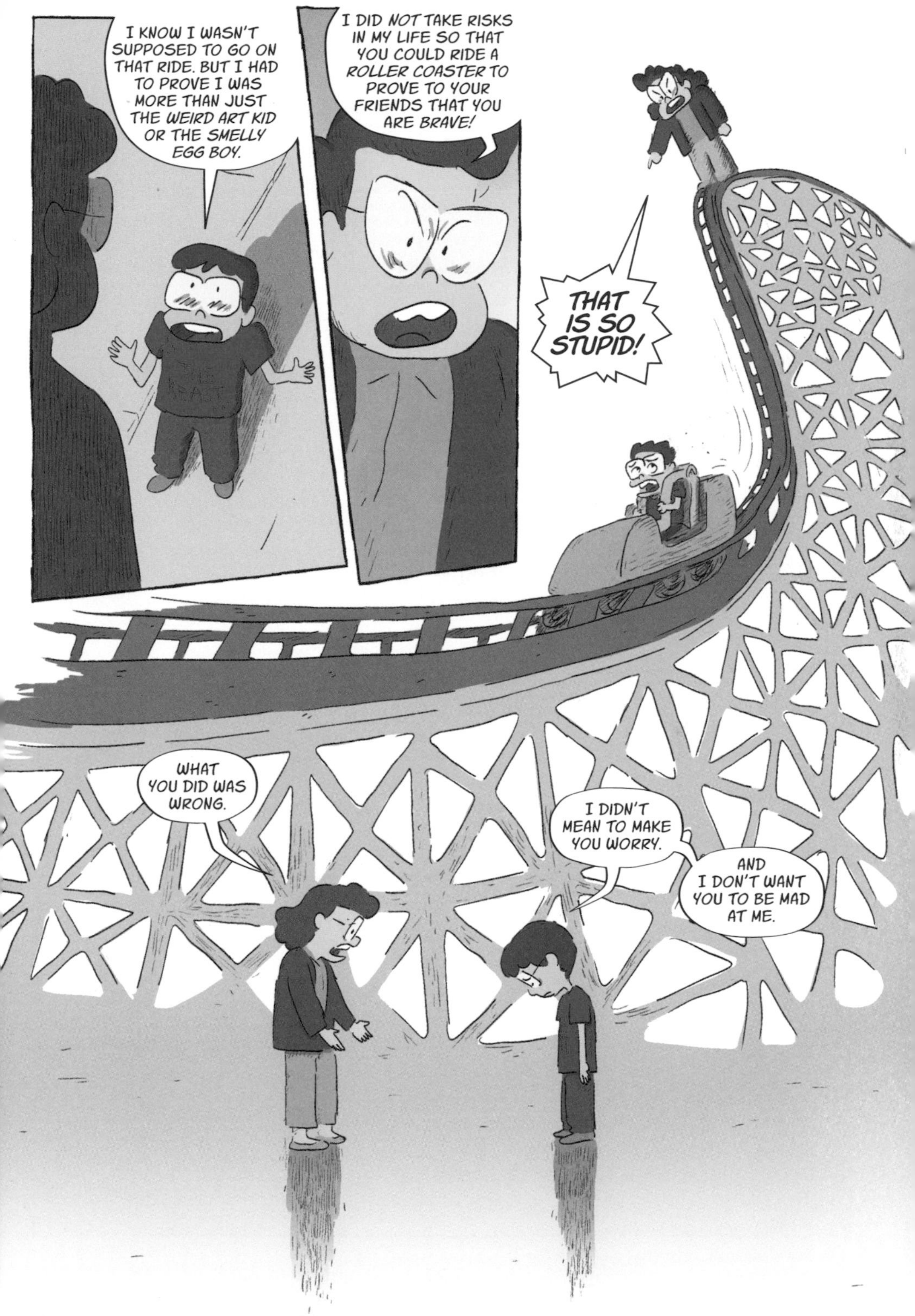

I KNOW I WASN'T SUPPOSED TO GO ON THAT RIDE. BUT I HAD TO PROVE I WAS MORE THAN JUST THE *WEIRD ART KID* OR THE *SMELLY EGG BOY*.
I DID *NOT* TAKE RISKS IN MY LIFE SO THAT YOU COULD RIDE A *ROLLER COASTER* TO PROVE TO YOUR FRIENDS THAT YOU ARE *BRAVE!*
THAT IS SO STUPID!
WHAT YOU DID WAS WRONG.
I DIDN'T MEAN TO MAKE YOU WORRY.
AND I DON'T WANT YOU TO BE MAD AT ME.

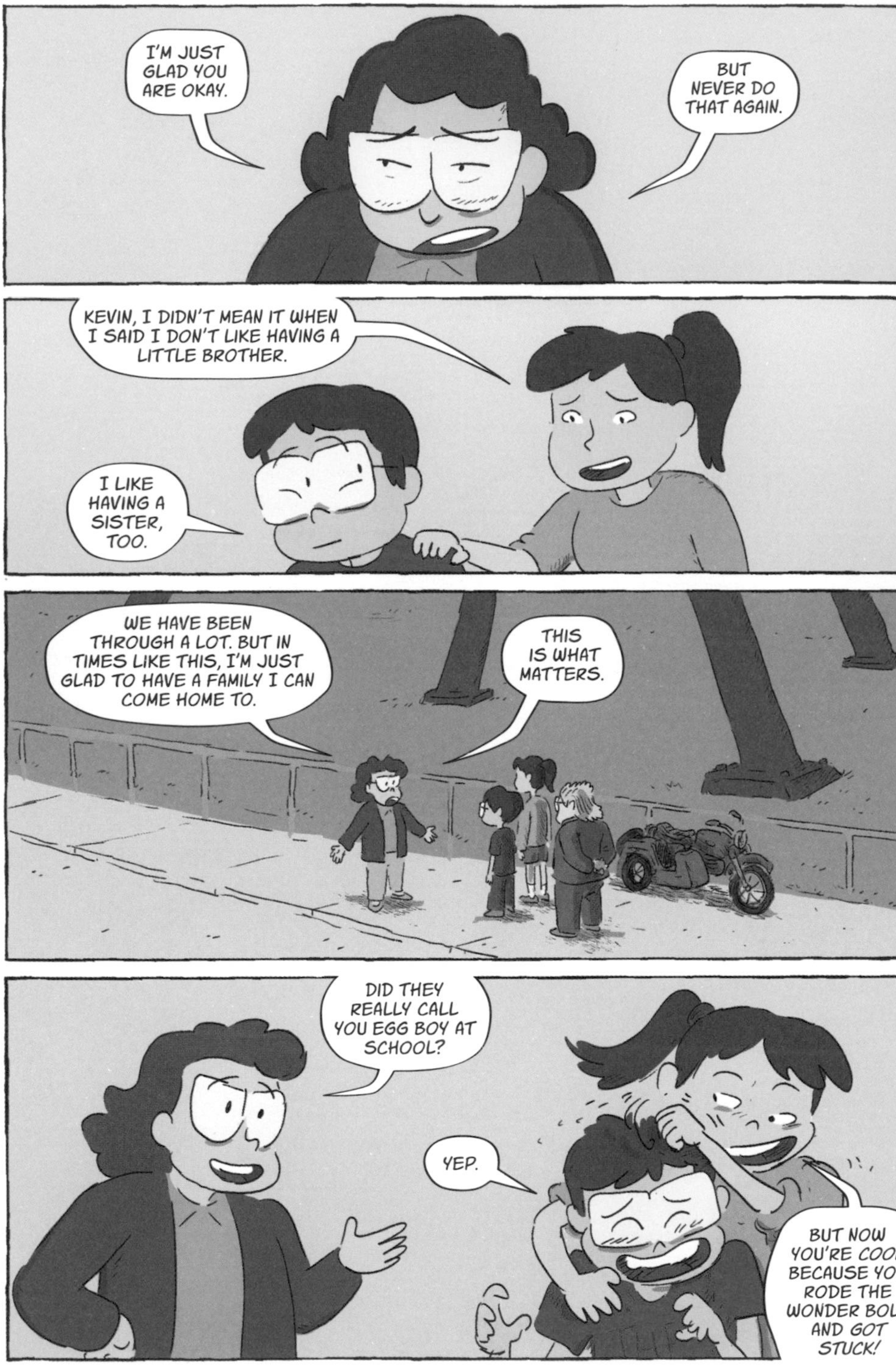
I'M JUST GLAD YOU ARE OKAY.
BUT NEVER DO THAT AGAIN.
KEVIN, I DIDN'T MEAN IT WHEN I SAID I DON'T LIKE HAVING A LITTLE BROTHER.
I LIKE HAVING A SISTER, TOO.
WE HAVE BEEN THROUGH A LOT. BUT IN TIMES LIKE THIS, I'M JUST GLAD TO HAVE A FAMILY I CAN COME HOME TO.
THIS IS WHAT MATTERS.
DID THEY REALLY CALL YOU EGG BOY AT SCHOOL?
YEP.
BUT NOW YOU'RE *COOL* BECAUSE YOU RODE THE WONDER BOLT AND GOT STUCK!

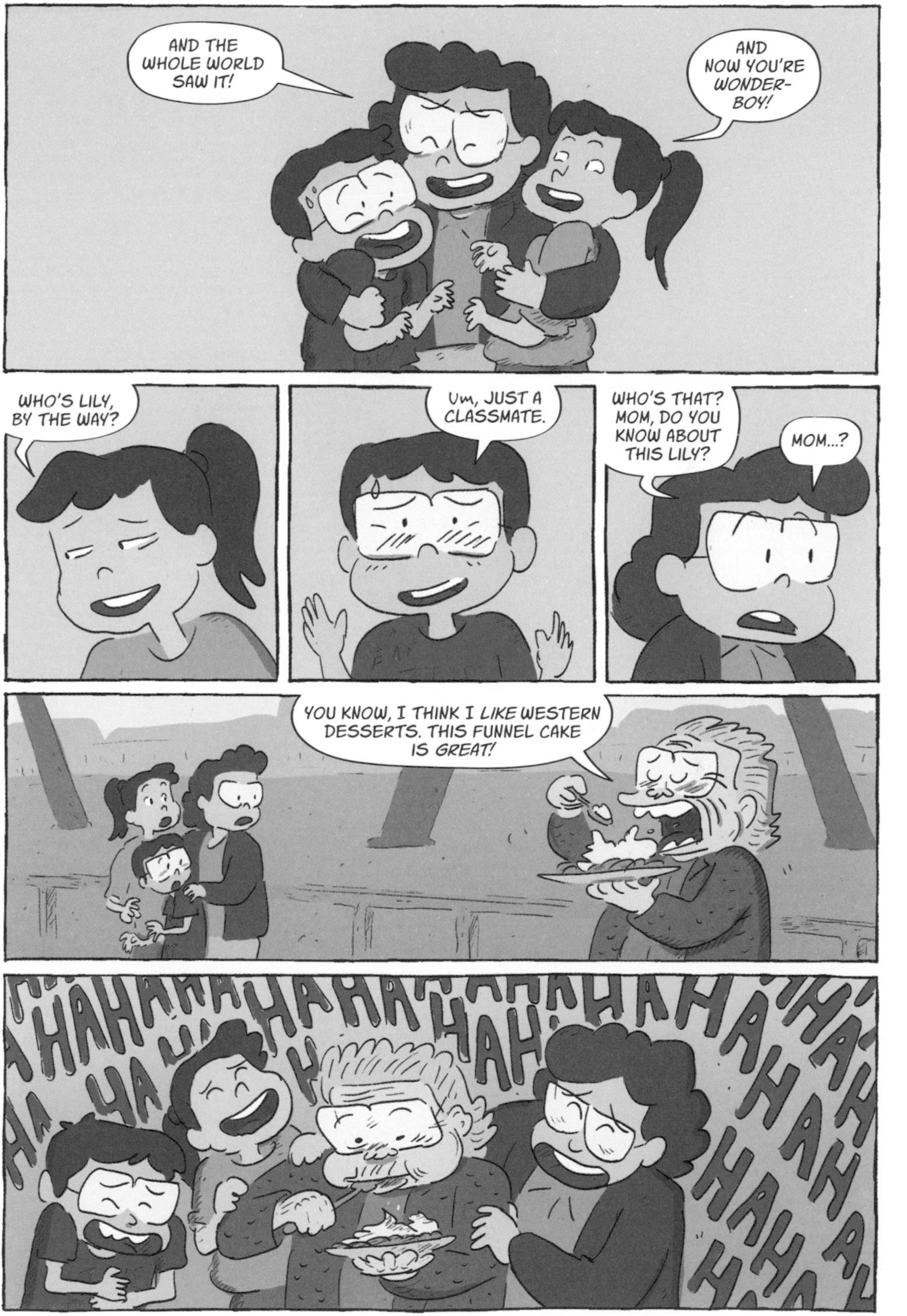
AND THE WHOLE WORLD SAW IT!
AND NOW YOU'RE WONDER-BOY!
WHO'S LILY, BY THE WAY?
UM, JUST A CLASSMATE.
WHO'S THAT? MOM, DO YOU KNOW ABOUT THIS LILY?
MOM...?
YOU KNOW, I THINK I LIKE WESTERN DESSERTS. THIS FUNNEL CAKE IS GREAT!
HAHAHAHAHAHAHAHAHAHA
HAH!

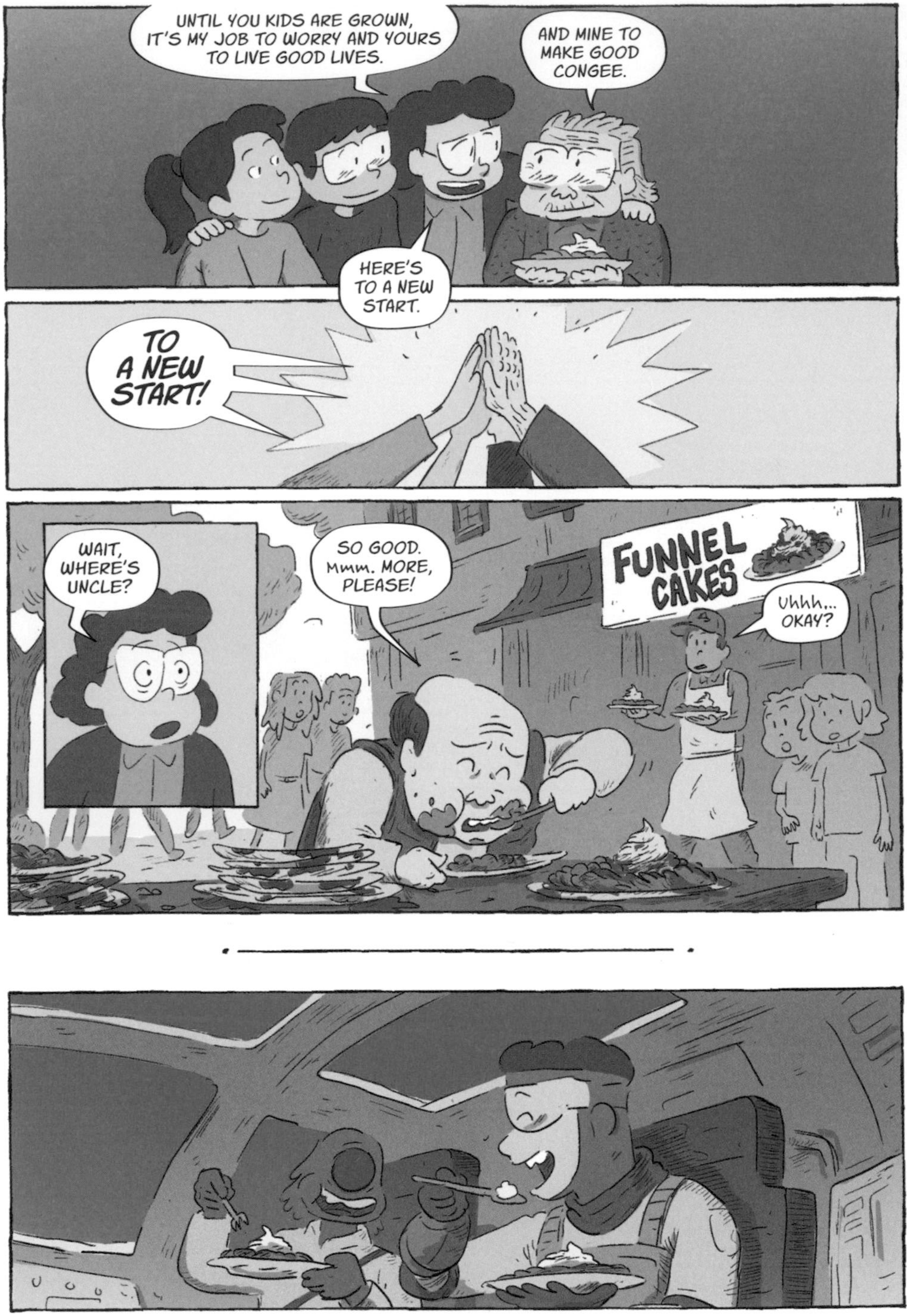
UNTIL YOU KIDS ARE GROWN, IT'S MY JOB TO WORRY AND YOURS TO LIVE GOOD LIVES.
AND MINE TO MAKE GOOD CONGEE.
HERE'S TO A NEW START.
TO A NEW START!
WAIT, WHERE'S UNCLE?
SO GOOD. Mmm. MORE, PLEASE!
FUNNEL CAKES
Uhhh... OKAY?

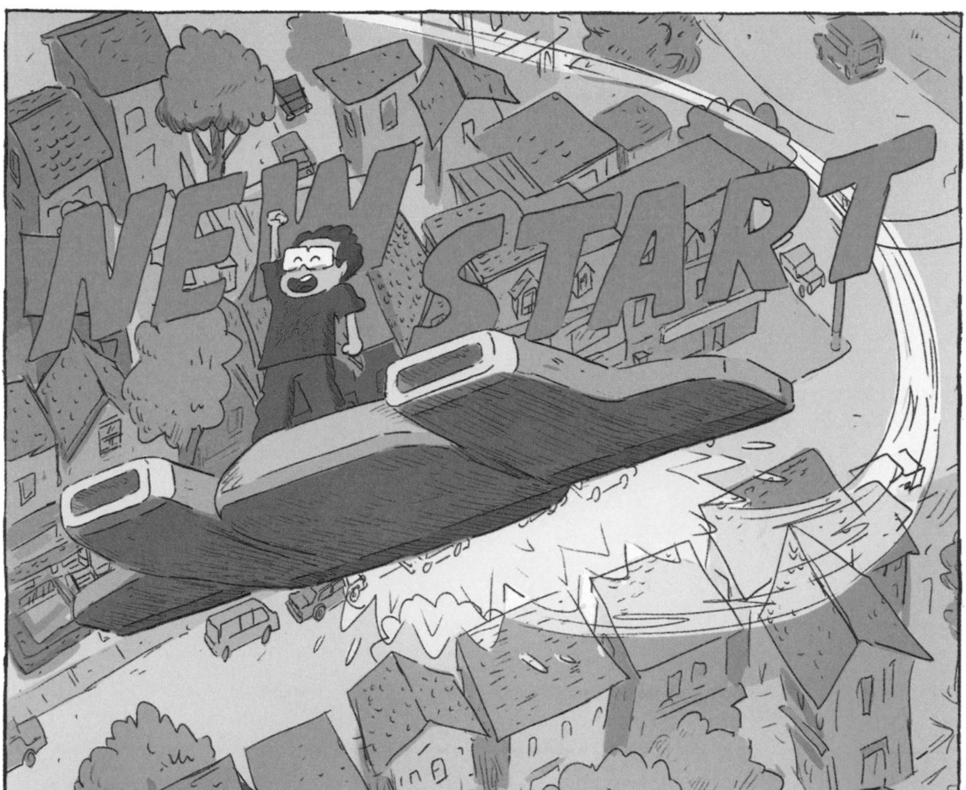
NEW START

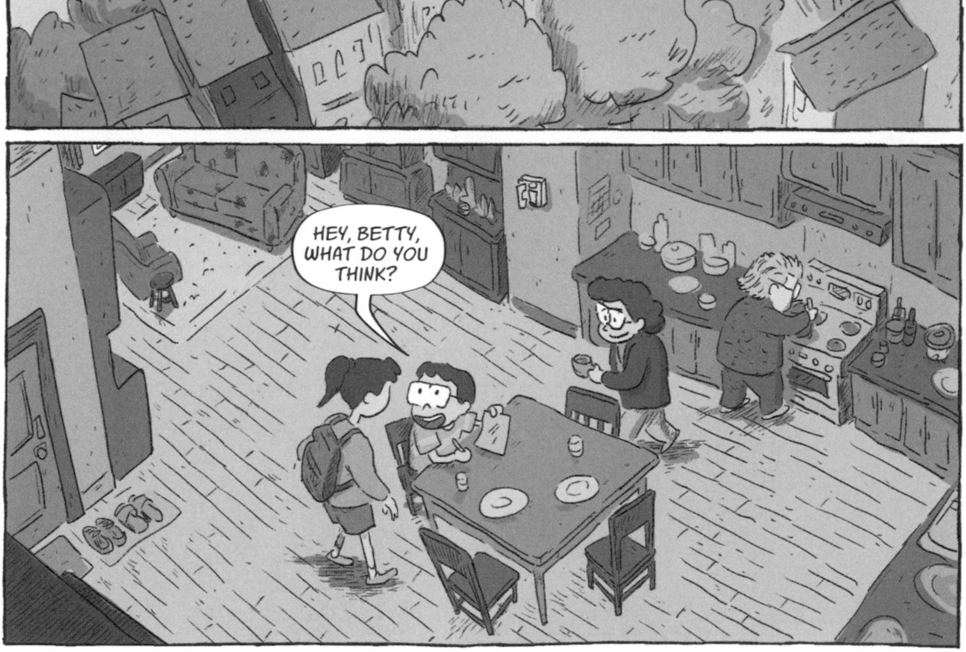
HEY, BETTY, WHAT DO YOU THINK?

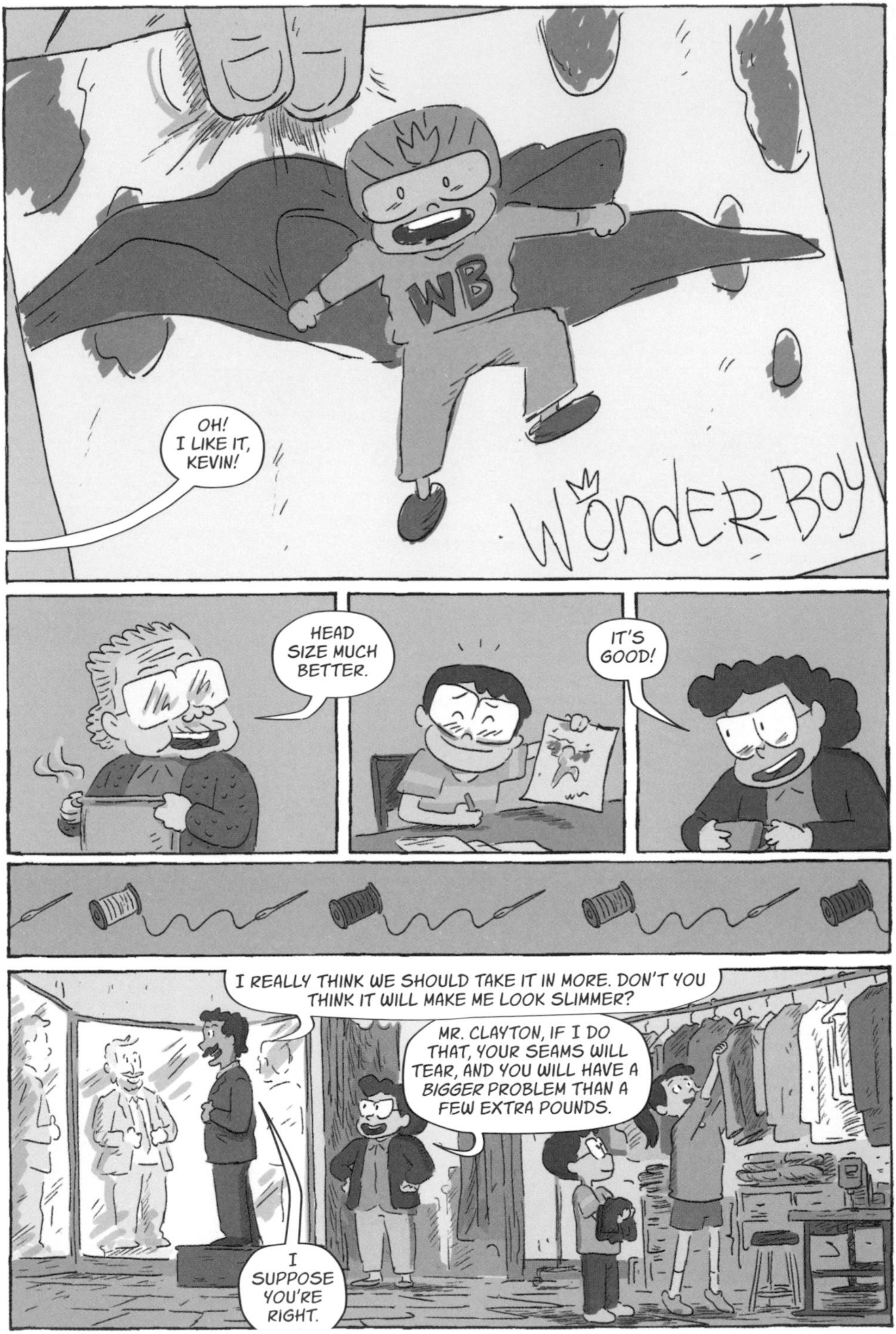

WB
OH! I LIKE IT, KEVIN!
WONDER-BOY
HEAD SIZE MUCH BETTER.
IT'S GOOD!
I REALLY THINK WE SHOULD TAKE IT IN MORE. DON'T YOU THINK IT WILL MAKE ME LOOK SLIMMER?
MR. CLAYTON, IF I DO THAT, YOUR SEAMS WILL TEAR, AND YOU WILL HAVE A *BIGGER* PROBLEM THAN A FEW EXTRA POUNDS.
I SUPPOSE YOU'RE RIGHT.

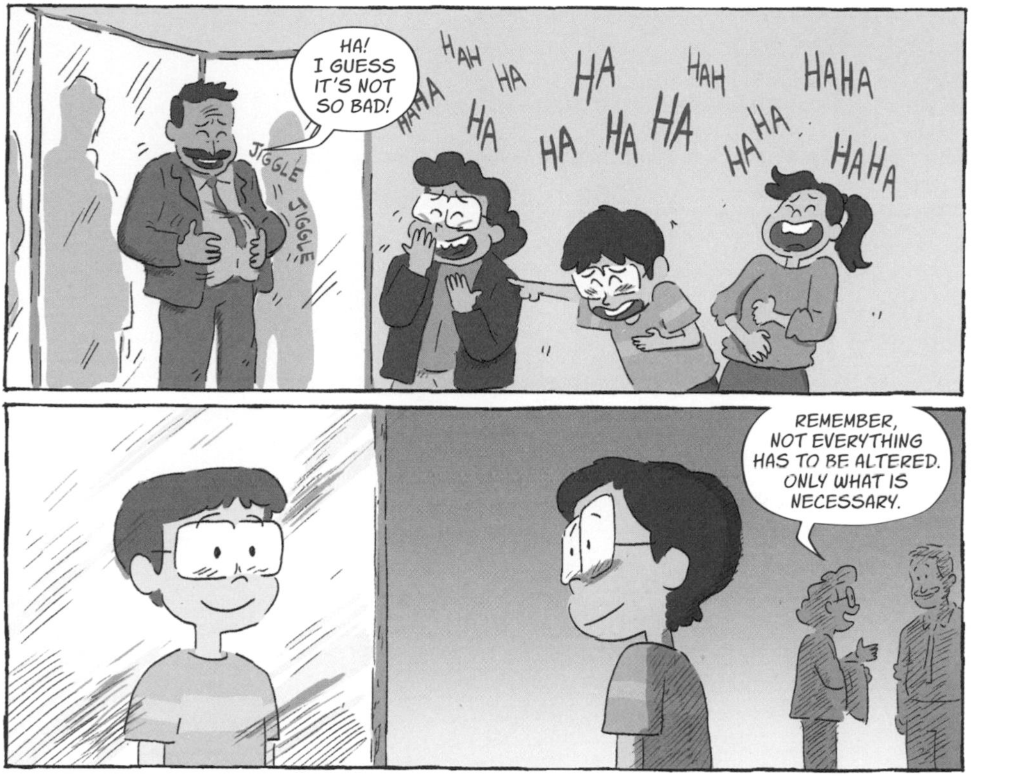
HA!
I GUESS
IT'S NOT
SO BAD!
JIGGLE
JIGGLE
HAHA HAH HA HA HA HAH HA HA HA HA HAHA HAHA HAHA
REMEMBER,
NOT EVERYTHING
HAS TO BE ALTERED.
ONLY WHAT IS
NECESSARY.

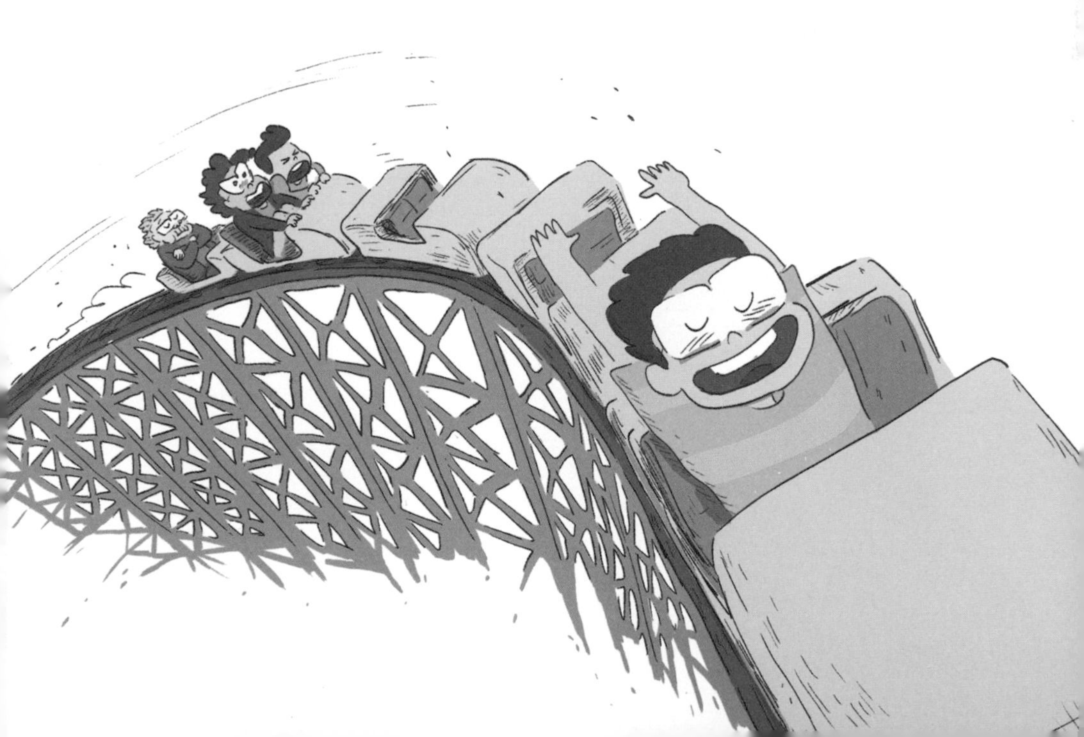

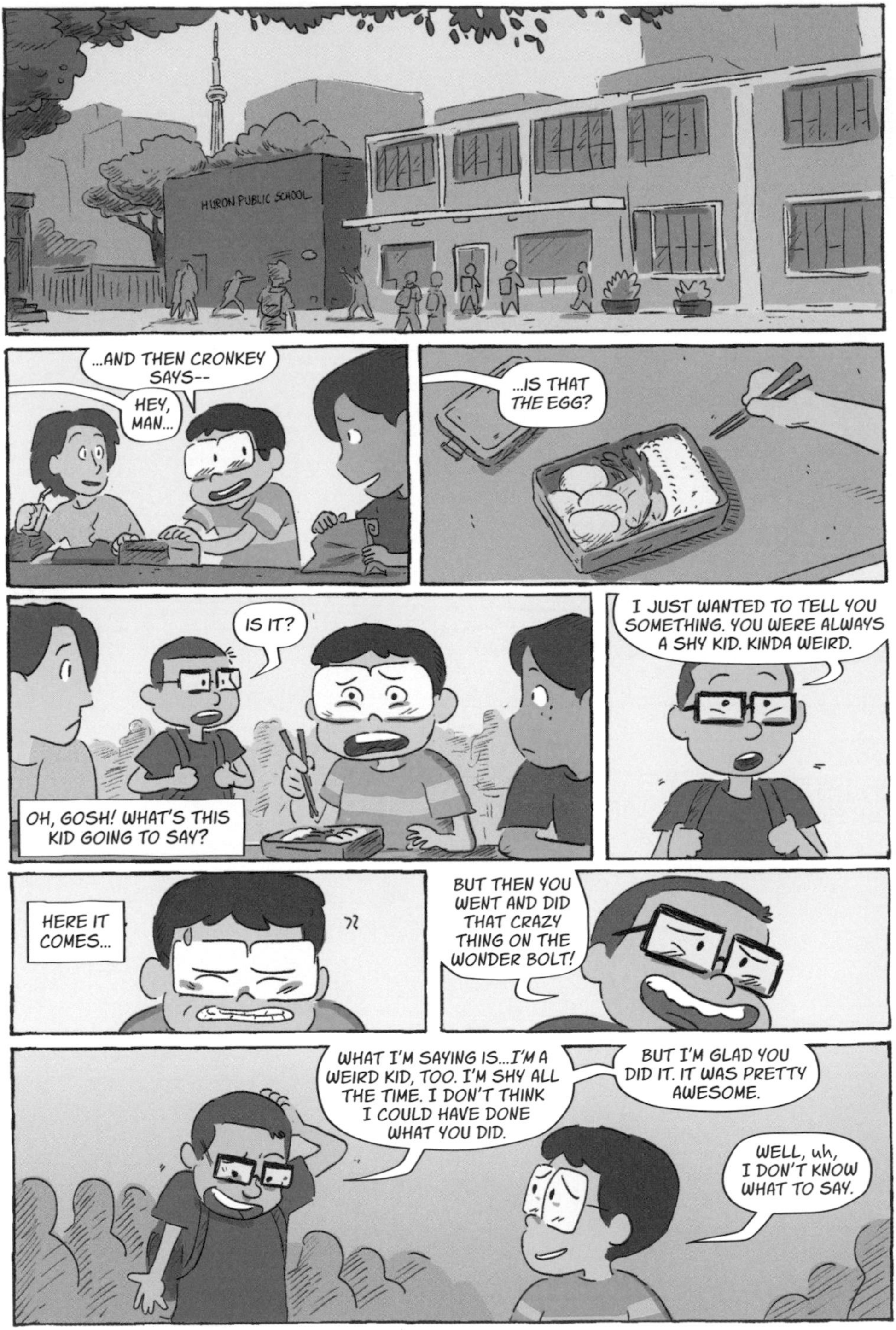
HURON PUBLIC SCHOOL
...AND THEN CRONKEY SAYS--
HEY, MAN...
...IS THAT THE EGG?
IS IT?
OH, GOSH! WHAT'S THIS KID GOING TO SAY?
I JUST WANTED TO TELL YOU SOMETHING. YOU WERE ALWAYS A SHY KID. KINDA WEIRD.
HERE IT COMES...
BUT THEN YOU WENT AND DID THAT CRAZY THING ON THE WONDER BOLT!
BUT I'M GLAD YOU DID IT. IT WAS PRETTY AWESOME.
WHAT I'M SAYING IS...I'M A WEIRD KID, TOO. I'M SHY ALL THE TIME. I DON'T THINK I COULD HAVE DONE WHAT YOU DID.
WELL, uh, I DON'T KNOW WHAT TO SAY.

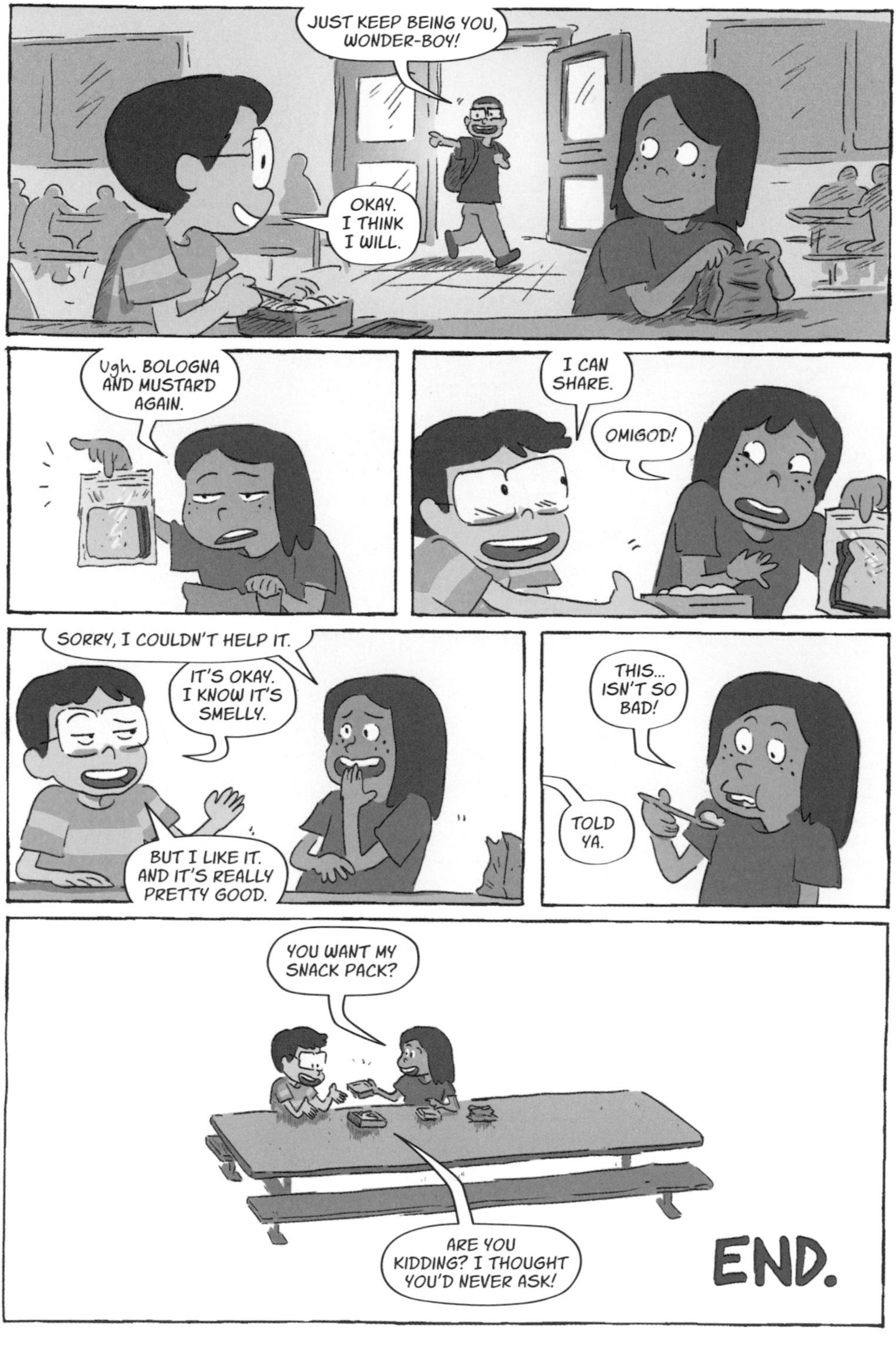
JUST KEEP BEING YOU, WONDER-BOY!
OKAY. I THINK I WILL.
Ugh. BOLOGNA AND MUSTARD AGAIN.
I CAN SHARE.
OMIGOD!
SORRY, I COULDN'T HELP IT.
IT'S OKAY. I KNOW IT'S SMELLY.
BUT I LIKE IT. AND IT'S REALLY PRETTY GOOD.
THIS... ISN'T SO BAD!
TOLD YA.
YOU WANT MY SNACK PACK?
ARE YOU KIDDING? I THOUGHT YOU'D NEVER ASK!
END.

ABOUT THE AUTHOR

Tobias Wang

RAY XU is a Toronto-based story artist for television and feature films. He has most recently worked on such hits as the 2021 Netflix animated movie *The Mitchells vs. The Machines, Teenage Mutant Ninja Turtles: Mutant Mayhem,* and more. He invites you to visit him online at raymond-xu.com.